THE
WIDE, WIDE
WORLD

THE
WIDE, WIDE
WORLD

by Susan Warner

Afterword by Jane Tompkins

Illustrated by Frederick Dielman

Here at the portal thou dost stand,
 And with thy little hand
Thou openest the mysterious gate.
 Into the future's undiscovered land
 I see its valves expand,
As at the touch of FATE!
Into those realms of Love and Hate.

LONGFELLOW

THE FEMINIST PRESS
at The City University of New York
New York

First Feminist Press edition
89 88 87 86 5 4 3 2 1

This publication is made possible, in part,
by a grant from the AT&T Foundation.

Library of Congress Cataloging-in-Publication Date

Warner, Susan, 1819–1885.
  The wide, wide world.

  Bibliography: p.
  Summary: Ellen has difficulty believing that God
will take care of her when her dying mother leaves her
with the unloving Mrs. Dunscombe.
  [1. Christian life—Fiction]   I. Tompkins, Jane P.
II. Title.
PZ7.W247Whi   1986   [Fic]   86-27062
ISBN 0-935312-65-X
ISBN 0-935312-66-8 (pbk.)

Cover art: Anonymous painting, used by permission of Jane Tompkins.

CONTENTS

List of Illustrations
A Note on the Text

THE WIDE, WIDE WORLD
Chapter

LIST OF ILLUSTRATIONS

A NOTE ON THE TEXT

This edition of *The Wide, Wide World* has been photo-offset from the 1892 J.B. Lippincott Company edition, illustrated by Frederick Dielman. Dielman's line drawings have been reproduced here, but not the plates. The original edition (G.P. Putnam's Sons, N,Y., 1850) appeared under the name Elizabeth Wetherell, a pen name which Susan Warner later dropped.

The final chapter, here published for the first time with the main text (by permission of the Huntington Library), was omitted from the original edition and all subsequent editions. Mabel Baker published it in 1978 as an appendix to her biography of Warner (*Light in the Morning: Memories of Susan and Anna Warner*, The Constitution Island Association, West Point, N.Y.). An unsigned note in the papers of The Constitution Island Association suggests that the manuscript had gone to Putnam without the last chapter and that Putnam urged omitting it since the book had run longer in galleys than he had expected and the last chapter, in his opinion, did not contribute substantially to the novel. No further information has yet come to light regarding this omission.

CHAPTER I.

Enjoy the spring of love and youth,
To some good angel leave the rest,
For time will teach thee soon the truth,
"There are no birds in last year's nest."

LONGFELLOW.

"MAMMA, what was that I heard papa saying to you this morning about his lawsuit?"

"I cannot tell you just now. Ellen, pick up that shawl, and spread it over me."

"Mamma!—are you cold in this warm room?"

"A little,—there, that will do. Now, my daughter, let me be quiet awhile—don't disturb me."

There was no one else in the room. Driven thus to her own resources, Ellen betook herself to the window and sought amusement there. The prospect without gave little promise of it. Rain was falling, and made the street and everything in it look dull and gloomy. The foot-passengers plashed through the water, and the horses and carriages plashed through the mud; gayety had forsaken the sidewalks, and equipages were few, and the people that were out were plainly there only because they could not help it. But yet Ellen, having seriously set herself to study everything that passed, presently became engaged in her occupation; and her thoughts travelling dreamily from one thing to another, she sat for a long time with her little face pressed against the window-frame, perfectly regardless of all but the moving world without.

Daylight gradually faded away, and the street wore a more and more gloomy aspect. The rain poured, and now only an occasional carriage or footstep disturbed the sound of its steady pattering. Yet still Ellen sat with her face glued to the window as if spellbound, gazing out at every dusky form that passed, as though it had some strange interest for her. At length, in the distance, light after light began to appear; presently Ellen could see the dim figure of the lamplighter crossing the street, from side to side, with his ladder; then he drew near enough for her to watch him as he hooked his ladder on the lamp-irons, ran up and lit the lamp, then shouldered the ladder and marched off quick, the light glancing on his wet oil-skin hat, rough great coat and lantern, and on the pavement and iron railings. The veriest moth could not have followed the light with more perseverance than did Ellen's eyes, till the lamplighter gradually disappeared from view, and the last lamp she could see was lit; and not till then did it occur to her that there was such a place as in-doors. She took her face from the window. The room was dark and cheerless; and Ellen felt stiff and chilly. However, she made her way to the fire, and having found the poker, she applied it gently to the Liverpool coal with such good effect that a bright ruddy blaze sprang up, and lighted the whole room. Ellen smiled at the result of her experiment. " That is something like," said she to herself; " who says I can't poke the fire ? Now, let us see if I can't do something else. Do but see how those chairs are standing—one would think we had had a sewing-circle here—there, go back to your places,— that looks a little better ; now these curtains must come down, and I may as well shut the shutters too ; and now this table-cloth must be content to hang straight, and mamma's box and the books must lie in their places, and not all helter-skelter. Now, I wish mamma would wake up; I should think she might. I don't believe she is asleep either, she don't look as if she was."

Ellen was right in this ; her mother's face did not wear the look of sleep, nor indeed of repose at all : the lips were compressed, and the brow not calm. To try, however, whether she was asleep or not, and with the half-acknowledged intent to rouse her at all events, Ellen knelt down by her side and laid her face close to her mother's on the pillow. But this failed to draw either word or sign. After a minute or two Ellen tried stroking her mother's cheek very gently ; and this succeeded, for Mrs. Montgomery arrested the little hand as it passed her lips, and kissed it fondly two or three times.

" I haven't disturbed you, mamma, have I ?" said Ellen.

Without replying, Mrs. Montgomery raised herself to a sitting posture, and lifting both hands to her face, pushed back the hair from her forehead and temples, with a gesture which Ellen knew meant that she was making up her mind to some disagreeable or painful effort. Then taking both Ellen's hands, as she still knelt before her, she gazed in her face with a look even more fond than usual, Ellen thought, but much sadder too; though Mrs. Montgomery's cheerfulness had always been of a serious kind.

"What question was that you were asking me awhile ago, my daughter?"

"I thought, mamma, I heard papa telling you this morning, or yesterday, that he had lost that lawsuit."

"You heard right, Ellen,—he has lost it," said Mrs. Montgomery, sadly.

"Are you sorry, mamma?—does it trouble you?"

"You know, my dear, that I am not apt to concern myself over-much about the gain or the loss of money. I believe my Heavenly Father will give me what is good for me."

"Then, mamma, why are you troubled?"

"Because, my child, I cannot carry out this principle in other matters, and leave quietly my *all* in His hands."

"What is the matter, dear mother? What makes you look so?"

"This lawsuit, Ellen, has brought upon us more trouble than I ever thought a lawsuit could,—the loss of it, I mean."

"How, mamma?"

"It has caused an entire change of all our plans. Your father says he is too poor now to stay here any longer; and he has agreed to go soon on some government or military business to Europe."

"Well, mamma, that is bad; but he has been away a great deal before, and I am sure we were always very happy."

"But, Ellen, he thinks now, and the doctor thinks too, that it is very important for my health that I should go with him."

"Does he, mamma?—and do you mean to go?"

"I am afraid I must, my dear child."

"Not, and leave *me*, mother?"

The imploring look of mingled astonishment, terror, and sorrow with which Ellen uttered these words, took from her mother all power of replying. It was not necessary; her little daughter understood only too well the silent answer of her eye. With a wild cry she flung her arms round her mother, and hiding her face in her lap, gave way to a violent burst of grief that seemed for a few moments as if it would rend soul and body in twain. For her passions were by nature very strong, and by education very imperfectly controlled; and time, "that rider that breaks youth," had not as yet tried his hand upon her. And Mrs. Montgomery, in spite of the fortitude and calmness to which she had steeled herself, bent down over her, and folding her arms about her, yielded to sorrow deeper still, and for a little while scarcely less violent in its expression than Ellen's own.

Alas! she had too good reason. She knew that the chance of her ever returning to shield the little creature who was nearest her heart from the future evils and snares of life was very, very small. She had at first absolutely refused to leave Ellen, when her husband proposed it: declaring that she would rather stay with her and die than take the chance of recovery at such a cost. But her physician assured her she could not live long without a change of climate; Captain Montgomery urged that it was better to submit to a temporary separation, than to cling obstinately to her child for a few months and then leave her for ever; said he must himself go speedily to France, and that now was her best opportunity; assuring her, however, that his circumstances would not permit him to take Ellen along, but that she would be secure of a happy home with his sister during her mother's absence; and to the pressure of argument Captain Montgomery added the weight of authority, insisting on her compliance. Conscience also asked Mrs. Montgomery whether she had a *right* to neglect any chance of life that was offered her; and at last she yielded to the combined influence of motives no one of which would have had power sufficient to move her, and, though with a secret consciousness it would be in vain, she consented to do as her friends wished. And it was for Ellen's sake she did it, after all.

Nothing but necessity had given her the courage to open the matter to her little daughter. She had foreseen and endeavored to prepare herself for Ellen's anguish; but nature was too strong for her, and they clasped each other in a convulsive embrace, while tears fell like rain.

It was some minutes before Mrs. Montgomery recollected herself, and then, though she struggled hard, she could not immediately regain her composure. But Ellen's deep sobs at length fairly alarmed her; she saw the necessity, for both their sakes, of putting a stop to this state of violent excitement; self-command was restored at once.

"Ellen! Ellen! listen to me," she said; "my child, this is not right. Remember, my darling, who it is that brings this sorrow upon us; though we *must* sorrow, we must not rebel."

Ellen sobbed more gently; but that and the mute pressure of her arms was her only answer.

"You will hurt both yourself and me, my daughter, if you cannot command yourself. Remember, dear Ellen, God sends no trouble upon his children but in love; and though we cannot see how, he will no doubt make all this work for our good."

"I know it, dear mother," sobbed Ellen, "but it's just as hard!"

Mrs. Montgomery's own heart answered so readily to the truth of Ellen's words that for the moment she could not speak.

"Try, my daughter," she said, after a pause,—"try to compose yourself. I am afraid you will make me worse, Ellen, if you cannot,—I am, indeed."

Ellen had plenty of faults, but amidst them all love to her mother was the strongest feeling her heart knew. It had power enough now to move her as nothing else could have done; and exerting all her self-command, of which she had sometimes a good deal, she *did* calm herself; ceased sobbing; wiped her eyes; arose from her crouching posture, and seating herself on the sofa by her mother, and laying her head on her bosom, she listened quietly to all the soothing words and cheering considerations with which Mrs. Montgomery endeavoured to lead her to take a more hopeful view of the subject. All she could urge, however, had but very partial success, though the conversation was prolonged far into the evening. Ellen said little, and did not weep any more; but in secret her heart refused consolation.

Long before this the servant had brought in the tea-things. Nobody regarded it at the time, but the little kettle hissing away on the fire now by chance attracted Ellen's attention, and she suddenly recollected her mother had had no tea. To make her mother's tea was Ellen's regular business. She treated it as a very grave affair, and loved it as one of the pleasantest in the course of the day. She used in the first place to make sure that the kettle really boiled; then she carefully poured some water into the teapot and rinsed it, both to make it clean and to make it hot; then she knew exactly how much tea to put into the tiny little tea-pot, which was just big enough to hold two cups of tea, and having poured a very little boiling water to it, she used to set it by the side of the fire while she made half a slice of toast. How careful Ellen was about that toast! The bread must not be cut too thick, nor too thin; the fire must, if possible, burn clear and bright, and she herself held the bread on a fork, just at the right distance from the coals to get nicely browned without burning. When this was done to her satisfaction (and if the first piece failed she would take another), she filled up the little tea-pot from the boiling kettle, and proceeded to make a cup of tea. She knew, and was very careful to put in, just the quantity of milk and sugar that her mother liked; and then she used to carry the tea and toast on a little tray to her mother's side, and very often held it there for her while she eat. All this Ellen did with the zeal that love gives, and though the same thing was to be gone over every night of the year, she was never wearied. It was a real pleasure; she had the greatest satisfaction in seeing that the little her mother could eat was prepared for her in the nicest possible manner; she knew her hands made it taste better; her mother often said so.

But this evening other thoughts had driven this important business quite out of poor Ellen's mind. Now, however, when her eyes fell upon the little kettle, she recollected her mother had not had her tea, and must want it very much ; and silently slipping off the sofa, she set about getting it as usual. There was no doubt this time whether the kettle boiled or no ; it had been hissing for an hour and more, calling as loud as it could to somebody to come and make the tea. So Ellen made it, and then began the toast. But she began to think, too, as she watched it, how few more times she would be able to do so,—how soon her pleasant tea-makings would be over,— and the desolate feeling of separation began to come upon her before the time. These thoughts were too much for poor Ellen ; the thick tears gathered so fast she could not see what she was doing ; and she had no more than just turned the slice of bread on the fork when the sickness of heart quite overcame her ; she could not go on. Toast and fork and all dropped from her hand into the ashes ; and rushing to her mother's side, who was now lying down again, and throwing herself upon her, she burst into another fit of sorrow ; not so violent as the former, but with a touch of hopelessness in it which went yet more to her mother's heart. Passion in the first said, " I cannot ;" despair now seemed to say, " I must."

But Mrs. Montgomery was too exhausted to either share or soothe Ellen's agitation. She lay in suffering silence ; till after some time she said, faintly, " Ellen, my love, I cannot bear this much longer."

Ellen was immediately brought to herself by these words. She arose, sorry and ashamed that she should have given occasion for them ; and tenderly kissing her mother, assured her most sincerely and resolutely that she would not do so again. In a few minutes she was calm enough to finish making the tea, and having toasted another piece of bread, she brought it to her mother. Mrs. Montgomery swallowed a cup of tea, but no toast could be eaten that night.

Both remained silent and quiet awhile after this, till the clock struck ten. " You had better go to bed, my daughter," said Mrs. Montgomery.

" I will, mamma."

" Do you think you can read me a little before you go ?"

" Yes, indeed, mamma ;" and Ellen brought the book. " Where shall I read ?"

" The twenty-third psalm."

Ellen began it, and went through it steadily and slowly, though her voice quavered a little.

" ' The Lord is my Shepherd ; I shall not want.

" ' He maketh me to lie down in green pastures : He leadeth me beside the still waters.

" ' He restoreth my soul : He leadeth me in the paths of right-eousness for his name's sake.

" ' Yea, though I walk through the valley of the shadow of

death, I will fear no evil: for Thou art with me; thy rod and thy staff they comfort me.

" 'Thou preparest a table before me in the presence of mine enemies: Thou anointest my head with oil; my cup runneth over.

" 'Surely goodness and mercy shall follow me all the days of my life: and I will dwell in the house of the Lord forever.' "

Long before she had finished, Ellen's eyes were full, and her heart too. " If I only could feel these words as mamma does!" she said to herself. She did not dare look up till the traces of tears had passed away; then she saw that her mother was asleep. Those first sweet words had fallen like balm upon the sore heart; and mind and body had instantly found rest together.

Ellen breathed the lightest possible kiss upon her forehead, and stole quietly out of the room to her own little bed.

CHAPTER II.

Not all the whispers that the soft winds utter
Speak earthly things—
There mingleth there, sometimes, a gentle flutter
Of angel's wings.

AMY LATHROP.

SORROW and excitement made Ellen's eyelids heavy, and she slept late on the following morning. The great dressing-bell waked her. She started up with a confused notion that something was the matter; there was a weight on her heart that was very strange to it. A moment was enough to bring it all back; and she threw herself again on her pillow, yielding helplessly to the grief she had twice been obliged to control the evening before. Yet love was stronger than grief still, and she was careful to allow no sound to escape her that could reach the ears of her mother, who slept in the next room. Her resolve was firm to grieve her no more with useless expressions of sorrow; to keep it to herself as much as possible. But this very thought that she must keep it to herself gave an edge to poor Ellen's grief, and the convulsive clasp of her little arms round the pillow plainly showed that it needed none.

The breakfast-bell again startled her, and she remembered she must not be too late down-stairs, or her mother might inquire and find out the reason. " I will *not* trouble mother—I will not—I will not," she resolved to herself as she got out of bed, though the tears fell faster as she said so. Dressing was sad work to Ellen to-day; it went on very heavily. Tears dropped into the water as she stooped her head to the basin; and she hid her face in the towel to cry, instead of making the ordinary use of it. But the usual duties were dragged through at last, and she went to the window. " I'll not go down till papa is gone," she thought; " he'll ask me what is the matter with my eyes."

Ellen opened the window. The rain was over; the lovely light of a fair September morning was beautifying everything it shone upon. Ellen had been accustomed to amuse herself a good deal at this window, though nothing was to be seen from it but an ugly city prospect of back walls of houses, with the yards belonging to them, and a bit of narrow street. But she had watched the people that showed themselves at the windows, and the children that played in the yards, and the women that went to the pumps, till she had become pretty well acquainted with the neighborhood ; and though they were for the most part dingy, dirty, and disagreeable,—women, children, houses, and all,—she certainly had taken a good deal of interest in their proceedings. It was all gone now. She could not bear to look at them ; she felt as if it made her sick ; and turning away her eyes, she lifted them to the bright sky above her head, and gazed into its clear depth of blue till she almost forgot that there was such a thing as a city in the world. Little white clouds were chasing across it, driven by the fresh wind that was blowing away Ellen's hair from her face, and cooling her hot cheeks. That wind could not have been long in coming from the place of woods and flowers, it was so sweet still. Ellen looked till, she didn't know why, she felt calmed and soothed,—as if somebody was saying to her, softly, " Cheer up, my child, cheer up ; things are not as bad as they might be ; things will be better." Her attention was attracted at length by voices below ; she looked down, and saw there, in one of the yards, a poor deformed child, whom she had often noticed before, and always with sorrowful interest. Besides his bodily infirmity, he had a further claim on her sympathy, in having lost his mother within a few months. Ellen's heart was easily touched this morning ; she felt for him very much. " Poor, poor little fellow !" she thought ; " he's a great deal worse off than I am. _His_ mother is dead ; mine is only going away for a few months—not forever ; oh, what a difference ! and then the joy of coming back again !" poor Ellen was weeping already at the thought—" and I will do, oh, how much ! while she is gone—I'll do more than she can possibly expect from me—I'll astonish her—I'll delight her—I'll work harder than ever I did in my life before, I'll mend all my faults, and give her so much pleasure ! But oh ! if she only needn't go away ! Oh, mamma !" Tears of mingled sweet and bitter were poured out fast, but the bitter had the largest share.

The breakfast-table was still standing, and her father gone, when Ellen went down-stairs. Mrs. Montgomery welcomed her with her usual quiet smile, and held out her hand. Ellen tried to smile in answer, but she was glad to hide her face in her mother's bosom ;

and the long, close embrace was too close and too long: it told of sorrow as well as love ; and tears fell from the eyes of each that the other did not see.

"Need I go to school to-day, mamma?" whispered Ellen.

"No ; I spoke to your father about that; you shall not go any more ; we will be together now while we can."

Ellen wanted to ask how long that would be, but could not make up her mind to it.

"Sit down, daughter, and take some breakfast."

"Have you done, mamma?"

"No ; I waited for you."

"Thank you, dear mamma," with another embrace ; "how good you are ; but I don't think I want any."

They drew their chairs to the table, but it was plain neither had much heart to eat; although Mrs. Montgomery with her own hands laid on Ellen's plate half of the little bird that had been broiled for her own breakfast. The half was too much for each of them.

"What made you so late this morning, daughter?"

"I got up late in the first place, mamma ; and then I was a long time at the window."

"At the window! were you examining into your neighbor's affairs as usual?" said Mrs. Mongomery, surprised that it should have been so.

"Oh, no, mamma, I didn't look at them at all,—except poor little Billy,—I was looking at the sky."

"And what did you see there that pleased you so much?"

"I don't know, mamma ; it looked so lovely and peaceful—that pure blue spread over my head, and the little white clouds flying across it—I loved to looked at it; it seemed to do me good."

"Could you look at it, Ellen, without thinking of Him who made it?"

"No, mamma," said Ellen, ceasing her breakfast, and now speaking with difficulty ; "I did think of Him ; perhaps that was the reason."

"And what did you think of Him, daughter?"

"I hoped, mamma—I felt—I thought—He would take care of me," said Ellen, bursting into tears, and throwing her arms again round her mother.

"He will, my dear daughter, He will, if you will only put your trust in Him, Ellen."

Ellen struggled hard to get back her composure, and after a few minutes succeeded.

"Mamma, will you tell me what you mean exactly by my ' putting my trust' in Him?"

"Don't you trust me, Ellen?"

"Certainly, mamma."

" How do you trust me ?—in what ?"

" Why, mamma,—in the first place I trust every word you say— entirely—I know nothing could be truer; if you were to tell me black is white, mamma, I should think my eyes had been mistaken. Then everything you tell or advise me to do, I know it is right, perfectly. And I always feel safe when you are near me, because I know you'll take care of me. And I am glad to think I belong to you, and you have the management of me entirely, and I needn't manage myself, because I know I can't; and if I could, I'd rather you would, mamma."

" My daughter, it is just so; it is *just* so: that I wish you to trust in God. He is truer, wiser, stronger, kinder, by far, than I am, even if I could always be with you; and what will you do when I am away from you?—and what would you do, my child, if I were to be parted from you forever?"

" Oh, mamma!" said Ellen, bursting into tears, and clasping her arms round her mother again,—" Oh, dear mamma, don't talk about it !"

Her mother fondly returned her caress, and one or two tears fell on Ellen's head as she did so, but that was all, and she said no more. Feeling severely the effects of the excitement and anxiety of the preceding day and night, she now stretched herself on the sofa and lay quite still. Ellen placed herself on a little bench at her side, with her back to the head of the sofa, that her mother might not see her face; and possessing herself of one of her hands, sat with her little head resting upon her mother, as quiet as she. They remained thus for two or three hours, without speaking; and Mrs. Montgomery was part of the time slumbering; but now and then a tear ran down the side of the sofa and dropped on the carpet where Ellen sat; and now and then her lips were softly pressed to the hand she held, as if they would grow there.

The doctor's entrance at last disturbed them. Doctor Green found his patient decidedly worse than he had reason to expect; and his sagacious eye had not passed back and forth many times between the mother and daughter before he saw how it was. He made no remark upon it, however, but continued for some moments a pleasant chatty conversation which he had begun with Mrs. Montgomery. He then called Ellen to him; he had rather taken a fancy to her.

" Well, Miss Ellen," he said, rubbing one of her hands in his; " what do you think of this fine scheme of mine?"

" What scheme, sir?"

" Why, this scheme of sending this sick lady over the water to get well; what do you think of it eh?"

" *Will* it make her quite well, do you think, sir?" asked Ellen, earnestly.

" 'Will it make her well !' to be sure it will; do you think I don't know better than to send people all the way across the ocean for nothing? Who do you think would want Dr. Green, if he sent people on wild-goose chases in that fashion?"

"Will she have to stay long there before she is cured, sir?" asked Ellen.

" Oh, that I can't tell ; that depends entirely on circumstances,— perhaps longer, perhaps shorter. But now, Miss Ellen, I've got a word of business to say to you ; you know you agreed to be my little nurse. Mrs. Nurse, this lady whom I put under your care the other day isn't quite as well as she ought to be this morning ; I'm afraid you haven't taken proper care of her ; she looks to me as if she had been too much excited. I've a notion she has been secretly taking half a bottle of wine, or reading some furious kind of a novel, or something of that sort, you understand? Now mind, Mrs. Nurse," said the doctor, changing his tone, " she *must not* be excited,—you must take care that she is not,—it isn't good for her. You mustn't let her talk much, or laugh much, or cry at all, on any account; she mustn't be worried in the least,—will you remember? Now you know what I shall expect of you ; you must be very careful—if that piece of toast of yours should chance to get burned, one of these fine evenings, I won't answer for the consequences. Good-by," said he, shaking Ellen's hand,—" you needn't look sober about it; all you have to do is to let your mamma be as much like an oyster as possible; you understand? Good-by." And Dr. Green took his leave.

" Poor woman !" said the doctor to himself as he went downstairs (he was a humane man). " I wonder if she'll live till she gets to the other side ! That's a nice little girl, too. Poor child! poor child !"

Both mother and daughter silently acknowledged the justice of the doctor's advice and determined to follow it. By common consent, as it seemed, each for several days avoided bringing the subject of sorrow to the other's mind ; though no doubt it was constantly present to both. It was not spoken of; indeed, little of any kind was spoken of, but that never. Mrs. Montgomery was doubtless employed during this interval in preparing for what she believed was before her ; endeavouring to resign herself and her child to Him in whose hands they were, and struggling to withdraw her affections from a world which she had a secret misgiving she was fast leaving. As for Ellen, the doctor's warning had served to strengthen the resolve she had already made, that she would not distress her mother with the sight of her sorrow ; and she kept it, as far as she could. She did not let her mother see but very few tears, and those were quiet ones ; though she dropped her head like a withered flower, and went about the house with an air of submissive sadness that tried her mother sorely. But when she was alone, and knew no one could see, sorrow had its way; and then there were sometimes agonies of grief that would almost have broken Mrs. Montgomery's resolution, had she known them.

This, however, could not last. Ellen was a child, and of most buoyant and elastic spirit naturally; it was not for one sorrow, however great, to utterly crush her. It would have taken years to do that. Moreover, she entertained not the slightest hope of being able by any means to alter her father's will. She regarded the dreaded evil as an inevitable thing. But though she was at first overwhelmed with sorrow, and for some days evidently pined under it sadly, hope at length *would* come back to her little heart; and no sooner in again, hope began to smooth the roughest, and soften the hardest, and touch the dark spots with light, in Ellen's future. The thoughts which had just passed through her head that first morning as she stood at her window, now came back again. Thoughts of wonderful improvement to be made during her mother's absence; of unheard-of efforts to learn and amend, which should all be crowned with success; and, above all, thoughts of that "coming home," when all these attainments and accomplishments should be displayed to her mother's delighted eyes, and her exertions receive their long-desired reward; they made Ellen's heart beat, and her eyes swim, and even brought a smile once more upon her lips. Mrs. Montgomery was rejoiced to see the change; she felt that as much time had already been given to sorrow as they could afford to lose, and she had not known exactly how to proceed. Ellen's amended looks and spirits greatly relieved her.

"What are you thinking about, Ellen?" said she, one morning. Ellen was sewing, and while busy at her work her mother had two or three times observed a light smile pass over her face. Ellen looked up, still smiling, and answered, "Oh, mamma, I was thinking of different things,—things that I mean to do while you are gone."

"And what are these things?" inquired her mother.

"Oh, mamma, it wouldn't do to tell you beforehand; I want to surprise you with them when you come back."

A slight shudder passed over Mrs. Montgomery's frame, but Ellen did not see it. Mrs. Montgomery was silent. Ellen presently introduced another subject.

"Mamma, what kind of a person is my aunt?"

"I do not know; I have never seen her."

"How has that happened, mamma?"

"Your aunt has always lived in a remote country town, and I have been very much confined to two or three cities, and your father's long and repeated absences made travelling impossible to me."

Ellen thought, but she didn't say it, that it was very odd her father should not sometimes, when he *was* in the country, have gone to see his relations, and taken her mother with him.

" What is my aunt's name, mamma ?"

" I think you must have heard that already, Ellen ; Fortune Emerson."

" Emerson ! I thought she was papa's sister !"

" So she is."

" Then how comes her name not to·be Montgomery ?"

" She is only his half-sister ; the daughter of his mother, not the daughter of his father."

" I am very sorry for that," said Ellen, gravely.

" Why, my daughter ?"

" I am afraid she will not be so likely to love me."

" You mustn't think so, my child. Her loving or not loving you will depend solely and entirely upon yourself, Ellen. Don't forget that. If you are a good child, and make it your daily care to do your duty, she cannot help liking you, be she what she may ; and on the other hand, if she have all the will in the world to love you, she cannot do it unless you will let her,—it all depends on your behaviour."

" Oh, mamma, I can't help wishing dear aunt Bessy was alive, and I was going to her."

Many a time the same wish had passed through Mrs. Montgomery's mind ! But she kept down her rising heart, and went on calmly.

" You must not expect, my child, to find anybody as indulgent as I am, or as ready to overlook and excuse your faults. It would be unreasonable to look for it ; and you must not think hardly of your aunt when you find she is not your mother ; but then it will be your own fault if she does not love you, in time, truly and tenderly. See that you render her all the respect and obedience you could render me ; that is your bounden duty ; she will stand in my place while she has the care of you,—remember that, Ellen ; and remember, too, that she will deserve more gratitude at your hands for showing you kindness than I do, because she cannot have the same feeling of love to make trouble easy."

" Oh, no, mamma," said Ellen, " I don't think so ; it's that very feeling of love that I am grateful for. I don't care a fig for anything people do for me without that."

" But you can make her love you, Ellen, if you try."

" Well, I'll try, mamma."

" And don't be discouraged. Perhaps you may be disappointed in first appearances, but never mind that ; have patience ; and let your motto be (if there's any occasion), overcome evil with good. Will you put that among the things you mean to do while I am gone ?" said Mrs. Montgomery, with a smile.

" I'll try, dear mamma."

" You will succeed if you try, dear, never fear; if you apply yourself in your trying to the old unfailing source of wisdom and strength ; to Him without whom you can do nothing."

There was silence for a little.

" What sort of a place is it where my aunt lives ?" asked Ellen.

" Your father says it is a very pleasant place ; he says the country is beautiful, and very healthy, and full of charming walks and rides. You have never lived in the country ; I think you will enjoy it very much."

" Then it is not in a town ?" said Ellen.

" No ; it is not a great way from the town of Thirlwall, but your aunt lives in the open country. Your father says she is a capital housekeeper, and that you will learn more and be in all respects a great deal happier and better off than you would be in a boarding-school here or anywhere."

Ellen's heart secretly questioned the truth of this last assertion very much.

" Is there any school near ?" she asked.

" Your father says there was an excellent one in Thirlwall when he was there."

" Mamma," said Ellen, " I think the greatest pleasure I shall have while you are gone will be writing to you. I have been think-ing of it a good deal. I mean to tell you everything,—absolutely everything, mamma. You know there will be nobody for me to talk to as I do to you ;" Ellen's word's came out with difficulty ; " and when I feel badly, I shall just shut myself up and write to you." She hid her face in her mother's lap.

" I count upon it, my dear daughter ; it will make quite as much the pleasure of my life, Ellen, as of yours."

" But then, mother," said Ellen, brushing away the tears from her eyes, " it will be so long before my letters can get to you ! The things I want you to know right away you won't know perhaps in a month."

" That's no matter, daughter ; they will just be as good when they do get to me. Never think of that ; write every day, and all manner of things that concern you,—just as particularly as if you were speaking to me."

" And you'll write to me too, mamma ?"

" Indeed I will, when I can. But, Ellen, you say that when I am away and cannot hear you, there will be nobody to supply my place. Perhaps it will be so, indeed ; but then, my daughter, let it make you seek that friend who is never far away, nor out of hearing. Draw nigh to God, and he will draw nigh to you. You know he has said of his children : ' Before they call, I will answer ; and while they are yet speaking, I will hear.' "

"But, mamma," said Ellen, her eyes filling instantly, "you know he is not my friend in the same way that he is yours." And hiding her face again, she added, "Oh, I wish he was!"

"You know the way to make him so, Ellen. *He* is willing, it only rests with you. Oh, my child, my child! if losing your mother might be the means of finding you that better friend, I should be quite willing—and glad to go—forever."

There was silence, only broken by Ellen's sobs. Mrs. Montgomery's voice had trembled, and her face was now covered with her hands; but she was not weeping; she was seeking a better relief where it had long been her habit to seek and find it. Both resumed their usual composure, and the employments which had been broken off, but neither chose to renew the conversation. Dinner, sleeping, and company prevented their having another opportunity during the rest of the day.

But when evening came, they were again left to themselves. Captain Montgomery was away, which indeed was the case most of the time; friends had taken their departure; the curtains were down, the lamp lit, the little room looked cosey and comfortable; the servant had brought the tea-things, and withdrawn, and the mother and daughter were happily alone. Mrs. Montgomery knew that such occasions were numbered, and fast drawing to an end, and she felt each one to be very precious. She now lay on her couch, with her face partially shaded, and her eyes fixed upon her little daughter, who was

now preparing the tea. She watched her, with thoughts and feelings not to be spoken, as the little figure went back and forward between the table and the fire ; and the light, shining full upon her busy face, showed that Ellen's whole soul was in her beloved duty. Tears would fall as she looked, and were not wiped away ; but when Ellen, having finished her work, brought with a satisfied face the little tray of tea and toast to her mother, there was no longer any sign of them left ; Mrs. Montgomery arose with her usual kind smile, to show her gratitude by honoring as far as possible what Ellen had provided."

" You have more appetite to-night, mamma."

" I am very glad, daughter," replied her mother, " to see that you have made up your mind to bear patiently this evil that has come upon us. I am glad for your sake, and I am glad for mine ; and I am glad too because we have a great deal to do and no time to lose in doing it."

" What have we so much to do, mamma ?" said Ellen.

" Oh, many things," said her mother ; " you will see. But now, Ellen, if there is anything you wish to talk to me about, any question you want to ask, anything you would like particularly to have, or to have done for you, I want you to tell it me as soon as possible, now while we can attend to it, for by and by perhaps we shall be hurried."

" Mamma," said Ellen, with brightening eyes, "there is one thing I have thought of that I should like to have ; shall I tell it you now ?"

" Yes."

" Mamma, you know I shall want to be writing a great deal ; wouldn't it be a good thing for me to have a little box with some pens in it, and an inkstand, and some paper and wafers ? Because, mamma, you know I shall be among strangers, at first, and I shan't feel like asking them for these things as often as I shall want them, and maybe they wouldn't want to let me have them if I did."

" I have thought of that already, daughter," said Mrs. Montgomery, with a smile and a sigh. " I will certainly take care that you are well provided in that respect before you go."

" How am I to go, mamma ?"

" What do you mean ?"

" I mean, who will go with me ? You know I can't go alone, mamma."

" No, my daughter, I'll not send you alone. But your father says it is impossible for *him* to take the journey at present, and it is yet more impossible for me. There is no help for it, daughter, but we must intrust you to the care of some friend going that way ; but He that holds the winds and waters in the hollow of his hand can take care of you without any of our help, and it is to his keeping, above all, that I shall commit you."

Ellen made no remark, and seemed much less surprised and

troubled than her mother had expected. In truth, the greater evil swallowed up the less. Parting from her mother, and for so long a time, it seemed to her comparatively a matter of little importance with whom she went, or how, or where. Except for this, the taking a long journey under a stranger's care would have been a dreadful thing to her.

"Do you know yet who it will be that I shall go with, mamma?"

"Not yet; but it will be necessary to take the first good opportunity, for I cannot go till I have seen you off; and it is thought very desirable that I should get to sea before the severe weather comes."

It was with a pang that these words were spoken, and heard, but neither showed it to the other.

"It has comforted me greatly, my dear child, that you have shown yourself so submissive and patient under this affliction. I should scarcely have been able to endure it if you had not exerted self-control. You have behaved beautifully."

This was almost too much for poor Ellen. It required her utmost stretch of self-control to keep within any bounds of composure; and for some moments her flushed cheek, quivering lip, and heaving bosom told what a tumult her mother's words had raised. Mrs. Montgomery saw she had gone too far, and, willing to give both Ellen and herself time to recover, she laid her head on the pillow again and closed her eyes. Many thoughts coming thick upon one another presently filled her mind, and half an hour had passed before she again recollected what she had meant to say. She opened her eyes; Ellen was sitting at a little distance, staring into the fire, evidently as deep in meditation as her mother had been.

"Ellen," said Mrs. Montgomery, "did you ever fancy what kind of a Bible you would like to have?"

"A Bible, mamma!" said Ellen, with sparkling eyes; "do you mean to give me a Bible?"

Mrs. Montgomery smiled.

"But, mamma," said Ellen, gently, "I thought you couldn't afford it?"

"I have said so, and truly," answered her mother; "and hitherto you have been able to use mine, but I will not leave you now without one. I will find ways and means," said Mrs. Montgomery, smiling again.

"Oh, mamma, thank you!" said Ellen, delighted; "how glad I shall be!" And after a pause of consideration, she added, "Mamma, I never thought much about what sort of a one I should like; couldn't I tell better if I were to see the different kinds in the store?"

"Perhaps so. Well, the first day that the weather is fine enough and I am well enough, I will go out with you and we will see about it."

" I am afraid Dr. Green won't let you, mamma."

" I shall not ask him. I want to get you a Bible, and some other things that I will not leave you without, and nobody can do it but myself. I shall go, if I possibly can."

" What other things, mamma ?" asked Ellen, very much interested in the subject.

" I don't think it will do to tell you to-night," said Mrs. Montgomery, smiling. " I foresee that you and I should be kept awake quite too late if we were to enter upon it just now. We will leave it till to-morrow. Now read to me, love, and then to bed."

Ellen obeyed ; and went to sleep with brighter visions dancing before her eyes than had been the case for some time.

CHAPTER III.

Sweetheart, we shall be rich ere we depart,
If fairings come thus plentifully in.—SHAKESPEARE.

ELLEN had to wait some time for the desired fine day. The equinoctial storms would have their way as usual, and Ellen thought they were longer than ever this year. But after many stormy days had tried her patience, there was at length a sudden change, both without and within doors. The clouds had done their work for that time, and fled away before a strong northerly wind, leaving the sky bright and fair. And Mrs. Montgomery's deceitful disease took a turn, and for a little space raised the hopes of her friends. All were rejoicing but two persons ; Mrs. Montgomery was not deceived, neither was the doctor. The shopping project was kept a profound secret from him and from everybody except Ellen.

Ellen watched now for a favourable day. Every morning as soon as she rose she went to the window to see what was the look of the weather ; and about a week after the change above noticed, she was greatly pleased one morning, on opening her window as usual, to find the air and sky promising all that could be desired. It was one of those beautiful days in the end of September, that sometimes herald October before it arrives,—cloudless, brilliant, and breathing balm. " This will do," said Ellen to herself, in great satisfaction. " I think this will do ; I hope mamma will think so."

Hastily dressing herself, and a good deal excited already, sne ran down-stairs ; and after the morning salutations, examined her mother's looks with as much anxiety as she had just done those of the weather. All was satisfactory there also, and Ellen ate her breakfast with an excellent appetite ; but she said not a word of the intended expedition till her father should be gone. She contented herself with strengthening her hopes by making constant fresh inspections of the weather and her mother's countenance alternately ; and her eyes, returning from the window on one of these excursions and meeting her mother's face, saw a smile there which said all she wanted. Breakfast went on more vigorously than ever. But after breakfast it seemed to Ellen that her father never would go away. He took the newspaper, an uncommon thing for him, and pored over it most perseveringly, while Ellen was in a perfect fidget of impatience. Her mother, seeing the state she was in, and taking pity on her, sent her up-stairs to do some little matters of business in her own room. These Ellen despatched with all possible zeal and speed ; and coming down again found her father gone and her mother alone. She flew to kiss her in the first place, and then make the inquiry, " Don't you think to-day will do, mamma ?"

" As fine as possible, daughter ; we could not have a better ; but I must wait till the doctor has been here."

" Mamma," said Ellen, after a pause, making a great effort of self-denial, " I am afraid you oughtn't to go out to get these things for me. Pray don't, mamma, if you think it will do you harm. I would rather go without them ; indeed I would."

" Never mind that, daughter," said Mrs. Montgomery, kissing her. " I am bent upon it ; it would be quite as much of a disappointment to me as to you not to go. We have a lovely day for it, and we will take our time and walk slowly, and we haven't far to go, either. But I must let Dr. Green make his visit first."

To fill up the time till he came, Mrs. Montgomery employed Ellen in reading to her as usual. And this morning's reading Ellen long after remembered. Her mother directed her to several passages in different parts of the Bible that speak of heaven and its enjoyments ; and though, when she began, her own little heart was full of excitement, in view of the day's plans, and beating with hope and pleasure, the sublime beauty of the words and thoughts, as she went on, awed her into quiet, and her mother's manner at length turned her attention entirely from herself. Mrs. Montgomery was lying on the sofa, and for the most part listened in silence, with her eyes closed, but sometimes saying a word or two that made Ellen feel how deep was the interest her mother had in the things she read of, and how pure and strong the pleasure she was even now taking in them ; and sometimes there was a smile on her face that Ellen scarce liked to see ; it gave her an indistinct feeling that her mother would not be long away from that heaven to which she seemed already to belong. Ellen had a sad consciousness, too, that she had no part with her mother in this matter. She could hardly go on. She came to that beautiful passage in the seventh of Revelation :

" And one of the elders answered, saying unto me, What are these which are arrayed in white robes? and whence came they? And I said unto him, Sir, thou knowest. And he said unto me, These are they which came out of great tribulation, and have washed their robes, and made them white in the blood of the Lamb. Therefore are they before the throne of God, and serve him day and night in his temple: and he that sitteth on the throne shall dwell among them. They shall hunger no more, neither thirst any more; neither shall the sun light on them, nor any heat. For the Lamb which is in the midst of the throne shall feed them, and shall lead them unto living fountains of waters: and God shall wipe away all tears from their eyes."

With difficulty, and a husky voice, Ellen got through it. Lifting then her eyes to her mother's face, she saw again the same singular sweet smile. Ellen felt that she could not read another word; to her great relief the door opened, and Dr. Green came in. His appearance changed the whole course of her thoughts. All that was grave or painful fled quickly away; Ellen's head was immediately full again of what had filled it before she began to read.

As soon as the doctor had retired and was fairly out of hearing, "Now, mamma, shall we go?" said Ellen. "You needn't stir, mamma; I'll bring all your things to you, and put them on; may I, mamma? then you won't be a bit tired before you set out."

Her mother assented; and with a great deal of tenderness and a great deal of eagerness, Ellen put on her stockings and shoes, arranged her hair, and did all that she could toward changing her dress and putting on her bonnet and shawl; and greatly delighted she was when the business was accomplished.

"Now, mamma, you look like yourself; I haven't seen you look so well this great while. I'm so glad you're going out again," said Ellen, putting her arms round her; "I do believe it will do you good. Now, mamma, I'll go and get ready; I'll be very quick about it; you shan't have to wait long for me."

In a few minutes the two set forth from the house. The day was as fine as could be; there was no wind, there was no dust; the sun was not oppressive; and Mrs. Montgomery did feel refreshed and strengthened during the few steps they had to take to their first stopping-place.

It was a jeweller's store. Ellen had never been in one before in her life, and her first feeling on entering was of dazzled wonderment at the glittering splendours around; this was presently forgotten in curiosity to know what her mother could possibly want there. She soon discovered that she had come to sell and not to buy. Mrs. Montgomery drew a ring from her finger, and after a little chaffering parted with it to the owner of the store for eighty dollars, being about three-quarters of its real value. The money was counted out, and she left the store.

"Mamma," said Ellen, in a low voice, "wasn't that grand-mamma's ring, which I thought you loved so much?"

"Yes, I did love it, Ellen, but I love you better."

"Oh, mamma, I am very sorry!" said Ellen.

"You need not be sorry, daughter. Jewels in themselves are the merest nothings to me; and as for the rest, it doesn't matter; I can remember my mother without any help from a trinket."

There were tears, however, in Mrs. Montgomery's eyes, that showed the sacrifice had cost her something; and there were tears in Ellen's that told it was not thrown away upon her.

"I am sorry you should know of this," continued Mrs. Montgomery; "you should not if I could have helped it. But set your heart quite at rest, Ellen; I assure you this use of my ring gives me more pleasure on the whole than any other I could have made of it."

A grateful squeeze of her hand and glance into her face was Ellen's answer.

Mrs. Montgomery had applied to her husband for the funds necessary to fit Ellen comfortably for the time they should be absent; and in answer he had given her a sum barely sufficient for her mere clothing. Mrs. Montgomery knew him better than to ask for a further supply, but she resolved to have recourse to other means to do what she had determined upon. Now that she was about to leave her little daughter, and it might be forever, she had set her heart upon providing her with certain things which she thought important to her comfort and improvement, and which Ellen would go very long without if *she* did not give them to her, and *now*, Ellen had had very few presents in her life, and those always of the simplest and cheapest kind; her mother resolved that in the midst of the bitterness of this time she would give her one pleasure, if she could; it might be the last.

They stopped next at a bookstore. "Oh, what a delicious smell of new books!" said Ellen, as they entered. "Mamma, if it wasn't for one thing, I should say I never was so happy in my life."

Children's books, lying in tempting confusion near the door, immediately fastened Ellen's eyes and attention. She opened one, and was already deep in the interest of it, when the word "*Bibles*" struck her ear. Mrs. Montgomery was desiring the shopman to show her various kinds and sizes that she might choose from among them. Down went Ellen's book, and she flew to the place, where a dozen different Bibles were presently displayed. Ellen's wits were ready to forsake her. Such beautiful Bibles she had never seen; she pored in ecstasy over their varieties of type and binding, and was very evidently in love with them all.

"Now, Ellen," said Mrs. Montgomery, "look and choose; take
your time, and see which you like best."

It was not likely that Ellen's "time" would be a short one.
Her mother, seeing this, took a chair at a little distance to await patiently
her decision; and while Ellen's eyes were riveted on the Bibles,
her own very naturally were fixed upon her. In the excitement and
eagerness of the moment, Ellen had thrown off her light bonnet,
and with flushed cheek and sparkling eye, and a brow grave with
unusual care, as though a nation's fate were deciding, she was weighing
the comparative advantages of large, small, and middle-sized;
black, blue, purple, and red; gilt and not gilt; clasp and no clasp.
Everything but the Bibles before her Ellen had forgotten utterly;
she was deep in what was to her the most important of business;
she did not see the bystanders smile; she did not know there were
any. To her mother's eye it was a most fair sight. Mrs. Montgomery
gazed with rising emotions of pleasure and pain that struggled
for the mastery, but pain at last got the better and rose very
high. "How can I give thee up!" was the one thought of her
heart. Unable to command herself, she rose and went to a distant
part of the counter, where she seemed to be examining books; but
tears, some of the bitterest she had ever shed, were falling thick
upon the dusty floor, and she felt her heart like to break. Her
little daughter at one end of the counter had forgotten there ever
was such a thing as sorrow in the world; and she at the other was
bowed beneath a weight of it that was nigh to crush her. But in
her extremity she betook herself to that refuge she had never
known to fail; it did not fail her now. She remembered the words
Ellen had been reading to her but that very morning, and they
came like the breath of heaven upon the fever of her soul. "Not
my will, but thine be done." She strove and prayed to say it, and
not in vain; and after a little while she was able to return to her
seat. She felt that she had been shaken by a tempest, but she was
calmer now than before.

Ellen was just as she had left her, and apparently just as far
from coming to any conclusion. Mrs. Montgomery was resolved
to let her take her way. Presently Ellen came over from the
counter with a large royal octavo Bible, heavy enough to be a good
lift for her. "Mamma," said she, laying it on her mother's lap
and opening it, "what do you think of that? isn't that splendid?"

"A most beautiful page, indeed; is this your choice, Ellen?"

"Well, mamma, I don't know; what do you think?"

"I think it is rather inconveniently large and heavy for every-
day use. It is quite a weight upon my lap. I shouldn't like to
carry it in my hands long. You would want a little table on purpose to hold it."

"Well, that wouldn't do at all," said Ellen, laughing; "I believe you are right, mamma; I wonder I didn't think of it. I might have known that myself."

She took it back; and there followed another careful examination of the whole stock; and then Ellen came to her mother with a beautiful miniature edition in two volumes, gilt and clasped, and very perfect in all respects, but of exceeding small print.

"I think I'll have this, mamma," said she; "isn't it a beauty? I could put it in my pocket, you know, and carry it anywhere with the greatest ease."

"It would have one great objection to me," said Mrs. Montgomery, "inasmuch as I cannot possibly see to read it."

"Cannot you, mamma! But I can read it perfectly."

"Well, my dear, take it; that is, if you will make up your mind to put on spectacles before your time."

"Spectacles, mamma! I hope I shall never wear spectacles."

"What do you propose to do when your sight fails, if you shall live so long?"

"Well, mamma,—if it comes to that,—but you don't advise me, then, to take this little beauty?"

"Judge for yourself; I think you are old enough."

"I know what you think, though, mamma, and I dare say you are right, too; I won't take it, though it's a pity. Well, I must look again."

Mrs. Montgomery came to her help, for it was plain Ellen had lost the power of judging amidst so many tempting objects. But she presently simplified the matter by putting aside all that were decidedly too large, or too small, or of too fine print. There remained three, of moderate size and sufficiently large type, but different binding. "Either of these I think will answer your purpose nicely," said Mrs. Montgomery.

"Then, mamma, if you please, I will have the red one. I like that best, because it will put me in mind of yours."

Mrs. Montgomery could find no fault with this reason. She paid for the red Bible, and directed it to be sent home. "Shan't I carry it, mamma?" said Ellen.

"No, you would find it in the way; we have several things to do yet."

"Have we, mamma? I thought we only came to get a Bible."

"That is enough for one day, I confess; I am a little afraid your head will be turned; but I must run the risk of it. I dare not lose the opportunity of this fine weather; I may not have such another. I wish to have the comfort of thinking, when I am away, that I have left you with everything necessary to the keeping up of good habits,—everything that will make them pleasant and easy. I wish you to be always neat, and tidy, and industrious; depending upon others as little as possible; and careful to improve yourself by every means, and especially by writing to me. I will leave you no excuse, Ellen, for failing in any of these duties. I trust you will not disappoint me in a single particular.''

Ellen's heart was too full to speak; she again looked up tearfully and pressed her mother's hand.

"I do not expect to be disappointed, love," returned Mrs. Montgomery.

They now entered a large fancy store. "What are we to get here, mamma?" said Ellen.

"A box to put your pens and paper in," said her mother, smiling.

"Oh, to be sure," said Ellen; "I had almost forgotten that." She quite forgot it a minute after. It was the first time she had ever seen the inside of such a store; and the articles displayed on every side completely bewitched her. From one thing to another she went, admiring and wondering; in her wildest dreams she had never imagined such beautiful things. The store was fairy-land.

Mrs. Montgomery meanwhile attended to business. Having chosen a neat little japanned dressing-box, perfectly plain, but well supplied with everything a child could want in that line, she called Ellen from the delightful journey of discovery she was making round the store, and asked her what she thought of it. "I think it's a little beauty," said Ellen; but I never saw such a place for beautiful things.''

"You think it will do, then?" said her mother.

"For me, mamma! You don't mean to give it to me? Oh, mother, how good you are! But I know what is the best way to thank you, and I'll do it. What a perfect little beauty! Mamma, I'm too happy.''

"I hope not," said her mother, "for you know I haven't got you the box for your pens and paper yet.''

"Well, mamma, I'll try and bear it," said Ellen, laughing. "But do get me the plainest little thing in the world, for you're giving me too much.''

Mrs. Montgomery asked to look at writing-desks, and was shown to another part of the store for the purpose. "Mamma," said Ellen, in a low tone, as they went, "you're not going to get me a writing-desk?''

"Why, that is the best kind of box for holding writing materials," said her mother, smiling; "don't you think so?''

"I don't know what to say!" exclaimed Ellen. "I can't thank you, mamma; I haven't any words to do it. I think I shall go crazy.''

She was truly overcome with the weight of happiness. Words failed her, and tears came instead.

From among a great many desks of all descriptions, Mrs. Montgomery with some difficulty succeeded in choosing one to her mind.

It was of mahogany, not very large, but thoroughly well made and finished, and very convenient and perfect in its internal arrangements. Ellen was speechless; occasional looks at her mother, and deep sighs, were all she had now to offer. The desk was quite empty. "Ellen," said her mother, "do you remember the furniture of Miss Allen's desk, that you were so pleased with a while ago."

"Perfectly, mamma ; I know all that was in it."

"Well, then, you must prompt me if I forget anything. Your desk will be furnished with every thing really useful. Merely showy matters we can dispense with. Now, let us see.—Here is a great empty place that I think wants some paper to fill it. Show me some of different sizes, if you please."

The shopman obeyed, and Mrs. Montgomery stocked the desk well with letter paper, large and small. Ellen looked on in great satisfaction. "That will do nicely," she said ;—"that large paper will be beautiful whenever I am writing to you, mamma, you know, and the other will do for other times when I haven't so much to say ; though I am sure I don't know who there is in the world I should ever send letters to except you."

"If there is nobody now, perhaps there will be at some future time," replied her mother. "I hope I shall not always be your only correspondent. Now what next?"

"Envelopes, mamma?"

"To be sure ; I had forgotten them. Envelopes of both sizes to match."

"Because, mamma, you know I might, and I certainly shall, want to write upon the fourth page of my letter, and I couldn't do it unless I had envelopes."

A sufficient stock of envelopes was laid in.

"Mamma," said Ellen, "what do you think of a little note-paper?"

"Who are the notes to be written to, Ellen?" said Mrs. Montgomery, smiling.

"You needn't smile, mamma; you know, as you said, if I don't now know, perhaps I shall by and by. Miss Allen's desk had note-paper; that made me think of it."

"So shall yours, daughter ; while we are about it we will do the thing well. And your note-paper will keep quite safely in this nice little place provided for it, even if you should not want to use a sheet of it in half a dozen years."

"How nice that is !" said Ellen, admiringly.

"I suppose the note-paper must have envelopes too," said Mrs. Montgomery.

"To be sure, mamma; I suppose so," said Ellen, smiling; "Miss Allen's had."

" Well now we have got all the paper we want, I think," said
Mrs. Montgomery ; " the next thing is ink,—or an inkstand rather."
Different kinds were presented for her choice.

" Oh, mamma, that one won't do," said Ellen, anxiously ; " you
know the desk will be knocking about in a trunk, and the ink
would run out, and spoil every thing. It should be one of those that
shut tight. I don't see the right kind here."

The shopman brought one.

" There, mamma, do you see ?" said Ellen ; " it shuts with a
spring, and nothing can possibly come out ; do you see, mamma ?
You can turn it topsy turvy."

" I see you are quite right, daughter ; it seems I should get on
very ill without you to advise me. Fill the inkstand, if you
please."

" Mamma, what shall I do when my ink is gone ? that inkstand
will hold but a little, you know."

" Your aunt will supply you, of course, my dear, when you are out."

" I'd rather take some of my own by half," said Ellen.

" You could not carry a bottle of ink in your desk without great
danger to every thing else in it. It would not do to venture."

" We have excellent ink-powder," said the shopman, " in small
packages, which can be very conveniently carried about. You see,
ma'am, there is a compartment in the desk for such things ; and
the ink is very easily made at any time."

" Oh, that will do nicely," said Ellen, " that is just the thing."

" Now what is to go in this other square place opposite the inkstand ?" said Mrs. Montgomery.

" That is the place for the box of lights, mamma."

" What sort of lights ?"

" For sealing letters, mamma, you know. They are not like your
wax taper at all ; they are little wax matches, that burn just long
enough to seal one or two letters ; Miss Allen showed me how she
used them. Hers were in a nice little box just like the inkstand
on the outside ; and there was a place to light the matches, and a
place to set them in while they are burning. There, mamma, that's
it," said Ellen, as the shopman brought forth the article which she
was describing, " that's it, exactly ; and that will just fit. Now,
mamma, for the wax."

" You want to seal your letter before you have written it," said
Mrs. Montgomery,—" we have not got the pens yet."

" That's true, mamma ; let us have the pens. And some quills
too, mamma ?"

" Do you know how to make a pen, Ellen ?"

" No, mamma, not yet ; but I want to learn very much. Miss
Pichegru says that every lady ought to know how to make her own
pens."

"Miss Pichegru is very right; but I think you are rather too young to learn. However, we will try. Now here are steel points enough to last you a great while,—and as many quills as it is needful you should cut up for one year at least;—we haven't a penhandle yet."

"Here, mamma," said Ellen, holding out a plain ivory one,— "don't you like this? I think that it is prettier than these that are all cut and fussed, or those other gay ones either."

"I think so too, Ellen; the plainer the prettier. Now what comes next?"

"The knife, mamma, to make the pens," said Ellen, smiling.

"True, the knife. Let us see some of your best pen-knives. Now, Ellen, choose. That one won't do, my dear; it should have two blades,—a large as well as a small one. You know you want to mend a pencil sometimes."

"So I do, mamma, to be sure, you're very right; here's a nice one. Now, mamma, the wax."

"There is a box full; choose your own colours." Seeing it was likely to be a work of time, Mrs. Montgomery walked away to another part of the store. When she returned Ellen had made up an assortment of the oddest colours she could find.

"I won't have any red, mamma, it is so common," she said.

"I think it is the prettiest of all," said Mrs. Montgomery.

"Do you, mamma? then I will have a stick of red on purpose to seal to you with."

"And who do you intend shall have the benefit of the other colours?" inquired her mother.

"I declare, mamma," said Ellen, laughing; "I never thought of that; I am afraid they will have to go to you. You must not mind, mamma, if you get green and blue and yellow seals once in a while."

"I dare say I shall submit myself to it with a good grace," said Mrs. Montgomery. "But come, my dear, have we got all that we want? This desk has been very long in furnishing."

"You haven't given me a seal yet, mamma."

"Seals! There are a variety before you; see if you can find one that you like. By the way, you cannot seal a letter, can you?"

"Not yet, mamma," said Ellen, smiling again; "that is another of the things I have got to learn."

"Then I think you had better have some wafers in the mean time."

While Ellen was picking out her seal, which took not a little time, Mrs. Montgomery laid in a good supply of wafers of all sorts; and then went on further to furnish the desk with an ivory leaf-cutter, a paper-folder, a pounce-box, a ruler, and a neat little silver pencil; also, some drawing-pencils, India-rubber, and sheets of drawing-paper. She took a sad pleasure in adding every thing she could think of that might be for Ellen's future use or advantage; but as with her own hands she placed in the desk one thing after another, the thought crossed her mind how Ellen would make drawings with those very pencils, on those very sheets of paper, which her eyes would never see! She turned away with a sigh, and receiving Ellen's seal from her hand, put that also in its place. Ellen had chosen one with her own name.

"Will you send these things *at once?*" said Mrs. Montgomery. "I particularly wish them at home as early in the day as possible." The man promised. Mrs. Montgomery paid the bill, and she and Ellen left the store.

They walked a little way in silence.

"I cannot thank you, mamma," said Ellen.

"It is not necessary, my dear child," said Mrs. Montgomery, returning the pressure of her hand; "I know all that you would say."

There was as much sorrow as joy at that moment in the heart of the joyfullest of the two.

"Where are we going now, mamma?" said Ellen again, after a while.

"I wished and intended to have gone to St. Clair and Fleury's, to get you some merino and other things; but we have been detained so long already that I think I had better go home. I feel somewhat tired."

"I am very sorry, dear mamma," said Ellen; I am afraid I kept you too long about that desk."

"You did not keep me, daughter, any longer than I chose to be kept. But I think I will go home now, and take the chance of another fine day for the merino."

CHAPTER IV.

How can I live without thee: how forego
Thy sweet converse, and love so dearly joined.—MILTON.

WHEN dinner was over and the table cleared away, the mother and daughter were left, as they always loved to be, alone. It was late in the afternoon and already somewhat dark, for clouds had gathered over the beautiful sky of the morning, and the wind, rising now and then, made its voice heard. Mrs. Montgomery was lying on the sofa, as usual, seemingly at ease; and Ellen was sitting on a little bench before the fire, very much at *her* ease, indeed, without any seeming about it. She smiled as she met her mother's eyes.

" You have made me very happy to-day, mamma."

" I am glad of it, my dear child. I hoped I should. I believe the whole affair has given me as much pleasure, Ellen, as it has you."

There was a pause.

" Mamma, I will take the greatest possible care of my new treasures."

" I know you will. If I had doubted it, Ellen, most assuredly I should not have given them to you, sorry as I should have been to leave you without them. So you see you have not established a character for carefulness in vain."

" And, mamma, I hope you have not given them to me in vain, either. I will try to use them in the way that I know you wish me to; that will be the best way I can thank you."

" Well, I have left you no excuse, Ellen. You know fully what I wish you to do and to be; and when I am away I shall please myself with thinking that my little daughter *is* following her mother's wishes; I shall believe so, Ellen. You will not let me be disappointed ?"

" Oh, no, mamma, " said Ellen, who was now in her mother's arms.

" Well, my child," said Mrs. Montgomery, in a lighter tone, " my gifts will serve as reminders for you if you are ever tempted to forget my lessons. If you fail to send me letters, or if those you send are not what they ought to be, I think the desk will cry shame upon you. And if you ever go an hour with a hole in your stocking, or a tear in your dress, or a string off your petticoat, I hope the sight of your work-box will make you blush."

" Work-box, mamma ?"

" Yes. Oh, I forgot; you've not seen that."

" No, mamma; what do you mean ?"

" Why, my dear, that was one of the things you most wanted, but I thought it best not to overwhelm you quite this morning; so while you were on an exploring expedition round the store I chose and furnished one for you."

" Oh, mamma, mamma !" said Ellen, getting up and clasping her hands; "what shall I do ? I don't know what to say; I can't say anything. Mamma, it's too much."

So it seemed, for Ellen sat down and began to cry. Her mother silently reached out a hand to her, which she squeezed and kissed with all the energy of gratitude, love, and sorrow; till gently drawn by the same hand she was placed again in her mother's arms and upon her bosom. And in that tried resting-place she lay, calmed and quieted, till the shades of afternoon deepened into evening, and evening into night, and the light of the fire was all that was left to them.

Though not a word had been spoken for a long time Ellen was not asleep; her eyes were fixed on the red glow of the coals in the grate, and she was busily thinking, but not of them. Many sober thoughts were passing through her little head, and stirring her heart; a few were of her new possessions and bright projects,— more of her mother. She was thinking how very, very precious was the heart she could feel beating where her cheek lay—she thought it was greater happiness to lie there than any thing else in life could be—she thought she had rather even die so, on her mother's breast, than live long without her in the world—she felt that in earth or in heaven there was nothing so dear. Suddenly she broke the silence.

"Mamma, what does that mean, ' He that loveth father or mother more than me, is not worthy of me?' "

"It means just what it says. If you love anybody or anything better than Jesus Christ, you cannot be one of his children."

" But then, mamma," said Ellen, raising her head; how *can* I be one of his children? I do love you a great deal better; how can I help it, mamma?"

" You cannot help it, I know, my dear," said Mrs. Montgomery, with a sigh, " except by His grace who has promised to change the hearts of his people—to take away the heart of stone and give them a heart of flesh."

" But is mine a heart of stone, then, mamma, because I cannot help loving you best?"

" Not to me, dear Ellen," replied Mrs. Montgomery, pressing closer the little form that lay in her arms; " I have never found it so. But yet I know that the Lord Jesus is far, far more worthy of your affection than I am, and if your heart were not hardened by sin you would see him so; it is only because you do not know him that you love me better. Pray, pray, my dear child, that he would take away the power of sin, and show you himself; that is all that is wanting."

" I will, mamma," said Ellen, tearfully. " Oh, mamma, what shall I do without you?"

Alas, Mrs. Montgomery's heart echoed the question; she had no answer.

" Mamma," said Ellen, after a few minutes, " can I have no true love to him at all unless I love him *best?*"

" I dare not say that you can," answered her mother, seriously.

" Mamma," said Ellen, after a little, again raising her head and looking her mother full in the face, as if willing to apply the severest test to this hard doctrine, and speaking with an indescribable expression, " do *you* love him *better than you do me?*"

She knew her mother loved the Saviour, but she thought it scarcely possible that herself could have but the second place in her heart; she ventured a bold question to prove whether her mother's practice would not contradict her theory.

But Mrs. Montgomery answered steadily, "I do, my daughter;" and with a gush of tears Ellen sunk her head again upon her bosom. She had no more to say; her mouth was stopped for ever as to the *right* of the matter, though she still thought it an impossible duty in her own particular case.

"I do indeed, my daughter," repeated Mrs. Montgomery; "that does not make my love to you the less, but the more, Ellen."

"Oh, mamma, mamma," said Ellen, clinging to her, "I wish you would teach me! I have only you, and I am going to lose you. What shall I do, mamma?"

With a voice that strove to be calm Mrs. Montgomery answered, "'I love them that love me, and they that seek me early shall find me.'" And after a minute or two she added, "He who says this, has promised too that he will 'gather the lambs with his arm, and carry them in his bosom.'"

The words fell soothingly on Ellen's ear, and the slight tremor in the voice reminded her also that her mother must not be agitated. She checked herself instantly, and soon lay as before, quiet and still on her mother's bosom, with her eyes fixed on the fire; and Mrs. Montgomery did not know that when she now and then pressed a kiss upon the forehead that lay so near her lips, it every time brought the water to Ellen's eyes and a throb to her heart. But after some half or three-quarters of an hour had passed away, a sudden knock at the door found both mother and daughter asleep; it had to be repeated once or twice before the knocker could gain attention.

"What is that, mamma?" said Ellen, starting up.

"Somebody at the door. Open it quickly, love."

Ellen did so, and found a man standing there, with his arms rather full of sundry packages.

"Oh, mamma, my things!" cried Ellen, clapping her hands; "here they are!"

The man placed his burden on the table, and withdrew.

"Oh, mamma, I am so glad they are come! Now if I only had a light—this is my desk, I know, for it's the largest; and I think this is my dressing-box, as well as I can tell by feeling—yes, it is, here's the handle on top; and this is my dear work-box—not so big as the desk, nor so little as the dressing-box. Oh, mamma, mayn't I ring for a light?"

There was no need, for a servant just then entered, bringing the wished-for candles and the not-wished-for *tea.* Ellen was capering about in the most fantastic style, but suddenly stopped short at sight of the tea-things, and looked very grave. "Well, mamma, I'll tell you what I'll do," she said after a pause of consideration; "I'll make the tea the first thing, before I untie a single knot; won't that be best, mamma? Because I know if I once begin to look, I shan't want to stop. Don't you think that is wise, mamma?"

But alas! the fire had got very low; there was no making the tea quickly; and the toast was a work of time. And when all was over at length, it was then too late for Ellen to begin to undo packages. She struggled with impatience a minute or two, and then gave up the point very gracefully, and went to bed.

She had a fine opportunity the next day to make up for the evening's disappointment. It was cloudy and stormy; going out was not to be thought of, and it was very unlikely that any body would come in. Ellen joyfully allotted the whole morning to the examination and trial of her new possessions; and as soon as breakfast was over and the room clear she set about it. She first went through the desk and every thing in it, making a running commentary on the excellence, fitness, and beauty of all it contained; then the dressing-box received a share, but a much smaller share, of attention; and lastly, with fingers trembling with eagerness she untied the packthread that was wound round the work-box, and slowly took off cover after cover; she almost screamed when the last was removed. The box was of satin-wood, beautifully finished, and lined with crimson silk; and Mrs. Montgomery had taken good care it should want nothing that Ellen might need to keep her clothes in perfect order.

"Oh, mamma, how beautiful! Oh, mamma, how good you are! Mamma, I promise you I'll never be a slattern. Here is more cotton than I can use up in a great while—every number, I do think; and needles, oh, the needles! what a parcel of them! and, mamma! what a lovely scissors! did you choose it, mamma, or did it belong to the box?"

"I chose it."

"I might have guessed it, mamma, it's just like you. And here's a thimble—fits me exactly; and an emery-bag! how pretty! —and a bodkin! this is a great deal nicer than yours, mamma— yours is decidedly the worse for wear;—and what's this?—Oh, to make eyelet holes with, I know. And oh, mamma! here is almost every thing, I think—here are tapes, and buttons, and hooks and eyes, and darning cotton, and silk-winders, and pins, and all sorts of things. What's this for, mamma?"

"That's a scissors to cut button-holes with. Try it on that piece of paper that lies by you, and you will see how it works."

"Oh, I see!" said Ellen, "how very nice that is. Well, I shall take great pains now to make my button-holes very handsomely."

One survey of her riches could by no means satisfy Ellen. For some time she pleased herself with going over and over the contents of the box, finding each time something new to like. At length she closed it, and keeping it still in her lap, sat awhile looking thoughtfully into the fire; till turning toward her mother she met her gaze, fixed mourntully, almost tearfully, on herself. The box was instantly shoved aside, and getting up and bursting into tears, Ellen went to her. "Oh, dear mother," she said, "I wish they were all back in the store, if I could only keep you!"

Mrs. Montgomery answered only by folding her to her heart.

"Is there no help for it, mamma?"

"There is none.—We know that all things shall work together for good to them that love God."

"Then it will be all good for you, mamma, but what will it be for me?" And Ellen sobbed bitterly.

"It will be all well, my precious child, I doubt not. I do not doubt it, Ellen. Do *you* not doubt it either, love; but from the hand that wounds, seek the healing. He wounds that he *may* heal. He does not afflict willingly. Perhaps he sees, Ellen, that you never would seek him while you had me to cling to."

Ellen clung to her at that moment! yet not more than her mother clung to her.

"How happy we were, mamma, only a year ago,—even a month."

"We have no continuing city here," answered her mother, with a sigh. "But there is a home, Ellen, where changes do not come; and they that are once gathered there are parted no more for ever; and all tears are wiped from their eyes. I believe I am going fast to that home; and now my greatest concern is, that my little Ellen —my precious baby—may follow me and come there too."

No more was said, nor could be said, till the sound of the doctor's steps upon the stair obliged each of them to assume an appearance of composure as speedily as possible. But they could not succeed perfectly enough to blind him. He did not seem very well satisfied, and told Ellen he believed he should have to get another nurse,—he was afraid she didn't obey orders.

While the doctor was there Ellen's Bible was brought in; and no sooner was he gone than it underwent as thorough an examination as the boxes had received. Ellen went over every part of it with the same great care and satisfaction; but mixed with a different feeling. The words that caught her eye as she turned over the leaves seemed to echo what her mother had been saying to her. It began to grow dear already. After a little she rose and brought it to the sofa.

"Are you satisfied with it, Ellen?"

"Oh, yes, mamma; it is perfectly beautiful, outside and inside. Now, mamma, will you please to write my name in this precious book—my name, and any thing else you please, mother. I'll

bring you my new pen to write it with, and I've got ink here;—
shall I?"

She brought it; and Mrs. Montgomery wrote Ellen's name, and
the date of the gift. The pen played a moment in her fingers,
and then she wrote below the date:

"'I love them that love me; and they that seek me early shall
find me.'"

This was for Ellen; but the next words were not for her; what
made her write them?—

"'I will be a God to thee, and to thy seed after thee.'"

They were written almost unconsciously, and as if bowed by an

unseen force Mrs. Montgomery's head sank upon the open page;
and her whole soul went up with her petition:

"Let these words be my memorial, that I have trusted in thee.
And oh, when these miserable lips are silent for ever, remember
the word unto thy servant, upon which thou hast caused me to
hope; and be unto my little one all thou hast been to me. Unto
thee lift I up mine eyes, O thou that dwellest in the heavens!"

She raised her face from the book, closed it, and gave it silently
to Ellen. Ellen had noticed her action, but had no suspicion of
the cause; she supposed that one of her mother's frequent feelings
of weakness or sickness had made her lean her head upon the
Bible, and she thought no more about it. However, Ellen felt
that she wanted no more of her boxes that day. She took her
old place by the side of her mother's sofa, with her head upon her
mother's hand, and an expression of quiet sorrow in her face that
it had not worn for several days.

CHAPTER V.

My child is yet a stranger in the world,
She hath not seen the change of fourteen years.
SHAKSPEARE.

THE next day would not do for the intended shopping; nor the next. The third day was fine, though cool and windy.

" Do you think you can venture out to-day, mamma?" said Ellen.

" I am afraid not. I do not feel quite equal to it; and the wind is a great deal too high for me besides."

" Well," said Ellen, in the tone of one who is making up her mind to something, " we shall have a fine day by and by, I suppose, if we wait long enough; we had to wait a great while for our first shopping day. I wish such another would come round."

" But the misfortune is," said her mother, " that we cannot afford to wait. November will soon be here, and your clothes may be suddenly wanted before they are ready, if we do not bestir ourselves. And Miss Rice is coming in a few days—I ought to have the merino ready for her."

" What will you do, mamma?"

" I do not know, indeed, Ellen; I am greatly at a loss."

" Couldn't papa get the stuffs for you, mamma?"

" No, he's too busy; and besides, he knows nothing at all about shopping for me; he would be sure to bring me exactly what I do not want. I tried that once."

" Well, what will you do, mamma? Is there nobody else you could ask to get the things for you? Mrs. Foster would do it, mamma!"

" I know she would, and I should ask her without any difficulty, but she is confined to her room with a cold. I see nothing for it but to be patient and let things take their course, though if a favorable opportunity should offer, you would have to go, clothes or no clothes; it would not do to lose the chance of a good escort."

And Mrs. Montgomery's face showed that this possibility, of Ellen's going unprovided, gave her some uneasiness. Ellen observed it.

" Never mind me, dearest mother; don't be in the least worried about my clothes. You don't know how little I think of them or care for them. It's no matter at all whether I have them or not."

Mrs. Montgomery smiled, and passed her hand fondly over her little daughter's head, but presently resumed her anxious look out of the window.

" Mamma!" exclaimed Ellen, suddenly starting up, " a bright thought has just come into my head! *I'll* do it for you, mamma!"

" Do what?"

" I'll get the merino and things for you, mamma. You needn't smile,—I will, indeed, if you will let me."

" My dear Ellen," said her mother, " I don't doubt you would if goodwill only were wanting ; but a great deal of skill and experience is necessary for a shopper, and what would you do without either?"

" But see, mamma," pursued Ellen, eagerly, " I'll tell you how I'll manage, and I know I can manage very well. You tell me exactly what coloured merino you want, and give me a little piece to show me how fine it should be, and tell me what price you wish to give, and then I'll go to the store and ask them to show me different pieces, you know, and if I see any I think you would like, I'll ask them to give me a little bit of it to show you ; and then I'll bring it home, and if you like it you can give me the money, and tell me how many yards you want, and I can go back to the store and get it. Why can't I, mamma?"

" Perhaps you could ; but my dear child I am afraid you wouldn't like the business."

" Yes I should ; indeed, mamma, I should like it dearly if I could help you so. Will you let me try, mamma?"

" I don't like, my child, to venture you alone on such an errand, among crowds of people ; I should be uneasy about you."

" Dear mamma, what would the crowds of people do to me ? I am not a bit afraid. You know, mamma, I have often taken walks alone,—that's nothing new ; and what harm should come to me while I am in the store ? You needn't be the least uneasy about me ;—may I go ?"

Mrs. Montgomery smiled, but was silent.

" May I go, mamma?" repeated Ellen. " Let me go at least and try what I can do. What do you say, mamma?"

" I don't know what to say, my daughter, but I am in difficulty on either hand. I will let you go and see what you can do. It would be a great relief to me to get this merino by any means."

" Then shall I go right away, mamma?"

" As well now as ever. *You* are not afraid of the wind?"

" I should think not," said Ellen ; and away she scampered up stairs to get ready. With eager haste she dressed herself; then with great care and particularity took her mother's instructions as to the article wanted ; and finally set out, sensible that a great trust was reposed in her, and feeling busy and important accordingly. But at the very bottom of Ellen's heart there was a little secret doubtfulness respecting her undertaking. She hardly knew it was there, but then she couldn't tell what it was that **made her** fingers so inclined to be tremulous while she was dressing, and that made her heart beat quicker than it ought, or than was pleasant, and one of her cheeks so much hotter than the other. However, she set forth upon her errand with a very brisk step, which she kept up till on turning a corner she came in sight of the place she was going to. Without thinking much about it, Ellen had directed her steps to St. Clair and Fleury's. It was one of the largest and best stores in the city, and the one she knew where her mother generally made her purchases ; and it did not occur to her that it might not be the best for her purpose on this occasion. But her steps slackened as soon as she came in sight of it, and continued to slacken as she drew nearer, and she went up the broad flight of marble steps in front of the store very slowly indeed, though they were exceeding low and easy. Pleasure was not certainly the uppermost feeling in her mind now ; yet she never thought of turning back. She knew that if she could succeed in the object of her mission her mother would be relieved from some anxiety ; that was enough ; she was bent on accomplishing it.

Timidly she entered the large hall of entrance. It was full of people, and the buzz of business was heard on all sides. Ellen had for some time past seldom gone a shopping with her mother, and had never been in this store but once or twice before. She had not the remotest idea where, or in what apartment of the building, the merino counter was situated, and she could see no one to speak to. She stood irresolute in the middle of the floor. Every body seemed to be busily engaged with somebody else ; and whenever an opening on one side or another appeared to promise her an opportunity, it was sure to be filled up before she could reach it, and disappointed and abashed she would return to her old station in the middle of the floor. Clerks frequently passed her, crossing the store in all directions, but they were always bustling along in a great hurry of business ; they did not seem to notice her at all, and were gone before poor Ellen could get her mouth open to speak to them. She knew well enough now, poor child, what it was that made her cheeks burn as they did, and her heart beat as if it would burst its bounds. She felt confused, and almost confounded, by the incessant hum of voices, and moving crowd of strange people all around her, while her little figure stood alone and unnoticed in the midst of them ; and there seemed no prospect that she would be able to gain the ear or the eye of a single person. Once she determined to accost a man she saw advancing toward her from a distance, and actually made up to him for the purpose, but with a hurried bow, and " I beg your pardon, miss !" he brushed past. Ellen almost burst into tears. She longed to turn and run out of the store, but a faint hope remaining, and an unwillingness to give up her undertaking, kept her fast. At length one of the clerks in the desk observed her, and remarked to Mr. St. Clair who stood by, " There is a little girl, sir, who seems to be looking for something, or waiting for somebody; she has been standing there a good while." Mr. St. Clair, upon this, advanced to poor Ellen's relief. " What do you wish, miss?" he said.

But Ellen had been so long preparing sentences, trying to utter them and failing in the attempt, that now, when an opportunity to speak and be heard was given her, the power of speech seemed to be gone.

" Do you wish any thing, miss?" inquired Mr. St. Clair again.

" Mother sent me," stammered Ellen,—" I wish, if you please, sir,—mamma wished me to look at merinoes, sir, if you please."

" Is your mamma in the store?"

" No, sir," said Ellen, " she is ill, and cannot come out, and she sent me to look at merinoes for her, if you please, sir."

" Here, Saunders," said Mr. St. Clair, " show this young lady the merinoes."

Mr. Saunders made his appearance from among a little group of clerks, with whom he had been indulging in a few jokes by way of relief from the tedium of business. " Come this way," he said to Ellen; and sauntering before her, with a rather dissatisfied air, led the way out of the entrance hall into another and much larger apartment. There were plenty of people here too, and just as busy as those they had quitted. Mr. Saunders having brought Ellen to the merino counter, placed himself behind it; and leaning over it and fixing his eyes carelessly upon her, asked what she wanted to look at. His tone and manner struck Ellen most unpleasantly, and made her again wish herself out of the store. He was a tall lank young man, with a quantity of fair hair combed down on each side of his face, a slovenly exterior, and the most disagreeable pair of eyes, Ellen thought, she had ever beheld. She could not bear to meet them, and cast down her own. Their look was bold, ill-bred, and ill-humoured; and Ellen felt, though she couldn't have told why, that she need not expect either kindness or politeness from him.

" What do you want to see, little one?" inquired this gentlemen, as if he had a business on hand he would like to be rid of. Ellen heartily wished he was rid of it, and she too. " Merinoes, if you please," she answered, without looking up.

" Well, what kind of merinoes? Here are all sorts and descriptions of merinoes, and I can't pull them all down, you know, for you to look at. What kind do you want?"

" I don't know without looking," said Ellen, " won't you please to show me some?"

He tossed down several pieces upon the counter, and tumbled them about before her.

"There," said he, "is that any thing like what you want? There's a pink one,—and there's a blue one,—and there's a green one. Is that the kind?"

"This is the kind," said Ellen; "but this isn't the colour I want."

"What colour do you want?"

"Something dark, if you please."

"Well, there, that green's dark; won't that do? See, that would make up very pretty for you."

"No," said Ellen, "mamma don't like green."

"Why don't she come and choose her stuffs herself, then? What colour *does* she like?"

"Dark blue, or dark brown, or a nice grey, would do," said Ellen, "if it is fine enough."

"'Dark blue,' or 'dark brown,' or a 'nice grey,' eh! Well, she's pretty easy to suit. A dark blue I've showed you already, —what's the matter with that?"

"It isn't dark enough," said Ellen.

"Well," said he discontentedly, pulling down another piece, "how'll that do? That's dark enough."

It was a fine and beautiful piece, very different from those he had showed her at first. Even Ellen could see that, and fumbling for her little pattern of merino, she compared it with the piece. They agreed perfectly as to fineness.

"What is the price of this?" she asked, with trembling hope that she was going to be rewarded by success for all the trouble of her enterprise.

"Two dollars a yard."

Her hopes and countenance fell together. "That's too high," she said with a sigh.

"Then take this other blue; come,—it's a great deal prettier than that dark one, and not so dear; and I know your mother will like it better."

Ellen's cheeks were tingling and her heart throbbing, but she couldn't bear to give up.

"Would you be so good as to show me some grey?"

He slowly and ill-humouredly complied, and took down an excellent piece of dark grey, which Ellen fell in love with at once; but she was again disappointed; it was fourteen shillings.

"Well, if you won't take that, take something else," said the man; "you can't have every thing at once; if you will have cheap goods of course you can't have the same quality that you like; but now here's this other blue, only twelve shillings, and I'll let you have it for ten if you'll take it."

"No, it is too light and too coarse," said Ellen, "mamma wouldn't like it."

"Let me see," said he, seizing her pattern and pretending to compare it; "it's quite as fine as this, if that's all you want."

"Could you," said Ellen timidly, "give me a little bit of this grey to show mamma?"

"Oh, no!" said he, impatiently, tossing over the cloths and throwing Ellen's pattern on the floor; "we can't cut up our goods; if people don't choose to buy of us they may go somewhere else, and if you cannot decide upon any thing I must go and attend to those that can. I can't wait here all day."

"What's the matter, Saunders?" said one of his brother clerks, passing him.

"Why, I've been here this half hour showing cloths to a child that doesn't know merino from a sheep's back," said he, laughing. And some other customers coming up at the moment, he was as good as his word, and left Ellen, to attend to them.

Ellen stood a moment stock still, just where he had left her, struggling with her feelings of mortification; she could not endure to let them be seen. Her face was on fire; her head was dizzy. She could not stir at first, and in spite of her utmost efforts she *could* not command back one or two rebel tears that forced their way; she lifted her hand to her face to remove them as quietly as possible. "What is all this about, my little girl?" said a strange voice at her side. Ellen started, and turned her face, with the tears but half wiped away, toward the speaker. It was an old gentleman, an odd old gentleman too, she thought; one she certainly would have been rather shy of if she had seen him under other circumstances. But though his face was odd, it looked kindly upon her, and it was a kind tone of voice in which his question had been put; so he seemed to her like a friend. "What is all this?" repeated the old gentleman. Ellen began to tell what it was, but the pride which had forbidden her to weep before strangers gave way at one touch of sympathy, and she poured out tears much faster than words as she related her story, so that it was some little time before the old gentleman could get a clear notion of her case. He waited very patiently till she had finished; but then he set himself in good earnest about righting the wrong. "Hallo! you, sir!" he shouted, in a voice that made every body look round; "you merino man! come and show your goods: why aren't you at your post, sir?"—as Mr. Saunders came up with an altered countenance—"here's a young lady you've left standing unattended-to I don't know how long; are these your manners?"

. "The young lady did not wish any thing, I believe, sir," returned Mr. Saunders softly.

"You know better, you scoundrel," retorted the old gentleman, who was in a great passion; "I saw the whole matter with my own eyes. You are a disgrace to the store, sir, and deserve to be sent out of it, which you are like enough to be."

"I really thought, sir," said Mr. Saunders, smoothly,—for he knew the old gentleman, and knew very well he was a person that must not be offended,—"I really thought—I was not aware, sir, that the young lady had any occasion for my services."

"Well, show your wares, sir, and hold your tongue. Now, my dear, what did you want?"

"I wanted a little bit of this grey merino, sir, to show to mamma;—I couldn't buy it, you know, sir, until I found out whether she would like it."

"Cut a piece, sir, without any words," said the old gentleman. Mr. Saunders obeyed.

"Did you like this best?" pursued the old gentleman.

"I like this dark blue very much, sir, and I thought mamma would; but it's too high."

"How much is it?" inquired he.

"Fourteen shillings," replied Mr. Saunders.

"He said it was two dollars!" exclaimed Ellen.

"I beg pardon," said the crest-fallen Mr. Saunders, "the young lady mistook me; I was speaking of another piece when I said two dollars."

"He said this was two dollars, and the grey fourteen shillings," said Ellen.

"Is the grey fourteen shillings," inquired the old gentleman.

"I think not, sir," answered Mr. Saunders—"I believe not, sir,—I think it's only twelve,—I'll inquire, if you please, sir."

"No, no," said the old gentleman, "I know it was only twelve —I know your tricks, sir. Cut a piece off the blue. Now, my dear, are there any more pieces of which you would like to take patterns, to show your mother?"

"No, sir," said the overjoyed Ellen; "I am sure she will like one of these."

"Now shall we go, then?"

"If you please, sir," said Ellen, "I should like to have my bit of merino that I brought from home; mamma wanted me to bring it back again."

"Where is it?"

"That gentleman threw it on the floor."

"Do you hear, sir?" said the old gentleman; "find it directly."

Mr. Saunders found and delivered it, after stooping in search of it till he was very red in the face; and he was left, wishing heartily that he had some safe means of revenge, and obliged to come to the conclusion that none was within his reach, and that he must stomach his indignity in the best manner he could. But Ellen and her protector went forth most joyously together from the store.

" Do you live far from here ?" asked the old gentleman.

" Oh, no, sir," said Ellen, " not very ; it's only at Green's Hotel, in Southing street."

" I'll go with you," said he, " and when your mother has decided which merino she will have, we'll come right back and get it. I do not want to trust you again to the mercy of that saucy clerk."

" Oh, thank you, sir!" said Ellen, " that is just what I was afraid of. But I shall be giving you a great deal of trouble, sir," she added, in another tone.

" No you won't," said the old gentleman, " I can't be troubled, so you needn't say any thing about that."

They went gayly along—Ellen's heart about five times as light as the one with which she had travelled that very road a little while before. Her old friend was in a very cheerful mood too, for he assured Ellen laughingly, that it was of no manner of use for her to be in a hurry, for he could not possibly set off and skip to Green's Hotel, as she seemed inclined to do. They got there at last. Ellen showed the old gentleman into the parlour, and ran up stairs in great haste to her mother. But in a few minutes she came down again, with a very April face, for smiles were playing in every feature, while the tears were yet wet upon her cheeks.

" Mamma hopes you'll take the trouble, sir, to come up stairs," she said, seizing his hand ; " she wants to thank you herself, sir."

" It is not necessary," said the old gentleman, " it is not necessary at all ;" but he followed his little conductor nevertheless to the door of her mother's room, into which she ushered him with great satisfaction.

Mrs. Montgomery was looking very ill—he saw that at a glance. She rose from her sofa, and extending her hand thanked him with glistening eyes for his kindness to her child.

" I don't deserve any thanks, ma'am," said the old gentleman ; " I suppose my little friend has told you what made us acquainted?"

" She gave me a very short account of it," said Mrs. Montgomery.

" She was very disagreeably tried," said the old gentleman. " I presume you do not need to be told, ma'am, that her behaviour was such as would have become any years. I assure you, ma'am, if I had had no kindness in my composition to feel for the *child*, my honour as a gentleman would have made me interfere for the *lady*."

Mrs. Montgomery smiled, but looked through glistening eyes again on Ellen. " I am *very* glad to hear it," she replied. " I was very far from thinking, when I permitted her to go on this errand, that I was exposing her to any thing more serious than the annoyance a timid child would feel at having to transact business with strangers."

" I suppose not," said the old gentleman ; " but it isn't a sort of thing that should be often done. There are all sorts of people in this world, and a little one alone in a crowd is in danger of being trampled upon.''

Mrs. Montgomery's heart answered this with an involuntary pang. He saw the shade that passed over her face as she said sadly :

"I know it, sir ; and it was with strong unwillingness that I allowed Ellen this morning to do as she had proposed ; but in truth I was but making a choice between difficulties. I am very sorry I chose as I did. If you are a father, sir, you know better than I can tell you, how grateful I am for your kind interference.''

"Say nothing about that, ma'am ; the less the better. I am an old man, and not good for much now, except to please young people. I think myself best off when I have the best chance to do that. So if you will be so good as to choose that merino, and let Miss Ellen and me go and despatch our business, you will be conferring and not receiving a favour. And any other errand that you please to intrust her with I'll undertake to see her safe through.''

His look and manner obliged Mrs. Montgomery to take him at his word. A very short examination of Ellen's patterns ended in favour of the grey merino ; and Ellen was commissioned not only to get and pay for this, but also to choose a dark dress of the same stuff, and enough of a certain article called nankeen for a coat ; Mrs. Montgomery truly opining that the old gentleman's care would do more than see her scathless,—that it would have some regard to the justness and prudence of her purchases.

In great glee Ellen set forth again with her new old friend. Her hand was fast in his, and her tongue ran very freely, for her heart was completely opened to him. He seemed as pleased to listen as she was to talk ; and by little and little Ellen told him all her history ; the troubles that had come upon her in consequence of her mother's illness, and her intended journey and prospects.

That was a happy day to Ellen. They returned to St. Clair and Fleury's ; bought the grey merino, and the nankeen, and a dark brown merino for a dress. "Do you want only one of these ?'' asked the old gentleman.

"Mamma said only one,'' said Ellen ; "that will last me all the winter.''

"Well,'' said he, "I think two will do better. Let us have another off the same piece, Mr. Shopman.''

"But I am afraid mamma won't like it, sir,'' said Ellen, gently.

"Pho, pho,'' said he, "your mother has nothing to do with this ; this is my affair.'' He paid for it accordingly. "Now, Miss Ellen,'' said he, when they left the store, "have you got any thing in the shape of a good warm winter bonnet ? For it's as cold as the mischief up there in Thirlwall ; your pasteboard things won't do ;

if you don't take good care of your ears you will lose them some fine frosty day. You must quilt and pad, and all sorts of things, to keep alive and comfortable. So you haven't a hood, eh? Do you think you and I could make out to choose one that your mother would think wasn't quite a fright? Come this way, and let us see. If she don't like it she can give it away, you know."

He led the delighted Ellen into a milliner's shop and after turning over a great many different articles chose her a nice warm hood, or quilted bonnet. It was of dark blue silk, well made and pretty. He saw with great satisfaction that it fitted Ellen well, and would protect her ears nicely; and having paid for it and ordered it home, he and Ellen sallied forth into the street again. But he wouldn't let her thank him. " It is just the very thing I wanted, sir," said Ellen ; " mamma was speaking about it the other day, and she did not see how I was ever to get one, because she did not feel at all able to go out, and I could not get one myself; I know she'll like it very much."

" Would you rather have something for yourself or your mother, Ellen, if you could choose, and have but one ?"

" Oh, for mamma, sir," said Ellen—" a great deal !"

" Come in here," said he ; " let us see if we can find anything she would like."

It was a grocery store. After looking about a little, the old gentleman ordered sundry pounds of figs and white grapes to be packed up in papers ; and being now very near home he took one parcel and Ellen the other till they came to the door of Green's Hotel, where he committed both to her care.

" Won't you come in, sir ?" said Ellen.

" No," said he, " I can't this time—I must go home to dinner."

"And shan't I see you any* more, sir ?" said Ellen, a shade coming over her face, which a minute before had been quite joyous.

" Well, I don't know," said he kindly; " I hope you will. You shall hear from me again at any rate I promise you. We've spent one pleasant morning together, haven't we ? Good-by, good-by."

Ellen's hands were full, but the old gentleman took them in both his, packages and all, and shook them after a fashion, and again bidding her good-by, walked away down the street.

The next morning Ellen and her mother were sitting quietly together, and Ellen had not finished her accustomed reading, when there came a knock at the door. " My old gentleman !" cried Ellen, as she sprung to open it. No—there was no old gentleman, but a black man with a brace of beautiful woodcock in his hand. He bowed very civilly, and said he had been ordered to leave the birds with Miss Montgomery. Ellen, in surprise, took them from him, and likewise a note which he delivered into her hand. Ellen asked from whom the birds came, but with another polite bow the man said the note would inform her, and went away. In great curiosity she carried them and the note to her mother, to whom the letter was directed. It read thus :—

"Will Mrs. Montgomery permit an old man to please himself in his own way, by showing his regard for her little daughter, and not feel that he is taking a liberty? The birds are *for Miss Ellen.*"

"Oh, mamma!" exclaimed Ellen, jumping with delight, "did you ever see such a dear old gentleman? Now I know what he meant yesterday, when he asked me if I would rather have something for myself or for you. How kind he is ! to do just the very thing for me that he knows would give me the most pleasure. Now, mamma, these birds are mine, you know, and I give them to you. You must pay me a kiss for them, mamma ; they are worth that. Aren't they beauties ?"

" They are very fine indeed," said Mrs. Montgomery; " This is
just the season for woodcock, and these are in beautiful condition."

" Do you like woodcocks, mamma?"

" Yes, very much."

" Oh, how glad I am!" said Ellen. " I'll ask Sam to have them
done very nicely for you, and then you will enjoy them so much."

The waiter was called, and instructed accordingly, and to him
the birds were committed, to be delivered to the care of the cook.

" Now, mamma," said Ellen, " I think these birds have made
me happy for all day."

" Then I hope, daughter, they will make you busy for all day.
You have ruffles to hem, and the skirts of your dresses to make,
we need not wait for Miss Rice to do that; and when she comes
you will have to help her, for I can do little. You can't be too
industrious."

" Well, mamma, I am as willing as can be."

This was the beginning of a pleasant two weeks to Ellen;
weeks to which she often looked back afterwards, so quietly and
swiftly the days fled away in busy occupation and sweet intercourse
with her mother. The passions which were apt enough to rise in
Ellen's mind upon occasion, were for the present kept effectually
in check. She could not forget that her days with her mother
would very soon be at an end, for a long time at least; and this
consciousness, always present to her mind, forbade even the wish
to do any thing that might grieve or disturb her. Love and tenderness had absolute rule for the time, and even had power to
overcome the sorrowful thoughts that would often rise, so that in
spite of them peace reigned. And perhaps both mother and
daughter enjoyed this interval the more keenly because they knew
that sorrow was at hand.

All this while there was scarcely a day that the old gentleman's
servant did not knock at their door, bearing a present of game.
The second time he came with some fine larks; next was a superb
grouse; then woodcock again. Curiosity strove with astonishment and gratitude in Ellen's mind. " Mamma," she said, after
she had admired the grouse for five minutes, " I cannot rest without finding out who this old gentleman is."

" I am sorry for that," replied Mrs. Montgomery gravely, "for
I see no possible way of your doing it."

" Why, mamma, couldn't I ask the man that brings the birds
what his name is? He must know it."

" Certainly not; it would be very dishonourable."

" Would it, mamma?—why?"

" This old gentleman has not chosen to tell you his name; he
wrote his note without signing it, and his man has obviously been
instructed not to disclose it; don't you remember, he did not tell

it when you asked him, the first time he came. Now this shows the old gentleman wishes to keep it secret, and to try to find it out in any way would be a very unworthy return for his kindness."

" Yes, it wouldn't be doing as I would be done by, to be sure; but would it be *dishonourable,* mamma ?"

" Very. It is very dishonourable to try to find out that about other people which does not concern you, and which they wish to keep from you. Remember that, my dear daughter."

" I will, mamma. I'll never do it, I promise you."

" Even in talking with people, if you discern in them any unwillingness to speak upon a subject, avoid it immediately, provided of course that some higher interest do not oblige you to go on. That is true politeness, and true kindness, which are nearly the same ; and *not* to do so, I assure you, Ellen, proves one wanting in true honour."

" Well, mamma, I don't care what his name is,—at least I won't try to find out:—but it does worry me that I cannot thank him. I wish he knew how much I feel obliged to him."

" Very well ; write and tell him so."

" Mamma !" said Ellen, opening her eyes very wide,—" can I? —would you ?"

" Certainly,—if you like. It would be very proper."

" Then I will ! I declare that is a good notion. I'll do it the first thing, and then I can give it to that man if he comes tomorrow, as I suppose he will. Mamma," said she, on opening her desk, " how funny ! don't you remember you wondered who I was going to write notes to ? here is one now, mamma ; it is very lucky I have got note-paper."

More than one sheet of it was ruined before Ellen had satisfied herself with what she wrote. It was a full hour from the time she began when she brought the following note for her mother's inspection :—

" Ellen Montgomery does not know how to thank the old gentleman who is so kind to her. Mamma enjoys the birds very much, and I think I do more ; for I have the double pleasure of giving them to mamma, and of eating them afterwards ; but your kindness is the best of all. I can't tell you how much I am obliged to you, sir, but I will always love you for all you have done for me.

" ELLEN MONTGOMERY."

This note Mrs. Montgomery approved ; and Ellen having with great care and great satisfaction enclosed it in an envelope, succeeded in sealing it according to rule and very well. Mrs. Montgomery laughed when she saw the direction, but let it go. Without consulting her, Ellen had written on the outside, " To the old gentleman." She sent it the next morning by the hands of the same servant, who this time was the bearer of a plump partridge " To Miss Montgomery ;" and her mind was a great deal easier on this subject from that time.

CHAPTER VI.

Mac. What is the night?
Lady Mac. Almost at odds with morning, which is which.
MACBETH.

OCTOBER was now far advanced. One evening, the evening of the last Sunday in the month, Mrs. Montgomery was lying in the parlour alone. Ellen had gone to bed some time before ; and now in the stillness of the Sabbath evening the ticking of the clock was almost the only sound to be heard. The hands were rapidly approaching ten. Captain Montgomery was abroad ; and he had been so,—according to custom,—or in bed, the whole day. The mother and daughter had had the Sabbath to themselves ; and most quietly and sweetly it had passed. They had read together, prayed together, talked together a great deal ; and the evening had been spent in singing hymns ; but Mrs. Montgomery s strength failed here, and Ellen sang alone. *She* was not soon weary. Hymn succeeded hymn, with fresh and varied pleasure ; and her mother could not tire of listening. The sweet words, and the sweet airs,—which were all old friends, and brought of themselves many a lesson of wisdom and consolation, by the mere force of association,—needed not the recommendation of the clear childish voice in which they were sung which was of all things the sweetest to Mrs. Montgomery's ear. She listened,—till she almost felt as if earth were left behind, and she and her child already standing within the walls of that city where sorrow and sighing shall be no more, and the tears shall be wiped from all eyes for ever. Ellen's next hymn, however, brought her back to earth again, but though her tears flowed freely while she heard it, all her causes of sorrow could not render them bitter.

> God in Israel sows the seeds
> Of affliction, pain, and toil;
> These spring up and choke the weeds
> Which would else o'erspread the soil.
> Trials make the promise sweet,—
> Trials give new life to prayer,—
> Trials bring me to his feet,
> Lay me low, and keep me there.

" It is so indeed, dear Ellen," said Mrs. Montgomery when she had finished, and holding the little singer to her breast,—" I have always found it so. God is faithful. I have seen abundant cause to thank him for all the evils he has made me suffer heretofore, and I do not doubt it will be the same with this last and worst one. Let us glorify him in the fires, my daughter ; and if earthly joys be stripped from us, and if we be torn from each other, let us cling the closer to him,—he can and he will in that case make up to us more than all we have lost."

Ellen felt her utter inability to join in her mother's expressions of confidence and hope ; to her there was no brightness on the cloud that hung over them,—it was all dark. She could only press her lips in tearful silence to the one and the other of her mother's cheeks alternately. How sweet the sense of the coming parting made every such embrace ! This one, for particular reasons, was often and long remembered. A few minutes they remained thus in each other's arms, cheek pressed against cheek, without speaking ; but then Mrs. Montgomery remembered that Ellen's bedtime was already past, and dismissed her.

For a while after Mrs. Montgomery remained just where Ellen had left her, her busy thoughts roaming over many things in the far past, and the sad present, and the uncertain future. She was unconscious of the passage of time, and did not notice how the silence deepened as the night drew on, till scarce a footfall was heard in the street, and the ticking of the clock sounded with that sad distinctness which seems to say,—" Time is going on—time is going on,—and you are going with it,—do what you will you can't help that." It was just upon the stroke of ten, and Mrs. Montgomery was still wrapped in her deep musings, when a sharp brisk footstep in the distance aroused her, rapidly approaching ;—and she knew very well whose it was, and that it would pause at the door, before she heard the quick run up the steps, succeeded by her husband's tread upon the staircase. And yet she saw him open the door with a kind of startled feeling which his appearance now invariably caused her ; the thought always darted through her head, " perhaps he brings news of Ellen's going." Something, it would have been impossible to say what, in his appearance or manner, confirmed this fear on the present occasion. Her heart felt sick, and she waited in silence to hear what he would say. *He* seemed very well pleased ; sat down before the fire rubbing his hands, partly with cold and partly with satisfaction ; and his first words were, " Well ! we have got a fine opportunity for her at last."

How little he was capable of understanding the pang this announcement gave his poor wife ! But she only closed her eyes and kept perfectly quiet, and he never suspected it."

He unbuttoned his coat, and taking the poker in his hand began to mend the fire, talking the while.

"I am very glad of it indeed," said he,—"it's quite a load off my mind. Now we'll be gone directly, and high time it is—I'll take passage in the England the first thing to-morrow. And this is the best possible chance for Ellen—every thing we could have desired. I began to feel very uneasy about it,—it was getting so late,—but I am quite relieved now."

"Who is it?" said Mrs. Montgomery, forcing herself to speak.

"Why, it's Mrs. Dunscombe," said the captain, flourishing his poker by way of illustration,—"you know her, don't you?—Captain Dunscombe's wife—she's going right through Thirlwall, and will take charge of Ellen as far as that, and there my sister will meet her with a wagon and take her straight home. Couldn't be any thing better. I write to let Fortune know when to expect her. Mrs. Duncombe is a lady of the first family and fashion—in the highest degree respectable; she is going on to Fort Jameson, with her daughter and a servant, and her husband is to follow her in a few days. I happened to hear of it to-day, and I immediately seized the opportunity to ask if she would not take Ellen with her as far as Thirlwall, and Dunscombe was only too glad to oblige me. I'm a very good friend of his, and he knows it."

"How soon does she go?"

"Why—that's the only part of the business I am afraid you won't like,—but there is no help for it;—and after all it is a great deal better so than if you had time to wear yourselves out with mourning—better and easier too, in the end."

"How soon?" repeated Mrs. Montgomery, with an agonized accent.

"Why—I'm a little afraid of startling you—Dunscombe's wife must go, he told me, to-morrow morning; and we arranged that she should call in the carriage at six o'clock to take up Ellen."

Mrs. Montgomery put her hands to her face and sank back against the sofa.

"I was afraid you would take it so," said her husband,—"but I don't think it is worth while. It is a great deal better as it is,—a great deal better than if she had a long warning. You would fairly wear yourself out if you had time enough; and you haven't any strength to spare."

It was some while before Mrs. Montgomery could recover composure and firmness enough to go on with what she had to do, though knowing the necessity, she strove hard for it. For several minutes she remained quite silent and quiet, endeavouring to collect her scattered forces; then sitting upright and drawing her shawl around her she exclaimed, "I must waken Ellen immediately!"

" Waken Ellen !" exclaimed her husband in his turn,—" what on earth for ? That's the very last thing to be done."

" Why you would not put off telling her until to-morrow morning ?" said Mrs. Montgomery.

" Certainly I would—that's the only proper way to do. Why in the world should you wake her up, just to spend the whole night in useless grieving ?—unfitting her utterly for her journey, and doing yourself more harm than you can undo in a week. No, no, —just let her sleep quietly, and you go to bed and do the same. Wake her up, indeed ! I thought you were wiser."

" But she will be so dreadfully shocked in the morning !"

" Not one bit more than she would be to-night, and she won't have so much time to feel it. In the hurry and bustle of getting off she will not have time to think about her feelings ; and once on the way she will do well enough ;—children always do."

Mrs. Montgomery looked undecided and unsatisfied.

" I'll take the responsibility of this matter on myself,—you must not waken her, absolutely. It would not do at all," said the captain, poking the fire very energetically,—" it would not do at all,—I cannot allow it."

Mrs. Montgomery silently arose and lit a lamp.

" You are not going into Ellen's room ?" said the husband.

" I must—I must put her things together."

" But you'll not disturb Ellen ?" said he, in a tone that required a promise.

" Not if I can help it."

Twice Mrs. Montgomery stopped before she reached the door of Ellen's room, for her heart failed her. But she *must* go on, and the necessary preparations for the morrow *must* be made ;—she knew it ; and repeating this to herself she gently turned the handle of the door and pushed it open, and guarding the light with her hand from Ellen's eyes, she set it where it would not shine upon her. Having done this, she set herself, without once glancing at her little daughter, to put all things in order for her early departure on the following morning. But it was a bitter piece of work for her. She first laid out all that Ellen would need to wear,—the dark merino, the new nankeen coat, the white bonnet, the clean frill that her own hands had done up, the little gloves and shoes, and all the etceteras, with the thoughtfulness and the carefulness of love ; but it went through and through her heart that it was the very last time a mother's fingers would ever be busy in arranging or preparing Ellen's attire ; the very last time she would ever see or touch even the little inanimate things that belonged to her ; and painful as the task was she was loth to have it come to an end. It was with a kind lingering unwillingness to quit her hold of them that one thing after another was stowed carefully and neatly away

in the trunk. She felt it was love's last act; words might indeed
a few times yet come over the ocean on a sheet of paper;—but
sight, and hearing, and touch must all have done henceforth for
ever. Keenly as Mrs. Montgomery felt this, she went on busily
with her work all the while; and when the last thing was safely
packed, shut the trunk and locked it without allowing herself to
stop and think, and even drew the straps. And then, having finished all her task, she went to the bedside; she had not looked
that way before.

Ellen was lying in the deep sweet sleep of childhood; the easy
position, the gentle breathing, and the flush of health upon the
cheek showed that all causes of sorrow were for the present far
removed. Yet not so far either;—for once when Mrs. Montgomery
stooped to kiss her, light as the touch of that kiss had been upon
her lips, it seemed to awaken a train of sorrowful recollections in
the little sleeper's mind. A shade passed over her face, and with
gentle but sad accent the word, " Mamma !" burst from the parted
lips. Only a moment,—and the shade passed away, and the expression of peace settled again upon her brow; but Mrs. Montgomery dared not try the experiment a second time. Long she
stood looking upon her, as if she knew she was looking her last;
then she knelt by the bedside and hid her face in the coverings,—
but no tears came ; the struggle in her mind and her anxious fear
for the morning's trial, made weeping impossible. Her husband
at length came to seek her, and it was well he did ; she would have
remained there on her knees all night. He feared something of
the kind, and came to prevent it. Mrs. Montgomery suffered herself to be led away without making any opposition ; and went to
bed as usual, but sleep was far from her. The fear of Ellen's distress when she would be awakened and suddenly told the truth,
kept her in an agony. In restless wakefulness she tossed and
turned uneasily upon her bed, watching for the dawn, and dreading
unspeakably to see it. The captain, in happy unconsciousness of
his wife's distress and utter inability to sympathize with it, was
soon in a sound sleep, and his heavy breathing was an aggravation
of her trouble ; it kept repeating, what indeed she knew already,
that the only one in the world who ought to have shared and soothed
her grief was not capable of doing either. Wearied with watching
and tossing to and fro, she at length lost herself a moment in uneasy slumber, from which she suddenly started in terror, and seizing her husband's arm to arouse him, exclaimed, " It is time to wake
Ellen !" but she had to repeat her efforts two or three times before
she succeeded in making herself heard.

" What is the matter?" said he heavily, and not over well
pleased at the interruption.

" It is time to wake Ellen."

" No it isn't," said he, relapsing,—" it isn't time yet this great while."

" Oh, yes it is," said Mrs. Montgomery;—" I am sure it is; I see the beginning of dawn in the east."

" Nonsense! it's no such thing; it's the glimmer of the lamp-light; what is the use of your exciting yourself so for nothing. It won't be dawn these two hours. Wait till I find my repeater, and I'll convince you."

He found and struck it.

" There! I told you so—only one quarter after four; it would be absurd to wake her yet. Do go to sleep and leave it to me; I'll take care it is done in proper time."

Mrs. Montgomery sighed heavily, and again arranged herself to watch the eastern horizon, or rather with her face in that direction; for she could see nothing. But more quietly now she lay gazing into the darkness which it was in vain to try to penetrate; and thoughts succeeding thoughts in a more regular train, at last fairly cheated her into sleep, much as she wished to keep it off. She slept soundly for near an hour; and when she awoke the dawn had really begun to break in the eastern sky. She again aroused Captain Montgomery, who this time allowed it might be as well to get up; but it was with unutterable impatience that she saw him lighting a lamp, and moving about as leisurely as if he had nothing more to do than to get ready for breakfast at eight o'clock.

" Oh, do speak to Ellen!" she said, unable to control herself. " Never mind brushing your hair till afterwards. She will have no time for any thing. Oh, do not wait any longer! what are you thinking of?"

" What are *you* thinking of?" said the captain;—" there's plenty of time. Do quiet yourself—you're getting as nervous as possible. I'm going immediately."

Mrs. Montgomery fairly groaned with impatience and an ago-nizing dread of what was to follow the disclosure to Ellen. But her husband coolly went on with his preparations, which indeed were not long in finishing; and then taking the lamp he at last went. He had in truth delayed on purpose, wishing the final leave-taking to be as brief as possible; and the grey streaks of light in the east were plainly showing themselves when he opened the door of his little daughter's room. He found her lying very much as her mother had left her,—in the same quiet sleep, and with the same expression of calmness and peace spread over her whole face and person. It touched even him,—and he was not readily touched by any thing;—it made him loth to say the word that would drive all that sweet expression so quickly and completely away. It must be said, however; the increasing light warned him he must not tarry; but it was with a hesitating and almost faltering voice that he said, " Ellen !"

She stirred in her sleep, and the shadow came over her face again.

" Ellen ! Ellen !"

She started up,—broad awake now ;—and both the shadow and the peaceful expression were gone from her face. It was a look of blank astonishment at first with which she regarded her father, but very soon indeed that changed into one of blank despair. He saw that she understood perfectly what he was there for, and that there was no need at all for him to trouble himself with making painful explanations.

" Come, Ellen," he said,—" that's a good child, make haste and dress. There's no time to lose now, for the carriage will soon be at the door ; and your mother wants to see you, you know."

Ellen hastily obeyed him, and began to put on her stockings and shoes.

" That's right—now you'll be ready directly. You are going with Mrs. Dunscombe—I have engaged her to take charge of you all the way quite to Thirlwall; she's the wife of Captain Dunscombe, whom you saw here the other day, you know; and her daughter is going with her, so you will have charming company. I dare say you will enjoy the journey very much ; and your aunt will meet you at Thirlwall. Now, make haste—I expect the carriage every minute. I meant to have called you before, but I overslept myself. Don't be long."

And nodding encouragement, her father left her.

" How did she bear it ?" asked Mrs. Montgomery when he returned.

" Like a little hero. She didn't say a word, or shed a tear. I expected nothing but that she would make a great fuss; but she has all the old spirit that you used to have,—and have yet, for any thing I know. She behaved admirably."

Mrs. Montgomery sighed deeply. She understood far better than her husband what Ellen's feelings were, and could interpret much more truly than he the signs of them ; the conclusions she drew from Ellen's silent and tearless reception of the news differed widely from his. She now waited anxiously and almost fearfully for her appearance, which did not come as soon as she expected it.

It was a great relief to Ellen when her father ended his talking, and left her to herself ; for she felt she could not dress herself so quick with him standing there and looking at her, and his desire that she should be speedy in what she had to do could not be greater than her own. Her fingers did their work as fast as they could, with every joint trembling. But though a weight like a mountain was upon the poor child's heart, she could not cry ; and she could not pray,—though true to her constant habit she fell on her knees by her bedside as she always did: it was in vain; all was in a whirl in her heart and head, and after a minute she rose again, clasping her little hands together with an expression of sorrow that it was well her mother could not see. She was dressed very soon, but she shrank from going to her mother's room while her father was there. To save time she put on her coat, and every thing but her bonnet and gloves; and then stood leaning against the bed-post, for she could not sit down, watching with most intense anxiety to hear her father's step come out of the room and go down stairs. Every minute seemed too long to be borne; poor Ellen began to feel as if she could not contain herself. Yet five had not passed away when she heard the roll of carriage-wheels which came to the door and then stopped, and immediately her father opening the door to come out. Without waiting any longer Ellen opened her own, and brushed past him into the room he had quitted. Mrs. Montgomery was still lying on the bed, for her husband had insisted on her not rising. She said not a word, but opened her arms to receive her little daughter; and with a cry of indescribable expression Ellen sprang upon the bed, and was folded in them. But then neither of them spoke or wept. What could words say? Heart met heart in that agony, for each knew all that was in the other. No,—not quite all. Ellen did not know that the whole of bitterness death had for her mother she was tasting then. But it was true. Death had no more power to give her pain after this parting should be over. His after-work,—the parting between soul and body,—would be welcome rather; yes, very welcome. Mrs. Montgomery knew it all well. She knew this was the last embrace between them. She knew it was the very last time that dear little form would ever lie on her bosom, or be pressed in her arms; and it almost seemed to her that soul and body must part company too when they should be rent asunder. Ellen's grief was not like this;—*she* did not think it was the last time;—but she was a child of very high spirit and violent passions, untamed at all by sorrow's discipline; and in proportion violent was the tempest excited by this first real trial. Perhaps, too, her sorrow was sharpened by a sense of wrong and a feeling of indignation at her father's cruelty in not waking her earlier.

Not many minutes had passed in this sad embrace, and no word had yet been spoken, no sound uttered, except Ellen's first inarticulate cry of mixed affection and despair, when Captain Montgomery's step was again heard slowly ascending the stairs. " He is coming to take me away!'' thought Ellen; and in terror lest she should go without a word from her mother, she burst forth with, " Mamma! speak!''

A moment before, and Mrs. Montgomery could not have spoken.

But she could now; and as clearly and calmly the words were uttered as if nothing had been the matter, only her voice fell a little toward the last.

"God bless my darling child! and make her his own,—and bring her to that home where parting cannot be."

Ellen's eyes had been dry until now; but when she heard the sweet sound of her mother's voice, it opened all the fountains of tenderness within her. She burst into uncontrollable weeping; it seemed as if she would pour out her very heart in tears; and she clung to her mother with a force that made it a difficult task for her father to remove her. He could not do it at first; and Ellen seemed not to hear any thing that was said to her. He was very unwilling to use harshness; and after a little, though she had paid no attention to his entreaties or commands, yet sensible of the necessity of the case, she gradually relaxed her hold and suffered him to draw her away from her mother's arms. He carried her down stairs, and put her on the front seat of the carriage, beside Mrs. Dunscombe's maid,—but Ellen could never recollect how she got there, and she did not feel the touch of her father's hand, nor hear him when he bid her good-by; and she did not know that he put a large paper of candies and sugar-plums in her lap. She knew nothing but that she had lost her mother.

"It will not be so long," said the captain, in a kind of apologizing way; "she will soon get over it, and you will not have any trouble with her."

"I hope so," returned the lady, rather shortly; and then, as the captain was making his parting bow, she added, in no very pleased tone of voice, "Pray, Captain Montgomery, is this young lady to travel without a bonnet?"

"Bless me! no," said the captain. "How is this? hasn't she a bonnet? I beg a thousand pardons, ma'am,—I'll bring it on the instant."

After a little delay, the bonnet was found, but the captain overlooked the gloves in his hurry.

"I am very sorry you have been delayed, ma'am," said he.

"I hope we may be able to reach the boat yet," replied the lady. "Drive on as fast as you can!"

A very polite bow from Captain Montgomery—a very slight one from the lady—and off they drove.

"Proud enough," thought the captain, as he went up the stairs again. "I reckon she don't thank me for her travelling companion. But Ellen's off—that's one good thing:—and now I'll go and engage berths in the England."

CHAPTER VII.

"So fair and foul a day I have not seen."
MACBETH.

THE long drive to the boat was only a sorrowful blank to Ellen's recollection. She did not see the frowns that passed between her companions on her account. She did not know that her white bonnet was such a matter of merriment to Margaret Dunscombe and the maid, that they could hardly contain themselves. She did not find out that Miss Margaret's fingers were busy with her paper of sweets, which only a good string and a sound knot kept her from rifling. Yet she felt very well that nobody there cared in the least for her sorrow. It mattered nothing; she wept on in her loneliness, and knew nothing that happened, till the carriage stopped on the wharf; even then she did not raise her head. Mrs. Dunscombe got out, and saw her daughter and servant do the same; then after giving some orders about the baggage, she returned to Ellen.

" Will you get out, Miss Montgomery? or would you prefer to remain in the carriage? We must go on board directly."

There was something, not in the words, but in the tone, that struck Ellen's heart with an entirely new feeling. Her tears stopped instantly, and wiping away quick the traces of them as well as she could, she got out of the carriage without a word, aided by Mrs. Dunscombe's hand. The party was presently joined by a fine-looking man, whom Ellen recognised as Captain Dunscombe.

" Dunscombe, do put these girls on board, will you? and then come back to me; I want to speak to you. Timmins, you may go along and look after them."

Captain Dunscombe obeyed. When they reached the deck, Margaret Dunscombe and the maid Timmins went straight to the cabin. Not feeling at all drawn toward their company, as indeed they had given her no reason, Ellen planted herself by the guards of the boat, not far from the gangway, to watch the busy scene that at another time would have had a great deal of interest and amusement for her. And interest it had now; but it was with a very, very grave little face that she looked on the bustling crowd. The weight on her heart was just as great as ever, but she felt this was not the time or the place to let it be seen; so for the present she occupied herself with what was passing before her, though it did not for one moment make her forget her sorrow.

At last the boat rang her last bell. Captain Dunscombe put his wife on board, and had barely time to jump off the boat again when the plank was withdrawn. The men on shore cast off the great

loops of ropes that held the boat to enormous wooden posts on the
wharf, and they were off!

At first it seemed to Ellen as if the wharf and the people upon
it were sailing away from them backwards; but she presently forgot to think of them at all.   She was gone!—she felt the bitterness of the whole truth;—the blue water already lay between her
and the shore, where she so much longed to be.   In that confused
mass of buildings at which she was gazing, but which would be so
soon beyond even gazing distance, was the only spot she cared for
in the world; her heart was there.   She could not see the place, to
be sure, nor tell exactly whereabouts it lay in all that wide-spread
city; but it was there, somewhere,—and every minute was making
it farther and farther off.   It's a bitter thing, that sailing away
from all one loves; and poor Ellen felt it so.   She stood leaning
both her arms upon the rail, the tears running down her cheeks,
and blinding her so that she could not see the place toward which
her straining eyes were bent.   Somebody touched her sleeve,—it
was Timmins.

"Mrs. Dunscombe sent me to tell you she wants you to come
into the cabin, miss."

Hastily wiping her eyes, Ellen obeyed the summons, and followed
Timmins into the cabin.   It was full of groups of ladies, children,
and nurses,—bustling and noisy enough.   Ellen wished she might
have stayed outside; she wanted to be by herself; but as the next
best thing, she mounted upon the bench which ran all round the
saloon, and kneeling on the cushion by one of the windows, placed
herself with the edge of her bonnet just touching the glass, so that
nobody could see a bit of her face, while she could look out near
by as well as from the deck.   Presently her ear caught, as she
thought, the voice of Mrs. Dunscombe, saying in rather an under-
tone, but laughing too, "What a figure she does cut in that outlandish bonnet!"

Ellen had no particular reason to think *she* was meant, and yet
she did think so.   She remained quite still, but with raised colour
and quickened 'breathing waited to hear what would come next.
Nothing came at first, and she was beginning to think she had perhaps been mistaken, when she plainly heard Margaret Dunscombe
say, in a loud whisper, "Mamma, I wish you could contrive some
way to keep her in the cabin—can't you? she looks so odd in that
queer sun-bonnet kind of a thing, that any body would think she
had come out of the woods, and no gloves too; I shouldn't like to
have the Miss M'Arthurs think she belonged to us—can't you,
mamma?"

If a thunderbolt had fallen at Ellen's feet, the shock would
hardly have been greater.   The lightning of passion shot through
every vein.   And it was not passion only; there was hurt feeling

and wounded pride, and the sorrow of which her heart was full
enough before, now wakened afresh. The child was beside herself.
One wild wish for a hiding-place was the most pressing thought,—
to be where tears could burst and her heart could break unseen.
She slid off her bench and rushed through the crowd to the red
curtain that cut off the far end of the saloon ; and from there down
to the cabin below,—people were everywhere. At last she spied a
nook where she could be completely hidden. It was in the far-back
end of the boat, just under the stairs by which she had come down.
Nobody was sitting on the three or four large mahogany steps that
ran round that end of the cabin and sloped up to the little cabin
window ; and creeping beneath the stairs, and seating herself on the
lowest of these steps, the poor child found that she was quite screened
and out of sight of every human creature. It was time indeed ; her
heart had been almost bursting with passion and pain, and now the
pent-up tempest broke forth with a fury that racked her little frame
from head to foot ; and the more because she strove to stifle every
sound of it as much as possible. It was the very bitterness of sorrow,
without any softening thought to allay it, and sharpened and made
more bitter by mortification and a passionate sense of unkindness and
wrong. And through it all, how constantly in her heart the poor
child was reaching forth longing arms toward her far-off mother,
and calling in secret on her beloved name. " Oh, mamma ! mamma !"
was repeated numberless times, with the unspeakable bitterness of
knowing that she would have been a sure refuge and protection
from all this trouble, but was now where she could neither reach
nor hear her. Alas ! how soon and how sadly missed.

Ellen's distress was not soon quieted, or, if quieted for a moment,
it was only to break out afresh. And then she was glad to sit still
and rest herself.

Presently she heard the voice of the chambermaid up stairs, at
a distance at first, and coming nearer and nearer. " Breakfast ready,
ladies—Ladies, breakfast ready !" and then came all the people in a
rush, pouring down the stairs over Ellen's head. She kept quite
still and close, for she did not want to see any body, and could not
bear that any body should see her. Nobody did see her ; they all
went off into the next cabin, where breakfast was set. Ellen began
to grow tired of her hiding-place, and to feel restless in her confinement ; she thought this would be a good time to get away ; so she
crept from her station under the stairs and mounted them as quick
and as quietly as she could. She found almost nobody left in the
saloon,—and breathing more freely, she possessed herself of her
despised bonnet, which she had torn off her head in the first burst
of her indignation, and passing gently out at the door, went up the
stairs which led to the promenade deck ;—she felt as if she could
not get far enough from Mrs. Dunscombe.

The promenade deck was very pleasant in the bright morning sun ; and nobody was there except a few gentlemen. Ellen sat down on one of the settees that were ranged along the middle of it, and, much pleased at having found herself such a nice place of retreat, she once more took up her interrupted amusement of watching the banks of the river.

It was a fair, mild day, near the end of October, and one of the loveliest of that lovely month. Poor Ellen, however, could not fairly enjoy it just now. There was enough darkness in her heart to put a veil over all nature's brightness. The thought did pass through her mind when she first went up, how very fair every thing was ;—but she soon forgot to think about it at all. They were now in a wide part of the river; and the shore toward which she was looking was low and distant, and offered nothing to interest her. She ceased to look at it, and presently lost all sense of every thing around and before her, for her thoughts went home. She remembered that sweet moment last night when she lay in her mother's arms, after she had stopped singing, could it be only last night? it seemed a long, long time ago. She went over again in imagination her shocked waking up that very morning,—how cruel that was!—her hurried dressing,—the miserable parting,—and those last words of her mother, that seemed to ring in her ears yet. " That home where parting cannot be." " Oh," thought Ellen, " how shall I ever get there ? who is there to teach me now? Oh, what shall I do without you? Oh, mamma! how much I want you already !"

While poor Ellen was thinking these things over and over, her little face had a deep sadness of expression it was sorrowful to see. She was perfectly calm ; her violent excitement had all left her ; her lip quivered a very little sometimes, but that was all ; and one or two tears rolled slowly down the side of her face. Her eyes were fixed upon the dancing water, but it was very plain her thoughts were not, nor on any thing else before her ; and there was a forlorn look of hopeless sorrow on her lip and cheek and brow, enough to move any body whose heart was not very hard. She was noticed, and with a feeling of compassion, by several people ; but they all thought it was none of their business to speak to her, or they didn't know how. At length, a gentleman who had been for some time walking up and down the deck, happened to look, as he passed, at her little pale face. He went to the end of his walk that time, but in coming back he stopped just in front of her, and bending down his face toward hers, said, " What is the matter with you, my little friend ?"

Though his figure had passed before her a great many times Ellen had not seen him at all; for " her eyes were with her heart, and that was far away." Her cheek flushed with surprise as she looked up. But there was no mistaking the look of kindness in the eyes that met hers, nor the gentleness and grave truthfulness of the whole countenance. It won her confidence immediately. All the floodgates of Ellen's heart were at once opened. She could not speak, but rising and clasping the hand that was held out to her in both her own, she bent down her head upon it, and burst into one of those uncontrollable agonies of weeping, such as the news of her mother's intended departure had occasioned that first sorrowful evening. He gently, and as soon as he could, drew her to a retired part of the deck where they were comparatively free from other people's eyes and ears; then taking her in his arms he endeavoured by many kind and soothing words to stay the torrent of her grief. This fit of weeping did Ellen more good than the former one; that only exhausted, this in some little measure relieved her.

" What is all this about?" said her friend kindly. " Nay, never mind shedding any more tears about it, my child. Let me hear what it is; and perhaps we can find some help for it."

" Oh, no you can't, sir," said Ellen sadly.

" Well, let us see," said he,—" perhaps I can. What is it that has troubled you so much ?"

" I have lost my mother, sir," said Ellen.

" Your mother ! Lost her !—how ?"

" She is very ill, sir, and obliged to go away over the sea to France to get well ; and papa could not take me with her," said poor Ellen, weeping again, " and I am obliged to go to be among strangers. Oh, what shall I do ?"

" Have you left your mother in the city ?"

" Oh, yes, sir ! I left her this morning."

" What is your name ?"

" Ellen Montgomery."

" Is your mother obliged to go to Europe for her health ?"

" Oh, yes, sir ; nothing else would have made her go, but the doctor said she would not live long if she didn't go, and that would cure her."

" Then you hope to see her come back by and by, don't you ?"

" Oh, yes, sir ; but it won't be this great, great, long while ; it seems to me as if it was for ever."

" Ellen, do you know who it is that sends sickness and trouble upon us ?"

" Yes, sir, I know ; but I don't feel that that makes it any easier."

" Do you know *why* he sends it ? He is the God of love,—he does not trouble us willingly,—he has said so ;—why does he ever make us suffer ? do you know ?"

" No, sir."

" Sometimes he sees that if he lets them alone, his children will love some dear thing on the earth better than himself, and he knows they will not be happy if they do so ; and then, because he loves them, he takes it away,—perhaps it is a dear mother, or a dear daughter,—or else he hinders their enjoyment of it ; that they may remember him, and give their whole hearts to him. He wants their whole hearts, that he may bless them. Are you one of his children, Ellen ?''

" No, sir," said Ellen, with swimming eyes, but cast down to the ground.

" How do you know that you are not ?''

" Because I do not love the Saviour."

" Do you not love him, Ellen ?''

" I am afraid not, sir."

" Why are you afraid not ? what makes you think so ?''

" Mamma said I could not love him at all if I did not love him best ; and oh, sir," said Ellen weeping, " I do love mamma a great deal better."

" You love your mother better than you do the Saviour ?''

" Oh, yes, sir," said Ellen ; " how can I help it ?''

" Then if he had left you your mother, Ellen, you would never have cared or thought about him ?''

Ellen was silent.

" Is it so ?—would you, do you think ?''

" I don't know, sir," said Ellen, weeping again,—" oh, sir, how can I help it ?''

" Then Ellen, can you not see the love of your Heavenly Father in this trial ? He saw that his little child was in danger of forgetting him, and he loved you, Ellen ; and so he has taken your dear mother, and sent you away where you will have no one to look to but him ; and now he says to you, ' My daughter, give *me* thy heart.'—Will you do it, Ellen ?''

Ellen wept exceedingly while the gentleman was saying these words, clasping his hands still in both hers ; but she made no answer. He waited till she had become calmer, and then went on in a low tone,—

" What is the reason that you do not love the Saviour, my child ?''

" Mamma says it is because my heart is so hard."

" That is true ; but you do not know how good and how lovely he is, or you could not help loving him. Do you often think of him, and think much of him, and ask him to show you himself that you may love him ?''

" No, sir," said Ellen,—" not often."

" You pray to him, don't you ?''

" Yes, sir ; but not so."

" But you ought to pray to him so. We are all blind by nature,

Ellen ;—we are all hard-hearted; none of us can see him or love him unless he opens our eyes and touches our hearts; but he has promised to do this for those that seek him. Do you remember what the blind man said when Jesus asked him what he should do for him ?—he answered, 'Lord, that I may receive my sight!' That ought to be your prayer now, and mine too; and the Lord is just as ready to hear us as he was to hear the poor blind man; and you know he cured him. Will you ask him, Ellen ?"

A smile was almost struggling through Ellen's tears as she lifted her face to that of her friend, but she instantly looked down again.

" Shall I put you in mind, Ellen, of some things about Christ that ought to make you love him with all your heart ?"

" Oh, yes, sir ! if you please."

" Then tell me first what it is that makes you love your mother so much ?"

" Oh, I can't tell you, sir ;—every thing, I think."

" I suppose the great thing is that she loves *you* so much ?"

" Oh, yes, sir," said Ellen strongly.

" But how do you know that she loves you ? how has she shown it ?"

Ellen looked at him, but could give no answer ; it seemed to her that she must bring the whole experience of her life before him to form one.

" I suppose," said her friend, " that, to begin with the smallest thing, she has always been watchfully careful to provide every thing that could be useful or necessary for you :—she never forgot your wants, or was careless about them ?"

" No indeed, sir."

" And perhaps you recollect that she never minded trouble or expense or pain where your good was concerned ;—she would sacrifice her own pleasure at any time for yours ?"

Ellen's eyes gave a quick and strong answer to this, but she said nothing.

" And in all your griefs and pleasures you were sure of finding her ready and willing to feel with you and for you, and to help you if she could ? And in all the times you have seen her tried, no fatigue ever wore out her patience, nor any naughtiness of yours ever lessened her love ; she could not be weary of waiting upon you when you were sick, nor of bearing with you when you forgot your duty,—more ready always to receive you than you to return. Isn't it so ?"

" Oh, yes, sir."

" And you can recollect a great many words and looks of kindness and love—many and many endeavours to teach you and lead you in the right way—all showing the strongest desire for your happiness in this world, and in the next ?"

" Oh, yes, sir," said Ellen tearfully ; and then added, " do you know my mother, sir ?"

" No," said he, smiling, " not at all ; but my own mother has been in many things like this to me, and I judged yours might have been such to you.   Have I described her right ?"

" Yes indeed, sir," said Ellen ;—" exactly."

" And in return for all this, you have given this dear mother the love and gratitude of your whole heart, haven't you ?"

" Indeed I have, sir ;" and Ellen's face said it more than her words.

" You are very right," he said gravely, "to love such a mother —to give her all possible duty and affection ;—she deserves it. But, Ellen, in all these very things I have been mentioning, Jesus Christ has shown that he deserves it far more.   Do you think, if you had never behaved like a child to your mother—if you had never made her the least return of love or regard—that she would have continued to love you as she does ?"

" No, sir," said Ellen,—" I do not think she would."

" Have you ever made any fit return to God for his goodness to you ?"

" No, sir," said Ellen, in a low tone.

" And yet there has been no change in *his* kindness.   Just look at it, and see what he has done and is doing for you.   In the first place, it is not your mother, but he, who has given you every good and pleasant thing you have enjoyed in your whole life.   You love your mother because she is so careful to provide for all your wants ; but who gave her the materials to work with ? she has only been, as it were, the hand by which he supplied you.   And who gave you such a mother ?—there are many mothers not like her ;—who put into her heart the truth and love that have been blessing you ever since you were born ?   It is all—all God's doing, from first to last ; but his child has forgotten him in the very gifts of his mercy."

Ellen was silent, but looked very grave.

" Your mother never minded her own ease or pleasure when your good was concerned.   Did Christ mind his ?   You know what he did to save sinners, don't you ?"

" Yes, sir, I know ; mamma often told me."

" ' Though he was rich, yet for our sake he became poor, that we through his poverty might be rich.'   He took your burden of sin upon himself, and suffered that terrible punishment—all to save you, and such as you.   And now he asks his children to leave off sinning and come back to him who has bought them with his own blood.   He did this because he *loved* you ; does he not deserve to be loved in return ?"

Ellen had nothing to say ; she hung down her head further and further.

"And patient and kind as your mother is, the Lord Jesus is kinder and more patient still. In all your life so far, Ellen, you have not loved or obeyed him ; and yet he loves you, and is ready to be your friend. Is he not even to-day taking away your dear mother for the very purpose that he may draw you gently to himself and fold you in his arms, as he has promised to do with his lambs? He knows you can never be happy anywhere else."

The gentleman paused again, for he saw that the little listener's mind was full.

" Has not Christ shown that he loves you better even than your mother does? And were there ever sweeter words of kindness than these?—

" 'Suffer the little children to come unto me, and forbid them not ; for of such is the kingdom of heaven.'

" 'I am the good shepherd ; the good shepherd giveth his life for the sheep.'

" 'I have loved thee with an everlasting love ; therefore with loving kindness have I drawn thee.' "

He waited a minute, and then added, gently, " Will you come to him, Ellen?"

Ellen lifted her tearful eyes to his ; but there were tears there too, and her own sank instantly. She covered her face with her hands, and sobbed out in broken words, " Oh, if I could—but I don't know how."

" Do you wish to be his child, Ellen?"

" Oh, yes, sir—if I could."

" I know, my child, that sinful heart of yours is in the way, but the Lord Jesus can change it, and will, if you will give it to him. He is looking upon you now, Ellen, with more kindness and love than any earthly father or mother could, waiting for you to give that little heart of yours to him, that he may make it holy and fill it with blessing. He says, you know, ' Behold I stand at the door and knock.' Do not grieve him away, Ellen."

Ellen sobbed, but all the passion and bitterness of her tears was gone. Her heart was completely melted.

" If your mother were here, and could do for you what you want, would you doubt her love to do it? would you have any difficulty in asking her?"

" Oh, no!"

" Then do not doubt his love who loves you better still. Come to Jesus. Do not fancy he is away up in heaven out of reach of hearing—he is here, close to you, and knows every wish and throb of your heart. Think you are in his presence and at his feet,— even now,—and say to him in your heart, ' Lord, look upon me— I am not fit to come to thee, but thou hast bid me come—take me and make me thine own—take this hard heart that I can do nothing with, and make it holy and fill it with thy love—I give it and myself into thy hands, oh, dear Saviour!' ''

These words were spoken very low, that only Ellen could catch them. Her bowed head sank lower and lower till he ceased speaking. He added no more for some time ; waited till she had resumed her usual attitude and appearance, and then said,—

" Ellen, could you join in heart with my words ?''

" I did, sir,—I couldn't help it, all but the last.''

" All but the last ?''

" Yes, sir.''

" But, Ellen, if you say the first part of my prayer with your whole heart, the Lord will enable you to say the last too,—do you believe that ?''

" Yes, sir.''

" Will you not make that your constant prayer till you are heard and answered ?''

" Yes, sir.''

And he thought he saw that she was in earnest.

" Perhaps the answer may not come at once,—it does not always ; —but it will come as surely as the sun will rise to-morrow morning. ' Then shall we know, if we *follow on* to know the Lord.' But then you must be in earnest. And if you are in earnest, is there nothing you have to do besides *praying ?*''

Ellen looked at him without making any answer.

" When a person is in earnest, how does he show it ?''

" By doing every thing he possibly can to get what he wants.''

" Quite right,'' said her friend, smiling ;—" and has God bidden us to do nothing besides pray for a new heart ?''

" Oh, yes, sir,—he has told us to do a great many things.''

" And will he be likely to grant that prayer, Ellen, if he sees that you do not care about displeasing him in those ' great many things ?'—will he judge that you are sincere in wishing for a new heart ?''

" Oh, no, sir.''

" Then if you are resolved to be a Christian, you will not be contented with praying for a new heart, but you will begin at once to be a servant of God. You can do nothing well without help, but you are sure the help will come ; and from this good day you will seek to know and to do the will of God, trusting in his dear Son to perfect that which concerneth you.—My little child,'' said the gentleman softly and kindly, " are you ready to say you will do this ?''

As she hesitated, he took a little book from his pocket, and turning over the leaves, said, " I am going to leave you for a little while—I have a few moments' business down stairs to attend to ;

and I want you to look over this hymn and think carefully of what
I have been saying, will you?—and resolve what you will do."

Ellen got off his knee, where she had been sitting all this while,
and silently taking the book, sat down in the chair he had quitted.
Tears ran fast again, and many thoughts passed through her mind,
as her eyes went over and over the words to which he had pointed:

> "Behold the Saviour at thy door,
> He gently knocks,—has knock'd before,—
> Has waited long,—is waiting still,—
> You treat no other friend so ill.

> "Oh, lovely attitude!—he stands
> With open heart and outstretch'd hands.
> Oh, matchless kindness!—and he shows
> This matchless kindness to his foes.

> "Admit him—for the human breast
> Ne'er entertain'd so kind a guest.
> Admit him—or the hour's at hand
> When at *his* door, denied, you'll stand.

> "Open my heart, Lord, enter in ;
> Slay every foe, and conquer sin.
> Here now to thee I all resign,—
> My body, soul, and all are thine."

The last two lines Ellen longed to say, but could not; the two
preceding were the very speech of her heart.

Not more than fifteen minutes had passed when her friend came
back again. The book hung in Ellen's hand ; her eyes were fixed
on the floor.

"Well," he said kindly, and taking her hand, "what's your decision ?"

Ellen looked up.

"Have you made up your mind on that matter we were talking
about?"

"Yes, sir," Ellen said in a low voice, casting her eyes down
again.

"And how have you decided, my child?"

"I will try to do as you said, sir."

"You will begin to follow your Saviour, and to please him, from
this day forward?"

"I will try, sir," said Ellen, meeting his eyes as she spoke.
Again the look she saw made her burst into tears. She wept
violently.

"God bless you and help you, my dear Ellen," said he, gently
passing his hand over her head ;—"but do not cry any more—you
have shed too many tears this morning already. We will not talk
about this any more now."

And he spoke only soothing and quieting words for a while to
her; and then asked if she would like to go over the boat and see
the different parts of it. Ellen's joyful agreement with this proposal was only qualified by the fear of giving him trouble. But
he put that entirely by.

CHAPTER VIII.

Time and the hour run through the roughest day.
                                                SHAKSPEARE.

THE going over the boat held them a long time, for Ellen's new
friend took kind pains to explain to her whatever he thought he
could make interesting; he was amused to find how far she pushed
her inquiries into the how and the why of things. For the time
her sorrows were almost forgotten.

"What shall we do now?" said he, when they had at last gone
through the whole;—"would you like to go to your friends?"

"I haven't any friends on board, sir," said Ellen, with a swelling
heart.

"Haven't any friends on board! what do you mean? Are you
alone?"

"No, sir," said Ellen,—"not exactly alone; my father put me
in the care of a lady that is going to Thirlwall;—but they are
strangers and not friends."

"Are they *un*friends? I hope you don't think, Ellen, that
strangers cannot be friends too?"

"No indeed, sir, I don't!" said Ellen, looking up with a face
that was fairly brilliant with its expression of gratitude and love.
But casting it down again, she added, "But they are not my
friends, sir."

"Well then," he said, smiling, "will you come with me?"

"Oh, yes, sir! if you will let me,—and if I shan't be a trouble
to you, sir."

"Come this way," said he, "and we'll see if we cannot find a
nice place to sit down, where no one will trouble us."

Such a place was found. And Ellen would have been quite
satisfied though the gentleman had done no more than merely permit her to remain there by his side; but he took out his little
Bible, and read and talked to her for some time, so pleasantly that
neither her weariness nor the way could be thought of.

When he ceased reading to her and began to read to himself,
weariness and faintness stole over her. She had had nothing to

eat, and had been violently excited that day. A little while she
sat in a dreamy sort of quietude,—then her thoughts grew misty,
—and the end of it was, she dropped her head against the arm of
her friend and fell fast asleep. He smiled at first, but one look at
the very pale little face changed the expression of his own. He
gently put his arm round her and drew her head to a better resting-
place than it had chosen.

And there she slept till the dinner-bell rang. Timmins was sent
out to look for her, but Timmins did not choose to meddle with the
grave protector Ellen seemed to have gained ; and Mrs. Dunscombe
declared herself rejoiced that any other hands should have taken
the charge of her.

After dinner, Ellen and her friend went up to the promenade
deck again, and there for a while they paced up and down, enjoying
the pleasant air and quick motion, and the lovely appearance of
every thing in the mild hazy sunlight. Another gentleman however joining them, and entering into conversation, Ellen silently
quitted her friend's hand and went and sat down at the side of the
boat. After taking a few turns more, and while still engaged in
talking, he drew his little hymn-book out of his pocket, and with
a smile put it into Ellen's hand as he passed. She gladly received

it, and spent an hour or more very pleasantly in studying and turning it over. At the end of that time, the stranger having left him, Ellen's friend came and sat down by her side.

" How do you like my little book?" said he.

" Oh, very much indeed, sir."

" Then you love hymns, do you?"

" Yes I do, sir, dearly."

" Do you sometimes learn them by heart?"

" Oh, yes, sir, often. Mamma often made me   I have learnt two since I have been sitting here."

" Have you?" said he ;—" which are they?"

" One of them is the one you showed me this morning, sir."

" And what is your mind now about the question I asked you this morning?"

Ellen cast down her eyes from his inquiring glance, and answered in a low tone, " Just what it was then, sir."

" Have you been thinking of it since?"

" I have thought of it the whole time, sir."

" And you are resolved you will obey Christ henceforth?"

" I am resolved to try, sir."

" My dear Ellen, if you are in earnest you will not try in vain. He never yet failed any that sincerely sought him. Have you a Bible?"

" Oh, yes sir! a beautiful one ; mamma gave it to me the other day."

He took the hymn-book from her hand, and turning over the leaves, marked several places in pencil.

" I am going to give you this," he said, " that it may serve to remind you of what we have talked of to-day, and of your resolution."

Ellen flushed high with pleasure.

" I have put this mark," said he, showing her a particular one, " in a few places of this book, for you ; wherever you find it, you may know there is something I want you to take special notice of. There are some other marks here too, but they are mine : *these* are for you."

" Thank you, sir," said Ellen, delighted ; " I shall not forget."

He knew from her face what she meant ;—not the *marks.*

The day wore on, thanks to the unwearied kindness of her friend, with great comparative comfort to Ellen. Late in the afternoon they were resting from a long walk up and down the deck.

" What have you got in this package that you take such care of?" said he, smiling.

" Oh! candies," said Ellen ; " I am always forgetting them. I meant to ask you to take some. Will you have some, sir?"

" Thank you. What are they?"

"Almost all kinds, I believe, sir; I think the almonds are the best."

He took one.

"Pray, take some more, sir," said Ellen;—"I don't care for them in the least."

"Then I am more of a child than you,—in this at any rate,—for I do care for them. But I have a little headache to-day; I mustn't meddle with sweets."

"Then take some for to-morrow, sir;—please do!" said Ellen, dealing them out very freely.

"Stop, stop!" said he,—"not a bit more; this won't do,—I must put some of these back again; you'll want them to-morrow too."

"I don't think I shall,' said Ellen;—"I haven't wanted to touch them to-day."

"Oh, you'll feel brighter to-morrow, after a night's sleep. But aren't you afraid of catching cold? This wind is blowing pretty fresh, and you've been bonnetless all day;—what's the reason?"

Ellen looked down, and coloured a good deal.

"What's the matter?" said he, laughing; "has any mischief befallen your bonnet?"

"No, sir," said Ellen in a low tone, her colour mounting higher and higher;—"it was laughed at this morning."

"Laughed at!—who laughed at it?"

"Mrs. Dunscombe and her daughter, and her maid."

"Did they! I don't see much reason in that, I confess. What did they think was the matter with it?"

"I don't know, sir;—they said it was outlandish, and what a figure I looked in it."

"Well, certainly that was not very polite. Put it on and let me see."

Ellen obeyed.

"I am not the best judge of ladies' bonnets, it is true," said he, "but I can see nothing about it that is not perfectly proper and suitable,—nothing in the world! So that is what has kept you bareheaded all day? Didn't your mother wish you to wear that bonnet?"

"Yes, sir."

"Then that ought to be enough for you. Will you be ashamed of what *she* approved, because some people that haven't probably half her sense choose to make merry with it?—is that right?" he said gently. "Is that honouring her as she deserves?"

"No, sir," said Ellen, looking up into his face, "but I never thought of that before;—I am sorry."

"Never mind being laughed at, my child. If your mother says a thing is right, that's enough for you—let them laugh!"

" I won't be ashamed of my bonnet any more," said Ellen, tying it on ; " but they made me very unhappy about it, and very angry too."

" I am sorry for that," said her friend, gravely. " Have you quite got over it, Ellen ?"

" Oh, yes, sir,—long ago."

" Are you sure ?"

" I am not angry now, sir."

" Is there no unkindness left toward the people who laughed at you ?"

" I don't like them much," said Ellen ;—" how can I ?"

" You cannot of course *like* the company of ill-behaved people, and I do not wish that you should ; but you can and ought to feel just as kindly disposed toward them as if they had never offended you—just as willing and inclined to please them or do them good. Now, could you offer Miss what's her name ?—some of your candies with as hearty good-will as you could before she laughed at you ?"

" No, sir, I couldn't. I don't feel as if I ever wished to see them again."

" Then, my dear Ellen, you have something to do, if you were in earnest in the resolve you made this morning. ' If ye forgive unto men their trespasses, my Heavenly Father will also forgive you ; but if you forgive not men their trespasses, neither will my father forgive your trespasses !' "

He was silent, and so was Ellen, for some time. His words had raised a struggle in her mind ; and she kept her face turned toward the shore, so that her bonnet shielded it from view ; but she did not in the least know what she was looking at. The sun had been some time descending through a sky of cloudless splendour, and now was just kissing the mountain tops of the western horizon. Slowly and with great majesty he sank behind the distant blue line, till only a glittering edge appeared,—and then that was gone. There were no clouds hanging over his setting, to be gilded and purpled by the parting rays, but a region of glory long remained, to show where his path had been.

The eyes of both were fixed upon this beautiful scene, but only one was thinking of it. Just as the last glimpse of the sun had disappeared Ellen turned her face, bright again, toward her companion. He was intently gazing toward the hills that had so drawn Ellen's attention a while ago, and thinking still more intently, it was plain ; so though her mouth had been open to speak, she turned her face away again as suddenly as it had just sought his. He saw the motion, however.

" What is it, Ellen ?" he said.

Ellen looked again with a smile.

" I have been thinking, sir, of what you said to me."

" Well ?" said he smiling in answer.

" I can't *like* Mrs. Dunscombe and Miss Dunscombe as well as if they hadn't done so to me, but I will try to behave as if nothing had been the matter, and be as kind and polite to them as if they had been kind and polite to me."

"And how about the sugar-plums ?"

" The sugar-plums ! Oh," said Ellen, laughing, " Miss Margaret may have them all if she likes—I'm quite willing. Not but I had rather give them to you, sir."

" You give me something a great deal better when I see you try to overcome a wrong feeling. You mustn't rest till you get rid of every bit of ill-will that you feel for this and any other unkindness you may suffer. You cannot do it yourself, but you know who can help you. I hope you have asked him, Ellen ?"

" I have, sir, indeed."

" Keep asking him, and he will do every thing for you."

A silence of some length followed. Ellen began to feel very much the fatigue of this exciting day, and sat quietly by her friend's side, leaning against him. The wind had changed about sundown, and now blew light from the south, so that they did not feel it all.

The light gradually faded away, till only a silver glow in the west showed where the sun had set, and the sober grey of twilight was gently stealing over all the bright colours of sky, and river, and hill ; now and then a twinkling light began to appear along the shores.

" You are very tired," said Ellen's friend to her,—" I see you are. A little more patience, my child ;—we shall be at our journey's end before a very great while."

" I am almost sorry," said Ellen, " though I *am* tired. We don't go in the steamboat to-morrow ; do we, sir."

" No,—in the stage."

" Shall *you* be in the stage, sir ?"

" No, my child. But I am glad you and I have spent this day together."

" Oh, sir !" said Ellen, " I don't know what I should have done if it hadn't been for you !"

There was silence again, and the gentleman almost thought his little charge had fallen asleep, she sat so still. But she suddenly spoke again, and in a tone of voice that showed sleep was far away.

" I wish I knew where mamma is now !"

" I do not doubt, my child, from what you told me, that it is well with her wherever she is. Let that thought comfort you whenever you remember her."

" She must want me so much," said poor Ellen, in a scarcely audible voice.

" She has not lost her best friend, my child."

"I know it, sir," said Ellen, with whom grief was now getting the mastery,—"but oh! it's just near the time when I used to make the tea for her—who'll make it now? she'll want me,—oh, what shall I do!" and overcome completely by this recollection, she threw herself into her friend's arms and sobbed aloud.

There was no reasoning against this. He did not attempt it; but with the utmost gentleness and tenderness endeavoured, as soon as he might, to soothe and calm her. He succeeded at last; with a sort of despairing submission, Ellen ceased her tears, and arose to her former position. But he did not rest from his kind endeavours till her mind was really eased and comforted; which, however, was not long before the lights of a city began to appear in the distance. And with them appeared a dusky figure ascending the stairs, which, upon nearer approach, proved by the voice to be Timmins.

"Is this Miss Montgomery?" said she;—"I can't see, I am sure, it's so dark. Is that you, Miss Montgomery?"

"Yes," said Ellen, "it is I; do you want me?"

"If you please, miss, Mrs. Dunscombe wants you to come right down; we're almost in, she says, miss."

"I'll come directly, Miss Timmins," said Ellen. "Don't wait for me,—I won't be a minute,—I'll come directly."

Miss Timmins retired, standing still a good deal in awe of the grave personage whose protection Ellen seemed to have gained.

"I must go," said Ellen, standing up and extending her hand;— "Good-by, sir."

She could hardly say it. He drew her toward him and kissed her cheek once or twice; it was well he did; for it sent a thrill of pleasure to Ellen's heart that she did not get over that evening, nor all the next day.

"God bless you, my child," he said, gravely but cheerfully; "and good-night!—you will feel better I trust when you have had some rest and refreshment."

He took care of her down the stairs, and saw her safe to the very door of the saloon, and within it; and there again took her hand and kindly bade her good-night!

Ellen entered the saloon only to sit down and cry as if her heart would break. She saw and heard nothing till Mrs. Dunscombe's voice bade her make haste and be ready, for they were going ashore in five minutes.

And in less than five minutes ashore they went.

"Which hotel, ma'am?" asked the servant who carried her baggage,—"the Eagle, or Foster's?"

"The Eagle," said Mrs. Dunscombe.

"Come this way then ma'am," said another man, the driver of the Eagle carriage,—"Now ma'am, step in, if you please."

Mrs. Dunscombe put her daughter in.

"But it's full!" said she to the driver; "there isn't room for another one!"

"Oh, yes, ma'am, there is," said the driver, holding the door open; "there's plenty of room for you, ma'am,—just get in, ma'am, if you please,—we'll be there in less than two minutes."

"Timmins, you'll have to walk," said Mrs. Dunscombe. "Miss Montgomery, would you rather ride, or walk with Timmins?"

"How far is it, ma'am?" said Ellen.

"Oh, bless me! how can I tell how far it is? I don't know, I am sure,—not far;—say quick,—would you rather walk or ride?"

"I would rather walk, ma'am, if you please," said Ellen.

"Very well," said Mrs. Dunscombe, getting in;—"Timmins, you know the way."

And off went the coach with its load; but tired as she was, Ellen did not wish herself along.

Picking a passage-way out of the crowd, she and Timmins now began to make their way up one of the comparatively quiet streets.

It was a strange place—that she felt. She had lived long enough in the place she had left to feel at home there; but here she came to no street or crossing that she had ever seen before; nothing looked familiar; all reminded her that she was a traveller. Only one pleasant thing Ellen saw on her walk, and that was the sky; and that looked just as it did at home; and very often Ellen's gaze was fixed upon it, much to the astonishment of Miss Timmins, who had to be not a little watchful for the safety of Ellen's feet while her eyes were thus employed. She had taken a great fancy to Ellen, however, and let her do as she pleased, keeping all her wonderment to herself.

"Take care, Miss Ellen!" cried Timmins, giving her arm a great pull,—"I declare I just saved you out of that gutter! poor child! you are dreadfully tired, ain't you?"

"Yes, I am very tired, Miss Timmins," said Ellen, "have we much further to go?"

"Not a great deal, dear; cheer up! we are almost there. I hope Mrs. Dunscombe will want to ride one of these days herself, and can't."

"Oh, don't say so, Miss Timmins," said Ellen,—"I don't wish so, indeed."

"Well, I should think you would," said Timmins,—"I should think you'd be fit to poison her;—*I* should, I know, if I was in your place."

"Oh, no," said Ellen, "that wouldn't be right,—that would be very wrong."

"Wrong!" said Timmins,—"why would it be wrong? she hasn't behaved good to you."

" Yes," said Ellen,—" but don't you know the Bible says if we
do not forgive people what they do to us, we shall not be forgiven
ourselves ?"

" Well, I declare !" said Miss Timmins, " you beat all ! But
here's the Eagle hotel at last,—and I am glad for your sake, dear."

Ellen was shown into the ladies' parlour. She was longing for
a place to rest, but she saw directly it was not to be there. The
room was large, and barely furnished ; and round it were scattered
part of the carriage-load of people that had arrived a quarter of
an hour before her. They were waiting till their rooms should be
ready. Ellen silently found herself a chair and sat down to wait
with the rest, as patiently as she might. Few of them had as
much cause for impatience ; but she was the only perfectly mute
and uncomplaining one there. Her two companions however
between them, fully made up her share of fretting. At length, a
servant brought the welcome news that their room was ready, and
the three marched up stairs. It made Ellen's very heart glad
when they got there, to find a good-sized, cheerful-looking bedroom, comfortably furnished, with a bright fire burning, large
curtains let down to the floor, and a nice warm carpet upon it.
Taking off her bonnet, and only that, she sat down on a low
cushion by the corner of the fireplace, and leaning her head against
the jamb fell fast asleep almost immediately. Mrs. Dunscombe
set about arranging herself for the tea-table.

" Well !" she said,—" one day of this precious journey is
over !"

" Does Ellen go with us to-morrow, mamma ?"

" Oh, yes !—quite to Thirlwall."

" Well, you haven't had much plague with her to-day, mamma."

" No—I am sure I am much obliged to whoever has kept her
out of my way."

" Where is she going to sleep to-night ?" asked Miss Margaret.

" I don't know, I am sure.—I suppose I shall have to have a cot
brought in here for her."

" What a plague !" said Miss Margaret. " It will lumber up
the room so ! There's no place to put it. Couldn't she sleep with
Timmins ?"

" Oh, she *could*, of course—just as well as not, only people
would make such a fuss about it ;—it wouldn't do ; we must bear
it for once. I'll try and not be caught in such a scrape again."

" How provoking !" said Miss Margaret ; " how came father to
do so without asking you about it ?"

" Oh, he was bewitched, I suppose,—men always are. Look
here, Margaret,—I can't go down to tea with a train of children
at my heels,—I shall leave you and Ellen up here, and I'll send
up your tea to you."

"Oh, no, mamma!" said Margaret eagerly; "I want to go down with you. Look here, mamma! she's asleep and you needn't wake her up—that's excuse enough; you can leave her to have her tea up here, and let me go down with you."

"Well," said Mrs. Dunscombe,—"I don't care—but make haste to get ready, for I expect every minute when the tea-bell will ring."

"Timmins! Timmins!" cried Margaret,—"come here and fix me—quick!—and step softly, will you?—or you'll wake that young one up, and then, you see, I shall have to stay up stairs."

This did not happen however. Ellen's sleep was much too deep to be easily disturbed. The tea-bell itself, loud and shrill as it was, did not even make her eyelids tremble. After Mrs. and Miss Dunscombe were gone down, Timmins employed herself a little while in putting all things about the room to rights; and then sat down to take *her* rest, dividing her attention between the fire and Ellen, toward whom she seemed to feel more and more kindness, as she saw that she was likely to receive it from no one else. Presently came a knock at the door;—"The tea for the young lady," on a waiter. Miss Timmins silently took the tray from the man and shut the door. "Well!" said she to herself,— "if that ain't a pretty supper to send up to a child that has gone two hundred miles to-day, and had no breakfast!—a cup of tea, cold enough I'll warrant,—bread and butter enough for a bird,— and two little slices of ham as thick as a wafer!—well, I just wish Mrs. Dunscombe had to eat it herself, and nothing else!—I'm not going to wake her up for that, I know, till I see whether something better ain't to be had for love or money. So just you sleep on, darling, till I see what I can do for you."

In great indignation, down stairs went Miss Timmins; and at the foot of the stairs she met a rosy-cheeked, pleasant-faced girl coming up.

"Are you the chambermaid?" said Timmins.

"I'm *one* of the chambermaids," said the girl smiling; "there's three of us in this house, dear."

"Well, I am a stranger here," said Timmins, "but I want you to help me, and I am sure you will. I've got a dear little girl up stairs that I want some supper for—she's a sweet child, and she's under the care of some proud folks here in the tea-room that think it's too much trouble to look at her; and they've sent her up about supper enough for a mouse,—and she's half starving; she lost her breakfast this morning by their ugliness. Now ask one of the waiters to give me something nice for her, will you?—there's a good girl."

"James!"—said the girl in a loud whisper to one of the waiters who was crossing the hall. He instantly stopped and came toward them, tray in hand, and making several extra polite bows as he drew near.

" What's on the supper-table, James?" said the smiling damsel.
" Every thing that ought to be there, Miss Johns," said the man,
with another flourish.

" Come, stop your nonsense," said the girl, " and tell me quick
—I'm in a hurry."

" It's a pleasure to perform your commands, Miss Johns. I'll
give you the whole bill of fare. There's a very fine beef-steak,
fricasseed chickens, stewed oysters, sliced ham, cheese, preserved
quinces,—with the usual complement of bread and toast and muffins,
and doughnuts, and new-year cake, and plenty of butter,—likewise
salt and pepper,—likewise tea and coffee, and sugar,—likewise,—"

" Hush !" said the girl. " Do stop, will you?"—and then laughing and turning to Miss Timmins, she added, " What will you
have?"

" I guess I'll have some of the chickens and oysters," said
Timmins ; " that will be the nicest for her,—and a muffin or two."

" Now, James, do you hear?" said the chambermaid ; " I want
you to get me now, right away, a nice little supper of chickens and
oysters and a muffin—it's for a lady up stairs. Be as quick as
you can."

" I should be very happy to execute impossibilities for you, Miss
Johns, but Mrs. Custers is at the table herself."

" Very well—that's nothing—she'll think it's for somebody up
stairs—and so it is."

" Ay, but the up-stairs people is Tim's business—I should be
hauled over the coals directly."

" Then ask Tim, will you? How slow you are ! Now, James,
if you don't, I won't speak to you again."

" Till to-morrow?—I couldn't stand that. It shall be done, Miss
Johns, instantum."

Bowing and smiling, away went James, leaving the girls giggling
on the staircase and highly gratified.

" He always does what I want him to," said the good-humoured
chambermaid, " but he generally makes a fuss about it first. He'll
be back directly with what you want."

Till he came, Miss Timmins filled up the time with telling her
new friend as much as she knew about Ellen and Ellen's hardships ;
with which Miss Johns was so much interested that she declared
she must go up and see her ; and when James in a few minutes
returned with a tray of nice things, the two women proceeded
together to Mrs. Dunscombe's room. Ellen had moved so far as to
put herself on the floor with her head on the cushion for a pillow,
but she was as sound asleep as ever.

" Just see now !" said Timmins ; " there she lies on the floor—
enough to give her her death of cold ; poor child, she's tired to
death ; and Mrs. Dunscombe made her walk up from the steamboat

to-night rather than do it herself;—I declare I wished the coach would break down, only for the other folks. I am glad I have got a good supper for her though,—thank *you*, Miss Johns."

"And I'll tell you what, I'll go and get you some nice hot tea," said the chambermaid, who was quite touched by the sight of Ellen's little pale face.

"Thank you," said Timmins,—"you're a darling. This is as cold as a stone."

While the chambermaid went forth on her kind errand, Timmins stooped down by the little sleeper's side. "Miss Ellen!" she said;—"Miss Ellen!—wake up, dear—wake up and get some supper—come! you'll feel a great deal better for it—you shall sleep as much as you like afterwards."

Slowly Ellen raised herself and opened her eyes. "Where am I?" she asked, looking bewildered.

"Here, dear," said Timmins;—"wake up and eat something—it will do you good."

With a sigh, poor Ellen arose and came to the fire. "You're tired to death, ain't you?" said Timmins.

"Not quite," said Ellen. "I shouldn't mind that if my legs would not ache so—and my head, too."

"Now I'm sorry!" said Timmins; "but your head will be better for eating, I know. See here—I've got you some nice chicken and oysters,—and I'll make this muffin hot for you by the fire; and here comes your tea. Miss Johns, I'm your servant, and I'll be your bridesmaid with the greatest pleasure in life. Now, Miss Ellen, dear, just you put yourself on that low chair, and I'll fix you off."

Ellen thanked her, and did as she was told. Timmins brought another chair to her side, and placed the tray with her supper upon it, and prepared her muffin and tea; and having fairly seen Ellen begin to eat, she next took off her shoes, and seating herself on the carpet before her, she made her lap the resting place for Ellen's feet, chafing them in her hands and heating them at the fire, saying there was nothing like rubbing and roasting to get rid of the leg-ache. By the help of the supper, the fire, and Timmins, Ellen mended rapidly. With tears in her eyes, she thanked the latter for her kindness.

"Now just don't say one word about that," said Timmins; "I never was famous for kindness, as I know; but people must be kind sometimes in their lives,—unless they happen to be made of stone, which I believe some people are. You feel better, don't you?"

"A great deal," said Ellen. "Oh, if I only could go to bed, now!"

"And you shall," said Timmins. "I know about your bed, and I'll go right away and have it brought in." And away she went.

While she was gone, Ellen drew from her pocket her little hymn-book, to refresh herself with looking at it. How quickly and freshly it brought back to her mind the friend who had given it, and his conversations with her, and the resolve she had made; and again Ellen's whole heart offered the prayer she had repeated many times that day,—

"Open my heart, Lord, enter in;
Slay every foe, and conquer sin."

Her head was still bent upon her little book when Timmins entered. Timmins was not alone; Miss Johns and a little cot bedstead came in with her. The latter was put at the foot of Mrs. Dunscombe's bed, and speedily made up by the chambermaid, while Timmins undressed Ellen; and very soon all the sorrows and vexations of the day were forgotten in a sound, refreshing sleep. But not till she had removed her little hymn-book from the pocket of her frock to a safe station under her pillow; it was with her hand upon it that Ellen went to sleep; and it was in her hand still when she was waked the next morning.

The next day was spent in a wearisome stage-coach, over a rough, jolting road. Ellen's companions did nothing to make her way pleasant, but she sweetened theirs with her sugar-plums. Somewhat mollified, perhaps, after that, Miss Margaret condescended to enter into conversation with her, and Ellen underwent a thorough cross-examination as to all her own and her parents' affairs, past, present, and future, and likewise as to all that could be known of her yesterday's friend, till she was heartily worried, and out of patience.

It was just five o'clock when they reached her stopping-place. Ellen knew of no particular house to go to; so Mrs. Dunscombe set her down at the door of the principal inn of the town, called the "Star" of Thirlwall.

The driver smacked his whip, and away went the stage again, and she was left standing alone beside her trunk before the piazza of the inn, watching Timmins, who was looking back at her out of the stage window, nodding and waving good by.

CHAPTER IX.

Gadshill.—Sirrah, carrier, what time do you mean to come to London?
2d Carrier.—Time enough to go to bed with a candle, I warrant thee.
KING HENRY IV.

ELLEN had been whirled along over the roads for so many hours, —the rattle of the stage-coach had filled her ears for so long,—that now, suddenly still and quiet, she felt half stunned. She stood with a kind of dreamy feeling, looking after the departing stage-coach. In it there were three people whose faces she knew, and she could not count a fourth within many a mile. One of those was a friend, too, as the fluttering handkerchief of poor Miss Timmins gave token still. Yet Ellen did not wish herself back in the coach, although she continued to stand and gaze after it as it rattled off at a great rate down the little street, its huge body lumbering up and down every now and then, reminding her of sundry uncomfortable jolts; till the horses making a sudden turn to the right, it disappeared round a corner. Still for a minute Ellen watched the whirling cloud of dust it had left behind; but then the feeling of strangeness and loneliness came over her, and her heart sank. She cast a look up and down the street. The afternoon was lovely; the slant beams of the setting sun came back from gilded windows, and the houses and chimney-tops of the little town were in a glow; but she saw nothing bright anywhere;—in all the glory of the setting sun the little town looked strange and miserable. There was no sign of her having been expected; nobody was waiting to meet her. What was to be done next? Ellen had not the slightest idea.

Her heart growing fainter and fainter, she turned again to the inn. A tall, awkward young countryman, with a cap set on one side of his head, was busying himself with sweeping off the floor of the piazza, but in a very leisurely manner; and between every two strokes of his broom he was casting long looks at Ellen, evidently wondering who she was and what she could want there. Ellen saw it, and hoped he would ask her in words, for she could not answer his *looks* of curiosity,—but she was disappointed. As he reached the end of the piazza and gave his broom two or three knocks against the edge of the boards to clear it of dust, he indulged himself with one good long finishing look at Ellen, and then she saw he was going to take himself and his broom into the house. So in despair she ran up the two or three low steps of the piazza and presented herself before him. He stopped short.

"Will you please to tell me, sir," said poor Ellen, "if Miss Emerson is here?"

"Miss Emerson?" said he,—"what Miss Emerson?"

"I don't know, sir,—Miss Emerson that lives not far from Thirlwall."

Eying Ellen from head to foot, the man then trailed his broom into the house. Ellen followed him.

"Mr. Forbes!" said he, "Mr. Forbes! do you know any thing of Miss Emerson?"

"What Miss Emerson?" said another man, with a big red face and a big round body, showing himself in a doorway which he nearly filled.

"Miss Emerson that lives a little way out of town."

" Miss Fortune Emerson ? yes, I know her. What of her ?"

" Has she been here to-day ?"

" Here ? what, in town ? No—not as I've seen or heerd. Why, who wants her ?"

" This little girl."

And the man with the broom stepping back, disclosed Ellen to the view of the red-faced landlord. He advanced a step or two toward her.

" What do you want with Miss Fortune, little one ?" said he.

" I expected she would meet me here, sir," said Ellen.

" Where have you come from ?"

" From New York."

" The stage set her down just now," put in the other man.

" And you thought Miss Fortune would meet you, did you ?"

" Yes, sir ; she was to meet me and take me home."

" Take you home ! Are you going to Miss Fortune's home ?"

" Yes, sir."

" Why, you don't belong to her any way, do you ?"

" No, sir," said Ellen, " but she's my aunt."

" She's your what ?"

" My aunt, sir,—my father's sister."

" Your father's sister ! You ben't the daughter of Morgan Montgomery, be you ?"

" Yes, I am," said Ellen, half smiling.

" And you are come to make a visit to Miss Fortune, eh ?"

" Yes," said Ellen, smiling no longer.

" And Miss Fortune ha'n't come up to meet you ;—that's real shabby of her ; and how to get you down.there to-night, I am sure is more than I can tell."—And he shouted, " Wife !"

" What's the matter, Mr. Forbes ?" said a fat landlady, appearing in the doorway, which she filled near as well as her husband would have done.

" Look here," said Mr. Forbes, " here's Morgan Montgomery's daughter come to pay a visit to her aunt, Fortune Emerson. Don't you think she'll be glad to see her ?"

Mr. Forbes put this question with rather a curious look at his wife. She didn't answer him. She only looked at Ellen, looked grave, and gave a queer little nod of her head, which meant, Ellen could not make out what.

" Now, what's to be done ?" continued Mr. Forbes. " Miss Fortune was to have come up to meet her, but she ain't here, and I don't know how in the world I can take the child down there to-night. The horses are both out to plough, you know ; and besides, the tire is come off that wagon wheel. I couldn't possibly use it. And then it's a great question in my mind what Miss Fortune would say to me. I should get paid, I s'pose ?"

"Yes, you'd get paid," said his wife, with another little shake of her head ; "but whether it would be the kind of pay you'd like, *I* don't know."

"Well, what's to be done, wife? Keep the child over-night, and send word down yonder?"

"No," said Mrs. Forbes, "I'll tell you. I think I saw Van Brunt go by two or three hours ago with the ox-cart, and I guess he's somewhere up town yet; I ha'n't seen him go back. He can take the child home with him. Sam!" shouted Mrs. Forbes,— "Sam!—here!—Sam, run up street directly, and see if you see Mr. Van Brunt's ox-cart standing anywhere—I dare say he's at Mr. Miller's, or maybe at Mr. Hammersley's, the blacksmith—and ask him to stop here before he goes home. Now hurry!—and don't run over him and then come back and tell me he ain't in town."

Mrs. Forbes herself followed Sam to the door, and cast an exploring look in every direction.

"I don't see no signs of him,—up nor down," said she, returning to Ellen ; "but I'm pretty sure he ain't gone home. Come in here —come in here, dear, and make yourself comfortable ; it'll be a while yet maybe 'afore Mr. Van Brunt comes, but he'll be along by and by ;—come in here and rest yourself."

She opened a door, and Ellen followed her into a large kitchen, where a fire was burning that showed wood must be plenty in those regions. Mrs. Forbes placed a low chair for her on the hearth, but herself remained standing by the side of the fire, looking earnestly and with a good deal of interest upon the little stranger. Ellen drew her white bonnet from her head, and sitting down with a wearied air, gazed sadly into the flames that were shedding their light upon her.

"Are you going to stop a good while with Miss Fortune?" said Mrs. Forbes.

"I don't know, ma'am,—yes, I believe so," said Ellen faintly.

"Ha'n't you got no mother?" asked Mrs. Forbes suddenly, after a pause.

"Oh, yes!" said Ellen, looking up. But the question had touched the sore spot. Her head sank on her hands, and "Oh, mamma!" was uttered with a bitterness that even Mrs. Forbes could feel.

"Now what made me ask you that!" said she. "Don't cry!— don't, love ; poor little dear! you're as pale as a sheet; you're tired, I know—ain't you? Now cheer up, do,—I can't bear to see you cry. You've come a great ways to-day, ha'n't you?"

Ellen nodded her head, but could give no answer.

"I know what will do you good," said Mrs. Forbes presently, getting up from the crouching posture she had taken to comfort Ellen ; "you want something to eat,—that's the matter. I'll warrant you're half starved;—no wonder you feel bad. Poor little thing! you shall have something good directly."

And away she bustled to get it. Left alone, Ellen's tears flowed a few minutes very fast. She felt forlorn; and she was besides, as Mrs. Forbes opined, both tired and faint. But she did not wish to be found weeping; she checked her tears, and was sitting again quietly before the fire when the landlady returned.

Mrs. Forbes had a great bowl of milk in one hand, and a plate of bread in the other, which she placed on the kitchen table, and setting a chair, called Ellen to come and partake of it.

"Come, dear,—here is something that will do you good. I thought there was a piece of pie in the buttery, and so there was, but Mr. Forbes must have got hold of it, for it ain't there now; and there ain't a bit of cake in the house for you; but I thought maybe you would like this as well as any thing. Come!"

Ellen thanked her, but said she did not want any thing.

"Oh, yes, you do," said Mrs. Forbes; "I know better. You're as pale as I don't know what. Come! this'll put roses in your cheeks. Don't you like bread and milk?"

"Yes, very much indeed, ma'am," said Ellen, "but I'm not hungry." She rose, however, and came to the table.

"Oh, well, try to eat a bit just to please me. It's real good country milk—not a bit of cream off. You don't get such milk as that in the city, I guess. That's right!—I see the roses coming back to your cheeks already. Is your pa in New York now?"

"Yes, ma'am."

"You expect your pa and ma up to Thirlwall by and by, don't you?"

"No, ma'am."

Mrs. Forbes was surprised, and longed to ask why not, and what Ellen had come for; but the shade that had passed over her face as she answered the last question warned the landlady she was getting upon dangerous ground.

"Does your aunt expect you to-night?'

"I believe so, ma'am,—I don't know,—she was to have met me; papa said he would write."

"Oh, well! maybe something hindered her from coming. It's no matter; you'll get home just as well. Mr. Van Brunt will be here soon, I guess; it's most time for him to be along."

She went to the front door to look out for him, but returned without any news. A few minutes passed in silence, for though full of curiosity, the good landlady dared not ask what she wanted to know, for fear of again exciting the sorrow of her little companion. She contented herself with looking at Ellen, who on her part, much rested and refreshed, had turned from the table and was again, though somewhat less sadly, gaxing into the fire.

Presently the great wooden clock struck half-past five, with a whirring, rickety voice, for all the world like a hoarse grasshopper. Ellen at first wondered where it came from, and was looking at the clumsy machine that reached nearly from the floor of the kitchen to the ceiling, when a door at the other end of the room opened, and " Good-day, Mrs. Forbes," in a rough but not un-pleasant voice, brought her head qu. kly round in that direction. There stood a large, strong-built man, with an ox-whip in his hand. He was well-made and rather handsome, but there was something of heaviness in the air of both face and person mixed with his certainly good-humoured expression. His dress was as rough as his voice—a coarse grey frock-coat, green velveteen pantaloons, and a fur cap that had seen its best days some time ago.

" Good-day, Mrs. Forbes," said this personage ; " Sam said you wanted me to stop as I went along."

" Ah, how d' ye do, Mr. Van Brunt ?" said the landlady, rising ; " you've got the ox-cart here with you, ha'n't you ?"

" Yes, I've got the ox-cart," said the person addressed. " I came in town for a barrel of flour, and then the near ox had lost both his fore shoes off, and I had to go over there, and Hammersley has kept me a precious long time. What's wanting, Mrs. Forbes ? I can't stop."

" You've no load in the cart, have you ?" said the landlady.

" No ; I should have had though, but Miller had no shorts nor fresh flour, nor won't till next week. What's to go down, Mrs. Forbes ?"

" The nicest load ever you carried, Mr. Van Brunt. Here's a little lady come to stay with Miss Fortune. She's a daughter of Captain Montgomery, Miss Fortune's brother, you know. She came by the stage a little while ago, and the thing is now to get her down to-night. She can go in the cart, can't she ?"

Mr. Van Brunt looked a little doubtful, and pulling off his cap with one hand, while he scratched his head with the other, he ex-amined Ellen from head to foot ; much as if she had been some great bale of goods, and he were considering whether his cart would hold her or not.

" Well," said he at length,—" I don't know but she can ; but there ain't nothing on 'arth for her to sit down upon."

" Oh, never mind ; I'll fix that," said Mrs. Forbes. " Is there any straw in the bottom of the cart?"

" Not a bit."

"Well, I'll fix it," said Mrs. Forbes. " You get her trunk into the cart, will you, Mr. Van Brunt ? and I'll see to the rest."

Mr. Van Brunt moved off without another word to do what was desired of him,—apparently quite confounded at having a passenger instead of his more wonted load of bags and barrels. And his face still continued to wear the singular doubtful expression it had put on at first hearing the news. Ellen's trunk was quickly hoisted in, however; and Mrs. Forbes presently appeared with a little arm-chair, which Mr. Van Brunt with an approving look bestowed in the cart, planting it with its back against the trunk to keep it steady. Mrs. Forbes then raising herself on tiptoe by the side of the cart, took a view of the arrangements.

"That won't do yet," said she; " her feet will be cold on that bare floor, and 'tain't over clean neither. Here, Sally! run up and fetch me that piece of carpet you'll find lying at the top of the back stairs. Now, hurry!—Now, Mr. Van Brunt, I depend upon you to get my things back again; will you see and bring 'em the first time you come in town?"

"I'll see about it. But what if I can't get hold of them?" answered the person addressed, with a half smile.

"Oh," said Mrs. Forbes, with another, "I leave that to you; you have your ways and means. Now, just spread this carpet down nicely under her chair; and then she'll be fixed. Now, my darling, you'll ride like a queen. But how are you going to get in? Will you let Mr. Van Brunt lift you up?"

Ellen's "Oh, no, ma'am, if you please!" was accompanied with such an evident shrinking from the proposal, that Mrs. Forbes did not press it. A chair was brought from the kitchen, and by making a long step from it to the top of the wheel, and then to the edge of the cart, Ellen was at length safely stowed in her place. Kind Mrs. Forbes then stretched herself up over the side of the cart to shake hands with her and bid her good-by, telling her again she would ride like a queen. Ellen answered only "Good-by, ma'am;" but it was said with a look of so much sweetness, and eyes swimming half in sadness and half in gratefulness, that the good landlady could not forget it.

"I do think," said she, when she went back to her husband, " that is the dearest little thing, about, I ever did see."

"Humph!" said her husband, " I reckon Miss Fortune will think so too."

The doubtful look came back to Mrs. Forbes' face, and with another little grave shake of her head, she went into the kitchen.

"How kind she is! how good every body is to me," thought little Ellen, as she moved off in state in her chariot drawn by oxen. Quite a contrast this new way of travelling was to the noisy stage and swift steamer. Ellen did not know at first whether to like or dislike it; but she came to the conclusion that it was very funny, and a remarkably amusing way of getting along. There was one disadvantage about it certainly,—their rate of travel was very slow. Ellen wondered her charioteer did not make his

animals go faster; but she soon forgot their lazy progress in the
interest of novel sights and new scenes.

Slowly, very slowly, the good oxen drew the cart and the little
queen in the arm-chair out of the town, and they entered upon the
open country. The sun had already gone down when they left
the inn, and the glow of his setting had faded a good deal by the
time they got quite out of the town; but light enough was left
still to delight Ellen with the pleasant look of the country. It
was a lovely evening, and quiet as summer; not a breath stirring.
The leaves were all off the trees; the hills were brown; but the
soft warm light that still lingered upon them forbade any look of
harshness or dreariness. These hills lay toward the west, and at

Thirlwall were not more than two miles distant, but sloping off
more to the west as the range extended in a southerly direction.
Between, the ground was beautifully broken. Rich fields and
meadows lay on all sides, sometimes level, and sometimes with a
soft wavy surface, where Ellen thought it must be charming to
run up and down. Every now and then these were varied by a
little rising ground capped with a piece of woodland; and beautiful trees, many of them, were seen standing alone, especially by
the road-side. All had a cheerful, pleasant look. The houses
were very scattered; in the whole way they passed but few.
Ellen's heart regularly began to beat when they came in sight of
one, and "I wonder if that is aunt Fortune's house!"—"perhaps

it is !''—or, " I hope it is not !'' were the thoughts that rose in her mind. But slowly the oxen brought her abreast of the houses, one after another, and slowly they passed on beyond, and there was no sign of getting home yet. Their way was through pleasant lanes toward the south, but constantly approaching the hills. About half a mile from Thirlwall, they crossed a little river, not more than thirty yards broad, and after that the twilight deepened fast. The shades gathered on field and hill: every thing grew brown, and then dusky ; and then Ellen was obliged to content herself with what was very near, for further than that she could only see dim outlines. She began again to think of their slow travelling, and to wonder that Mr. Van Brunt could be content with it. She wondered too what made him walk, when he might just as well have sat in the cart; the truth was he had chosen that for the very purpose that he might have a good look at the little queen in the arm-chair. Apparently, however, he too now thought it might be as well to make a little haste, for he thundered out some orders to his oxen, accompanied with two or three strokes of his heavy lash, which, though not cruel by any means, went to Ellen's heart.

" Them lazy critters won't go fast anyhow," said he to Ellen,— " they will take their own time ; it ain't no use to cut them.''

" Oh, no ! pray don't, if you please !'' said Ellen, in a voice of earnest entreaty.

" 'Tain't fair neither,'' continued Mr. Van Brunt, lashing his great whip from side to side without touching any thing. " I have seen critters that would take any quantity of whipping to make them go, but them 'ere ain't of that kind ; they'll work as long as they can stand, poor fellows !''

There was a little silence, during which Ellen eyed her rough charioteer, not knowing exactly what to make of him.

" I guess this is the first time you ever rid in an ox-cart, ain't it ?''

" Yes,'' said Ellen ; " I never saw one before.''

" Ha'n't you never seen an ox-cart ! Well—how do you like it ?''

" I like it very much indeed. Have we much farther to go before we get to aunt Fortune's house ?''

" ' Aunt Fortune's house !' a pretty good bit yet. You see that mountain over there ?''—pointing with his whip to a hill directly west of them, and about a mile distant.

" Yes,'' said Ellen.

" That's the Nose. Then you see that other ?''—pointing to one that lay some two miles further south ;—" Miss Fortune's house is just this side of that ; it's all of two miles from here.''

And urged by this recollection, he again scolded and cheered the patient oxen, who for the most part kept on their steady way without any reminder. But perhaps it was for Ellen's sake that he scarcely touched them with the whip.

" That don't hurt them, not a bit," he remarked to Ellen,—" it only lets them know that I'm here, and they must mind their business. So you're Miss Fortune's niece, eh ?"

" Yes," said Ellen.

" Well," said Mr. Van Brunt, with a desperate attempt at being complimentary, " I shouldn't care if you was mine too."

Ellen was somewhat astounded, and so utterly unable to echo the wish, that she said nothing. She did not know it, but Mr. Van Brunt had made, for him, most extraordinary efforts at sociability. Having quite exhausted himself, he now mounted into the cart and sat silent, only now and then uttering energetic " Gee's !" and " Haw's !" which greatly excited Ellen's wonderment. She discovered they were meant for the ears of the oxen, but more than that she could not make out.

They plodded along very slowly, and the evening fell fast. As they left behind the hill which Mr. Van Brunt had called " the Nose," they could see, through an opening in the mountains, a bit of the western horizon, and some brightness still lingering there ; but it was soon hid from view, and darkness veiled the whole country. Ellen could amuse herself no longer with looking about ; she could see nothing very clearly but the outline of Mr. Van Brunt's broad back, just before her. But the stars had come out ! —and, brilliant and clear, they were looking down upon her with their thousand eyes. Ellen's heart jumped when she saw them with a mixed feeling of pleasure and sadness. They carried her right back to the last evening when she was walking up the hill with Timmins ; she remembered her anger against Mrs. Dunscombe, and her kind friend's warning not to indulge it, and all his teaching that day ; and tears came with the thought, how glad she should be to hear him speak to her again. Still looking up at the beautiful quiet stars, she thought of her dear far-off mother,—how long it was already since she had seen her ;—faster and faster the tears dropped ;—and then she thought of that glorious One who had made the stars, and was above them all, and who could and did see her mother and her, though ever so far apart, and could hear and bless them both. The little face was no longer upturned —it was buried in her hands, and bowed to her lap, and tears streamed as she prayed that God would bless her dear mother and take care of her. Not once nor twice ;—the fulness of Ellen's heart could not be poured out in one asking. Greatly comforted at last, at having as it were laid over the care of her mother upon One who was able, she thought of herself, and her late resolution to serve him. She was in the same mind still. She could not call herself a Christian yet, but she was resolved to be one; and she earnestly asked the Saviour she sought, to make her and keep her his child. And then Ellen felt happy.

Quiet, and weariness, and even drowsiness succeeded. It was well the night was still, for it had grown quite cool, and a breeze would have gone through and through Ellen's nankeen coat. As it was she began to be chilly, when Mr. Van Brunt, who since he got into the cart had made no remarks except to his oxen, turned round a little and spoke to her again.

"It's only a little bit of way we've got to go now," said he; "we're turning the corner."

The words seemed to shoot through Ellen's heart. She was wide awake instantly, and quite warm; and leaning forward in her little chair, she strove to pierce the darkness on either hand of her, to see whereabouts the house stood, and how things looked. She could discern nothing but misty shadows, and outlines of she could not tell what, the starlight was too dim to reveal any thing to a stranger.

"There's the house," said Mr. Van Brunt, after a few minutes more,—"do you see it yonder?"

Ellen strained her eyes, but could make out nothing,—not even a glimpse of white. She sat back in her chair, her heart beating violently. Presently Mr. Van Brunt jumped down and opened a gate at the side of the road; and with a great deal of "gee"-ing the oxen turned to the right, and drew the cart a little way up hill, then stopped on what seemed level ground.

"Here we are!" cried Mr. Van Brunt, as he threw his whip on the ground,—"and late enough! You must be tired of that little arm-cheer by this time. Come to the side of the cart and I'll lift you down."

Poor Ellen! There was no help for it. She came to the side of the cart, and taking her in his arms her rough charioteer set her very gently and carefully on the ground.

"There!" said he, "now you can run right in; do you see that little gate?"

"No," said Ellen, "I can't see any thing."

"Well, come here," said he, "and I'll show you. Here—you're running agin the fence—this way!"

And he opened a little wicket, which Ellen managed to stumble through.

"Now," said he, "go straight up to that door yonder, and open it, and you'll see where to go. Don't knock, but just pull the latch and go in."

And he went off to his oxen. Ellen at first saw no door, and did not even know where to look for it; by degrees, as her head became clearer, the large dark shadow of the house stood before her, and a little glimmering line of a path seemed to lead onward from where she stood. With unsteady steps, Ellen pursued it till her foot struck against the stone before the door. Her trembling fingers found the latch—lifted it—and she entered. All was dark there; but at the right a window showed light glimmering within. Ellen made toward it, and groping, came to another door-latch. This was big and clumsy; however, she managed it, and pushing open the heavy door, went in.

It was a good-sized, cheerful-looking kitchen. A fine fire was burning in the enormous fireplace; the white walls and ceiling were yellow in the light of the flame. No candles were needed, and none were there. The supper table was set, and with its snow-white table-cloth and shining furniture, looked very comfortable indeed. But the only person there was an old woman, sitting by the side of the fire, with her back toward Ellen. She seemed to be knitting, but did not move nor look round. Ellen had come a step or two into the room, and there she stood, unable to speak or to go any farther. "Can that be aunt Fortune?" she thought; "she can't be as old as that?"

In another minute a door opened at her right, just behind the old woman's back, and a second figure appeared at the top of a flight of stairs which led down from the kitchen. She came in, shutting the door behind her with her foot; and indeed both hands were full, one holding a lamp and a knife, and the other a plate of butter. The sight of Ellen stopped her short.

"What is this?—and what do you leave the door open for, child?" she said.

She advanced toward it, plate and lamp in hand, and setting her back against the door, shut it vigorously.

"Who are you?—and what's wanting?"

"I am Ellen Montgomery, ma'am," said Ellen, timidly.

"*What?*" said the lady, with some emphasis

"Didn't you expect me, ma'am?" said Ellen; "papa said he would write."

"Why, is this Ellen Montgomery?" said Miss Fortune, apparently forced to the conclusion that it must be.

"Yes, ma'am," said Ellen.

Miss Fortune went to the table and put the butter and the lamp in their places.

"Did you say your father wrote to tell me of your coming?"

"He said he would, ma'am," said Ellen.

"He didn't! Never sent me a line. Just like him! I never yet knew Morgan Montgomery do a thing when he promised he would."

Ellen's face flushed, and her heart swelled. She stood motionless.

"How did you get down here to-night?"

"I came in Mr. Van Brunt's ox-cart," said Ellen.

"Mr. Van Brunt's ox-cart! Then he's got home, has he?" And hearing this instant a noise outside, Miss Fortune swept to the door, saying, as she opened it, "Sit down, child, and take off your things."

The first command, at least, Ellen obeyed gladly; she did not feel enough at home to comply with the second. She only took off her bonnet.

"Well, Mr. Van Brunt," said Miss Fortune at the door, "have you brought me a barrel of flour?"

"No, Miss Fortune," said the voice of Ellen's charioteer, "I've brought you something better than that."

"Where did you find her?" said Miss Fortune, something shortly.

"Up at Forbes's."

"What have you got there?"

"A trunk. Where is it to go?"

"A trunk! Bless me! it must go up stairs; but how it is ever to get there, I am sure I don't know."

"I'll find a way to get it there, I'll engage, if you'll be so good as to open the door for me, ma'am."

"Indeed you won't! That'll never do! With your shoes!" said Miss Fortune, in a tone of indignant house wifery.

"Well—without my shoes, then," said Mr. Van Brunt, with a half giggle, as Ellen heard the shoes kicked off. "Now, ma'am, out of my way! give me a road."

Miss Fortune seized the lamp, and opening another door, ushered Mr. Van Brunt and the trunk out of the kitchen, and up, Ellen saw not whither. In a minute or two they returned, and he of the ox-cart went out.

"Supper's just ready, Mr. Van Brunt," said the mistress of the house.

"Can't stay, ma'am;—it's so late; must hurry home." And he closed the door behind him.

"What made you so late?" asked Miss Fortune of Ellen.

"I don't know, ma'am—I believe Mr. Van Brunt said the blacksmith had kept him."

Miss Fortune bustled about a few minutes in silence, setting some things on the table and filling the tea-pot.

"Come," she said to Ellen, "take off your coat and come to the table. You must be hungry by this time. It's a good while since you had your dinner, ain't it? Come, mother."

The old lady rose, and Miss Fortune, taking her chair, set it by the side of the table next the fire. Ellen was opposite to her, and now for the first time, the old lady seemed to know that she was in the room. She looked at her very attentively, but with an expressionless gaze which Ellen did not like to meet, though otherwise her face was calm and pleasant.

" Who is that?" inquired the old lady presently of Miss Fortune, in a half whisper.

" That's Morgan's daughter," was the answer.

" Morgan's daughter! Has Morgan a daughter?"

" Why, yes, mother; don't you remember I told you a month ago he was going to send her here?"

The old lady turned again with a half shake of her head toward Ellen. " Morgan's daughter," she repeated to herself softly, " she's a pretty little girl,—very pretty. Will you come round here and give me a kiss, dear?"

Ellen submitted. The old lady folded her in her arms and kissed her affectionately. " That's your grandmother, Ellen," said Miss Fortune, as Ellen went back to her seat.

Ellen had no words to answer. Her aunt saw her weary, down look, and soon after supper proposed to take her up stairs. Ellen gladly followed her. Miss Fortune showed her to her room, and first asking if she wanted any thing, left her to herself. It was a relief. Ellen's heart had been brimful and ready to run over for some time, but the tears could not come then. They did not now, till she had undressed and laid her weary little body on the bed; then they broke forth in an agony. " She did not kiss me! she didn't say she was glad to see me!" thought poor Ellen. But weariness this time was too much for sorrow and disappointment. It was but a few minutes, and Ellen's brow was calm again, and her eyelids still, and with the tears wet upon her cheeks, she was fast asleep.

CHAPTER X.

Nimble mischance, that com'st so swift of foot!
SHAKSPEARE.

THE morning sun was shining full and strong in Ellen's eyes when she awoke. Bewildered at the strangeness of every thing around her, she raised herself on her elbow, and took a long look at her new home. It could not help but seem cheerful. The bright beams of sunlight streaming in through the windows lighted on the wall and the old wainscoting, and paintless and rough as they were, nature's own gilding more than made amends for their want of comeliness. Still Ellen was not much pleased with the result of her survey. The room was good-sized, and perfectly neat and clean ; it had two large windows opening to the east, through which, morning by morning, the sun looked in—that was another blessing. But the floor was without the sign of a carpet, and the bare boards looked to Ellen very comfortless. The hard-finished walls were not very smooth nor particularly white. The doors and wood-work, though very neat, and even carved with some attempt at ornament, had never known the touch of paint, and had grown in the course of years to be of a light-brown colour. The room was very bare of furniture too. A dressing-table, pier-table, or whatnot, stood between the windows, but it was only a half-circular top of pine board set upon three very long, bare-looking legs— altogether of a most awkward and unhappy appearance, Ellen thought, and quite too high for her to use with any comfort. No glass hung over it, nor anywhere else. On the north side of the room was a fireplace ; against the opposite wall stood Ellen's trunk and two chairs ;—that was all, except the cot bed she was lying on, and which had its place opposite the windows. The coverlid of that came in for a share of her displeasure, being of home-made white and blue worsted mixed with cotton, exceeding thick and heavy.

"I wonder what sort of a blanket is under it," said Ellen, "if I can ever get it off to see !—pretty good ; but the sheets are cotton, and so is the pillow-case !"

She was still leaning on her elbow, looking around her with a rather discontented face, when some door being opened down stairs, a great noise of hissing and sputtering came to her ears, and presently after there stole to her nostrils a steaming odour of something very savoury from the kitchen. It said as plainly as any dressing-bell that she had better get up. So up she jumped, and set about the business of dressing with great alacrity. Where was the distress of last night? Gone—with the darkness. She had slept well ; the bracing atmosphere had restored strength and spirits ; and the bright morning light made it impossible to be dull or downhearted, in spite of the new cause she thought she had found. She went on quick with the business of the toilet ; but when it came to the washing, she suddenly discovered that there were no conveniences for it in her room—no sign of pitcher or basin, or stand to hold them. Ellen was slightly dismayed ; but presently recollected her arrival had not been looked for so soon, and probably the preparations for it had not been completed. So she finished dressing, and then set out to find her way to the kitchen. On opening the door, there was a little landing-place from which the stairs descended just in front of her, and at the left hand another door, which she supposed must lead to her aunt's room. At the foot of the stairs Ellen found herself in a large square room or hall, for one of its doors, on the east, opened to the outer air, and was in fact the front door of the house. Another Ellen tried on the south side; it would not open. A third, under the stairs, admitted her to the kitchen.

The noise of hissing and sputtering now became quite violent, and the smell of the cooking, to Ellen's fancy, rather too strong to be pleasant. Before a good fire stood Miss Fortune, holding the end of a very long iron handle by which she was kept in communication with a flat vessel sitting on the fire, in which Ellen soon discovered all this noisy and odorous cooking was going on. A tall tin coffee-pot stood on some coals in the corner of the fireplace, and another little iron vessel in front also claimed a share of Miss Fortune's attention, for she every now and then leaned forward to give a stir to whatever was in it, making each time quite a spasmodic effort to do so without quitting her hold of the end of the long handle. Ellen drew near and looked on with great curiosity, and not a little appetite; but Miss Fortune was far too busy to give her more than a passing glance. At length the hissing pan was brought to the hearth for some new arrangement of its contents, and Ellen seized the moment of peace and quiet to say, "Good-morning, aunt Fortune."

Miss Fortune was crouching by the pan turning her slices of pork. "How do you do this morning?" she answered, without looking up.

Ellen replied she felt a great deal better.

"Slept warm, did you?" said Miss Fortune, as she set the pan back on the fire. And Ellen could hardly answer. "Quite warm, ma'am," when the hissing and sputtering began again as loud as ever.

"I must wait," thought Ellen, "till this is over before I say what I want to. I can't scream out to ask for a basin and towel."

In a few minutes the pan was removed from the fire, and Miss Fortune went on to take out the brown slices of nicely-fried pork and arrange them in a deep dish, leaving a small quantity of clear fat in the pan. Ellen, who was greatly interested, and observing every step most attentively, settled in her own mind that certainly this would be thrown away, being fit for nothing but the pigs. But Miss Fortune didn't think so, for she darted into some pantry close by, and returning with a cup of cream in her hand emptied it all into the pork fat. Then she ran into the pantry again for a little round tin box, with a cover full of holes, and shaking this gently over the pan, a fine white shower of flour fell upon the cream. The pan was then replaced on the fire and stirred; and to Ellen's astonishment the whole changed, as if by magic, to a thick, stiff, white froth. It was not till Miss Fortune was carefully pouring this over the fried slices in the dish, that Ellen suddenly recollected that breakfast was ready, and she was not.

"Aunt Fortune," she said timidly, "I haven't washed yet,—there's no basin in my room."

Miss Fortune made no answer nor gave any sign of hearing; she went on dishing up breakfast. Ellen waited a few minutes.

"Will you please, ma'am, to show me where I can wash myself."

"Yes," said Miss Fortune, suddenly standing erect, you'll have to go down to the spout."

"The spout, ma'am," said Ellen,—"what's that?"

"You'll know it when you see it, I guess," answered her aunt, again stooping over her preparations. But in another moment she arose and said, "Just open that door there behind you, and go down the stairs and out at the door, and you'll see where it is, and what it is too."

Ellen still lingered. "Would you be so good as to give me a towel, ma'am," she said timidly.

Miss Fortune dashed past her and out of another door, whence she presently returned with a clean towel which she threw over Ellen's arm, and then went back to her work.

Opening the door by which she had first seen her aunt enter the night before, Ellen went down a steep flight of steps, and found herself in a lower kitchen, intended for common purposes. It seemed not to be used at all, at least there was no fire there, and a cellar-like feeling and smell instead. That was no wonder, for beyond the fireplace on the left hand was the opening to the cellar, which running under the other part of the house, was on a level with this kitchen. It had no furniture but a table and two chairs. The thick heavy door stood open. Passing out, Ellen looked around her for water,—in what shape or form it was to present itself she had no very clear idea. She soon spied, a few yards distant a little stream of water pouring from the end of a pipe or trough raised about a foot and a half from the ground, and a well-worn path leading to it, left no doubt of its being "the spout." But when she had reached it Ellen was in no small puzzle as to how she should manage. The water was clear and bright, and poured very fast into a shallow wooden trough underneath, whence it ran off into the meadow and disappeared.

" But what shall I do without a basin," thought Ellen, " I can't catch any water in my hands, it runs too fast. If I only could get my face under there—that would be fine !"

Very carefully and cautiously she tried it, but the continual spattering of the water had made the board on which she stood so slippery that before her face could reach the stream she came very near tumbling headlong, and so taking more of a cold bath than she wished for. So she contented herself with the drops her hands could bring to her face,—a scanty supply ; but those drops were deliciously cold and fresh. And afterwards she pleased herself with holding her hands in the running water, till they were red with the cold. On the whole Ellen enjoyed her washing very much. The morning air came playing about her ; its cool breath was on her cheek with health in its touch. The early sun was shining on tree and meadow and hill ; the long shadows stretched over the grass, and the very brown outhouses, looked bright. She thought it was the loveliest place she ever had seen. And that sparkling trickling water was certainly the purest and sweetest she had ever tasted. Where could it come from ? It poured from a small trough made of the split trunk of a tree with a little groove or channel two inches wide hollowed out in it. But at the end of one of these troughs, another lapped on, and another at the end of that, and how many there were Ellen could not see, nor where the beginning of them was. Ellen stood gazing and wondering, drinking in the fresh air, hope and spirits rising every minute, when she suddenly recollected breakfast! She hurried in. As she expected, her aunt was at the table; but to her surprise, and not at all to her gratification, there was Mr. Van Brunt at the other end of it, eating away, very much at home indeed. In silent dismay Ellen drew her chair to the side of the table.

" Did you find the spout?" asked Miss Fortune.

" Yes, ma'am."

" Well, how do you like it?"

" Oh, I like it very much indeed," said Ellen. " I think it is beautiful."

Miss Fortune's face rather softened at this, and she gave Ellen an abundant supply of all that was on the table. Her journey, the bracing air, and her cool morning wash, altogether, had made Ellen very sharp, and she did justice to the breakfast. She thought never was coffee so good as this country coffee; nor any thing so excellent as the brown bread and butter, both as sweet as bread and butter could be; neither was any cookery so entirely satisfactory as Miss Fortune's fried pork and potatoes. Yet her tea-spoon was not silver; her knife could not boast of being either sharp or bright; and her fork was certainly made for any thing else in the world but comfort and convenience, being of only two prongs, and those so far apart that Ellen had no small difficulty to carry the potato safely from her plate to her mouth. It mattered nothing; she was now looking on the bright side of things, and all this only made her breakfast taste the sweeter.

Ellen rose from the table when she had finished, and stood a few minutes thoughtfully by the fire.

" Aunt Fortune," she said at length timidly, " if you've no objection, I should like to go and take a good look all about."

" Oh, yes," said Miss Fortune, " go where you like; I'll give you a week to do what you please with yourself."

" Thank you, ma'am," said Ellen, as she ran off for her bonnet; " a week's a long time. I suppose," thought she, " I shall go to school at the end of that."

Returning quickly with her white bonnet, Ellen opened the heavy kitchen door by which she had entered last night, and went out. She found herself in a kind of long shed. It had very rough walls and floor, and overhead showed the brown beams and rafters; two little windows and a door were on the side. All manner of rubbish lay there, especially at the farther end. There was scattered about and piled up various boxes, boards, farming and garden tools, old pieces of rope and sheepskin, old iron, a cheese-press, and what not. Ellen did not stay long to look, but went out to find something pleasanter. A few yards from the shed door was the little gate through which she had stumbled in the dark, and outside of that Ellen stood still a while. It was a fair, pleasant day, and the country scene she looked upon was very pretty. Ellen thought so. Before her, at a little distance, rose the great gable end of the barn, and a long row of outhouses stretched away from it toward the left. The ground was strewn thick with chips; and the reason was not hard to find, for a little way off, under an old stunted apple-tree, lay a huge log, well chipped on the upper surface, with the axe resting against it; and close by were some sticks of wood both chopped and unchopped. To the right the ground descended gently to a beautiful plane meadow, skirted on the hither side by a row of fine apple-trees. The smooth green flat tempted Ellen to a run, but first she looked to the left. There was the garden, she guessed, for there was a paling fence which enclosed a pretty large piece of ground; and between the garden and the house a green slope ran down to the spout. That reminded her that she intended making a journey of discovery up the course of the long trough. No time could be better than now, and she ran down the slope.

The trough was supported at some height from the ground by little heaps of stones placed here and there along its whole course. Not far from the spout it crossed a fence. Ellen must cross it too to gain her object, and how that could be done was a great question; she resolved to try, however. But first she played awhile with the water, which had great charms for her. She dammed up the little channel with her fingers, forcing the water to flow over the side of the trough; there was something very pleasant in stopping the supply of the spout, and seeing the water trickling over where it had no business to go; and she did not heed that some of the drops took her frock in their way. She stooped her lips to the trough and drank of its sweet current,—only for fun's sake, for she was not thirsty. Finally she set out to follow the stream up to its head. But poor Ellen had not gone more than half way toward the fence when she all at once plunged into the mire. The green grass growing there had looked fair enough, but there was running water and black mud under the green grass, she found to her sorrow. Her shoes, her stockings, were full. What was to be done, now? The journey of discovery must be given up. She forgot to think about where the water came from, in the more pressing question, " What will aunt Fortune say ?"—and the quick wish came that she had her mother to go to. However, she got out of the slough, and wiping her shoes as well as she could on the grass, she hastened back to the house.

The kitchen was all put in order, the hearth swept, the irons at the fire, and Miss Fortune just pinning her ironing blanket on the table. " Well,—what's the matter ? " she said, when she saw Ellen's face ; but as her glance reached the floor, her brow darkened. " Mercy on me ! " she exclaimed, with slow emphasis,— " what on earth have you been about ? where have you been ? "

Ellen explained.

" Well, you *have* made a figure of yourself ! Sit down ! " said her aunt, shortly, as she thrust a chair down on the hearth before the fire ; " I should have thought you'd have wit enough at your age to keep out of the ditch."

" I didn't see any ditch," said Ellen.

" No, I suppose not," said Miss Fortune, who was energetically twitching off Ellen's shoes and stockings with her fore finger and thumb ; " I suppose not ! you were staring up at the moon or stars, I suppose."

" It all looked green and smooth," said poor Ellen ; " one part just like another ; and the first thing I knew I was up to my ankles."

" What were you there at all for ? " said Miss Fortune, shortly enough.

" I couldn't see where the water came from, and I wanted to find out."

" Well you've found out enough for one day I hope. Just look at those stockings ! Ha'n't you got never a pair of coloured stockings, that you must go poking into the mud with white ones ? "

" No, ma'am."

" Do you mean to say you never wore any but white ones at home ? "

" Yes, ma'am ; I never had any others."

Miss Fortune's thoughts seemed too much for speech, from the way in which she jumped up and went off without saying any thing more. She presently came back with an old pair of grey socks, which she bade Ellen put on as soon as her feet were dry.

" How many of those white stockings have you ? " she said.

" Mamma bought me half a dozen pair of new ones just before I came away, and I had as many as that of old ones besides."

" Well, now go up to your trunk and bring 'em all down to me —every pair of white stockings you have got. There's a pair of old slippers you can put on till your shoes are dry," she said, flinging them to her ;—" They arn't much too big for you."

" They're not much too big for the *socks*—they're a great deal too big for me," thought Ellen. But she said nothing. She gathered all her stockings together and brought them down stairs, as her aunt had bidden her.

" Now you may run out to the barn, to Mr. Van Brunt,—you'll

find him there,—and tell him I want him to bring me some white maple bark, when he comes home to dinner,—white maple bark, do you hear?"

Away went Ellen, but in a few minutes came back. "I can't get in," she said.

"What's the matter?"

"Those great doors are shut, and I can't open them. I knocked, but nobody came."

"Knock at a barn door!" said Miss Fortune. "You must go in at the little cowhouse door, at the left, and go round. He's in the lower barn-floor."

The barn stood lower than the level of the chip-yard, from which a little bridge led to the great doorway of the second floor. Passing down the range of outhouses, Ellen came to the little door her aunt had spoken of. "But what in the world should I do if there should be cows inside there?" said she to herself. She peeped in;—the cowhouse was perfectly empty; and cautiously, and with many a fearful glance to the right and left, lest some terrible horned animal should present itself, Ellen made her way across the cowhouse, and through the barn-yard, littered thick with straw wet and dry, to the lower barn-floor. The door of this stood wide open. Ellen looked with wonder and pleasure when she got in. It was an immense room—the sides showed nothing but hay up to the ceiling, except here and there an enormous upright post; the floor was perfectly clean, only a few locks of hay and grains of wheat scattered upon it; and a pleasant sweet smell was there, Ellen could not tell of what. But no Mr. Van Brunt. She looked about for him, she dragged her disagreeable slippers back and forth over the floor, in vain.

"Hilloa! what's wanting?" at length cried a rough voice she remembered very well. But where was the speaker? On every side, to every corner, her eyes turned without finding him. She looked up at last. There was the round face of Mr. Van Brunt peering down at her through a large opening or trap-door, in the upper floor.

"Well!" said he, "have you come out here to help me thrash wheat!"

Ellen told him what she had come for.

"White maple bark,—well,"—said he, in his slow way, "I'll bring it. I wonder what's in the wind now."

So Ellen wondered, as she slowly went back to the house; and yet more, when her aunt set her to tacking her stockings together by two and two.

"What are you going to do with them, aunt Fortune?" she at last ventured to say.

"You'll see, —when the time comes."

" Mayn't I keep out one pair?" said Ellen, who had a vague notion that by some mysterious means her stockings were to be prevented from ever looking white any more.

" No ;—just do as I tell you."

Mr. Van Brunt came at dinner-time with the white maple bark. It was thrown forthwith into a brass kettle of water which Miss Fortune had already hung over the fire. Ellen felt sure this had something to do with her stockings, but she could ask no questions; and as soon as dinner was over she went up to her room. It didn't look pleasant now. The brown wood-work and rough dingy walls had lost their gilding. The sunshine was out of it; and what was more, the sunshine was out of Ellen's heart too. She went to the window and opened it, but there was nothing to keep it open ; it slid down again as soon as she let it go. Baffled and sad, she stood leaning her elbows on the window-sill, looking out on the grass-plat that lay before the door, and the little gate that opened on the lane, and the smooth meadow, and rich broken country beyond. It was a very fair and pleasant scene in the soft sunlight of the last of October ; but the charm of it was gone for Ellen ; it was dreary. She looked without caring to look, or knowing what she was looking at ; she felt the tears rising to her eyes ; and sick of the window, turned away. Her eye fell on her trunk ; her next thought was of her desk inside of it ; and suddenly her heart sprang ;—" I will write to mamma!" No sooner said than done. The trunk was quickly open, and hasty hands pulled out one thing after another till the desk was reached.

" But what shall I do ?" thought she,—" there isn't a sign of a table. Oh, what a place ! I'll shut my trunk and put it on that. But here are all these things to put back first."

They were eagerly stowed away ; and then kneeling by the side of the trunk, with loving hands Ellen opened her desk. A sheet of paper was drawn from her store, and properly placed before her ; the pen dipped in the ink, and at first with a hurried, then with a trembling hand, she wrote, " My dear Mamma." But Ellen's heart had been swelling and swelling, with every letter of those three words, and scarcely was the last " a" finished, when the pen was dashed down, and flinging away from the desk, she threw herself on the floor in a passion of grief. It seemed as if she had her mother again in her arms, and was clinging with a death-grasp not to be parted from her. And then the feeling that she was parted !—As much bitter sorrow as a little heart can know was in poor Ellen's now. In her childish despair she wished she could die, and almost thought she should. After a time, however, though not a short time, she rose from the floor and went to her writing again ; her heart a little eased by weeping, yet the tears kept coming all the time, and she could not quite keep her paper from

being blotted. The first sheet was spoiled before she was aware;
she took another.

"MY DEAREST MAMMA,

"It makes me so glad and so sorry to write to you, that I don't
know what to do. I want to see you so much, mamma, that it
seems to me sometimes as if my heart would break. Oh, mamma,
if I could just kiss you once more, I would give any thing in the
whole world. I can't be happy as long as you are away, and I am
afraid I can't be good either; but I will try. Oh, I will try,
mamma. I have so much to say to you that I don't know where
to begin. I am sure my paper will never hold it all. You will
want to know about my journey. The first day was on the steamboat, you know. I should have had a dreadful time that day,
mamma, but for something I'll tell you about. I was sitting up on
the upper deck, thinking about you, and feeling very badly indeed,
when a gentleman came and spoke to me, and asked me what was
the matter. Mamma, I can't tell you how kind he was to me. He
kept me with him the whole day. He took me all over the boat,
and showed me all about a great many things, and he talked to me
a great deal. Oh, mamma, how he talked to me. He read in the
Bible to me, and explained it, and he tried to make me a Christian.
And oh, mamma, when he was talking to me, how I wanted to do
as he said, and I resolved I would. I did, mamma, and I have not
forgotten it. I will try indeed, but I am afraid it will be very
hard without you or him, or any body else to help me. You
couldn't have been kinder yourself, mamma; he kissed me at night
when I bid him good-by, and I was very sorry indeed. I wish I
could see him again. Mamma, I will always love that gentleman
if I never see him again in the world. I wish there was somebody here that I could love, but there is not. You will want to
know what sort of a person my aunt Fortune is. I think she is
very good looking, or she would be if her nose was not quite so
sharp: but, mamma, I can't tell you what sort of a feeling I have
about her; it seems to me as if she was sharp all over. I am sure
her eyes are as sharp as two needles. And she don't walk like
other people; at least sometimes. She makes queer little jerks
and starts and jumps, and flies about like I don't know what. I
am afraid it is not right for me to write so about her; but may I not
tell you, mamma? There's nobody else for me to talk to. I can't
like aunt Fortune much yet, and I am sure she don't like me; but
I will try to make her. I have not forgotten what you said to me
about that. Oh, dear mamma, I will try to mind every thing you
ever said to me in your life. I am afraid you won't like what I
have written about aunt Fortune; but indeed I have done nothing
to displease her, and I will try not to. If you were only here,

mamma, I should say it was the loveliest place I ever saw in my life. Perhaps, after all, I shall feel better, and be quite happy by and by; but, oh, mamma, how glad I shall be when I get a letter from you. I shall begin to look for it soon, and I think I shall go out of my wits with joy when it comes. I had the funniest ride down here from Thirlwall that you can think; how do you guess I came? In a cart drawn by oxen. They went so slow we were an age getting here; but I liked it very much. There was a good-natured man driving the oxen, and he was kind to me; but, mamma, what do you think? he eats at the table. I know what you would tell me; you would say I must not mind trifles. Well, I will try not, mamma. Oh, darling mother, I can't think much of any thing but you. I think of you the whole time. Who makes tea for you now? Are you better? Are you going to leave New York soon? It seems dreadfully long since I saw you. I am tired, dear mamma, and cold; and it is getting dark. I must stop. I have a good big room to myself; that is a good thing. I should not like to sleep with aunt Fortune. Good-night, dear mamma. I wish I could sleep with you once more. Oh, when will that be again, mamma? Good-night. Good-night.

"Your affectionate ELLEN."

The letter finished was carefully folded, enclosed, and directed; and then with an odd mixture of pleasure and sadness, Ellen lit one of her little wax matches, as she called them, and sealed it very nicely. She looked at it fondly a minute when all was done, thinking of the dear fingers that would hold and open it; her next movement was to sink her face in her hands, and pray most earnestly for a blessing upon her mother, and help for herself,— poor Ellen felt she needed it. She was afraid of lingering lest tea should be ready; so, locking up her letter, she went down stairs.

The tea was ready. Miss Fortune and Mr. Van Brunt were at the table, and so was the old lady, whom Ellen had not seen before that day. She quietly drew up her chair to its place.

"Well," said Miss Fortune, "I hope you feel better for your long stay up stairs."

"I do, ma'am," said Ellen; "a great deal better."

"What have you been about?"

"I have been writing, ma'am."

"Writing what?"

"I have been writing to mamma."

Perhaps Miss Fortune heard the trembling of Ellen's voice, or her sharp glance saw the lip quiver and eyelid droop. Something softened her. She spoke in a different tone; asked Ellen if her tea was good; took care she had plenty of the bread and butter, and excellent cheese, which was on the table; and lastly cut her a large piece of the pumpkin pie. Mr. Van Brunt too looked once or twice at Ellen's face as if he thought all was not right there. He was not so sharp as Miss Fortune, but the swollen eyes and tear-stains were not quite lost upon him.

After tea, when Mr. Van Brunt was gone, and the tea-things cleared away, Ellen had the pleasure of finding out the mystery of the brass kettle and the white maple bark. The kettle now stood in the chimney corner. Miss Fortune, seating herself before it, threw in all Ellen's stockings except one pair, which she flung over to her, saying, "There—I don't care if you keep that one." Then, tucking up her sleeves to the elbows, she fished up pair after pair out of the kettle, and wringing them out hung them on chairs to dry. But, as Ellen had opined, they were no longer white, but of a fine slate colour. She looked on in silence, too much vexed to ask questions.

"Well, how do you like that?" said Miss Fortune at length, when she had got two or three chairs round the fire pretty well hung with a display of slate-coloured cotten legs.

"I don't like it at all," said Ellen.

"Well, *I* do. How many pair of white stockings would you like to drive into the mud and let me wash out every week?"

"*You* wash!" said Ellen in surprise; "I didn't think of *your* doing it."

"Who did you think *was* going to do it? There's nothing in this house but goes through my hand, I can tell you, and so must you. I suppose you've lived all your life among people that thought a great deal of wetting their little finger; but I'm not one of 'em, I guess you'll find."

Ellen was convinced of that already.

"Well, what are you thinking of?" said Miss Fortune presently.

"I'm thinking of my nice white darning-cotton," said Ellen. "I might just as well not have had it."

"Is it wound or in the skein?"

"In the skein."

"Then just go right up and get it. I'll warrant I'll fix it so that you'll have a use for it."

Ellen obeyed, but musing rather uncomfortably what else there was of hers that Miss Fortune could lay hands on. She seemed in imagination to see all her white things turning brown. She resolved she would keep her trunk well locked up; but what if her keys should be called for?

She was dismissed to her room soon after the dyeing business was completed. It was rather a disagreeable surprise to find her bed still unmade; and she did not at all like the notion that the making of it in future must depend entirely upon herself; Ellen had no fancy for such handiwork. She went to sleep in somewhat the same dissatisfied mood with which the day had been begun; displeasure at her coarse heavy coverlid and cotton sheets again taking its place among weightier matters;—and dreamed of tying them together into a rope by which to let herself down out of the window; but when she had got so far, Ellen's sleep became sound, and the end of the dream was never known.

CHAPTER XI.

Downward, and ever farther,
And ever the brook beside;
And ever fresher murmured,
And ever clearer, the tide.
                    LONGFELLOW. *From the German.*

CLOUDS and rain and cold winds kept Ellen within doors for several days. This did not better the state of matters between herself and her aunt. Shut up with her in the kitchen from morning till night, with the only variety of the old lady's company part of the time, Ellen thought neither of them improved upon acquaintance. Perhaps they thought the same of her; she was certainly not in her best mood. With nothing to do, the time hanging very heavy on her hands, disappointed, unhappy, frequently irritated, Ellen became at length very ready to take offence, and nowise disposed to pass it over or smooth it away. She seldom showed this in words, it is true, but it rankled in her mind. Listless and brooding, she sat day after day, comparing the present with the past, wishing vain wishes, indulging bootless regrets, and looking upon her aunt and grandmother with an eye of more settled aversion. The only other person she saw was Mr. Van Brunt, who came in regularly to meals; but he never said any thing unless in answer to Miss Fortune's questions and remarks about the farm concerns. These did not interest her; and she was greatly wearied with the sameness of her life. She longed to go out again; but Thursday, and Friday, and Saturday, and Sunday passed, and the weather still kept her close prisoner. Monday brought a change, but though a cool, drying wind blew all day, the ground was too wet to venture out.

On the evening of that day, as Miss Fortune was setting the table for tea, and Ellen sitting before the fire, feeling weary of every thing, the kitchen door opened, and a girl somewhat larger and older than herself came in. She had a pitcher in her hand, and marching straight up to the tea-table, she said,

"Will you let granny have a little milk to-night, Miss Fortune? I can't find the cow. I'll bring it back to-morrow."

" You ha'n't lost her, Nancy ?"

" Have, though," said the other; " she's been away these two days."

" Why didn't you go somewhere nearer for milk ?"

" Oh ! I don't know—I guess your'n is the sweetest," said the girl, with a look Ellen did not understand.

Miss Fortune took the pitcher and went into the pantry. While she was gone, the two children improved the time in looking very hard at each other. Ellen's gaze was modest enough, though it showed a great deal of interest in the new object; but the broad, searching stare of the other seemed intended to take in all there was of Ellen from her head to her feet, and keep it, and find out what sort of a creature she was at once. Ellen almost shrank from the bold black eyes, but they never wavered, till Miss Fortune's voice broke the spell.

" How's your grandmother, Nancy ?"

" She's tolerable, ma'am, thank you."

" Now if you don't bring it back to-morrow, you won't get any more in a hurry," said Miss Fortune, as she handed the pitcher back to the girl.

" I'll mind it," said the latter, with a little nod of her head, which seemed to say there was no danger of her forgetting.

" Who is that, aunt Fortune ?" said Ellen, when she was gone.

" She is a girl that lives up on the mountain yonder."

" But what's her name ?"

" I had just as lief you wouldn't know her name. She ain't a good girl. Don't you never have any thing to do with her."

Ellen was in no mind to give credit to all her aunt's opinions, and she set this down as in part at least coming from ill-humour.

The next morning was calm and fine, and Ellen spent nearly the whole of it out of doors. She did not venture near the ditch, but in every other direction she explored the ground, and examined what stood or grew upon it as thoroughly as she dared. Toward noon she was standing by the little gate at the back of the house, unwilling to go in, but not knowing what more to do, when Mr. Van Brunt came from the lane with a load of wood. Ellen watched the oxen toiling up the ascent, and thought it looked like very hard work ; she was sorry for them.

" Isn't that a very heavy load ?" she asked of their driver, as he was throwing it down under the apple-tree.

" Heavy ? Not a bit of it. It ain't nothing at all to 'em. They'd take twice as much any day with pleasure."

" I shouldn't think so," said Ellen ; " they don't look as if there was much pleasure about it. What makes them lean over so against each other when they are coming up hill ?"

" Oh, that's just a way they've got. They're so fond of each other, I suppose. Perhaps they've something particular to say, and want to put their heads together for the purpose."

"No," said Ellen, half laughing, "it can't be that; they wouldn't take the very hardest time for that; they would wait till they got to the top of the hill; but there they stand just as if they were asleep, only their eyes are open. Poor things!"

"They're not very poor any how," said Mr. Van Brunt; "there ain't a finer yoke of oxen to be seen than them are, nor in better condition."

He went on throwing the wood out of the cart, and Ellen stood looking at him.

"What'll you give me if I'll make you a scup one of these days?" said Mr. Van Brunt.

"A scup?" said Ellen

"Yes—a scup! how would you like it?"

"I don't know what it is," said Ellen.

"A scup!—may be you don't know it by that name; some folks call it a swing."

"A swing! oh, yes," said Ellen, "now I know. Oh, I like it very much."

"Would you like to have one?"

"Yes, indeed I should, very much."

"Well, what'll you give me, if I'll fix you one?"

"I don't know," said Ellen, "I have nothing to give; I'll be very much obliged to you, indeed."

"Well now, come, I'll make a bargain with you; I'll engage to fix up a scup for you, if you'll give me a kiss."

Poor Ellen was struck dumb. The good-natured Dutchman had taken a fancy to the little pale-faced, sad-looking stranger, and really felt very kindly disposed toward her, but she neither knew, nor at the moment cared about that. She stood motionless, utterly astounded at his unheard-of proposal, and not a little indignant; but when, with a good-natured smile upon his round face, he came near to claim the kiss he no doubt thought himself sure of, Ellen shot from him like an arrow from a bow. She rushed to the house, and bursting open the door, stood with flushed face and sparkling eyes in the presence of her astonished aunt.

"What in the world is the matter?" exclaimed that lady.

"He wanted to kiss me!" said Ellen, scarce knowing whom she was talking to, and crimsoning more and more.

"Who wanted to kiss you?"

"That man out there."

"What man?"

"The man that drives the oxen."

"What, Mr. Van Brunt?" And Ellen never forgot the loud ha! ha! which burst from Miss Fortune's wide-open mouth.

" Well, why didn't you let him kiss you?"

The laugh, the look, the tone, stung Ellen to the very quick. In a fury of passion she dashed away out of the kitchen, and up to her own room. And there, for a while, the storm of anger drove over her with such violence that conscience had hardly time to whisper. Sorrow came in again as passion faded, and gentler but very bitter weeping took the place of convulsive sobs of rage and mortification, and then the whispers of conscience began to be heard a little. " Oh, mamma! mamma!" cried poor Ellen in her heart, " how miserable I am without you! I never can like aunt Fortune—it's of no use—I never can like her; I hope I shan't get to hate her!—and that isn't right. I am forgetting all that is good and there's nobody to put me in mind. Oh, mamma! if I could lay my head in your lap for a minute!" Then came thoughts of her Bible and hymn-book, and the friend who had given it; sorrowful thoughts they were; and at last, humbled and sad, poor Ellen sought that great friend she knew she had displeased, and prayed earnestly to be made a good child; she felt and owned she was not one now.

It was long after mid-day when Ellen rose from her knees. Her passion was all gone; she felt more gentle and pleasant than she had done for days; but at the bottom of her heart resentment was not all gone. She still thought she had cause to be angry, and she could not think of her aunt's look and tone without a thrill of painful feeling. In a very different mood, however, from that in which she had flown up stairs two or three hours before, she now came softly down, and went out by the front door, to avoid meeting her aunt. She had visited that morning a little brook which ran through the meadow on the other side of the road. It had great charms for her; and now crossing the lane and creeping under the fence, she made her way again to its banks. At a particular spot, where the brook made one of its sudden turns, Ellen sat down upon the grass, and watched the dark water,—whirling, brawling over the stones, hurrying past her, with ever the same soft pleasant sound, and she was never tired of it. She did not hear footsteps drawing near, and it was not till some one was close beside her, and a voice spoke almost in her ears, that she raised her startled eyes and saw the little girl who had come the evening before for a pitcher of milk.

" What are you doing?" said the latter.

" I'm watching for fish," said Ellen.

" Watching for fish!" said the other, rather disdainfully.

" Yes," said Ellen,—" there, in that little quiet place they come sometimes; I've seen two."

" You can look for fish another time. Come now and take a walk with me."

"Where?" said Ellen.

"Oh, you shall see. Come! I'll take you all about and show you where people live; you ha'n't been anywhere yet, have you?"

"No," said Ellen,—"and I should like dearly to go, but——"

She hesitated. Her aunt's words came to mind, that this was not a good girl, and that she must have nothing to do with her; but she had not more than half believed them, and she could not possibly bring herself now to go in and ask Miss Fortune's leave to take this walk. "I am sure," thought Ellen, "she would refuse me if there was no reason in the world." And then the delight of rambling through the beautiful country, and being for awhile in other company than that of her aunt Fortune and the old grandmother! The temptation was too great to be withstood.

"Well, what are you thinking about?" said the girl; "what's the matter? won't you come?"

"Yes," said Ellen, "I'm ready. Which way shall we go?"

With the assurance from the other that she would show her plenty of ways, they set off down the lane; Ellen with a secret fear of being seen and called back, till they had gone some distance, and the house was hid from view. Then her pleasure became great. The afternoon was fair and mild, the footing pleasant, and Ellen felt like a bird out of a cage. She was ready to be delighted with every trifle; her companion could not by any means understand or enter into her bursts of pleasure at many a little thing which she of the black eyes thought not worthy of notice. She tried to bring Ellen back to higher subjects of conversation.

"How long have you been here?" she asked.

"Oh, a good while," said Ellen,—"I don't know exactly; it's a week, I believe."

"Why, do you call that a good while?" said the other.

"Well, it seems a good while to me," said Ellen, sighing; "it seems as long as four, I am sure."

"Then you don't like to live here much, do you?"

"I had rather be at home, of course."

"How do you like your aunt Fortune?"

"How do I like her?" said Ellen, hesitating,—"I think she's good-looking, and very smart."

"Yes, you needn't tell me she's smart,—every body knows that; that ain't what I ask you;—how do you *like* her?"

"How do I like her?" said Ellen, again; "how can I tell how I shall like her? I haven't lived with her but a week yet."

"You might just as well ha' spoke out," said the other, somewhat scornfully;—"do you think I don't know you half hate her already? and it'll be whole hating in another week more. When I first heard you'd come, I guessed you'd have a sweet time with her."

" Why ?" said Ellen.

" Oh, don't ask me why," said the other, impatiently, " when you know as well as I do. Every soul that speaks of you says ' poor child !' and ' I'm glad I ain't her.' You needn't try to come cunning over me. I shall be too much for you, I tell you."

" I don't know what you mean," said Ellen.

" Oh, no, I suppose you don't," said the other, in the same tone, —" of course you don't ; I suppose you don't know whether your tongue is your own or somebody's else. You think Miss Fortune is an angel, and so do I ; to be sure she is !"

Not very pleased with this kind of talk, Ellen walked on for a while in grave silence. Her companion mean time recollected herself ; when she spoke again it was with an altered tone.

" How do you like Mr. Van Brunt ?"

" I don't like him at all," said Ellen, reddening.

" Don't you !" said the other surprised,—" why every body likes him. What don't you like him for ?"

" I don't like him," repeated Ellen.

" Ain't Miss Fortune queer to live in the way she does ?"

" What way ?" said Ellen.

" Why, without any help,—doing all her own work, and living all alone, when she's so rich as she is."

" Is she rich ?" asked Ellen.

" Rich ! I guess she is ! she's one of the very best farms in the country, and money enough to have a dozen help, if she wanted 'em. Van Brunt takes care of the farm, you know ?"

" Does he ?" said Ellen.

" Why, yes, of course he does ; didn't you know that ? what did you think he was at your house all the time for ?"

" I am sure I don't know," said Ellen. " And are those aunt Fortune's oxen that he drives ?"

" To be sure they are. Well, I do think you *are* green, to have been there all this time, and not found that out. Mr. Van Brunt does just what he pleases over the whole farm though ; hires what help he wants, manages every thing ; and then he has his share of all that comes off it. I tell you what—you'd better make friends with Van Brunt, for if any body can help you when your aunt gets one of her ugly fits, it's him ; she don't care to meddle with him much."

Leaving the lane, the two girls took a foot-path leading across the fields. The stranger was greatly amused here with Ellen's awkwardness in climbing fences. Where it was a possible thing, she was fain to crawl under ; but once or twice that could not be done, and having with infinite difficulty mounted to the top rail, poor Ellen sat there in a most tottering condition, uncertain on which side of the fence she should tumble over, but seeing no other possible way of getting down. The more she trembled the more her companion laughed, standing aloof meanwhile, and insisting she should get down by herself. Necessity enabled her to do this at last, and each time the task became easier ; but Ellen secretly made up her mind that her new friend was not likely to prove a very good one.

As they went along, she pointed out to Ellen two or three houses in the distance, and gave her not a little gossip about the people who lived in them; but all this Ellen scarcely heard, and cared nothing at all about. She had paused by the side of a large rock standing alone by the wayside, and was looking very closely at its surface.

" What is this curious brown stuff," said Ellen, " growing all over the rock?—like shrivelled and dried-up leaves ? Isn't it curious ? part of it stands out like a leaf, and part of it sticks fast; I wonder if it grows here, or what it is."

" Oh, never mind," said the other ; " it always grows on the rocks everywhere ; I don't know what it is, and what's more I don't care. 'Tain't worth looking at. Come !"

Ellen followed her. But presently the path entered an open woodland, and now her delight broke forth beyond bounds.

" Oh, how pleasant this is ! how lovely this is ! Isn't it beautiful ?" she exclaimed.

" Isn't *what* beautiful ? I do think you are the queerest girl, Ellen."

" Why, every thing," said Ellen, not minding the latter part of the sentence; " the ground is beautiful, and those tall trees, and that beautiful blue sky—only look at it."

' The ground is all covered with stones and rocks—is that what you call beautiful ? and the trees are as homely as they can be, with their great brown stems and no leaves. Come ! what *are* you staring at ?"

Ellen's eyes were fixed on a string of dark spots which were rapidly passing overhead.

" Hark !" said she ; " do you hear that noise ? what is that ? what is that ?"

" Isn't it only a flock of ducks," said the other, contemptuously ; " come ! do come !"

But Ellen was rooted to the ground, and her eyes followed the airy travellers till the last one had quitted the piece of blue sky which the surrounding woods left to be seen. And scarcely were these gone when a second flight came in view, following exactly in the track of the first.

" Where are they going ?" said Ellen.

" I am sure I don't know where they are going ; they never told me. I know where *I* am going ; I should like to know whether you are going along with me."

Ellen, however, was in no hurry. The ducks had disappeared, but her eye had caught something else that charmed it.

" What is this ?" said Ellen.

" Nothing but moss."

" Is that moss ! How beautiful ! how green and soft it is ! I declare it's as soft as a carpet."

" As soft as a carpet !" repeated the other : " I should like to see a carpet as soft as that ! *you* never did, I guess."

" Indeed I have, though," said Ellen, who was gently jumping up and down on the green moss to try its softness, with a face of great satisfaction.

" I don't believe it a bit," said the other ; " all the carpets I ever saw were as hard as a board, and harder ; as soft as that, indeed !"

" Well," said Ellen, still jumping up and down, with bonnet off, and glowing cheek, and hair dancing about her face, " you may believe what you like ; but I've seen a carpet as soft as this, and softer too ; only one, though."

" What was it made of ?"

" What other carpets are made of, I suppose. Come, I'll go with you now. I do think this is the loveliest place I ever did see. Are there any flowers here in the spring ?"

" I don't know—yes, lots of 'em."

" Pretty ones ?" said Ellen.

" *You'd* think so, I suppose ; I never look at 'em."

" Oh, how lovely that will be !" said Ellen, clasping her hands ; " how pleasant it must be to live in the country !"

" Pleasant, indeed !" said the other ; " I think it's hateful. You'd think so, too, if you lived where I do. It makes me mad at granny every day because she won't go to Thirlwall. Wait till we get out of the wood, and I'll show you where I live. You can't see it from here."

Shocked a little at her companion's language, Ellen again walked on in sober silence. Gradually the ground became more broken, sinking rapidly from the side of the path, and rising again in a steep bank on the other side of a narrow dell ; both sides were thickly wooded, but stripped of green, now, except where here and there a hemlock flung its graceful branches abroad and stood in lonely beauty among its leafless companions. Now the gurgling of waters was heard.

" Where is that ?" said Ellen, stopping short.

" 'Way down, down, at the bottom there. It's the brook."

" What brook ? Not the same that goes by aunt Fortune's ?"

" Yes, it's the very same. It's the crookedest thing you ever saw. It runs over there," said the speaker, pointing with her arm, " and then it takes a turn and goes that way, and then it comes round so, and then it shoots off in that way again and passes by your house; and after that the dear knows where it goes, for I don't. But I don't suppose it could run straight if it was to try to."

" Can't we get down to it ?" asked Ellen.

" To be sure we can, unless you're as afraid of steep banks as you are of fences."

Very steep indeed it was, and strewn with loose stones, but Ellen did not falter here, and though once or twice in imminent danger of exchanging her cautious stepping for one long roll to the bottom, she got there safely on her two feet. When there, every thing was forgotten in delight. It was a wild little place. The high, close sides of the dell left only a little strip of sky overhead; and at their feet ran the brook, much more noisy and lively here than where Ellen had before made its acquaintance; leaping from rock to rock, eddying round large stones, and boiling over the small ones, and now and then pouring quietly over some great trunk of a tree that had fallen across its bed and dammed up the whole stream. Ellen could scarcely contain herself at the magnificence of many of the waterfalls, the beauty of the little quiet pools where the water lay still behind some large stone, and the variety of graceful tiny cascades.

" Look here, Nancy !" cried Ellen, "that's the Falls of Niagara —do you see ?—that large one ; Oh, that is splendid ! And this will do for Trenton Falls—what a fine foam it makes—isn't it a beauty ?—and what shall we call this ? I don't know what to call it ; I wish we could name them all. But there's no end to them. Oh, just look at that one ! that's too pretty not to have a name ; what shall it be ?"

" Black Falls," suggested the other.

" Black," said Ellen, dubiously, " why !—I don't like that."

" Why the water's all dark and black, don't you see ?"

" Well," said Ellen, " let it be Black, then ; but I don't like it. Now remember,—this is Niagara,—that is Black,—and this is Trenton,—and what is this ?"

" If you are a-going to name them all," said Nancy, " we shan't get home to-night ; you might as well name all the trees ; there's a hundred of 'em, and more. I say, Ellen ! suppos'n we follow the brook instead of climbing up yonder again ; it will take us out to the open fields by and by."

" Oh, do let's !" said Ellen ; " that will be lovely."

It proved a rough way ; but Ellen still thought and called it "lovely." Often by the side of the stream there was no footing at all, and the girls picked their way over the stones, large and small, wet and dry, which strewed its bed ; against which the water foamed and fumed and fretted, as if in great impatience. It was ticklish work getting along over these stones ; now tottering on an unsteady one ; now slipping on a wet one ; and every now and then making huge leaps from rock to rock, which there was no other method of reaching, at the imminent hazard of falling in. But they laughed at the danger ; sprang on in great glee, delighted with the exercise and the fun ; didn't stay long enough anywhere to lose their balance, and enjoyed themselves amazingly. There was many a hair-breadth escape ; many an *almost* sousing ; but that made it all the more lively. The brook formed, as Nancy had said, a constant succession of little waterfalls, its course being quite steep and very rocky ; and in some places there were pools quite deep enough to have given them a thorough wetting, to say no more, if they had missed their footing and tumbled in. But this did not happen. In due time, though with no little difficulty, they reached the spot where the brook came forth from the wood into the open day, and thence making a sharp turn to the right, skirted along by the edge of the trees, as if unwilling to part company with them.

"I guess we'd better get back into the lane now," said Miss Nancy, "we're a pretty good long way from home."

CHAPTER XII.

"Behind the door stand bags o' meal,
And in the ark is plenty.
And good hard cakes his mither makes,
And mony a sweeter dainty.
A good fat sow, a sleeky cow
Are standing in the byre ;
While winking puss, wi' mealy mou,
Is playing round the fire."

SCOTCH SONG.

THEY left the wood and the brook behind them, and crossed a large stubble-field ; then got over a fence into another. They were in the midst of this when Nancy stopped Ellen, and bade her look up toward the west, where towered a high mountain, no longer hid from their view by the trees.

"I told you I'd show you where I live," said she. "Look up now,—clear to the top of the mountain, almost, and a little to the right ; do you see that little mite of a house there ? Look sharp, —it's a'most as brown as the rock,—do you see it ?—it's close by that big pine-tree, but it don't look big from here—it's just by that little dark spot near the top ?"

"I see it," said Ellen,—"I see it now : do you live 'way up there ?"

"That's just what I do; and that's just what I wish I didn't. But granny likes it; she will live there. I'm blessed if I know what for, if it ain't to plague me. Do you think you'd like to live up on the top of a mountain like that?"

"No, I don't think I should," said Ellen. "Isn't it very cold up there?"

"Cold! you don't know any thing about it. The wind comes there, I tell you! enough to cut you in two; I have to take and hold on to the trees sometimes to keep from being blowed away. And then granny sends me out every morning before it's light, no matter how deep the snow is, to look for the cow; and it's so bitter cold I expect nothing else but I'll be froze to death some time."

"Oh," said Ellen, with a look of horror, "how can she do so?"

"Oh, she don't care," said the other; "she sees my nose freeze off every winter, and it don't make no difference."

"Freeze your nose off!" said Ellen.

"To be sure," said the other nodding gravely,—"every winter; it grows out again when the warm weather comes."

"And is that the reason why it is so little?" said Ellen, innocently, and with great curiosity.

"Little!" said the other, crimsoning in a fury,—"what do you mean by that? it's as big as yours any day, I can tell you."

Ellen involuntarily put her hand to her face to see if Nancy spoke true. Somewhat reassured to find a very decided ridge where her companion's nose was wanting in the line of beauty, she answered in her turn,—

"It's no such thing, Nancy! you oughtn't to say so; you know better."

"I *don't* know better! I *ought* to say so!" replied the other, furiously. "If I had your nose, I'd be glad to have it freeze off; I'd a sight rather have none. I'd pull it every day, if I was you, to make it grow."

"I shall believe what aunt Fortune said of you was true," said Ellen. She had coloured very high, but she added no more, and walked on in dignified silence. Nancy stalked before her in silence that was meant to be dignified too, though it had not exactly that air. By degrees each cooled down, and Nancy was trying to find out what Miss Fortune had said of her, when on the edge of the next field they met the brook again. After running a long way to the right, it had swept round, and here was flowing gently in the opposite direction. But how were they ever to cross it? The brook ran in a smooth current between them and a rising bank on the other side, so high as to prevent their seeing what lay beyond. There were no stepping stones now. The only thing that looked like a bridge was an old log that had fallen across the brook, or perhaps had at some time or other been put there on purpose; and that lay more than half in the water; what remained of its surface was green with moss and slippery with slime. Ellen was sadly afraid to trust herself on it; but what to do?—Nancy soon settled the question as far as she was concerned. Pulling off her thick shoes, she ran fearlessly upon the rude bridge; her clinging bare feet carried her safely over, and Ellen soon saw her reshoeing herself in triumph on the opposite side; but thus left behind and alone, her own difficulty increased.

"Pull off your shoes, and do as I did," said Nancy.

"I can't," said Ellen; "I'm afraid of wetting my feet; I know mamma wouldn't let me."

"Afraid of wetting your feet!" said the other; "what a chickaninny you are! Well, if you try to come over with your shoes on you'll fall in, I tell you; and then you'll wet more than your feet. But come along somehow, for I won't stand waiting here much longer."

Thus urged, Ellen set out upon her perilous journey over the bridge. Slowly and fearfully, and with as much care as possible, she set step by step upon the slippery log. Already half of the danger was passed, when, reaching forward to grasp Nancy's outstretched hand, she missed it,—*perhaps* that was Nancy's fault,—poor Ellen lost her balance and went in head foremost. The water was deep enough to cover her completely as she lay, though not enough to prevent her getting up again. She was greatly frightened, but managed to struggle up first to a sitting posture, and then to her feet, and then to wade out to the shore; though, dizzy and sick, she came near falling back again more than once. The water was very cold; and, thoroughly sobered, poor Ellen felt chill enough in body and mind too; all her fine spirits were gone; and not the less because Nancy had risen to a great pitch of delight at her misfortune. The air rang with her laughter; she likened Ellen to every ridiculous thing she could think of. Too miserable to be angry, Ellen could not laugh, and would not cry, but she exclaimed in distress,—

"Oh, what shall I do! I am so cold!"

"Come along," said Nancy; "give me your hand; we'll run right over to Mrs. Van Brunt's—'tain't far—its just over here. There," said she, as they got to the top of the bank, and came within sight of a house standing only a few fields off,—"there it is! Run, Ellen, and we'll be there directly."

"Who is Mrs. Van Brunt?" Ellen contrived to say, as Nancy hurried her along.

"Who is she?—run, Ellen!—why she's just Mrs. Van Brunt —your Mr. Van Brunt's mother you know,—make haste, Ellen— we had rain enough the other day; I'm afraid it wouldn't be good for the grass if you stayed too long in one place;—hurry! I'm afraid you'll catch cold,—you got your feet wet after all, I'm sure."

Run they did; and a few minutes brought them to Mrs. Van Brunt's door. The little brick walk leading to it from the court-yard gate was as neat as a pin; so was every thing else the eye could rest on; and when Nancy went in poor Ellen stayed *her* foot at the door, unwilling to carry her wet shoes and dripping garments any further. She could hear, however, what was going on.

"Hillo! Mrs. Van Brunt," shouted Nancy,—"where are you?—oh! Mrs. Van Brunt, are you out of water? 'cos if you are I've brought you a plenty; the person that has it don't want it; she's just at the door; she wouldn't bring it in till she knew you wanted it; oh, Mrs. Van Brunt, don't look so or you'll kill me with laughing. Come and see! come and see."

The steps within drew near the door, and first Nancy showed herself, and then a little old woman, not very old either, of very kind, pleasant countenance.

"What is all this?" said she in great surprise. "Bless me! poor little dear! what is this?"

"Nothing in the world but a drowned rat, Mrs. Van Brunt, don't you see?" said Nancy.

"Go home, Nancy Vawse! go home," said the old lady, "you're a regular bad girl. I do believe this is some mischief o' yourn, go right off home; it's time you were after your cow a great while ago."

As she spoke, she drew Ellen in, and shut the door.

"Poor little dear," said the old lady, kindly, "what has happened to you? Come to the fire, love, you're trembling with the cold. Oh, dear! dear! your soaking wet; this is all along of Nancy somehow, I know; how was it, love? Ain't you Miss Fortune's little girl? Never mind, don't talk, darling; there ain't one bit of colour in your face, not one bit."

Good Mrs. Van Brunt had drawn Ellen to the fire, and all this while she was pulling off as fast as possible her wet clothes. Then sending a girl who was in waiting, for clean towels, she rubbed Ellen dry from head to foot, and wrapping her in a blanket, left her in a chair before the fire, while she went to seek something for her to put on. Ellen had managed to tell who she was, and how her mischance had come about, but little else, though the kind old lady had kept on pouring out words of sorrow and pity during the whole time. She came trotting back directly with one of her own short gowns, the only thing that she could lay hands on that was anywhere near Ellen's length. Enormously big it was for her, but Mrs. Van Brunt wrapped it round and round, and the blanket over it again, and then she bustled about till she had prepared a tumbler of hot drink, which she said was to keep Ellen from catching cold. It was any thing but agreeable, being made from some bitter herb, and sweetened with molasses; but Ellen swallowed it, as she would any thing else at such kind hands, and the old lady carried her herself into a little room opening out of the kitchen, and laid her in a bed that had been warmed for her. Excessively tired and weak as she was, Ellen scarcely needed the help of the hot herb tea to fall into a very deep sleep; perhaps it might not have lasted so very long as it did, but for that. Afternoon changed for evening, evening grew quite dark, still Ellen did not stir; and after every little journey into the bedroom to see how she was doing, Mrs. Van Brunt came back saying how glad she was to see her sleeping so finely. Other eyes looked on her for a minute—kind and gentle eyes; though Mrs. Van Brunt's were kind and gentle too; once a soft kiss touched her forehead, there was no danger of waking her.

It was perfectly dark in the little bedroom, and had been so a good while, when Ellen was aroused by some noise, and then a rough voice she knew very well. Feeling faint and weak, and not more than half awake yet, she lay still and listened. She heard the outer door open and shut, and then the voice said,

"So mother, you've got my stray sheep here, have you?"

"Ay, ay," said the voice of Mrs. Van Brunt, "have you been looking for her? how did you know she was here?"

"Looking for her! ay, looking for her ever since sundown. She has been missing at the house since some time this forenoon. I believe her aunt got a bit scared about her; any how I did. She's a queer little chip as ever I see."

"She's a dear little soul, *I* know," said his mother; "you needn't say nothin' agin her, I ain't a going to believe it."

"No more am I—I'm the best friend she's got, if she only knowed it; but don't you think," said Mr. Van Brunt, laughing, "I asked her to give me a kiss this forenoon, and if I'd been an owl she couldn't ha' been more scared; she went off like a streak, and Miss Fortune said she was as mad as she could be, and that's the last of her."

"How did you find her out?"

"I met that mischievous Vawse girl, and I made her tell me; she had no mind to at first. It'll be the worse for Ellen if she takes to that wicked thing."

"She won't. Nancy has been taking her a walk, and worked it so as to get her into the brook, and then she brought her here, just as dripping wet as she could be. I gave her something hot and put her to bed, and she'll do, I reckon; but I tell you it gave me queer feelings to see the poor little thing just as white as ashes, and all of a tremble, and looking so sorrowful too. She's sleeping finely now; but it ain't right to see a child's face look so;—it ain't right," repeated Mrs. Van Brunt, thoughtfully.—" You ha'n't had supper, have you?"

" No, mother, and I must take that young one back.   Ain't she awake yet?"

" I'll see directly; but she ain't going home, nor you neither, 'Brahm, till you've got your supper; it would be a sin to let her. She shall have a taste of my splitters this very night; I've been makin' them o' purpose for her.   So you may just take off your hat and sit down."

" You mean to let her know where to come when she wants good things, mother.   Well, I won't say splitters ain't worth waiting for."

Ellen heard him sit down, and then she guessed from the words that passed that Mrs. Van Brunt and her little maid were busied in making the cakes; she lay quiet.

" You're a good friend, 'Brahm," began the old lady again, " nobody knows that better than me; but I hope that poor little thing has got another one to-day that'll do more for her than you can."

" What, yourself, mother?   I don't know about that."

" No, no; do you think I mean myself?—there, turn it quick, Sally!—Miss Alice has been here."

" How? this evening?"

" Just a little before dark, on her grey pony.   She came in for a minute, and I took her—that'll burn, Sally!—I took her in to see the child while she was asleep, and I told her all you told me about her.   She didn't say much, but she looked at her very sweet, as she always does, and I guess,—there—now I'll see after my little sleeper."

And presently Mrs. Van Brunt came to the bedside with a light, and her arm full of Ellen's dry clothes.   Ellen felt as if she could have put her arms round her kind old friend and hugged her with all her heart; but it was not her way to show her feelings before strangers.   She suffered Mrs. Van Brunt to dress her in silence, only saying with a sigh, " How kind you are to me, ma'am!" to which the old lady replied with a kiss, and telling her she mustn't say a word about that.

The kitchen was bright with firelight and candlelight; the tea-table looked beautiful with its piles of white splitters, besides plenty of other and more substantial things; and at the corner of the hearth sat Mr. Van Brunt.

" So," said he, smiling, as Ellen came in and took her stand at the opposite corner,—" so I drove you away this morning?   You ain't mad with me yet, I hope."

Ellen crossed directly over to him, and putting her little hand in his great rough one, said, " I'm very much obliged to you, Mr.

Van Brunt, for taking so much trouble to come and look after me."

She said it with a look of gratitude and trust that pleased him very much.

"Trouble, indeed!" said he, good-humouredly, "I'd take twice as much any day for what you wouldn't give me this forenoon. But never fear, Miss Ellen, I ain't a going to ask you that again.

He shook the little hand; and from that time Ellen and her rough charioteer were firm friends.

Mrs. Van Brunt now summoned them to table; and Ellen was well feasted with the splitters, which were a kind of rich short-cake baked in irons, very thin and crisp, and then split in two and buttered, whence their name. A pleasant meal was that. Whatever an epicure might have thought of the tea, to Ellen in her famished state it was delicious; and no epicure could have found fault with the cold ham and the butter and the cakes; but far better than all was the spirit of kindness that was there. Ellen feasted on that more than on any thing else. If her host and hostess were not very polished, they could not have been outdone in their kind care of her and kind attention to her wants. And when the supper was at length over, Mrs. Van Brunt declared a little colour had come back to the pale cheeks. The colour came back in good earnest a few minutes after, when a great tortoise-shell cat walked into the room. Ellen jumped down from her chair, and presently was bestowing the tenderest caresses upon pussy, who stretched out her head and purred as if she liked them very well.

"What a nice cat!" said Ellen.

"She has five kittens," said Mrs. Van Brunt.

"Five kittens!" said Ellen. "Oh, may I come some time and see them?"

"You shall see 'em right away, dear, and come as often as you like too. Sally, just take a basket, and go fetch them kittens here."

Upon this, Mr. Van Brunt began to talk about its being time to go, if they were going. But his mother insisted that Ellen should stay where she was; she said she was not fit to go home that night, that she oughtn't to walk a step, and that 'Brahm' should go and tell Miss Fortune the child was safe and well, and would be with her early in the morning. Mr. Van Brunt shook his head two or three times, but finally agreed, to Ellen's great joy. When he came back, she was sitting on the floor before the fire, with all the five kittens in her lap, and the old mother cat walking around and over her and them. But she looked up with a happier face then he had ever seen her wear, and told him she was "so much obliged to him for taking such a long walk for her;" and Mr. Van Brunt felt that, like his oxen, he could have done a great deal more with pleasure.

CHAPTER XIII.

It's hardly in a body's pow'r,
To keep at times frae being sour.
                              BURNS.

BEFORE the sun was up the next morning, Mrs. Van Brunt came into Ellen's room and aroused her.

"It's a real shame to wake you up," she said, "when you were sleeping so finely; but 'Brahm wants to be off to his work, and won't stay for breakfast. Slept sound, did you?"

"Oh, yes, indeed; as sound as a top," said Ellen, rubbing her eyes;—"I am hardly awake yet."

"I declare it's too bad," said Mrs. Van Brunt,—"but there's no help for it. You don't feel no headache, do you, nor pain in your bones?"

"No, ma'am, not a bit of it; I feel nicely."

"Ah! well," said Mrs. Van Brunt, "then your tumble into the brook didn't do you any mischief; I thought it wouldn't. Poor little soul!"

"I am very glad I did fall in," said Ellen, "for if I hadn't I shouldn't have come here, Mrs. Van Brunt."

The old lady instantly kissed her.

"Oh! mayn't I just take one look at the kitties?" said Ellen, when she was ready to go.

"Indeed you shall," said Mrs. Van Brunt, "if 'Brahm's hurry was ever so much ;—and it ain't, besides. Come here, dear."

She took Ellen back to a waste lumber-room, where in a corner, on some old pieces of carpet, lay pussy and her family. How fondly Ellen's hand was passed over each little soft back! how hard it was for her to leave them!

"Wouldn't you like to take one home with you, dear?" said Mrs. Van Brunt, at length.

"Oh! may I?" said Ellen, looking up in delight; "are you in earnest? Oh, thank you, dear Mrs. Van Brunt! Oh, I shall be so glad!"

"Well, choose one then, dear,—choose the one you like best, and 'Brahm shall carry it for you."

The choice was made, and Mrs. Van Brunt and Ellen returned to the kitchen, where Mr. Van Brunt had already been waiting some time. He shook his head when he saw what was in the basket his mother handed to him.

"That won't do," said he; "I can't go that, mother. I'll undertake to see Miss Ellen safe home, but the cat 'ud be more than I could manage. I think I'd hardly get off with a whole skin 'tween the one and t'other."

" Well, now !" said Mrs. Van Brunt.

Ellen gave a longing look at her little black-and-white favourite, which was uneasily endeavouring to find out the height of the basket, and mewing at the same time with a most ungratified expression. However, though sadly disappointed, she submitted with a very good grace to what could not be helped. First setting down the little cat out of the basket it seemed to like so ill, and giving it one farewell pat and squeeze, she turned to the kind old lady who stood watching her, and throwing her arms around her neck, silently spoke her gratitude in a hearty hug and kiss.

" Good-by, ma'am," said she ; " I may come and see them some time again, and see you, mayn't I ?"

" Indeed you shall, my darling," said the old woman, "just as often as you like ;—just as often as you can get away. I'll make 'Brahm bring you home sometimes. 'Brahm, you'll bring her, won't you ?"

" There's two words to that bargain, mother, I can tell you ; but if I don't, I'll know the reason on't."

And away they went. Ellen drew two or three sighs at first, but she could not help brightening up soon. It was early—not sunrise ; the cool freshness of the air was enough to give one new life and spirit ; the sky was fair and bright ; and Mr. Van Brunt marched along at a quick pace. Enlivened by the exercise, Ellen speedily forgot every thing disagreeable ; and her little head was filled with pleasant things. She watched where the silver light in the east foretold the sun's coming. She watched the silver change to gold, till a rich yellow tint was flung over the whole landscape ; and then broke the first rays of light upon the tops of the western hills, —the sun was up. It was a new sight to Ellen.

" How beautiful ! Oh, how beautiful !" she exclaimed.

" Yes," said Mr. Van Brunt, in his slow way, " it'll be a fine day for the field. I guess I'll go with the oxen over to that 'ere big meadow."

" Just look," said Ellen, " how the light comes creeping down the side of the mountain,—now it has got to the wood,—Oh, do look at the tops of the trees ! Oh, I wish mamma was here."

Mr. Van Brunt didn't know what to say to this. He rather wished so too, for her sake.

" There," said Ellen, " now the sunshine is on the fence, and the road, and every thing. I wonder what is the reason that the sun shines first upon the top of the mountain, and then comes so slowly down the side ; why don't it shine on the whole at once ?"

Mr. Van Brunt shook his head in ignorance. " He guessed it always did so," he said.

" Yes," said Ellen, " I suppose it does, but that's the very thing,
—I want to know the reason why. And I noticed just now, it
shone in my face before it touched my hands. Isn't it queer?"

" Humph!—there's a great many queer things, if you come to
that," said Mr. Van Brunt, philosophically.

But Ellen's head ran on from one thing to another, and her next
question was not so wide of the subject as her companion might
have thought.

" Mr. Van Brunt, are there any schools about here?"

" Schools?" said the person addressed, " yes—there's plenty of
schools."

" Good ones?" said Ellen.

" Well, I don't exactly know about that; there's Captain Conklin's, that had ought to be a good 'un; he's a regular smart man,
they say."

" Whereabouts is that?" said Ellen.

" His school? it's a mile or so the other side of my house."

" And how far is it from your house to aunt Fortune's?"

" A good deal better than two mile, but we'll be there before
long. You ain't tired, be you?"

" No," said Ellen. But this reminder gave a new turn to her
thoughts, and her spirits were suddenly checked. Her former
brisk and springing step changed to so slow and lagging a one, that
Mr. Van Brunt more than once repeated his remark that he saw
she was tired.

If it was that, Ellen grew tired very fast; she lagged more
and more as they neared the house, and at last quite fell behind,
and allowed Mr. Van Brunt to go in first.

Miss Fortune was busy about the breakfast, and as Mr. Van Brunt
afterwards described it, " looking as if she could have bitten off a
tenpenny nail," and indeed as if the operation would have been
rather gratifying than otherwise. She gave them no notice at first,
bustling to and fro with great energy, but all of a sudden she
brought up directly in front of Ellen, and said,

" Why didn't you come home last night?"

The words were jerked out rather than spoken.

" I got wet in the brook," said Ellen, " and Mrs. Van Brunt was
so kind as to keep me."

" Which way did you go out of the house yesterday?"

" Through the front door."

" The front door was locked."

" I unlocked it."

" What did you go out that way for?"

" I didn't want to come this way."

" Why not?"

Ellen hesitated.

" Why not ?" demanded Miss Fortune still more emphatically than before.

" I did't want to see you, ma'am," said Ellen flushing.

" If ever you do so again !" said Miss Fortune in a kind of cold fury ; " I've a great mind to whip you for this, as ever I had to eat."

The flush faded on Ellen's cheek, and a shiver visibly passed over her—not from fear. She stood with downcast eyes and compressed lips, a certain instinct of childish dignity warning her to be silent. Mr. Van Brunt put himself in between.

" Come, come !" said he, " this is getting to be too much of a good thing. Beat your cream, ma'am, as much as you like, or if you want to try your hand on something else you'll have to take me first, I promise you."

" Now don't *you* meddle, Van Brunt," said the lady sharply, " with what ain't no business o' yourn."

" I don't know about that," said Mr. Van Brunt,—" maybe it *is* my business ; but meddle or no meddle, Miss Fortune, it is time for me to be in the field ; and if you ha'n't no better breakfast for Miss Ellen and me than all this here, we'll just go right away hum again ; but there's something in your kettle there that smells uncommonly nice, and I wish you'd just let us have it and no more words."

No more words did Miss Fortune waste on any one that morning. She went on with her work and dished up the breakfast in silence, and with a face that Ellen did not quite understand ; only she thought she had never in her life seen one so disagreeable. The meal was a very solemn and uncomfortable one. Ellen could scarcely swallow, and her aunt was near in the same condition. Mr. Van Brunt and the old lady alone despatched their breakfast as usual ; with no other attempts at conversation than the common mumbling on the part of the latter, which nobody minded, and one or two strange grunts from the former, the meaning of which, if they had any, nobody tried to find out.

There was a breach now between Ellen and her aunt that neither could make any effort to mend. Miss Fortune did not renew the disagreeable conversation that Mr. Van Brunt had broken off ; she left Ellen entirely to herself, scarcely speaking to her, or seeming to know when she went out or came in. And this lasted day after day. Wearily they passed. After one or two, Mr. Van Brunt seemed to stand just where he did before in Miss Fortune's good graces ;—but not Ellen. To her, when others were not by, her face wore constantly something of the same cold, hard, disagreeable expression it had put on after Mr. Van Brunt's interference,—a look that Ellen came to regard with absolute abhorrence. She kept away by herself as much as she could ; but she did not know what to do with her time, and for want of something better often spent it in tears. She went to bed cheerless night after night, and arose spiritless morning after morning; and this lasted till Mr. Van Brunt more than once told his mother that "that poor little thing was going wandering about like a ghost, and growing thinner and paler every day; and he didn't know what she would come to if she went on so."

Ellen longed now for a letter with unspeakable longing,—but none came;—day after day brought new disappointment, each day more hard to bear. Of her only friend, Mr. Van Brunt, she saw little; he was much away in the fields during the fine weather, and when it rained Ellen herself was prisoner at home, whither he never came but at meal times. The old grandmother was very much disposed to make much of her; but Ellen shrank, she hardly knew why, from her fond caresses, and never found herself alone with her if she could help it; for then she was regularly called to the old lady's side and obliged to go through a course of kissing, fondling, and praising, she would gladly have escaped. In her aunt's presence this was seldom attempted, and never permitted to go on. Miss Fortune was sure to pull Ellen away and bid her mother "stop that palavering,"—avowing that "it made her sick." Ellen had one faint hope that her aunt would think of sending her to school, as she employed her in nothing at home, and certainly took small delight in her company; but no hint of the kind dropped from Miss Fortune's lips; and Ellen's longing look for this as well as for a word from her mother was daily doomed to be ungratified and to grow more keen by delay.

One pleasure only remained to Ellen in the course of the day, and that one she enjoyed with the carefulness of a miser. It was seeing the cows milked, morning and evening. For this she got up very early and watched till the men came for the pails; and then away she bounded out of the house and to the barnyard. There were the milky mothers, five in number, standing about, each in her own corner of the yard or cowhouse, waiting to be relieved of their burden of milk. They were fine gentle animals, in excellent condition, and looking every way happy and comfortable; nothing living under Mr. Van Brunt's care was ever suffered to look otherwise. He was always in the barn or barnyard at milking time, and under his protection Ellen felt safe and looked on at her ease. It was a very pretty scene—at least she thought so. The gentle cows standing quietly to be milked as if they enjoyed it, and munching the cud; and the white stream of milk foaming into the pails; then there was the interest of seeing whether Sam or Johnny would get through first; and how near Jane or Dolly would come to rivalling Streaky's fine pailful; and at last Ellen allowed Mr. Van Brunt to teach herself how to milk. She began with trembling, but learnt fast enough; and more than one pailful of milk that Miss Fortune strained had been, unknown to her, drawn by Ellen's fingers. These minutes in the farmyard were the pleasantest in Ellen's day. While they lasted every care was forgotten and her little face was as bright as the morning; but the milking was quickly over, and the cloud gathered on Ellen's brow almost as soon as the shadow of the house fell upon it.

"Where is the post-office, Mr. Van Brunt?" she asked one morning, as she stood watching the sharpening of an axe upon the grindstone. The axe was in that gentleman's hand, and its edge carefully laid to the whirling-stone, which one of the farm-boys was turning.

"Where is the post-office? Why, over to Thirlwall to be sure," replied Mr. Van Brunt, glancing up at her from his work.— "Faster, Johnny."

"And how often do the letters come here?" said Ellen.

"Take care, Johnny!—some more water,—mind your business, will you!—Just as often as I go to fetch 'em, Miss Ellen, and no oftener."

"And how often do you go, Mr. Van Brunt?"

"Only when I've some other errand Miss Ellen; my grain would never be in the barn if I was running to the post-office every other thing,—and for what ain't there too. I don't get a letter but two or three times a year I s'pose, though I call,—I guess,—half a dozen times."

"Ah but there's one there now, or soon will be, I know, for me," said Ellen. "When do you think you will go again, Mr. Van Brunt?"

"Now if I'd ha' knowed that I'd ha' gone to Thirlwall yesterday—I was within a mile of it. I don't see as I can go this week anyhow in the world; but I'll make some errand there the first day I can, Miss Ellen, that you may depend on. You shan't wait for your letter a bit longer than I can help."

"Oh, thank you, Mr. Van Brunt—you're very kind. Then the letters never come except when you go after them?"

"No;—yes—they do come once in a while by old Mr. Swaim, but he ha'n't been here this great while."

"And who's he?" said Ellen.

"Oh, he's a queer old chip that goes round the country on all sorts of errands; he comes along once in a while. That'll do, Johnny,—I believe this here tool is as sharp as I have any occasion for."

"What's the use of pouring water upon the grindstone?" said Ellen; "why wouldn't it do as well dry?"

"I can't tell, I am sure," replied Mr. Van Brunt, who was slowly drawing his thumb over the edge of the axe; "your questions are a good deal too sharp for me, Miss Ellen; I only know it would spoil the axe, or the grindstone, or both most likely."

"It's very odd," said Ellen, thoughtfully; "I wish I knew every thing. But, oh dear! I am not likely to know any thing," said she, her countenance suddenly changing from its pleased inquisitive look to a cloud of disappointment and sorrow. Mr. Van Brunt noticed the change.

"Ain't your aunt going to send you to school, then?" said he.

"I don't know," said Ellen, sighing; "she never speaks about it, nor about any thing else. But I declare I'll make her!" she exclaimed, changing again. "I'll go right in and ask her, and then she'll have to tell me. I will! I am tired of living so. I'll know what she means to do, and then I can tell what *I* must do."

Mr. Van Brunt, seemingly dubious about the success of this line of conduct, stroked his chin and his axe alternately two or three times in silence, and finally walked off. Ellen, without waiting for her courage to cool, went directly into the house.

Miss Fortune, however, was not in the kitchen; to follow her into her secret haunts, the dairy, cellar, or lower kitchen was not to be thought of. Ellen waited awhile, but her aunt did not come, and the excitement of the moment cooled down. She was not quite so ready to enter upon the business as she had felt at first; she had even some qualms about it.

"But I'll do it," said Ellen to herself; "it will be hard, but I'll do it!"

CHAPTER XIV.

For my part, he keeps me here rustically
At home, or, to speak more properly, stays
Me here at home unkept.

As You Like It.

THE next morning after breakfast Ellen found the chance she rather dreaded than wished for. Mr. Van Brunt had gone out; the old lady had not left her room, and Miss Fortune was quietly seated by the fire, busied with some mysteries of cooking. Like a true coward, Ellen could not make up her mind to bolt at once into the thick of the matter, but thought to come to it gradually, —always a bad way.

"What is that, aunt Fortune?" said she, after she had watched her with a beating heart for about five minutes.

"What is what?"

"I mean, what is that you are straining through the colander into that jar?"

"Hop-water."

"What is it for?"

"I'm scalding this meal with it to make turnpikes."

"Turnpikes!" said Ellen; "I thought turnpikes were high, smooth roads with toll-gates every now and then—that's what mamma told me they were."

"That's all the kind of turnpikes your mamma knew any thing about, I reckon," said Miss Fortune, in a tone that conveyed the notion that Mrs. Montgomery's education had been very incomplete. "And indeed," she added immediately after, "if she had made more turnpikes and paid fewer tolls, it would have been just as well, I'm thinking."

Ellen felt the tone, if she did not thoroughly understand the words. She was silent a moment; then remembering her purpose, she began again.

"What are these then, aunt Fortune?"

"Cakes, child, cakes!—turnpike cakes—what I raise the bread with."

"What, those little brown cakes I have seen you melt in water and mix in the flour when you make bread?"

"Mercy on us! yes! you've seen hundreds of 'em since you've been here if you never saw one before."

"I never did," said Ellen. "But what are they called turnpikes for?"

"The land knows!—I don't. For mercy's sake stop asking me questions, Ellen; I don't know what's got into you; you'll drive me crazy."

"But there's one more question I want to ask very much," said Ellen, with her heart beating.

"Well, ask it then quick, and have done, and take yourself off. I have other fish to fry than to answer all your questions."

Miss Fortune, however, was still quietly seated by the fire stirring her meal and hop-water, and Ellen could not be quick; the words stuck in her throat,—came out at last.

"Aunt Fortune, I wanted to ask you if I may go to school?"

"Yes."

Ellen's heart sprang with a feeling of joy, a little qualified by the peculiar dry tone in which the word was uttered.

"When may I go?"

"As soon as you like."

"Oh, thank you, ma'am. To which school shall I go, aunt Fortune?"

"To whichever you like."

"But I don't know any thing about them," said Ellen;—"how can I tell which is best?"

Miss Fortune was silent.

"What schools are there near here?" said Ellen.

"There's Captain Conklin's down at the Cross, and Miss Emerson's at Thirlwall."

Ellen hesitated. The name was against her, but nevertheless she concluded on the whole that the lady's school would be the pleasantest.

"Is Miss Emerson any relation of yours?" she asked.

"No."

"I think I should like to go to her school the best. I will go there if you will let me,—may I?"

"Yes."

"And I will begin next Monday,—may I?"

"Yes."

Ellen wished exceedingly that her aunt would speak in some other tone of voice; it was a continual damper to her rising hopes.

"I'll get my books ready," said she,—"and look 'em over a little too, I guess. But what will be the best way for me to go, aunt Fortune?"

"I don't know."

"I couldn't walk so far, could I?"

" You know best."

" I couldn't I am sure," said Ellen;—" it's four miles to Thirlwall, Mr. Van Brunt said ; that would be too much for me to walk twice a day ; and I should be afraid besides."

A dead silence.

" But aunt Fortune, do please tell me what I am to do. How can I know unless you tell me ? What way is there that I can go to school ?"

" It is unfortunate that I don't keep a carriage," said Miss Fortune,—" but Mr. Van Brunt can go for you morning and evening in the ox-cart, if that will answer."

" The ox-cart ! But dear me ! it would take him all day, aunt Fortune. It takes hours and hours to go and come with the oxen ; —Mr. Van Brunt wouldn't have time to do any thing but carry me to school and bring me home."

" Of course,—but that's of no consequence," said Miss Fortune, in the same dry tone.

" Then I can't go—there's no help for it," said Ellen despondingly. " Why didn't you say so before ? When you said yes I thought you meant yes."

She covered her face. Miss Fortune rose with a half smile and carried her jar of scalded meal into the pantry. She then came back and commenced the operation of washing up the breakfast things.

" Ah, if I only had a little pony," said Ellen, " that would carry me there and back, and go trotting about with me everywhere,— how nice that would be !"

" Yes, that would be very nice ! And who do you think would go trotting about after the pony ? I suppose you would leave that to Mr. Van Brunt ; and I should have to go trotting about after you, to pick you up in case you broke your neck in some ditch or gully ;—it would be a very nice affair altogether I think."

Ellen was silent. Her hopes had fallen to the ground, and her disappointment was unsoothed by one word of kindness or sympathy. With all her old grievances fresh in her mind, she sat thinking her aunt was the very most disagreeable person she ever had the misfortune to meet with. No amiable feelings were working within her ; and the cloud on her brow was of displeasure and disgust, as well as sadness and sorrow. Her aunt saw it.

" What are you thinking of?" said she, rather sharply.

" I am thinking," said Ellen, " I am very sorry I cannot go to school."

" Why, what do you want to learn so much ? you know how to read and write and cipher, don't you ?"

" Read and write and cipher ?" said Ellen,—" to be sure I do ; but that's nothing ;—that's only the beginning."

" Well, what do you want to learn besides ?"

" Oh, a great many things."

" Well what ?''

" Oh, a great many things," said Ellen ;—" French, and Italian, and Latin, and music, and arithmetic and chemistry, and all about animals and plants and insects,—I forget what it's called,—and— Oh, I can't recollect ; a great many things. Every now and then I think of something I want to learn ; I can't remember them now. But I'm doing nothing," said Ellen sadly,—" learning nothing—I am not studying and improving myself as I meant to ; mamma will be disappointed when she comes back, and I meant to please her so much !''

The tears were fast coming ; she put her hand upon her eyes to force them back.

" If you are so tired of being idle," said Miss Fortune, " I'll warrant I'll give you something to do ; and something to learn too, that you want enough more than all those crinkumcrankums ; I wonder what good they'd ever do you! That's the way your mother was brought up I suppose. If she had been trained to use her hands and do something useful instead of thinking herself above it, maybe she wouldn't have had to go to sea for her health just now ; it doesn't do for women to be bookworms.''

" Mamma isn't a bookworm !'' said Ellen indignantly ;—" I don't know what you mean ; and she never thinks herself above being useful ; it's very strange you should say so when you don't know any thing about her.''

" I know she ha'n't brought you up to know manners, anyhow," said Miss Fortune. " Look here, I'll give you something to do,— just you put those plates and dishes together ready for washing, while I am down stairs.''

Ellen obeyed, unwillingly enough. She had neither knowledge of the business nor any liking for it ; so it is no wonder Miss Fortune at her return was not well pleased.

" But I never did such a thing before,'' said Ellen.

" There it is now !'' said Miss Fortune. " I wonder where your eyes have been every single time that I have done it since you have been here. I should think your own sense might have told you ! But you're too busy learning of Mr. Van Brunt to know what's going on in the house. Is that what you call made ready for washing ? Now just have the goodness to scrape every plate clean off and put them nicely in a pile here ; and turn out the slops out of the tea-cups and saucers and set them by themselves. —Well ! what makes you handle them so ? are you afraid they'll burn you ?''

" I don't like to take hold of things people have drunk out of,'' said Ellen, who was indeed touching the cups and saucers very delicately with the tips of her fingers.

"Look here," said Miss Fortune,—"don't you let me hear no more of that, or I vow I'll give you something to do you won't like. Now put the spoons here, and the knives and forks together here; and carry the salt-cellar and the pepper-box and the butter and the sugar into the buttery."

"I don't know where to put them," said Ellen.

"Come along, then, and I'll show you; it's time you did. I reckon you'll feel better when you've something to do, and you shall have plenty. There—put them in that cupboard, and set the butter up here, and put the bread in this box, do you see? now don't let me have to show you twice over."

This was Ellen's first introduction to the buttery; she had never dared to go in there before. It was a long, light closet or pantry, lined on the left side, and at the further end, with wide shelves up to the ceiling. On these shelves stood many capacious pans and basins of tin and earthenware, filled with milk, and most of them coated with superb yellow cream. Midway was the window, before which Miss Fortune was accustomed to skim her milk; and at the side of it was the mouth of a wooden pipe, or covered trough, which conveyed the refuse milk down to an enormous hogshead standing at the lower kitchen door, whence it was drawn as wanted for the use of the pigs. Beyond the window in the buttery, and on the higher shelves, were rows of yellow cheeses; forty or fifty were there at least. On the right hand of the door was the cupboard, and a short range of shelves, which held in ordinary all sorts of matters for the table, both dishes and eatables. Floor and shelves were well painted with thick yellow paint, hard and shining, and clean as could be; and there was a faint pleasant smell of dairy things.

Ellen did not find out all this at once, but in the course of a day or two, during which her visits to the buttery were many. Miss Fortune kept her word, and found her plenty to do; Ellen's life soon became a pretty busy one. She did not like this at all; it was a kind of work she had no love for; yet no doubt it was a good exchange for the miserable moping life she had lately led. Any thing was better than that. One concern, however, lay upon poor Ellen's mind with pressing weight,—her neglected studies and wasted time; for no better than wasted she counted it. "What shall I do?" she said to herself, after several of these busy days had passed; "I am doing nothing—I am learning nothing—I shall forget all I have learnt, directly. At this rate I shall not know any more than all these people around me; and what *will* mamma say?—Well, if I can't go to school I know what I will do," she said, taking a sudden resolve, "I'll study by myself! I'll see what I can do; it will be better than nothing, any way. I'll begin this very day!"

With new life Ellen sprang up stairs to her room, and forthwith

began pulling all the things out of her trunk to get at her books.
They were at the very bottom; and by the time she had reached
them half the floor was strewn with the various articles of her
wardrobe; without minding them in her first eagerness, Ellen
pounced at the books.

"Here you are, my dear Numa Pompilius," said she, drawing
out a little French book she had just begun to read, "and here *you*
are, old grammar and dictionary,—and here is my history,—very
glad to see you, Mr. Goldsmith!—and what in the world's this?—
wrapped up as if it was something great,—Oh, my expositor; I am
not glad to see *you*, I am sure; never want to look at your face, or
your back again. My copy-book—I wonder who'll set copies for
me now;—my arithmetic, that's you!—geography and atlas—all
right;—and my slate; but dear me! I don't believe I've such a
thing as a slate-pencil in the world; where shall I get one, I wonder?
—well, I'll manage. And that's all,—that's all, I believe."

With all her heart Ellen would have begun her studying at once,
but there were all her things on the floor, silently saying, " Put us
up first."

"I declare," said she to herself, " it's too bad to have nothing
in the shape of a bureau to keep one's clothes in. I wonder if I
am to live in a trunk, as mamma says, all the time I am here, and
have to go down to the bottom of it every time I want a pocket-
handkerchief or a pair of stockings. How I do despise those grey
stockings!—But what can I do? it's too bad to squeeze my nice
things up so. I wonder what is behind those doors. I'll find out,
I know, before long."

On the north side of Ellen's room were three doors. She had
never opened them, but now took it into her head to see what was
there, thinking she might possibly find what would help her out of
her difficulty. She had some little fear of meddling with any thing
in her aunt's domain; so she fastened her own door, to guard against
interruption while she was busied in making discoveries.

At the foot of her bed, in the corner, was one large door fastened
by a button, as indeed they were all. This opened, she found, upon
a flight of stairs, leading as she supposed to the garret, but Ellen
did not care to go up and see. They were lighted by half of a
large window, across the middle of which the stairs went up. She
quickly shut that door, and opened the next, a little one. Here she
found a tiny closet under the stairs, lighted by the other half of the
window. There was nothing in it but a broad low shelf or step
under the stairs, where Ellen presently decided she could stow
away her books very nicely. "It only wants a little brushing out,"
said Ellen, "and it will do very well." The other door, in the
other corner, admitted her to a large light closet, perfectly empty.
" Now if there were only some hooks or pegs here," thought Ellen,

" to hang up dresses on—but why shouldn't I drive some nails ?—
I will ! I will ! Oh, that'll be fine."

Unfastening her door in a hurry, she ran down stairs, and her
heart beating, between pleasure and the excitement of daring so far
without her aunt's knowledge, she ran out and crossed the chip-
yard to the barn, where she had some hope of finding Mr. Van
Brunt. By the time she got to the little cowhouse door a great
noise of knocking or pounding in the barn made her sure he was
there, and she went on to the lower barn-floor. There he was, he
and the two farm boys (who, by the by, were grown men), all three
threshing wheat. Ellen stopped at the door, and for a minute forgot what she had come for in the pleasure of looking at them. The
clean floor was strewn with grain, upon which the heavy flails came
down one after another, with quick regular beat,—one—two—three
—one—two—three,—keeping perfect time. The pleasant sound
could be heard afar off ; though, indeed, where Ellen stood it was
rather too loud to be pleasant. Her little voice had no chance of
being heard ; she stood still and waited. Presently Johnny who
was opposite caught a sight of her, and without stopping his work,
said to his leader, " Somebody there for you, Mr. Van Brunt."
That gentleman's flail ceased its motion, then he threw it down,
and went to the door to help Ellen up the high step.

" Well," said he, " have you come out to see what's going
on ?"

" No," said Ellen, " I've been looking—but Mr. Van Brunt,
could you be so good as to let me have a hammer and half-a-dozen
nails ?"

" A hammer and half-a-dozen nails ;—come this way," said he.

They went out of the barnyard and across the chip-yard to an
outhouse below the garden and not far from the spout, called the
poultry-house ; though it was quite as much the property of the
hogs, who had a regular sleeping apartment there, where corn was
always fed out to the fatting ones. Opening a kind of granary
store-room, where the corn for this purpose was stored, Mr. Van
Brunt took down from a shelf a large hammer and a box of nails,
and asked Ellen what size she wanted.

" Pretty large."

" So ?"

" No, a good deal bigger yet I should like."

" ' A good deal bigger yet,'—who wants 'em ?"

" I do," said Ellen, smiling.

" You do ! do you think your little arms can manage that big
hammer ?"

" I don't know ; I guess so ; I'll try."

" Where do you want 'em driv ?"

" Up in a closet in my room," said Ellen, speaking as softly as if she had feared her aunt was at the corner; "I want 'em to hang up dresses and things."

Mr. Van Brunt half smiled, and put up the hammer and nails on the shelf again.

"Now I'll tell you what we'll do," said he;—"you can't manage them big things; "I'll put 'em up for you to-night when I come in to supper."

"But I'm afraid she won't let you," said Ellen doubtfully.

"Never you mind about that," said he, "I'll fix it. Maybe we won't ask her."

"Oh, thank you!" said Ellen joyfully, her face recovering its full sunshine in answer to his smile; and clapping her hands she ran back to the house, while more slowly Mr. Van Brunt returned to the threshers. Ellen seized dust-pan and brush and ran up to her room; and setting about the business with right good will, she soon had her closets in beautiful order. The books, writing-desk, and work-box were then bestowed very carefully in the one; in the other her coats and dresses neatly folded up in a pile on the floor, waiting till the nails should be driven. Then the remainder of her things were gathered up from the floor and neatly arranged in the trunk again. Having done all this, Ellen's satisfaction was unbounded. By this time dinner was ready. As soon after dinner as she could escape, from Miss Fortune's calls upon her, Ellen stole up to her room and her books, and began work in earnest. The whole afternoon was spent over sums and verbs and maps and pages of history. A little before tea, as Ellen was setting the table, Mr. Van Brunt came into the kitchen with a bag on his back.

"What have you got there, Mr. Van Brunt?" said Miss Fortune.

"A bag of seed corn."

"What are you going to do with it?"

"Put it up in the garret for safe keeping."

"Set it down in the corner and I'll take it up to-morrow."

"Thank you, ma'am,—rather go myself, if it's all the same to you. You needn't be scared, I've left my shoes at the door. Miss Ellen, I believe I've got to go through your room."

Ellen was glad to run before to hide her laughter. When they reached her room Mr. Van Brunt produced a hammer out of the bag, and taking a handful of nails from his pocket, put up a fine row of them along her closet wall; then while she hung up her dresses he went on to the garret, and Ellen heard him hammering there too. Presently he came down and they returned to the kitchen.

"What's all that knocking?" said Miss Fortune.

"I've been driving some nails," said Mr. Van Brunt coolly.

"Up in the garret?"

"Yes, and in Miss Ellen's closet; she said she wanted some."

"You should ha' spoke to *me* about it," said Miss Fortune to Ellen. There was displeasure enough in her face; but she said no more, and the matter blew over much better than Ellen had feared.

Ellen steadily pursued her plan of studying, in spite of some discouragements.

A letter written about ten days after gave her mother an account of her endeavours and of her success. It was a despairing account. Ellen complained that she wanted help to understand, and lacked time to study; that her aunt kept her busy, and, she believed, took pleasure in breaking her off from her books; and she bitterly said her mother must expect to find an ignorant little daughter when she came home. It ended with, "Oh, if I could just see you, and kiss you, and put my arms round you, mamma, I'd be willing to die!"

This letter was despatched the next morning by Mr. Van Brunt; and Ellen waited and watched with great anxiety for his return from Thirlwall in the afternoon.

CHAPTER XV.

An ant dropped into the water; a wood-pigeon took pity of her and threw her a little bough.—L'ESTRANGE.

THE afternoon was already half spent when Mr. Van Brunt's ox-cart was seen returning. Ellen was standing by the little gate that opened on the chip-yard; and with her heart beating anxiously she watched the slow-coming oxen;—how slowly they came! At last they turned out of the lane and drew the cart up the ascent; and stopping beneath the apple tree Mr. Van Brunt leisurely got down, and flinging back his whip came to the gate. But the little face that met him there, quivering with hope and fear, made his own quite sober. "I'm really *very* sorry, Miss Ellen,—" he began.

That was enough. Ellen waited to hear no more, but turned away, the cold chill of disappointment coming over her heart. She had borne the former delays pretty well, but this was one too many, and she felt sick. She went round to the front stoop, where scarcely ever any body came, and sitting down on the steps wept sadly and despairingly.

It might have been half an hour or more after, that the kitchen door slowly opened and Ellen came in. Wishing her aunt should not see her swollen eyes, she was going quietly through to her own room when Miss Fortune called her. Ellen stopped. Miss

Fortune was sitting before the fire with an open letter lying in her lap and another in her hand. The latter she held out to Ellen, saying " Here, child, come and take this."

" What is it?" said Ellen, slowly coming toward her.

" Don't you see what it is?" said Miss Fortune, still holding it out.

" But who is it from?" said Ellen.

" Your mother."

" A letter from mamma, and not to me!" said Ellen with changing colour. She took it quick from her aunt's hand. But her colour changed more as her eye fell upon the first words, " My dear Ellen," and turning the paper she saw upon the back, " Miss Ellen Montgomery." Her next look was to her aunt's face, with her eye fired and her cheek paled with anger, and when she spoke her voice was not the same.

" This is *my* letter," she said trembling ;—" who opened it?"

Miss Fortune's conscience must have troubled her a little, for her eye wavered uneasily. Only for a second though.

" Who opened it?" she answered; " *I* opened it. I should like to know who has a better right. And I shall open every one that comes to serve you for looking so ;—that you may depend upon."

The look and the words and the injury together, fairly put Ellen beside herself. She dashed the letter to the ground, and livid and trembling with various feelings—rage was not the only one,—she ran from her aunt's presence. She did not shed any tears now ; she could not ; they were absolutely burnt up by passion. She walked her room with trembling steps, clasping and wringing her hands now and then, wildly thinking what *could* she do to get out of this dreadful state of things, and unable to see any thing but misery before her. She walked, for she could not sit down ; but presently she felt that she could not breathe the air of the house ; and taking her bonnet she went down, passed through the kitchen and went out. Miss Fortune asked where she was going, and bade her stay within doors, but Ellen paid no attention to her.

She stood still a moment outside the little gate. She might have stood long to look. The mellow light of an Indian-summer afternoon lay upon the meadow and the old barn and chip-yard ; there was beauty in them all under its smile. Not a breath was stirring. The rays of the sun struggled through the blue haze, which hung upon the hills and softened every distant object; and the silence of nature all around was absolute, made more noticeable by the far-off voice of somebody, it might be Mr. Van Brunt, calling to his oxen, very far off and not to be seen ; the sound came softly to her ear through the stillness. " Peace," was the whisper of nature to her troubled child ; but Ellen's heart was in a whirl; she could not hear the whisper. It was a relief however to be out of the house and in the sweet open air. Ellen breathed more freely, and pausing a moment there, and clasping her hands together once more in sorrow, she went down the road and out at the gate, and exchanging her quick broken step for a slow measured one, she took the way toward Thirlwall. Little regarding the loveliness which that day was upon every slope and roadside, Ellen presently quitted the Thirlwall road and half unconsciously turned into a path on the left which she had never taken before,—perhaps for that reason. It was not much travelled evidently; the grass grew green on both sides and even in the middle of the way, though here and there the track of wheels could be seen. Ellen did not care about where she was going; she only found it pleasant to walk on and get further from home. The road or lane led toward a mountain somewhat to the northwest of Miss Fortune's; the same which Mr. Van Brunt had once named to Ellen as "the Nose." After three quarters of an hour the road began gently to ascend the mountain, rising toward the north. About one-third of the way from the bottom Ellen came to a little foot-path on the left which allured her by its promise of prettiness, and she forsook the lane for it. The promise was abundantly fulfilled; it was a most lovely wild woodway path; but withal not a little steep and rocky. Ellen began to grow weary. The lane went on toward the north; the path rather led off toward the southern edge of the mountain, rising all the while; but before she reached that Ellen came to what she thought a good resting-place, where the path opened upon a small level platform or ledge of the hill. The mountain rose steep behind her, and sank very steep immediately before her, leaving a very superb view of the open country from the northeast to the southeast. Carpeted with moss, and furnished with fallen stones and pieces of rock, this was a fine resting-place for the wayfarer, or loitering place for the lover of nature. Ellen seated herself on one of the stones, and looked sadly and wearily toward the east, at first very careless of the exceeding beauty of what she beheld there.

For miles and miles, on every side but the west, lay stretched before her a beautifully broken country. The November haze hung over it now like a thin veil, giving great sweetness and softness to the scene. Far in the distance a range of low hills showed like a misty cloud; near by, at the mountain's foot, the fields and farm-houses a d roads lay a pictured map. About a mile and a half to the south rose the mountain where Nancy Vawse lived, craggy and bare; but the leafless trees and stern jagged rocks were wrapped in the haze; and through this the sun, now near the setting, threw his mellowing rays, touching every slope and ridge with a rich warm glow.

Poor Ellen did not heed the picturesque effect of all this, yet the sweet influences of nature reached her, and softened while they increased her sorrow. She felt her own heart sadly out of tune with the peace and loveliness of all she saw. Her eye sought those distant hills,—how very far off they were! and yet all that wide tract of country was but a little piece of what lay between her and her mother. Her eye sought those hills,—but her mind overpassed them and went far beyond, over many such a tract, till it reached the loved one at last. But oh! how much between! "I cannot reach her!—she cannot reach me!" thought poor Ellen. Her eyes had been filling and dropping tears for some time, but now came the rush of the pent-up storm, and the floods of grief were kept back no longer.

When once fairly excited, Ellen's passions were always extreme. During the former peaceful and happy part of her life the occasions of such excitement had been very rare. Of late unhappily they had occurred much oftener. Many were the bitter fits of tears she had known within a few weeks. But now it seemed as if all the scattered causes of sorrow that had wrought those tears were gathered together and pressing upon her at once; and that the burden would crush her to the earth. To the earth it brought her literally. She slid from her seat at first, and embracing the stone on which she had sat, she leaned her head there; but presently in her agony quitting her hold of that, she cast herself down upon the moss, lying at full length upon the cold ground, which seemed to her childish fancy the best friend she had left. But Ellen was wrought up to the last pitch of grief and passion. Tears brought no relief. Convulsive weeping only exhausted her. In the extremity of her distress and despair, and in that lonely place, out of hearing of every one, she sobbed aloud, and even screamed, for almost the first time in her life; and these fits of violence were succeeded by exhaustion, during which she ceased to shed tears and lay quite still, drawing only long sobbing sighs now and then.

How long Ellen had lain there, or how long this would have gone on before her strength had been quite worn out, no one can tell. In one of these fits of forced quiet, when she lay as still as the rocks around her, she heard a voice close by say, "What is the matter, my child?"

The silver sweetness of the tone came singularly upon the tempest in Ellen's mind. She got up hastily, and brushing away the tears from her dimmed eyes, she saw a young lady standing there, and a face whose sweetness well matched the voice looking upon her with grave concern. She stood motionless and silent.

"What is the matter, my dear?"

The tone found Ellen's heart and brought the water to her eyes again, though with a difference. She covered her face with her hands. But gentle hands were placed upon hers and drew them away; and the lady sitting down on Ellen's stone, took her in her arms; and Ellen hid her face in the bosom of a better friend than the cold earth had been like to prove her. But the change overcame her; and the soft whisper, "Don't cry any more," made it impossible to stop crying. Nothing further was said for some time;

the lady waited till Ellen grew calmer. When she saw her able to answer, she said gently,

"What does all this mean, my child? What troubles you? Tell me, and I think we can find a way to mend matters."

Ellen answered the tone of voice with a faint smile, but the words with another gush of tears.

"You are Ellen Montgomery, aren't you?"

"Yes, ma'am."

"I thought so. This isn't the first time I have seen you; I have seen you once before."

Ellen looked up surprised.

"Have you, ma'am?—I am sure I have never seen you."

"No, I know that. I saw you when you didn't see me. Where do you think?"

"I can't tell, I am sure," said Ellen,—"I can't guess; I haven't seen you at aunt Fortune's, and I haven't been anywhere else."

"You have forgotten," said the lady. "Did you never hear of a little girl who went to take a walk once upon a time, and had an unlucky fall into a brook?—and then went to a kind old lady's house where she was dried and put to bed and went to sleep."

"Oh, yes," said Ellen. "Did you see me there, ma'am, and when I was asleep?"

"I saw you there when you were asleep; and Mrs. Van Brunt told me who you were and where you lived; and when I came here a little while ago I knew you again very soon. And I knew what the matter was too, pretty well; but nevertheless tell me all about it, Ellen; perhaps I can help you."

Ellen shook her head dejectedly. "Nobody in this world can help me," she said.

"Then there's one in heaven that can," said the lady steadily. "Nothing is too bad for him to mend. Have you asked *his* help, Ellen?"

Ellen began to weep again. "Oh, if I could I would tell you all about it, ma'am," she said; "but there are so many things, I don't know where to begin, I don't know when I should ever get through."

"So many things that trouble you, Ellen?"

"Yes, ma'am."

"I am sorry for that indeed. But never mind, dear, tell me what they are. Begin with the worst, and if I haven't time to hear them all now I'll find time another day. Begin with the worst."

But she waited in vain for an answer, and became distressed herself at Ellen's distress, which was extreme.

"Don't cry so, my child,—don't cry so," she said, pressing her in her arms. "What *is* the matter? hardly any thing in this world is so bad it can't be mended. I think I know what troubles you so —it is that your dear mother is away from you, isn't it?"

"Oh, no, ma'am!"—Ellen could scarcely articulate. But struggling with herself for a minute or two, she then spoke again and more clearly.

"The worst is,—oh the worst is—that I meant—I meant—to be

a good child, and I have been worse than ever I was in my life before."

Her tears gushed forth.

" But how, Ellen ?" said her surprised friend after a pause. " I don't quite understand you. When did you ' mean to be a good child ?' Didn't you always mean so ? and what have you been doing ?"

Ellen made a great effort and ceased crying ; straightened herself ; dashed away her tears as if determined to shed no more ; and presently spoke calmly, though a choking sob every now and then threatened to interrupt her.

" I will tell you, ma'am. That first day I left mamma—when I was on board the steamboat and feeling as badly as I could feel, a kind, kind gentleman, I don't know who he was, came to me and spoke to me, and took care of me the whole day. Oh, if I could see him again ! He talked to me a great deal ; he wanted me to be a Christian ; he wanted me to make up my mind to begin that day to be one ; and ma'am, I did. I did resolve with my whole heart, and I thought I should be different from that time from what I had ever been before. But I think I have never been so bad in my life as I have been since then. Instead of feeling right I have felt wrong all the time, almost,—and I can't help it. I have been passionate and cross, and bad feelings keep coming, and I know it's wrong, and it makes me miserable. And yet, oh ! ma'am, I haven't changed my mind a bit,—I think just the same as I did that day ; I want to be a Christian more than any thing else in the world, but I am not,—and what shall I do !"

Her face sank in her hands again.

" And this is your great trouble ?" said her friend.

" Yes."

" Do you remember who said, ' Come unto me all ye that labour and are heavy laden, and I will give you rest' ?"

Ellen looked up inquiringly.

" You are grieved to find yourself so unlike what you would be. You wish to be a child of the dear Saviour and to have your heart filled with his love, and to do what will please him. Do you ?— Have you gone to him day by day, and night by night, and told him so ?—have you begged him to give you strength to get the better of your wrong feelings, and asked him to change you and make you his child ?"

" At first I did, ma'am,"—said Ellen in a low voice.

" Not lately ?"

" No ma'am ;" in a low tone still and looking down.

" Then you have neglected your Bible and prayer for some time past ?"

Ellen hardly uttered, " Yes."

" Why, my child ?"

" I don't know, ma'am," said Ellen weeping,—" that is one of the things that made me think myself so very wicked. I couldn't like to read my Bible or pray either, though I always used to before. My Bible lay down quite at the bottom of my trunk, and I even didn't like to raise my things enough to see the cover of it. I was so full of bad feelings I didn't feel fit to pray or read either."

" Ah ! that is the way with the wisest of us," said her companion ; " how apt we are to shrink most from our Physician just when we are in most need of him. But Ellen, dear, that isn't right. No hand but his can touch that sickness you are complaining of. Seek it, love, seek it. He will hear and help you, no doubt of it, in every trouble you carry simply and humbly to his feet ;—he has *promised*, you know."

Ellen was weeping very much, but less bitterly than before ; the clouds were breaking and light beginning to shine through.

" Shall we pray together now ?" said her companion after a few minutes' pause.

" Oh, if you please, ma'am, do !" Ellen answered through her tears.

And they knelt together there on the moss beside the stone, where Ellen's head rested and her friend's folded hands were laid. It might have been two children speaking to their father, for the simplicity of that prayer ; difference of age seemed to be forgotten, and what suited one suited the other. It was not without difficulty that the speaker carried it calmly through, for Ellen's sobs went nigh to check her more than once. When they rose Ellen silently sought her friend's arms again, and laying her face on her shoulder and putting both arms round her neck, she wept still,—but what different tears ! It was like the gentle rain falling through sunshine, after the dark cloud and the thunder and the hurricane have passed by. And they kissed each other before either of them spoke.

" You will not forget your Bible and prayer again, Ellen ?"

" Oh, no, ma'am."

" Then I am sure you will find your causes of trouble grow less. I will not hear the rest of them now. In a day or two I hope you will be able to give me a very different account from what you would have done an hour ago ; but besides that it is getting late, and it will not do for us to stay too long up here ; you have a good way to go to reach home. Will you come and see me to-morrow afternoon ?"

" Oh, yes, ma'am, indeed I will !—if I can ;—and if you will tell me where."

" Instead of turning up this little rocky path you must keep straight on in the road,—that's all; and it's the first house you come to. It isn't very far from here. Where were you going on the mountain?"

"Nowhere, ma'am."

"Have you been any higher up than this?"

"No, ma'am."

"Then before we go away I want to show you something. I'll take you over the Bridge of the Nose; it isn't but a step or two more; a little rough to be sure, but you musn't mind that."

"What is the 'Bridge of the Nose,' ma'am?" said Ellen, as they left her resting-place, and began to toil up the path which grew more steep and rocky than ever.

"You know this mountain is called the Nose. Just here it runs out to a very thin sharp edge. We shall come to a place presently where you turn a very sharp corner to get from one side of the hill to the other; and my brother named it jokingly the Bridge of the Nose."

"Why do they give the mountain such a queer name?" said Ellen.

"I don't know I'm sure. The people say that from one point of view this side of it looks very like a man's nose; but I never could find it out, and have some doubt about the fact. But now here we are! Just come round this great rock,—mind how you step, Ellen,—now look there!"

The rock they had just turned was at their backs, and they looked toward the west. Both exclaimed at the beauty before them. The view was not so extended as the one they had left. On the north and south the broken wavy outline of mountains closed in the horizon; but far to the west stretched an opening between the hills through which the setting sun sent his long beams, even to their feet. In the distance all was a golden haze; nearer, on the right and left the hills were lit up singularly, and there was a most beautiful mingling of deep hazy shadow and bright glowing mountain sides and ridges. A glory was upon the valley. Far down below at their feet lay a large lake gleaming in the sunlight; and at the upper end of it a village of some size showed like a cluster of white dots.

"How beautiful!" said the lady again. "Ellen, dear,—he whose hand raised up those mountains and has painted them so gloriously is the very same One who has said, to you and to me, 'Ask and it shall be given you.'"

Ellen looked up; their eyes met; her answer was in that grateful glance.

The lady sat down and drew Ellen close to her. "Do you see that little white village yonder, down at the far end of the lake? that is the village of Carra-carra; and that is Carra-carra lake;

that is where I go to church; you cannot see the little church from
here.   My father preaches there every Sunday morning.

"You must have a long way to go," said Ellen.

"Yes—a pretty long way, but it's very pleasant though.   I
mount my little grey pony, and he carries me there in quick time,
when I will let him.   I never wish the way shorter.   I go in all
sorts of weathers too, Ellen; Sharp and I don't mind frost and
snow."

"Who is Sharp?" said Ellen.

"My pony.   An odd name, isn't it.   It wasn't of my choosing,
Ellen, but he deserves it if ever pony did.   He's a very cunning
little fellow.   Where do you go, Ellen? to Thirlwall?"

"To church, ma'am?—I don't go anywhere."

"Doesn't your aunt go to church?"

"She hasn't since I have been here."

"What do you do with yourself on Sunday?"

"Nothing, ma'am; I don't know what to do with myself all the
day long.   I get tired of being in the house, and I go out of doors,
and then I get tired of being out of doors and come in again.   I
wanted a kitten dreadfully, but Mr. Van Brunt said aunt Fortune
would not let me keep one."

"Did you want a kitten to help you keep Sunday, Ellen?" said
her friend smiling.

"Yes I did, ma'am," said Ellen, smiling again;—"I thought it
would be a great deal of company for me.   I got very tired of
reading all day long, and I had nothing to read but the Bible; and
you know, ma'am, I told you I have been all wrong ever since I
came here, and I didn't like to read that much."

"My poor child!" said the lady,—"you have been hardly
bestead I think.   What if you were to come and spend next Sunday with me?   Don't you think I should do instead of a kitten?"

"Oh, yes, ma'am, I am sure of it," said Ellen clinging to her.
"Oh, I'll come gladly if you will let me,—and if aunt Fortune
will let me; and I hope she will, for she said last Sunday I was
the plague of her life."

"What did you do to make her say so?" said her friend gravely.

"Only asked her for some books, ma'am."

"Well, my dear, I see I am getting upon another of your
troubles, and we haven't time for that now.   By your own account
you have been much in fault yourself; and I trust you will find all
things mend with your own mending.   But now there goes the sun!
—and you and I must follow his example."

The lake ceased to gleam, and the houses of the village were
less plainly to be seen; still the mountain heads were as bright as
ever.   Gradually the shadows crept up their sides while the grey
of evening settled deeper and deeper upon the valley.

"There," said Ellen,—"that's just what I was wondering at the other morning; only then the light shone upon the top of the mountains first and walked down, and now it leaves the bottom first and walks up. I asked Mr. Van Brunt about it and he could not tell me. That's another of my troubles,—there's nobody that can tell me any thing."

"Put me in mind of it to-morrow, and I'll try to make you understand it," said the lady, "but we must not tarry now. I see you are likely to find me work enough, Ellen."

"I'll not ask you a question, ma'am, if you don't like it," said Ellen earnestly.

"I do like, I do like," said the other. "I spoke laughingly, for I see you will be apt to ask me a good many. As many as you please, my dear."

"Thank you, ma'am," said Ellen, as they ran down the hill; "they keep coming into my head all the while."

It was easier going down than coming up. They soon arrived at the place where Ellen had left the road to take the wood-path.

"Here we part," said the lady. "Good-night!"

"Good-night, ma'am."

There was a kiss and a squeeze of the hand, but when Ellen would have turned away the lady still held her fast.

"You are an odd little girl," said she. "I gave you liberty to ask me questions."

"Yes, ma'am," said Ellen, doubtfully.

"There is a question you have not asked me that I have been expecting. Do you know who I am?"

"No, ma'am."

"Don't you want to know?"

"Yes, ma'am, very much," said Ellen, laughing at her friend's look, "but mamma told me never to try to find out any thing about other people that they didn't wish me to know, or that wasn't my business."

"Well, I think this is your business decidedly. Who are you going to ask for when you come to see me to-morrow? Will you ask for 'the young lady that lives in this house?' or will you give a description of my nose and eyes and inches?"

Ellen laughed.

"My dear Ellen," said the lady, changing her tone, "do you know you please me very much? For one person that shows herself well-bred in this matter there are a thousand I think that ask impertinent questions. I am very glad you are an exception to the common rule. But, dear Ellen, I am quite willing you should know my name—it is Alice Humphreys. Now kiss me again and run home; it is quite, quite time; I have kept you too late. Good-night, my dear! Tell your aunt I beg she will allow you to take tea with me to-morrow."

They parted; and Ellen hastened homewards, urged by the rapidly growing dusk of the evening. She trod the green turf with a step lighter and quicker than it had been a few hours before, and she regained her home in much less time than it had taken her to come from thence to the mountain. Lights were in the kitchen, and the table set; but though weary and faint she was willing to forego her supper rather than meet her aunt just then; so she stole quietly up to her room. She did not forget her friend's advice. She had no light; she could not read; but Ellen did pray. She did carry all her heart-sickness, her wants, and her woes, to that Friend whose ear is always open to hear the cry of those who call upon him in truth; and then, relieved, refreshed, almost healed, she went to bed and slept sweetly.

CHAPTER XVI.

After long storms and tempests overblowne,
The sunne at length his joyous face doth cleare;
So when as fortune all her spight hath showne,
Some blissfull houres at last must needs appeare;
Else should afflicted wights oft-times despeire.
                                    FAERIE QUEENE.

EARLY next morning Ellen awoke with a sense that something pleasant had happened. Then the joyful reality darted into her mind, and jumping out of bed she set about her morning work with a better heart than she had been able to bring to it for many a long day. When she had finished she went to the window. She had found out how to keep it open now, by means of a big nail stuck in a hole under the sash. It was very early, and in the perfect stillness the soft gurgle of the little brook came distinctly to her ear. Ellen leaned her arms on the window-sill, and tasted the morning air; almost wondering at its sweetness and at the loveliness of field and sky and the bright eastern horizon. For days and days all had looked dark and sad.

There were two reasons for the change. In the first place Ellen had made up her mind to go straight on in the path of duty; in the second place, she had found a friend. Her little heart bounded with delight and swelled with thankfulness at the thought of Alice Humphreys. She was once more at peace with herself, and had even some notion of being by and by at peace with her aunt; though a sad twinge came over her whenever she thought of her mother's letter.

"But there is only one way for me," she thought; "I'll do as that dear Miss Humphreys told me—it's good and early, and I shall have a fine time before breakfast yet to myself. And I'll get up so every morning and have it!—that'll be the very best plan I can hit upon."

As she thought this she drew forth her Bible from its place at the bottom of her trunk; and opening it at hazard she began to read the 18th chapter of Matthew. Some of it she did not quite understand; but she paused with pleasure at the 14th verse. "That means me," she thought. The 21st and 22d verses struck her a good deal, but when she came to the last she was almost startled.

"There it is again!" she said. "That is exactly what that gentleman said to me. I thought I was forgiven, but how can I be, for I feel I have not forgiven aunt Fortune."

Laying aside her book, Ellen kneeled down; but this one thought so pressed upon her mind that she could think of scarce any thing else; and her prayer this morning was an urgent and repeated petition that she might be enabled "from her heart" to forgive her aunt Fortune "all her trespasses." Poor Ellen! she felt it was very hard work. At the very minute she was striving to feel at peace with her aunt, one grievance after another would start up to remembrance, and she knew the feelings that met them were far enough from the spirit of forgiveness. In the midst of this she was called down. She rose with tears in her eyes, and "What shall I do?" in her heart. Bowing her head once more she earnestly prayed that if she could not yet *feel* right toward her aunt, she might be kept at least from acting or speaking wrong. Poor Ellen! In the heart is the spring of action; and she found it so this morning.

Her aunt and Mr. Van Brunt were already at the table. Ellen took her place in silence, for one look at her aunt's face told her that no "good-morning" would be accepted. Miss Fortune was in a particularly bad humour, owing among other things to Mr. Van Brunt's having refused to eat his breakfast unless Ellen were called. An unlucky piece of kindness. She neither spoke to Ellen nor looked at her; Mr. Van Brunt did what in him lay to make amends. He helped her very carefully to the cold pork and potatoes, and handed her the well-piled platter of griddle-cakes.

"Here's the first buckwheats of the season," said he,—"and I told Miss Fortune I warn't a going to eat one on 'em if you didn't come down to enjoy 'em along with us. Take two—take two!— you want 'em to keep each other hot."

Ellen's look and smile thanked him, as following his advice she covered one generous "buckwheat" with another as ample.

"That's the thing! Now here's some prime maple. You like 'em, I guess, don't you?"

"I don't know yet—I have never seen any," said Ellen.

"Never seen buckwheats! why, they're most as good as my mother's splitters. Buckwheat cakes and maple molasses,—that's food fit for a king, *I* think—when they're good; and Miss Fortune's are always first-rate."

Miss Fortune did not relent at all at this compliment.

"What makes you so white this morning?" Mr. Van Brunt presently went on;—"you ain't well, be you?"

"Yes,"—said Ellen doubtfully,—"I'm well——"

"She's as well as I am, Mr. Van Brunt, if you don't go and put her up to any notions!" Miss Fortune said in a kind of choked voice.

Mr. Van Brunt hemmed, and said no more to the end of breakfast-time.

Ellen rather dreaded what was to come next, for her aunt's look was ominous. In dead silence the things were put away, and put up, and in course of washing and drying, when Miss Fortune suddenly broke forth.

"What did you do with yourself yesterday afternoon?"

"I was up on the mountain," said Ellen.

"What mountain?"

"I believe they call it the 'Nose.'"

"What business had you up there?"

"I hadn't any business there."

"What did you go there for?"

"Nothing."

"Nothing!—you expect me to believe that? you call yourself a truth-teller, I suppose?"

"Mamma used to say I was," said poor Ellen, striving to swallow her feelings.

"Your mother!—I dare say—mothers always are blind. I dare say she took every thing you said for gospel!"

Ellen was silent, from sheer want of words that were pointed enough to suit her.

"I wish Morgan could have had the gumption to marry in his own country; but he must go running after a Scotch woman! A Yankee would have brought up his child to be worth something. Give me Yankees!"

Ellen set down the cup she was wiping.

"You don't know any thing about my mother," she said. "You oughtn't to speak so—it's not right."

"Why ain't it right, I should like to know?" said Miss Fortune; —"this is a free country, I guess. Our tongues ain't tied—we're all free here."

"I wish we were," muttered Ellen;—"I know what I'd do."

"What would you do?" said Miss Fortune.

Ellen was silent. Her aunt repeated the question in a sharper tone.

"I oughtn't to say what I was going to," said Ellen;—"I'd rather not."

"I don't care," said Miss Fortune, "you began, and you shall finish it. I will hear what it was."

"I was going to say, if we were all free I would run away."

"Well, that *is* a beautiful, well-behaved speech! I am glad to have heard it. I admire it very much. Now what were you doing yesterday up on the Nose? Please to go on wiping. There's a pile ready for you. What were you doing yesterday afternoon?"

Ellen hesitated.

"Were you alone or with somebody?"

"I was alone part of the time."

"And who were you with the rest of the time?"

"Miss Humphreys."

"Miss Humphreys!—what were you doing with her?"

"Talking."

"Did you ever see her before?"

"No, ma'am."

"Where did you find her?"

"She found me, up on the hill."

"What were you talking about?"

Ellen was silent.

"What were you talking about?" repeated Miss Fortune.

"I had rather not tell."

"And I had rather you *should* tell—so out with it."

"I was alone with Miss Humphreys," said Ellen; "and it is no matter what we were talking about—it doesn't concern any body but her and me."

"Yes it does, it concerns me," said her aunt, "and I choose to know;—what were you talking about?"

Ellen was silent.

"Will you tell me?"

"No," said Ellen, low but resolutely.

"I vow you're enough to try the patience of Job! Look here," said Miss Fortune, setting down what she had in her hands,—"I *will* know! I don't care what it was, but you shall tell me or I'll find a way to make you. I'll give you such a——"

"Stop! stop!" said Ellen wildly,—"you must not speak to me so! Mamma never did, and you have no *right* to! If mamma or papa were here you would not *dare* talk to me so."

The answer to this was a sharp box on the ear from Miss Fortune's wet hand. Half stunned, less by the blow than the tumult of feeling it roused, Ellen stood a moment, and then throwing down her towel she ran out of the room, shivering with passion, and brushing off the soapy water left on her face as if it had been her aunt's very hand. Violent tears burst forth as soon as she reached her own room,—tears at first of anger and mortification only; but conscience presently began to whisper, "You are wrong! you are wrong!"—and tears of sorrow mingled with the others.

"Oh," said Ellen, "why couldn't I keep still!—when I had resolved so this morning, why couldn't I be quiet!—But she ought not to have provoked me so dreadfully,—I couldn't help it." "You are wrong," said conscience again, and her tears flowed faster. And then came back her morning trouble—the duty and the difficulty of forgiving. Forgive her aunt Fortune!—with her whole heart in a passion of displeasure against her. Alas! Ellen began to feel and acknowledge that indeed all was wrong. But what to do? There was just one comfort, the visit to Miss Humphreys in the afternoon. "She will tell me," thought Ellen; "she will help me. But in the mean while?"

Ellen had not much time to think; her aunt called her down and set her to work. She was very busy till dinner-time, and very unhappy; but twenty times in the course of the morning did Ellen pause for a moment, and covering her face with her hands pray that a heart to forgive might be given her.

As soon as possible after dinner she made her escape to her room that she might prepare for her walk. Conscience was not quite easy that she was going without the knowledge of her aunt. She had debated the question with herself, and could not make up her mind to hazard losing her visit.

So she dressed herself very carefully. One of her dark merinos was affectionately put on; her single pair of white stockings; shoes, ruffle, cape,—Ellen saw that all was faultlessly neat, just as her mother used to have it; and the nice blue hood lay upon the bed ready to be put on the last thing, when she heard her aunt's voice calling.

"Ellen!—come down and do your ironing—right away, now! the irons are hot."

For one moment Ellen stood still in dismay; then slowly undressed, dressed again, and went down stairs.

"Come! you've been an age," said Miss Fortune; "now make haste; there ain't but a handful; and I want to mop up."

Ellen took courage again; ironed away with right good will; and as there was really but a handful of things she had soon done, even to taking off the ironing blanket and putting up the irons. In the mean time she had changed her mind as to stealing off without leave; conscience was too strong for her; and though with a beating heart, she told of Miss Humphreys' desire and her half engagement.

"You may go where you like—I am sure I do not care what you do with yourself," was Miss Fortune's reply.

Full of delight at this ungracious permission, Ellen fled up
stairs, and dressing much quicker than before, was soon on her
way.

But at first she went rather sadly. In spite of all her good
resolves and wishes, every thing that day had gone wrong; and
Ellen felt that the root of the evil was in her own heart. Some
tears fell as she walked. Further from her aunt's house, however,
her spirits began to rise; her foot fell lighter on the greensward.
Hope and expectation quickened her steps; and when at length
she passed the little wood-path it was almost on a run. Not very
far beyond that her glad eyes saw the house she was in quest of.

It was a large white house; not very white either, for its last
dress of paint had grown old long ago. It stood close by the road,
and the trees of the wood seemed to throng round it on every side.
Ellen mounted the few steps that led to the front door, and knocked;
but as she could only just reach the high knocker, she was not
likely to alarm any body with the noise she made. After a great
many little faint raps, which if any body heard them might easily
have been mistaken for the attacks of some rat's teeth upon the
wainscot, Ellen grew weary of her fruitless toil of standing on tiptoe, and resolved, though doubtfully, to go round the house and
see if there was any other way of getting in. Turning the far
corner, she saw a long, low out-building or shed jutting out from
the side of the house. On the further side of this Ellen found an
elderly woman standing in front of the shed, which was there open
and paved, and wringing some clothes out of a tub of water. She
was a pleasant woman to look at, very trim and tidy, and a good-
humoured eye and smile when she saw Ellen. Ellen made up to
her and asked for Miss Humphreys.

" Why, where in the world did you come from?" said the woman.
" I don't receive company at the back of the house."

" I knocked at the front door till I was tired," said Ellen, smiling
in return.

" Miss Alice must ha' been asleep. Now, honey, you have come
so far round to find me, will you go a little further and find Miss
Alice? Just go round this corner and keep straight along till you
come to the glass door—there you'll find her. Stop!—maybe she's
asleep; I may as well go along with you myself."

She wrung the water from her hands and led the way.

A little space of green grass stretched in front of the shed, and
Ellen found it extended all along that side of the house like a very
narrow lawn; at the edge of it shot up the high forest trees;
nothing between them and the house but the smooth grass and a
narrow worn foot-path. The woods were now all brown stems,
except here and there a superb hemlock and some scattered sil-
very birches. But the grass was still green, and the last day of

the Indian summer hung its soft veil over all; the foliage of the
forest was hardly missed. They passed another hall door, opposite
the one where Ellen had tried her strength and patience upon the
knocker; a little further on they paused at the glass door. One
step led to it. Ellen's conductress looked in first through one of
the panes, and then opening the door motioned her to enter.

"Here you are, my new acquaintance," said Alice, smiling and
kissing her. "I began to think something was the matter, you
tarried so late. We don't keep fashionable hours in the country,
you know. But I'm very glad to see you. Take off your things
and lay them on that settee by the door. You see I've a settee for
summer and a sofa for winter; for here I am, in this room, at all
times of the year; and a very pleasant room I think it, don't
you?"

"Yes, indeed I do, ma'am," said Ellen, pulling off her last
glove.

"Ah, but wait till you have taken tea with me half a dozen times,
and then see if you don't say it is pleasant. Nothing can be so
pleasant that is quite new. But now come here and look out of
this window, or door, whichever you choose to call it. Do you see
what a beautiful view I have here? The wood was just as thick
all along as it is on the right and left; I felt half smothered to be
so shut in, so I got my brother and Thomas to take axes and go to
work there; and many a large tree they cut down for me, till you
see they opened a way through the woods for the view of that
beautiful stretch of country. I should grow melancholy if I had
that wall of trees pressing on my vision all the time; it always
comforts me to look off, far away, to those distant blue hills."

"Aren't those the hills I was looking at yesterday?" said Ellen.

"From up on the mountain?—the very same; this is part of
the very same view, and a noble view it is. Every morning, Ellen,
the sun rising behind those hills shines in through this door and
lights up my room; and in winter he looks in at that south window,
so I have him all the time. To be sure if I want to see him set I
must take a walk for it, but that isn't unpleasant; and you know
we cannot have every thing at once."

It was a very beautiful extent of woodland, meadow, and hill,
that was seen picture-fashion through the gap cut in the forest;—
the wall of trees on each side serving as a frame to shut it in, and
the descent of the mountain, from almost the edge of the lawn,
being very rapid. The opening had been skilfully cut; the effect
was remarkable and very fine; the light on the picture being often
quite different from that on the frame or on the hither side of the
frame.

"Now, Ellen," said Alice turning from the window, "take a
good look at my room. I want you to know it and feel at home in

it; for whenever you can run away from your aunt's this is your home,—do you understand?"

A smile was on each face. Ellen felt that she was understanding it very fast.

"Here, next the door, you see, is my summer settee; and in summer it very often walks out of doors to accommodate people on the grass plat. I have a great fancy for taking tea out of doors, Ellen, in warm weather; and if you do not mind a mosquito or two I shall be always happy to have your company. That door opens into the hall; look out and see, for I want you to get the geography of the house.—That odd-looking, lumbering, painted concern, is my cabinet of curiosities. I tried my best to make the carpenter man at Thirlwall understand what sort of a thing I wanted, and did all but show him how to make it; but as the southerners say, 'he hasn't made it right no how!' There I keep my dried flowers, my minerals, and a very odd collection of curious things of all sorts that I am constantly picking up. I'll show you them some day, Ellen. Have you a fancy for curiosities?"

"Yes, ma'am, I believe so."

"Believe so!—not more sure than that? Are you a lover of dead moths, and empty beetle-skins, and butterflies' wings, and dry tufts of moss, and curious stones, and pieces of ribbon-grass, and strange bird's nests? These are some of the things I used to delight in when I was about as old as you."

"I don't know, ma'am," said Ellen. "I never was where I could get them."

"Weren't you! Poor child! Then you have been shut up to brick walls and paving-stones all your life?"

"Yes, ma'am, all my life."

"But now you have seen a little of the country,—don't you think you shall like it better?"

"Oh, a great deal better!"

"Ah, that's right. I am sure you will. On that other side, you see, is my winter sofa. It's a very comfortable resting-place I can tell you, Ellen, as I have proved by many a sweet nap; and its old chintz covers are very pleasant to me, for I remember them as far back as I remember any thing."

There was a sigh here; but Alice passed on and opened a door near the end of the sofa.

"Look in here, Ellen; this is my bedroom."

"Oh, how lovely!" Ellen exclaimed.

The carpet covered only the middle of the floor; the rest was painted white. The furniture was common but neat as wax. Ample curtains of white dimity clothed the three windows, and lightly draped the bed. The toilet-table was covered with snow-white muslin, and by the toilet-cushion stood, late as it was, a glass of flowers. Ellen thought it must be a pleasure to sleep there.

"This," said Alice when they came out,—"between my door and the fireplace, is a cupboard. Here be cups and saucers, and so forth. In that other corner beyond the fireplace you see my flower-stand. Do you love flowers, Ellen?"

"I love them dearly, Miss Alice."

"I have some pretty ones out yet, and shall have one or two in the winter; but I can't keep a great many here; I haven't room for them. I have hard work to save these from frost. There's a beautiful daphne that will be out by and by, and make the whole house sweet. But here, Ellen, on this side between the windows, is my greatest treasure—my precious books. All these are mine. —Now, my dear, it is time to introduce you to my most excellent of easy chairs—the best things in the room, aren't they? Put yourself in that—now do you feel at home?"

"Very much indeed, ma'am," said Ellen laughing, as Alice placed her in the deep easy chair.

There were two things in the room that Alice had not mentioned, and while she mended the fire Ellen looked at them. One was the portrait of a gentleman, grave and good-looking; this had very little of her attention. The other was the counter-portrait of a lady; a fine dignified countenance that had a charm for Ellen. It hung over the fireplace in an excellent light; and the mild eye and somewhat of a peculiar expression about the mouth bore such like-ness to Alice, though older, that Ellen had no doubt whose it was.

Alice presently drew a chair close to Ellen's side, and kissed her.

"I trust, my child," she said, "that you feel better to-day than you did yesterday?"

"Oh, I do, ma'am,—a great deal better," Ellen answered.

"Then I hope the reason is that you have returned to your duty, and are resolved, not to be a Christian by and by, but to lead a Christian's life now?"

"I have resolved so, ma'am,—I did resolve so last night and this morning,—but yet I have been doing nothing but wrong all to-day."

Alice was silent. Ellen's lips quivered for a moment, and then she went on,

"Oh, ma'am, how I have wanted to see you to-day to tell me what I *should* do! I resolved and resolved this morning, and then as soon as I got down stairs I began to have bad feelings toward aunt Fortune, and I have been full of bad feelings all day; and I couldn't help it."

"It will not do to say that we cannot help what is wrong, Ellen. —What is the reason that you have bad feelings toward your aunt?"

"She don't like me, ma'am."

"But how happens that, Ellen? I am afraid you don't like her."

"No, ma'am, I don't to be sure; how can I?"

"Why cannot you, Ellen?"

"Oh, I can't, ma'am! I wish I could. But oh, ma'am, I should have liked her—I might have liked her, if she had been kind, but she never has. Even that first night I came she never kissed me, nor said she was glad to see me."

"That was failing in kindness certainly, but is she *un*kind to you, Ellen?"

"Oh, yes, ma'am, indeed she is. She talks to me, and talks to me, in a way that almost drives me out of my wits; and to-day she even struck me! She has no right to do it," said Ellen, firing with passion,—"she has no *right* to!—and she has no right to talk as she does about mamma. She did it to-day, and she has done it before;—I can't bear it!—and I can't bear *her!* I can't *bear* her!"

"Hush, hush," said Alice, drawing the excited child to her arms, for Ellen had risen from her seat;—"you must not talk so, Ellen;—you are not feeling right now."

"No, ma'am, I am not," said Ellen coldly and sadly. She sat a moment, and then turning to her companion put both arms round her neck, and hid her face on her shoulder again; and without raising it she gave her the history of the morning.

"What has brought about this dreadful state of things?" said Alice after a few minutes. "Whose fault is it, Ellen?"

"I think it is aunt Fortune's fault," said Ellen raising her head; "I don't think it is mine. If she had behaved well to me I should have behaved well to her. I meant to, I am sure."

"Do you mean to say you do not think you have been in fault at all in the matter?"

"No, ma'am—I do not mean to say that. I have been very much in fault—very often—I know that. I get very angry and vexed, and sometimes I say nothing, but sometimes I get out of all patience and say things I ought not. I did so to-day; but it is so very hard to keep still when I am in such a passion;—and now I have got to feel so toward aunt Fortune that I don't like the sight of her; I hate the very look of her bonnet hanging up on the wall. I know it isn't right; and it makes me miserable; and I can't help it, for I grow worse and worse every day;—and what shall I do?"

Ellen's tears came faster than her words.

"Ellen, my child," said Alice after a while,—"There is but one way. You know what I said to you yesterday?"

"I know it, but dear Miss Alice, in my reading this morning I came to that verse that speaks about not being forgiven if we do not forgive others; and oh! how it troubles me; for I can't feel that I forgive aunt Fortune; I feel vexed whenever the thought of her comes into my head; and how can I behave right to her while I feel so?"

"You are right there, my dear; you cannot indeed; the heart must be set right before the life can be."

"But what shall I do to set it right?"

"Pray."

"Dear Miss Alice, I have been praying all this morning that I might forgive aunt Fortune, and yet I cannot do it."

"Pray, still, my dear," said Alice, pressing her closer in her arms,—"pray still; if you are in earnest the answer will come. But there is something else you can do, and must do, Ellen, besides praying, or praying may be in vain."

"What do you mean, Miss Alice?"

"You acknowledge yourself in fault—have you made all the amends you can? Have you, as soon as you have seen yourself in the wrong, gone to your aunt Fortune and acknowledged it, and humbly asked her pardon?"

Ellen answered "no" in a low voice.

"Then, my child, your duty is plain before you. The next thing after doing wrong is to make all the amends in your power; confess your fault, and ask forgiveness, both of God and man. Pride struggles against it,—I see yours does,—but my child, 'God resisteth the proud, but giveth grace unto the humble.'"

Ellen burst into tears and cried heartily.

"Mind your own wrong doings, my child, and you will not be half so disposed to quarrel with those of other people. But, Ellen dear, if you will not humble yourself to this you must not count upon an answer to your prayer. 'If thou bring thy gift to the altar, and there rememberest that thy brother hath aught against thee,'—what then?—'Leave there thy gift before the altar;' go first and be reconciled to thy brother, and then come."

"But it is so hard to forgive?" sobbed Ellen.

"Hard? yes it is hard when our hearts are so. But there is little love to Christ and no just sense of his love to us in the heart that finds it hard. Pride and selfishness make it hard; the heart full of love to the dear Saviour *cannot* lay up offences against itself."

"I have said quite enough," said Alice after a pause; "you know what you want, my dear Ellen, and what you ought to do. I shall leave you for a little while to change my dress, for I have been walking and riding all the morning. Make a good use of the time while I am gone."

Ellen did make good use of the time. When Alice returned she met her with another face than she had worn all that day, humbler and quieter; and flinging her arms around her, she said,

"I will ask aunt Fortune's forgiveness;—I feel I can do it now."

"And how about *forgiving*, Ellen?"

"I think God will help me to forgive her," said Ellen; "I have asked him. At any rate I will ask her to forgive me. But oh, Miss Alice! what would have become of me without you."

"Don't lean upon me, dear Ellen; remember you have a better friend than I always near you; trust in him; if I have done you any good, don't forget it was he brought me to you yesterday afternoon."

"There's just one thing that troubles me now," said Ellen,— "mamma's letter. I am thinking of it all the time; I feel as if I should fly to get it!"

"We'll see about that. Cannot you ask your aunt for it?"

"I don't like to."

"Take care, Ellen; there is some pride there yet."

"Well, I will try," said Ellen, "but sometimes, I know, she would not give it to me if I were to ask her. But I'll try, if I can."

"Well, now to change the subject—at what o'clock did you dine to-day?"

"I don't know, ma'am,—at the same time we always do, I believe."

"And that is twelve o'clock, isn't it?"

"Yes, ma'am; but I was so full of coming here and other things that I couldn't eat."

"Then I suppose you would have no objection to an early tea?"

"No, ma'am,—whenever you please," said Ellen laughing.

"I shall please it pretty soon. I have had no dinner at all to-day, Ellen; I have been out and about all the morning, and had just taken a little nap when you came in. Come this way and let me show you some of my housekeeping."

She led the way across the hall to the room on the opposite side; a large, well-appointed, and spotlessly neat kitchen. Ellen could not help exclaiming at its pleasantness.

"Why, yes—I think it is. I have been in many a parlour that I do not like as well. Beyond this is a lower kitchen where Margery does all her rough work; nothing comes up the steps that lead from that to this but the very nicest and daintiest of kitchen matters. Margery, is my father gone to Thirlwall?"

"No, Miss Alice—he's at Carra-carra—Thomas heard him say he wouldn't be back early."

"Well, I shall not wait for him. Margery, if you will put the kettle on and see to the fire, I'll make some of my cakes for tea."

"I'll do it, Miss Alice; it's not good for you to go so long without eating."

Alice now rolled up her sleeves above the elbows, and tying a large white apron before her, set about gathering the different things she wanted for her work,—to Ellen's great amusement. A white moulding-board was placed upon a table as white; and round it soon grouped the pail of flour, the plate of nice yellow butter, the bowl of cream, the sieve, tray, and sundry etceteras. And then, first sifting some flour into the tray, Alice began to throw in the other things one after another and toss the whole about with a carelessness that looked as if all would go wrong, but with a confidence that seemed to say all was going right. Ellen gazed in comical wonderment.

"Did you think cakes were made without hands?" said Alice, laughing at her look. "You saw me wash mine before I began."

"Oh, I'm not thinking of that," said Ellen; "I am not afraid of your hands."

"Did you never see your mother do this?" said Alice, who was now turning and rolling about the dough upon the board in a way that seemed to Ellen curious beyond expression.

"No, never," she said. "Mamma never kept house, and I never saw any body do it."

"Then your aunt does not let you into the mysteries of bread-and butter-making!"

"Butter-making! Oh," said Ellen with a sigh, "I have enough of that!"

Alice now applied a smooth wooden roller to the cake, with such quickness and skill that the lump forthwith lay spread upon the board in a thin even layer, and she next cut it into little round cakes with the edge of a tumbler. Half the board was covered with the nice little white things, which Ellen declared looked good enough to eat already, and she had quite forgotten all possible causes of vexation, past, present, or future,—when suddenly a large grey cat jumped upon the table, and coolly walking upon the moulding-board planted his paw directly in the middle of one of his mistress's cakes.

"Take him off—Oh, Ellen!" cried Alice,—"take him off! I can't touch him."

But Ellen was a little afraid.

Alice then tried gently to shove puss off with her elbow; but he seemed to think that was very good fun,—purred, whisked his great tail over Alice's bare arm, and rubbed his head against it, having evidently no notion that he was not just where he ought to be. Alice and Ellen were too much amused to try any violent method of relief, but Margery happily coming in seized puss in both hands and set him on the floor.

"Just look at the print of his paw in that cake," said Ellen.

"He has set his mark on it certainly. I think it is his now, by the right of possession if not the right of discovery."

"I think he discovered the cakes too," said Ellen laughing.

"Why, yes. He shall have that one baked for his supper."

"Does he like cakes?"

"Indeed he does. He is very particular and delicate about his eating, is Captain Parry."

"Captain Parry!" said Ellen,—"is that his name?"

"Yes," said Alice laughing; "I don't wonder you look astonished, Ellen. I have had that cat five years, and when he was first given me by my brother Jack, who was younger then than he is now, and had been reading Captain Parry's Voyages, he gave him that name and would have him called so. Oh, Jack!"—said Alice, half laughing and half crying.

Ellen wondered why. But she went to wash her hands, and when her face was again turned to Ellen it was unruffled as ever.

"Margery, my cakes are ready," said she, "and Ellen and I are ready too."

"Very well, Miss Alice—the kettle is just going to boil; you shall have tea in a trice. I'll do some eggs for you."

"Something—any thing," said Alice; "I feel one cannot live without eating. Come, Ellen, you and I will go and set the tea-table."

Ellen was very happy arranging the cups and saucers and other things that Alice handed her from the cupboard; and when a few minutes after the tea and the cakes came in, and she and Alice were cosily seated at supper, poor Ellen hardly knew herself in such a pleasant state of things.

CHAPTER XVII.

The very sooth of it is, that an ill-habit has the force of an ill-fate.
L'ESTRANGE.

"ELLEN dear," said Alice as she poured out Ellen's second cup of tea, "have we run through the list of your troubles?"

"Oh, no, Miss Alice, indeed we haven't; but we have got through the worst."

"Is the next one so bad it would spoil our supper?"

"No," said Ellen, "it couldn't do that, but it's bad enough though; it's about my not going to school. Miss Alice, I promised myself I would learn so much while mamma was away, and surprise her when she came back, and instead of that I am not learning any thing. I don't mean not learning *any thing*," said Ellen correcting herself;—"but I can't do much. When I found aunt Fortune wasn't going to send me to school I determined I would try to study by myself; and I have tried; but I can't get along."

"Well now don't lay down your knife and fork and look so doleful," said Alice smiling; "this is a matter I can help you in. What are you studying?"

"Some things I can manage well enough," said Ellen, "the easy things; but I cannot understand my arithmetic without some one to explain it to me, and French I can do nothing at all with, and that is what I wanted to learn most of all; and often I want to ask questions about my history."

"Suppose," said Alice, "you go on studying by yourself as much and as well as you can, and bring your books up to me two or three times a week; I will hear and explain and answer questions to your heart's content, unless you should be too hard for me. What do you say to that?"

Ellen said nothing to it, but the colour that rushed to her cheeks, —the surprised look of delight,—were answer enough.

"It will do then," said Alice, "and I have no doubt we shall untie the knot of those arithmetical problems very soon. But, Ellen, my dear, I cannot help you in French, for I do not know it myself? What will you do about that?"

"I don't know, ma'am; I am sorry."

"So am I, for your sake. I can help you in Latin, if that would be any comfort to you."

"It wouldn't be much comfort to me," said Ellen, laughing; "mamma wanted me to learn Latin, but I wanted to learn French a great deal more; I don't care about Latin, except to please her."

"Permit me to ask if you know English?"

"Oh, yes, ma'am, I hope so; I knew that a great while ago."

"Did you? I am very happy to make your acquaintance then, for the number of young ladies who *do* know English is in my opinion remarkably small. Are you sure of the fact, Ellen?"

"Why yes, Miss Alice."

"Will you undertake to write me a note of two pages that shall not have one fault of grammar, nor one word spelt wrong, nor any thing in it that is not good English? You may take for a subject the history of this afternoon."

"Yes, ma'am, if you wish it. I hope I can write a note that long without making mistakes."

Alice smiled.

"I will not stop to inquire," she said, "whether *that long* is Latin or French; but Ellen, my dear, it is not English."

Ellen blushed a little, though she laughed too.

"I believe I have got into the way of saying that by hearing aunt Fortune and Mr. Van Brunt say it; I don't think I ever did before I came here."

"What are you so anxious to learn French for?"

"Mamma knows it, and I have often heard her talk French with a great many people; and papa and I always wanted to be able to talk it too; and mamma wanted me to learn it; she said there were a great many French books I ought to read."

"That last is true, no doubt. Ellen, I will make a bargain with you,—if you will study English with me, I will study French with you."

"Dear Miss Alice," said Ellen, caressing her, "I'll do it without that; I'll study any thing you please."

"Dear Ellen, I believe you would. But I should like to know it for my own sake; we'll study it together; we shall get along nicely, I have no doubt; we can learn to read it, at least, and that is the main point."

" But how shall we know what to call the words ?" said Ellen, doubtfully.

" That is a grave question," said Alice, smiling. " I am afraid we should hit upon a style of pronunciation that a Frenchman would make nothing of. I have it !'' she exclaimed, clapping her hands,—" where there's a will there's a way,—it always happens so. Ellen, I have an old friend upon the mountain who will give us exactly what we want, unless I am greatly mistaken. We'll go and see her; that is the very thing !—my old friend Mrs. Vawse."

" Mrs. Vawse !" repeated Ellen ;—" not the grandmother of that Nancy Vawse ?''

" The very same. Her name is not Vawse ; the country people call it so, and I being one of the country people have fallen into the way of it ; but her real name is Vosier. She was born a Swiss, and brought up in a wealthy French family, as the personal attendant of a young lady to whom she became exceedingly attached. This lady finally married an American gentleman ; and so great was Mrs. Vawse's love to her, that she left country and family to follow her here. In a few years her mistress died ; she married ; and since that time she has been tossed from trouble to trouble ;— a perfect sea of troubles ;—till now she is left like a wreck upon this mountain top. A fine wreck she is ! I go to see her very often, and next time I will call for you, and we will propose our French plan ; nothing will please her better, I know. By the way, Ellen, are you as well versed in the other common branches of education as you are in your mother tongue ?''

" What do you mean, Miss Alice ?''

" Geography, for instance ; do you know it well ?''

" Yes, ma'am ; I believe so ; I am sure I have studied it till I am sick of it.''

" Can you give me the boundaries of Great Thibet or Peru ?''
Ellen hesitated.

" I had rather not try," she said,—" I am not sure. I can't remember those queer countries in Asia and South America half so well as Europe and North America.''

" Do you know any thing about the surface of the country in Italy or France ; the character and condition of the people ; what kind of climate they have, and what grows there most freely ?''

" Why no, ma'am," said Ellen ; " nobody ever taught me that.''

" Would you like to go over the Atlas again, talking about all these matters, as well as the mere outlines of the countries you have studied before ?''

" Oh, yes, dearly !'' exclaimed Ellen.

" Well, I think we may let Margery have the tea-things. But here is Captain's cake.''

" Oh, may I give him his supper ?'' said Ellen.

" Certainly. You must carve it for him ; you know I told you he is very particular. Give him some of the egg, too—he likes that. Now where is the Captain ?''

Not far off ; for scarcely had Alice opened the door and called him once or twice, when with a queer little note of answer, he came hurriedly trotting in.

" He generally has his supper in the outer kitchen,'' said Alice, —" but I grant him leave to have it here to-night as a particular honour to him and you.''

" How handsome he is ! and how large !'' said Ellen.

" Yes, he is very handsome, and more than that he is very sensible, for a cat. Do you see how prettily his paws are marked? Jack used to say he had white gloves on.''

" And white boots too,'' said Ellen. " No, only one leg is white ; pussy's boots aren't mates. Is he good-natured ?''

" Very—if you don't meddle with him.''

" I don't call that being good-natured,'' said Ellen laughing.

" Nor I ; but truth obliges me to say the Captain does not permit any body to take liberties with him. He is a character, Captain Parry. Come out on the lawn, Ellen, and we will let Margery clear away.''

" What a pleasant face Margery has,'' said Ellen, as the door closed behind them ; " and what a pleasant way she has of speaking. I like to hear her,—the words come out so clear, and I don't know how, but not like other people.''

" You have a quick ear, Ellen ; you are very right. Margery had lived too long in England before she came here to lose her trick of speech afterwards. But Thomas speaks as thick as a Yankee, and always did.''

" Then Margery is English ?'' said Ellen.

" To be sure. She came over with us twelve years ago for the pure love of my father and mother ; and I believe now she looks upon John and me as her own children. I think she could scarcely love us more if we were so in truth. Thomas—you haven't seen Thomas yet, have you ?''

" No.''

" He is an excellent good man in his way, and as faithful as the day is long ; but he isn't equal to his wife. Perhaps I am partial ; Margery came to America for the love of us, and Thomas came for the love of Margery ; there's a difference.''

" But, Miss Alice !—''

" What, Miss Ellen ?''

" You said Margery came over *with you* ?''

" Yes ; is that what makes you look so astonished ?''

" But then you are English, too ?''

" Well, what of that ? you won't love me the less, will you ?''

"Oh, no," said Ellen; "my own mother came from Scotland, aunt Fortune says."

"I am English born, Ellen, but you may count me half American if you like, for I have spent rather more than half my life here. Come this way, Ellen, and I'll show you my garden. It is some distance off, but as near as a spot could be found fit for it."

They quitted the house by a little steep path leading down the mountain, which in two or three minutes brought them to a clear bit of ground. It was not large, but lying very prettily among the trees, with an open view to the east and southeast. On the extreme edge and at the lower end of it was fixed a rude bench, well sheltered by the towering forest trees. Here Alice and Ellen sat down.

It was near sunset; the air cool and sweet; the evening light upon field and sky.

"How fair it is!" said Alice musingly; "how fair and lovely! Look at those long shadows of the mountains, Ellen; and how bright the light is on the far hills. It won't be so long. A little while more, and our Indian summer will be over; and then the clouds, the frost, and the wind, and the snow. Well, let them come."

"I wish they wouldn't, I am sure," said Ellen. "I am sorry enough they are coming."

"Why?—all seasons have their pleasures. I am not sorry at all; I like the cold very much."

"I guess you wouldn't, Miss Alice, if you had to wash every morning where I do."

"Why, where is that?"

"Down at the spout."

"At the *spout*—what is that, pray?"

"The spout of water, ma'am, just down a little way from the kitchen door. The water comes in a little long, very long, trough from a spring at the back of the pig-field, and at the end of the trough, where it pours out, is the spout."

"Have you no conveniences for washing in your room?"

"Not a sign of such a thing, ma'am. I have washed at the spout ever since I have been here," said Ellen, laughing in spite of her vexation.

"And do the pigs share the water with you?"

"The pigs? Oh, no, ma'am; the trough is raised up from the ground on little heaps of stones; they can't get at the water,— unless they drink at the spring, and I don't think they do that, so many big stones stand around it."

"Well, Ellen, I must say that is rather uncomfortable, even without any danger of four-footed society."

"It isn't so bad just now," said Ellen, "in this warm weather, but in that cold time we had a week or two back, do you remember, Miss Alice?—just before the Indian summer began?—oh, how disagreeable it was! Early in the morning, you know,—the sun scarcely up, and the cold wind blowing my hair and my clothes all about; and then that board before the spout, that I have to stand on, is always kept wet by the spattering of the water, and it's muddy besides and very slippery,—there's a kind of green stuff comes upon it; and I can't stoop down for fear of muddying myself; I have to tuck my clothes round me and bend over as well as I can, and fetch up a little water to my face in the hollow of my hand, and of course I have to do that a great many times before I get enough. I can't help laughing," said Ellen, " but it isn't a laughing matter for all that."

" So you wash your face in your hands and have no pitcher but a long wooden trough?—Poor child! I am sorry for you; I think you must have some other way of managing before the snow comes."

" The water is bitter cold already," said Ellen, " it's the coldest water I ever saw. Mamma gave me a nice dressing-box before I came away, but I found very soon this was a queer place for a dressing-box to come to. Why, Miss Alice, if I take out my brush or comb I haven't any table to lay them on but one that's too high, and my poor dressing-box has to stay on the floor. And I haven't a sign of a bureau,—all my things are tumbling about in my trunk."

" I think if I were in your place I would not permit *that* at any rate," said Alice; " if my things were confined to my trunk I would have them keep good order there at least."

" Well, so they do," said Ellen,—" pretty good order; I didn't mean ' tumbling about' exactly."

" Always try to say what you mean *exactly.*"

" But now, Ellen, love, do you know I must send you away? Do you see the sunlight has quitted those distant hills? and it will be quite gone soon. You must hasten home."

Ellen made no answer. Alice had taken her on her lap again, and she was nestling there with her friend's arms wrapped around her. Both were quite still for a minute.

" Next week, if nothing happens, we will begin to be busy with our books. You shall come to me Tuesday and Friday; and all the other days you must study as hard as you can at home, for I am very particular, I forewarn you."

" But suppose aunt Fortune should not let me come?" said Ellen without stirring.

" Oh, she will. You need not speak about it; I'll come down and ask her myself, and nobody ever refuses me any thing."

" I shouldn't think they would," said Ellen.

"Then don't you set the first example," said Alice laughingly.
"I ask you to be cheerful and happy and grow wiser and better
every day."

"Dear Miss Alice!—How can I promise that?"

"Dear Ellen, it is very easy.   There is One who has promised
to hear and answer you when you cry to him; he will make you
in his own likeness again; and to know and love him and not be
happy, is impossible.   That blessed Saviour!"—said Alice,—"oh,
what should you and I do without him, Ellen?—' as rivers of
waters in a dry place; as the shadow of a great rock in a weary
land;'—how beautiful! how true! how often I think of that."

Ellen was silent, though entering into the feeling of the words.

"Remember him dear Ellen;—remember your best friend.
Learn more of Christ, our dear Saviour, and you can't help but
be happy.   Never fancy you are helpless and friendless while you
have him to go to.   Whenever you feel wearied and sorry, flee to
the shadow of that great rock; will you?—and do you understand
me?"

"Yes, ma'am,—yes, ma'am," said Ellen, as she lifted her lips
to kiss her friend.   Alice heartily returned the kiss, and pressing
Ellen in her arms said,

"Now Ellen, dear, you *must* go; I dare not keep you any
longer.   It will be too late now, I fear, before you reach home."

Quick they mounted the little path again, and soon were at the
house; and Ellen was putting on her things.

"Next Tuesday remember,—but before that! Sunday,—you are
to spend Sunday with me; come bright and early."

"How early?"

"Oh, as early as you please—before breakfast—and our Sunday
morning breakfasts aren't late, Ellen; we have to set off betimes
to go to church."

Kisses and good-by's; and then Ellen was running down the
road at a great rate, for twilight was beginning to gather, and she
had a good way to go.

She ran till out of breath; then walked a while to gather
breath; then ran again.   Running down hill is a pretty quick
way of travelling; so before very long she saw her aunt's house
at a distance.   She walked now.   She had come all the way in
good spirits, though with a sense upon her mind of something
disagreeable to come; when she saw the house this disagreeable
something swallowed up all her thoughts, and she walked leisurely
on, pondering what she had to do and what she was like to meet
in the doing of it.

"If aunt Fortune should be in a bad humour—and say something to vex me,—but I'll not be vexed.   But it will be very hard
to help it;—but I *will not* be vexed;—I have done wrong, and I'll

tell her so, and ask her to forgive me ;—it will be hard,—but I'll do it—I'll say what I ought to say, and then however she takes it I shall have the comfort of knowing I have done right." "But," said conscience, "you must not say it stiffly and proudly; you must say it humbly and as if you really felt and meant it." "I will," said Ellen.

She paused in the shed and looked through the window to see what was the promise of things within. Not good; her aunt's step sounded heavy and ominous; Ellen guessed she was not in a pleasant state of mind. She opened the door,—no doubt of it,— the whole air of Miss Fortune's figure, to the very handkerchief that was tied round her head, spoke displeasure.

"She isn't in a good mood," said Ellen, as she went up stairs to leave her bonnet and cape there ;—"I never knew her to be good-humoured when she had that handkerchief on."

She returned to the kitchen immediately. Her aunt was busied in washing and wiping the dishes.

"I have come home rather late," said Ellen pleasantly ;—"shall I help you, aunt Fortune?"

Her aunt cast a look at her.

"Yes, you may help me. Go and put on a pair of white gloves and a silk apron, and then you'll be ready."

Ellen looked down at herself. "Oh, my merino! I forgot about that. I'll go and change it."

Miss Fortune said nothing, and Ellen went.

When she came back the things were all wiped, and as she was about to put some of them away, her aunt took them out of her hands, bidding her "go and sit down!"

Ellen obeyed and was mute ; while Miss Fortune dashed round with a display of energy there seemed to be no particular call for, and speedily had every thing in its place and all straight and square about the kitchen. When she was, as a last thing, brushing the crumbs from the floor into the fire she broke the silence again. The old grandmother sat in the chimney corner, but she seldom was very talkative in the presence of her stern daughter.

"What did you come home for to-night? Why didn't you stay at Mr. Humphreys'?"

"Miss Alice didn't ask me."

"That means I suppose that you would if she had?"

"I don't know, ma'am ; Miss Alice wouldn't have asked me to do any thing that wasn't right."

"Oh, no !—of course not ;—Miss Alice is a piece of perfection ; every body says so ; and I suppose you'd sing the same song who haven't seen her three times."

"Indeed I would," said Ellen ; "I could have told that in one seeing. I'd do any thing in the world for Miss Alice."

" Ay—I dare say—that's the way of it. You can show not one bit of goodness or pleasantness to the person that does the most for you and has all the care of you,—but the first stranger that comes along you can be all honey to them, and make yourself out too good for common folks, and go and tell great tales how you are used at home I suppose. I am sick of it !" said Miss Fortune, setting up the andirons and throwing the tongs and shovel into the corner, in a way that made the iron ring again. " One might as good be a stepmother at once, and done with it ! Come, mother, it's time for you to go to bed."

The old lady rose with the meekness of habitual submi‗‗ion, and went up stairs with her daughter. Ellen had time to bethink herself while they were gone, and resolved to lose no time when her aunt came back in doing what she had to do. She would fain have persuaded herself to put it off. " It is late," she said to herself, " it isn't a good time. It will be better to go to bed now, and ask aunt Fortune's pardon to-morrow." But conscience said, " *First* be reconciled to thy brother."

Miss Fortune came down stairs presently. But before Ellen could get any words out, her aunt prevented her.

" Come, light your candle and be off; I want you out of the way ; I can't do any thing with half a dozen people about."

Ellen rose. " I want to say something to you first, aunt Fortune."

" Say it and be quick ; I haven't time to stand talking."

" Aunt Fortune," said Ellen, stumbling over her words,—" I want to tell you that I know I was wrong this morning, and I am sorry, and I hope you'll forgive me."

A kind of indignant laugh escaped from Miss Fortune's lips.

" It's easy talking ; I'd rather have acting. I'd rather see people mend their ways than stand and make speeches about them. Being sorry don't help the matter much."

" But I will try not to do so any more," said Ellen.

" When I see you don't I shall begin to think there is something in it. Actions speak louder than words. I don't believe in this jumping into goodness all at once."

" Well, I will try not to, at any rate," said Ellen sighing.

" I shall be very glad to see it. What has brought you into this sudden fit of dutifulness and fine talking ?"

" Miss Alice told me I ought to ask your pardon for what I had done wrong," said Ellen, scarce able to keep from crying; " and I know I did wrong this morning, and I did wrong the other day about the letter ; and I am sorry, whether you believe it or no."

" Miss Alice told you, did she ? So all this is to please Miss Alice. I suppose you were afraid your friend Miss Alice would hear of some of your goings on, and thought you had better make up with me. Is that it ?"

Ellen answered, " No, ma'am," in a low tone, but had no voice to say more.

" I wish Miss Alice would look after her own affairs, and let other people's houses alone. That's always the way with your pieces of perfection ;—they're eternally finding out something that isn't as it ought to be among their neighbours. I think people that don't set up for being quite such great things get along quite as well in the world."

Ellen was strongly tempted to reply, but kept her lips shut.

" I'll tell you what," said Miss Fortune,—" if you want me to believe that all this talk means something I'll tell you what you shall do,—you shall just tell Mr. Van Brunt to-morrow about it all, and how ugly you have been these two days, and let him know you were wrong and I was right. I believe he thinks you cannot do any thing wrong, and I should like him to know it for once."

Ellen struggled hard with herself before she could speak ; Miss Fortune's lips began to wear a scornful smile.

" I'll tell him !" said Ellen, at length ; " I'll tell him I was wrong, if you wish me to."

" I *do* wish it. I like people's eyes to be opened. It'll do him good, I guess, and you too. Now, have you any thing more to say ?"

Ellen hesitated ;—the colour came and went ;—she knew it wasn't a good time, but how could she wait ?

" Aunt Fortune," she said, " you know I told you I behaved very ill about that letter,—won't you forgive me ?"

" Forgive you ? yes, child ; I don't care any thing about it."

" Then you will be so good as to let me have my letter again ?" said Ellen, timidly.

" Oh, I can't be bothered to look for it now ; I'll see about it some other time ; take your candle and go to bed now if you've nothing more to say."

Ellen took her candle and went. Some tears were wrung from her by hurt feeling and disappointment ; but she had the smile of conscience, and as she believed of Him whose witness conscience is. She remembered that " great rock in a weary land," and she went to sleep in the shadow of it.

The next day was Saturday. Ellen was up early, and after carefully performing her toilet duties, she had a nice long hour before it was time to go down stairs. The use she made of this hour had fitted her to do cheerfully and well her morning work ; and Ellen would have sat down to breakfast in excellent spirits if it had not been for her promised disclosure to Mr. Van Brunt. It vexed her a little. " I told aunt Fortune,—that was all right ; but why I should be obliged to tell Mr. Van Brunt I don't know. But if it convinces aunt Fortune that I am in earnest, and meant what I say?—then I had better."

Mr. Van Brunt looked uncommonly grave, she thought; her aunt, uncommonly satisfied. Ellen had more than half a guess at the reason of both; but make up her mind to speak, she could not, during all breakfast time. She eat without knowing what she was eating.

Mr. Van Brunt at length, having finished his meal without saying a syllable, arose and was about to go forth, when Miss Fortune stopped him. "Wait a minute, Mr. Van Brunt," she said, "Ellen has something to say to you. Go ahead, Ellen."

Ellen *felt*, rather than saw, the smile with which these words were spoken. She crimsoned and hesitated.

"Ellen and I had some trouble yesterday," said Miss Fortune, "and she wants to tell you about it."

Mr. Van Brunt stood gravely waiting.

Ellen raised her eyes, which were full, to his face. "Mr. Van Brunt," she said, "aunt Fortune wants me to tell you what I told her last night,—that I knew I behaved as I ought not to her yesterday, and the day before, and other times."

"And what made you do that?" said Mr. Van Brunt.

"Tell him," said Miss Fortune, colouring, "that you were in the wrong and I was in the right—then he'll believe it, I suppose."

"I was wrong," said Ellen.

"And I was right," said Miss Fortune.

Ellen was silent. Mr. Van Brunt looked from one to the other.

"Speak," said Miss Fortune; "tell him the whole if you mean what you say."

"I can't," said Ellen.

"Why, you said you were wrong," said Miss Fortune; "that's only half of the business; if you were wrong I was right; why don't you say so, and not make such a shilly-shally piece of work of it?"

"I said I was wrong," said Ellen, "and so I was; but I never said you were right, aunt Fortune, and I don't think so."

These words, though moderately spoken, were enough to put Miss Fortune in a rage.

"What did I do that was wrong?" she said; "come, I should like to know. What was it, Ellen? Out with it; say every thing you can think of; stop and hear it, Mr. Van Brunt; come, Ellen, let's hear the whole!"

"Thank you, ma'am, I've heerd quite enough," said that gentleman, as he went out and closed the door.

"And I have said too much," said Ellen. "Pray, forgive me, aunt Fortune. I shouldn't have said that if you hadn't pressed me so; I forgot myself a moment. I am sorry I said that."

"Forgot yourself!" said Miss Fortune; "I wish you'd forget yourself out of my house. Please to forget the place where I am for to-day, anyhow; I've got enough of you for one while. You had better go to Miss Alice and get a new lesson; and tell her you are coming on finely."

Gladly would Ellen indeed have gone to Miss Alice, but as the next day was Sunday she thought it best to wait. She went sorrowfully to her own room. "Why couldn't I be quiet?" said Ellen. "If I had only held my tongue that unfortunate minute! what possessed me to say that?"

Strong passion—strong pride,—both long unbroken; and Ellen had yet to learn that many a prayer and many a tear, much watchfulness, much help from on high, must be hers before she could be thoroughly dispossessed of these evil spirits. But she knew her sickness; she had applied to the Physician;—she was in a fair way to be well.

One thought in her solitary room that day drew streams of tears down Ellen's cheeks. "My letter—my letter! what shall I do to get you!" she said to herself. "It serves me right; I oughtn't to have got in a passion; oh, I have got a lesson this time!"

CHAPTER XVIII.

Tranquilitie
So purely sate there, that waves great nor small
Did ever rise to any height at all.

CHAPMAN.

THE Sunday with Alice met all Ellen's hopes. She wrote a very long letter to her mother giving the full history of the day. How pleasantly they had ridden to church on the pretty grey pony,—she half the way, and Alice the other half, talking to each other all the while; for Mr. Humphreys had ridden on before. How lovely the road was, "winding about round the mountain, up and down," and with such a wide, fair view, and "part of the time close along by the edge of the water." This had been Ellen's first ride on horseback. Then the letter described the little Carra-carra church—Mr. Humphreys' excellent sermon, "every word of which she could understand;" Alice's Sunday School, in which she was sole teacher, and how Ellen had four little ones put under *her* care; and told how while Mr. Humphreys went on to hold a second service at a village some six miles off, his daughter ministered to two infirm old women at Carra-carra,—reading and explaining the Bible to the one, and to the other, who was blind, repeating the whole substance of her father's sermon. "Miss Alice told me that nobody could enjoy a sermon better than that old woman, but she cannot go out, and every Sunday Miss Alice goes and preaches to her, she says." How Ellen went home in the boat with Thomas and Margery, and spent the rest of the day and night also at the parsonage; and how polite and kind Mr. Humphreys had been. "He's a very grave-looking man indeed," said the letter, "and not a bit like Miss Alice; he is a great deal older than I expected."

This letter was much the longest Ellen had ever written in her life; but she had set her heart on having her mother's sympathy in her new pleasures, though not to be had but after the lapse of many weeks and beyond a sad interval of land and sea. Still, she must have it; and her little fingers travelled busily over the paper hour after hour, as she found time, till the long epistle was finished. She was hard at work at it Tuesday afternoon when her aunt called her down; and obeying the call, to her great surprise and delight she found Alice seated in the chimney corner and chatting away with her old grandmother, who looked remarkably pleased. Miss Fortune was bustling round as usual, looking at nobody, though putting in her word now and then.

"Come, Ellen," said Alice, "get your bonnet; I am going up the mountain to see Mrs. Vawse, and your aunt has given leave for you to go with me. Wrap yourself up well, for it is not warm."

Without waiting for a word of answer, Ellen joyfully ran off.

"You have chosen rather an ugly day for your walk, Miss Alice."

"Can't expect pretty days in December, Miss Fortune. I am only too happy it doesn't storm; it will by to-morrow, I think. But I have learned not to mind weathers."

"Yes, I know you have," said Miss Fortune. "You'll stop up on the mountain till supper-time, I guess, won't you?"

"Oh, yes; I shall want something to fortify me before coming home after such a long tramp. You see I have brought a basket along. I thought it safest to take a loaf of bread with me, for no one can tell what may be in Mrs. Vawse's cupboard, and to lose our supper is not a thing to be thought of."

"Well, have you looked out for butter, too? for you'll find none where you're going. I don't know how the old lady lives up there, but it's without butter, I reckon."

"I have taken care of that, too, thank you, Miss Fortune. You see I'm a far-sighted creature."

"Ellen," said her aunt, as Ellen now, cloaked and hooded, came in, "go into the buttery and fetch out one of them pumpkin pies to put in Miss Alice's basket."

"Thank you, Miss Fortune," said Alice, smiling, "I shall tell

Mrs. Vawse who it comes from. Now, my dear, let's be off; we have a long walk before us."

Ellen was quite ready to be off. But no sooner had she opened the outer shed door than her voice was heard in astonishment.

" A cat!—What cat is this? Miss Alice! look here;—here's the Captain I do believe."

" Here is the Captain, indeed," said Alice. " Oh, pussy, pussy, what have you come for!"

Pussy walked up to his mistress, and stroking himself and his great tail against her dress, seemed to say that he had come for her sake, and that it made no difference to him where she was going.

" He was sitting as gravely as possible," said Ellen, " on the stone just outside the door, waiting for the door to be opened. How could he have come here?"

" Why, he has followed me," said Alice; " he often does; but I came quick and I thought I had left him at home to-day. This is too long an expedition for him. Kitty—I wish you had stayed at home."

Kitty did not think so; he was arching his neck and purring in acknowledgment of Alice's soft touch.

" Can't you send him back?" said Ellen.

" No, my dear; he is the most sensible of cats no doubt, but he could by no means understand such an order. No, we must let him trot on after us, and when he gets tired I'll carry him; it won't be the first time by a good many."

They set off with a quick pace, which the weather forbade them to slacken. It was somewhat as Miss Fortune had said, an ugly afternoon. The clouds hung cold and grey, and the air had a raw chill feeling that betokened a coming snow. The wind blew strong too, and seemed to carry the chillness through all manner of wrappers. Alice and Ellen however did not much care for it; they walked and ran by turns, only stopping once in a while when poor Captain's uneasy cry warned them they had left him too far behind. Still he would not submit to be carried, but jumped down whenever Alice attempted it, and trotted on most perseveringly. As they neared the foot of the mountain they were somewhat sheltered from the wind, and could afford to walk more slowly.

" How is it between you and your aunt Fortune now?" said Alice.

" Oh, we don't get on well at all, Miss Alice, and I don't know exactly what to do. You know I said I would ask her pardon. Well I did, the same night after I got home, but it was very disagreeable. She didn't seem to believe I was in earnest, and wanted me to tell Mr. Van Brunt that I had been wrong. I thought that was rather hard; but at any rate I said I would; and next morning I did tell him so; and I believe all would have gone well if I could

only have been quiet; but aunt Fortune said something that vexed
me, and almost before I knew it I said something that vexed her
dreadfully. It was nothing very bad, Miss Alice, though I ought
not to have said it; and I was sorry two minutes after, but I just
got provoked; and what shall I do, for it's so hard to prevent it?"

"The only thing I know," said Alice with a slight smile, "is to
be full of that charity which among other lovely ways of showing
itself has this,—that it is 'not easily provoked.'"

"I am easily provoked," said Ellen.

"Then you know one thing at any rate that is to be watched and
prayed and guarded against; it is no little matter to be acquainted
with one's own weak points."

"I tried so hard to keep quiet that morning," said Ellen, "and
if I only could have let that unlucky speech alone—but somehow
I forgot myself, and I just told her what I thought."

"Which it is very often best not to do."

"I do believe," said Ellen, "aunt Fortune would like to have
Mr. Van Brunt not like me."

"Well," said Alice,—"what then?"

"Nothing, I suppose, ma'am."

"I hope you are not going to lay it up against her?"

"No, ma'am,—I hope not."

"Take care, dear Ellen, don't take up the trade of suspecting
evil; you could not take up a worse; and even when it is forced
upon you, see as little of it as you can, and forget as soon as you
can what you see. Your aunt, it may be, is not a very happy
person, and no one can tell but those that are unhappy how hard it
is not to be unamiable too. Return good for evil as fast as you
can; and you will soon either have nothing to complain of or be
very well able to bear it."

They now began to go up the mountain, and the path became in
places steep and rugged enough. "There is an easier way on the
other side," said Alice, "but this is the nearest for us." Captain
Parry now showed signs of being decidedly weary, and permitted
Alice to take him up. But he presently mounted from her arms
to her shoulder, and to Ellen's great amusement kept his place there,
passing from one shoulder to the other, and every now and then
sticking his nose up into her bonnet as if to kiss her.

"What *does* he do that for?" said Ellen.

"Because he loves me and is pleased," said Alice. "Put your
ear close, Ellen, and hear the quiet way he is purring to himself—
do you hear?—that's his way; he very seldom purrs aloud."

"He's a very funny cat," said Ellen laughing.

"Cat," said Alice,—"there isn't such a cat as this to be seen.
He's a cat to be respected, my old Captain Parry. He is not to be
laughed at Ellen, I can tell you"

The travellers went on with good will; but the path was so steep
and the way so long that when about half way up the mountain
they were fain to follow the example of their four-footed companion
and rest themselves. They sat down on the ground. They had
warmed themselves with walking, but the weather was as chill and
disagreeable and gusty as ever; every now and then the wind came
sweeping by, catching up the dried leaves at their feet and whirling
and scattering them off to a distance,—winter's warning voice.

" I never was in the country before when the leaves were off the
trees," said Ellen. " It isn't so pretty, Miss Alice, do you think
so ?"

" So pretty ? No, I suppose not, if we were to have it all the
while; but I like the change very much."

" Do you like to see the leaves off the trees ?"

" Yes—in the time of it. There's beauty in the leafless trees
that you cannot see in summer. Just look, Ellen—no, I cannot
find you a nice specimen here, they grow too thick ; but where they
have room the way the branches spread and ramify, or branch out
again, is most beautiful. There's first the trunk—then the large
branches—then those divide into smaller ones ; and those part and
part again into smaller and smaller twigs, till you are canopied as it
were with a network of fine stems. And when the snow falls gently on
them—Oh, Ellen, winter has its own beauties. I love it all ; the
cold, and the wind, and the snow, and the bare forests, and our
little river of ice. What pleasant sleigh-rides to church I have
had upon that river. And then the evergreens,—look at them ;
you don't know in summer how much they are worth ; wait till you
see the hemlock branches bending with a weight of snow, and then
if you don't say the winter is beautiful I'll give you up as a young
lady of bad taste."

" I dare say I shall," said Ellen ; " I am sure I shall like what
you like. But, Miss Alice, what makes the leaves fall when the
cold weather comes ?"

" A very pretty question, Ellen, and one that can't be answered
in a breath."

" I asked aunt Fortune the other day," said Ellen, laughing very
heartily,—"and she told me to hush up and not be a fool; and I
told her I really wanted to know, and she said she wouldn't make
herself a simpleton if she was in my place ; so I thought I might
as well be quiet."

" By the time the cold weather comes, Ellen, the leaves have
done their work and are no more needed. Do you know what work
they have to do ?—do you know what is the use of leaves ?"

" Why, for prettiness, I suppose," said Ellen, " and to give
shade ;—I don't know anything else."

" Shade is one of their uses, no doubt, and prettiness too ; he who made the trees made them 'pleasant to the eyes' as well as good for food.' So we have an infinite variety of leaves; one shape would have done the work just as well for every kind of tree, but then we should have lost a great deal of pleasure. But, Ellen, the tree could not live without leaves. In the spring the thin sap which the roots suck up from the ground is drawn into the leaves; there by the help of the sun and air it is thickened and prepared in a way you cannot understand, and goes back to supply the wood with the various matters necessary for its growth and hardness. After this has gone on some time the little vessels of the leaves become clogged and stopped up with earthy and other matter; they cease to do their work any longer; the hot sun dries them up more and more, and by the time the frost comes they are as good as dead. That finishes them, and they drop off from the branch that needs them no more. Do you understand all this?"

" Yes, ma'am, very well," said Ellen; "and it's exactly what I wanted to know, and very curious. So the trees couldn't live without leaves?"

" No more than you could without a heart and lungs."

" I am very glad to know that," said Ellen. " Then how is it with the evergreens, Miss Alice? Why don't their leaves die and drop off too?"

" They do; look how the ground is carpeted under that pine tree."

" But they stay green all winter, don't they?"

" Yes; their leaves are fitted to resist frost; I don't know what the people in cold countries would do else. They have the fate of all other leaves however; they live awhile, do their work, and then die; not all at once though; there is always a supply left on the tree. Are we rested enough to begin again?"

" I am," said Ellen; " I don't know about the Captain. Poor fellow! he's fast asleep. I declare it's too bad to wake you up, pussy. Haven't we had a pleasant little rest, Miss Alice? I have learnt something while we have been sitting here."

" *That* is pleasant, Ellen," said Alice, as they began their upward march;—" I would I might be all the while learning something."

" But you have been teaching, Miss Alice, and that's as good. Mamma used to say it is more blessed to give than to receive."

" Thank you, Ellen," said Alice, smiling; " that ought to satisfy me certainly."

They bent themselves against the steep hill again and pressed on. As they rose higher they felt it grow more cold and bleak; the woods gave them less shelter, and the wind swept round the mountain-head and over them with great force, making their way quite difficult.

" Courage, Ellen !" said Alice, as they struggled on ; " we shall soon be there."

" I wonder," said the panting Ellen, as making an effort she came up alongside of Alice—" I wonder why Mrs. Vawse will live in such a disagreeable place."

" It is not disagreeable to her, Ellen ; though I must say I should not like to have too much of this wind."

" But does she really like to live up here better than down below where it is warmer ?—and all alone too ?"

" Yes, she does. Ask her why, Ellen, and see what she will tell you. She likes it so much better that this little cottage was built on purpose for her near ten years ago, by a good old friend of hers, a connection of the lady whom she followed to this country."

" Well," said Ellen, " she must have a queer taste—that is all I can say."

They were now within a few easy steps of the house, which did not look so uncomfortable when they came close to it. It was small and low, of only one story, though it is true the roof ran up very steep to a high and sharp gable. It was perched so snugly in a niche of the hill that the little yard was completely sheltered with a high wall of rock. The house itself stood out more boldly and caught pretty well near all the winds that blew ; but so, Alice informed Ellen, the inmate liked to have it.

" And that roof," said Alice,—" she begged Mr. Marshman when the cottage was building that the roof might be high and pointed ; she said her eyes were tired with the low roofs of this country, and if he would have it made so it would be a great relief to them."

The odd roof Ellen thought was pretty. But they now reached the door, protected with a deep porch. Alice entered and knocked at the other door. They were bade to come in. A woman was there stepping briskly back and forth before a large spinning-wheel. She half turned her head to see who the comers were, then stopped her wheel instantly, and came to meet them with open arms.

" Miss Alice ! dear Miss Alice, how glad I am to see you."

" And I you, dear Mrs. Vawse," said Alice kissing her. " Here's another friend you must welcome for my sake—little Ellen Montgomery."

" I am very glad to see Miss Ellen," said the old woman, kissing her also ; and Ellen did not shrink from the kiss, so pleasant were the lips that tendered it ; so kind and frank the smile, so winning the eye ; so agreeable the whole air of the person. She turned from Ellen again to Miss Alice.

" It's a long while that I have not seen you, dear,—not since you went to Mrs. Marshman's. And what a day you have chosen to come at last !"

" I can't help that," said Alice, pulling off her bonnet,—" I couldn't wait any longer. I wanted to see you dolefully, Mrs. Vawse."

" Why, my dear? what's the matter? I have wanted to see *you*, but not dolefully."

" That's the very thing, Mrs. Vawse ; I wanted to see you to get a lesson of quiet contentment."

" I never thought you wanted such a lesson, Miss Alice. What's the matter ?"

" I can't get over John's going away."

Her lip trembled and her eye was swimming as she said so. The old woman passed her hands over the gentle head and kissed her brow.

" So I thought—so I felt, when my mistress died ; and my husband; and my sons, one after the other. But now I think I can say with Paul, ' I have learned in whatsoever state I am therewith to be content.' I think so; maybe that I deceive myself; but they are all gone, and I am certain that I am content now."

" Then surely I ought to be," said Alice.

" It is not till one looses one's hold of other things and looks to Jesus alone that one finds how much he can do. ' There is a friend that sticketh closer than a brother;' but I never knew all that meant till I had no other friends to lean upon;—nay, I should not say *no* other friends;—but my dearest were taken away. You have *your* dearest still, Miss Alice."

" Two of them," said Alice faintly;—" and hardly that now."

" I have not one," said the old woman,—" I have not one; but my home is in heaven, and my Saviour is there preparing a place for me. I know it—I am sure of it—and I can wait a little while, and rejoice all the while I am waiting. Dearest Miss Alice— ' none of them that trust in him shall be desolate;' don't you believe that?"

" I do surely, Mrs. Vawse," said Alice, wiping away a tear or two, " but I forget it sometimes; or the pressure of present pain is too much for all that faith and hope can do."

" It hinders faith and hope from acting—that is the trouble. ' They that seek the Lord shall not want any good thing.' I know that is true, of my own experience; so will you, dear."

" I know it, Mrs. Vawse—I know it all; but it does me good to hear you say it. I thought I should become accustomed to John's absence, but I do not at all; the autumn winds all the while seem to sing to me that he is away."

" My dear love," said the old lady, " it sorrows me much to hear you speak so; I would take away this trial from you if I could; but He knows best. Seek to live nearer to the Lord, dear Miss Alice, and he will give you much more than he has taken away."

Alice again brushed away some tears.

" I felt I must come and see you to-day," said she, " and you have comforted me already. The sound of your voice always does me good. I catch courage and patience from you I believe."

" ' As iron sharpeneth iron, so a man sharpeneth the countenance of his friend.' How did you leave Mr. and Mrs. Marshman? and has Mr. George returned yet?"

Drawing their chairs together, a close conversation began. Ellen had been painfully interested and surprised by what went before, but the low tone of voice now seemed to be not meant for her ear, and turning away her attention, she amused herself with taking a general survey.

It was easy to see that Mrs. Vawse lived in this room, and probably had no other to live in. Her bed was in one corner; cupboards filled the deep recesses on each side of the chimney, and in the wide fireplace the crane and the hooks and trammels hanging upon it showed that the bedroom and sitting-room was the kitchen too. Most of the floor was covered with a thick rag carpet; where the boards could be seen they were beautifully clean and white, and every thing else in the room in this respect matched with the boards. The panes of glass in the little windows were clean and bright as panes of glass could be made; the hearth was clean swept up; the cupboard doors were unstained and unsoiled, though fingers had worn the paint off; dust was nowhere. On a little stand by the chimney corner lay a large Bible and another book; close beside stood a cushioned arm chair. Some other apartment there probably was where wood and stores were kept; nothing was to be seen here that did not agree with a very comfortable face of the whole. It looked as if one might be happy there; it looked as if somebody *was* happy there; and a glance at the old lady of the house would not alter the opinion. Many a glance Ellen gave her as she sat talking with Alice; and with every one she felt more and more drawn toward her. She was somewhat under the common size and rather stout; her countenance most agreeable; there was sense, character, sweetness in it. Some wrinkles no doubt were there too; lines deep-marked that spoke of sorrows once known. Those storms had all passed away; the last shadow of a cloud had departed; her evening sun was shining clear and bright toward the setting; and her brow was beautifully placid, not as though it never had been, but as if it never could be ruffled again. Respect no one could help feeling for her; and more than respect one felt would grow with acquaintance. Her dress was very odd, Ellen thought. It was not American, and what it was she did not know, but supposed Mrs. Vawse must have a lingering fancy for the costume as well as for the roofs of her fatherland. More than all her eye turned again and again to the face, which seemed to her in its changing expression winning and pleasant exceedingly. The mouth had not forgotten to smile, nor the eye to laugh; and though this was not often seen, the constant play of feature showed a deep and lively sympathy in all Alice was saying, and held Ellen's charmed gaze; and when the old lady's looks and words were at length turned to herself she blushed to think how long she had been looking steadily at a stranger.

"Little Miss Ellen, how do you like my house on the rock here?"

"I don't know, ma'am," said Ellen; "I like it very much, only I don't think I should like it so well in winter."

"I am not certain that I don't like it then best of all. Why would you not like it in winter?"

"I shouldn't like the cold, ma'am, and to be alone."

"I like to be alone, but cold? I am in no danger of freezing, Miss Ellen. I make myself very warm—keep good fires,—and my house is too strong for the wind to blow it away. Don't you want to go out and see my cow? I have one of the best cows that ever you saw; her name is Snow; there is not a black hair upon her; she is all white. Come, Miss Alice; Mr. Marshman sent her to me a month ago; she's a great treasure and worth looking at."

They went across the yard to the tiny barn or outhouse, where they found Snow nicely cared for. She was in a warm stable, a nice bedding of straw upon the floor, and plenty of hay laid up for her. Snow deserved it, for she was a beauty, and a very well-behaved cow, letting Alice and Ellen stroke her and pat her and feel of her thick hide, with the most perfect placidity. Mrs. Vawse meanwhile went to the door to look out.

"Nancy ought to be home to milk her," she said; "I must give you supper and send you off. I've no feeling nor smell if snow isn't thick in the air somewhere; we shall see it here soon."

"I'll milk her," said Alice.

"I'll milk her!" said Ellen; "I'll milk her! Ah, do let me; I know how to milk; Mr. Van Brunt taught me, and I have done it several times. May I? I should like it dearly."

"You shall do it surely, my child," said Mrs. Vawse. "Come with me, and I'll give you the pail and the milking stool."

When Alice and Ellen came in with the milk they found the kettle on, the little table set, and Mrs. Vawse very busy at another table.

"What are you doing, Mrs. Vawse, may I ask?" said Alice.

"I'm just stirring up some Indian meal for you; I find I have not but a crust left."

"Please to put that away, ma'am, for another time. Do you think I didn't know better than to come up to this mountain-top without bringing along something to live upon while I am here? Here's a basket, ma'am, and in it are divers things; I believe Margery and I between us have packed up enough for two or three suppers; to say nothing of Miss Fortune's pie. There it is—sure to be good, you know; and here are some of my cakes that you like so much, Mrs. Vawse," said Alice, as she went on pulling the things out of the basket,—"there is a bowl of butter—that's not wanted, I see—and here is a loaf of bread; and that's all. Ellen, my dear, this basket will be lighter to carry down than it was to bring up."

"I am glad of it, I am sure," said Ellen; "my arm hasn't done aching yet, though I had it so little while."

"Ah, I am glad to hear that kettle singing," said their hostess. "I can give you good tea, Miss Alice; you'll think so, I know,

for it's the same Mr. John sent me. It is very fine tea; and he
sent me a noble supply, like himself," continued Mrs. Vawse,
taking some out of her little caddy. "I ought not to say I have
no friends left; I cannot eat a meal that I am not reminded of two
good ones. Mr. John knew one of my weak points when he sent
me that box of Souchong."

The supper was ready, and the little party gathered round the
table. The tea did credit to the judgment of the giver and the
skill of the maker, but they were no critics that drank it. Alice
and Ellen were much too hungry and too happy to be particular.
Miss Fortune's pumpkin pie was declared to be very fine, and so
were Mrs. Vawse's cheese and butter. Eating and talking went
on with great spirit, their old friend seeming scarce less pleased or
less lively than themselves. Alice proposed the French plan, and
Mrs. Vawse entered into it very frankly; it was easy to see that
the style of building and of dress to which she had been accustomed in early life were not the only things remembered kindly for
old time's sake. It was settled they should meet as frequently as
might be, either here or at the parsonage, and become good French-
women with all convenient speed.

"Will you wish to walk so far to see me again, little Miss
Ellen?"

"Oh, yes, ma'am!"

"You won't fear the deep snow, and the wind and cold, and the
steep hill?"

"Oh, no, ma'am, I won't mind them a bit; but, ma'am, Miss
Alice told me to ask you why you loved better to live up here than
down where it is warmer. I shouldn't ask if she hadn't said I
might."

"Ellen has a great fancy for getting at the reason of every thing,
Mrs. Vawse," said Alice, smiling.

"You wonder any body should choose it, don't you, Miss Ellen?"
said the old lady.

"Yes, ma'am, a little."

"I'll tell you the reason, my child. It is for the love of my
old home and the memory of my young days. Till I was as old
as you are, and a little older, I lived among the mountains and
upon them; and after that, for many a year, they were just
before my eyes every day, stretching away for more than *one*
hundred miles, and piled up one above another, fifty times as big
as any you ever saw; these are only molehills to them. I loved
them—oh, how I love them still! If I have one unsatisfied wish,"
said the old lady, turning to Alice, "it is to see my Alps again;
but that will never be. Now, Miss Ellen, it is not that I fancy,
when I get to the top of this hill that I am among my own mountains, but I can breathe better here than down in the plain. I

feel more free; and in the village I would not live for gold, unless that duty bade me.''

" But all alone so far from every body," said Ellen.

" I am never lonely; and old as I am I don't mind a long walk or a rough road any more than your young feet do.''

" But isn't it very cold?" said Ellen.

" Yes, it is very cold;—what of that? I make a good blazing fire, and then I like to hear the wind whistle.''

" Yes, but you wouldn't like to have it whistling inside as well as out," said Alice. " I will come and do the listing and caulking for you in a day or two. Oh, you have it done without me! I am sorry.''

" No need to be sorry, dear—I am glad; you don't look fit for any troublesome jobs.''

" I am fit enough," said Alice. " Don't put up the curtains; I'll come and do it.''

" You must come with a stronger face, then," said her old friend; " have you wearied yourself with walking all this way?"

" I was a little weary," said Alice, " but your nice tea has made me up again.''

" I wish I could keep you all night," said Mrs. Vawse, looking out, " but your father would be uneasy. I am afraid the storm will catch you before you get home; and you aren't fit to breast it. Little Ellen too don't look as if she was made of iron. Can't you stay with me ?''

" I must not—it wouldn't do," said Alice, who was hastily putting on her things; " we'll soon run down the hill. But we are leaving you alone ;—where's Nancy?''

" She'll not come if there's a promise of a storm," said Mrs. Vawse ; " she often stays out all night.''

" And leaves you alone !''

" I am never alone," said the old lady quietly ; " I have nothing to fear; but I am uneasy about you, dear. Mind my words; don't try to go back the way you came; take the other road; it's easier; and stop when you get to Mrs. Van Brunt's; Mr. Van Brunt will take you the rest of the way in his little wagon.''

" Do you think it is needful?" said Alice doubtfully.

" I am sure it is best. Hasten down. Adieu, mon enfant.''

They kissed and embraced her and hurried out.

CHAPTER XIX.

November chill blaws loud wi' angry sough;
The shortening winter day is near a close.
BURNS.

THE clouds hung thick and low; the wind was less than it had been. They took the path Mrs. Vawse had spoken of; it was broader and easier than the other, winding more gently down the mountain; it was sometimes, indeed, travelled by horses, though far too steep for any kind of carriage. Alice and Ellen ran along without giving much heed to any thing but their footing,—down, down,—running and bounding, hand in hand, till want of breath obliged them to slacken their pace.

"Do you think it will snow?—soon?" asked Ellen.

"I think it will snow,—how soon I cannot tell. Have you had a pleasant afternoon?"

"Oh, very!"

"I always have when I go there. Now, Ellen, there is an example of contentment for you. If ever a woman loved husband and children and friends Mrs. Vawse loved hers; I know this from those who knew her long ago; and now look at her. Of them all she has none left but the orphan daughter of her youngest son, and you know a little what sort of a child that is."

"She must be a very bad girl," said Ellen; "you can't think what stories she told me about her grandmother."

"Poor Nancy!" said Alice. "Mrs. Vawse has no money nor property of any kind, except what is in her house; but there is not a more independent woman breathing. She does all sorts of things to support herself. Now, for instance, Ellen, if any body is sick within ten miles round, the family are too happy to get Mrs. Vawse for a nurse. She is an admirable one. Then she goes out tailoring at the farmers' houses; she brings home wool and returns it spun into yarn; she brings home yarn and knits it up into stockings and socks; all sorts of odd jobs. I have seen her picking hops; she isn't above doing any thing, and yet she never forgets her own dignity. I think wherever she goes and whatever she is about, she is at all times one of the most truly lady-like persons I have ever seen. And every body respects her; every body likes to gain her good-will; she is known all over the country; and all the country are her friends."

"They pay her for doing these things, don't they?"

"Certainly; not often in money; more commonly in various

kinds of matters that she wants,—flour, and sugar, and Indian meal, and pork, and ham, and vegetables, and wool,—any thing; it is but a little of each that she wants. She has friends that would not permit her to earn another sixpence if they could help it, but she likes better to live as she does. And she is always as you saw her to-day—cheerful and happy, as a little girl."

Ellen was turning over Alice's last words and thinking that little girls were not *always* the cheerfullest and happiest creatures in the world, when Alice suddenly exclaimed, " It is snowing! Come, Ellen, we must make haste now !"—and set off at a quickened pace. Quick as they might, they had gone not a hundred yards when the whole air was filled with the falling flakes, and the wind which had lulled for a little now rose with greater violence and swept round the mountain furiously. The storm had come in good earnest and promised to be no trifling one. Alice and Ellen ran on, holding each other's hands and strengthening themselves against the blast, but their journey became every moment more difficult. The air was dark with the thick-falling snow ; the wind seemed to blow in every direction by turns, but chiefly against them, blinding their eyes with the snow and making it necessary to use no small effort to keep on their way. Ellen hardly knew where she went, but allowed herself to be pulled along by Alice, or as well pulled *her* along ; it was hard to say which hurried most. In the midst of this dashing on down the hill Alice all at once came to a sudden stop.

" Where's the Captain ?" said she.

" I don't know," said Ellen,—" I haven't thought of him since we left Mrs. Vawse's."

Alice turned her back to the wind and looked up the road they had come,—there was nothing but wind and snow there ; how furiously it blew ! Alice called, " Pussy !—"

" Shall we walk up the road a little way, or shall we stand and wait for him here ?" said Ellen, trembling half from exertion and half from a vague fear of she knew not what.

Alice called again ;—no answer, but a wild gust of wind and snow that drove past.

" I can't go on and leave him," said Alice ; " he might perish in the storm." And she began to walk slowly back, calling at intervals, " Pussy !—kitty !—pussy !"—and listening for an answer that came not. Ellen was very unwilling to tarry, and nowise inclined to prolong their journey by going backwards ! She thought the storm grew darker and wilder every moment.

" Perhaps Captain staid up at Mrs. Vawse's," she said, " and didn't follow us down."

" No," said Alice,—" I am sure he did. Hark !—wasn't that he ?"

"I don't hear any thing," said Ellen, after a pause of anxious listening.

Alice went a few steps further.

"I hear him!" she said;—"I hear him! poor kitty!"—and she set off at a quick pace up the hill. Ellen followed, but presently a burst of wind and snow brought them both to a stand. Alice faltered a little at this, in doubt whether to go up or down. But then to their great joy Captain's far-off cry was heard, and both Alice and Ellen strained their voices to cheer and direct him. In a few minutes he came in sight, trotting hurriedly along through the snow, and on reaching his mistress he sat down immediately on the ground without offering any caress; a sure sign that he was tired. Alice stooped down and took him up in her arms.

"Poor kitty!" she said, "you've done your part for to-day, I think; I'll do the rest. Ellen, dear, it's of no use to tire ourselves out at once; we will go moderately. Keep hold of my cloak, my child; it takes both of my arms to hold this big cat. Now, never mind the snow; we can bear being blown about a little; are you very tired?"

"No," said Ellen,—"not very;—I am a little tired; but I don't care for that if we can only get home safe."

"There's no difficulty about that I hope. Nay, there may be some *difficulty*, but we shall get there I think in good safety after a while. I wish we were there now, for your sake, my child."

"Oh, never mind me," said Ellen gratefully; "I am sorry for *you*, Miss Alice; you have the hardest time of it with that heavy load to carry; I wish I could help you."

"Thank you, my dear, but nobody could do that; I doubt if Captain would lie in any arms but mine."

"Let me carry the basket then," said Ellen,—"do, Miss Alice."

"No, my dear, it hangs very well on my arm. Take it gently; Mrs. Van Brunt's isn't very far off; we shall feel the wind less when we turn."

But the road seemed long. The storm did not increase in violence, truly there was no need of that, but the looked-for turning was not soon found, and the gathering darkness warned them day was drawing toward a close. As they neared the bottom of the hill Alice made a pause.

"There's a path that turns off from this and makes a shorter cut to Mrs. Van Brunt's, but it must be above here; I must have missed it, though I have been on the watch constantly."

She looked up and down. It would have been a sharp eye indeed that had detected any slight opening in the woods on either side of the path, which the driving snow-storm blended into one continuous wall of trees. They could be seen stretching darkly before and behind them ; but more than that,—where they stood near together and where scattered apart,—was all confusion, through that fast-falling shower of flakes.

"Shall we go back and look for the path ?" said Ellen.

"I am afraid we shouldn't find it if we did," said Alice ; "we should only lose our time, and we have none to lose. I think we had better go straight forward."

"Is it much further this way than the other path we have missed ?"

"A good deal—all of half-a-mile. I am sorry ; but courage, my child! we shall know better than to go out in snowy weather next time,—on long expeditions at least."

They had to shout to make each other hear, so drove the snow and wind through the trees and into their very faces and ears. They plodded on. It was plodding; the snow lay thick enough now to make their footing uneasy, and grew deeper every moment ; their shoes were full ; their feet and ankles were wet; and their steps began to drag heavily over the ground. Ellen clung as close to Alice's cloak as their hurried travelling would permit ; sometimes one of Alice's hands was loosened for a moment to be passed round Ellen's shoulders, and a word of courage or comfort in the clear calm tone cheered her to renewed exertion. The night fell fast ; it was very darkling by the time they reached the bottom of the hill, and the road did not yet allow them to turn their faces toward Mrs. Van Brunt's. A wearisome piece of the way this was, leading them *from* the place they wished to reach. They could not go fast either ; they were too weary and the walking too heavy. Captain had the best of it ; snug and quiet he lay wrapped in Alice's cloak and fast asleep, little wotting how tired his mistress's arms were.

The path at length brought them to the long-desired turning ; but it was by this time so dark that the fences on each side of the road showed but dimly. They had not spoken for a while ; as they turned the corner a sigh of mingled weariness and satisfaction escaped from Ellen's lips. It reached Alice's ear.

"What's the matter, love ?" said the sweet voice. No trace of weariness was allowed to come into it.

"I am so glad we have got here at last," said Ellen, looking up with another sigh, and removing her hand for an instant from its grasp on the cloak to Alice's arm.

"My poor child! I wish I could carry you too. Can you hold on a little longer ?"

"Oh, yes, dear Miss Alice ; I can hold on."

But Ellen's voice was not so well guarded. It was like her steps, a little unsteady. She presently spoke again.

"Miss Alice——are you afraid ?"

" I am afraid of your getting sick, my child, and a little afraid of it for myself;—of nothing else. What is there to be afraid of ?''

" It is very dark,'' said Ellen ; " and the storm is so thick,—do you think you can find the way ?''

" I know it perfectly ; it is nothing but to keep straight on ; and the fences would prevent us from getting out of the road. It is hard walking I know, but we shall get there by and by ; bear up as well as you can, dear. I am sorry I can give you no help but words. Don't you think a nice bright fire will look comfortable after all this ?''

" Oh, dear, yes !'' answered Ellen, rather sadly.

" Are *you* afraid, Ellen ?''

" No, Miss Alice—not much—I don't like its being so dark, I can't see where I am going.''

" The darkness makes our way longer and more tedious ; it will do us no other harm, love. I wish I had a hand to give you, but this great cat must have both of mine. The darkness and the light are both alike to our Father ; we are in his hands ; we are safe enough, dear Ellen.''

Ellen's hand left the cloak again for an instant to press Alice's arm in answer; her voice failed at the minute. Then clinging anew as close to her side as she could get, they toiled patiently on. The wind had somewhat lessened of its violence, and besides it blew not now in their faces, but against their backs, helping them on. Still the snow continued to fall very fast, and already lay thick upon the ground ; every half hour increased the heaviness and painfulness of their march ; and darkness gathered till the very fences could no longer be seen. It was pitch dark ; to hold the middle of the road was impossible ; their only way was to keep along by one of the fences ; and for fear of hurting themselves against some outstanding post or stone it was necessary to travel quite gently. They were indeed in no condition to travel otherwise if light had not been wanting. Slowly and patiently, with painful care groping their way, they pushed on through the snow and the thick night. Alice could *feel* the earnestness of Ellen's grasp upon her clothes ; and her close pressing up to her made their progress still slower and more difficult than it would otherwise have been.

" Miss Alice,''—said Ellen.

" What, my child ?''

" I wish you would speak to me once in a while.''

Alice freed one of her hands and took hold of Ellen's.

" I have been so busy picking my way along, I have neglected you, haven't I ?''

" Oh, no, ma'am. But I like to hear the sound of your voice sometimes, it makes me feel better.''

"This is an odd kind of travelling, isn't it?" said Alice cheerfully;—"in the dark, and feeling our way along? This will be quite an adventure to talk about, won't it?"

"Quite," said Ellen.

"It is easier going this way, don't you find it so? The wind helps us forward."

"It helps me too much," said Ellen; "I wish it wouldn't be quite so very kind. Why, Miss Alice, I have enough to do to hold myself together sometimes. It almost makes me run, though I am so very tired."

"Well, it is better than having it in our faces at any rate. Tired you are, I know, and must be. We shall want to rest all day to-morrow, shan't we?"

"Oh, I don't know!" said Ellen sighing; "I shall be glad when we begin. How long do you think it will be, Miss Alice, before we get to Mrs. Van Brunt's?"

"My dear child I cannot tell you. I have not the least notion whereabouts we are. I can see no waymarks, and I cannot judge at all of the rate at which we have come."

"But what if we should have passed it in this darkness?" said Ellen.

"No, I don't think that," said Alice, though a cold doubt struck her mind at Ellen's words;—"I think we shall see the glimmer of Mrs. Van Brunt's friendly candle by and by."

But more uneasily and more keenly now she strove to see that glimmer through the darkness; strove till the darkness seemed to press painfully upon her eyeballs, and she almost doubted her being able to see any light if light there were; it was all blank thick darkness still. She began to question anxiously with herself which side of the house was Mrs. Van Brunt's ordinary sitting-room;—whether she should see the light from it before or after passing the house; and now her glance was directed often behind her, that they might be sure in any case of not missing their desired haven. In vain she looked forward or back; it was all one; no cheering glimmer of lamp or candle greeted her straining eyes. Hurriedly now from time to time the comforting words were spoken to Ellen, for to pursue the long stretch of way that led onward from Mr. Van Brunt's to Miss Fortune's would be a very serious matter; Alice wanted comfort herself.

"Shall we get there soon, do you think, Miss Alice?" said poor Ellen, whose wearied feet carried her painfully over the deepening snow. The tone of voice went to Alice's heart.

"I don't know, my darling,—I hope so," she answered, but it was spoken rather patiently than cheerfully. "Fear nothing, dear Ellen; remember who has the care of us; darkness and light are both alike to him; nothing will do us any real harm."

"How tired you must be, dear Miss Alice, carrying pussy!" Ellen said with a sigh.

For the first time Alice echoed the sigh; but almost immediately Ellen exclaimed in a totally different tone, "There's a light!—but it isn't a candle—it is moving about;—what is it? what is it, Miss Alice?"

They stopped and looked. A light there certainly was, dimly seen, moving at some little distance from the fence on the opposite side of the road. All of a sudden it disappeared.

"What is it?" whispered Ellen fearfully.

"I don't know, my love, yet; wait—"

They waited several minutes.

"What could it be?" said Ellen. "It was certainly a light,—I saw it as plainly as ever I saw any thing;—what can it have done with itself—there it is again!—going the other way!"

Alice waited no longer, but screamed out, "Who's there?"

But the light paid no attention to her cry; it travelled on.

"Halloo!" called Alice again as loud as she could.

"Halloo!" answered a rough deep voice. The light suddenly stopped.

"That's he! that's he!" exclaimed Ellen in an ecstasy and almost dancing.—"I know it,—it's Mr. Van Brunt! it's Mr. Van Brunt!—oh, Miss Alice!——"

Struggling between crying and laughing Ellen could not stand it, but gave way to a good fit of crying. Alice felt the infection, but controlled herself, though her eyes watered as her heart sent up its grateful tribute; as well as she could she answered the halloo.

The light was seen advancing toward them. Presently it glimmered faintly behind the fence, showing a bit of the dark rails covered with snow, and they could dimly see the figure of a man getting over them. He crossed the road to where they stood. It was Mr. Van Brunt.

"I am very glad to see you, Mr. Van Brunt," said Alice's sweet voice; but it trembled a little.

That gentleman, at first dumb with astonishment, lifted his lantern to survey them, and assure his eyes that his ears had not been mistaken.

"Miss Alice!—My goodness alive!—How in the name of wonder!—And my poor little lamb!—But what on 'arth, ma'am! you must be half dead. Come this way,—just come back a little bit,—why, where were you going, ma'am?"

"To your house, Mr. Van Brunt; I have been looking for it with no little anxiety, I assure you."

"Looking for it! Why how on 'arth! you wouldn't see the biggest house ever was built half a yard off such a plaguy night as this."

" I thought I should see the light from the windows, Mr. Van Brunt."

" The light from the windows ! Bless my soul ! the storm rattled so again' the windows that mother made me pull the great shutters to. I won't have 'em shut again of a stormy night, that's a fact; you'd ha' gone far enough afore you'd ha' seen the light through them shutters."

" Then we had passed the house already, hadn't we ?"

" Indeed had you, ma'am. I guess you saw my light, ha'n't you ?"

" Yes, and glad enough we were to see it, too."

" I suppose so. It happened so to-night—now that is a queer thing—I minded that I hadn't untied my horse; he's a trick of being untied at night, and won't sleep well if he ain't; and mother wanted me to let him alone 'cause of the awful storm, but I couldn't go to my bed in peace till I had seen him to his'n. So that's how my lantern came to be going to the barn in such an awk'ard night as this."

They had reached the little gate, and Mr. Van Brunt with some difficulty pulled it open. The snow lay thick upon the neat brick walk which Ellen had trod the first time with wet feet and dripping garments. A few steps further, and they came to the same door that had opened then so hospitably to receive her. As the faint light of the lantern was thrown upon the old latch and door-posts, Ellen felt at home, and a sense of comfort sank down into her heart which she had not known for some time.

CHAPTER XX.

True is, that whilome that good poet said,
The gentle minde by gentle deeds is knowne:
For a man by nothing is so well bewrayed
As by his manners, in which plaine is showne
Of what degree and what race he is growne.
                                        FAERIE QUEENE.

MR. VAN BRUNT flung open the door and the two wet and weary travellers stepped after him into the same cheerful, comfort-able-looking kitchen that had received Ellen once before. Just the same, tidy, clean swept up, a good fire, and the same old red-backed chairs standing round on the hearth in most cosey fashion. It seemed to Ellen a perfect storehouse of comfort; the very walls had a kind face for her. There were no other faces however ; the chairs were all empty. Mr. Van Brunt put Alice in one and Ellen

in another, and shouted, " Mother !—here !"—muttering that she
had taken herself off with the light somewhere. Not very far ;
for in half a minute answering the call Mrs. Van Brunt and the
light came hurriedly in.

" What's the matter, 'Brahm ?—who's this ?—why, 'tain't Miss
Alice ! My gracious me !—and all wet !—oh, dear, dear ! poor
lamb ! Why, Miss Alice, dear, where have you been ?—and if that
ain't my little Ellen ! oh, dear ! what a fix you are in ;—well,
darling, I'm glad to see you again a'most any way."

She crossed over to kiss Ellen as she said this ; but surprise was
not more quickly alive than kindness and hospitality. She fell to
work immediately to remove Alice's wet things, and to do whatever
their joint prudence and experience might suggest to ward off any
ill effects from the fatigue and exposure the wanderers had suffered ;
and while she was thus employed Mr. Van Brunt busied himself
with Ellen, who was really in no condition to help herself. It was
curious to see him carefully taking off Ellen's wet hood (not the
blue one) and knocking it gently to get rid of the snow ; evidently
thinking that ladies' things must have delicate handling. He tried
the cloak next, but boggled sadly at the fastening of that, and at
last was fain to call in help.

" Here, Nancy !—where are you ? step here and see if you can
undo this here thing, whatever you call it ; I believe my fingers
are too big for it."

It was Ellen's former acquaintance who came forward in obedience to this call. Ellen had not seen before that she was in the
room. Nancy grinned a mischievous smile of recognition as she
stooped to Ellen's throat and undid the fastening of the cloak, and
then shortly enough bade her " get up, that she might take it off !"
Ellen obeyed, but was very glad to sit down again. While Nancy
went to the door to shake the cloak, Mr. Van Brunt was gently
pulling off Ellen's wet gloves, and on Nancy's return he directed
her to take off the shoes, which were filled with snow. Nancy sat
down on the floor before Ellen to obey this order ; and tired and
exhausted as she was, Ellen felt the different manner in which her
hands and feet were waited upon.

" How did you get into this scrape ?" said Nancy ; " *this* was
none of my doings any how. It'll never be dry weather, Ellen,
where you are. I won't put on my Sunday-go-to-meeting clothes
when I go a walking with you. You had ought to ha' been a duck
or a goose, or something like that.—What's that for, Mr. Van
Brunt !"

This last query, pretty sharply spoken, was in answer to a light
touch of that gentleman's hand upon Miss Nancy's ear, which came
rather as a surprise. He deigned no reply.

" You're a fine gentleman !" said Nancy, tartly.

"Have you done what I gave you to do?" said Mr. Van Brunt coolly.

"Yes—there!" said Nancy, holding up Ellen's bare feet on one hand, while the fingers of the other secretly applied in ticklish fashion to the soles of them caused Ellen suddenly to start and scream.

"Get up!" said Mr. Van Brunt; Nancy didn't think best to disobey;—"Mother, ha'n't you got nothing you want Nancy to do?"

"Sally," said Mrs. Van Brunt, "you and Nancy go and fetch here a couple of pails of hot water,—right away."

"Go, and mind what you are about," said Mr. Van Brunt; "and after that keep out of this room and don't whisper again till I give you leave. Now Miss Ellen dear, how do you feel?"

Ellen said in words that she felt "nicely." But the eyes and the smile said a great deal more; Ellen's heart was running over.

"Oh, she'll feel nicely directly, I'll be bound," said Mrs. Van Brunt; "wait till she gets her feet soaked, and then !——"

"I do feel nicely now," said Ellen. And Alice smiled in answer to their inquiries, and said if she only knew her father was easy there would be nothing wanting to her happiness.

The bathing of their feet was a great refreshment, and their kind hostess had got ready a plentiful supply of hot herb tea, with which both Alice and Ellen were well dosed. While they sat sipping this, toasting their feet before the fire, Mrs. Van Brunt and the girls meanwhile preparing their room, Mr. Van Brunt suddenly entered. He was cloaked and hatted and had a riding-whip in his hand.

"Is there any word you'd like to get home, Miss Alice? I'm going to ride a good piece that way, and I can stop as good as not."

"To-night, Mr. Van Brunt!" exclaimed Alice in astonishment.

Mr. Van Brunt's silence seemed to say that to-night was the time and no other.

"But the storm is too bad," urged Alice. "Pray don't go till to-morrow."

"Pray don't, Mr. Van Brunt!" said Ellen.

"Can't help it—I've got business; must go. What shall I say, ma'am."

"I should be *very* glad," said Alice, "to have my father know where I am. Are you going very near the Nose?"

"Very near."

"Then I shall be greatly obliged if you will be so kind as to stop and relieve my father's anxiety. But how *can* you go in such weather? and so dark as it is."

"Never fear," said Mr. Van Brunt. "We'll be back in half

an hour, if 'Brahm and me don't come across a snowdrift a *leetle* too deep. Good night, ma'am." And out he went.

" ' Back in half an hour,' " said Alice musing. " Why, he said he had been to untie his horse for the night! He must be going on our account, I am sure, Ellen!"

" On *your* account," said Ellen smiling. " Oh, I knew that all the time, Miss Alice. I don't think he'll stop to relieve aunt Fortune's anxiety."

Alice sprang to call him back; but Mrs. Van Brunt assured her it was too late, and that she need not be uneasy, for her son " didn't mind the storm no more than a weatherboard." 'Brahm and 'Brahm could go anywhere in any sort of a time. " He was a going without speaking to you, but I told him he had better, for maybe you wanted to send some word particular. And your room's ready now, dear, and you'd better go to bed and sleep as long as you can."

They went thankfully. " Isn't this a pleasant room?" said Ellen, who saw every thing in rose-colour; " and a nice bed? But I feel as if I could sleep on the floor to-night. Isn' it a'most worth while to have such a time, Miss Alice, for the sake of the pleasure afterwards?"

" I don't know, Ellen," said Alice smiling; " I won't say that; though it *is* worth paying a price for to find how much kindness there is in some people's hearts. As to sleeping on the floor, I must say I never felt less inclined to it."

" Well, I am tired enough too," said Ellen as they laid themselves down. " Two nights with you in a week! Oh, those weeks before I saw you, Miss Alice!"

One earnest kiss for good-night; and Ellen's sigh of pleasure on touching the pillow was scarcely breathed when sleep deep and sound fell upon her eyelids.

It was very late next morning when they awoke, having slept rather heavily than well. They crawled out of bed feeling stiff and sore in every limb; each confessing to more evil effects from their adventure than she had been aware of the evening before. All the rubbing and bathing and drinking that Mrs. Van Brunt had administered had been too little to undo what wet and cold and fatigue had done. But Mrs. Van Brunt had set her breakfast-table with every thing her house could furnish that was nice; a bountifully spread board it was. Mr. Humphreys was there too; and no bad feelings of two of the party could prevent that from being a most cheerful and pleasant meal. Even Mr. Humphreys and Mr. Van Brunt, two persons not usually given to many words, came out wonderfully on this occasion; gratitude and pleasure in the one, and generous feeling on the part of the other, untied their tongues; and Ellen looked from one to the other in some amazement to see how agreeable they could be. Kindness and hospitality always kept Mrs. Van Brunt in full flow; and Alice, whatever she felt, exerted herself and supplied what was wanting everywhere; like the transparent glazing which painters use to spread over the dead colour of their pictures; unknown, it was she gave life and harmony to the whole. And Ellen in her enjoyment of every thing and every body, forgot or despised aches and pains, and even whispered to Alice that coffee was making her well again.

But happy breakfasts must come to an end, and so did this, prolonged though it was. Immediately after, the party whom circumstances had gathered for the first and probably the last time, scattered again; but the meeting had left pleasant effects on all minds. Mrs. Van Brunt was in general delight that she had entertained so many people she thought a great deal of, and particularly glad of the chance of showing her kind feelings toward two of the number. Mr. Humphreys remarked upon "that very sensible, good-hearted man, Mr. Van Brunt, toward whom he felt himself under great obligation." Mr. Van Brunt said " the minister warn't such a grum man as people called him;" and moreover said, " it was a good thing to have an education, and he had a notion to read more." As for Alice and Ellen, they went away full of kind feeling for every one and much love to each other. This was true of them before; but their late troubles had drawn them closer together and given them fresh occasion to value their friends.

Mr. Humphreys had brought the little one-horse sleigh for his daughter, and soon after breakfast Ellen saw it drive off with her. Mr. Van Brunt then harnessed his own and carried Ellen home. Ill though she felt, the poor child made an effort and spent part of the morning in finishing the long letter to her mother which had been on the stocks since Monday. The effort became painful toward the last; and the aching limbs and trembling hand of which she complained were the first beginnings of a serious fit of illness. She went to bed that same afternoon, and did not leave it again for two weeks. Cold had taken violent hold of her system; fever set in and ran high; and half the time little Ellen's wits were roving in delirium. Nothing however could be too much for Miss Fortune's energies; she was as much at home in a sick room as in a well one. She flew about with increased agility; was up stairs and down stairs twenty times in the course of a day, and kept all straight everywhere. Ellen's room was always the picture of neatness; the fire, the wood-fire, was taken care of; Miss Fortune seemed to know by instinct when it wanted a fresh supply, and to be on the spot by magic to give it. Ellen's medicines were dealt out in proper time; her gruels and drinks perfectly well made and arranged with appetizing nicety on a little

table by the bedside where she could reach them herself; and Miss
Fortune was generally at hand when she was wanted. But in
spite of all this there was something missing in that sick room,—
there was a great want; and whenever the delirium was upon her
Ellen made no secret of it. She was never violent; but she
moaned, sometimes impatiently and sometimes plaintively, for her
mother. It was a vexation to Miss Fortune to hear her. The
name of her mother was all the time on her lips; if by chance
her aunt's name came in, it was spoken in a way that generally
sent her bouncing out of the room.

"Mamma," poor Ellen would say, "just lay your hand on my
forehead, will you? it's so hot. Oh, do, mamma!—where are
you? Do put your hand on my forehead, won't you?—Oh, do
speak to me, why don't you, mamma? Oh, why don't she come
to me!"

Once when Ellen was uneasily calling in this fashion for her
mother's hand, Miss Fortune softly laid her own upon the child's
brow; but the quick sudden jerk of the head from under it told
her how well Ellen knew the one from the other; and little as she
cared for Ellen it was wormwood to her.

Miss Fortune was not without offers of help during this sick
time. Mrs. Van Brunt, and afterwards Mrs. Vawse, asked leave
to come and nurse Ellen; but Miss Fortune declared it was more
plague than profit to her; and she couldn't be bothered with having strangers about. Mrs. Van Brunt she suffered, much against
her will, to come for a day or two: at the end of that Miss Fortune found means to get rid of her civilly. Mrs. Vawse she would
not allow to stay an hour. The old lady got leave however to go
up to the sick room for a few minutes. Ellen, who was then in a
high fever, informed her that her mother was down stairs, and her
aunt Fortune would not let her come up; she pleaded with tears
that she might come, and entreated Mrs. Vawse to take her aunt
away and send her mother. Mrs. Vawse tried to soothe her.
Miss Fortune grew impatient.

"What on earth's the use," said she, "of talking to a child
that's out of her head? She can't hear reason; that's the way
she gets into whenever the fever's on her. I have the pleasure of
hearing that sort of thing all the time. Come away, Mrs. Vawse,
and leave her; she can't be better any way than alone, and I am
in the room every other thing;—she's just as well quiet. Nobody
knows," said Miss Fortune, on her way down stairs,—"nobody
knows the blessing of taking care of other people's children that
ha'n't tried it. *I've* tried it, to my heart's content."

Mrs Vawse sighed, but departed in silence.

It was not when the fever was on her and delirium high that
Ellen most felt the want she then so pitifully made known. There

were other times,—when her head was aching, and weary and weak she lay still there,—Oh, how she longed then for the dear wonted face; the old quiet smile that carried so much of comfort and assurance with it; the voice that was like heaven's music; the touch of that loved hand to which she had clung for so many years! She could scarcely bear to think of it sometimes. In the still wakeful hours of night, when the only sound to be heard was the heavy breathing of her aunt asleep on the floor by her side, and in the long solitary day, when the only variety to be looked for was Miss Fortune's flitting in and out, and there came to be a sameness about that,—Ellen mourned her loss bitterly. Many and many were the silent tears that rolled down and wet her pillow; many a long-drawn sigh came from the very bottom of Ellen's heart; she was too weak and subdued now for violent weeping. She wondered sadly why Alice did not come to see her; it was another great grief added to the former. She never chose, however, to mention her name to her aunt. She kept her wonder and her sorrow to herself,—all the harder to bear for that. After two weeks Ellen began to mend, and then she became exceedingly weary of being alone and shut up to her room. It was a pleasure to have her Bible and hymn-book lying upon the bed, and a great comfort when she was able to look at a few words; but that was not very often, and she longed to see somebody, and hear something besides her aunt's dry questions and answers.

One afternoon Ellen was sitting, alone as usual, bolstered up in bed. Her little hymn-book was clasped in her hand; though not equal to reading, she felt the touch of it a solace to her. Half dozing, half waking, she had been perfectly quiet for some time, when the sudden and not very gentle opening of the room door caused her to start and open her eyes. They opened wider than usual, for instead of her aunt Fortune it was the figure of Miss Nancy Vawse that presented itself. She came in briskly, and shutting the door behind her advanced to the bedside.

"Well!" said she, "there you are! Why, you look smart enough. I've come to see you."

"Have you?" said Ellen, uneasily.

"Miss Fortune's gone out, and she told me to come and take care of you; so I'm a going to spend the afternoon."

"Are you?" said Ellen again.

"Yes—ain't you glad! I knew you must be lonely, so I thought I'd come."

There was a mischievous twinkle in Nancy's eyes. Ellen for once in her life wished for her aunt's presence.

"What are you doing?"

"Nothing," said Ellen.

"Nothing indeed! It's a fine thing to lie there and do nothing.

You won't get well in a hurry, I guess, will you? You look as well as I do this minute. Oh, I always knew you was a sham."

" You are very much mistaken," said Ellen, indignantly; " I have been very sick, and I am not at all well yet."

" Fiddle-de-dee! it's very nice to think so; I guess you're lazy. How soft and good those pillows do look to be sure. Come, Ellen, try getting up a little. _I_ believe you hurt yourself with sleeping. It'll do you good to be out of bed awhile; come! get up."

She pulled Ellen's arm as she spoke.

" Stop, Nancy, let me alone!" cried Ellen, struggling with all her force,—" I musn't—I can't! I musn't get up; what do you mean? I'm not able to sit up at all; let me go!"

She succeeded in freeing herself from Nancy's grasp.

" Well, you're an obstinate piece," said the other; " have your own way. But mind, I'm left in charge of you; is it time for you to take your physic?"

" I am not taking any," said Ellen.

" What are you taking?"

" Nothing but gruel and little things."

" ' Gruel and little things;' little things means something good, I s'pose. Well, is it time for you to take some gruel or one of the little things?"

" No, I don't want any."

" Oh, that's nothing; people never know what's good for them; I'm your nurse now, and I'm going to give it to you when I think you want it. Let me feel your pulse—yes, your pulse says gruel is wanting. I shall put some down to warm right away."

" I shan't take it," said Ellen.

" That's a likely story! You'd better not say so. I rather s'pose you will if I give it to you. Look here, Ellen, you'd better mind how you behave; you're going to do just what I tell you. I know how to manage you; if you make any fuss I shall just tickle you finely," said Nancy, as she prepared a bed of coals, and set the cup of gruel on it to get hot,—" I'll do it in no time at all, my young lady—so you'd better mind."

Poor Ellen involuntarily curled up her feet under the bed-clothes, so as to get them as far as possible out of harm's way. She judged the best thing was to keep quiet if she could; so she said nothing. Nancy was in great glee; with something of the same spirit of mischief that a cat shows when she has a captured mouse at the end of her paws. While the gruel was heating she spun round the room in quest of amusement; and her sudden jerks and flings from one place and thing to another had so much of lawlessness that Ellen was in perpetual terror as to what she might take it into her head to do next.

" Where does that door lead to?"

"I believe that one leads to the garret," said Ellen.

"You *believe so?* why don't you say it does, at once?"

"I haven't been up to see."

"You haven't! you expect me to believe that, I s'pose? I am not quite such a gull as you take me for. What's up there?"

"I don't know, of course."

"Of course! I declare I don't know what you are up to exactly; but if you won't tell me I'll find out for myself pretty quick,—that's one thing."

She flung open the door and ran up; and Ellen heard her feet trampling overhead from one end of the house to the other; and sounds too of pushing and pulling things over the floor; it was plain Nancy was rummaging.

"Well," said Ellen, as she turned uneasily upon her bed, "it's no affair of mine; I can't help it, whatever she does. But oh! won't aunt Fortune be angry!"

Nancy presently came down with her frock gathered up into a bag before her.

"What do you think I have got here?" said she. "I s'pose you didn't know there was a basket of fine hickory nuts up there in the corner? Was it you or Miss Fortune that hid them away so nicely? I s'pose she thought nobody would ever think of looking behind the great blue chest and under the feather bed, but it takes me!—Miss Fortune was afraid of your stealing 'em, I guess, Ellen?"

"She needn't have been," said Ellen, indignantly.

"No, I s'pose you wouldn't take 'em if you saw 'em; you wouldn't eat 'em if they were cracked for you, would you?"

She flung some on Ellen's bed as she spoke. Nancy had seated herself on the floor, and using for a hammer a piece of old iron she had brought down with her from the garret, she was cracking the nuts on the clean white hearth.

"Indeed I wouldn't!" said Ellen, throwing them back; "and you oughtn't to crack them there, Nancy,—you'll make a dreadful muss."

"What do you think I care?" said the other, scornfully. She leisurely cracked and eat as many as she pleased of the nuts, bestowing the rest in the bosom of her frock. Ellen watched fearfully for her next move. If she should open the little door and get among her books and boxes.

Nancy's first care however was the cup of gruel. It was found too hot for any mortal lips to bear, so it was set on one side to cool. Then taking up her rambling examination of the room, she went from window to window.

"What fine big windows! one might get in here easy enough. I declare, Ellen, some night I'll set the ladder up against here, and the first thing you'll see will be me coming in. You'll have me to sleep with you before you think."

" I'll fasten my windows," said Ellen.

" No, you won't. You'll do it a night or two, maybe, but then you'll forget it. I shall find them open when I come. Oh, I'll come !"

" But I could call aunt Fortune," said Ellen.

" No, you couldn't, 'cause if you spoke a word I'd tickle you to death ; that's what I'd do. I know how to fix you off. And if you did call her I'd just whap out of the window and run off with my ladder, and then you'd get a fine combing for disturbing the house. What's in this trunk ?"

" Only my clothes and things," said Ellen.

" Oh, goody ! that's fine ; now I'll have a look at 'em. That's just what I wanted, only I didn't know it. Where's the key ? Oh, here it is sticking in,—that's good !"

" Oh, please, don't !" said Ellen, raising herself on her elbow, " they're all in nice order and you'll get them all in confusion. Oh, do let them alone !"

" You'd best be quiet or I'll come and see you," said Nancy ; " I'm just going to look at every thing in it, and if I find any thing out of sorts, you'll get it.—What's this ? ruffles, I declare ! ain't you fine ! I'll see how they look on me. What a plague ! you haven't a glass in the room. Never mind,—I am used to dressing without a glass."

" Oh, I wish you wouldn't," said Ellen, who was worried to the last degree at seeing her nicely done-up ruffles round Nancy's neck ; —" they're so nice, and you'll muss them all up."

" Don't cry about it," said Nancy coolly, " I ain't a going to eat 'em. My goodness ! what a fine hood ! ain't that pretty."

The nice blue hood was turning about in Nancy's fingers, and well looked at inside and out. Ellen was in distress for fear it would go on Nancy's head, as well as the ruffles round her neck ; but it didn't ; she flung it at length on one side, and went on pulling out one thing after another, strewing them very carelessly about the floor.

" What's here ? a pair of dirty stockings, as I am alive. Ain't you ashamed to put dirty stockings in your trunk ?"

" They are no such thing," said Ellen, who in her vexation was in danger of forgetting her fear,—" I've worn them but once."

" They've no business in here any how," said Nancy, rolling them up in a hard ball and giving them a sudden fling at Ellen. They just missed her face and struck the wall beyond. Ellen seized them to throw back, but her weakness warned her she was not able, and a moment reminded her of the folly of doing any thing to rouse Nancy, who for the present was pretty quiet. Ellen lay upon her pillow and looked on, ready to cry with vexation. All her nicely stowed piles of white clothes were ruthlessly hurled out and tumbled about; her capes tried on; her summer dresses unfolded, displayed, criticised. Nancy decided one was too short; another very ugly; a third horribly ill-made; and when she had done with each it was cast out of her way on one side or the other as the case might be.

The floor was littered with clothes in various states of disarrangement and confusion. The bottom of the trunk was reached at last, and then Nancy suddenly recollected her gruel, and sprang to it. But it had grown cold again.

"This won't do," said Nancy, as she put it on the coals again,— "it must be just right; it'll warm soon, and then, Miss Ellen, you're a going to take it, whether or no. I hope you won't give me the pleasure of pouring it down."

Meanwhile she opened the little door of Ellen's study closet and went in there, though Ellen begged her not. She pulled the door to, and stayed some time perfectly quiet. Not able to see or hear what she was doing, and fretted beyond measure that her work-box and writing-desk should be at Nancy's mercy, or even feel the touch of her fingers, Ellen at last could stand it no longer but threw herself out of the bed, weak as she was, and went to see what was going on. Nancy was seated quietly on the floor, examining with much seeming interest the contents of the work-box; trying on the thimble, cutting bits of thread with the scissors, and marking the ends of the spools; with whatever like pieces of mischief her restless spirit could devise; but when Ellen opened the door she put the box from her and started up.

"My goodness me!" said she, "this'll never do. What are you out here for? you'll catch your death with those dear little bare feet, and we shall have the mischief to pay."

As she said this she caught up Ellen in her arms as if she had been a baby and carried her back to the bed, where she laid her with two or three little shakes, and then proceeded to spread up the clothes and tuck her in all round. She then ran for the gruel. Ellen was in great question whether to give way to tears or vexation; but with some difficulty determined upon vexation as the best plan. Nancy prepared the gruel to her liking, and brought it to the bedside; but to get it swallowed was another matter. Nancy was resolved Ellen should take it. Ellen had less strength but quite as much obstinacy as her enemy, and she was equally resolved not to drink a drop. Between laughing on Nancy's part, and very serious anger on Ellen's, a struggle ensued. Nancy tried to force it down, but Ellen's shut teeth were as firm as a vice, and the end was that two-thirds were bestowed on the sheet. Ellen burst into tears. Nancy laughed.

" Well, I *do* think," said she, " you are one of the hardest customers ever I came across. I shouldn't want to have the managing of you when you get a little bigger. Oh, the way Miss Fortune will look when she comes in here will be a caution ! Oh, what fun !"

Nancy shouted and clapped her hands. " Come, stop crying !" said she, " what a baby you are ! what are you crying for ? come, stop !—I'll make you laugh if you don't."

Two or three little applications of Nancy's fingers made her words good, but laughing was mixed with crying, and Ellen writhed in hysterics. Just then came a little knock at the door. Ellen did not hear it, but it quieted Nancy. She stood still a moment ; and then as the knock was repeated she called out boldly " Come in !" Ellen raised her head " to see who there might be ;" and great was the surprise of both and the joy of one as the tall form and broad shoulders of Mr. Van Brunt presented themselves.

" Oh, Mr. Van Brunt," sobbed Ellen, " I am so glad to see you ! won't you please send Nancy away ?"

" What are you doing here ?" said the astonished Dutchman.

" Look and see, Mr. Van Brunt," said Nancy with a smile of mischief's own curling ; " you won't be long finding out I guess."

" Take yourself off, and don't let me hear of your being caught here again."

" I'll go when I'm ready, thank you," said Nancy ; " and as to the rest I haven't been caught the first time yet ; I don't know what you mean."

She sprang as she finished her sentence, for Mr. Van Brunt made a sudden movement to catch her then and there. He was foiled ; and then began a running chase round the room, in the course of which Nancy dodged, pushed, and sprang, with the power of squeezing by impassables and overleaping impossibilities, that to say the least of it was remarkable. The room was too small for her and she was caught at last.

" I vow !" said Mr. Van Brunt as he pinioned her hands, " I should like to see you play blind-man's-buff for once, if I warn't the blind man."

" How'd you see me if you was ?" said Nancy, scornfully.

" Now, Miss Ellen," said Mr. Van Brunt, as he brought her to Ellen's bedside, " here she is safe ; what shall I do with her ?"

" If you will only send her away, and not let her come back, Mr. Van Brunt !" said Ellen, " I'll be so much obliged to you !"

" Let me go !" said Nancy. " I declare you're a real mean Dutchman, Mr. Van Brunt."

He took both her hands in one, and laid the other lightly over her ears.

"I'll let you go," said he. "Now, don't you be caught here again if you know what is good for yourself."

He saw Miss Nancy out of the door, and then came back to Ellen, who was crying heartily again from nervous vexation.

"She's gone," said he. "What has that wicked thing been doing, Miss Ellen? what's the matter with you?"

"Oh, Mr. Van Brunt," said Ellen, "you can't think how she has worried me; she has been here this great while; just look at all my things on the floor, and that isn't the half."

Mr. Van Brunt gave a long whistle as his eye surveyed the tokens of Miss Nancy's mischief-making, over and through which both she and himself had been chasing at full speed, making the state of matters rather worse than it was before.

"I do say," said he, slowly, "that is too bad. I'd fix them up again for you, Miss Ellen, if I knew how; but my hands are a'most as clumsy as my feet, and I see the marks of them there; it's too bad I declare; I didn't know what I was going on."

"Never mind, Mr. Van Brunt," said Ellen,—"I don't mind what you have done a bit. I'm *so* glad to see you!"

She put out her little hand to him as she spoke. He took it in his own silently, but though he said and showed nothing of it, Ellen's look and tone of affection thrilled his heart with pleasure.

"How do you do?" said he kindly.

"I'm a great deal better," said Ellen. "Sit down, won't you, Mr. Van Brunt? I want to see you a little."

Horses wouldn't have drawn him away after that. He sat down.

"Ain't you going to be up again some of these days?" said he.

"Oh, yes, I hope so," said Ellen sighing; "I am very tired of lying here."

He looked round the room; got up and mended the fire; then came and sat down again.

"I was up yesterday for a minute," said Ellen, "but the chair tired me so I was glad to get back to bed again."

It was no wonder; harder and straighter-backed chairs never were invented. Probably Mr. Van Brunt thought so.

"Wouldn't you like to have a rocking-cheer?" said he suddenly, as if a bright thought had struck him.

"Oh, yes, how much I should!" said Ellen, with another long-drawn breath, "but there isn't such a thing in the house that ever I saw."

"Ay, but there is in other houses though," said Mr. Van Brunt, with as near an approach to a smile as his lips commonly made;— we'll see!"

Ellen smiled more broadly. "But don't you give yourself any trouble for me," said she.

"Trouble indeed!" said Mr. Van Brunt; "I don't know any thing about that. How came that wicked thing up here to plague you?"

"She said aunt Fortune left her to take care of me."

"That's one of her lies. Your aunt's gone out, I know; but she's a trifle wiser than to do such a thing as that. She has plagued you badly, ha'n't she?"

He might have thought so. The colour which excitement brought into Ellen's face had faded away, and she had settled herself back against her pillow with an expression of weakness and weariness that the strong man saw and felt.

"What is there I can do for you?" said he, with a gentleness that seemed almost strange from such lips.

"If you would," said Ellen faintly,—"if you *could* be so kind as to read me a hymn?—I should be so glad. I've had nobody to read to me."

Her hand put the little book toward him as she said so.

Mr. Van Brunt would vastly rather any one had asked him to plough an acre. He was to the full as much confounded as poor Ellen had once been at a request of his. He hesitated, and looked toward Ellen wishing for an excuse. But the pale little face that lay there against the pillow,—the drooping eyelids,—the meek helpless look of the little child, put all excuses out of his head; and though he would have chosen to do almost any thing else, he took the book and asked her "Where?" She said anywhere; and he took the first he saw.

> "Poor, weak, and worthless though I am,
> I have a rich almighty friend;
> Jesus the Saviour is his name,
> He freely loves, and without end."

"Oh," said Ellen with a sigh of pleasure, and folding her hands on her breast,—"how lovely that is!"

He stopped and looked at her a moment, and then went on with increased gravity.

> "He ransom'd me from hell with blood,
> And by his pow'r my foes controll'd;
> He found me wand'ring far from God,
> And brought me to his chosen fold."

"Fold?" said Ellen, opening her eyes; "what is that?"

"It's where sheep are penned, ain't it?" said Mr. Van Brunt, after a pause.

"Oh, yes!" said Ellen, "that's it; I remember; that's like what he said, 'I am the good shepherd,' and 'the Lord is my shepherd;' I know now. Go on, please."

He finished the hymn without more interruption. Looking
again toward Ellen, he was surprised to see several large tears
finding their way down her cheeks from under the wet eyelash.
But she quickly wiped them away.

"What do you read them things for," said he, "if they make
you feel bad?"

"Feel bad!" said Ellen. "Oh, they don't; they make me
happy; I love them dearly. I never read that one before. You
can't think how much I am obliged to you for reading it to me.
Will you let me see where it is?"

He gave it her.

"Yes, there's his mark!" said Ellen, with sparkling eyes.
"Now, Mr. Van Brunt, would you be so very good as to read it
once more?"

He obeyed. It was easier this time. She listened as before
with closed eyes, but the colour came and went once or twice.

"Thank you very much," she said, when he had done. "Are
you going?"

"I must; I have some things to look after."

She held his hand still.

"Mr. Van Brunt,—don't *you* love hymns?"

"I don't know much about 'em, Miss Ellen."

"Mr. Van Brunt, are you one of that fold?"

"What fold?"

"The fold of Christ's people."

"I'm afeard not, Miss Ellen," said he soberly, after a minute's pause.

"Because," said Ellen, bursting into tears, "I wish you were, very much."

She carried the great brown hand to her lips before she let it go. He went without saying a word. But when he got out he stopped and looked at a little tear she had left on the back of it. And he looked till one of his own fell there to keep it company.

CHAPTER XXI.

Oh, that *had*, how sad a passage 'tis!

SHAKSPEARE.

THE next day, about the middle of the afternoon, a light step crossed the shed, and the great door opening gently, in walked Miss Alice Humphreys. The room was all "redd up," and Miss Fortune and her mother sat there at work ; one picking over white beans at the table, the other in her usual seat by the fire, and at her usual employment, which was knitting. Alice came forward, and asked the old lady how she did.

"Pretty well—Oh, pretty well !" she answered, with the look of bland good-humour her face almost always wore,—"and glad to see you, dear. Take a chair."

Alice did so, quite aware that the other person in the room was *not* glad to see her.

"And how goes the world with you, Miss Fortune ?"

"Humph ! it's a queer kind of world, I think," answered that lady dryly, sweeping some of the picked beans into her pan ;—" I get a'most sick of it sometimes."

"Why, what's the matter?" said Alice, pleasantly; "may I ask ? Has any thing happened to trouble you ?"

"Oh, no !" said the other somewhat impatiently ; "nothing that's any matter to any one but myself; it's no use speaking about it."

"Ah ! Fortune never would take the world easy," said the old woman, shaking her head from side to side ; "never would ;— I never could get her."

"Now do hush, mother, will you !" said the daughter, turning round upon her with startling sharpness of look and tone ;— "'take the world easy !' you always did. I am glad I ain't like you."

"I don't think it's a bad way after all," said Alice; "what's the use of taking it hard, Miss Fortune?"

"The way one goes on!" said that lady, picking away at her beans very fast and not answering Alice's question,—"I'm tired of it;—toil, toil, and drive, drive,—from morning to night; and what's the end of it all?"

"Not much," said Alice gravely, "if our toiling looks no further than *this* world. When we go we shall carry nothing away with us. I should think it would be very wearisome to toil only for what we cannot keep nor stay long to enjoy."

"It's a pity you warn't a minister, Miss Alice," said Miss Fortune dryly.

"Oh, no, Miss Fortune," said Alice smiling, "the family would be overstocked. My father is one and my brother will be another; a third would be too much. You must be so good as to let me preach without taking orders."

"Well, I wish every minister was as good a one as you'd make," said Miss Fortune, her hard face giving way a little;—"at any rate nobody'd mind any thing you'd say Miss Alice."

"That would be unlucky, in one sense," said Alice; "but I believe I know what you mean. But, Miss Fortune, no one would dream the world went very hard with you. I don't know any body I think lives in more independent comfort and plenty, and has things more to her mind. I never come to the house that I am not struck with the fine look of the farm and all that belongs to it."

"Yes," said the old lady, nodding her head two or three times, "Mr. Van Brunt is a good farmer—very good—there's no doubt about that."

"I wonder what *he'd* do," said Miss Fortune, quickly and sharply as before, "if there warn't a head to manage for him! — Oh, the farm's well enough, Miss Alice,—tain't that; every one knows where his own shoe pinches."

"I wish you'd let me into the secret then, Miss Fortune; I'm a cobbler by profession."

Miss Fortune's ill-humour was giving way, but something disagreeable seemed again to cross her mind. Her brow darkened.

"I say it's a poor kind of world and I'm sick of it! One may slave and slave one's life out for other people, and what thanks do you get?—I'm sick of it."

"There's a little body up-stairs, or I'm much mistaken, who will give you very sincere thanks for every kindness shown her."

Miss Fortune tossed her head, and brushing the refuse beans into her lap, she pushed back her chair with a jerk to go to the fire with them.

"Much you know about her, Miss Alice! Thanks, indeed! I

haven't seen the sign of such a thing since she's been here, for all I have worked and worked and had plague enough with her I am sure. Deliver me from other people's children, say I!"

"After all, Miss Fortune," said Alice soberly, "it is not what we *do* for people that makes them love us,—or at least every thing depends on the way things are done. A look of love, a word of kindness, goes further toward winning the heart than years of service or benefactions mountain-high without them."

"Does she say I am unkind to her?" asked Miss Fortune fiercely.

"Pardon me," said Alice, "words on her part are unnecessary; it is easy to see from your own that there is no love lost between you, and I am very sorry it is so."

"Love, indeed!" said Miss Fortune with great indignation; "there never was any to lose I can assure you. She plagues the very life out of me. Why, she hadn't been here three days before she went off with that girl Nancy Vawse that I had told her never to go near, and was gone all night; that's the time she got in the brook. And if you'd seen her face when I was scolding her about it!—it was like seven thunder clouds. Much you know about it! I dare say she's very sweet to you; that's the way she is to every body beside me—they all think she's too good to live; and it just makes me mad!"

"She told me herself," said Alice, "of her behaving ill another time, about her mother's letter."

"Yes—that was another time. I wish you'd seen her!"

"I believe she saw and felt her fault in that case. Didn't she ask your pardon? she said she would."

"Yes," said Miss Fortune dryly, "after a fashion."

"Has she had her letter yet?"

"No."

"How is she to-day?"

"Oh, she's well enough—she's sitting up. You can go up and see her."

"I will directly," said Alice. "But now, Miss Fortune, I am going to ask a favour of you,—will you do me a great pleasure?"

"Certainly, Miss Alice,—if I can?"

"If you think Ellen has been sufficiently punished for her ill behaviour—if you do not think it right to withhold her letter still, —will you let me have the pleasure of giving it to her? I should take it as a great favour to myself."

Miss Fortune made no kind of reply to this, but stalked out of the room, and in a few minutes stalked in again with the letter, which she gave to Alice, only saying shortly, "It came to me in a letter from her father."

"You are willing she should have it?" said Alice.

" Oh, yes !—do what you like with it."

Alice now went softly up stairs. She found Ellen's door a little ajar, and looking in could see Ellen seated in a rocking-chair between the door and the fire, in her double-gown, and with her hymnbook in her hand. It happened that Ellen had spent a good part of that afternoon in crying for her lost letter; and the face that she turned to the door on hearing some slight noise outside was very white and thin indeed. And though it was placid too, her eye searched the crack of the door with a keen wistfulness that went to Alice's heart. But as the door was gently pushed open, and the eye caught the figure that stood behind it, the sudden and entire change of expression took away all her powers of speech. Ellen's face became radiant; she rose from her chair, and as Alice came silently in and kneeling down to be near her took her in her arms, Ellen put both hers round Alice's neck and laid her face there;—one was too happy and the other too touched to say a word.

" My poor child !" was Alice's first expression.

" No I ain't," said Ellen, tightening the squeeze of her arms round Alice's neck ; " I am not poor at all now."

Alice presently rose, sat down in the rocking chair and took Ellen in her lap; and Ellen rested her head on her bosom as she had been wont to do of old time on her mother's.

" I am too happy," she murmured. But she was weeping, and the current of tears seemed to gather force as it flowed. What was little Ellen thinking of just then? Oh, those times gone by !—when she had sat just so; her head pillowed on another as gentle a breast; kind arms wrapped round her, just as now; the same little old double-gown ; the same weak helpless feeling; the same committing herself to the strength and care of another ;—how much the same, and oh ! how much not the same !—and Ellen knew both. Blessing as she did the breast on which she leaned and the arms whose pressure she felt, they yet reminded her sadly of those most loved and so very far away; and it was an odd mixture of relief and regret, joy and sorrow, gratified and ungratified affection, that opened the sluices of her eyes. Tears poured.

" What is the matter, my love ?" said Alice softly.

" I don't know," whispered Ellen.

" Are you so glad to see me? or so sorry? or what is it?"

" Oh, glad and sorry both, I think," said Ellen with a long breath, and sitting up.

" Have you wanted me so much, my poor child ?"

" I cannot tell you how much," said Ellen, her words cut short.

" And didn't you know that I have been sick too? What did you think had become of me? Why, Mrs. Vawse was with me a whole week, and this is the very first day I have been able to go out. It is so fine to-day I was permitted to ride Sharp down."

"Was that it?" said Ellen. "I did wonder, Miss Alice, I did wonder very much why you did not come to see me. but I never liked to ask aunt Fortune, because——"

"Because what?"

"I don't know as I ought to say what I was going to ;—I had a feeling she would be glad about what I was sorry about."

"Don't know *that* you ought to say," said Alice. "Remember, you are to study English with me."

Ellen smiled a glad smile.

"And you have had a weary two weeks of it, haven't you, dear?"

"Oh," said Ellen, with another long-drawn sigh, "how weary! Part of that time, to be sure, I was out of my head; but I have got *so* tired lying here all alone; aunt Fortune coming in and out was just as good as nobody."

"Poor child!" said Alice, "you have had a worse time than I."

"I used to lie and watch that crack in the door at the foot of my bed," said Ellen, "and I got so tired of it I hated to see it, but when I opened my eyes I couldn't help looking at it, and watching all the little ins and outs in the crack till I was as sick of it as could be. And that button too that fastens the door, and the little round mark the button has made, and thinking how far the button went round. And then if I looked toward the windows I would go right to counting the panes, first up and down and then across; and I didn't want to count them, but I couldn't help it; and watching to see through which pane the sky looked brightest. Oh, I got so sick of it all! There was only the fire that I didn't get tired of looking at; I always liked to lie and look at that, except when it hurt my eyes. And oh, how I wanted to see you, Miss Alice! You can't think how sad I felt that you didn't come to see me. I couldn't think what could be the matter."

"I should have been with you, dear, and not have left you, if I had not been tied at home myself."

"So I thought; and that made it seem so very strange. But Oh! don't you think," said Ellen, her face suddenly brightening, —"don't you think Mr. Van Brunt came up to see me last night? Wasn't it good of him? He even sat down and read to me; only think of that. And isn't he kind? he asked if I would like a rocking-chair; and of course I said yes, for these other chairs are dreadful, they break my back; and there wasn't such a thing as a rocking-chair in aunt Fortune's house, she hates 'em, she says; and this morning, the first thing I knew, in walked Mr. Van Brunt with this nice rocking-chair. Just get up and see how nice it is;

—you see the back is cushioned, and the elbows, as well as the seat; — it's queer-looking, ain't it? but it's very comfortable. Wasn't it good of him?"

"It was very kind, I think. But do you know, Ellen, I am going to have a quarrel with you?"

"What about?" said Ellen. "I don't believe it's any thing very bad, for you look pretty good-humoured, considering."

"Nothing *very* bad," said Alice, "but still enough to quarrel about. You have twice said ' *ain't* ' since I have been here."

"Oh," said Ellen, laughing, "is that all?"

"Yes," said Alice, "and my English ears don't like it at all."

"Then they shan't hear it," said Ellen, kissing her. "I don't know what makes me say it; I never used to. But I've got more to tell you; I've had more visitors. Who do you think came to see me?—you'd never guess—Nancy Vawse!—Mr. Van Brunt came in the very nick of time, when I was almost worried to death with her. Only think of *her* coming up here! unknown to every body. And she stayed an age, and how she *did* go on. She cracked nuts on the hearth;—she got every stitch of my clothes out of my trunk and scattered them over the floor;—she tried to make me drink gruel till between us we spilled a great parcel on the bed; and she had begun to tickle me when Mr. Van Brunt came. Oh, wasn't I glad to see him! And when aunt Fortune came up and saw it all she was as angry as she could be; and she scolded and scolded, till at last I told her it was none of my doing, —I couldn't help it at all,—and she needn't talk so to me about it; and then she said it was my fault the whole of it! that if I hadn't scraped acquaintance with Nancy when she had forbidden me all this would never have happened."

"There is some truth in that, isn't there, Ellen?"

"Perhaps so; but I think it might all have happened whether or no; and at any rate it is a little hard to talk so to me about it now when it's all over and can't be helped. Oh, I have been so tired to-day, Miss Alice!—aunt Fortune has been in such a bad humour."

"What put her in a bad humour?"

"Why, all this about Nancy in the first place; and then I know she didn't like Mr. Van Brunt's bringing the rocking-chair for me; she couldn't say much, but I could see by her face. And then Mrs. Van Brunt's coming—I don't think she liked that. Oh, Mrs. Van Brunt came to see me this morning, and brought me a custard. How many people are kind to me!—everywhere I go."

"I hope, dear Ellen, you don't forget whose kindness sends them all."

"I don't, Miss Alice; I always think of that now; and it seems you can't think how pleasant to me sometimes."

" Then I hope you can bear unkindness from one poor woman,—
who after all isn't as happy as you are,—without feeling any ill-will
toward her in return."

" I don't think I feel ill-will toward her," said Ellen ; " I always
try as hard as I can not to ; but I can't *like* her, Miss Alice ; and
I do get out of patience. It's very easy to put me out of patience,
I think ; it takes almost nothing sometimes."

" But remember, ' charity suffereth long and is kind.' "

" And I try all the while, dear Miss Alice, to keep down my bad
feelings," said Ellen, her eyes watering as she spoke ; " I try and
pray to get rid of them, and I hope I shall by and by ; I believe I
am very bad."

Alice drew her closer.

" I have felt very sad part of to-day," said Ellen presently ;
" aunt Fortune, and my being so lonely, and my poor letter,
altogether ;—but part of the time I felt a great deal better. I was
learning that lovely hymn,—do you know it, Miss Alice ?—' Poor,
weak, and worthless, though I am ?'——"

Alice went on :—

> " I have a rich almighty friend,
> Jesus the Saviour is his name,
> He freely loves, and without end."

" Oh, dear Ellen, whoever can say that, has no right to be
unhappy. No matter what happens, we have enough to be glad
of."

" And then I was thinking of those words in the Psalms,—
' Blessed is the man'—stop, I'll find it ; I don't know exactly how
it goes ;—' Blessed is he whose transgression is forgiven ; whose sin
is covered.' "

" Oh, yes indeed !" said Alice. " It is a shame that any trifles
should worry much those whose sins are forgiven them and who are
the children of the great King. Poor Miss Fortune never knew
the sweetness of those words. We ought to be sorry for her, and
pray for her, Ellen ; and never, never, even in thought, return evil
for evil. It is not like Christ to do so."

" I will not, I will not, if I can help it," said Ellen.

" You can help it ; but there is only one way. Now, Ellen dear,
I have three pieces of news for you that I think you will like.
One concerns you, another myself, and the third concerns both you
and myself. Which will you have first ?"

" Three pieces of good news !" said Ellen with opening eyes ;—
" I think I'll have my part first."

Directing Ellen's eyes to her pocket, Alice slowly made the corner
of the letter show itself. Ellen's colour came and went quick as
it was drawn forth ; but when it was fairly out and she knew it
again, she flung herself upon it with a desperate eagerness Alice

had not looked for; she was startled at the half frantic way in which the child clasped and kissed it, weeping bitterly at the same time. Her transport was almost hysterical. She had opened the letter, but she was not able to read a word; and quitting Alice's arms she threw herself upon the bed, sobbing in a mixture of joy and sorrow that seemed to take away her reason. Alice looked on surprised a moment, but only a moment, and turned away.

When Ellen was able to begin her letter the reading of it served to throw her back into fresh fits of tears. Many a word of Mrs. Montgomery's went so to her little daughter's heart that its very inmost cords of love and tenderness were wrung. It is true the letter was short and very simple; but it came from her mother's heart; it was written by her mother's hand; and the very old remembered handwriting had mighty power to move her. She was so wrapped up in her own feelings that through it all she never noticed that Alice was not near her, that Alice did not speak to comfort her. When the letter had been read time after time, and wept over again and again, and Ellen at last was folding it up for the present, she bethought herself of her friend and turned to look after her. Alice was sitting by the window, her face hid in her hands, and as Ellen drew near she was surprised to see that *her* tears were flowing and her breast heaving. Ellen came quite close, and softly laid her hand on Alice's shoulder. But it drew no attention.

"Miss Alice," said Ellen almost fearfully,—" *dear* Miss Alice," —and her own eyes filled fast again, " what is the matter?—won't you tell me?—Oh, don't do so! please don't!"

"I will not," said Alice lifting her head; "I am sorry I have troubled you dear; I am sorry I could not help it."

She kissed Ellen, who stood anxious and sorrowful by her side, and brushed away her tears. But Ellen saw she had been shedding a great many.

"What is the matter, dear Miss Alice? what has happened to trouble you?—won't you tell me?"—Ellen was almost crying herself.

Alice came back to the rocking-chair, and took Ellen in her arms again; but she did not answer her. Leaning her face against Ellen's forehead she remained silent. Ellen ventured to ask no more questions; but lifting her hand once or twice caressingly to Alice's face she was distressed to find her cheek wet still. Alice spoke at last.

"It isn't fair not to tell you what is the matter, dear Ellen, since I have let you see me sorrowing. It is nothing new, nor anything I would have otherwise if I could. It is only that I have had a mother once, and have lost her; and you brought back the old time so strongly that I could not command myself."

Ellen felt a hot tear drop upon her forehead, and again ventured to speak her sympathy only by silently stroking Alice's cheek.

"It is all past now," said Alice; "it is all well. I would not have her back again. I shall go to her I hope by and by."

"Oh, no! you must stay with me," said Ellen, clasping both arms round her.

There was a long silence, during which they remained locked in each other's arms.

"Ellen dear," said Alice at length, "we are both motherless, for the present at least,—both of us almost alone; I think God has brought us together to be a comfort to each other. We will be sisters while he permits us to be so. Don't call me Miss Alice any more. You shall be my little sister and I will be your elder sister, and my home shall be your home as well."

Ellen's arms were drawn very close round her companion at this, but she said nothing, and her face was laid in Alice's bosom. There was another very long pause. Then Alice spoke in a livelier tone.

"Come, Ellen! look up! you and I have forgotten ourselves; it isn't good for sick people to get down in the dumps. Look up and let me see these pale cheeks. Don't you want something to eat?"

"I don't know," said Ellen faintly.

"What would you say to a cup of chicken broth?"

"Oh, I should like it very much!" said Ellen with new energy.

"Margery made me some particularly nice, as she always does; and I took it into my head a little might not come amiss to you; so I resolved to stand the chance of Sharp's jolting it all over me, and I rode down with a little pail of it on my arm. Let me rake open these coals and you shall have some directly."

"And did you come without being spattered?" said Ellen.

"Not a drop. Is this what you use to warm things in? Never mind, it has had gruel in it; I'll set the tin pail on the fire; it won't hurt it."

"I am so much obliged to you," said Ellen, "for do you know I have got quite tired of gruel, and panada I can't bear."

"Then I am very glad I brought it."

While it was warming Alice washed Ellen's gruel cup and spoon; and presently she had the satisfaction of seeing Ellen eating the broth with that keen enjoyment none know but those that have been sick and are getting well. She smiled to see her gaining strength almost in the very act of swallowing.

"Ellen," said she presently, "I have been considering your dressing-table. It looks rather doleful. I'll make you a present of some dimity, and when you come to see me you shall make a cover for it that will reach down to the floor and hide those long legs."

" That wouldn't do at all," said Ellen ; " aunt Fortune would go off into all sorts of fits."

" What about ?"

" Why the washing, Miss Alice—to have such a great thing to wash every now and then. You can't think what a fuss she makes if I have more than just so many white clothes in the wash every week."

" That's too bad," said Alice. " Suppose you bring it up to me —it wouldn't be often—and I'll have it washed for you,—if you care enough about it to take the trouble."

" Oh, indeed I do !" said Ellen ; " I should like it very much, and I'll get Mr. Van Brunt to—no I can't, aunt Fortune won't let me ; I was going to say I would get him to saw off the legs and make it lower for me, and then my dressing-box would stand so nicely on the top. Maybe I can yet. Oh, I never showed you my boxes and things."

Ellen brought them all out and displayed their beauties. In the course of going over the writing-desk she came to the secret drawer and a little money in it.

" Oh, that puts me in mind !" she said. " Miss Alice, this money is to be spent for some poor child ;—now I've been think-ing Nancy has behaved so to me I should like to give her some-thing to show her that I don't feel unkindly about it—what do you think will be a good thing ?"

" I don't know, Ellen—I'll take the matter into consideration."

" Do you think a Bible would do ?"

" Perhaps that would do as well as any thing ;—I'll think about it."

" I should like to do it very much," said Ellen, " for she has vexed me wonderfully."

" Well, Ellen, would you like to hear my other pieces of news ? or have you no curiosity ?"

" Oh, yes, indeed," said Ellen ; " I had forgotten it entirely ; what is it, Miss Alice ?"

" You know I told you one concerns only myself, but it is great news to me. I learnt this morning that my brother will come to spend the holidays with me. It is many months since I have seen him."

" Does he live far away ?" said Ellen.

" Yes,—he has gone far away to pursue his studies, and cannot come home often. The other piece of news is that I intend, if you have no objection, to ask Miss Fortune's leave to have you spend the holidays with me too."

" Oh, delightful !" said Ellen, starting up and clapping her hands, and then throwing them round her adopted sister's neck ;—" dear Alice, how good you are !"

"Then I suppose I may reckon upon your consent," said Alice, "and I'll speak to Miss Fortune without delay."

"Oh, thank you, dear Miss Alice;—how glad I am! I shall be happy all the time from now till then thinking of it. You aren't going?"

"I must."

"Ah, don't go yet! Sit down again; you know you're my sister,—don't you want to read mamma's letter?"

"If you please, Ellen, I should like it very much."

She sat down, and Ellen gave her the letter, and stood by while she read it, watching her with glistening eyes; and though as she saw Alice's fill her own overflowed again, she hung over her still to the last; going over every line this time with a new pleasure.

"New York, Saturday, Nov. 22, 18—.

"My Dear Ellen,

"I meant to have written to you before, but have been scarcely able to do so. I did make one or two efforts which came to nothing; I was obliged to give it up before finishing any thing that could be called a letter. To-day I feel much stronger than I have at any time since your departure.

"I have missed you, my dear child, very much. There is not an hour in the day, nor a half hour, that the want of you does not come home to my heart; and I think I have missed you in my very dreams. This separation is a very hard thing to bear. But the hand that has arranged it does nothing amiss; we must trust Him, my daughter, that all will be well. I feel it *is* well; though sometimes the thought of your dear little face is almost too much for me. I will thank God I have had such a blessing so long, and I now commit my treasure to Him. It is an unspeakable comfort to me to do this, for nothing committed to his care is ever forgotten or neglected. Oh, my daughter, never forget to pray; never slight it. It is almost my only refuge, now I have lost you, and it bears me up. How often—how often,—through years gone by,—when heart-sick and faint,—I have fallen on my knees, and presently there have been as it were drops of cool water sprinkled upon my spirit's fever. Learn to love prayer, dear Ellen, and then you will have a cure for all the sorrows of life. And keep this letter, that if ever you are like to forget it, your mother's testimony may come to mind again.

"My tea, that used to be so pleasant, has become a sad meal to me. I drink it mechanically and set down my cup, remembering only that the dear little hand which used to minister to my wants is near me no more. My child—my child!—words are poor to express the heart's yearnings,—my spirit is near you all the time.

"Your old gentleman has paid me several visits. The day after you went came some beautiful pigeons. I sent word back that you were no longer here to enjoy his gifts, and the next day he came to see me. He has shown himself very kind. And all this, dear Ellen, had for its immediate cause your proper and ladylike behaviour in the store. That thought has been sweeter to me than all the old gentleman's birds and fruit. I am sorry to inform you that though I have seen him so many times I am still perfectly ignorant of his name.

" We set sail Monday in the England. Your father has secured a nice state-room for me, and I have a store of comforts laid up for the voyage. So next week you may imagine me out on the broad ocean, with nothing but sky and clouds and water to be seen around me, and probably much too sick to look at those. Never mind that; the sickness is good for me.

" I will write you as soon as I can again, and send by the first conveyance.

" And now my dear baby—my precious child—farewell. May the blessing of God be with you !

" Your affectionate mother,

" E. MONTGOMERY."

" You ought to be a good child, Ellen," said Alice, as she dashed away some tears. " Thank you for letting me see this; it has been a great pleasure to me."

" And now," said Ellen, " you feel as if you knew mamma a little."

" Enough to honour and respect her very much. Now good-by, my love; I must be at home before it is late. I will see you again before Christmas comes."

CHAPTER XXII.

When icicles hang by the wall,
And Dick the shepherd blows his nail,
And Tom bears logs into the hall,
And milk comes frozen home in pail.
                              SHAKSPEARE.

To Ellen's sorrow she was pronounced next morning well enough to come down stairs; her aunt averring that " it was no use to keep a fire burning up there for nothing." She must get up and dress in the cold again; and winter had fairly set in now; the 19th of December rose clear and keen. Ellen looked sighingly at the heap of ashes and the dead brands in the fireplace where the bright little fire had blazed so cheerfully the evening before. But regrets did not help the matter; and shivering she began to dress as fast as she could. Since her illness a basin and pitcher had been brought into her room, so the washing at the spout was ended for the present; and though the basin had no place but a chair, and the pitcher must stand on the floor, Ellen thought herself too happy. But how cold it was! The wind swept past her windows, giving wintry shakes to the panes of glass, and through many an opening in the wooden frame-work of the house it came in and saluted Ellen's bare arms and neck. She hurried to finish her dressing, and wrapping her double-gown over all, went down to the kitchen. It was another climate there. A great fire was burning that it quite cheered Ellen's heart to look at; and the air seemed to be full of coffee and buckwheat cakes; Ellen almost thought she should get enough breakfast by the sense of smell.

"Ah! here you are," said Miss Fortune. "What have you got that thing on for?"

"It was so cold up stairs," said Ellen, drawing up her shoulders. The warmth had not got inside of her wrapper yet.

"Well, 'tain't cold here; you'd better pull it off right away. I've no notion of people's making themselves tender. You'll be warm enough directly. Breakfast 'll warm you."

Ellen felt almost inclined to quarrel with the breakfast that was offered in exchange for her comfortable wrapper; she pulled it off however and sat down without saying any thing. Mr. Van Brunt put some cakes on her plate.

"If breakfast's a going to warm you," said he, "make haste and get something down; or drink a cup of coffee; you're as blue as skim milk."

"Am I?" said Ellen laughing; "I feel blue; but I can't eat such a pile of cakes as that, Mr. Van Brunt."

As a general thing the meals at Miss Fortune's were silent solemnities; an occasional consultation, or a few questions and remarks about farm affairs, being all that ever passed. The breakfast this morning was a singular exception to the common rule.

"I am in a regular quandary," said the mistress of the house, when the meal was about half over.

Mr. Van Brunt looked up for an instant, and asked "what about?"

"Why, how I am ever going to do to get those apples and sausage-meat done. If I go to doing 'em myself I shall about get through by spring."

"Why don't you make a bee?" said Mr. Van Brunt.

"Ain't enough of either on 'em to make it worth while. I ain't a going to have all the bother of a bee without some thing to show for't."

"Turn 'em both into one," suggested her counsellor, going on with his breakfast.

"Both?"

"Yes—let 'em pare apples in one room and cut pork in t'other."

"But I wonder who ever heard of such a thing before," said Miss Fortune, pausing with her cup of coffee half way to her lips. Presently, however, it was carried to her mouth, drunk off, and set down with an air of determination.

"I don't care," said she, "if it never was heard of. I'll do it for once anyhow. I'm not one of them to care what folks say. I'll have it so ! But I won't have 'em to tea, mind you ; I'd rather throw apples and all into the fire at once. I'll have but one plague of setting tables, and that I won't have 'em to tea. I'll make it up to 'em in the supper though."

"I'll take care to publish that," said Mr. Van Brunt.

"Don't you go and do such a thing," said Miss Fortune earnestly. "I shall have the whole country on my hands. I won't have but just as many on 'em as'll do what I want done ; that'll be as much as I can stand under. Don't you whisper a word of it to a living creature. I'll go round and ask 'em myself to come Monday evening."

"Monday evening—then I suppose you'd like to have up the sleigh this afternoon. Who's a-coming?"

"I don't know ; I ha'n't asked 'em yet."

"They'll every soul come that's asked, that you may depend ; there ain't one on 'em that would miss of it for a dollar."

Miss Fortune bridled a little at the implied tribute to her housekeeping.

"If I was some folks I wouldn't let people know I was in such a mighty hurry to get a good supper," she observed rather scornfully.

"Humph !" said Mr. Van Brunt ; "I think a good supper ain't a bad thing ; and I've no objection to folk's knowing it."

"Pshaw ! I didn't mean *you,*" said Miss Fortune ; "I was thinking of those Lawsons, and other folks."

"If you're a going to ask *them* to your bee you ain't of my mind."

"Well, I am though," replied Miss Fortune ; "there's a good many hands of 'em ; they can turn off a good lot of work in an evening ; and they always take care to get me to *their* bees. I may as well get something out of them in return if I can."

"They'll reckon on getting as much as they can out o' *you,* if they come, there's no sort of doubt in my mind. It's my belief Mimy Lawson will kill herself some of these days upon green corn. She was at home to tea one day last summer, and I declare I thought——"

What Mr. Van Brunt thought he left his hearers to guess.

" Well, let them kill themselves if they like," said Miss Fortune; " I am sure I am willing; there'll be enough; I ain't a going
to mince matters when once I begin. Now, let me see. There's
five of the Lawsons to begin with—I suppose they'll all come;—
Bill Huff, and Jany, that's seven;—"

" That Bill Huff is as good-natured a fellow as ever broke
ground," remarked Mr. Van Brunt. " Ain't better people in the
town than them Huffs are."

" They're well enough," said Miss Fortune. " Seven—and the
Hitchcocks, there's three of them, that'll make ten,—"

" Dennison's ain't far from there," said Mr. Van Brunt. " Dan
Dennison's a fine hand at a'most any thing, in doors or out."

" That's more than you can say for his sister. Cilly Dennison
gives herself so many airs it's altogether too much for plain
country folks. I should like to know what she thinks herself.
It's a'most too much for my stomach to see her flourishing that
watch and chain."

" What's the use of troubling yourself about other people's
notions?" said Mr. Van Brunt. " If folks want to take the road
let 'em have it. That's my way. I am satisfied, provided they
don't run me over."

" 'Tain't *my* way, then, I'd have you to know," said Miss Fortune; " I despise it! And 'tain't your way neither, Van Brunt;
what did you give Tom Larkens a cowhiding for?"

" 'Cause he deserved it, if ever a man did," said Mr. Van
Brunt, quite rousing up;—" he was treating that little brother of
his'n in a way a boy shouldn't be treated, and I am glad I did it.
I gave him notice to quit before I laid a finger on him. He warn't
doing nothing to *me*."

" And how much good do you suppose it did?" said Miss
Fortune rather scornfully.

" It did just the good I wanted to do. He has seen fit to let
little Billy alone ever since."

" Well, I guess I'll let the Dennisons come," said Miss Fortune;
" that makes twelve, and you and your mother are fourteen. I
suppose that man Marshchalk will come dangling along after the
Hitchcocks."

" To be sure he will; and his aunt, Miss Janet, will come with
him most likely."

" Well—there's no help for it," said Miss Fortune. " That
makes sixteen."

" Will you ask Miss Alice?"

" Not I! she's another of your proud set. I don't want to see
any body that thinks she's going to do me a great favour by
coming."

Ellen's lips opened, but wisdom came in time to stop the words that were on her tongue. It did not, however, prevent the quick little turn of her head which showed what she thought, and the pale cheeks were for a moment bright enough.

"She is, and I don't care who hears it," repeated Miss Fortune. "I suppose she'd look as sober as a judge too if she saw cider on the table; they say she won't touch a drop ever, and thinks it's wicked; and if that ain't setting oneself up for better than other folks I don't know what is."

"I saw her paring apples at the Huffs though," said Mr. Van Brunt, "and as pleasant as any body; but she didn't stay to supper."

"I'd ask Mrs. Vawse if I could get word to her," said Miss Fortune,—"but I can never travel up that mountain. If I get a sight of Nancy I'll tell her."

"There she is, then," said Mr. Van Brunt, looking toward the little window that opened into the shed. And there indeed was the face of Miss Nancy pressed flat against the glass, peering into the room. Miss Fortune beckoned to her.

"That is the most impudent, shameless, outrageous piece of—— What were you doing at the window?" said she as Nancy came in.

"Looking at you, Miss Fortune," said Nancy coolly. "What have you been talking about this great while? If there had only been a pane of glass broken I needn't have asked."

"Hold your tongue," said Miss Fortune, "and listen to me."

"I'll listen, ma'am," said Nancy, "but it's of no use to hold my tongue. I do try, sometimes, but I never could keep it long."

"Have you done?"

"I don't know, ma'am," said Nancy, shaking her head; "it's just as it happens."

"You tell your granny I am going to have a bee here next Monday evening, and ask her if she'll come to it."

Nancy nodded. "If it's good weather," she added conditionally.

"Stop, Nancy!" said Miss Fortune, "here!"—for Nancy was shutting the door behind her.—"As sure as you come here Monday night without your grandma you'll go out of the house quicker than you come in; see if you don't!"

With another gracious nod and smile Nancy departed.

"Well," said Mr. Van Brunt, rising, "I'll despatch this business down stairs, and then I'll bring up the sleigh. The pickle's ready I suppose."

"No it ain't," said Miss Fortune, "I couldn't make it yesterday; but it's all in the kettle, and I told Sam to make a fire down stairs, so you can put it on when you go down. The kits are all ready, and the salt and every thing else."

Mr. Van Brunt went down the stairs that led to the lower kitchen; and Miss Fortune, to make up for lost time, set about her morning's work with even an uncommon measure of activity. Ellen, in consideration of her being still weak, was not required to do any thing. She sat and looked on, keeping out of the way of her bustling aunt as far as it was possible; but Miss Fortune's gyrations were of that character that no one could tell five minutes beforehand what she might consider " in the way." Ellen wished for her quiet room again. Mr. Van Brunt's voice sounded down stairs in tones of business; what could he be about? it must be very uncommon business that kept him in the house. Ellen grew restless with the desire to go and see, and to change her aunt's company for his; and no sooner was Miss Fortune fairly shut up in the buttery at some secret work than Ellen gently opened the door at the head of the lower stairs and looked down. Mr. Van Brunt was standing at the bottom and he looked up.

" May I come down there, Mr. Van Brunt?" said Ellen softly.

" Come down here? to be sure you may! You may always come straight where I am without asking any questions."

Ellen went down. But before she reached the bottom stair she stopped with almost a start, and stood fixed with such a horrified face that neither Mr. Van Brunt nor Sam Larkens, who was there, could help laughing.

" What's the matter?" said the former,—" they're all dead enough, Miss Ellen; you needn't be scared."

Three enormous hogs which had been killed the day before greeted Ellen's eyes. They lay in different parts of the room, with each a cob in his mouth. A fourth lay stretched upon his back on the kitchen table, which was drawn out into the middle of the floor. Ellen stood fast on the stair.

" Have they been killed!" was her first astonished exclamation, to which Sam responded with another burst.

" Be quiet, Sam Larkens!" said Mr. Van Brunt. " Yes, Miss Ellen, they've been killed sure enough."

" Are these the same pigs I used to see you feeding with corn, Mr. Van Brunt?"

" The identical same ones," replied that gentleman, as laying hold of the head of the one on the table and applying his long sharp knife with the other hand, he while he was speaking severed it neatly and quickly from the trunk. " And very fine porkers they are; I ain't ashamed of 'em."

" And what's going to be done with them now?" said Ellen.

" I am just going to cut them up and lay them down. Bless my heart! you never see nothing of the kind before, did you?"

" No," said Ellen. " What do you mean by ' laying them down,' Mr. Van Brunt?"

"Why, laying 'em down in salt for pork and hams. You want to see the whole operation, don't you ? Well, here's a seat for you. You'd better fetch that painted coat o' yourn and wrap round you, for it ain't quite so warm here as up stairs ; but it's getting warmer. Sam, just you shut that door to, and throw on another log."

Sam built up as large a fire as could be made under a very large kettle that hung in the chimney. When Ellen came down in her wrapper she was established close in the chimney corner ; and when Mr. Van Brunt, not thinking her quite safe from the keen currents of air that would find their way into the room, despatched Sam for an old buffalo robe that lay in the shed. This he himself with great care wrapped round her, feet and chair and all, and secured it in various places with old forks. He declared then she looked for all the world like an Indian, except her face, and in high good-humour both, he went to cutting up the pork, and Ellen from out of her buffalo robe watched him.

It was beautifully done. Even Ellen could see that, although she could not have known if it had been done ill. The knife guided by strength and skill seemed to go with the greatest ease and certainty just where he wished it; the hams were beautifully trimmed out; the pieces fashioned clean ; no ragged cutting ; and his quick-going knife disposed of carcass after carcass with admirable neatness and celerity. Sam meanwhile arranged the pieces in different parcels at his direction, and minded the kettle, in which a great boiling and scumming was going on. Ellen was too much amused for a while to ask any questions. When the cutting up was all done the hams and shoulders were put in a cask by themselves and Mr. Van Brunt began to pack down the other pieces in the kits, strewing them with an abundance of salt.

"What's the use of putting all that salt with the pork, Mr. Van Brunt ?" said Ellen.

"It wouldn't keep good without that ; it would spoil very quick."

"Will the salt make it keep ?'

"All the year round—as sweet as a nut."

"I wonder what is the reason of that," said Ellen. "Will salt make every thing keep ?"

"Every thing in the world—if it only has enough of it, and is kept dry and cool."

"Are you going to do the hams in the same way ?"

"No ;—they're to go in that pickle over the fire."

"In this kettle ? what is in it ?" said Ellen.

"You must ask Miss Fortune about that ;—sugar and salt and saltpetre and molasses, and I don't know what all."

"And will this make the hams so different from the rest of the pork ?"

" No ; they've got to be smoked after they have laid in that for a while."

" Smoked!" said Ellen; " how ?"

" Why ha'n't you been in the smoke-house ? The hams has to be taken out of the pickle and hung up there ; and then we make a little fire of oak chips and keep it burning night and day."

" And how long must they stay in the smoke ?"

" Oh, three or four weeks or so."

" And then they are done."

" Then they are done."

" How very curious!" said Ellen. " Then it's the smoke that gives them that nice taste ? I never knew smoke was good for any thing before."

" Ellen !" said the voice of Miss Fortune from the top of the stairs,—" come right up here this minute ! you'll catch your death !"

Ellen's countenance fell.

" There's no sort of fear of that, ma'am," said Mr. Van Brunt, quietly, " and Miss Ellen is fastened up so she can't get loose ; and I can't let her out just now."

The upper door was shut again pretty sharply, but that was the only audible expression of opinion with which Miss Fortune favoured them.

" I guess my leather curtains keep off the wind, dont't they ?" said Mr. Van Brunt.

" Yes, indeed they do," said Ellen, " I don't feel a breath ; I am as warm as a toast,—too warm almost. How nicely you have fixed me up, Mr. Van Brunt."

" I thought that 'ere old buffalo had done its work," he said, " but I'll never say any thing is good for nothing again. Have you found out where the apples are yet ?"

" No," said Ellen.

" Ha'n't Miss Fortune showed you ! Well, it's time you'd know. Sam, take that little basket and go fill it at the bin ; I guess you know where they be, for I believe you put 'em there."

Sam went into the cellar, and presently returned with the basket nicely filled. He handed it to Ellen.

" Are all these for me ?" she said in surprise.

" Every one of 'em," said Mr. Van Brunt.

" But I don't like to," said Ellen ;—" what will aunt Fortune say ?"

" She won't say a word," said Mr. Van Brunt; " and don't you say a word neither, but whenever you want apples just go to the bin and take 'em. *I* give you leave. It's right at the end of the far cellar, at the left-hand corner ; there are the bins and all sorts of apples in 'em. You've got a pretty variety there, ha'n't you ?"

" Oh, all sorts," said Ellen,—" and what beauties! and I love apples very much,—red, and yellow, and speckled, and green.— What a great monster!"

" That's a Swar; that ain't as good as most of the others;— those are Seek-no-furthers."

" Seek-no-further!" said Ellen;—" what a funny name. It ought to be a mighty good apple. *I* shall seek further at any rate. What is this?"

" That's as good an apple as you've got in the basket; that's a real Orson pippin; a very fine kind. I'll fetch you some up from home some day though that are better than the best of those."

The pork was all packed; the kettle was lifted off the fire; Mr. Van Brunt was wiping his hands from the salt.

" And now I suppose I must go," said Ellen with a little sigh.

" Why *I* must go," said he,—" so I suppose I may as well let you out of your tent first."

" I have had such a nice time," said Ellen; " I had got *so* tired of doing nothing up stairs. I am *very* much obliged to you, Mr. Van Brunt. But," said she, stopping as she had taken up her basket to go,—" aren't you going to put the hams in the pickle?"

"No," said he, laughing, "it must wait to get cold first. But you'll make a capital farmer's wife, there's no mistake."

Ellen blushed, and ran up stairs with her apples. To bestow them safely in her closet was her first care; the rest of the morning was spent in increasing weariness and listlessness. She had brought down her little hymn-book, thinking to amuse herself with learning a hymn, but it would not do; eyes and head both refused their part of the work; and when at last Mr. Van Brunt came in to a late dinner, he found Ellen seated flat on the hearth before the fire, her right arm curled round upon the hard wooden bottom of one of the chairs, and her head pillowed upon that, fast asleep.

"Bless my soul!" said Mr. Van Brunt, "what's become of that 'ere rocking-cheer?"

"It's up stairs, I suppose. You can go fetch it if you've a mind to," answered Miss Fortune dryly enough.

He did so immediately; and Ellen barely waked up to feel herself lifted from the floor, and placed in the friendly rocking-chair; Mr. Van Brunt remarking at the same time that "it might be well enough to let well folks lie on the floor, and sleep on cheers, but cushions warn't a bit too soft for sick ones."

Among the cushions Ellen went to sleep again with a much better prospect of rest; and either sleeping or dozing passed away the time for a good while.

CHAPTER XXIII.

O that I were an Orange tree,
    That busy plant!
Then should I always laden be,
    And never want
Some fruit for him that dresseth me.
                        G. HERBERT.

SHE was thoroughly roused at last by the slamming of the house-door after her aunt. She and Mr. Van Brunt had gone forth on their sleighing expedition, and Ellen waked to find herself quite alone.

She could not long have doubted that her aunt was away, even if she had not caught a glimpse of her bonnet going out of the shed door,—the stillness was so uncommon. No such quiet could be with Miss Fortune anywhere about the premises. The old grandmother must have been abed and asleep too, for a cricket under the hearth and the wood fire in the chimney had it all to themselves, and made the only sounds that were heard; the first singing out every now and then in a very contented and cheerful style, and the latter giving occasional little snaps and sparks that just served to make one take notice how very quietly and steadily it was burning.

Miss Fortune had left the room put up in the last extreme of neatness. Not a speck of dust could be supposed to lie on the shining painted floor; the back of every chair was in its place against the wall. The very hearth-stones shone and the heads of the large iron nails in the floor were polished to steel. Ellen sat a while listening to the soothing chirrup of the cricket and the pleasant crackling of the flames. It was a fine cold winter's day. The two little windows at the far end of the kitchen looked out upon an expanse of snow; and the large lilac bush that grew close by the wall, moved lightly by the wind, drew its icy fingers over the panes of glass. Wintry it was without; but that made the warmth and comfort within seem all the more. Ellen would have enjoyed it very much if she had had any one to talk to; as it was she felt rather lonely and sad. She had begun to learn a hymn; but it had set her off upon a long train of thought; and with her head resting on her hand, her fingers pressed into her cheek, the other hand with the hymn-book lying listlessly in her lap, and eyes staring into the fire, she was sitting the very picture of meditation when the door opened and Alice Humphreys came in. Ellen started up.

"Oh, I'm so glad to see you! I'm all alone."

"Left alone, are you?" said Alice, as Ellen's warm lips were pressed again and again to her cold cheeks.

"Yes, aunt Fortune's gone out. Come and sit down here in the rocking-chair. How cold you are. Oh, do you know she is going to have a great bee here Monday evening? What is a *bee?*"

Alice smiled. "Why," said she, "when people here in the country have so much of any kind of work to do that their own hands are not enough for it, they send and call in their neighbours to help them,—that's a bee. A large party in the course of a long evening can do a great deal."

"But why do they call it a *bee?*"

"I don't know, unless they mean to be like a hive of bees for the time. 'As busy as a bee,' you know."

"Then they ought to call it a hive and not a bee, I should think. Aunt Fortune is going to ask sixteen people. I wish you were coming!"

"How do you know but I am?"

"Oh, I know you aren't. Aunt Fortune isn't going to ask you."

"You are sure of that, are you?"

"Yes, I wish I wasn't. Oh, how she vexed me this morning by something she said!"

" You mustn't get vexed so easily, my child. Don't let every little untoward thing roughen your temper."

" But I couldn't help it, dear Miss Alice; it was about you. I don't know whether I ought to tell you; but I don't think you'll mind it, and I know it isn't true. She said she didn't want you to come because you were one of the proud set."

" And what did *you* say ?"

" Nothing. I had it just on the end of my tongue to say, ' It's no such thing;' but I didn't say it."

" I am glad you were so wise. Dear Ellen, that is nothing to be vexed about. If it were true, indeed, you might be sorry. I trust Miss Fortune is mistaken. I shall try and find some way to make her change her mind. I am glad you told me."

" I am *so* glad you are come, dear Alice !" said Ellen again. " I wish I could have you always !" And the long, very close pressure of her two arms about her friend said as much. There was a long pause. The cheek of Alice rested on Ellen's head which nestled against her ; both were busily thinking ; but neither spoke ; and the cricket chirped and the flames crackled without being listened to.

" Miss Alice," said Ellen, after a long time,—" I wish you would talk over a hymn with me."

" How do you mean, my dear ?" said Alice rousing herself.

" I mean, read it over and explain it. Mamma used to do it sometimes. I have been thinking a great deal about her to-day ; and I think I'm very different from what I ought to be. I wish you would talk to me and make me better, Miss Alice."

Alice pressed an earnest kiss upon the tearful little face that was uplifted to her, and presently said,

" I am afraid I shall be a poor substitute for your mother, Ellen. What hymn shall we take ?"

" Any one—this one if you like. Mamma likes it very much. I was looking it over to-day.

> " ' A charge to keep I have—
>   A God to glorify ;
>   A never-dying soul to save,
>   And fit it for the sky.' "

Alice read the first line and paused.

" There now," said Ellen,—" what is a charge ?"

" Don't you know that ?"

" I think I do, but I wish you would tell me."

" Try to tell me first."

" Isn't it something that is given one to do ?—I don't know exactly."

" It is something given one in trust, to be done or taken care of.

I remember very well once when I was about your age my mother had occasion to go out for half an hour, and she left me in charge of my little baby sister; she gave me a *charge* not to let anything disturb her while she was away and to keep her asleep if I could. And I remember how I kept my charge too. I was not to take her out of the cradle, but I sat beside her the whole time; I would not suffer a fly to light on her little fair cheek; I scarcely took my eyes from her; I made John keep pussy at a distance; and whenever one of the little round dimpled arms was thrown out upon the coverlet I carefully drew something over it again."

"Is she dead?" said Ellen timidly, her eyes watering in sympathy with Alice's.

"She is dead, my dear; she died before we left England."

"I understand what a charge is," said Ellen after a little; "but what is this charge the hymn speaks of? What charge have I to keep?"

"The hymn goes on to tell you. The next line gives you part of it. 'A God to glorify.'"

"To glorify?" said Ellen doubtfully.

"Yes—that is to honour,—to give him all the honour that belongs to him."

"But can *I* honour *Him?*"

"Most certainly; either honour or dishonour; you cannot help doing one."

"I!" said Ellen again.

"Must not your behaviour speak either well or ill for the mother who has brought you up?"

"Yes—I know that."

"Very well; when a child of God lives as he ought to do, people cannot help having high and noble thoughts of that glorious One whom he serves, and of that perfect law he obeys. Little as they may love the ways of religion, in their own secret hearts they *cannot help* confessing that there is a God and that they ought to serve him. But a worldling, and still more an unfaithful Christian, just helps people to forget there is such a Being, and makes them think either that religion is a sham, or that they may safely go on despising it. I have heard it said, Ellen, that Christians are the only Bible some people ever read; and it is true; all they know of religion is what they get from the lives of its professors; and oh! were the world but full of the right kind of example, the kingdom of darkness could not stand. 'Arise. shine!' is a word that every Christian ought to take home."

"But how can I shine?" asked Ellen.

"My dear Ellen!—in the faithful, patient, self-denying performance of every duty as it comes to hand—'whatsoever thy hand findeth to do, do it with thy might.'"

"It is very little that *I* can do," said Ellen.

"Perhaps more than you think, but never mind that. All are not great stars in the church; you may be only a little rushlight; —see you burn well!"

"I remember," said Ellen, musing,—"mamma once told me when I was going somewhere, that people would think strangely of *her* if I didn't behave well."

"Certainly. Why, Ellen, I formed an opinion of her very soon after I saw you."

"Did you!" said Ellen, with a wonderfully brightened face,— "what was it? was it good? ah! do tell me!"

"I am not quite sure of the wisdom of that," said Alice, smiling; "you might take home the praise that is justly her right and not yours."

"Oh, no indeed," said Ellen, "I had rather she should have it than I. Please tell me what you thought of her, dear Alice,—I know it was good, at any rate."

"Well, I will tell you," said Alice, "at all risks. I thought your mother was a lady, from the honourable notions she had given you; and from your ready obedience to her, which was evidently the obedience of love, I judged she had been a good mother in the true sense of the term. I thought she must be a refined and cultivated person from the manner of your speech and behaviour; and I was sure she was a Christian, because she had taught you the truth, and evidently had tried to lead you in it."

The quivering face of delight with which Ellen began to listen gave way, long before Alice had done, to a burst of tears.

"It makes me so glad to hear you say that," she said.

"The praise of it is your mother's, you know, Ellen."

"I know it,—but you make me so glad!" And hiding her face in Alice's lap, she fairly sobbed.

"You understand now, don't you, how Christians may honour or dishonour their Heavenly Father?"

"Yes, I do; but it makes me afraid to think of it."

"Afraid? It ought rather to make you glad. It is a great honour and happiness for us to be permitted to honour him.—

> "'A never-dying soul to save,
> And fit it for the sky.'

"Yes—that is the great duty you owe yourself. Oh, never forget it, dear Ellen! And whatever would hinder you, have nothing to do with it. 'What will it profit a man though he gain the whole world, and lose his own soul?'

> "'To serve the present age,
> My calling to fulfil—'"

" What is ' the present age ?' " said Ellen.

" All the people who are living in the world at this time."

" But, dear Alice !—what can I do to the present age ?"

" Nothing to the most part of them certainly ; and yet, dear Ellen, if your little rushlight shines well there is just so much the less darkness in the world,—though perhaps you light only a very little corner. Every Christian is a blessing to the world ; another grain of salt to go toward sweetening and saving the mass."

" That is very pleasant to think of," said Ellen, musing.

" Oh, if we were but full of love to our Saviour, how pleasant it would be to do any thing for him ! how many ways we should find of honouring him by doing good."

" I wish you would tell me some of the ways that I can do it," said Ellen.

" You will find them fast enough if you seek them, Ellen. No one is so poor or so young but he has one talent at least to use for God."

" I wish I knew what mine is," said Ellen.

" Is your daily example as perfect as it can be ?"

Ellen was silent and shook her head.

" Christ pleased not himself, and went about doing good ; and he said, ' If any man serve me, let him *follow me.*' Remember that. Perhaps your aunt is unreasonable and unkind ;—see with how much patience and perfect sweetness of temper you can bear and forbear ; see if you cannot win her over by untiring gentleness, obedience, and meekness. Is there no improvement to be made here ?"

" Oh, me, yes !" answered Ellen with a sigh.

" Then your old grandmother. Can you do nothing to cheer her life in her old age and helplessness ? can't you find some way of giving her pleasure ? some way of amusing a long tedious hour now and then ?"

Ellen looked very grave ; in her inmost heart she knew this was a duty she shrank from.

" He ' went about doing good.' Keep that in mind. A kind word spoken,—a little thing done to smooth the way of one, or lighten the load of another,—teaching those who need teaching,—entreating those who are walking in the wrong way,—oh ! my child, there is work enough !

> " ' To serve the present age,
> My calling to fulfil ;
> Oh, may it all my powers engage
> To do my Maker's will.
>
> " ' Arm me with jealous care,
> As in thy sight to live ;
> And oh ! thy servant, Lord, prepare
> A strict account to give.' "

" An account of what?'' said Ellen.''

" You know what an account is. If I give Thomas a dollar to spend for me at Carra-carra, I expect he will give me an exact *account* when he comes back, what he has done with every. shilling of it. So must we give an account of what we have done with every thing our Lord has committed to our care,—our hands, our tongues, our time, our minds, our influence ; how much we have honoured him, how much good we have done to others, how fast and how far we have grown holy and fit for heaven.''

" It almost frightens me to hear you talk, Miss Alice.''

" Not *frighten*, dear Ellen,—that is not the word ; *sober* we ought to be ;—mindful to do nothing we shall not wish to remember in the great day of account. Do you recollect how that day is described?   Where is your Bible ?''

She opened to the 20th chapter of the Revelation.

" And I saw a great white throne, and Him that sat on it, from whose face the earth and the heaven flew away ; and there was found no place for them.

" And I saw the dead, small and great, stand before God ; and the books were opened ; and another book was opened, which is the book of life : and the dead were judged out of those things which were written in the books, according to their works.   And the sea gave up the dead which were in it ; and death and hell delivered up the dead which were in them ; and they were judged every man according to their works.   And death and hell were cast into the lake of fire.   This is the second death.

" And whosoever was not found written in the book of life was cast into the lake of fire.' '

Ellen shivered.   " That is dreadful !'' she said.

" It will be a dreadful day to all but those whose names are written in the Lamb's book of life ;—not dreadful to them, dear Ellen.''

" But how shall I be sure, dear Alice, that *my* name is written there ? and I can't be happy if I am not sure.''

" My dear child,'' said Alice tenderly, as Ellen's anxious face and glistening eyes were raised to hers, " if you love Jesus Christ you may know you are his child, and none shall pluck you out of his hand.''

" But how can I tell whether I do love him really ? sometimes I think I do, and then again sometimes I am afraid I don't at all.''

Alice answered in the words of Christ ;—" He that hath my commandments and keepeth them, he it is that loveth me.''

" Oh, I don't keep his commandments !'' said Ellen, the tears running down her cheeks.

" *Perfectly*, none of us do. But, dear Ellen, *that* is not the question. Is it your heart's desire and effort to keep them ?   Are you grieved when you fail?—There is the point. You cannot love Christ without loving to please him."

Ellen rose and putting both arms round Alice's neck laid her head there, as her manner sometimes was, tears flowing fast.

"I sometimes think I do love him a little," she said, "but I do so many wrong things. But he will teach me to love him if I ask him, won't he, dear Alice?"

"Indeed he will, dear Ellen," said Alice, folding her arms round her little adopted sister,—" *indeed* he will. He has promised that. Remember what he told somebody who was almost in despair,— 'Fear not; only believe.'"

Alice's neck was wet with Ellen's tears; and after they had ceased to flow her arms kept their hold and her head its resting-place on Alice's shoulder for some time. It was necessary at last for Alice to leave her.

Ellen waited till the sound of her horse's footsteps died away on the road; and then sinking on her knees beside her rocking-chair she poured forth her whole heart in prayers and tears. She confessed many a fault and short-coming that none knew but herself; and most earnestly besought help that "her little rushlight might shine bright." Prayer was to little Ellen what it is to all that know it,—the satisfying of doubt, the soothing of care, the quieting of trouble. She had knelt down very uneasy; but she knew that God has promised to be the hearer of prayer, and she rose up very comforted, her mind fixing on those most sweet words Alice had brought to her memory,—" Fear not—only believe." When Miss Fortune returned, Ellen was quietly asleep again in her rocking-chair, with a face very pale but calm as an evening sunbeam.

"Well, I declare if that child ain't sleeping her life away!" said Miss Fortune. "She's slept this whole blessed forenoon; I suppose she'll want to be alive and dancing the whole night to pay for it."

"I can tell you what she'll want a sight more," said Mr. Van Brunt, who had followed her in; it must have been to see about Ellen, for he was never known to do such a thing before or since; —"I'll tell you what she'll want, and that's a right hot supper. She eat as nigh as possible nothing at all this noon. There ain't much danger of her dancing a hole in your floor this some time."

CHAPTER XXIV.

Is supper ready, the house trimmed, rushes strewed, cobwebs swept?
TAMING OF THE SHREW.

GREAT preparations were making all Saturday and Monday for the expected gathering. From morning till night Miss Fortune was in a perpetual bustle. The great oven was heated no less than three several times on Saturday alone. Ellen could hear the breaking of eggs in the buttery, and the sound of beating or whisking for a long time together; and then Miss Fortune would come out with floury hands, and plates of empty egg-shells made their appearance. But Ellen saw no more. Whenever the coals were swept out of the oven and Miss Fortune had made sure that the heat was just right for her purposes, Ellen was sent out of the way, and when she got back there was nothing to be seen but the fast-shut oven door. It was just the same when the dishes in all their perfection were to come out of the oven again. The utmost Ellen was permitted to see was the napkin covering some stray cake or pie that by chance had to pass through the kitchen where she was.

As she could neither help nor look on, the day passed rather wearily. She tried studying; a very little she found was enough to satisfy both mind and body in their present state. She longed to go out again and see how the snow looked, but a fierce wind all the fore part of the day made it unfit for her. Toward the middle of the afternoon she saw with joy that it had lulled, and though very cold, was so bright and calm that she might venture. She had eagerly opened the kitchen door to go up and get ready, when a long weary yawn from her old grandmother made her look back. The old lady had laid her knitting in her lap and bent her face down to her hand, which she was rubbing across her brow as if to clear away the tired feeling that had settled there. Ellen's conscience instantly brought up Alice's words,—" Can't you do something to pass away a tedious hour now and then?" The first feeling was of vexed regret that they should have come into her head at that moment; then conscience said that was very selfish. There was a struggle. Ellen stood with the door in her hand, unable to go out or come in. But not long. As the words came back upon her memory,—" A charge to keep I have,"—her mind was made up; after one moment's prayer for help and forgiveness she shut the door, came back to the fireplace, and spoke in a cheerful tone.

" Grandma, wouldn't you like to have me read something to you ?"

" Read !" answered the old lady, " Laws a me ! *I* don't read nothing, deary."

" But wouldn't you like to have *me* read to you, grandma ?"

The old lady in answer to this laid down her knitting, folded both arms round Ellen, and kissing her a great many times declared she should like any thing that came out of that sweet little mouth. As soon as she was set free Ellen brought her Bible, sat down close beside her, and read chapter after chapter ; rewarded even then by seeing that though her grandmother said nothing she was listening with fixed attention, bending down over her knitting as if in earnest care to catch every word. And when at last she stopped, warned by certain noises down stairs that her aunt would presently be bustling in, the old lady again hugged her close to her bosom, kissing her forehead and cheeks and lips, and declaring that she was " a great deal sweeter than any sugar-plums ;" and Ellen was very much surprised to feel her face wet with a tear from her grandmother's cheek. Hastily kissing her again (for the first time in her life) she ran out of the room, her own tears starting and her heart swelling big. " Oh ! how much pleasure," she thought, " I might have given my poor grandma, and how I have let her alone all this while ! How wrong I have been. But it shan't be so in future !"

It was not quite sundown, and Ellen thought she might yet have two or three minutes in the open air. So she wrapped up very warm and went out to the chip-yard.

Ellen's heart was very light ; she had just been fulfilling a duty that cost her a little self-denial, and the reward had already come ; and now it seemed to her that she had never seen any thing so perfectly beautiful as the scene before her ;—the brilliant snow that lay in a thick carpet over all the fields and hills, and the pale streaks of sunlight stretching across it between the long shadows that reached now from the barn to the house. One moment the light tinted the snow-capped fences and whitened barn-roofs ; then the lights and the shadows vanished together, and it was all one cold dazzling white. Oh, how glorious !—Ellen almost shouted to herself. It was too cold to stand still ; she ran to the barnyard to see the cows milked. There they were,—all her old friends,—Streaky and Dolly and Jane and Sukey and Betty Flynn,—sleek and contented ; winter and summer were all the same to them. And Mr. Van Brunt was very glad to see her there again, and Sam Larkens and Johnny Low looked as if they were too, and Ellen told them with great truth she was very glad indeed to be there ; and then she went in to supper with Mr. Van Brunt and an amazing appetite.

That was Saturday. Sunday passed quietly, though Ellen could not help suspecting it was not entirely a day of rest to her aunt; there was a savoury smell of cooking in the morning which nothing that came on the table by any means accounted for, and Miss Fortune was scarcely to be seen the whole day.

With Monday morning began a grand bustle, and Ellen was well enough now to come in for her share.   The kitchen, parlour, hall, shed, and lower kitchen, must all be thoroughly swept and dusted; this was given to her, and a morning's work pretty near she found it.   Then she had to rub bright all the brass handles of the doors, and the big brass andirons in the parlour, and the brass candlesticks on the parlour mantelpiece.   When at last she got through and came to the fire to warm herself, she found her grandmother lamenting that her snuff-box was empty, and asking her daughter to fill it for her.

"Oh, I can't be bothered to be running up stairs to fill snuff-boxes!" answered that lady; "you'll have to wait."

"I'll get it, grandma," said Ellen, "if you'll tell me where."

"Sit down and be quiet!" said Miss Fortune.   "You go into my room just when I bid you, and not till then."

Ellen sat down.   But no sooner was Miss Fortune hid in the buttery than the old lady beckoned her to her side, and nodding her head a great many times, gave her the box, saying softly,

"You can run up now, she won't see you, deary.   It's in a jar in the closet.   Now's the time."

Ellen could not bear to say no.   She hesitated a minute, and then boldly opened the buttery door.

"Keep out!—what do you want?"

"She wanted me to go for the snuff," said Ellen in a whisper; "please do let me—I won't look at any thing nor touch any thing, but just get the snuff."

With an impatient gesture her aunt snatched the box from her hand, pushed Ellen out of the buttery and shut the door.   The old lady kissed and fondled her as if she had done what she had only tried to do; smoothed down her hair, praising its beauty, and whispered,

"Never mind deary,—you'll read to grandma, won't you?"

It cost Ellen no effort now.   With the beginning of kind offices to her poor old parent, kind feeling had sprung up fast; instead of disliking and shunning she had begun to love her.

There was no dinner for any one this day.   Mr. and Mrs. Van Brunt came to an early tea; after which Ellen was sent to dress herself, and Mr. Van Brunt to get some pieces of board for the meat-choppers.   He came back presently with an armful of square bits of wood; and sitting down before the fire began to whittle the rough sawn ends over the hearth.   His mother grew nervous.   Miss Fortune bore it as she would have borne it from no one else, but vexation was gathering in her breast for the first occasion. Presently Ellen's voice was heard singing down the stairs.

"I'd give something to stop that child's pipe!" said Miss Fortune; "she's eternally singing the same thing over and over—something about 'a charge to keep'—I'd a good notion to give her a charge to keep this morning; it would have been to hold her tongue."

"That would have been a public loss, *I* think," said Mr. Van Brunt gravely.

"Well, you *are* making a precious litter!" said the lady, turning short upon him.

"Never mind," said he in the same tone,—"it's nothing but what the fire'll burn up anyhow; don't worry yourself about it."

Just as Ellen came in, so did Nancy by the other door.

"What are you here for?" said Miss Fortune with an ireful face.

"Oh!—Come to see the folks and get some peaches," said Nancy;—"come to help along, to be sure."

"Ain't your grandma coming?"

"No, ma'am, she ain't. I knew she wouldn't be of much use, so I thought I wouldn't ask her."

Miss Fortune immediately ordered her out. Half laughing, half serious, Nancy tried to keep her ground, but Miss Fortune was in no mood to hear parleying. She laid violent hands on the passive Nancy, and between pulling and pushing at last got her out and shut the door. Her next sudden move was to haul off her mother to bed. Ellen looked her sorrow at this, and Mr. Van Brunt whistled *his* thoughts; but that either made nothing, or made Miss Fortune more determined. Off she went with her old mother under her arm. While she was gone Ellen brought the broom to sweep up the hearth, but Mr. Van Brunt would not let her.

"No," said he,—"it's more than you nor I can do. You know," said he with a sly look, "we might sweep up the shavings into the wrong corner!"

This entirely overset Ellen's gravity, and unluckily she could not get it back again, even though warned by Mrs. Van Brunt that her aunt was coming. Trying only made it worse, and Miss Fortune's entrance was but the signal for a fresh burst of hearty merriment. What she was laughing at was of course instantly asked, in no pleased tone of voice. Ellen could not tell; and her silence and blushing only made her aunt more curious.

"Come, leave bothering her," said Mr. Van Brunt at last, "she was only laughing at some of my nonsense, and she won't tell on me."

"Will you swear to that?" said the lady sharply.

" Humph !—no, I won't swear ; unless you will go before a mag-
istrate with me ;—but it is true."

" I wonder if you think I am as easy blinded as all that comes
to !" said Miss Fortune, scornfully.

And Ellen saw that her aunt's displeasure was all gathered upon
her for the evening. She was thinking of Alice's words and trying to arm herself with patience and gentleness, when the door
opened, and in walked Nancy as demurely as if nobody had ever
seen her before.

" Miss Fortune, granny sent me to tell you she is sorry she can't
come to-night—she don't think it would do for her to be out so late,
—she's a little touch of the rheumatics, she says."

" Very well," said Miss Fortune. " Now clear out !"

" You had better not say so, Miss Fortune—I'll do as much for
you as any two of the rest,—see if I don't !"

" I don't care—if you did as much as fifty !" said Miss Fortune,
impatiently. " I won't have you here ; so go, or I'll give you
something to help you along."

Nancy saw she had no chance with Miss Fortune in her present
humour, and went quickly out. A little while after Ellen was
standing at the window, from which through the shed window she
had a view of the chip-yard, and there she saw Nancy lingering
still, walking round and round in a circle, and kicking the snow
with her feet in a discontented fashion.

" I am very glad she isn't going to be here," thought Ellen.
" But, poor thing ! I dare say she is very much disappointed.
And how sorry she will feel going back all that long, long way
home !—what if I should get her leave to stay ? wouldn't it be a
fine way of returning good for evil ?—But oh, dear ! I don't want
her here ! But that's no matter—"

The next minute Mr. Van Brunt was half startled by Ellen's
hand on his shoulder, and the softest of whispers in his ear. He
looked up, very much surprised.

" Why, do *you* want her ?" said he, likewise in a low tone.

" No," said Ellen, " but I know I should feel very sorry if I
was in her place."

Mr. Van Brunt whistled quietly to himself. " Well !" said he,
" you *are* a good-natured piece."

" Miss Fortune," said he presently, " if that mischievous girl
comes in again I recommend you to let her stay."

" Why ?"

" 'Cause it's true what she said—she'll do you as much good as
half a dozen. She'll behave herself this evening, I'll engage,
or if she don't I'll make her."

" She's too impudent to live ! But I don't care—her grandmother is another sort,—but I guess she is gone by this time."

Ellen waited only till her aunt's back was turned. She slipped down stairs and out at the kitchen door, and ran up the slope to the fence of the chip-yard.

"Nancy—Nancy!"

"What?" said Nancy, wheeling about.

"If you go in now I guess aunt Fortune will let you stay."

"What makes you think so?" said the other surlily.

"'Cause Mr. Van Brunt was speaking to her about it. Go in and you'll see."

Nancy looked doubtfully at Ellen's face, and then ran hastily in. More slowly Ellen went back by the way she came. When she reached the upper kitchen she found Nancy as busy as possible,—as much at home already as if she had been there all day; helping to set the table in the hall, and going to and fro between that and the buttery with an important face. Ellen was not suffered to help, nor even to stand and see what was doing; so she sat down in the corner by her old friend Mrs. Van Brunt, and with her head in her lap watched by the firelight the busy figures that went back and forward, and Mr. Van Brunt who still sat working at his bits of board. There were pleasant thoughts in Ellen's head that kept the dancing blaze company. Mr. Van Brunt once looked up and asked what she was smiling at; the smile brightened at his question, but he got no more answer.

At last the supper was all set out in the hall so that it could very easily be brought into the parlour when the time came; the waiter with the best cups and saucers, which always stood covered with a napkin on the table in the front room, was carried away; the great pile of wood in the parlour fireplace, built ever since morning, was kindled; all was in apple-pie order, and nothing was left but to sweep up the shavings that Mr. Van Brunt had made. This was done; and then Nancy seized hold of Ellen.

"Come along," said she, pulling her to the window,—"come along, and let us watch the folks come in."

"But it isn't time for them to be here yet," said Ellen, "the fire is only just burning."

"Fiddle-de-dee! they won't wait for the fire to burn, I can tell you. They'll be along directly, some of them. I wonder what Miss Fortune is thinking of,—that fire had ought to have been burning this long time ago,—but they won't set to work till they all get here, that's one thing. Do you know what's going to be for supper?"

"No."

"Not a bit?"

"No."

"Ain't that funny! Then I'm better off than you. I say, Ellen, any one would think *I* was Miss Fortune's niece and you was somebody else, wouldn't they? Goodness! I'm glad I ain't. I am going to make part of the supper myself,—what do you think of that? Miss Fortune always has grand suppers—when she has 'em at all; 'tain't very often, that's one thing. I wish she'd have a bee every week, I know, and let me come and help. Hark!—didn't I tell you? there's somebody coming this minute; don't you hear the sleigh-bells? I'll tell you who it is now; it's the Lawsons; you see if it ain't. It's good it's such a bright night—we can see 'em first-rate. There—here they come—just as I told you—here's Mimy Lawson the first one—if there's any body I do despise it's Mimy Lawson."

"Hush!" said Ellen. The door opened and the lady herself walked in followed by three others—large, tall women, muffled from head to foot against the cold. The quiet kitchen was speedily changed into a scene of bustle. Loud talking and laughing—a vast deal of unrobing—pushing back and pulling up chairs on the hearth—and Nancy and Ellen running in and out of the room with countless wrappers, cloaks, shawls, comforters, hoods, mittens, and moccasins.

"What a precious muss it will be to get 'em all their own things when they come to go away again," said Nancy. "Throw 'em all down there, Ellen, in that heap. Now come quick—somebody else 'll be here directly."

"Which is Miss Mimy?" said Ellen.

"That big ugly woman in a purple frock. The one next her is Kitty—the black-haired one is Mary, and t'other is Fanny. Ugh! don't look at 'em; I can't bear 'em."

"Why?"

"'Cause I don't, I can tell you; reason good. They are as stingy as they can live. Their way is to get as much as they can out of other folks, and let other folks get as little as they can out of them. I know 'em. Just watch that purple frock when it comes to the eating. There's Mr. Bob."

"Mr. who?"

"Bob—Bob Lawson. He's a precious small young man, for such a big one. There—go take his hat. Miss Fortune," said Nancy coming forward, "mayn't the gentlemen take care of their own things in the stoop, or must the young ladies wait upon them too? t'other room won't hold every thing neither."

This speech raised a general laugh, in the midst of which Mr. Bob carried his own hat and cloak into the shed as desired. Before Nancy had done chuckling came another arrival; a tall, lank gentleman, with one of those unhappy-shaped faces that are very broad at the eyes and very narrow across the chops, and having a particularly grave and dull expression. He was welcomed with such a shout of mingled laughter, greeting, and jesting, that the room was in a complete hurly-burly; and a plain-looking stout elderly lady, who had come in just behind him, was suffered to stand unnoticed.

"It's Miss Janet," whispered Nancy,—" Mr. Marshchalk's aunt. Nobody wants to see her here; she's one of your pious kind, and that's a kind your aunt don't take to."

Instantly Ellen was at her side, offering gently to relieve her of hood and cloak, and with a tap on his arm drawing Mr. Van Brunt's attention to the neglected person.

Quite touched by the respectful politeness of her manner, the old lady inquired of Miss Fortune as Ellen went off with a load of mufflers, "who was that sweet little thing?"

"It's a kind of sweetmeats that is kept for company, Miss Janet," replied Miss Fortune with a darkened brow.

"She's too good for every-day use, that's a fact," remarked Mr. Van Brunt.

Miss Fortune coloured and tossed her head, and the company were for a moment still with surprise. Another arrival set them agoing again.

"Here come the Hitchcocks, Ellen," said Nancy. "Walk in, Miss Mary—walk in, Miss Jenny—Mr. Marshchalk has been here this great while."

Miss Mary Hitchcock was in nothing remarkable. Miss Jenny when her wrappers were taken off showed a neat little round figure, and a round face of very bright and good-humoured expression. It fastened Ellen's eye, till Nancy whispered her to look at Mr. Juniper Hitchcock, and that young gentleman entered dressed in the last style of elegance. His hair was arranged in a faultless manner—unless perhaps it had a *little* too much of the tallow candle; for when he had sat for a while before the fire it had somewhat the look of being excessively wet with perspiration. His boots were as shiny as his hair; his waistcoat was of a startling pattern; his pantaloons were very tightly strapped down; and at the end of a showy watch-ribbon hung some showy seals.

The kitchen was now one buzz of talk and good-humour. Ellen stood half smiling herself to see the universal smile, when Nancy twitched her.

"Here's more coming—Cilly Dennison, I guess—no, it's too tall;—*who* is it?"

But Ellen flung open the door with a half-uttered scream and threw herself into the arms of Alice, and then led her in; her face full of such extreme joy that it was perhaps one reason why her aunt's wore a very doubtful air as she came forward. That could not stand however against the graceful politeness and pleasantness of Alice's greeting. Miss Fortune's brow smoothed, her voice cleared, she told Miss Humphreys she was very welcome, and she meant it. Clinging close to her friend as she went from one to another, Ellen was delighted to see that every one echoed the welcome. Every face brightened at meeting hers, every eye softened, and Jenny Hitchcock even threw her arms round Alice and kissed her.

Ellen left now the window to Nancy and stood fast by her adopted sister, with a face of satisfaction it was pleasant to see, watching her very lips as they moved. Soon the door opened again, and various voices hailed the new-comer as " Jane," " Jany," and " Jane Huff." She was a decidedly plain-looking country girl, but when she came near, Ellen saw a sober sensible face and a look of thorough good nature which immediately ranked her next to Jenny Hitchcock in her fancy. Mr. Bill Huff followed, a sturdy young man; quite as plain and hardly so sensible-looking, he was still more shining with good-nature. He made no pretension to the elegance of Mr. Juniper Hitchcock; but before the evening was over, Ellen had a vastly greater respect for him.

Last, not least, came the Dennisons; it took Ellen some time to make up her mind about them. Miss Cilly, or Cecelia, was certainly very elegant indeed. Her hair was in the extremest state of nicety, with a little round curl plastered in front of each ear; how she coaxed them to stay there Ellen could not conceive. She wore a real watch, there was no doubt of that, and there was even a ring on one of her fingers with two or three blue or red stones in it. Her dress was smart, and so was her figure, and her face was pretty; and Ellen overheard one of the Lawsons whisper to Jenny Hitchcock that " there wasn't a greater lady in the land than Cilly Dennison." Her brother was very different; tall and athletic, and rather handsome, *he* made no pretension to be a gentleman. He valued his fine farming and fine cattle a great deal higher than Juniper Hitchcock's gentility.

CHAPTER XXV.

Wi' merry sangs, an' friendly cracks
I wat they didna weary :
An' unco tales, an' funnie jokes,
    Their sports were cheap an' cheery.
                                 BURNS.

As the party were all gathered it was time to set to work. The fire in the front room was burning up finely now, but Miss Fortune had no idea of having pork-chopping or apple-paring done there. One party was despatched down stairs into the lower kitchen; the others made a circle round the fire. Every one was furnished with a sharp knife, and a basket of apples was given to each two or three. Now it would be hard to say whether talking or working went on best. Not faster moved the tongues than the fingers; not smoother went the knives than the flow of talk; while there was a constant leaping of quarters of apples from the hands that had prepared them into the bowls, trays, or what-not, that stood on the hearth to receive them. Ellen had nothing to do; her aunt had managed it so, though she would gladly have shared the work that looked so pretty and pleasant in other people's hands. Miss Fortune would not let her; so she watched the rest, and amused herself as well as she could with hearing and seeing; and standing between Alice and Jenny Hitchcock, she handed them the apples out of the basket as fast as they were ready for them. It was a pleasant evening that. Laughing and talking went on merrily; stories were told; anecdotes, gossip, jokes, passed from mouth to mouth; and not one made himself so agreeable, or had so much to do with the life and pleasure of the party, as Alice. Ellen saw it, delighted. The pared apples kept dancing into the bowls and trays; the baskets got empty surprisingly fast; Nancy and Ellen had to run to the barrels in the shed again and again for fresh supplies.

"Do they mean to do all these to-night?" said Ellen to Nancy on one of these occasions.

"I don't know what *they* mean, I am sure," replied Nancy, diving down into the barrel to reach the apples; "if you had asked me what *Miss Fortune* meant, I might ha' given a guess."

"But only look," said Ellen,—"only so many done, and all these to do!—Well, I know what 'busy as a bee' means now, if I never did before."

"You'll know it better to-morrow, I can tell you."

"Why?"

"Oh, wait till you see. I wouldn't be you to-morrow for something though. Do you like sewing?"

"Sewing!" said Ellen. But "Girls! girls!—what *are* you leaving the door open for!"—sounded from the kitchen, and they hurried in.

"'Most got through, Nancy?" inquired Bob Lawson. (Miss Fortune had gone down stairs.)

"Ha'n't begun to, Mr. Lawson. There's every bit as many to do as there was at your house t'other night."

"What on airth does she want with such a sight of 'em," inquired Dan Dennison.

"Live on pies and apple-sass till next summer," suggested Mimy Lawson.

"That's the stuff for my money!" replied her brother; "'taters and apple-sass is my sass in the winter."

"It's good those is easy got," said his sister Mary; "the sass is the most of the dinner to Bob most commonly."

"Are they fixing for more apple-sass down stairs?" Mr. Dennison went on rather dryly.

"No—hush!"—said Juniper Hitchcock,—"sassages!"

"Humph!" said Dan, as he speared up an apple out of the basket on the point of his knife,—"ain't that something like what you call killing two——"

"Just that exactly," said Jenny Hitchcock, as Dan broke off short, and the mistress of the house walked in. "Ellen," she whispered, "don't you want to go down stairs and see when the folks are coming up to help us? And tell the doctor he must be spry, for we ain't a go'ng to get through in a hurry," she added, laughing.

"Which is the doctor, ma'am?"

"The doctor—Doctor Marshchalk—don't you know?"

"Is he a doctor?" said Alice.

"No, not exactly, I suppose, but he's just as good as the real. He's a natural knack at putting bones in their places and all that sort of thing. There was a man broke his leg horribly at Thirlwall the other day, and Gibson was out of the way, and Marshchàlk set it, and did it famously they said. So go, Ellen, and bring us word what they are all about."

Mr. Van Brunt was head of the party in the lower kitchen. He stood at one end of the table, cutting with his huge knife the hard-frozen pork into very thin slices, which the rest of the company took and before they had time to thaw cut up into small dice on the little boards Mr. Van Brunt had prepared. As large a fire as the chimney would hold was built up and blazing finely; the room looked as cosey and bright as the one up stairs, and the people as busy and as talkative. They had less to do, however, or they had been more smart, for they were drawing to the end of their chopping; of which Miss Janet declared herself very glad, for she said, "the wind came sweeping in under the doors and freezing her feet the whole time, and she was sure the biggest fire ever was built couldn't warm that room;" an opinion in which Mrs. Van Brunt agreed perfectly. Miss Janet no sooner spied Ellen standing in the chimney-corner than she called her to her side, kissed her, and talked to her a long time, and finally fumbling in her pocket brought forth an odd little three-cornered pincushion which she gave her for a keepsake. Jane Huff and her brother also took kind notice of her; and Ellen began to think the world was full of nice people. About half-past eight the choppers went up and joined the company who were paring apples; the circle was a very large one now, and the buzz of tongues grew quite furious.

"What are you smiling at?" asked Alice of Ellen, who stood at her elbow.

" Oh, I don't know," said Ellen, smiling more broadly; and presently added,—" they're all so kind to me."

" Who ?"

" Oh, every body—Miss Jenny, and Miss Jane Huff, and Miss Janet, and Mrs. Van Brunt, and Mr. Huff,—they all speak so kindly and look so kindly at me. But it's very funny what a notion people have for kissing—I wish they hadn't—I've run away from three kisses already, and I'm so afraid somebody else will try next."

" You don't seem very bitterly displeased," said Alice smiling.

" I am, though,—I can't bear it," said Ellen, laughing and blushing. " There's Mr. Dennison caught me in the first place and tried to kiss me, but I tried so hard to get away I believe he saw I was really in good earnest and let me go. And just now,—only think of it,—while I was standing talking to Miss Jane Huff down stairs, her brother caught me and kissed me before I knew what he was going to do. I declare it's too bad!" said Ellen, rubbing her cheek very hard as if she would rub off the affront.

" You must let it pass, my dear; it is one way of expressing kindness. They feel kindly toward you or they would not do it."

" Then I wish they wouldn't feel quite so kindly," said Ellen—" that's all. Hark !—what was that ?"

" What is that ?" said somebody else, and instantly there was silence, broken again after a minute or two by the faint blast of a horn.

" It's old Father Swaim, I reckon," said Mr. Van Brunt. " I'll go fetch him in."

" Oh, yes! bring him in—bring him in," was heard on all sides.

" That horn makes me think of what happened to me once," said Jenny Hitchcock to Ellen. " I was a little girl at school, not so big as you are,—and one afternoon when we were all as still as mice and studying away, we heard Father Swaim's horn"—

" What does he blow it for ?" said Ellen, as Jenny stooped for her knife which she had let fall.

" Oh, to let people know he's there, you know; did you never see Father Swaim ?"

" No."

" La ! he's the funniest old fellow ! He goes round and round the country carrying the newspapers; and we get him to bring us our letters from the post-office, when there are any. He carries 'em in a pair of saddle-bags hanging across that old white horse of his—I don't think that horse will ever grow old, no more than his master,—and in summer he has a stick—so long—with a horse's tail tied to the end of it, to brush away the flies, for the poor horse has had *his* tail cut off pretty short. I wonder if it isn't the very same," said Jenny, laughing heartily; "Father Swaim thought he could manage it best, I guess."

"But what was it that happened to you that time at school?" said Ellen.

"Why, when we heard the horn blow, our master, the schoolmaster you know, went out to get a paper; and I was tired with sitting still, so I jumped up and ran across the room and then back again, and over and back again five or six times; and when he came in one of the girls up and told of it. It was Fanny Lawson," said Jenny in a whisper to Alice, "and I think she ain't much different now from what she was then. I can hear her now,—'Mr. Starks, Jenny Hitchcock's been running all round the room.' Well, what do you think he did to me? He took hold of my two hands and swung me round and round by the arms till I didn't know which was head and which was feet."

"What a queer schoolmaster!" said Ellen.

"Queer enough; you may say that. His name was Starks;— the boys used to call him Starksification. We did hate him, that's a fact. I'll tell you what he did to a black boy of ours—you know our black Sam, Alice?—I forget what he had been doing; but Starks took him so—by the rims of the ears, and danced him up and down upon the floor."

"But didn't that hurt him?"

"Hurt him! I guess it did! he meant it should. He tied me under the table once. Sometimes when he wanted to punish two boys at a time he would set them to spit in each other's faces."

"Oh, don't tell me about him!" cried Ellen, with a face of horror; "I don't like to hear it."

Jenny laughed; and just then the door opened and Mr. Van Brunt and the old news-carrier came in.

He was a venerable mild-looking old man, with thin hair as white as snow. He wore a long snuff-coloured coat, and a broad-brimmed hat, the sides of which were oddly looped up to the crown with twine; his tin horn or trumpet was in his hand. His saddle bags were on Mr. Van Brunt's arm. As soon as she saw him Ellen was fevered with the notion that perhaps he had something for her, and she forgot every thing else. It would seem that the rest of the company had the same hope, for they crowded round him shouting out welcomes and questions and inquiries for letters, all in a breath.

"Softly—softly," said the old man, sitting down slowly; "not all at once; I can't attend to you all at once;—one at a time—one at a time."

"Don't attend to 'em at all till you're ready," said Miss Fortune,—"let 'em wait." And she handed him a glass of cider.

He drank it off at a breath, smacking his lips as he gave back the glass to her hand, and exclaiming, "That's prime!" Then taking up his saddle-bags from the floor, he began slowly to undo the fastenings.

"You are going to our house to-night, ain't you, Father Swaim?" said Jenny.

"That's where I *was* going," said the old man; "I *was* a going to stop with your father, Miss Jenny; but since I've got into far-mer Van Brunt's hands, I don't know any more what's going to become of me;—and after that glass of cider I don't much care! Now let's see,—let's see—'Miss Jenny Hitchcock,"—here's some-thing for you. I should like very much to know what's inside of that letter—there's a blue seal to it. Ah, young folks!—young folks!"

Jenny received her letter amidst a great deal of laughing and joking, and seemed herself quite as much amused as any body.

"'Jedediah B. Lawson,'—there's for your father, Miss Mimy; that saves me a long tramp—if you've twenty-one cents in your pocket, that is; if you ha'n't, I shall be obleeged to tramp after that. Here's something for 'most all of you, I'm thinking. 'Miss Cecilia Dennison,'—your fair hands—how's the Squire?—rheuma-tism, eh? I think I'm a younger man now than your father, Cecilly; and yet I must ha' seen a good many years more than Squire Dennison;—I must surely. 'Miss Fortune Emerson,'—that's for you; a double letter, ma'am."

Ellen, with a beating heart, had pressed nearer and nearer to the old man, till she stood close by his right hand, and could see every letter as he handed it out. A spot of deepening red was on each cheek as her eye eagerly scanned letter after letter; it spread to a sudden flush when the last name was read. Alice watched in some anxiety her keen look as it followed the letter from the old man's hand to her aunt's, and thence to the pocket, where Miss Fortune coolly bestowed it. Ellen could not stand this; she sprang for-ward across the circle.

"Aunt Fortune, there's a letter inside of that for me—won't you give it to me?—won't you give it to me?" she repeated trem-bling.

Her aunt did not notice her by so much as a look; she turned away and began talking to some one else. The red had left Ellen's face when Alice could see it again;—it was livid and spotted from stifled passion. She stood in a kind of maze. But as her eye caught Alice's anxious and sorrowful look she covered her face with her hands, and as quick as possible made her escape out of the room.

For some minutes Alice heard none of the hubbub around her. Then came a knock at the door, and the voice of Thomas Grimes saying to Mr. Van Brunt that Miss Humphreys' horse was there.

"Mr. Swaim," said Alice rising, "I don't like to leave you with these gay friends of ours; you'll stand no chance of rest with them to-night. Will you ride home with me?"

Many of the party began to beg Alice would stay to supper, but she said her father would be uneasy. The old news-carrier concluded to go with her, for he said "there was a p'int he wanted to mention to parson Humphreys that he had forgotten to bring

for'ard when they were talking on that 'ere subject two months ago." So Nancy brought her things from the next room and helped her on with them, and looked pleased, as well she might, at the smile and kind words with which she was rewarded. Alice lingered at her leave-taking, hoping to see Ellen; but it was not till the last moment that Ellen came in. She did not say a word; but the two little arms were put around Alice's neck and held her with a long, close earnestness which did not pass from her mind all the evening afterwards.

When she was gone the company sat down again to business ; and apple-paring went on more steadily than ever for a while, till the bottom of the barrels was seen, and the last basketful of apples was duly emptied. Then there was a general shout ; the kitchen was quickly cleared, and every body's face-brightened, as much as to say, "Now for fun !" While Ellen and Nancy and Miss Fortune and Mrs. Van Brunt were running all ways with trays, pans, baskets, knives, and buckets, the fun began by Mr. Juniper Hitchcock's whistling in his dog and setting him to do various feats for the amusement of the company. There followed such a rushing, leaping, barking, laughing, and scolding, on the part of the dog and his admirers, that the room was in an uproar. He jumped over a stick ; he got into a chair and sat up on two legs ; he kissed the ladies' hands ; he suffered an apple-paring to be laid across his nose, then threw it up with a jerk and caught it in his mouth. Nothing very remarkable certainly, but, as Miss Fortune observed to somebody, " if he had been the learned pig there couldn't ha' been more fuss made over him."

Ellen stood looking on, smiling partly at the dog and his master, and partly at the antics of the company. Presently Mr. Van Brunt, bending down to her, said,

" What is the matter with your eyes ?"

" Nothing," said Ellen starting,—" at least nothing that's any matter, I mean."

" Come here," said he, drawing her on one side ; " tell me all about it—what is the matter ?"

" Never mind—please don't ask me, Mr. Van Brunt—it's nothing I ought to tell you—it isn't any matter."

But her eyes were full again, and he still held her fast doubtfully.

" *I'll* tell you about it, Mr. Van Brunt," said Nancy as she came past them,—" you let her go, and I'll tell you by and by."

And Ellen tried in vain afterwards to make her promise she would not.

" Come, June," said Miss Jenny, " we have got enough of you and Jumper—turn him out; we are going to have the cat now. Come !—Puss, puss in the corner ! Go off in t'other room, will you, every body that don't want to play. Puss, puss?—"

Now the fun began in good earnest, and few minutes had passed before Ellen was laughing with all her heart, as if she never had had any thing to cry for in her life. After "puss, puss in the corner" came " blind-man's-buff;" and this was played with great spirit, the two most distinguished being Nancy and Dan Dennison, though Miss Fortune played admirably well. Ellen had seen Nancy

play before; but she forgot her own part of the game in sheer
amazement at the way Mr. Dennison managed his long body, which
seemed to go where there was no room for it, and vanish into air
just when the grasp of some grasping "blind man" was ready to
fasten upon him. And when *he* was blinded, he seemed to know
by instinct where the walls were, and keeping clear of them he
would swoop like a hawk from one end of the room to the other,
pouncing upon the unlucky people who could by no means get out
of the way fast enough. When this had lasted a while there was
a general call for "the fox and the goose;" and Miss Fortune was
pitched upon for the latter; she having in the other game showed
herself capable of good generalship. But who for the fox? Mr.
Van Brunt?

"Not I," said Mr. Van Brunt,—"there ain't nothing of the
fox about me; Miss Fortune would beat me all hollow."

"Who then, farmer?" said Bill Huff;—"come, who is the fox?
Will I do?"

"Not you, Bill; the goose 'ud be too much for you."

There was a general shout, and cries of "who then?" "who
then?"

"Dan Dennison," said Mr. Van Brunt. "Now look out for a
sharp fight."

Amidst a great deal of laughing and confusion the line was
formed, each person taking hold of a handkerchief or band passed
round the waist of the person before him, except when the women
held by each other's skirts. They were ranged according to height,
the tallest being next their leader the "goose." Mr. Van Brunt
and the elder ladies, and two or three more, chose to be lookers-on,
and took post outside the door.

Mr. Dennison began by taking off his coat, to give himself
more freedom in his movements; for his business was to catch the
train of the goose, one by one, as each in turn became the hind-
most; while *her* object was to baffle him and keep her family
together, meeting him with outspread arms at every rush he made
to seize one of her brood; while the long train behind her, following her quick movements and swaying from side to side to get
out of the reach of the furious fox, was sometimes in the shape of
the letter C, and sometimes in that of the letter S, and sometimes
looked like a long snake with a curling tail. Loud was the laughter, shrill the shrieks, as the fox drove them hither and thither,
and seemed to be in all parts of the room at once. He was a
cunning fox that, as well as a bold one. Sometimes, when they
thought him quite safe, held at bay by the goose, he dived under
or leaped over her outstretched arms and *almost* snatched hold of
little Ellen, who being the least was the last one of the party.
But Ellen played very well, and just escaped him two or three

times, till he declared she gave him so much trouble that when he caught her he would " kiss her the worst kind." Ellen played none the worse for that; however she was caught at last, and kissed too; there was no help for it; so she bore it as well as she could. Then she watched, and laughed till the tears ran down her cheeks to see how the fox and the goose dodged each other, what tricks were played, and how the long train pulled each other about. At length Nancy was caught; and then Jenny Hitchcock; and then Cecilia Dennison; and then Jane Huff, and so on, till at last the fox and the goose had a long struggle for Mimy Lawson, which would never have come to an end if Mimy had not gone over to the enemy.

There was a general pause. The hot and tired company were seated round the room, panting and fanning themselves with their pocket-handkerchiefs, and speaking in broken sentences; glad to rest even from laughing. Miss Fortune had thrown herself down on a seat close by Ellen, when Nancy came up and softly asked, " Is it time to beat the eggs now?" Miss Fortune nodded, and then drew her close to receive a long low whisper in her ear, at the end of which Nancy ran off.

" Is there anything *I* can do, aunt Fortune?" said Ellen, so gently and timidly that it ought to have won a kind answer.

" Yes," said her aunt,—" you may go and put yourself to bed; it's high time long ago." And looking round as she moved off she added "Go!"—with a little nod that as much as said, "I am in earnest."

Ellen's heart throbbed; she stood doubtful. One word to Mr. Van Brunt and she need not go,—that she knew. But as surely too that word would make trouble and do harm. And then she remembered " A charge to keep I have!"—She turned quick and quitted the room.

Ellen sat down on the first stairs she came to, for her bosom was heaving up and down, and she was determined not to cry. The sounds of talking and laughing came to her ear from the parlour, and there at her side stood the covered-up supper;—for a few minutes it was hard work to keep her resolve. The thick breath came and went very fast. Through the fanlights of the hall door, opposite to which she was sitting, the bright moonlight streamed in;— and presently, as Ellen quieted, it seemed to her fancy like a gentle messenger from its Maker, bidding his child remember him;—and then came up some words in her memory that her mother's lips had fastened there long ago;—" I love them that love me, and they that seek me early shall find me." She remembered her mother had told her it is Jesus who says this. Her lost pleasure was well nigh forgotten; and yet as she sat gazing into the moonlight Ellen's eyes were gathering tears very fast.

" Well, I *am* seeking him," she thought,—" can it be that he loves me?—Oh, I'm so glad!"

And they were glad tears that little Ellen wiped away as she went up stairs; for it was too cold to sit there long if the moon was ever so bright.

She had her hand on the latch of the door when her grandmother called out from the other room to know who was there.

" It's I, grandma."

" Ain't somebody there? Come in here—who is it?"

" It's I, grandma," said Ellen, coming to the door.

" Come in here, deary," said the old woman in a lower tone,— " what is it all? what's the matter? who's down stairs?"

" It's a bee, grandma; there's nothing the matter."

" A bee! who's been stung? what's all the noise about?"

" 'Tisn't that kind of bee, grandma; don't you know? there's a parcel of people that came to pare apples, and they've been playing games in the parlour—that's all."

" Paring apples, eh? Is there company below?"

" Yes, ma'am; a whole parcel of people."

" Dear me!" said the old lady, " I oughtn't to ha' been abed! Why ha'n't Fortune told me? I'll get right up. Ellen, you go in that fur closet and bring me my paddysoy that hangs there, and then help me on with my things; I'll get right up. Dear me! what was Fortune thinking about?"

The moonlight served very well instead of candles. After twice bringing the wrong dresses Ellen at last hit upon the " paddysoy," which the old lady knew immediately by the touch. In haste, and not without some fear and trembling on Ellen's part, she was arrayed in it; her best cap put on, not over hair in the best order Ellen feared, but the old lady would not stay to have it made better; Ellen took care of her down the stairs, and after opening the door for her went back to her room.

A little while had passed, and Ellen was just tying her nightcap strings and ready to go peacefully to sleep, when Nancy burst in.

" Ellen! Hurry! you must come right down stairs."

" Down stairs!—why, I am just ready to go to bed."

" No matter—you must come right away down. There's Mr. Van Brunt says he won't begin supper till you come."

" But does aunt Fortune want me to?"

" Yes, I tell you! and the quicker you come the better she'll be pleased. She sent me after you in all sorts of a hurry. She said she didn't know where you was."

" Said she didn't know where I was! Why, she told me herself——" Ellen began and stopped short.

" Of course!" said Nancy, " don't you think I know that? But *he* don't, and if you want to plague her you'll just tell him. Now come and be quick, will you? The supper's splendid."

Ellen lost the first view of the table, for every thing had begun to be pulled to pieces before she came in. The company were all crowded round the table, eating and talking and helping themselves; and ham and bread and butter, pumpkin pies and mince pies and apple pies, cake of various kinds, and glasses of egg-nogg and cider were in every body's hands. One dish in the middle of the big table had won the praise of every tongue; nobody could guess and many asked how it was made, but Miss Fortune kept a satisfied silence, pleased to see the constant stream of comers to the big dish till it was near empty. Just then Mr. Van Brunt seeing Ellen had nothing gathered up all that was left and gave it to her.

It was sweet and cold and rich. Ellen told her mother afterwards it was the best thing she had ever tasted except the ice-cream she once gave her in New York. She had taken, however, but one spoonful when her eye fell upon Nancy, standing back of all the company, and forgotten. Nancy had been upon her good behaviour all the evening, and it was a singular proof of this that she had not pushed in and helped herself among the first. Ellen's eye went once or twice from her plate to Nancy, and then she crossed over and offered it to her. It was eagerly taken, and a little disappointed Ellen stepped back again. But she soon forgot the disappointment. "She'll know now that I don't bear her any grudge," she thought.

"Ha'n't you got nothing?" said Nancy, coming up presently; "that wasn't your'n that you gave me, was it?"

Ellen nodded smilingly.

"Well, there ain't no more of it," said Nancy. "The bowl is empty."

"I know it," said Ellen.

"Why, didn't you like it?"

"Yes—very much."

"Why, you're a queer little fish," said Nancy. "What did you get Mr. Van Brunt to let me in for?"

"How did you know I did?"

"'Cause he told me. Say—what did you do it for? Mr. Dennison, won't you give Ellen a piece of cake or something? Here —take this," said Nancy, pouncing upon a glass of egg-nogg which a gap in the company enabled her to reach; "I made it more than half myself. Ain't it good?"

"Yes, very," said Ellen, smacking her lips; "what's in it?"

"Oh, plenty of good things. But what made you ask Mr. Van Brunt to let me stop to-night? you didn't tell me—did you want me to stay?"

"Never mind," said Ellen; "don't ask me any questions."

"Yes but I will though, and you've got to answer me. Why did you? Come!—do you like me?—say?"

"I should like you, I dare say, if you would be different."

"Well, I don't care," said Nancy, after a little pause,—"I like *you*, though you're as queer as you can be. I don't care whether you like me or not. Look here, Ellen, *that* cake there is the best —I know it is, for I've tried 'em all.—You know I told Van Brunt I would tell him what you were crying about?"

"Yes, and I asked you not. Did you?"

Nancy nodded, being at the moment still further engaged in "trying" the cake.

"I am sorry you did. What did he say?"

"He didn't say much to *me*—somebody else will hear of it, I guess. He *was* mad about it, or I am mistaken. What makes you sorry?"

"It will only do harm and make aunt Fortune angry."

"Well, that's just what I should like if I were you. I can't make you out."

"I'd a great deal rath_r have her like me," said Ellen. "Was she vexed when grandma came down?"

"I don't know, but she had to keep it to herself if she was; every body else was so glad, and Mr. Van Brunt made such a fuss. Just look at the old lady, how pleased she is. I declare, if the folks ain't talking of going! Come, Ellen! now for the cloaks! you and me 'll finish our supper afterwards."

That, however, was not to be. Nancy was offered a ride home to Mrs. Van Brunt's and a lodging there. They were ready cloaked and shawled, and Ellen was still hunting for Miss Janet's things in the moonlit hall, when she heard Nancy close by, in a lower tone than common, say,

"Ellen—will you kiss me?"

Ellen dropped her armful of things, and taking Nancy's hands, gave her truly the kiss of peace.

When she went up to undress for the second time, she found on her bed—her letter! And with tears Ellen kneeled down and gave earnest thanks for this blessing, and that she had been able to gain Nancy's good-will.

CHAPTER XXVI.

"He was a gentleman on whom I built an absolute trust."
MACBETH.

IT was Tuesday the 22d of December, and late in the day. Not a pleasant afternoon. The grey snow-clouds hung low; the air was keen and raw. It was already growing dark, and Alice was sitting alone in the firelight, when two little feet came running round the corner of the house; the glass door opened and Ellen rushed in.

"I have come! I have come!" she exclaimed. "Oh, dear Alice! I'm so glad!"

So was Alice if her kiss meant any thing.

"But how late, my child! how late you are."

"Oh, I thought I never was going to get done," said Ellen, pulling off her things in a great hurry and throwing them on the sofa, —"but I am here at last. Oh, I'm so glad!"

"Why, what has been the matter?" said Alice, folding up what Ellen laid down.

"Oh, a great deal of matter—I couldn't think what Nancy meant last night—I know very well now. I shan't want to see any more apples all winter. What do you think I have been about all to-day, dear Miss Alice?"

"Nothing that has done you much harm," said Alice smiling— "if I am to guess from your looks. You are as rosy as a good Spitzenberg yourself."

"That's very funny," said Ellen laughing, "for aunt Fortune said awhile ago that my cheeks were just the colour of two mealy potatoes."

"But about the apples?" said Alice.

"Why, this morning I was thinking I would come here so early, when the first thing I knew aunt Fortune brought out all those heaps and heaps of apples into the kitchen, and made me sit down on the floor, and then she gave me a great big needle and set me to stringing them all together, and as fast as I strung them she hung them up all round the ceiling. I tried very hard to get through before, but I could not, and I am so tired! I thought I never *should* get to the bottom of that big basket."

"Never mind, love—come to the fire—we'll try and forget all disagreeable things while we are together."

"I have forgotten it almost already," said Ellen, as she sat down in Alice's lap and laid her face against hers;—"I don't care for it at all now."

But her cheeks were fast fading into the uncomfortable colour Miss Fortune had spoken of; and weariness and weakness kept her for a while quiet in Alice's arms, overcoming even the pleasure of talking. They sat so till the clock struck half-past five; then Alice proposed they should go into the kitchen and see Margery, and order the tea made, which she had no doubt Ellen wanted. Margery welcomed her with great cordiality. She liked any body that Alice liked, but she had besides declared to her husband that Ellen was "an uncommon, well-behaved child." She said she would put the tea to draw, and they should have it in a very few minutes.

"But, Miss Alice, there's an Irish body out by, waiting to speak to you. I was just coming in to tell you; will you please to see her now?"

"Certainly—let her come in. Is she in the cold, Margery?"

"No, Miss Alice—there's a fire there this evening. I'll call her."

The woman came up from the lower kitchen at the summons. She was young, rather pretty, and with a pleasant countenance, but unwashed, uncombed, untidy,—no wonder Margery's nicety had shrunk from introducing her into her spotless upper kitchen. The unfailing Irish cloak was drawn about her, the hood brought over her head, and on the head and shoulders the snow lay white, not yet melted away.

"Did you wish to speak to me, my friend?" said Alice pleasantly.

"If ye plase, ma'am, it's the master I'm wanting," said the woman, dropping a curtsey.

"My father? Margery, will you tell him?"

Margery departed.

"Come nearer the fire," said Alice,—"and sit down: my father will be here presently. It is snowing again, is it not?"

"It is, ma'am;—a bitter storm."

"Have you come far?"

"It's a good bit, my lady—it's more nor a mile beyant Carra— just right forgin the ould big hill they call the Catchback;—in Jemmy Morrison's woods—where Pat M'Farren's clearing is—it's there I live, my lady."

"That is a long distance indeed for a walk in the snow," said Alice kindly; "sit down and come nearer the fire. Margery will give you something to refresh you."

"I thank ye, my lady, but I want nothing man can give me the night; and when one's on an arrant of life and death, it's little the cold or the storm can do to put out the heart's fire."

"Life and death? who is sick?" said Alice.

"It's my own child, ma'am,—my own boy—all the child I have —and I'll have none by the morning light."

" Is he so ill ?" said Alice ; " what is the matter with him ?"
" Myself doesn't know."

The voice was fainter ; the brown cloak was drawn over her face ; and Alice and Ellen saw her shoulders heaving with the grief she kept from bursting out. They exchanged glances.

" Sit down," said Alice again presently, laying her hand upon the wet shoulder ;—" sit down and rest; my father will be here directly. Margery—oh, that's right,—a cup of tea will do her good. What do you want with my father ?"

" The Lord bless ye !—I'll tell you, my lady."

She drank off the tea, but refused something more substantial that Margery offered her.

" The Lord bless ye ! I couldn't. My lady, there wasn't a stronger, nor a prettier, nor a swater child, nor couldn't be, nor he was when we left it—it'll be three years come the fifteenth of April next; but I'm thinking the bitter winters o' this cowld country has chilled the life out o' him,—and troubles cowlder than all," she added in a lower tone. " I seed him grow waker an' waker an' his daar face grow thinner an' thinner, and the red all left it, only two burning spots was on it some days; an' I worried the life out o' me for him, an' all I could do I couldn't do nothing at all to help him, for he just growed waker an' waker. I axed the father wouldn't he see the doctor about him, but he's an' 'asy kind o' man, my lady, an' he said he would, an' he never did to this day ; an' John he always said it was no use sinding for the doctor, an' looked so swate at me, an' said for me not to fret, for sure he'd be better soon, or he'd go to a better place. An' I thought he was like a heavenly angel itself already, an' always was, but then more nor ever. Och! it's soon that he'll be one entirely !—let Father Shannon say what he will."

She sobbed for a minute, while Alice and Ellen looked on, silent and pitying.

" An' to-night, my lady, he's very bad," she went on, wiping away the tears that came quickly again,—" an' I seed he was going fast from me, an' I was breaking my heart wid the loss of him, whin I heard one of the men that was in it say, ' What's this he's saying ?' says he. ' An' what is it thin ?' says I. ' About the jantleman that praaches at Carra,' says he,—' he's a calling for him,' says he. I knowed there wasn't a praast at all at Carra, an' I thought he was draaming, or out o' his head, or crazy wid his sickness, like; an' I went up close to him, an' says I, ' John,' says I, ' what is it you want,' says I,—' an' sure if it's any thing in heaven above or in earth beneath that yer own mother can get for ye,' says I,—' ye shall have it,' says I. An' he put up his two arms to my neck an' pulled my face down to his lips, that was hot wid the faver, an' kissed me—he did—an' says he, ' Mother daar,'

says he,—'if ye love me,' says he, 'fetch me the good jantleman
that praaches at Carra till I spake to him.' 'Is it the praast you
want, John my boy?' says I,—'sure he's in it,' says I;—for
Michael had been for Father Shannon, an' he had come home wid
him half an hour before. 'Oh, no, mother,' says he, 'it's not him
at all that I maan—it's the jantleman that spakes in the little white
church at Carra,—he's not a praast at all,' says he. 'An' who is
he thin?' says I, getting up from the bed, 'or where will I find
him, or how will I get to him?' 'Ye'll not stir a fut for him thin
the night Kitty Dolan,' says my husband,—'are ye mad,' says he;
'sure it's not his own head the child has at all at all, or it's a little
hiritic he is,' says he; 'an' ye won't show the disrespect to the
praast in yer own house.' 'I'm maaning none,' says I,—'nor
more he isn't a hiritic, but if he was, he's a born angel to you
Michael Dolan anyhow,' says I; 'an' wid the kiss of his lips on
my face wouldn't I do the arrant of my own boy, an' he a dying?
by the blessing, an' I will, if twenty men stud between me an' it.
So tell me where I'll find him, this praast, if there's the love o'
mercy in any sowl o' ye,' says I. But they wouldn't spake a word
for me, not one of them; so I axed an' axed at one place an' other,
till here I am. An' now, my lady, will the master go for me to
my poor boy?—for he'd maybe be dead while I stand here."

"Surely I will," said Mr. Humphreys, who had come in while
she was speaking. "Wait but one moment."

In a moment he came back ready, and he and the woman set
forth to their walk. Alice looked out anxiously after them.

"It storms very hard," she said,—"and he has not had his tea!
But he couldn't wait. Come, Ellen, love, we'll have ours. How
will he ever get back again! it will be so deep by that time."

There was a cloud on her fair brow for a few minutes, but it
passed away, and quiet and calm as ever she sat down at the little
tea-table with Ellen. From *her* face all shadows seemed to have
flown for ever. Hungry and happy, she enjoyed Margery's good
bread and butter, and the nice honey, and from time to time cast
very bright looks at the dear face on the other side of the table,
which could not help looking bright in reply. Ellen was well
pleased for her part that the third seat was empty. But Alice
looked thoughtful sometimes as a gust of wind swept by, and once
or twice went to the window.

After tea Alice took out her work, and Ellen put herself contentedly down on the rug, and sat leaning back against her. Silent for very contentment for a while, she sat looking gravely into
the fire; while Alice's fingers drove a little steel hook through and
through some purse silk in a mysterious fashion that no eye could
be quick enough to follow, and with such skill and steadiness that
the work grew fast under her hand.

"I had such a funny dream last night," said Ellen.

"Did you? what about?"

"It was pleasant too," said Ellen, twisting herself round to talk, —"but very queer. I dreamed about that gentleman that was so kind to me on board the boat—you know?—I told you about him?"

"Yes, I remember."

"Well, I dreamed of seeing him somewhere, I don't know where, —and he didn't look a bit like himself, only I knew who it was; and I thought I didn't like to speak to him for fear he wouldn't know *me*, but then I thought he did, and came up and took my hand, and seemed so glad to see me; and he asked me if I had been *pious* since he saw me."

Ellen stopped to laugh.

"And what did you tell him?"

"I told him yes. And/ then I thought he seemed so very pleased."

"Dreamers do not always keep close to the truth, it seems."

"*I* didn't," said Ellen. "But then I thought I had, in my dream."

"Had what? kept close to the truth?"

"No, no ;—been what he said."

"Dreams are queer things," said Alice.

"I have been far enough from being good to-day," said Ellen, thoughtfully.

"How so, my dear?"

"I don't know, Miss Alice—because I never *am* good, I suppose."

"But what has been the matter to-day?"

"Why, those apples! I thought I would come here so early, and then when I found I must do all those baskets of apples first I was very ill-humoured; and aunt Fortune saw I was and said something that made me worse. And I tried as hard as I could to get through before dinner, and when I found I couldn't I said I wouldn't come to dinner, but she made me, and that vexed me more, and I wouldn't eat scarcely any thing, and then when I got back to the apples again I sewed so hard that I ran the needle into my finger ever so far,—see there? what a mark it left?—and aunt Fortune said it served me right and she was glad of it, and that made me angry. I knew I was wrong afterwards, and I was very sorry. Isn't it strange, dear Alice, I should do so when I have resolved so hard I wouldn't?"

"Not very, my darling, as long as we have such evil hearts as ours are—it *is* strange they should be so evil."

"I told aunt Fortune afterwards I was sorry, but she said ' actions speak louder than words, and words are cheap.' If she only wouldn't say that just as she does! it does worry me so."

" Patience !" said Alice, passing her hand over Ellen's hair as she sat looking sorrowfully up at her ; " you must try not to give her occasion. Never mind what she says, and overcome evil with good."

" That is just what mamma said !" exclaimed Ellen, rising to throw her arms round Alice's neck, and kissing her with all the energy of love, gratitude, repentance, and sorrowful recollection.

" Oh, what do you think !" she said suddenly, her face changing again,—" I got my letter last night !"

" Your letter !"

" Yes, the letter the old man brought—don't you know ? and it was written on the ship, and there was only a little bit from mamma, and a little bit from papa, but so good ! papa says she is a great deal better, and he has no doubt he will bring her back in the spring or summer quite well again. Isn't that good ?"

" Very good, dear Ellen. I am very glad for you."

" It was on my bed last night. I can't think how it got there, —and I don't care either, so long as I have got it. What are you making ?"

" A purse," said Alice, laying it on the table for her inspection.

" It will be very pretty. Is the other end to be like this ?"

" Yes, and these tassels to finish them off."

" Oh, that's beautiful," said Ellen, laying them down to try the effect ;—" and these rings to fasten it with. Is it black ?"

" No, dark green. I am making it for my brother John."

" A Christmas present !" exclaimed Ellen.

" I am afraid not ; he will hardly be here by that time. It may do for New Year."

" How pleasant it must be to make Christmas and New Year presents !" said Ellen, after she had watched Alice's busy fingers for a few minutes. " I wish I could make something for some-body. Oh, I wonder if I couldn't make something for Mr. Van Brunt ! Oh, I should like to very much."

Alice smiled at Ellen's very wide-open eyes.

" What could you make for him ?"

" I don't know—that's the thing. He keeps his money in his pocket,—and besides, I don't know how to make purses."

" There are other things besides purses. How would a watch-guard do ? Does he wear a watch ?"

" I don't know whether he does or not ; he doesn't every day, I am sure, but I don't know about Sundays."

" Then we won't venture upon that. You might knit him a nightcap."

" A nightcap !—you're joking, Alice, aren't you ? I don't think a nightcap would be pretty for a Christmas present, do you ?"

" Well, what shall we do, Ellen ?" said Alice laughing. " I

made a pocket-pincushion for papa once when I was a little girl, but I fancy Mr. Van Brunt would not know exactly what use to make of such a convenience. I don't think you could fail to please him though, with any thing you should hit upon.''

" I have got a dollar,'' said Ellen, " to buy stuff with ; it came in my letter last night. If I only knew what !''

Down she went on the rug again, and Alice worked in silence, while Ellen's thoughts ran over every possible and impossible article of Mr. Van Brunt's dress.

" I have some nice pieces of fine linen,'' said Alice ; " suppose I cut out a collar for him, and you can make it and stitch it, and then Margery will starch and iron it for you, all ready to give to him. How will that do ? Can you stitch well enough ?''

" Oh, yes, I guess I can,'' said Ellen. " Oh, thank you, dear Alice ! you are the best help that ever was. Will he like that, do you think ?''

" I am sure he will—very much.''

" Then that will do nicely,'' said Ellen, much relieved. " And now what do you think about Nancy's Bible ?''

" Nothing could be better, only that I am afraid Nancy would either sell it for something else, or let it go to destruction very quickly. I never heard of her spending five minutes over a book, and the Bible, I am afraid, last of all.''

" But I think,'' said Ellen slowly, " I think she would not spoil it or sell it either, if *I* gave it to her.''

And she told Alice about Nancy's asking for the kiss last night.

" That's the most hopeful thing I have heard about Nancy for a long time,'' said Alice. " We will get her the Bible by all means, my dear,—a nice one,—and I hope you will be able to persuade her to read it.''

She rose as she spoke and went to the glass door. Ellen followed her, and they looked out into the night. It was very dark. She opened the door a moment, but the wind drove the snow into their faces, and they were glad to shut it again.

" It's almost as bad as the night we were out, isn't it ?'' said Ellen.

" Not such a heavy fall of snow I think, but it is very windy and cold. Papa will be late getting home.''

" I am sorry you are worried, dear Alice.''

" I am not *much* worried, love. I have often known papa out late before, but this is rather a hard night for a long walk. Come, we'll try to make a good use of the time while we are waiting. Suppose you read to me while I work.''

She took down a volume of Cowper and found his account of the three pet hares. Ellen read it, and then several of his smaller pieces of poetry. Then followed a long talk about hares and other animals ; about Cowper and his friends and his way of life. Time passed swiftly away ; it was getting late.

" How weary papa will be," said Alice, " he has had nothing to eat since dinner. I'll tell you what we'll do, Ellen," she exclaimed as she threw her work down, " we'll make some chocolate for him —that'll be the very thing. Ellen, dear, run into the kitchen and ask Margery to bring me the little chocolate pot and a pitcher of night's milk."

Margery brought them. The pot was set on the coals, and Alice had cut up the chocolate that it might melt the quicker. Ellen watched it with great interest, till it was melted, and the boiling water stirred in, and the whole was simmering quietly on the coals.

" Is it done now ?"

" No, it must boil a little while, and then the milk must be put in, and when that has boiled, the eggs—and then it will be done."

With Margery and the chocolate pot the cat had walked in. Ellen immediately endeavoured to improve his acquaintance ; that was not so easy. The Captain chose the corner of the rug furthest from her, in spite of all her calling and coaxing, paying her no more attention than if he had not heard her. Ellen crossed over to him and began most tenderly and respectfully to stroke his head and back, touching his soft fur with great care. Parry presently lifted up his head uneasily, as much as to say, " I wonder how long this is going to last,"—and finding there was every prospect of its lasting some time, he fairly got up and walked over to the other end of the rug. Ellen followed him and tried again, with exactly the same effect.

" Well cat ! you aren't very kind," said she at length ;—" Alice, he won't let me have any thing to do with him !"

" I am sorry, my dear, he is so unsociable ; he is a cat of very bad taste—that is all I can say."

" But I never saw such a cat ! he won't let me touch him ever so softly ; he lifts up his head and looks as cross !—and then walks off."

" He don't know you yet, and truth is, Parry has no fancy for extending the circle of his acquaintance. Oh, kitty, kitty !" said Alice, fondly stroking his head, " why don't you behave better ?"

Parry lifted his head, and opened and shut his eyes, with an expression of great satisfaction very different from that he had bestowed on Ellen. Ellen gave him up for the present as a hopeless case, and turned her attention to the chocolate, which had now received the milk and must be watched lest it should run over, which Alice said it would very easily do when once it began to boil again. Meanwhile Ellen wanted to know what chocolate was made of—where it came from—where it was made best,—burning her little face in the fire all the time lest the pot should boil over while she was not looking. At last the chocolate began to gather a rich froth, and Ellen called out,

"Oh, Alice! look here quick! here's the shape of the spoon on the top of the chocolate! do look at it."

An iron spoon was in the pot, and its shape was distinctly raised on the smooth frothy surface. As they were both bending forward

to watch it, Alice waiting to take the pot off the moment it began to boil, Ellen heard a slight click of the lock of the door, and turning her head was a little startled to see a stranger there, standing still at the far end of the room. She touched Alice's arm without looking round. But Alice started to her feet with a slight scream, and in another minute had thrown her arms round the stranger and was locked in his. Ellen knew what it meant now very well. She turned away as if she had nothing to do with what was going on there, and lifted the pot of chocolate off the fire with infinite difficulty; but it was going to boil over, and she would have broken her back rather than not do it. And then she stood with her back to the brother and sister, looking into the fire, as if she was determined not to see them till she couldn't help it. But what she was thinking of, Ellen could not have told, then or after-wards. It was but a few minutes, though it seemed to her a great many, before they drew near the fire. Curiosity began to be strong, and she looked round to see if the new-comer was like Alice. No, not a bit,—how different!—darker hair and eyes—not a bit like her; handsome enough, too, to be her brother. And Alice did not look like herself; her usually calm sweet face was quivering and sparkling now,—lit up as Ellen had never seen it,—oh, how bright! Poor Ellen herself had never looked duller in her life; and when Alice said gayly, "This is my brother, Ellen,"—her con-fusion of thoughts and feelings resolved themselves into a flood of tears; she sprang and hid her face in Alice's arms.

Ellen's were not the only eyes that were full just then, but of course she didn't know that.

"Come, Ellen," whispered Alice, presently, "look up!—what kind of a welcome is this? come!—we have no business with tears just now,—won't you run into the kitchen for me, love," she added more low, "and ask Margery to bring some bread and butter, and any thing else she has that is fit for a traveller?"

Glad of an escape, Ellen darted away that her wet face might not be seen. The brother and sister were busily talking when she returned.

"John," said Alice, "this is my little sister that I wrote you about—Ellen Montgomery. Ellen, this is your brother as well as mine, you know."

"Stop! stop!" said her brother. "Miss Ellen, this sister of mine is giving us away to each other at a great rate,—I should like to know first what you say to it. Are you willing to take a strange brother upon her recommendation?"

Half inclined to laugh, Ellen glanced at the speaker's face, but meeting the grave though somewhat comical look of two very keen eyes, she looked down again, and merely answered "yes."

"Then if I am to be your brother you must give me a brother's right, you know," said he, drawing her gently to him, and kissing her gravely on the lips.

Probably Ellen thought there was a difference between John Humphreys and Mr. Van Brunt, or the young gentlemen of the apple-paring; for though she coloured a good deal, she made no objection and showed no displeasure. Alice and she now busied themselves with getting the cups and saucers out of the cupboard, and setting the table ; but all that evening, through whatever was doing, Ellen's eyes sought the stranger as if by fascination. She watched him whenever she could without being noticed. At first she was in doubt what to think of him ; she was quite sure from that one look into his eyes that he was a person to be feared ;— there was no doubt of that; as to the rest she didn't know.

" And what have my two sisters been doing to spend the evening ?" said John Humphreys, one time that Alice was gone into the kitchen on some kind errand for him.

" Talking, sir,"—said Ellen doubtfully.

" Talking ! this whole evening ? Alice must have improved. What have you been talking about ?"

" Hares—and dogs—and about Mr. Cowper—and some other things,——"

" Private affairs, eh ?" said he, with again the look Ellen had seen before.

" Yes, sir," said Ellen, nodding and laughing.

" And how came you upon Mr. Cowper ?"

" Sir ?"

" How came you to be talking about Mr. Cowper ?"

" I was reading about his hares, and about John Gilpin; and then Alice told me about Mr. Cowper and his friends."

" Well I don't know after all that you have had a pleasanter evening than I have had," said her questioner, " though I have been riding hard, with the cold wind in my face, and the driving snow doing all it could to discomfit me. I have had this very bright fireside before me all the way."

He fell into a fit of grave musing which lasted till Alice came in. Then suddenly fell a fumbling in his pocket.

" Here's a note for you," said he, throwing it into her lap.

" A note !—Sophia Marshman !—where did you get it ?"

" From her own hand. Passing there to-day I thought I must stop a moment to speak to them, and had no notion of doing more ; but Mrs. Marshman was very kind, and Miss Sophia in despair, so the end of it was I dismounted and went in to await the preparing of that billet, while my poor nag was led off to the stables and a fresh horse supplied me,—I fancy that tells you on what conditions."

" Charming !" said Alice, " to spend Christmas,—I am very glad ; I should like to very much—with you dear. If I can only get papa—but I think he will ; it will do him a great deal of good. To-morrow, she says, we must come ; but I doubt the weather will not let us ; we shall see."

" I rode Prince Charlie down. He is a good traveller, and the sleighing will be fine if the snow be not too deep. The old sleigh is in being yet, I suppose ?"

" Oh, yes ! in good order.   Ellen what are you looking so grave about ? you are going too."

" I !" said Ellen, a great spot of crimson coming in each cheek.

" To be sure ; do you think I am going to leave you behind ?"

" But——"

" But what ?"

" There won't be room."

" Room in the sleigh ?   Then we'll put John on Prince Charlie, and let him ride there, postilion-fashion."

" But—Mr. Humphreys ?"

" He always goes on horseback ; he will ride Sharp or old John."

In great delight Ellen gave Alice an earnest kiss ; and then they all gathered round the table to take their chocolate, or rather to see John take his, which his sister would not let him wait for any longer.   The storm had ceased, and through the broken clouds the moon and stars were looking out, so they were no more uneasy for Mr. Humphreys and expected him every moment.   Still the supper was begun and ended without him, and they had drawn round the fire again before his welcome step was at last heard.

There was new joy then ; new embracing, and questioning and answering ; the little circle opened to let him in ; and Alice brought the corner of the table to his side, and poured him out a cup of hot chocolate.   But after drinking half of it, and neglecting the eatables beside him, he sat with one hand in the other, his arm leaning on his knee, with a kind of softened gravity upon his countenance.

" Is your chocolate right, papa ?" said Alice at length.

" *Very* good, my daughter !"

He finished the cup, but then went back to his old attitude and look.   Gradually they ceased their conversation, and waited with respectful affection and some curiosity for him to speak ; something of more than common interest seemed to be in his thoughts.   He sat looking earnestly in the fire, sometimes with almost a smile on his face, and gently striking one hand in the palm of the other. And sitting so, without moving or stirring his eyes, he said at last, as though the words had been forced from him, " Thanks be unto God for his unspeakable gift !"

As he added no more, Alice said gently, " What have you seen to-night, papa ?"

He roused himself and pushed the empty cup toward her.

" A little more, my daughter :—I have seen the fairest sight, almost, a man can see in this world.   I have seen a little ransomed spirit go home to its rest.   Oh, that ' unspeakable gift !' "—

He pressed his lips thoughtfully together while he stirred his chocolate ; but having drunk it he pushed the table from him and drew up his chair.

" You had a long way to go, papa," observed Alice again.

" Yes—a long way there—I don't know what it was coming home; I never thought of it. How independent the spirit can be of externals! I scarcely felt the storm to-night."

" Nor I," said his son.

" I had a long way to go," said Mr. Humphreys; " that poor woman — that Mrs. Dolan—she lives in the woods behind the Cat's Back, a mile beyond Carra-carra, or more—it seemed a long mile to-night; and a more miserable place I never saw yet. A little rickety shanty, the storm was hardly kept out of it, and no appearance of comfort or nicety anywhere or in any thing. There were several men gathered round the fire, and in a corner, on a miserable kind of bed, I saw the sick child. His eye met mine the moment I went in, and I thought I had seen him before, but couldn't at first make out where. Do you remember, Alice, a little ragged boy, with a remarkably bright pleasant face, who has planted himself regularly every Sunday morning for some time past in the south aisle of the church, and stood there all service time ?"

Alice said no.

" I have noticed him often, and noticed him as paying a most fixed and steady attention. I have repeatedly tried to catch him on his way out of church, to speak to him, but always failed. I asked him to night, when I first went in, if he knew me. ' I do, sir,' he said. I asked him where he had seen me. He said, ' In the church beyant.' ' So,' said I, ' you are the little boy I have seen there so regularly; what did you come there for?"

" ' To hear yer honor spake the good words.'

" ' What good words?' said I; ' about what?'

" He said, ' About Him that was slain and washed us from our sins in his own blood.'

" ' And do you think he has washed away yours?' I said.

" He smiled at me very expressively. I suppose it was some-what difficult for him to speak; and to tell the truth so it was for me, for I was taken by surprise; but the people in the hut had gathered round, and I wished to hear him say more, for their sake as well as my own. I asked him why he thought his sins were washed away. He gave me for answer part of the verse, ' Suffer little children to come unto me,' but did not finish it. ' Do you think you are very sick, John ?' I asked.

" ' I am, sir,' he said,—' I'll not be long here.'

" ' And where do you think you are going then ?' said I.

" He lifted one little thin bony arm from under his coverlid, and through all the dirt and pallor of his face the smile of heaven I am sure was on it, as he looked and pointed upward and answered, ' Jesus !'

"I asked him presently, as soon as I could, what he had wished to see me for. I don't know whether he heard me or not; he lay with his eyes half closed, breathing with difficulty. I doubted whether he would speak again; and indeed, for myself, I had heard and seen enough to satisfy me entirely;—for the sake of the group around the bed I could have desired something further. They kept perfect stillness; awed, I think, by a profession of faith such as they had never heard before. They and I stood watching him, and at the end of a few minutes, not more than ten or fifteen, he opened his eyes and with sudden life and strength rose up half way in bed, exclaiming, 'Thanks be to God for his unspeakable gift!'—and then fell back—just dead."

The old gentleman's voice was husky as he finished, for Alice and Ellen were both weeping, and John Humphreys had covered his face with his hands.

"I have felt," said the old gentleman presently,—"as if I could have shouted out his words—his dying words—all the way as I came home. My little girl," said he, drawing Ellen to him, "do you know the meaning of those sweet things of which little John Dolan's mind was so full?"

Ellen did not speak.

"Do you know what it is to be a sinner?—and what it is to be a forgiven child of God?"

"I believe I do, sir," Ellen said.

He kissed her forehead and blessed her; and then said, "Let us pray."

It was late; the servants had gone to bed, and they were alone. Oh, what a thanksgiving Mr. Humphreys poured forth for that "unspeakable gift;"—that they, every one there, had been made to know and rejoice in it; for the poor little boy, rich in faith, who had just gone home in the same rejoicing; for their own loved one who was there already; and for the hope of joining them soon in safety and joy, to sing with them the "new song" for ever and ever.

There were no dry eyes in the room. And when they arose, Mr. Humpreys, after giving his daughter the usual kiss for good night, gave one to Ellen too, which he had never done before, and then going to his son and laying both hands on his shoulders, kissed his cheek also; then silently took his candle and went.

They lingered a little while after he was gone, standing round the fire as if loth to part, but in grave silence, each busy with his own thoughts. Alice's ended by fixing on her brother, for laying her hand and her head carelessly on his shoulder, she said, "And so you have been well all this time, John?"

He turned his face toward her without speaking, but Ellen as well as his sister saw the look of love with which he answered her question, rather of endearment than inquiry; and from that min-ute Ellen's mind was made up as to the doubt which had troubled her. She went to bed quite satisfied that her new brother was a decided acquisition.

CHAPTER XXVII.

The night was winter in his roughest mood,
The morning sharp and clear . . .
. . . The vault is blue
Without a cloud, and white without a speck
The dazzling splendour of the scene below.
COWPER.

BEFORE Ellen's eyes were open the next morning—almost before she awoke—the thought of the Christmas visit, the sleigh-ride, John Humphreys, and the weather, all rushed into her mind at once, and started her half up in the bed to look out of the window. Well frosted the panes of glass were, but at the corners and edges unmistakable bright gleams of light came in.

"Oh, Alice, it's beautiful!" exclaimed Ellen; "look how the sun is shining! and 'tisn't very cold. Are we going to-day?"

"I don't know yet, Ellie, but we shall know very soon. We'll settle that at breakfast."

At breakfast it was settled. They were to go, and set off di-rectly. Mr. Humphreys could not go with them, because he had promised to bury little John Dolan; the priest had declared *he* would have nothing to do with it; and the poor mother had applied to Mr. Humphreys, as being the clergyman her child had most trusted and loved to hear. It seemed that little John had per-suaded her out of half her prejudices by his affectionate talk and blameless behaviour during some time past. Mr. Humphreys, therefore, must stay at home that day. He promised, however, to follow them the next, and would by no means permit them to wait for him. He said the day was fine, and they must improve it; and he should be pleased to have them with their friends as long as possible.

So the little travelling bag was stuffed, with more things than it seemed possible to get into it. Among the rest Ellen brought her little red Bible, which Alice decided should go in John's pocket; —the little carpet-bag could not take it. Ellen was afraid it never would be locked. By dint of much pushing and crowding, how-ever, locked it was; and they made themselves ready. Over Ellen's merino dress and coat went an old fur tippet; a little shawl was tied round her neck; her feet were cased in a pair of warm moc-

casins, which belonging to Margery were of course a world too big
for her, but "any thing but cold," as their owner said. Her nice
blue hood would protect her head well, and Alice gave her a green
veil to save her eyes from the glare of the snow. When Ellen
shuffled out of Alice's room in this trim, John gave her one of his
grave looks, and saying she looked like Mother Bunch, begged to
know how she expected to get to the sleigh; he said she would
want a *foot*man indeed to wait upon her, to pick up her slippers, if
she went in that fashion. However he ended by picking *her* up,
carried her and set her down safely in the sleigh. Alice followed,
and in another minute they were off.

Ellen's delight was unbounded. Presently they turned round a
corner and left the house behind out of sight; and they were
speeding away along a road that was quite new to her. Ellen's
heart felt like dancing for joy. Nobody would have thought it,
she sat so still and quiet between Alice and her brother; but her
eyes were very bright as they looked joyously about her, and every
now and then she could not help smiling to herself. Nothing was
wanting to the pleasure of that ride. The day was of winter's
fairest; the blue sky as clear as if clouds had never dimmed or
crossed it. None crossed it now. It was cold, but not bitterly
cold, nor windy; the sleigh skimmed along over the smooth frozen
surface of the snow as if it was no trouble at all to Prince Charlie
to draw it; and the sleigh-bells jingled and rang, the very music
for Ellen's thoughts to dance to. And then with somebody she
liked very much on each side of her, and pleasures untold in the
prospect, no wonder she felt as if her heart could not hold any more.
The green veil could not be kept on, every thing looked so beautiful in that morning's sun. The long wide slopes of untrodden and
unspotted snow too bright sometimes for the eye to look at; the
shadows that here and there lay upon it, of woodland and scattered
trees; the very brown fences, and the bare arms and branches of
the leafless trees showing sharp against the white ground and clear
bright heaven;—all seemed lovely in her eyes. For

> "It is content of heart
> Gives nature power to please."

She could see nothing that was not pleasant. And besides they
were in a nice little red sleigh, with a warm buffalo robe, and Prince
Charlie was a fine spirited grey that scarcely ever needed to be
touched with the whip; at a word of encouragement from his
driver he would toss his head and set forward with new life, making
all the bells jingle again. To be sure she would have been just as
happy if they had had the poorest of vehicles on runners, with old
John instead; but still it was pleasanter so.

Their road at first was through a fine undulating country like that between the Nose and Thirlwall; farmhouses and patches of woodland scattered here and there. It would seem that the minds of all the party were full of the same thoughts, for after a very long silence Alice's first word, almost sigh, was,

"This is a beautiful world, John!"

"Beautiful!—wherever you can escape from the signs of man's presence and influence."

"Isn't that almost too strong?" said Alice.

He shook his head, smiling somewhat sadly, and touched Prince Charlie, who was indulging himself in a walk.

"But there are bright exceptions," said Alice.

"I believe it;—never so much as when I come home."

"Are there none around you, then, in whom you can have confidence and sympathy?"

He shook his head again. "Not enough, Alice. I long for you every day of my life."

Alice turned her head quick away.

"It must be so, my dear sister," he said presently; "we can never expect to find it otherwise. There are, as you say, bright exceptions,—many of them; but in almost all I find some sad want. We must wait till we join the spirits of the just made perfect, before we see society that will be all we wish for."

"What is Ellen thinking of all this while?" said Alice presently, bending down to see her face. "As grave as a judge!—what are you musing about?"

"I was thinking," said Ellen, "how men could help the world's being beautiful."

"Don't trouble your little head with that question," said John smiling;—"long may it be before you are able to answer it. Look at those snow-birds!"

By degrees the day wore on. About one o'clock they stopped at a farm-house to let the horse rest, and to stretch their own limbs, which Ellen for her part was very glad to do. The people of the house received them with great hospitality and offered them pumpkin pies and sweet cider. Alice had brought a basket of sandwiches, and Prince Charlie was furnished with a bag of corn Thomas had stowed away in the sleigh for him; so they were all well refreshed and rested and warmed before they set off again.

From home to Ventnor, Mr. Marshman's place, was more than thirty miles, and the longest, because the most difficult, part of the way was still before them. Ellen, however, soon became sleepy, from riding in the keen air; she was content now to have the green veil over her face, and sitting down in the bottom of the sleigh, her head leaning against Alice, and covered well with the buffalo robe, she slept in happy unconsciousness of hill and dale, wind and sun, and all the remaining hours of the way.

It was drawing toward four o'clock when Alice with some difficulty roused her to see the approach to the house and get wide awake before they should reach it. They turned from the road and entered by a gateway into some pleasure-grounds, through which a short drive brought them to the house. These grounds were fine, but the wide lawns were a smooth spread of snow now ; the great skeletons of oaks and elms were bare and wintry ; and patches of shrubbery offered little but tufts and bunches of brown twigs and stems. It might have looked dreary, but that some

well-grown evergreens were clustered round the house, and others scattered here and there relieved the eye ;—a few holly bushes, singly and in groups, proudly displayed their bright dark leaves and red berries ;—and one unrivalled hemlock on the west threw its graceful shadow quite across the lawn, on which, as on itself, the white chimney tops, and the naked branches of oaks and elms, was the faint smile of the afternoon sun.

A servant came to take the horse, and Ellen, being first rid of her moccasins, went with John and Alice up the broad flight of steps and into the house. They entered a large handsome square hall with a blue and white stone floor, at one side of which the staircase went winding up. Here they were met by a young lady, very lively and pleasant-faced, who threw her arms round Alice and kissed her a great many times, seeming very glad indeed to see her. She welcomed Ellen too with such warmth that she began to feel almost as if she had been sent for and expected; told Mr. John he had behaved admirably; and then led them into a large room where was a group of ladies and gentlemen.

The welcome they got here was less lively but quite as kind. Mr. and Mrs. Marshman were fine handsome old people, of stately presence, and most dignified as well as kind in their deportment. Ellen saw that Alice was at home here, as if she had been a daughter of the family. Mrs. Marshman also stooped down and kissed herself, telling her she was very glad she had come, and that there were a number of young people there who would be much pleased to have her help them keep Christmas. Ellen could not make out yet who any of the rest of the company were. John and Alice seemed to know them all, and there was a buzz of pleasant voices and a great bustle of shaking hands.

The children had all gone out to walk, and as they had had their dinner a great while ago it was decided that Ellen should take hers that day with the elder part of the family. While they were waiting to be called to dinner and every body else was talking and laughing, old Mr. Marshman took notice of little Ellen, and drawing her from Alice's side to his own, began a long conversation. He asked her a great many questions, some of them such funny ones that she could not help laughing, but she answered them all, and now and then so that she made him laugh too. By the time the butler came to say dinner was ready she had almost forgotten she was a stranger. Mr. Marshman himself led her to the dining-room, begging the elder ladies would excuse him, but he felt bound to give his attention to the greatest stranger in the company. He placed her on his right hand and took the greatest care of her all dinner-time; once sending her plate the whole length of the table for some particular little thing he thought she would like. On the other side of Ellen sat Mrs. Chauncey, one of Mr. Marshman's daughters; a lady with a sweet, gentle, quiet face and manner that made Ellen like to sit by her. Another daughter, Mrs. Gillespie, had more of her mother's stately bearing; the third, Miss Sophia, who met them first in the hall, was very unlike both the others, but lively and agreeable and good-humoured.

Dinner gave place to the dessert, and that in its turn was removed with the cloth. Ellen was engaged in munching almonds and raisins, admiring the brightness of the mahogany, and the richly cut and coloured glass, and silver decanter stands, which were reflected in it, when a door at the further end of the room half opened, a little figure came partly in, and holding the door in her hand stood looking doubtfully along the table, as if seeking for some one.

"What is the matter, Ellen?" said Mrs. Chauncey.

"Mrs. Bland told me,—mamma,—" she began, her eye not ceasing its uneasy quest, but then breaking off and springing to Alice's side she threw her arms round her neck, and gave her certainly the warmest of all the warm welcomes she had had that day.

"Hallo!" cried Mr. Marshman rapping on the table; "that's too much for any one's share. Come here, you baggage, and give me just such another."

The little girl came near accordingly and hugged and kissed him with a very good will, remarking, however, "Ah, but I've seen you before to-day, grandpapa!"

"Well, here's somebody you've not seen before," said he good-humouredly, pulling her round to Ellen,—"here's a new friend for you,—a young lady from the great city, so you must brush up your country manners—Miss Ellen Montgomery, come from— pshaw! what is it?—come from——"

"London, grandpapa?" said the little girl, as with a mixture of simplicity and kindness she took Ellen's hand and kissed her on the cheek.

"From Carra-carra, sir," said Ellen smiling.

"Go along with you," said he, laughing and pinching her cheek. "Take her away, Ellen, take her away, and mind you take good care of her. Tell Mrs. Bland she is one of grandpapa's guests."

The two children had not however reached the door when Ellen Chauncey exclaimed, "Wait, oh! wait a minute! I must speak to aunt Sophia about the bag." And flying to her side there followed an earnest whispering, and then a nod and smile from aunt Sophia; and satisfied, Ellen returned to her companion and led her out of the dining-room.

"We have both got the same name," said she as they went along a wide corridor; "how shall we know which is which?"

"Why," said Ellen laughing, "when you say Ellen I shall know you mean me, and when I say it you will know I mean you. I shouldn't be calling myself, you know."

"Yes, but when somebody else calls Ellen, we shall both have to run. Do you run when you are called?"

"Sometimes," said Ellen laughing.

"Ah, but I do always; mamma always makes me. I thought perhaps you were like Marianne Gillespie—she waits often as much as half a minute before she stirs when any body calls her. Did you come with Miss Alice?"

" Yes."

" Do you love her ?"

" Very much !—oh, very much !"

Little Ellen looked at her companion's rising colour with a glance of mixed curiosity and pleasure in which lay a strong promise of growing love.

"So do I," she answered gayly; " I am very glad she is come, and I am very glad you are come, too."

The little speaker pushed open a door and led Ellen into the presence of a group of young people rather older than themselves.

" Marianne," said she to one of them, a handsome girl of fourteen, " this is Miss Ellen Montgomery—she came with Alice, and she is come to keep Christmas with us—aren't you glad ? There'll be quite a parcel of us when what's-her-name comes—won't there ?"

Marianne shook hands with Ellen.

"She is one of grandpapa's guests, I can tell you," said little Ellen Chauncey; " and he says we must brush up our country manners—she's come from the great city."

" Do you think we are a set of ignoramuses, Miss Ellen ?" inquired a well-grown boy of fifteen, who looked enough like Marianne Gillespie to prove him her brother.

" I don't know what that is," said Ellen.

" Well, do they do things better in the great city than we do here ?"

" I don't know how you do them here," said Ellen.

"Don't you?—Come ! Stand out of my way, right and left, all of you, will you, and give me a chance ? Now then !"

Conscious that he was amusing most of the party, he placed himself gravely at a little distance from Ellen, and marching solemnly up to her bowed down to her knees—then slowly raising his head stepped back.

" Miss Ellen Montgomery, I am rejoiced to have the pleasure of seeing you at Ventnor.—Isn't that polite, now ? Is that like what you have been accustomed to, Miss Montgomery ?"

" No, sir—thank you," said Ellen, who laughed in spite of herself. The mirth of the others redoubled.

" May I request to be informed then," continued Gillespie, " what is the fashion of making bows in the great city ?"

" I don't know," said Ellen; " I never saw a boy make a bow before."

" Humph !—I guess country manners will do for you," said William, turning on his heel.

" You're giving her a pretty specimen of 'em, Bill," said another boy.

" For shame, William !" cried little Ellen Chauncey ;—" didn't

I tell you she was one of grandpapa's guests? Come here, Ellen, I'll take you somewhere else."

She seized Ellen's hand and pulled her toward the door, but suddenly stopped again.

"Oh, I forgot to tell you!" she said,—"I asked aunt Sophia about the bag of moroccos, and she said she would have 'em early to-morrow morning, and then we can divide 'em right away."

"We mustn't divide 'em till Maggie comes," said Marianne.

"Oh, no—not till Maggie comes," said little Ellen; and then ran off again.

"I am so glad you are come," said she;—"the others are all so much older, and they have all so much to do together—and now you can help me think what I will make for mamma. Hush! don't say a word about it!"

They entered the large drawing-room, where old and young were gathered for tea. The children, who had dined early, sat down to a well-spread table, at which Miss Sophia presided; the elder persons were standing or sitting in different parts of the room. Ellen, not being hungry, had leisure to look about her, and her eye soon wandered from the tea-table in search of her old friends. Alice was sitting by Mrs. Marshman, talking with two other ladies; but Ellen smiled presently as she caught her eye from the far end of the room, and got a little nod of recognition. John came up just then to set down his coffee-cup, and asked her what she was smiling at.

"That's city manners," said William Gillespie, "to laugh at what's going on."

"I have no doubt we shall all follow the example," said John Humphreys gravely, "if the young gentleman will try to give us a smile."

The young gentleman had just accommodated himself with an outrageously large mouthful of bread and sweetmeats, and if ever so well-disposed, compliance with the request was impossible. None of the rest, however, not even his sister, could keep their countenances, for the eye of the speaker had pointed and sharpened his words; and William, very red in the face, was understood to mumble, as soon as mumbling was possible, that "he wouldn't laugh unless he had a mind to," and a threat to "do something" to his tormentor.

"Only not eat me," said John, with a shade of expression in his look and tone which overcame the whole party, himself and poor William alone retaining entire gravity.

"What's all this—what's all this? What's all this laughing about?" said old Mr. Marshman, coming up.

"This young gentleman, sir," said John, "has been endeavouring—with a mouthful of arguments—to prove to us the inferiority of city manners to those learned in the country."

" Will?" said the old gentleman, glancing doubtfully at William's discomfited face; then added sternly, " I don't care where your manners were learnt, sir, but I advise you to be very particular as to the sort you bring with you here. Now, Sophia, let us have some music."

He set the children a dancing, and as Ellen did not know how, he kept her by him, and kept her very much amused too, in his own way; then he would have her join in the dancing and bade Ellen Chauncey give her lessons. There was a little backwardness at first, and then Ellen was jumping away with the rest, and thinking it perfectly delightful, as Miss Sophia's piano rattled out merry jigs and tunes, and little feet flew over the floor as light as the hearts they belonged to. At eight o'clock the young ones were dismissed, and bade good-night to their elders; and pleased with the kind kiss Mrs. Marshman had given her as well as her little granddaughter, Ellen went off to bed very happy.

The room to which her companion led her was the very picture of comfort. It was not too large, furnished with plain old-fashioned furniture, and lighted and warmed by a cheerful wood-fire. The very old brass-headed andirons that stretched themselves out upon the hearth with such a look of being at home, seemed to say, " You have come to the right place for comfort." A little dark mahogany book-case in one place—an odd toilet-table of the same stuff in another; and opposite the fire an old-fashioned high-post bedstead with its handsome Marseilles quilt and ample pillows looked very tempting. Between this and the far side of the room, in the corner, another bed was spread on the floor.

" This is aunt Sophia's room," said little Ellen Chauncey;— " this is where you are to sleep."

" And where will Alice be?" said the other Ellen.

" Oh, she'll sleep here, in this bed, with aunt Sophia; that is because the house is so full, you know;—and here is your bed, here on the floor. Oh, delicious! I wish I was going to sleep here. Don't you love to sleep on the floor? I do. I think it's fun."

Anybody might have thought it fun to sleep on that bed, for instead of a bedstead it was luxuriously piled on mattresses. The two children sat down together on the foot of it.

" This is aunt Sophia's room," continued little Ellen, " and next to it, out of that door, is our dressing-room, and next to that is where mamma and I sleep. Do you undress and dress yourself?"

" To be sure I do," said Ellen,—" always."

" So do I; but Marianne Gillespie won't even put on her shoes and stockings for herself."

"Who does it, then ?" said Ellen.

"Why, Lester—aunt Matilda's maid. Mamma sent away her maid when we came here, and she says if she had fifty she would like me to do every thing I can for myself. I shouldn't think it was pleasant to have any one put on one's shoes and stockings for you, should you ?"

"No, indeed," said Ellen. "Then you live here all the time ?"

"Oh, yes—ever since papa didn't come back from that long voyage—we live here since then."

"Is he coming back soon ?"

"No," said little Ellen gravely—"he never came back—he never will come back any more."

Ellen was sorry she had asked, and both children were silent for a minute.

"I'll tell you what !" said little Ellen, jumping up,—"mamma said we mustn't sit up too long talking, so I'll run and get my things and bring 'em here, and we can undress together ; won't that be a nice way ?"

CHAPTER XXVIII.

He that loses any thing, and gets wisdom by it, is a gainer by the loss.
L'Estrange.

LEFT alone in the strange room with the flickering fire, how quickly Ellen's thoughts left Ventnor and flew over the sea. They often travelled that road it is true, but now perhaps the very home look of every thing, where yet *she* was not at home, might have sent them. There was a bitter twinge or two, and for a minute Ellen's head drooped. "To-morrow will be Christmas eve—last Christmas eve—oh, mamma !"

Little Ellen Chauncey soon came back, and sitting down beside her on the foot of the bed began the business of undressing.

"Don't you love Christmas time ?" said she ; "I think it's the pleasantest in all the year ; we always have a houseful of people, and such fine times. But then in summer I think *that's* the pleasantest. I s'pose they're all pleasant. Do you hang up your stocking ?"

"No," said Ellen.

"Don't you ! why I always did ever since I can remember. I used to think, when I was a little girl you know," said she laughing,—"I used to think that Santa Claus came down the chimney, and I used to hang up my stocking as near the fireplace as I could ;

but I know better than that now; I don't care where I hang it. You know who Santa Claus is, don't you?"

"He's nobody," said Ellen.

"Oh, yes he is—he's a great many people—he's whoever gives you any thing. *My* Santa Claus is mamma, and grandpapa, and grandmamma, and aunt Sophia, and aunt Matilda; and I thought I should have had uncle George too this Christmas, but he couldn't come. Uncle Howard never gives me any thing. I am sorry uncle George couldn't come; I like him the best of all my uncles."

"I never had any body but mamma to give me presents," said Ellen, "and she never gave me much more at Christmas than at other times."

"I used to have presents from mamma and grandpapa too, both Christmas and New Year, but now I have grown so old mamma only gives me something Christmas and grandpapa only New Year. It would be too much, you know, for me to have both when my presents are so big. I don't believe a stocking will hold 'em much longer. But oh! we've got such a fine plan in our heads," said little Ellen, lowering her voice and speaking with open eyes and great energy,—"*we* are going to make presents this year!—we children—won't it be fine?—we are going to make what we like for any body we choose, and let nobody know any thing about it; and then New Year's morning, you know, when the things are all under the napkins we will give ours to somebody to put where they belong, and nobody will know any thing about them till they see them there. Won't it be fine? I'm so glad you are here, for I want you to tell me what I shall make."

"Who is it for?" said Ellen.

"Oh, mamma; you know I can't make for every body, so I think I had rather it should be for mamma. I *thought* of making her a needlebook with white backs, and getting Gilbert Gillespie to paint them—he can paint beautifully,—and having her name and something else written very nicely inside—how do you think that would do?"

"I should think it would do very nicely," said Ellen,—"very nicely indeed."

"I wish uncle George was at home though to write it for me,—he writes so beautifully; I can't do it well enough."

"I am afraid I can't either," said Ellen. "Perhaps somebody else can."

"I don't know who. Aunt Sophia scribbles and scratches, and besides I don't want her to know any thing about it. But there's another thing I don't know how to fix, and that's the edges of the leaves—the leaves for the needles—they must be fixed—somehow."

"I can show you how to do that," said Ellen brightening; "mamma had a needlebook that was given to her that had the edges beautifully fixed; and I wanted to know how it was done, and she showed me. I'll show you that. It takes a good while, but that's no matter."

" Oh, thank you; how nice that is. Oh, no, that's no matter. And then it will do very well, won't it? Now if I can only catch Gilbert in a good humour—he isn't my cousin—he's Marianne's cousin—that big boy you saw down stairs—he's so big he won't have any thing to say to me sometimes, but I guess I'll get him to do this. Don't you want to make something for somebody?"

Ellen *had* had one or two feverish thoughts on this subject since the beginning of the conversation; but she only said,—

" It's no matter—you know I haven't got any thing here; and besides I shall not be here till New Year."

" Not here till New Year! yes you shall," said little Ellen, throwing herself upon her neck; "indeed you aren't going away before that. I *know* you aren't—I heard grandmamma and aunt Sophia talking about it. Say you will stay here till New Year—do!"

" I should like to very much indeed," said Ellen, "if Alice does."

In the midst of half a dozen kisses with which her little companion rewarded this speech, somebody close by said pleasantly,—

" What time of night do you suppose it is?"

The girls started;—there was Mrs. Chauncey.

" Oh, mamma," exclaimed her little daughter, springing to her feet, " I hope you haven't heard what we have been talking about?"

" Not a word," said Mrs. Chauncey, smiling, " but as to-morrow will be long enough to talk in, hadn't you better go to bed now?"

Her daughter obeyed her immediately, after one more hug to Ellen and telling her she was *so* glad she had come. Mrs. Chauncey stayed to see Ellen in bed and press one kind motherly kiss upon her face, so tenderly that Ellen's eyes were moistened as she withdrew. But in her dreams that night the rosy sweet face, blue eyes, and little plump figure of Ellen Chauncey played the greatest part.

She slept till Alice was obliged to waken her the next morning; and then got up with her head in a charming confusion of pleasures past and pleasures to come,—things known and unknown to be made for every body's New Year presents,—linen collars and painted needlebooks; and no sooner was breakfast over than she was showing and explaining to Ellen Chauncey a particularly splendid and mysterious way of embroidering the edges of needle-book leaves. Deep in this they were still an hour afterwards, and in the comparative merits of purple and rose-colour, when a little hubbub arose at the other end of the room on the arrival of a new-comer. Ellen Chauncey looked up from her work, then dropped it, exclaiming, "There she is!—now for the bag!"—and pulled Ellen along with her toward the party. A young lady was in the midst of it, talking so fast that she had not time to take off her cloak and bonnet. As her eye met Ellen's however she came to a sudden pause. It was Margaret Dunscombe. Ellen's face certainly showed no pleasure; Margaret's darkened with a very disagreeable surprise.

"My goodness!—Ellen Montgomery!—how on earth did you get *here?*"

"Do you know her?" asked one of the girls, as the two Ellens went off after "aunt Sophia."

"Do I know her? Yes—just enough,—exactly. How did she get here?"

"Miss Humphreys brought her."

"Who's Miss Humphreys?"

"Hush!" said Marianne, lowering her tone,—"that's her brother in the window."

"Whose brother?—hers or Miss Humphreys' ?"

"Miss Humphreys'. Did you never see her? she is here, or has been here, a great deal of the time. Grandma calls her her fourth daughter; and she is just as much at home as if she was; and she brought her here."

"And she's at home too, I suppose. Well, it's no business of mine."

"What do you know of her?"

"Oh, enough—that's just it—don't want to know any more."

"Well, you needn't; but what's the matter with her?"

"Oh, I don't know—I'll tell you some other time—she's a conceited little piece. We had the care of her coming up the river, that's how I come to know about her; 'ma said it was the last child she would be bothered with in that way."

Presently the two girls came back, bring word to clear the table, for aunt Sophia was coming with the moroccos. As soon as she came Ellen Chauncey sprang to her neck and whispered an earnest question. "Certainly!" aunt Sophia said, as she poured out the contents of the bag; and her little niece delightedly told Ellen *she* was to have her share as well as the rest.

The table was now strewn with pieces of morocco of all sizes and colours, which were hastily turned over and examined with eager hands and sparkling eyes. Some were mere scraps, to be sure; but others showed a breadth and length of beauty which was declared to be "first-rate," and "fine;" and one beautiful large piece of blue morocco in particular was made up in imagination by two or three of the party in as many different ways. Marianne wanted it for a book-cover; Margaret declared she could make a make a very pretty needle-box, such a one as she had seen in the possession of one of the girls, and longed to make for Alice.

" Well, what's to be done now?" said Miss Sophia,—" or am I not to know?"

" Oh, you're not to know—you're not to know, aunt Sophy," cried the girls ;—" you mustn't ask."

" I'll tell you what they are going to do with 'em," said George Walsh coming up to her with a mischievous face, and adding in a loud whisper, shielding his mouth with his hand,—" they're going to make pr——"

He was laid hold of forcibly by the whole party screaming and laughing, and stopped short from finishing his speech.

" Well then I'll take my departure," said Miss Sophia ;—" but how will you manage to divide all these scraps?"

" Suppose we were to put them in the bag again, and you hold the bag, and we were to draw them out without looking," said Ellen Chauncey,—" as we used to do with the sugar-plums."

As no better plan was thought of this was agreed upon ; and little Ellen shutting up her eyes very tight stuck in her hand and pulled out a little bit of green morocco about the size of a dollar.   Ellen Montgomery came next ; then Margaret, then Marianne, then their mutual friend Isabel Hawthorn.   Each had to take her turn a great many times ; and at the end of the drawing the pieces were found to be pretty equally divided among the party, with the exception of Ellen, who besides several other good pieces had drawn the famous blue.

" That will do very nicely," said little Ellen Chauncey ;—" I am glad you have got that, Ellen.   Now, aunt Sophy !—one thing more—you know the silks and ribbons you promised us."

" Bless me ! I haven't done yet, eh ?   Well you shall have them, but we are all going out to walk now ; I'll give them to you this afternoon.   Come ! put these away and get on your bonnets and cloaks."

A hard measure ! but it was done.   After the walk came dinner : after dinner aunt Sophia had to be found and waited on, till she had fairly sought out and delivered to their hands the wished-for bundles of silks and satins.   It gave great satisfaction.

" But how shall we do about dividing these?" said little Ellen ; " shall we draw lots again?"

" No, Ellen," said Marianne, " that won't do, because we might every one get just the thing we do not want.   I want one colour or stuff to go with my morocco, and you want another to go with yours ; and you might get mine and I might get yours.   We had best each choose in turn what we like, beginning at Isabel."

" Very well," said little Ellen, " I'm agreed."

" Any thing for a quiet life," said George Walsh.

But this business of choosing was found to be very long and very difficult, each one was so fearful of not taking the exact piece she wanted most. The elder members of the family began to gather for dinner, and several came and stood round the table where the children were; little noticed by them, they were so wrapped up in silks and satins. Ellen seemed the least interested person at table, and had made her selections with the least delay and difficulty; and now as it was not her turn sat very soberly looking on with her head resting on her hand.

"I declare it's too vexatious!" said Margaret Dunscombe;— "here I've got this beautiful piece of blue satin, and can't do any thing with it; it just matches that blue morocco—it's a perfect match—I could have made a splendid thing of it, and I have got some cord and tassels that would just do—I declare it's too bad."

Ellen's colour changed.

"Well, choose, Margaret," said Marianne.

"I don't know what to choose—that's the thing. What can one do with red and purple morocco and blue satin? I might as well give up. I've a great notion to take this piece of yellow satin and dress up a Turkish doll to frighten the next young one I meet with."

"I wish you would, Margaret, and give it to me when it's done," cried little Ellen Chauncey.

"'Tain't made yet," said the other dryly.

Ellen's colour had changed and changed; her hand twitched nervously, and she glanced uneasily from Margaret's store of finery to her own.

"Come, choose, Margaret," said Ellen Chauncey;—"I dare say Ellen wants the blue morocco as much as you do."

"No, I don't!" said Ellen abruptly, throwing it over the table to her;—"take it, Margaret,—you may have it."

"What do you mean?" said the other astounded.

"I mean you may have it," said Ellen,—"I don't want it."

"Well, I'll tell you what," said the other,—"I'll give you yellow satin for it—or some of my red morocco?"

"No,—I had rather not," repeated Ellen;—"I don't want it— you may have it."

"Very generously done," remarked Miss Sophia; "I hope you'll all take a lesson in the art of being obliging."

"Quite a noble little girl," said Mrs. Gillespie.

Ellen crimsoned. "No, ma'am, I am not, indeed," she said, looking at them with eyes that were filling fast,—"please don't say so—I don't deserve it."

"I shall say what I think, my dear," said Mrs. Gillespie smiling, "but I am glad you add the grace of modesty to that of generosity; it is the more uncommon of the two."

lovely reticule with it; and Ellen could not help thinking it would

" I am not modest! I am not generous! you mustn't say so,"
cried Ellen. She struggled; the blood rushed to the surface, suf-
fusing every particle of skin that could be seen;—then left it, as
with eyes cast down she went on—" I don't deserve to be praised,
—it was more Margaret's than mine. I oughtn't to have kept it
at all—for I saw a little bit when I put my hand in. I didn't
mean to, but I did!"

Raising her eyes hastily to Alice's face, they met those of John,
who was standing behind her. She had not counted upon him for
one of her listeners; she knew Mrs. Gillespie, Mrs. Chauncey, Miss
Sophia, and Alice had heard her; but this was the one drop too
much. Her head sunk; she covered her face a moment, and then
made her escape out of the room before even Ellen could follow
her.

There was a moment's silence. Alice seemed to have some difficulty not to follow Ellen's example. Margaret pouted; Mrs.
Chauncey's eyes filled with tears, and her little daughter seemed
divided between doubt and dismay. Her first move however was
to run off in pursuit of Ellen. Alice went after her.

" Here's a beautiful example of honour and honesty for you!"
said Margaret Dunscombe. at length.

" I think it is," said John, quietly.

" An uncommon instance," said Mrs. Chauncey.

" I am glad every body thinks so," said Margaret, sullenly; " I
hope I shan't copy it, that's all."

" I think you are in no danger," said John, again.

" Very well!" said Margaret, who between her desire of speaking and her desire of concealing her vexation did not know what
to do with herself;—" every body must judge for himself, I suppose; I've got enough of her, for my part."

" Where did you ever see her before?" said Isabel Hawthorn.

" Oh, she came up the river with us—mamma had to take care
of her—she was with us two days."

" And didn't you like her?"

" No, I guess I didn't! she was a perfect plague. All the day
on board the steamboat she scarcely came near us; we couldn't
pretend to keep sight of her; mamma had to send her maid out to
look after her I don't know how many times. She scraped acquaintance with some strange man on board and liked his company
better than ours, for she stayed with him the whole blessed day,
waking and sleeping; of course mamma didn't like it at all. She
didn't go to a single meal with us; you know of course that wasn't
proper behaviour."

" No indeed," said Isabel.

" I suppose," said John, coolly, " she chose the society she thought the pleasantest. Probably Miss Margaret's politeness was more than she had been accustomed to."

Margaret coloured, not quite knowing what to make of the speaker or his speech.

"It would take much to make me believe," said gentle Mrs. Chauncey, "that a child of such refined and delicate feeling as that little girl evidently has, could take pleasure in improper company."

Margaret had a reply at her tongue's end, but she had also an uneasy feeling that there were eyes not far off too keen of sight to be baffled; she kept silence till the group dispersed and she had an opportunity of whispering in Marianne's ear that "*that* was the very most disagreeable man she had ever seen in her life."

"What a singular fancy you have taken to this little pet of Alice's, Mr. John," said Mrs. Marshman's youngest daughter. "You quite surprise me."

"Did you think me a misanthrope, Miss Sophia?"

"Oh, no, not at all; but I always had a notion you would not be easily pleased in the choice of favourites."

"*Easily!* When a simple intelligent child of twelve or thirteen is a common character, then I will allow that I am easily pleased."

"Twelve or thirteen!" said Miss Sophia; "what are you thinking about? Alice says she is only ten or eleven."

"In years—perhaps."

"How gravely you take me up!" said the young lady, laughing. "My dear Mr. John, 'in years perhaps,' you may call yourself twenty, but in every thing else you might much better pass for thirty or forty."

As they were called to dinner Alice and Ellen Chauncey came back; the former looking a little serious, the latter crying, and wishing aloud that all the moroccos had been in the fire. They had not been able to find Ellen. Neither was she in the drawing-room when they returned to it after dinner; and a second search was made in vain. John went to the library which was separate from the other rooms, thinking she might have chosen that for a hiding-place. She was not there; but the pleasant light of the room where only the fire was burning, invited a stay. He sat down in the deep window, and was musingly looking out into the moonlight, when the door softly opened and Ellen came in. She stole in noiselessly, so that he did not hear her, and *she* thought the room empty; till in passing slowly down toward the fire she came upon him in the window. Her start first let him know she was there; she would have run, but one of her hands was caught, and she could not get it away.

"Running away from your brother, Ellie!" said he, kindly; "what is the matter?"

Ellen shrunk from meeting his eye and was silent.

"I know all, Ellie," said he, still very kindly,—"I have seen all ;—why do you shun me ?"

Ellen said nothing ; the big tears began to run down her face and frock.

"You are taking this matter too hardly, dear Ellen," he said, drawing her close to him ;—"you did wrong, but you have done all you could to repair the wrong ;—neither man nor woman can do more than that."

But though encouraged by his manner, the tears flowed faster than ever.

"Where have you been ? Alice was looking for you, and little Ellen Chauncey was in great trouble. I don't know what dreadful thing she thought you had done with yourself. Come !—lift up your head and let me see you smile again."

Ellen lifted her head, but could not her eyes, though she tried to smile.

"I want to talk to you a little about this," said he. "You know you gave me leave to be your brother,—will you let me ask you a question or two ?"

"Oh, yes—whatever he pleased," Ellen said.

"Then sit down here," said he, making room for her on the wide window-seat, but still keeping hold of her hand and speaking very gently. "You said you saw when you took the morocco—I don't quite understand—how was it ?"

"Why," said Ellen, "we were not to look, and we had gone three times round and nobody had got that large piece yet, and we all wanted it ; and I did not mean to look at all, but I don't know how it was, just before I shut my eyes I happened to see the corner of it sticking up, and then I took it."

"With your eyes open ?"

"No, no, with them shut. And I had scarcely got it when I was sorry for it and wished it back."

"You will wonder at me perhaps, Ellie," said John, "but I am not very sorry this has happened. You are no worse than before ; —it has only made you see what you are—very, very weak,—quite unable to keep yourself right without constant help. Sudden temptation was too much for you—so it has many a time been for me, and so it has happened to the best men on earth. I suppose if you had had a minute's time to think you would not have done as you did ?"

"No, indeed !" said Ellen. "I was sorry a minute after."

"And I dare say the thought of it weighed upon your mind ever since ?"

"Oh, yes !" said Ellen ;—"it wasn't out of my head a minute the whole day."

"Then let it make you very humble, dear Ellie, and let it make you in future keep close to our dear Saviour, without whose help we cannot stand a moment."

Ellen sobbed; and he allowed her to do so for a few minutes, then said,

"But you have not been thinking much about Him, Ellie."

The sobs ceased; he saw his words had taken hold.

"Is it right," he said softly, "that we should be more troubled about what people will think of us, than for having displeased or dishonoured Him?"

Ellen now looked up, and in her look was all the answer he wished.

"You understand me, I see," said he. "Be humbled in the dust before him—the more the better; but whenever we are greatly concerned, for our own sakes, about other people's opinion, we may be sure we are thinking too little of God and what will please him."

"I am very sorry," said poor Ellen, from whose eyes the tears began to drop again,—"I am very wrong—but I couldn't bear to think what Alice would think—and you—and all of them——"

"Here's Alice to speak for herself," said John.

As Alice came up with a quick step and knelt down before her, Ellen sprang to her neck, and they held each other very fast indeed. John walked up and down the room. Presently he stopped before them.

"All's well again," said Alice, "and we are going in to tea."

He smiled and held out his hand, which Ellen took, but he would not leave the library, declaring they had a quarter of an hour still. So they sauntered up and down the long room, talking of different things, so pleasantly that Ellen near forgot her troubles. Then came in Miss Sophia to find them, and then Mr. Marshman, and Marianne to call them to tea; so the going into the drawing-room was not half so bad as Ellen thought it would be.

She behaved very well; her face was touchingly humble that night; and all the evening she kept fast by either Alice or John, without budging an inch. And as little Ellen Chauncey and her cousin George Walsh chose to be where she was, the young party was quite divided; and not the least merry portion of it was that mixed with the older people. Little Ellen was half beside herself with spirits; the secret of which perhaps was the fact, which she several times in the course of the evening whispered to Ellen as a great piece of news, that "it was Christmas eve!"

CHAPTER XXIX.

As bees flee hame wi' lades o' treasure,
The minutes winged their way wi' pleasure.
Kings may be blest, but *they* were glorious,
O'er all the ills o' life victorious.

BURNS.

CHRISTMAS morning was dawning grey, but it was still far from broad daylight, when Ellen was awakened. She found little Ellen Chauncey pulling and pushing at her shoulders, and whispering " Ellen! Ellen!''—in a tone that showed a great fear of waking somebody up. There she was, in night-gown and nightcap, and barefooted too, with a face brimfull of excitement and as wide awake as possible. Ellen roused herself in no little surprise and asked what the matter was.

" I am going to look at my stocking,'' whispered her visitor,— "don't you want to get up and come with me? it's just here in the other room,—come!—don't make any noise.''

" But what if you should find nothing in it?'' said Ellen laughingly, as she bounded out of bed.

" Ah, but I shall, I know ;—I always do ;—never fear. Hush! step ever so softly—I don't want to wake any body.''

" It's hardly light enough for you to see,'' whispered Ellen, as the two little barefooted white figures glided out of the room.

" Oh, yes it is—that's all the fun. Hush!—don't make a bit of noise—I know where it hangs—mamma always puts it at the back of her big easy chair—come this way—here it is! Oh, Ellen! there's two of 'em! There's one for you! there's one for you.''

In a tumult of delight one Ellen capered about the floor on the tips of her little bare toes, while the other, not less happy, stood still for pleasure. The dancer finished by hugging and kissing her with all her heart, declaring she was so glad she didn't know what to do.

" But how shall we know which is which?''

" Perhaps they are both alike,'' said Ellen.

" No—at any rate one's for me, and t'other's for you. Stop! here are pieces of paper, with our names on I guess—let's turn the chair a little bit to the light—there—yes!—Ellen—M-o-n,—there, that's yours; my name doesn't begin with an M; and this is mine!''

Another caper round the room, and then she brought up in front of the chair where Ellen was still standing.

"I wonder what's in 'em," she said; "I want to look, and I *don't* want to. Come, you begin."

"But that's no stocking of mine," said Ellen, a smile gradually breaking upon her sober little face; "my leg never was as big as that."

"Stuffed, isn't it?" said Ellen Chauncey. "Oh, do make haste, and see what is in yours. I want to know so I don't know what to do."

"Well, will you take out of yours as fast as I take out of mine?"

"Well!"——

Oh, mysterious delight, and delightful mystery, of the stuffed stocking! Ellen's trembling fingers sought the top, and then very suddenly left it.

"I can't think what it is," said she laughing,—"it feels so funny."

"Oh, never mind! make haste," said Ellen Chauncey; "it won't hurt you, I guess."

"No, it won't hurt me," said Ellen,—"but——"

She drew forth a great bunch of white grapes.

"Splendid! isn't it?" said Ellen Chauncey. "Now for mine."

It was the counterpart of Ellen's bunch.

"So far, so good," said she. "Now for the next."

The next thing in each stocking was a large horn of sugar-plums.

"Well, that's fine, isn't it?" said Ellen Chauncey;—"yours is tied with white ribbon and mine with blue; that's all the difference. Oh, and your paper's red and mine is purple."

"Yes, and the pictures are different," said Ellen.

"Well, I had rather they would be different, wouldn t you? I think it's just as pleasant. One's as big as the other, at any rate. Come—what's next?"

Ellen drew out a little bundle, which being opened proved to be a nice little pair of dark kid gloves.

"Oh, I wonder who gave me this!" she said,—"it's just what I wanted. How pretty! Oh, I'm so glad. I guess who it was."

"Oh, look here," said the other Ellen, who had been diving into *her* stocking,—"I've got a ball—this is just what I wanted too; George told me if I'd get one he'd show me how to play. Isn't it pretty? Isn't it funny we should each get just what we wanted? Oh, this is a very nice ball. I'm glad I've got it. Why, here is another great round thing in my stocking!—what can it be? they wouldn't give me *two* balls," said she, chuckling.

"So there is in mine!" said Ellen. "Maybe they're apples?"

"They aren't! they wouldn't give us apples; besides, it is soft. Pull it out and see."

"Then they are oranges," said Ellen laughing.

"*I* never felt such a soft orange," said little Ellen Chauncey. "Come Ellen! stop laughing, and let's see."

They were two great scarlet satin pincushions, with E. C. and E. M. very neatly stuck in pins.

"Well, we shan't want pins for a good while, shall we?" said Ellen. "Who gave us these?"

"I know," said little Ellen Chauncey,—"Mrs. Bland."

"She was very kind to make one for me," said Ellen. "Now for the next!"

Her next thing was a little bottle of Cologne water.

"I can tell who put that in," said her friend,—"aunt Sophia.

I know her little bottles of Cologne water. Do you love Cologne water? Aunt Sophia's is delicious."

Ellen did like it very much, and was extremely pleased. Ellen Chauncey had also a new pair of scissors which gave entire satisfaction.

"Now I wonder what all this toe is stuffed with," said she,— "raisins and almonds, I declare! and yours the same, isn't it? Well, don't you think we have got enough sweet things? Isn't this a pretty good Christmas?"

"What are you about, you monkeys?" cried the voice of aunt Sophia from the dressing-room door. "Alice, Alice! do look at them. Come, right back to bed both of you. Crazy pates! It is lucky it is Christmas day—if it was any other in the year we should have you both sick in bed; as it is I suppose you will go scot free."

Laughing, and rosy with pleasure, they came back and got into bed together; and for an hour afterwards the two kept up a most animated conversation, intermixed with long chuckles and bursts of merriment, and whispered communications of immense importance. The arrangement of the painted needlebook was entirely decided upon in this consultation; also two or three other matters; and the two children seemed to have already lived a day since daybreak by the time they came down to breakfast.

After breakfast Ellen applied secretly to Alice to know if she could write *very* beautifully; she exceedingly wanted something done.

"I should not like to venture, Ellie, if it must be so superfine; but John can do it for you."

"Can he? Do you think he would?"

"I am sure he will if you ask him."

"But I don't like to ask him," said Ellen, casting a doubtful glance at the window.

"Nonsense! he's only reading the newspaper. You won't disturb him."

"Well, you won't say any thing about it?"

"Certainly not."

Ellen accordingly went near and said gently, "Mr. Humphreys," —but he did not seem to hear her. "Mr. Humphreys!"—a little louder.

"He has not arrived yet," said John, looking round gravely.

He spoke so gravely that Ellen could not tell whether he were joking or serious. Her face of extreme perplexity was too much for his command of countenance. "Whom do you want to speak to?" said he, smiling.

"I wanted to speak to you, sir," said Ellen, "if you are not too busy."

" *Mr. Humphreys* is always busy," said he, shaking his head; " but *Mr. John* can attend to you at any time, and *John* will do for you whatever you please to ask him."

" Then, Mr. John," said Ellen laughing, " if you please, I wanted to ask you to do something for me very much indeed, if you are not too busy ; Alice said I shouldn't disturb you."

" Not at all ; I've been long enough over this stupid newspaper. What is it ?"

" I want you, if you will be so good," said Ellen, " to write a little bit for me on something, very beautifully."

" ' Very beautifully !' Well—come to the library ; we will see."

" But it is a great secret," said Ellen ; " you won't tell any body ?"

" Tortures shan't draw it from me—when I know what it is," said he, with one of his comical looks.

In high glee Ellen ran for the pieces of Bristol board which were to form the backs of the needlebook, and brought them to the library ; and explained how room was to be left in the middle of each for a painting, a rose on one, a butterfly on the other ; the writing to be as elegant as possible, above, beneath, and round-about, as the fancy of the writer should choose.

" Well, what is to be inscribed on this most original of needle-books ?" said John, as he carefully mended his pen.

" Stop !"—said Ellen,—" I'll tell you in a minute—on this one, the front you know, is to go, ' To my dear mother, many happy New Years ;'—and on this side, ' From her dear little daughter, Ellen Chauncey.' You know," she added, " Mrs. Chauncey isn't to know any thing about it till New Year's Day ; nor any body else."

" Trust me," said John. " If I am asked any questions they shall find me as obscure as an oracle."

" What is an oracle, sir ?"

" Why," said John smiling, " this pen won't do yet—the old heathens believed there were certain spots of earth to which some of their gods had more favour than to others, and where they would permit mortals to come nearer to them and would even deign to answer their questions."

" And did they ?" said Ellen.

" Did they what?"

" Did they answer their questions ?"

" Did *who* answer their questions ?"

" The—oh ! to be sure," said Ellen,—" there were no such gods. But what made people think they answered them ? and how could they ask questions ?"

" I suppose it was a contrivance of the priests to increase their power and wealth. There was always a temple built near, with priests and priestesses; the questions were put through them; and they would not ask them except on great occasions, or for people of consequence who could pay them well by making splendid gifts to the god."

"But I should think the people would have thought the priest or priestess had made up the answers themselves."

"Perhaps they did sometimes. But people had not the Bible then, and did not know as much as we know. It was not unnatural to think the gods would care a little for the poor people that lived on the earth. Besides, there was a good deal of management and trickery about the answers of the oracle that helped to deceive."

"How was it?" said Ellen;—"how could they manage? and what was *the oracle?*"

"The oracle was either the answer itself, or the god who was supposed to give it, or the place where it was given; and there were different ways of managing. At one place the priest hid himself in the hollow body or among the branches of an oak tree, and people thought the tree spoke to them. Sometimes the oracle was delivered by a woman who pretended to be put into a kind of fit—tearing her hair and beating her breast."

"But suppose the oracle made a mistake?—what would the people think then?"

"The answers were generally contrived so that they would seem to come true in any event."

"I don't see how they could do that," said Ellen.

"Very well—just imagine that I am an oracle, and come to me with some question;—I'll answer you."

"But you can't tell what's going to happen?"

"No matter—you ask me truly and I'll answer you oracularly."

"That means, like an oracle, I suppose?" said Ellen. "Well— Mr. John, will Alice be pleased with what I am going to give her New Year?"

"She will be pleased with what she will receive on that day."

"Ah, but," said Ellen laughing, "that isn't fair; you haven't answered me; perhaps somebody else will give her something, and then she might be pleased with that and not with mine."

"Exactly—but the oracle never means to be understood."

"Well, I won't come to you," said Ellen. "I don't like such answers. Now for the needlebook!"

Breathlessly she looked on while the skilful pen did its work; and her exclamations of delight and admiration when the first cover was handed to her were not loud but deep.

"It will do, then, will it? Now let us see—'From her dear little daughter,'—there—now 'Ellen Chauncey' I suppose must be in hieroglyphics."

"In what?" said Ellen.

" I mean written in some difficult character."

" Yes," said Ellen.   " But what was that you said ?"

" Hieroglyphics ?"

Ellen added no more, though she was not satisfied.   He looked up and smiled.

" Do you want to know what that means ?"

" Yes, if you please," said Ellen.

The pen was laid down while he explained, to a most eager little listener.   Even the great business of the moment was forgotten. From hieroglyphics they went to the pyramids ; and Ellen had got to the top of one and was enjoying the prospect (in imagination), when she suddenly came down to tell John of her stuffed stocking and its contents.   The pen went on again, and came to the end of the writing by the time Ellen had got to the toe of the stocking.

" Wasn't it very strange they should give me so many things ?" said she ;—" people that don't know me ?"

" Why, no," said John smiling,—" I cannot say I think it was *very* strange.   Is this all the business you had for my hands ?"

" This is all ; and I am *very* much obliged to you, Mr. John." Her grateful affectionate eye said much more, and he felt well paid.

Gilbert was next applied to, to paint the rose and the butterfly, which, finding so excellent a beginning made in the work, he was very ready to do.   The girls were then free to set about the embroidery of the leaves, which was by no means the business of an hour.

A very happy Christmas day was that.   With their needles and thimbles, and rose-coloured silk, they kept by themselves in a corner, or in the library, out of the way ; and sweetening their talk with a sugar-plum now and then, neither tongues nor needles knew any flagging.   It was wonderful what they found so much to say, but there was no lack.   Ellen Chauncey especially was inexhaustible.   Several times too that day the Cologne bottle was handled, the gloves looked at and fondled, the ball tried, and the new scissors extolled as " just the thing for their work."   Ellen attempted to let her companion into the mystery of oracles and hieroglyphics, but was fain to give it up; little Ellen showed a decided preference for American, not to say Ventnor, subjects, where she felt more at home.

Then came Mr. Humphreys ; and Ellen was glad, both for her own sake and because she loved to see Alice pleased.   Then came the great merry Christmas dinner, when the girls had, not talked themselves out, but tired themselves with working.   Young and old dined together to-day, and the children not set by themselves, but scattered among the grown-up people ; and as Ellen was nicely placed between Alice and little Ellen Chauncey, she enjoyed it all very much.   The large long table surrounded with happy faces ; tones of cheerfulness and looks of kindness, and lively talk ; the superb display of plate and glass and china; the stately dinner; and last but not least, the plum pudding. There was sparkling wine too, and a great deal of drinking of healths; but Ellen noticed that Alice and her brother smilingly drank all theirs in water; so when old Mr. Marshman called to her to "hold out her glass," she held it out to be sure and let him fill it, but she lifted her tumbler of water to her lips instead, after making him a very low bow. Mr. Marshman laughed at her a great deal, and asked her if she was "a proselyte to the new notions;" and Ellen laughed with him, without having the least idea what he meant, and was extremely happy. It was very pleasant too when they went into the drawing-room to take coffee. The young ones were permitted to have coffee to-night as a great favour. Old Mrs. Marshman had the two little ones on either side of her; and was so kind, and held Ellen's hand in her own, and talked to her about her mother, till Ellen loved her.

After tea there was a great call for games, and young and old joined in them. They played the Old Curiosity Shop; and Ellen thought Mr. John's curiosities could not be matched. They played the Old Family Coach, Mr. Howard Marshman being the manager, and Ellen laughed till she was tired; she was the coach door, and he kept her opening and shutting and swinging and breaking, it seemed all the while, though most of the rest were worked just as hard. When they were well tired they sat down to rest and hear music, and Ellen enjoyed that exceedingly. Alice sang, and Mrs. Gillespie, and Miss Sophia, and another lady, and Mr. Howard; sometimes alone, sometimes three or four or all together.

At last came ten o'clock and the young ones were sent off; and from beginning to end that had been a Christmas day of unbroken and unclouded pleasure. Ellen's last act was to take another look at her Cologne bottle, gloves, pincushion, grapes, and paper of sugar-plums, which were laid side by side carefully in a drawer.

CHAPTER XXX.

But though life's valley be a vale of tears,
A brighter scene beyond that vale appears,
Whose glory, with a light that never fades,
Shoots between scattered rocks and opening shades.

COWPER.

MR. HUMPHREYS was persuaded to stay over Sunday at Ventnor; and it was also settled that his children should not leave it till after New Year. This was less their own wish than his; he said Alice wanted the change, and he wished she looked a little fatter. Besides, the earnest pleadings of the whole family were not to be denied. Ellen was very glad of this, though there was one drawback to the pleasures of Ventnor,—she could not feel quite at home with any of the young people but only Ellen Chauncey and her cousin George Walsh. This seemed very strange to her; she almost thought Margaret Dunscombe was at the bottom of it all, but she recollected she had felt something of this before Margaret came. She tried to think nothing about it; and in truth it was not able to prevent her from being very happy. The breach however was destined to grow wider.

About four miles from Ventnor was a large town called Randolph. Thither they drove to church Sunday morning, the whole family; but the hour of dinner and the distance prevented any one from going in the afternoon. The members of the family were scattered in different parts of the house, most in their own rooms. Ellen with some difficulty made her escape from her young companions, whose manner of spending the time did not satisfy her notions of what was right on that day, and went to look in the library for her friends. They were there, and alone; Alice half reclining on the sofa, half in her brother's arms; he was reading or talking to her; there was a book in his hand.

"Is any thing the matter?" said Ellen, as she drew near; "aren't you well, dear Alice?—Headache? oh, I am sorry. Oh! I know——"

She darted away. In two minutes she was back again with a pleased face, her bunch of grapes in one hand, her bottle of Cologne water in the other.

"Won't you open that, please, Mr. John," said she;—"I can't open it; I guess it will do her good, for Ellen says it's delicious. Mamma used to have Cologne water for her headaches. And here, dear Alice, won't you eat these?—do!—try one."

"Hasn't that bottle been open yet?" said Alice, as she smilingly took a grape.

"Why no, to be sure it hasn't. I wasn't going to open it till I wanted it. Eat them all, dear Alice,—please do!"

"But I don't think you have eaten one yourself, Ellen, by the look of the bunch. And here are a great many too many for me."

"Yes I have, I've eaten two; I don't want 'em. I give them all to you and Mr. John. I had a great deal rather!"

Ellen took however as precious payment Alice's look and kiss; and then with a delicate consciousness that perhaps the brother and sister might like to be alone, she left the library. She did not know where to go, for Miss Sophia was stretched on the bed in her room, and she did not want any company. At last with her little Bible she placed herself on the old sofa in the hall above stairs, which was perfectly well warmed, and for some time she was left

there in peace. It was pleasant, after all the hubbub of the morning, to have a little quiet time that seemed like Sunday; and the
sweet Bible words came, as they often now came to Ellen, with a
healing breath. But after half an hour or so, to her dismay she
heard a door open and the whole gang of children come trooping
into the hall below, where they soon made such a noise that reading or thinking was out of the question.

"What a bother it is that one can't play games on a Sunday!"
said Marianne Gillespie.

"One *can* play games on a Sunday," answered her brother.
"Where's the odds? It's all Sunday's good for, *I* think."

"William!—William!" sounded the shocked voice of little
Ellen Chauncey,—"you're a real wicked boy!"

"Well now!" said William,—"how am I wicked? Now say,—
I should like to know. How is it any more wicked for us to play
games than it is for aunt Sophia to lie abed and sleep, or for uncle
Howard to read novels, or for grandpa to talk politics, or for mother
to talk about the fashions?—there were she and Miss What's-her-
name for ever so long this morning doing every thing but *make*
a dress. Now which is the worst?"

"Oh, William!—William!—for shame! for shame!" said little
Ellen again.

"Do hush, Ellen Chauncey! will you?" said Marianne, sharply;
—"and you had better hush too, William, if you know what is
good for yourself. I don't care whether it's right or wrong, I do
get dolefully tired with doing nothing."

"Oh, so do I!" said Margaret, yawning. "I wish one could
sleep all Sunday."

"I'll tell you what," said George, "I know a game we can play,
and no harm, either, for it's all out of the Bible."

"Oh, do you? let's hear it, George," cried the girls.

"I don't believe it is good for anything if it is out of the Bible,"
said Margaret. "Now stare, Ellen Chauncey, do!"

"I *ain't* staring," said Ellen indignantly,—"but I don't believe
it is right to play it, if it *is* out of the Bible."

"Well it is though," said George. "Now listen;—I'll think of
somebody in the Bible,—some man or woman, you know; and you
all may ask me twenty questions about him to see if you can find
out who it is."

"What kind of questions?"

"Any kind of questions—whatever you like."

"That will improve your knowledge of scripture history," said
Gilbert.

"To be sure; and exercise our memory," said Isabel Hawthorn.

"Yes, and then we are thinking of good people and what they
did, all the time," said little Ellen.

"Or bad people and what they did," said William.

"But I don't know enough about people and things in the Bible," said Margaret; "I couldn't guess."

"Oh, never mind—it will be all the more fun," said George. "Come! let's begin. Who'll take somebody?"

"Oh, I think this will be fine!" said little Ellen Chauncey;—"but Ellen—where's Ellen?—we want her."

"No we don't want her!—we've enough without her—she won't play!" shouted William, as the little girl ran up stairs. She persevered however. Ellen had left her sofa before this, and was found seated on the foot of her bed. As far and as long as she could she withstood her little friend's entreaties, and very unwillingly at last yielded and went with her down stairs.

"Now we are ready," said little Ellen Chauncey; "I have told Ellen what the game is; who's going to begin?"

"We have begun," said William. "Gilbert has thought of somebody. Man or woman?"

"Man."

"Young or old?"

"Why—he was young first and old afterwards."

"Pshaw, William! what a ridiculous question," said his sister. "Besides you mustn't ask more than one at a time. Rich or poor, Gilbert?"

"Humph!—why I suppose he was moderately well off. I dare say I should think myself a lucky fellow if I had as much."

"Are you answering truly, Gilbert?"

"Upon my honour!"

"Was he in a high or low station of life?" asked Miss Hawthorn.

"Neither at the top nor the bottom of the ladder—a very respectable person indeed."

"But we are not getting on," said Margaret; "according to you he wasn't any thing in particular; what kind of a person was he, Gilbert?"

"A very good man."

"Handsome or ugly?"

"History don't say."

"Well, what *does* it say?" said George,—"what did he do?"

"He took a journey once upon a time."

"What for?"

"Do you mean *why* he went, or what was the *object* of his going?"

"Why the one's the same as the other, ain't it?"

"I beg your pardon."

"Well, what was the object of his going?"

"He went after a wife."

"Samson! Samson!" shouted William and Isabel and Ellen Chauncey.

"No—it wasn't Samson either."

"I can't think of any body else that went after a wife," said George. "That king—what's his name?—that married Esther?"

The children screamed. "*He* didn't go after a wife, George,—his wives were brought to him. Was it Jacob?"

"No—he didn't go after a wife either," said Gilbert; "he married two of them, but he didn't go to his uncle's to find them. You had better go on with your questions. You have had eight already. If you don't look out you won't catch me. Come!"

"Did he get the wife that he went after?" asked Ellen Chauncey.

"He was never married that I know of," said Gilbert.

"What was the reason he failed?" said Isabel.

"He did not fail."

"Did he bring home his wife then? you said he wasn't married."

"He never was, that I know of; but he brought home a wife notwithstanding."

"But how funny you are, Gilbert," said little Ellen,—"he had a wife and he hadn't a wife;—what became of her?"

"She lived and flourished. Twelve questions;—take care."

"Nobody asked what country he was of," said Margaret,—"what was he, Gilbert?"

"He was a Damascene."

"A *what?*"

"Of Damascus—of Damascus. You know where Damascus is, don't you?"

"Fiddle!" said Marianne,—"I thought he was a Jew. Did he live before or after the flood?"

"After. I should think you might have known that."

"Well, I can't make out any thing about him," said Marianne. "We shall have to give it up."

"No, no,—not yet," said William. "Where did he go after his wife?"

"Too close a question."

"Then that don't count. Had he ever seen her before?"

"Never."

"Was she willing to go with him?"

"Very willing. Ladies always are when they go to be married."

"And what became of her?"

"She was married and lived happily,—as I told you."

"But you said *he* wasn't married?"

"Well, what then? I didn't say she married *him.*"

"Whom did she marry?"

"Ah that is asking the whole; I can't tell you."

" Had they far to go ?'' asked Isabel.

" Several days' journey,—I don't know how far.''

" How did they travel ?''

" On camels.''

" Was it the Queen of Sheba !'' said little Ellen.

There was a roar of laughter at this happy thought, and poor little Ellen declared she forgot all but about the journey ; she remembered the Queen of Sheba had taken a journey, and the camels in the picture of the Queen of Sheba, and that made her think of her.

The children gave up. Questioning seemed hopeless ; and Gilbert at last told them his thought. It was Eleazar, Abraham's steward, whom he sent to fetch a wife for his son Isaac.

" Why haven't *you* guessed, little mumchance ?'' said Gilbert to Ellen Montgomery.

" I have guessed,'' said Ellen ;—" I knew who it was some time ago.''

" Then why didn't you say so ? and you haven't asked a single question,'' said George.

" No, you haven't asked a single question,'' said Ellen Chauncey.

" She is a great deal too good for that,'' said William ; " she thinks it is wicked, and that we are not at all nice proper-behaved boys and girls to be playing on Sunday ; she is very sorry she could not help being amused.''

" *Do* you think it is wicked, Ellen ?'' asked her little friend.

" Do you think it isn't right ?'' said George Walsh.

Ellen hesitated ; she saw they were all waiting to hear what she would say. She coloured, and looked down at her little Bible which was still in her hand. It encouraged her.

" I don't want to say any thing rude,'' she began ;—" I don't think it is quite right to play such plays, or any plays.''

She was attacked with impatient cries of " Why not ?'' " Why not ?''

" Because,'' said Ellen, trembling with the effort she made,— " I think Sunday was meant to be spent in growing better and learning good things ; and I don't think such plays would help one at all to do that ; and I have a kind of *feeling* that I ought not to do it.''

" Well I hope you'll act according to your *feelings* then,'' said William ; " I am sure nobody has any objection. You had better go somewhere else though, for we are going on ; we have been learning to be good long enough for one day. Come ! I have thought of somebody.''

Ellen could not help feeling hurt and sorry at the half sneer she saw in the look and manner of the others as well as in William's words. She wished for no better than to go away, but as she did so her bosom swelled and the tears started and her breath came quicker. She found Alice lying down and asleep, Miss Sophia beside her; so she stole out again and went down to the library. Finding nobody, she took possession of the sofa and tried to read again; reading somehow did not go well, and she fell to musing on what had just passed. She thought of the unkindness of the children; how sure she was it was wrong to spend any part of Sunday in such games; what Alice would think of it, and John, and her mother; and how the Sundays long ago used to be spent, when that dear mother was with her; and then she wondered how *she* was passing this very one,—while Ellen was sitting here in the library alone, what *she* was doing in that faraway land; and she thought if there only *were* such things as oracles that could tell truly, how much she would like to ask about her.

"Ellen!" said the voice of John from the window.

She started up; she had thought she was alone; but there he was lying in the window seat.

"What are you doing?"

"Nothing," said Ellen.

"Come here. What are you thinking about? I didn't know you were there till I heard two or three very long sighs. What is the matter with my little sister?"

He took her hand and drew her fondly up to him. "What were you thinking about?"

"I was thinking about different things,—nothing is the matter," said Ellen.

"Then what are those tears in your eyes for?"

"I don't know," said she laughing,—"there weren't any till I came here. I was thinking just now about mamma."

He said no more, still however keeping her beside him.

"I should think," said Ellen presently, after a few minutes' musing look out of the window,—"it would be very pleasant if there were such things as oracles—don't you, Mr. John?"

"No."

"But wouldn't you like to know something about what's going to happen?"

"I do know a great deal about it."

"About what is going to happen!"

He smiled.

"Yes—a great deal, Ellie,—enough to give me work for all the rest of my life."

"Oh, you mean from the Bible!—I was thinking of other things."

"It is best not to know the other things, Ellie;—I am very glad to know those the Bible teaches us."

"But it doesn't tell us much, does it? What does it tell us?"

"Go to the window and tell me what you see."

"I don't see any thing in particular," said Ellen, after taking a grave look-out.

"Well, what in general?"

"Why there is the lawn covered with snow, and the trees and bushes; and the sun is shining on every thing just as it did the

day we came; and there's the long shadow of that hemlock across the snow, and the blue sky."

"Now look out again, Ellie, and listen. I know that a day is to come when those heavens shall be wrapped together as a scroll—they shall vanish away like smoke, and the earth shall wax old like a garment;—and it and all the works that are therein shall be burned up."

As he spoke Ellen's fancy tried to follow,—to picture the ruin and desolation of all that stood so fair and seemed to stand so firm before her;—but the sun shone on, the branches waved gently in the wind, the shadows lay still on the snow, and the blue heaven was fair and cloudless. Fancy was baffled. She turned from the window.

"Do you believe it?" said John.

"Yes," said Ellen,—"I know it; but I think it is very disagreeable to think about it."

"It would be, Ellie," said he, bringing her again to his side,— "very disagreeable—very miserable indeed, if we knew no more than that. But we know more—read here."

Ellen took his little Bible and read at the open place.

"'Behold, I create new heavens and a new earth, and the former shall not be remembered, neither come into mind.'"

"Why won't they be remembered?" said Ellen; "shall we forget all about them."

"No, I do not think that is meant. The new heavens and the new earth will be so much more lovely and pleasant that we shall not want to think of these."

Ellen's eye sought the window again.

"You are thinking that it is hardly possible?" said John with a smile.

"I suppose it is *possible*," said Ellen,—"but——"

"But lovely as this world is, Ellie, man has filled it with sin, and sin has everywhere brought its punishment, and under the weight of both the earth groans. There will be no sin *there;* sorrow and sighing shall flee away; love to each other and love to their blessed King will fill all hearts, and his presence will be with them. Don't you see that even if that world shall be in itself no better than this, it will yet be far, far more lovely than this can ever be with the shadow of sin upon it?"

"Oh, yes!" said Ellen. "I know whenever I feel wrong in any way nothing seems pretty or pleasant to me, or not half so much."

"Very well," said John,—"I see you understand me. I like to think of that land, Ellen,—very much."

"Mr. John," said Ellen,—"don't you think people will know each other again?"

"Those that love each other here?—I have no doubt of it."

Before either John or Ellen had broken the long musing fit that followed these words, they were joined by Alice. Her head was better; and taking her place in the window-seat, the talk began again, between the brother and sister now; Ellen too happy to sit with them and listen. They talked of that land again, of the happy company preparing for it; of their dead mother, but not much of her; of the glory of their King, and the joy of his service, even here;—till thoughts grew too strong for words, and silence again stole upon the group. The short winter day came to an end; the sunlight faded away into moonlight. No shadows lay now on the lawn; and from where she sat Ellen could see the great hemlock all silvered with the moonlight which began to steal in at the window. It was very, very beautiful;—yet she could think now without sorrow that all this should come to an end; because of that new heaven and new earth wherein righteousness should dwell.

"We have eaten up all your grapes, Ellie," said Alice,—" or rather *I* have, for John didn't help me much. I think I never ate so sweet grapes in my life; John said the reason was because every one tasted of you."

"I am very glad," said Ellen laughing.

"There is no evil without some good," Alice went on;—" except for my headache John would not have held my head by the hour as he did; and you couldn't have given me the pleasure you did, Ellie. Oh, Jack!—there has been many a day lately when I would gladly have had a headache for the power of laying my head on your shoulder!"

"And if mamma had not gone away I should never have known you," said Ellen. "I wish she never *had* gone, but I am very, very glad for this!"

She had kneeled upon the window-seat and clasped Alice round the neck, just as they were called to tea. The conversation had banished every disagreeable feeling from Ellen's mind. She met her companions in the drawing-room almost forgetting that she had any cause of complaint against them. And this appeared when in the course of the evening it came in her way to perform some little office of politeness for Marianne. It was done with the gracefulness that could only come from a spirit entirely free from ungrateful feelings. The children felt it, and for the time were shamed into better behaviour. The evening passed pleasantly, and Ellen went to bed very happy.

CHAPTER XXXI.

"The ancient heroes were illustrious,
For being benign, and not blustrous."
HUDIBRAS.

THE next day it happened that the young people were amusing themselves with talking in a room where John Humphreys, walking up and down, was amusing *himself* with thinking. In the course of his walk, he began to find their amusement rather disturbing to his. The children were all grouped closely around

Margaret Dunscombe, who was entertaining them with a long and very detailed account of a wedding and great party at Randolph which she had had the happiness of attending. Eagerly fighting her battles over again, and pleased with the rapt attention of her hearers, the speaker forgot herself and raised her voice much more than she meant to do. As every turn of his walk brought John near, there came to his ears sufficient bits and scraps of Margaret's story to give him a very fair sample of the whole ; and he was sorry to see Ellen among the rest, and as the rest, hanging upon her lips and drinking in what seemed to be very poor nonsense. " Her gown was all blue satin, trimmed here,—and so,—you know, with the most *exquisite* lace, as deep as that,—and on the shoulders and here—you know, it was looped up with the most lovely bunches of"—here John lost the sense. When he came near again she had got upon a different topic—" ' Miss Simmons,' says I, ' what did you do that for ?' ' Why,' says she, ' how could I help it ? I saw Mr. Payne coming, and I thought I'd get behind you, and so——.' " The next time the speaker was saying with great animation, " And lo, and behold, when I was in the midst of all my pleasure, up comes a little gentleman of about his dimensions——." He had not taken many turns when he saw that Margaret's nonsense was branching out right and left into worse than nonsense.

" Ellen !" said he suddenly,—" I want you in the library."

" My conscience !" said Margaret as he left the room,—" King John the Second, and no less."

" Don't go on till I come back," said Ellen ; " I won't be three minutes ; just wait for me."

She found John seated at one of the tables in the library sharpening a pencil.

" Ellen," said he in his usual manner,—" I want you to do something for me."

She waited eagerly to hear what, but instead of telling her he took a piece of drawing paper and began to sketch something. Ellen stood by, wondering and impatient to the last degree ; not caring however to show her impatience, though her very feet were twitching to run back to her companions.

" Ellen," said John as he finished the old stump of a tree with one branch left on it, and a little bit of ground at the bottom, " did you ever try your hand at drawing ?"

" No," said Ellen.

" Then sit down here," said he rising from his chair, " and let me see what you can make of that."

" But I don't know how," said Ellen.

" I will teach you. There is a piece of paper, and this pencil is sharp enough. Is that chair too low for you ?"

He placed another, and with extreme unwillingness and some displeasure Ellen sat down.   It was on her tongue to ask if another time would not do, but somehow she could not get the words out.   John showed her how to hold her pencil, how to place her paper, where to begin, and how to go on; and then went to the other end of the room and took up his walk again.   Ellen at first felt more inclined to drive her pencil *through* the paper than to make quiet marks upon it.   However necessity was upon her. She began her work; and once fairly begun it grew delightfully interesting.   Her vexation went off entirely; she forgot Margaret and her story; the wrinkles on the old trunk smoothed those on her brow, and those troublesome leaves at the branch end brushed away all thoughts of every thing else.   Her cheeks were burning with intense interest, when the library door burst open and the whole troop of children rushed in; they wanted Ellen for a round game in which all their number were needed; she must come directly.

" I can't come just yet," said she; " I must finish this first."

" Afterwards will do just as well," said George;—" come Ellen, do!—you can finish it afterwards."

" No I can't," said Ellen,—" I can't leave it till it's done.   Why, I thought Mr. John was here!   I didn't see him go out.   I'll come in a little while."

" Did *he* set you about that precious piece of business?" said William.

" Yes."

" I declare," said Margaret,—" he's fitter to be the Grand Turk than any one else I know of."

" I don't know who the Grand Turk is," said Ellen.

" I'll tell you," said William, putting his mouth close to her ear, and speaking in a disagreeable loud whisper,—" it's the biggest gobbler in the yard."

" Ain't you ashamed, William!" cried little Ellen Chauncey.

" That's it exactly," said Margaret,—" always strutting about."

" He isn't a bit," said Ellen very angry; " I've seen people a great deal more like gobblers than he is."

" Well," said William, reddening in his turn, " I had rather at any rate be a good turkey gobbler than one of those outlandish birds that have an appetite for stones and glass and bits of morocco, and such things.   Come, let us leave her to do the Grand Turk's bidding.   Come, Ellen Chauncey—you mustn't stay to interrupt her—we want you!"

They left her alone.   Ellen had coloured, but William's words did not hit very sore; since John's talk with her about the matter referred to she had thought of it humbly and wisely; it is only pride that makes such fault-finding very hard to bear.   Sho was very sorry however that they had fallen out again, and that her own passion, as she feared, had been the cause. A few tears had to be wiped away before she could see exactly how the old tree stood, —then taking up her pencil she soon forgot every thing in her work. It was finished, and with head now on one side, now on the other, she was looking at her picture with very great satisfaction, when her eye caught the figure of John standing before her.

"Is it done?" said he.

"It is done," said Ellen smiling, as she rose up to let him come. He sat down to look at it.

"It is very well, he said,—"better than I expected,—it is very well indeed. Is this your *first* trial, Ellen?"

"Yes—the first."

"You found it pleasant work?"

"Oh, very!—very pleasant. I like it dearly."

"Then I will teach you. This shows you have a taste for it, and that is precisely what I wanted to find out. I will give you an easier copy next time. I rather expected when you sat down," said he, smiling a little, that the old tree would grow a good deal more crooked under your hands than I meant it to be."

Ellen blushed exceedingly. "I do believe, Mr. John," she said, stammering, "that you know every thing I am thinking about."

"I might do that, Ellen, without being as wise as an oracle. But I do not expect to make any very painful discoveries in that line."

Ellen thought, if he did not, it would not be her fault. She truly repented her momentary anger and hasty speech to William. Not that he did not deserve it, or that it was not true; but it was unwise, and had done mischief, and "it was not a bit like peace-making, nor meek at all," Ellen said to herself. She had been reading that morning the fifth chapter of Matthew, and it ran in her head, "Blessed are the meek,"—"Blessed are the peacemakers: for they shall be called the children of God." She strove to get back a pleasant feeling toward her young companions, and prayed that she might not be angry at any thing they should say. She was tried again at tea-time.

Miss Sophia had quitted the table, bidding William hand the doughnuts to those who could not reach them. Marianne took a great while to make her choice. Her brother grew impatient.

"Well, I hope you have suited yourself," said he. "Come, Miss Montgomery, don't you be as long; my arm is tired. Shut your eyes, and then you'll be sure to get the biggest one in the basket."

"No, Ellen," said John, who none of the children thought was near,—"it would be ungenerous—I wouldn't deprive Master William of his best arguments."

" What do you mean by my arguments?" said William sharply.

" Generally, those which are the most difficult to take in," answered his tormentor with perfect gravity.

Ellen tried to keep from smiling, but could not; and others of the party did not try. William and his sister were enraged, the more because John had said nothing they could take hold of, or even repeat. Gilbert made common cause with them.

" I wish I was grown up for once," said William.

" Will you fight *me*, sir?" asked Gilbert, who was a matter of three years older, and well grown enough.

His question received no answer, and was repeated.

" No, sir."

" Why not, sir?"

" I am afraid you'd lay me up with a sprained ankle," said John, " and I should not get back to Doncaster as quickly as I must."

" It is very mean of him," said Gilbert, as John walked away,— " I could whip him I know."

" Who's that?" said Mr. Howard Marshman.

" John Humphreys."

" John Humphreys! You had better not meddle with him, my dear fellow. It would be no particular proof of wisdom."

" Why, he is no such great affair," said Gilbert; " he's tall enough to be sure, but I don't believe he is heavier than I am."

" You don't know, in the first place, how to judge of the size of a perfectly well-made man; and in the second place *I* was not a match for him a year ago; so you may judge. I do not know precisely," he went on to the lady he was walking with, " what it takes to rouse John Humphreys, but when he *is* roused he seems to me to have strength enough for twice his bone and muscle. I have seen him do curious things once or twice!"

" That quiet Mr. Humphreys?"

" Humph!" said Mr. Howard,—" gunpowder is pretty quiet stuff so long as it keeps cool."

The next day another matter happened to disturb Ellen. Margaret had received an elegant pair of ear-rings as a Christmas present, and was showing them for the admiration of her young friends. Ellen's did not satisfy her.

" Ain't they splendid," said she. " Tell the truth now, Ellen Montgomery, wouldn't you give a great deal if somebody would send you such a pair?"

" They are very pretty," said Ellen, " but I don't think I care much for such things,—I would rather have the money."

" Oh, you avaricious!—Mr. Marshman!" cried Margaret, as the old gentleman was just then passing through the room,—" here's

Ellen Montgomery says she'd rather have money than any thing else for *her* present."

He did not seem to hear her, and went out without making any reply.

"Oh, Margaret!" said Ellen, shocked and distressed,—"how could you! how could you! What will Mr. Marshman think?"

Margaret answered she didn't care what he thought. Ellen could only hope he had not heard.

But a day or two after, when neither Ellen nor her friends were present, Mr. Marshman asked who it was that had told him Ellen Montgomery would like money better than any thing else for her New Year's present.

"It was I, sir," said Margaret.

"It sounds very unlike her to say so," remarked Mrs. Chauncey.

"Did she say so?" inquired Mr. Marshman.

"I understood her so," said Margaret,—"I understood her to say she wouldn't care for any thing else."

"I am disappointed in her," said the old gentleman; "I wouldn't have believed it."

"I do not believe it," said Mrs. Chauncey quietly; "there has been some mistake."

It was hard for Ellen now to keep to what she thought right. Disagreeable feelings would rise when she remembered the impoliteness, the half sneer, the whole taunt, and the real unkindness of several of the young party. She found herself ready to be irritated, inclined to dislike the sight of those, even wishing to visit some sort of punishment upon them. But Christian principle had taken strong hold in little Ellen's heart; she fought her evil tempers manfully. It was not an easy battle to gain. Ellen found that resentment and pride had roots deep enough to keep her pulling up the shoots for a good while. She used to get alone when she could, to read a verse, if no more, of her Bible, and pray; she could forgive William and Margaret more easily then. Solitude and darkness saw many a prayer and tear of hers that week. As she struggled thus to get rid of sin and to be more like what would please God, she grew humble and happy. Never was such a struggle carried on by faith in him, without success. And after a time, though a twinge of the old feeling might come, it was very slight; she would bid William and Margaret good-morning, and join them in any enterprise of pleasure or business, with a brow as unclouded as the sun. They, however, were too conscious of having behaved unbecomingly toward their little stranger guest to be over fond of her company. For the most part she and Ellen Chauncey were left to each other.

Meanwhile the famous needlebook was in a fair way to be finished. Great dismay had at first been excited in the breast of the intended giver, by the discovery that Gilbert had consulted what seemed to be a very extraordinary fancy, in making the rose a yellow one. Ellen did her best to comfort her. She asked Alice, and found there were such things as yellow roses, and they were very beautiful too ; and besides it would match so nicely the yellow butterfly on the other leaf.

" I had rather it wouldn't match !" said Ellen Chauncey ;—" and it don't match the rose-coloured silk besides. Are the yellow roses sweet ?"

" No," said Ellen,—" but *this* couldn't have been a sweet rose at any rate, you know."

" Oh, but," said the other, bursting out into a fresh passion of inconsolable tears,—" I wanted it should be the *picture* of a sweet rose !—And I think he might have put a purple butterfly—yellow butterflies are so common ! I had a great deal rather have had a purple butterfly and a red rose !"

What cannot be cured, however, must be endured. The tears were dried, in course of time, and the needlebook with its yellow pictures and pink edges was very neatly finished. Ellen had been busy too on her own account. Alice had got a piece of fine linen for her from Miss Sophia ; the collar for Mr. Van Brunt had been cut out, and Ellen with great pleasure had made it. The stitching, the strings, and the very button-hole, after infinite pains, were all finished by Thursday night. She had also made a needlecase for Alice, not of so much pretension as the other one ; this was green morocco lined with crimson satin ; no leaves, but ribbon stitched in to hold papers of needles, and a place for a bodkin. Ellen worked very hard at this ; it was made with the extremest care, and made beautifully. Ellen Chauncey admired it very much, and anew lamented the uncouth variety of colours in her own. It was a grave question whether pink or yellow ribbon should be used for the latter ; Ellen Montgomery recommended pink, she herself inclined to yellow ; and tired of doubting, at last resolved to split the difference and put one string of each colour. Ellen thought that did not mend matters, but wisely kept her thoughts to herself. Besides the needlecase for Alice, she had snatched the time whenever she could get away from Ellen Chauncey to work at something for her. She had begged Alice's advice and help ; and between them, out of Ellen's scraps of morocco and silk, they had manufactured a little bag of all the colours of the rainbow, and very pretty and tasteful withal. Ellen thought it a chef-d'œuvre, and was unbounded in her admiration. It lay folded up in white paper in a locked drawer ready for New Year's day. In addition to all these pieces of business John had begun to give her drawing lessons, according to his promise. These became Ellen's delight. She would willingly have spent much more time upon them than he would allow her. It was the most loved employment of the day. Her teacher's skill was not greater than the perfect gentleness and kindness with which he taught. Ellen thought of Mr. Howard's speech about gunpowder,—she could not understand it.

"What is your conclusion on the whole?" asked John one day, as he stood beside her mending a pencil.

"Why," said Ellen, laughing and blushing,—" how *could* you guess what I was thinking about, Mr. John?"

"Not very difficult, when you are eying me so hard."

"I was thinking," said Ellen,—" I don't know whether it is right in me to tell it—because somebody said you——"

"Well?"

"Were like gunpowder."

"Very kind of somebody! And so you have been in doubt of an explosion?"

"No—I don't know—I wondered what he meant."

"Never believe what you hear said of people, Ellen; judge for yourself. Look here—that house has suffered from a severe gale of wind, I should think—all the uprights are slanting off to the right—can't you set it up straight?"

Ellen laughed at the tumble-down condition of the house as thus pointed out to her, and set about reforming it.

It was Thursday afternoon that Alice and Ellen were left alone in the library, several of the family having been called out to receive some visitors; Alice had excused herself, and Ellen as soon as they were gone nestled up to her side.

"How pleasant it is to be alone together, dear Alice!—I don't have you even at night now."

"It is very pleasant, dear Ellie! Home will not look disagreeable again, will it? even after all our gayety here."

"No indeed!—at least *your* home won't—I don't know what mine will. Oh, me! I had almost forgotten aunt Fortune!—"

"Never mind, dear Ellie! You and I have each something to bear—we must be brave and bear it manfully. There is a friend that sticketh closer than a brother, you know. We shan't be unhappy if we do our duty and love Him."

"How soon is Mr. John going away?"

"Not for all next week. And so long as he stays, I do not mean that you shall leave me."

Ellen cried for joy.

"I can manage it with Miss Fortune I know," said Alice. "These fine drawing lessons must not be interrupted. John is very much pleased with your performances."

"Is he?" said Ellen delighted;—" I have taken all the pains I could."

"That is the sure way to success, Ellie. But, Ellie, I want to

ask you about something. What was that you said to Margaret
Dunscombe about wanting money for a New Year's present?"

"You know it then!" cried Ellen, starting up. "Oh, I'm so
glad! I wanted to speak to you about it so I didn't know what
to do, and I thought I oughtn't to. What shall I do about it,
dear Alice? How did you know? George said you were not
there."

"Mrs. Chauncey told me; she thought there had been some
mistake, or something wrong;—how was it, Ellen?"

"Why," said Ellen, "she was showing us her ear-rings, and
asking us what we thought of them, and she asked me if I
wouldn't like to have such a pair; and I thought I would a great
deal rather have the money they cost, to buy other things with,
you know, that I would like better; and I said so; and just then
Mr. Marshman came in, and she called out to him, loud, that I
wanted money for a present, or would like it better than any thing
else, or something like that. Oh, Alice, how I felt! I was
frightened;—but then I hoped Mr. Marshman did not hear her,
for he did not say any thing; but the next day George told me all
about what she had been saying in there, and oh, it made me so
unhappy!" said poor Ellen, looking very dismal. "What *will* Mr.
Marshman think of me? he will think I expected a present, and I
never *dreamed* of such a thing! it makes me ashamed to speak of
it even; and I *can't bear* he should think so—I can't bear it!
What shall I do, dear Alice?"

"I don't know what you can do, dear Ellie, but be patient.
Mr. Marshman will not think anything very hard of you, I dare
say."

"But I think he does already; he hasn't kissed me since that
as he did before; I know he does, and I don't know what to do.
How could Margaret say that! oh, how could she! it was very
unkind.—What can I do?" said Ellen again, after a pause, and
wiping away a few tears. "Couldn't Mrs. Chauncey tell Mr.
Marshman not to give me any thing, for that I never expected it,
and would a great deal rather not?"

"Why no, Ellie, I do not think that would be exactly the best
or most dignified way."

"What then, dear Alice? I'll do just as you say."

"I would just remain quiet."

"But Ellen says the things are all put on the plates in the
morning; and if there should be money on mine—I don't know
what I should do, I should feel so badly. I couldn't keep it, Alice!
—I couldn't!"

"Very well—you need not—but remain quiet in the meanwhile;
and if it should be so, then say what you please, only take care
that you say it in the right spirit and in a right manner. Nobody

can hurt you much, my child, while you keep the even path of duty; poor Margaret is her own worst enemy."

" Then if there should be money in the morning, I may tell Mr. Marshman the truth about it ?"

" Certainly.—only do not be in haste; speak gently."

" Oh, I wish every body would be kind and pleasant always !" said poor Ellen, but half comforted.

" What a sigh was there !" said John, coming in. " What is the matter with my little sister ?"

" Some of the minor trials of life, John," said Alice with a smile.

" What is the matter, Ellie ?"

" Oh, something you can't help," said Ellen.

" And something I mustn't know. Well, to change the scene,— suppose you go with me to visit the greenhouse and hothouses. Have you seen them yet ?"

" No," said Ellen, as she eagerly sprang forward to take his hand ;—" Ellen promised to go with me, but we have been so busy."

" Will you come, Alice ?"

" Not I," said Alice,—" I wish I could, but I shall be wanted elsewhere."

" By whom I wonder so much as by me," said her brother. " However, after to-morrow I will have you all to myself."

As he and Ellen were crossing the hall they met Mrs. Marshman.

" Where are you going, John ?" said she.

" Where I ought to have been before ma'am,—to pay my respects to Mr. Hutchinson."

" You've not seen him yet ! that is very ungrateful of you. Hutchinson is one of your warmest friends and admirers. There are few people he mentions with so much respect, or that he is so glad to see, as Mr. John Humphreys."

" A distinction I owe, I fear, principally to my English blood," said John shaking his head.

" It is not altogether that," said Mrs. Marshman laughing ; " though I do believe I am the only Yankee good Hutchinson has ever made up his mind entirely to like. But go and see him, do, he will be very much pleased."

" Who is Mr. Hutchinson ?" said Ellen as they went on.

" He is the gardener, or rather the head gardener. He came out with his master some thirty or forty years ago, but his old English prejudice will go to the grave with him, I believe."

" But why don't he like the Americans ?"

John laughed. " It would never do for me to attempt to answer that question, Ellie, fond of going to the bottom of things as you are. We should just get to hard fighting about tea-time, and should barely make peace by mid-day to-morrow at the most moderate calculation. You shall have an answer to your question however."

Ellen could not conceive what he meant, but resolved to wait for his promised answer.

As they entered the large and beautifully kept greenhouse Hutchinson came from the further end of it to meet them ; an old man, of most respectable appearance. He bowed very civilly, and then slipped his pruning knife into his left hand to leave the right at liberty for John, who shook it cordially.

"And why 'aven't you been to see me before, Mr. John ? I 'ave thought it rather 'ard of you, Miss h'Alice has come several times."

"The ladies have more leisure, Mr. Hutchinson. You look flourishing here."

" Why yes, sir,—pretty middling within doors ; but I don't like the climate, Mr. John, I don't the climate, sir. There's no country like h'England, I believe, for my business. 'Ere's a fine rose, sir, —if you'll step a bit this way—quite a new kind—I got it over last h'autumn—the Palmerston it is. Those are fine buds, sir."

The old man was evidently much pleased to see his visitor, and presently plunged him deep into English politics, for which he seemed to have lost no interest by forty years life in America. As Ellen could not understand what they were talking about, she quitted John's side and went wandering about by herself. From the moment the sweet aromatic smell of the plants had greeted her she had been in a high state of delight ; and now lost to all the world beside, from the mystery of one beautiful and strange green thing to another, she went wondering and admiring, and now and then timidly advancing her nose to see if something glorious was something sweet too. She could hardly leave a superb cactus, in the petals of which there was such a singular blending of scarlet and crimson as almost to dazzle her sight ; and if the pleasure of smell could intoxicate she would have *reeled* away from a luxuriant daphne odorata in full flower, over which she feasted for a long time. The variety of green leaves alone was a marvel to her ; some rough and brown-streaked, some shining as if they were varnished, others of hair-like delicacy of structure,—all lovely. At last she stood still with admiration and almost held her breath before a white camellia.

" What does that flower make you think of, Ellen ?" said John coming up ; his friend the gardener had left him to seek a news-paper in which he wished to show him a paragraph.

" I don't know," said Ellen,—" I couldn't think of any thing but itself."

" It reminds me of what I ought to be—and of what I shall be if I ever see heaven ; it seems to me the emblem of a sinless pure spirit,—looking up in fearless spotlessness. Do you remember what was said to the old Church of Sardis?—'Thou hast a few names that have not defiled their garments; and they shall walk with me in white, for they are worthy.'"

The tears rushed to Ellen's eyes, she felt she was so very unlike this; but Mr. Hutchinson coming back prevented any thing more from being said. She looked at the white camellia; it seemed to speak to her.

"That's the paragraph, sir," said the old gardener, giving the paper to John. "'Ere's a little lady that is fond of flowers, if I don't make a mistake; this is somebody I've not seen before. Is this the little lady little Miss h'Ellen was telling me about?"

"I presume so," said John;—"she is Miss Ellen Montgomery, a sister of mine, Mr. Hutchinson, and Mr. Marshman's guest."

"By both names h'entitled to my greatest respect," said the old man, stepping back and making a very low bow to Ellen with his hand upon his heart, at which she could not help laughing. "I am very glad to see Miss h'Ellen; what can I do to make her remember old 'Utchinson? Would Miss h'Ellen like a bouquet?"

Ellen did not venture to say yes, but her blush and sparkling eyes answered him. The old gardener understood her, and was as good as his word. He began with cutting a beautiful sprig of a large purple geranium, then a slip of lemon myrtle. Ellen watched him as the bunch grew in his hand, and could hardly believe her eyes as one beauty after another was added to what became a most elegant bouquet. And most sweet too; to her joy the delicious daphne and fragrant lemon blossom went to make part of it. Her thanks, when it was given her, were made with few words but with all her face; the old gardener smiled, and was quite satisfied that his gift was not thrown away. He afterwards showed them his hothouses, where Ellen was astonished and very much interested to see ripe oranges and lemons in abundance, and pines too, such as she had been eating since she came to Ventnor, thinking nothing less than that they grew so near home. The grapes had all been cut.

There was to be quite a party at Ventnor in the evening of New Year's day. Ellen knew this, and destined her precious flowers for Alice's adornment. How to keep them in the meanwhile? She consulted Mr. John, and according to his advice took them to Mrs. Bland the housekeeper, to be put in water and kept in a safe place for her till the time. She knew Mrs. Bland, for Ellen Chauncey and she had often gone to her room to work where none of the children would find and trouble them. Mrs. Bland promised to take famous care of the flowers, and said she would do it with the greatest pleasure. Mr. Marshman's guests, she added smiling,—must have every thing they wanted.

"What does that mean, Mrs. Bland?" said Ellen.

"Why, you see, Miss Ellen, there's a deal of company always coming, and some is Mrs. Gillespie's friends, and some Mr. Howard's, and some to see Miss Sophia more particularly, and some belong to Mrs. Marshman, or the whole family maybe; but now and then *Mr.* Marshman has an old English friend or so, that he sets the greatest store by; and them he calls *his* guests; and the best in the house is hardly good enough for them, or the country either."

"And so I am one of Mr. Marshman's guests!" said Ellen, "I didn't know what it meant."

She saved out one little piece of rose-geranium from her flowers, for the gratification of her own nose; and skipped away through the hall to rejoin her companions, very light-hearted indeed.

CHAPTER XXXII.

This life, sae far's I understand,
Is a' enchanted fairy-land,
Where pleasure is the magic wand,
    That wielded right,
Makes hours like minutes, hand in hand,
    Dance by fu' light.

BURNS.

NEW YEAR'S morning dawned.

"How I wish breakfast was over!"—thought Ellen as she was dressing. However, there is no way of getting *over* this life but by going through it; so when the bell rang she went down as usual. Mr. Marshman had decreed that he would not have a confusion of gifts at the breakfast table; other people might make presents in their own way; they must not interfere with his. Needlecases, bags, and so forth, must therefore wait another opportunity; and Ellen Chauncey decided it would just make the pleasure so much longer, and was a great improvement on the old plan. "Happy New Years" and pleasant greetings were exchanged as the party gathered in the breakfast room; pleasure sat on all faces, except Ellen's, and many a one wore a broad smile as they sat down to table. For the napkins were in singular disarrangement this morning; instead of being neatly folded up on the plates, in their usual fashion, they were in all sorts of disorder,—sticking up in curious angles, some high, some low, some half folded, some quite unfolded, according to the size and shape of that which they covered. It was worth while to see that long tableful, and the faces of the company, before yet a napkin was touched. An anxious glance at her own showed Ellen that it lay quite flat; Alice's, which was next, had an odd little rising in the middle, as if there were a small dumpling under it. Ellen was in an agony for this pause to come to an end. It was broken by some of the older persons, and then in a trice every plate was uncovered. And then what a buzz!—pleasure and thanks and admiration, and even laughter. Ellen dreaded at first to look at her plate; she bethought her, however, that if she waited long she would have to do it with all eyes upon her; she lifted the napkin slowly—yes—just as she feared—there lay a clean bank-note—of what value she could not see, for confusion covered her; the blood rushed to her cheeks and the tears to her eyes. She could not have spoken, and happily it was no time then; every body else was speaking; she could not have been heard. She had time to cool and recollect herself; but she sat with her eyes cast down, fastened upon her plate and the unfortunate bank-bill, which she detested with all her heart. She did not know what Alice had received; she understood nothing that was going on, till Alice touched her and said gently, "Mr. Marshman is speaking to you, Ellen."

"Sir!" said Ellen, starting.

"You need not look so terrified," said Mr. Marshman, smiling; —"I only asked you if your bill was a counterfeit—something seems to be wrong about it."

Ellen looked at her plate and hesitated. Her lip trembled.

"What is it?" continued the old gentleman. "Is any thing the matter."

Ellen desperately took up the bill, and with burning cheeks marched to his end of the table.

"I am very much obliged to you, sir, but I had a great deal rather not;—if you please—if you will please to be so good as to let me give it back to you—I should be very glad."—

"Why hoity toity!" said the old gentleman,—"what's all this? what's the matter? don't you like it? I thought I was doing the very thing that would please you best of all."

"I am very sorry you should think so, sir," said Ellen, who had recovered a little breath, but had the greatest difficulty to keep back her tears;—"I never thought of such a thing as your giving me any thing, sir, till somebody spoke of it, and I had rather never have any thing in the world than that you should think what you thought about me."

"What did I think about you?"

"George told me that somebody told you, sir, I wanted money for my present."

"And didn't you say so?"

"Indeed I didn't, sir!" said Ellen with a sudden fire. "I never thought of such a thing!"

"What *did* you say then?"

" Margaret was showing us her ear-rings, and she asked me if I wouldn't like to have some like them ; and I couldn't help thinking I would a great deal rather have the money they would cost to buy something for Alice ; and just when I said so you came in, sir, and she said what she did. I was very much ashamed. I wasn't thinking of you, sir, at all, nor of New Year."

" Then you would like something else better than money."

" No, sir, nothing at all if you please. If you'll only be so good as not to give me this I will be very much obliged to you indeed ; and please not to think I could be so shameful as you thought I was."

Ellen's face was not to be withstood. The old gentleman took the bill from her hand.

" I will never think any thing of you," said he, " but what is the very tip-top of honourable propriety. But you make *me* ashamed now—what am I going to do with this ? Here have you come and made me a present, and I feel very awkward indeed."

" I don't care what you do with it, sir," said Ellen, laughing, though in imminent danger of bursting into tears ;—" I am very glad it is out of *my* hands."

" But you needn't think I am going to let you off so," said he ; " you must give me half-a-dozen kisses at least to prove that you have forgiven me for making so great a blunder."

" Half-a-dozen is too many at once," said Ellen, gayly ; " three now and three to-night."

So she gave the old gentleman three kisses, but he caught her in his arms and gave her a dozen at least ; after which he found out that the waiter was holding a cup of coffee at his elbow, and Ellen went back to her place with a very good appetite for her breakfast.

After breakfast the needlecases were delivered. Both gave the most entire satisfaction. Mrs. Chauncey assured her daughter that she would quite as lief have a yellow as a red rose on the cover, and that she liked the inscription extremely ; which the little girl acknowledged to have been a joint device of her own and Ellen's. Ellen's bag gave great delight, and was paraded all over the house.

After the bustle of thanks and rejoicing was at last over, and when she had a minute to herself, which Ellen Chauncey did not give her for a good while, Ellen bethought her of her flowers,—a sweet gift still to be made. Why not make it now ? why should not Alice have the pleasure of them all day ? A bright thought ! Ellen ran forthwith to the housekeeper's room, and after a long admiring look at her treasures, carried them glass and all to the library, where Alice and John often were in the morning alone. Alice thanked her in the way she liked best, and then the flowers were smelled and admired afresh.

"Nothing could have been pleasanter to me, Ellie, except Mr. Marshman's gift."

"And what was that, Alice? I haven t seen it yet."

Alice pulled out of her pocket a small round morocco case, the very thing that Ellen had thought looked like a dumpling under the napkin, and opened it.

"It's Mr. John!" exclaimed Ellen. "Oh, how beautiful!" Neither of her hearers could help laughing.

"It is very fine, Ellie," said Alice; "you are quite right. Now I know what was the business that took John to Randolph every day, and kept him there so long, while I was wondering at him unspeakably. Kind, kind Mr. Marshman."

"Did Mr. John get any thing?"

"Ask him, Ellie."

"Did you get any thing, Mr. John?" said Ellen, going up to him where he was reading on the sofa.

"I got this," said John, handing her a little book which lay beside him.

"What is this? Wime's—Wiem's—Life of Washington— Washington? he was—May I look at it?"

"Certainly!"

She opened the book, and presently sat down on the floor where she was by the side of the sofa. Whatever she had found within the leaves of the book, she had certainly lost herself. An hour passed. Ellen had not spoken or moved except to turn over leaves.

"Ellen!" said John.

She looked up, her cheeks coloured high.

"What have you found there?" said he, smiling.

"Oh, a great deal! But—did Mr. Marshman give you this?"

"No."

"Oh!" said Ellen, looking puzzled,—"I thought you said you got this this morning."

"No, I got it last night. I got it for you, Ellie."

"For me!" said Ellen, her colour deepening very much,—"for me! did you? Oh, thank you!—oh, I'm so much obliged to you, Mr. John."

"It is only an answer to one of your questions."

"This! is it?—I don't know what, I am sure. Oh, I wish I could do something to please you, Mr. John!"

"You shall, Ellie; you shall give me a brother's right again."

Blushingly Ellen approached her lips to receive one of his grave kisses; and then, not at all displeased, went down on the floor and was lost in her book.

Oh, the long joy of that New Year's day!—how shall it be told? The pleasure of that delightful book, in which she was

wrapped the whole day ; even when called off, as she often was,
by Ellen Chauncey to help her in fifty little matters of business or
pleasure.   These were attended to, and faithfully and cheerfully,·
but *the book* was in her head all the while.   And this pleasure
was mixed with Alice's pleasure, the flowers and the miniature,
and Mr. Marshman's restored kindness.   She never met John's
or Alice's eye that day without a smile.   Even when she went
to be dressed her book went with her, and was laid on the bed
within sight, ready to be taken up the moment she was at liberty.
Ellen Chauncey lent her a white frock which was found to answer
very well with a tuck let out; and Alice herself dressed her.
While this was doing, Margaret Dunscombe put her head in at
the door to ask Anne, Miss Sophia's maid, if she was almost ready
to come and curl her hair.

"Indeed I can't say that I am, Miss Margaret," said Anne.
"I've something to do for Miss Humphreys, and Miss Sophia
hasn't so much as done the first thing toward beginning to get
ready yet.   It'll be a good hour and more."

Margaret went away exclaiming impatiently that she could get
nobody to help her, and would have to wait till every body was
down stairs.

A few minutes after she heard Ellen's voice at the door of her
room asking if she might come in.

"Yes—who's that ?—what do you want?"

"I'll fix your hair if you'll let me," said Ellen.

"You ?   I don't believe you can."

"Oh, yes I can; I used to do mamma's very often; I am not
afraid if you'll trust me."

"Well, thank you, I don't care if you try then," said Margaret,
seating herself,—"it won't do any harm at any rate ; and I want
to be down stairs before anybody gets here ; I think it's half the
fun to see them come in.   Bless me ! you're dressed and all ready."

Margaret's hair was in long thick curls; it was not a trifling
matter to dress them.   Ellen plodded through it patiently and
faithfully, taking great pains, and doing the work well ; and then
went back to Alice.   Margaret's thanks, not very gracefully given,
would have been a poor reward for the loss of three-quarters of an
hour of pleasure.   But Ellen was very happy in having done right.
It was no longer time to read ; they must go down stairs.

The New Year's party was a nondescript,—young and old
together; a goodly number of both were gathered from Randolph
and the neighbouring country.   There were games for the young,
dancing for the gay, and a superb supper for all ; and the big
bright rooms were full of bright faces.   It was a very happy evening to Ellen.   For a good part of it Mr. Marshman took possession
of her, or kept her near him ; and his extreme kindness would

alone have made the evening pass pleasantly ; she was sure he was her firm friend again.

In the course of the evening Mrs. Chauncey found occasion to ask her about her journey up the river, without at all mentioning Margaret or what she had said. Ellen answered that she had come with Mrs. Dunscombe and her daughter.

" Did you have a pleasant time ?" asked Mrs. Chauncey.

" Why, no, ma'am," said Ellen,—" I don't know—it was partly pleasant and partly unpleasant."

" What made it so, love ?"

" I had left mamma that morning, and that made me unhappy."

" But you said it was partly pleasant ?"

" Oh, that was because I had such a good friend on board,"said Ellen, her face lighting up as his image came before her.

" Who was that ?"

" I don't know, ma'am, who he was."

" A stranger to you ?"

" Yes, ma'am—I never saw him before—I wish I could see him again."

" Where did you find him ?"

" I didn't find him—he found me, when I was sitting up on the highest part of the boat."

" And your friends with you ?"

" What friends ?"

" Mrs. Dunscombe and her daughter."

" No, ma'am—they were down in the cabin."

" And what business had you to be wandering about the boat alone ?" said Mr. Marshman, good-humouredly.

" They were strangers, sir," said Ellen, colouring a little.

" Well, so was this man—your friend—a stranger too, wasn't he ?"

" Oh, he was a very different stranger," said Ellen, smiling,— " and he wasn't a stranger long, besides."

" Well, you must tell me more about him,—come, I'm curious ; —what sort of a strange friend was this ?"

" He wasn't a *strange* friend," said Ellen, laughing ;—" he was a very, very good friend ; he took care of me the whole day ; he was very good and very kind."

" What kind of a man ?" said Mrs. Chauncey ;—" a gentleman ?"

" Oh, yes, ma'am !" said Ellen, looking surprised at the question. " I am sure he was."

" What did he look like ?"

Ellen tried to tell, but the portrait was not very distinct.

" What did he wear ? Coat or cloak ?"

" Coat—dark brown, I think."

" This was in the end of October, wasn't it ?"

Ellen thought a moment and answered " yes."

" And you don't know his name ?"

" No, ma'am ; I wish I did."

" I can tell you," said Mrs. Chauncey,　iling ;—" he is one of my best friends too, Ellen ; it is my brother, Mr. George Marshman."

How Ellen's face crimsoned ! Mr. Marshman asked how she knew.

" It was then he came up the river, you know, sir ; and don't you remember his speaking of a little girl on board the boat who was travelling with strangers, and whom he endeavoured to befriend ? I had forgotten it entirely till a minute or two ago."

" Miss Margaret Dunscombe !" cried George Walsh, " what kind of a person was that you said Ellen was so fond of when you came up the river ?"

" I don't know, nor care," said Margaret. " Somebody she picked up somewhere."

" It was Mr. George Marshman !"

" It wasn't."

" Uncle George !" exclaimed Ellen Chauncey, running up to the group her cousin had quitted ;—" *My* uncle George ? Do you know uncle George, Ellen ?"

" Very much—I mean—yes," said Ellen.

Ellen Chauncey was delighted. So was Ellen Montgomery. It seemed to bring the whole family nearer to her, and they felt it too. Mrs. Marshman kissed her when she heard it, and said she remembered very well her son's speaking of her, and was very glad to find who it was. And now, Ellen thought, she would surely see him again some time.

The next day they left Ventnor. Ellen Chauncey was very sorry to lose her new friend, and begged she would come again " as soon as she could." All the family said the same. Mr. Marshman told her she must give him a large place in her heart, or he should be jealous of her " strange friend ;" and Alice was charged to bring her whenever she came to see them.

The drive back to Carra-carra was scarcely less pleasant than the drive out had been ; and home, Ellen said, looked lovely. That is, Alice's home, which she began to think more her own than any other. The pleasure of the past ten days, though great, had not been unmixed ; the week that followed was one of perfect enjoyment. In Mr. Humphreys' household there was an atmosphere of peace and purity that even a child could feel, and in which such a child as Ellen throve exceedingly. The drawing lessons went on with great success ; other lessons were begun ; there were fine long walks, and charming sleigh-rides, and more than one visit to Mrs.

Vawse ; and what Ellen perhaps liked the best of all, the long evenings of conversation and reading aloud, and bright fire-lights, and brighter sympathy and intelligence and affection. That week did them all good, and no one more than Ellen.

It was a little hard to go back to Miss Fortune's and begin her old life there. She went on the evening of the day John had departed. They were at supper.

" Well !" said Miss Fortune, as Ellen entered,—" have you got enough of visiting ? I should be ashamed to go where I wasn't wanted, for my part."

" I haven't, aunt Fortune," said Ellen.

" She's been nowhere but what's done her good," said Mr. Van Brunt ; " she's reely growed handsome since she's been away."

" Grown a fiddlestick !" said Miss Fortune.

" She couldn't grow handsomer than she was before,' said the old grandmother, hugging and kissing her little grand-daughter with great delight ;—" the sweetest posie in the garden she always was !"

Mr. Van Brunt looked as if he entirely agreed with the old lady. That, while it made some amends for Miss Fortune's dryness, perhaps increased it. She remarked, that " she thanked Heaven she could always make herself contented at home ;" which Ellen could not help thinking was a happiness for the rest of the world.

In the matter of the collar, it was hard to say whether the giver or receiver had the most satisfaction. Ellen had begged him not to speak of it to her aunt ; and accordingly one Sunday when he came there with it on, both he and she were in a state of exquisite delight. Miss Fortune's attention was at last aroused ; she made a particular review of him, and ended it by declaring that " he looked uncommonly dandified, but she could not make out what he had done to himself ;" a remark which transported Mr. Van Brunt and Ellen beyond all bounds of prudence.

Nancy's Bible, which had been purchased for her at Randolph, was given to her the first opportunity. Ellen anxiously watched her as she slowly turned it over, her face showing, however, very decided approbation of the style of the gift. She shook her head once or twice, and then said,

" What did you give this to me for, Ellen ?"

" Because I wanted to give you something for New Year," said Ellen,—" and I thought that would be the best thing,—if you would only read it,—it would make you so happy and good."

" *You* are good, I believe," said Nancy, " but I don't expect ever to be myself—I don't think I *could* be. You might as well teach a snake not to wriggle."

" I am not good at all," said Ellen,—" we're none of us good," —and the tears rose to her eyes,—" but the Bible will teach us

how to be. If you'll only read it!—please Nancy, do! say you
will read a little every day."

" You don't want me to make a promise I shouldn't keep, I
guess, do you?"

" No," said Ellen.

" Well, I shouldn't keep that, so I won't promise it; but I tell
you what I *will* do,—I'll take precious fine care of it, and keep it
always for your sake."

" Well," said Ellen sighing,—" I am glad you will even do so
much as that. But Nancy—before you begin to read the Bible
you may have to go where you never can read it, nor be happy
nor good neither."

Nancy made no answer, but walked away, Ellen thought, rather
more soberly than usual.

This conversation had cost Ellen some effort. It had not been
made without a good deal of thought and some prayer. She
could not hope she had done much good, but she had done her
duty. And it happened that Mr. Van Brunt, standing behind the
angle of the wall, had heard every word.

CHAPTER XXXIII.

If erst he wished, now he longed sore.
FAIRFAX.

ELLEN's life had nothing to mark it for many months. The
rest of the winter passed quietly away, every day being full of
employment. At home the state of matters was rather bettered.
Either Miss Fortune was softened by Ellen's gentle inoffensive
ways and obedient usefulness, or she had resolved to bear what
could not be helped, and make the best of the little inmate she
could not get rid of. She was certainly resolved to make the
most of her. Ellen was kept on the jump a great deal of the
time; she was runner of errands and maid of all work; to set the
table and clear it was only a trifle in the list of her every-day
duties; and they were not ended till the last supper dish was put
away and the hearth swept up. Miss Fortune never spared herself
and never spared Ellen, so long as she had any occasion for her.

There were however long pieces of time that were left free;
these Ellen seized for her studies and used most diligently.
Urged on by a three or four-fold motive. For the love of them,
and for her own sake,—that John might think she had done well,
—that she might presently please and satisfy Alice,—above all,

that her mother's wishes might be answered. This thought, whenever it came, was a spur to her efforts ; so was each of the others; and Christian feeling added another and kept all the rest in force. Without this, indolence might have weakened, or temptation surprised her resolution ; little Ellen was open to both ; but if ever she found herself growing careless, from either cause, conscience was sure to smite her; and then would rush in all the motives that called upon her to persevere. Soon faithfulness began to bring its reward. With delight she found herself getting the better of difficulties, beginning to see a little through the mists of ignorance, making some sensible progress on the long road of learning. Study grew delightful ; her lessons with Alice one of her greatest enjoyments. And as they were a labour of love to both teacher and scholar, and as it was the aim of each to see quite to the bottom of every matter, where it was possible, and to leave no difficulties behind them on the road which they had not cleared away, no wonder Ellen went forward steadily and rapidly. Reading also became a wonderful pleasure. Wiems' Life of Washington was read, and read, and read over again, till she almost knew it by heart; and from that she went to Alice's library, and ransacked it for what would suit her. Happily it was a well-picked one, and Ellen could not light upon many books that would do her mischief. For those, Alice's wish was enough ;— she never opened them. Furthermore Alice insisted that when Ellen had once fairly begun a book she should go through with it ; not capriciously leave it for another, nor have half a dozen about at a time. But when Ellen had read it once she commonly wanted to go over it again, and seldom laid it aside until she had sucked the sweetness all out of it.

As for drawing, it could not go on very fast while the cold weather lasted. Ellen had no place at home where she could spread out her paper and copies without danger of being disturbed. Her only chance was at the parsonage. John had put all her pencils in order before he went, and had left her an abundance of copies, marked as she was to take them. They, or some of them, were bestowed in Alice's desk ; and whenever Ellen had a spare hour or two, of a fine morning or afternoon, she made the best of her way to the mountain ; it made no difference whether Alice were at home or not ; she went in, coaxed up the fire, and began her work. It happened many a time that Alice, coming home from a walk or a run in the woods, saw the little hood and cloak on the settee before she opened the glass door, and knew very well how she should find Ellen, bending intently over her desk. These runs to the mountain were very frequent ; sometimes to draw, sometimes to recite, always to see Alice and be happy. Ellen grew rosy and hardy, and in spite of her separation from her

mother, she was very happy too. Her extreme and varied occupation made this possible. She had no time to indulge useless sorrow ; on the contrary, her thoughts were taken up with agreeable
matters, either doing or to be done ; and at night she was far too
tired and sleepy to lie awake musing. And besides, she hoped
that her mother would come back in the spring, or the summer at
farthest. It is true Ellen had no liking for the kind of business
her aunt gave her ; it was oftentimes a trial of temper and
patience. Miss Fortune was not the pleasantest work-mistress in
the world, and Ellen was apt to wish to be doing something else ;
but after all this was not amiss. Besides the discipline of character, these trials made the pleasant things with which they were
mixed up seem doubly pleasant ; the disagreeable parts of her life
relished the agreeable wonderfully. After spending the whole
morning with Miss Fortune in the depths of housework, how delightful it was to forget all in drawing some nice little cottage
with a bit of stone wall and a barrel in front ; or to go with Alice,
in thought, to the south of France, and learn how the peasants
manage their vines and make the wine from them ; or run over the
Rock of Gibraltar with the monkeys ; or at another time, seated
on a little bench in the chimney corner, when the fire blazed up
well, before the candles were lighted, to forget the kitchen and the
supper and her bustling aunt, and sail round the world with
Captain Cook. Yes—these things were all the sweeter for being
tasted by snatches.

Spring brought new occupation ; household labours began to
increase in number and measure ; her leisure times were shortened.
But pleasures were increased too. When the snow went off, and
spring-like days began to come, and birds' notes were heard again,
and the trees put out their young leaves, and the brown mountains
were looking soft and green, Ellen's heart bounded at the sight.
The springing grass was lovely to see ; dandelions were marvels of
beauty ; to her each wild wood-flower was a never to be enough
admired and loved wonder. She used to take long rambles with
Mr. Van Brunt when business led him to the woods, sometimes
riding part of the way on the ox-sled. Always a basket for
flowers went along ; and when the sled stopped, she would wander
all around seeking among the piled-up dead leaves for the white
wind-flower, and pretty little hang-head Uvularia, and delicate
blood-root, and the wild geranium and columbine ; and many
others the names of which she did not know. They were like
friends to Ellen ; she gathered them affectionately as well as admiringly into her little basket, and seemed to purify herself in
their pure companionship. Even Mr. Van Brunt came to have an
indistinct notion that Ellen and flowers were made to be together.
After he found what a pleasure it was to her to go on these expe-

ditions, he made it a point, whenever he was bound to the woods of a fine day, to come to the house for her. Miss Fortune might object as she pleased; he always found an answer; and at last Ellen to her great joy would be told, "Well! go get your bonnet

and be off with yourself." Once under the shadow of the big trees, the dried leaves crackling beneath her feet, and alone with her kind conductor,—and Miss Fortune and all in the world that was disagreeable was forgotten—forgotten no more to be remembered till the walk should come to an end. And it would have surprised any body to hear the long conversations she and Mr. Van Brunt kept up,—he, the silentest man in Thirlwall! Their talk often ran upon trees, among which Mr. Van Brunt was at home. Ellen wanted to become acquainted with them, as well as with the little flowers that grew at their feet; and he tried to teach her how to know each separate kind by the bark and leaf and manner of growth. The pine and hemlock and fir were easily learnt; the white birch too; beyond those at first she was perpetually confounding one with another. Mr. Van Brunt had to go over and over his instructions; never weary, always vastly amused. Pleasant lessons these were! Ellen thought so, and Mr. Van Brunt thought so too.

Then there were walks with Alice, pleasanter still, if that could be. And even in the house Ellen managed to keep a token of spring-time. On her toilet-table, the three uncouth legs of which were now hidden by a neat dimity cover, there always stood a broken tumbler with a supply of flowers. The supply was very varied, it is true; sometimes only a handful of dandelions, sometimes a huge bunch of lilac flowers, which could not be persuaded to stay in the glass without the help of the wall, against which it leaned in very undignified style; sometimes the bouquet was of really delicate and beautiful wild flowers. All were charming in Ellen's eyes.

As the days grew long and the weather warm, Alice and she began to make frequent trips to the Cat's back, and French came very much into fashion. They generally took Sharp to ease the long way, and rested themselves with a good stay on the mountain. Their coming was always a joy to the old lady. She was dearly fond of them both, and delighted to hear from their lips the language she loved best. After a time they spoke nothing else when with her. She was well qualified to teach them; and, indeed, her general education had been far from contemptible, though nature had done more for her. As the language grew familiar to them, she loved to tell and they to hear long stories of her youth and native country,—scenes and people so very different from all Ellen had ever seen or heard of; and told in a lively simple style which she could not have given in English, and with a sweet colouring of Christian thought and feeling. Many things made these visits good and pleasant. It was not the least of Alice's and Ellen's joy to carry their old friend something that might be for her comfort in her lonely way of life. For even Miss Fortune now and then told Ellen " she might take a piece of that cheese along with her;" or " she wondered if the old lady would like a little fresh meat?—she guessed she'd cut her a bit of that nice lamb; she wouldn't want but a little piece." A singular testimony this was to the respect and esteem of Mrs. Vawse had from every body. Miss Fortune very, very seldom was known to take a bit from her own comforts to add to those of another. The ruling passion of this lady was thrift; her next, good housewifery. First, to gather to herself and heap up of what the world most esteems; after that, to be known as the most thorough housekeeper and the smartest woman in Thirl-wall.

Ellen made other visits she did not like so well. In the course of the winter and summer she became acquainted with most of the neighbourhood. She sometimes went with her aunt to a formal tea-drinking, one, two, three, or four miles off, as the case might be. They were not very pleasant. To some places she was asked by herself; and though the people invariably showed themselves very kind, and did their best to please her, Ellen seldom cared to go a second time; liked even home and Miss Fortune better. There were a few exceptions; Jenny Hitchcock was one of her favourites, and Jane Huff was another; and all of their respective families came in, with good reason, for a share of her regard, Mr. Juniper indeed excepted. Once they went to a quilting at Squire Dennison's; the house was spotlessly neat and well-ordered; the people all kind; but Ellen thought they did not seem to know how to be pleasant. Dan Dennison alone had no stiffness about him. Miss Fortune remarked with pride that even in this family of pretension, as she thought it, the refreshments could bear no comparison with hers. Once they were invited to tea at the Lawsons'; but Ellen told Alice, with much apparent disgust, that she never wanted to go again. Mrs. Van Brunt she saw often. To Thirlwall Miss Fortune never went.

Twice in the course of the summer Ellen had a very great pleasure in the company of little Ellen Chauncey. Once Miss Sophia brought her, and once her mother; and the last time they made a visit of two weeks. On both occasions Ellen was sent for to the parsonage and kept while they stayed; and the pleasure that she and her little friend had together cannot be told. It was unmixed now. Rambling about through the woods and over the fields, no matter where, it was all enchanting; helping Alice garden; helping Thomas make hay, and the mischief they did his haycocks by tumbling upon them, and the patience with which he bore it; the looking for eggs; the helping Margery churn, and the helping each other set tables; the pleasant mornings and pleasant evenings and pleasant mid-days,—it cannot be told. Long to be remembered, sweet and pure, was the pleasure of those summer days, unclouded by a shade of discontent or disagreement on either brow. Ellen loved the whole Marshman family now, for the sake of one, the one she had first known; and little Ellen Chauncey repeatedly told her mother in private that Ellen Montgomery was the very nicest girl she had ever seen. They met with joy and parted with sorrow, entreating and promising, if possible, a speedy meeting again.

Amidst all the improvement and enjoyment of these summer months, and they had a great deal of both for Ellen, there was one cause of sorrow she could not help feeling, and it began to press more and more. Letters—they came slowly,—and when they came they were not at all satisfactory. Those in her mother's hand dwindled and dwindled, till at last there came only mere scraps of letters from her; and sometimes after a long interval one from Captain Montgomery would come alone. Ellen's heart sickened with long-deferred hope. She wondered what could make her mother neglect a matter so necessary for her happiness; sometimes she fancied they were travelling about, and it might be inconvenient to write; sometimes she thought perhaps they were coming home without letting her know, and would suddenly surprise her some day and make her half lose her wits with joy. But they did not come, nor write; and whatever was the reason, Ellen felt it was very sad, and sadder and sadder as the summer went on. Her own letters became pitiful in their supplications for letters; they had been very cheerful and filled with encouraging matter, and in part they were still.

For a while her mind was diverted from this sad subject, and her brow cleared up, when John came home in August. As before, Alice gained Miss Fortune's leave to keep her at the parsonage the whole time of his stay, which was several weeks. Ellen wondered that it was so easily granted, but she was much too happy to spend time in thinking about it. Miss Fortune had several reasons. She was unwilling to displease Miss Humphreys, and conscious that it would be a shame to her to stand openly in the way of Ellen's good. Besides, though Ellen's services were lost for a time, yet she said she got tired of setting her to work; she liked to dash round the house alone, without thinking what somebody else was doing or ought to be doing. In short she liked to have her out of the way for a while. Furthermore, it did not please her that Mr. Van Brunt and her little handmaid were, as she expressed it, "so thick." His first thought and his last thought, she said, she believed were for Ellen, whether she came in or went out; and Miss Fortune was accustomed to be chief, not only in her own house, but in the regards of all who came to it. At any rate the leave was granted and Ellen went.

And now was repeated the pleasure of the first week in January. It would have been increased, but that increase was not possible. There was only the difference between lovely winter and lovely summer weather; it was seldom very hot in Thirlwall. The fields and hills were covered with green instead of white; fluttering leaves had taken the place of snow-covered sprays and sparkling icicles; and for the keen north and brisk northwester, soft summer airs were blowing. Ellen saw no other difference,—except that perhaps, if it could be, there was something more of tenderness in the manner of Alice and her brother toward her. No little sister could have been more cherished and cared for. If there was a change, Mr. Humphreys shared it. It is true he seldom took much part in the conversation, and seldomer was with them in any of their pursuits or pleasures. He generally kept by himself in his study. But whenever he did speak to Ellen his tone was particularly gentle and his look kind. He sometimes called her " My little daughter," which always gave Ellen great pleasure; she would jump at such times with double zeal to do any thing he asked her.

Now drawing went on with new vigour under the eye of her master. And many things beside. John took a great deal of pains with her in various ways. He made her read to him; he helped her and Alice with their French; he went with them to Mrs. Vawse's; and even Mr. Humphreys went there too one afternoon to tea. How much Ellen enjoyed that afternoon! They took with them a great basket of provisions, for Mrs. Vawse could not be expected to entertain so large a party; and borrowed Jenny Hitchcock's pony, which with old John and Sharp mounted three of the company; they took turns in walking. Nobody minded that. The fine weather, the beautiful mountain-top, the general pleasure, Mr. Humphreys' uncommon spirits and talkableness, the oddity of their way of travelling, and of a tea-party up on the " Cat's back," and furthermore, the fact that Nancy stayed at home and behaved very well the whole time, all together filled Ellen's cup of happiness, for the time, as full as it could hold. She never forgot that afternoon. And the ride home was the best of all. The sun was low by the time they reached the plain; long shadows lay across their road; the soft air just stirred the leaves on the branches; stillness and loveliness were over all things; and down the mountain and along the roads through the open country, the whole way, John walked at her bridle; so kind in his care of her, so pleasant in his talk to her, teaching her how to sit in the saddle and hold the reins and whip, and much more important things too, that Ellen thought a pleasanter thing could not be than to ride so. After that they took a great many rides, borrowing Jenny's pony or some other, and explored the beautiful country far and near. And almost daily John had up Sharp and gave Ellen a regular lesson. She often thought, and sometimes looked, what she had once said to him, " I wish I could do something for *you*, Mr. John ;"—but he smiled at her and said nothing.

At last he was gone. And in all the week he had been at home, and in many weeks before, no letter had come for Ellen. The thought had been kept from weighing upon her by the thousand pleasures that filled up every moment of his stay; she could not be sad then, or only for a minute; hope threw off the sorrow as soon as it was felt; and she forgot how time flew. But when his visit was over, and she went back to her old place and her old life at her aunt's, the old feeling came back in greater strength. She began again to count the days and the weeks; to feel the bitter unsatisfied longing. Tears would drop down upon her Bible; tears streamed from her eyes when she prayed that God would make her mother well and bring her home to her quickly,—oh, quickly!—and little Ellen's face began to wear once more something of its old look.

CHAPTER XXXIV.

All was ended now, the hope, and the fear, and the sorrow,
All the aching of heart, the restless, unsatisfied longing,
All the dull deep pain, and constant anguish of patience!
LONGFELLOW.

ONE day in the early part of September, she was standing in front of the house at the little wicket that opened on the road. With her back against the open gate, she was gently moving it to and fro, half enjoying the weather and the scene, half indulging the melancholy mood which drove her from the presence of her bustling aunt. The gurgling sound of the brook a few steps off was a great deal more soothing to her ear than Miss Fortune's sharp tones. By and by a horseman came in sight at the far end of the road, and the brook was forgotten. What made Ellen look at him so sharply? Poor child, she was always expecting news. At first she could only see that the man rode a white horse; then, as he came nearer, an odd looped-up hat showed itself,—and something queer in his hand,—what was it? who is it?—The old newsman! Ellen was sure. Yes—she could now see his saddle-bags, and the white horse-tail set in a handle with which he was brushing away the flies from his horse; the tin trumpet was in his other hand, to blow withal. He was a venerable old figure with all his oddities; clad in a suit of snuff brown, with a neat quiet look about him, he and the saddle-bags and the white horse jogged on together as if they belonged to nothing else in the world but each other. In an ecstasy of fear and hope Ellen watched the pace of the old horse to see if it gave any sign of slackening near the gate. Her breath came short, she hardly breathed at all, she was trembling from head to foot. *Would* he stop, or was he going on! Oh, the long agony of two minutes!—He stopped. Ellen went toward him.

"What little gal is this?" said he.

"I am Ellen Montgomery, sir," said Ellen eagerly;—"Miss Fortune's niece—I live here."

"Stop a bit," said the old man, taking up his saddle-bags,—

" Miss Fortune's niece, eh ?   Well—I believe—as I've got somethin' for her—somethin' here—aunt well, eh ?"

" Yes, sir."

" That's more than you be, ain't it ?" said he, glancing sideways
at Ellen's face.   " How do you know but I've got a letter for you
here, eh ?"

The colour rushed to that face, and she clasped her hands.

" No, dear, no," said he,—" I ha'n't got any for you—it's for
the old lady—there, run in with it, dear."

But Ellen knew before she touched it that it was a foreign letter,
and dashed into the house with it.   Miss Fortune coolly sent her
back to pay the postage.

When she came in again her aunt was still reading the letter.
But her look, Ellen *felt*, was unpromising.   She did not venture to
speak ; expectation was chilled.   She stood till Miss Fortune began
to fold up the paper.

" Is there nothing for me ?" she said then timidly.

" No."

" Oh, why don't she write to me !" cried Ellen, bursting into
tears.

Miss Fortune stalked about the room without any particular purpose, as far as could be seen.

" It is very strange !" said Ellen sorrowfully,—" I am afraid she
is worse—does papa say she is worse ?"

" No."

" Oh, if she had only sent me a message !   I should think she
might ; oh, I wish she had !—three words !—does papa say why she
don't write ?"

" No."

" It is very strange !" repeated poor Ellen.

" Your father talks of coming home," said Miss Fortune, after
a few minutes, during which Ellen had been silently weeping.

" Home !—Then she must be better !" said Ellen with new life ;
" does papa say she is better ?"

" No."

" But what does he mean ?" said Ellen uneasily ;—" I don't see
what he means ; he doesn't say she is worse, and he doesn't say she
is better,—what *does* he say ?"

" He don't say much about any thing."

" Does he say when they are coming home ?"

Miss Fortune mumbled something about " Spring," and whisked
off to the buttery ; Ellen thought no more was to be got out of her.
She felt miserable.   Her father and her aunt both seemed to act
strangely ; and where to find comfort she scarcely knew.   She had
one day been telling her doubts and sorrows to John.   He did not
try to raise her hopes, but said, " Troubles will come in this world,

Ellie ; the best is to trust them and ourselves to our dear Saviour, and let trials drive us to him. Seek to love him more and to be patient under his will ; the good Shepherd means nothing but kindness to any lamb in his flock,—you may be sure of that, Ellie."

Ellen remembered his words and tried to follow them now, but she could not be "patient under his will" yet,—not quite. It was very hard to be patient in such uncertainty. With swimming eyes she turned over her Bible in search of comfort, and found it. Her eye lit upon words she knew very well, but that were like the fresh sight of a friend's face for all that,—"Let not your heart be troubled ; ye believe in God, believe also in me. In my Father's house are many mansions." There is no parting there, thought little Ellen. She cried a long time ; but she was comforted nevertheless. The heart that rests on the blessed One who said those words can never be quite desolate.

For several days things went on in the old train, only her aunt, she thought, was sometimes rather queer,—not quite as usual in her manner toward her. Mr. Van Brunt was not *rather* but *very* queer ; he scarce spoke or looked at Ellen ; bolted down his food and was off without a word ; and even stayed away entirely from two or three meals. She saw nobody else. Weather and other circumstances prevented her going to the mountain.

One afternoon she was giving her best attention to a French lesson, when she heard herself called. Miss Fortune was in the lower kitchen dipping candles. Ellen ran down.

" I don't know what's got into these candles," said Miss Fortune. —" I can't make 'em hang together ; the tallow ain't good, I guess. Where's the nearest place they keep bees ?"

" They have got bees at Mrs. Hitchcock's," said Ellen.

" So they have in Egypt, for any thing I know," said her aunt ; —" one would be about as much good now as t'other. Mrs. Lowndes !—that ain't far off. Put on your bonnet, Ellen, and run over there, and ask her to let me have a little bees-wax. I'll pay her in something she likes best."

" Does Mrs. Lowndes keep bee-hives ?" said Ellen doubtfully.

" No—she makes the bees-wax herself," said Miss Fortune, in the tone she always took when any body presumed to suppose she might be mistaken in any thing.

" How much shall I ask for ?" said Ellen.

" Oh, I don't know—a pretty good piece."

Ellen was not very clear what quantity this might mean. However she wisely asked no more questions, and set out upon her walk. It was hot and disagreeable ; just the time of day when the sun had most power, and Mrs. Lowndes' house was about half way on the road to Alice's. It was not a place where Ellen liked to go, though the people always made much of her ; she did not fancy them, and regularly kept out of their way when she could. Miss Mary Lawson was sitting with Mrs. Lowndes and her daughter when Ellen came in and briefly gave her aunt's message.

"Bees-wax," said Mrs. Lowndes,—"well, I don't know—How much does she want?"

"I don't know, ma'am, exactly; she said a pretty good piece."

"What's it for? do you know, honey?"

"I believe it's to put in some tallow for candles," said Ellen;—"the tallow was too soft she said."

"I didn't know Miss Fortune's tallow was ever any thing but the hardest," said Sarah Lowndes.

"You had better not let your aunt know you've told on her, Ellen," remarked Mary Lawson; "she won't thank you."

"Had she a good lot of taller to make up?" inquired the mother, preparing to cut her bees-wax.

"I don't know, ma'am; she had a big kettle, but I don't know how full it was."

"You may as well cut a good piece, ma, while you are about it," said the daughter;—"and ask her to let us have a piece of her sage cheese, will you?"

"Is it worth while to weigh it?" whispered Mrs. Lowndes.

Her daughter answered in the same tone, and Miss Mary joining them, a conversation of some length went on over the bees-wax which Ellen could not hear. The tones of the speakers became lower and lower; till at length her own name and an incautious sentence were spoken more distinctly and reached her.

"Shouldn't you think Miss Fortune might put a black ribbon at least on her bonnet?"

"Any body but her would."

"Hush!——" They whispered again under breath.

The words entered Ellen's heart like cold iron. She did not move, hand or foot; she sat motionless with pain and fear, yet what she feared she dared not think. When the bees-wax was given her she rose up from her chair and stood gazing into Mrs. Lowndes' face as if she had lost her senses.

"My goodness, child, how you look!" said that lady. "What ails you, honey?"

"Ma'am," said Ellen,—"what was that you said, about——"

"About what, dear?" said Mrs. Lowndes, with a startled look at the others.

"About—a ribbon—" said Ellen, struggling to get the words out of white lips.

"My goodness!" said the other;—"did you ever hear any thing like that?—I didn't say nothing about a ribbon, dear."

"Do you suppose her aunt ha'n't told her?" said Miss Mary in an under tone.

" Told me what ?" cried Ellen ;—" Oh, what ?—what ?"

" I wish I was a thousand miles off !" said Mrs. Lowndes ;—" I don't know, dear—I don't know what it is—Miss Alice knows."

" Yes, ask Miss Alice," said Mary Lawson ;—" she knows better than we do."

Ellen looked doubtfully from one to the other ; then as " Go ask Miss Alice," was repeated on all sides, she caught up her bonnet and flinging the bees-wax from her hand darted out of the house. Those she had left looked at each other a minute in silence.

" Ain't that too bad now !" exclaimed Mrs. Lowndes, crossing the room to shut the door. " But what could I say ?"

" Which way did she go ?"

" I don't know I am sure—I had no head to look, or any thing else. I wonder if I had ought to ha' told her.—But I couldn't ha' done it."

" Just look at her bees-wax !" said Sarah Lowndes.

" She will kill herself if she runs up the mountain at that rate," said Mary Lawson.

They all made a rush to the door to look after her.

" She ain't in sight," said Mrs. Lowndes ;—" if she's gone the way to the Nose she's got as far as them big poplars already, or she'd be some where this side of 'em where we could see her."

" You hadn't ought to ha' let her go, 'ma, in all this sun," said Miss Lowndes.

" I declare," said Mrs. Lowndes, " she scared me so I hadn't three idees left in my head. I wish I knew where she was, though, poor little soul !"

Ellen was far on her way to the mountain, pressed forward by a fear that knew no stay of heat or fatigue ; they were little to her that day. She saw nothing on her way ; all within and without were swallowed up in that one feeling ; yet she dared not think what it was she feared. She put that by. Alice knew, Alice would tell her ; on that goal her heart fixed, to that she pressed on ; but oh, the while, what a cloud was gathering over her spirit, and growing darker and darker. Her hurry of mind and hurry of body made each other worse ; it must be so ; and when she at last ran round the corner of the house and burst in at the glass door she was in a frightful state.

Alice started up and faced her as she came in, but with a look that stopped Ellen short. She stood still ; the colour in her cheeks, as her eyes read Alice's, faded quite away ; words and the power to speak them were gone together. Alas ! the need to utter them was gone too. Alice burst into tears and held out her arms, saying only, " My poor child !" Ellen reached her arms, and strength and spirit seemed to fail there. Alice thought she had fainted ; she laid her on the sofa, called Margery, and tried the usual things, weeping bitterly herself as she did so. It was not fainting however; Ellen's senses soon came back; but she seemed like a person stunned with a great blow, and Alice wished grief had had any other effect upon her. It lasted for days. A kind of stupor hung over her; tears did not come; the violent strain of every nerve and feeling seemed to have left her benumbed. She would sleep long heavy sleeps the greater part of the time, and seemed to have no power to do any thing else.

Her adopted sister watched her constantly, and for those days lived but to watch her. She had heard all Ellen's story from Mary Lawson and Mr. Van Brunt; who had both been to the parsonage, one on Mrs. Lowndes' part, the other on his own, to ask about her; and she dreaded that a violent fit of illness might be brought on by all Ellen had undergone. She was mistaken, however. Ellen was not ill; but her whole mind and body bowed under the weight of the blow that had come upon her. As the first stupor wore off there were indeed more lively signs of grief; she would weep till she wept her eyes out, and that often, but it was very quietly; no passionate sobbing, no noisy crying; sorrow had taken too strong hold to be struggled with, and Ellen meekly bowed her head to it. Alice saw this with the greatest alarm. She had refused to let her go back to her aunt's; it was impossible to do otherwise; yet it may be that Ellen would have been better there. The busy industry to which she would have been forced at home might have roused her; as it was, nothing drew her, and nothing could be found to draw her, from her own thoughts. Her interest in every thing seemed to be gone. Books had lost their charm. Walks and drives and staying at home were all one, except indeed that she rather liked best the latter. Appetite failed; her cheek grew colourless; and Alice began to fear that if a stop were not soon put to this gradual sinking it would at last end with her life. But all her efforts were without fruit; and the winter was a sorrowful one not to Ellen alone.

As it wore on, there came to be one thing in which Ellen again took pleasure, and that was her Bible. She used to get alone or into a corner with it, and turn the leaves over and over; looking out its gentle promises and sweet comforting words to the weak and the sorrowing. She loved to read about Christ,—all he said and did; all his kindness to his people and tender care of them; the love shown them here and the joys prepared for them hereafter. She began to cling more to that one unchangeable friend from whose love neither life nor death can sever those that believe in him; and her heart, tossed and shaken as it had been, began to take rest again in that happy resting-place with stronger affection and even with greater joy than ever before. Yet for all that, this joy often kept company with bitter weeping; the stirring of any thing like pleasure roused sorrow up afresh ; and though Ellen's look of sadness grew less dark, Alice could not see that her face was at all less white and thin. She never spoke of her mother after once hearing when and where she had died ; she never hinted at her loss, except exclaiming in an agony, " I shall get no more letters !" and Alice dared not touch upon what the child seemed to avoid so carefully ; though Ellen sometimes wept on her bosom, and often sat for hours still and silent with her head in her lap.

The time drew nigh when John was expected home for the holidays. In the mean while they had had many visits from other friends. Mr. Van Brunt had come several times, enough to set the whole neighbourhood a wondering if they had only known it ; his good old mother oftener still. Mrs. Vawse as often as possible. Miss Fortune once ; and that because, as she said to herself, " every body would be talking about what was none of their business if she didn't." As neither she nor Ellen knew in the least what to say to each other, the visit was rather a dull one, spite of all Alice could do. Jenny Hitchcock and the Huffs and the Dennisons, and others, came now and then ; but Ellen did not like to see any of them all but Mrs. Vawse. Alice longed for her brother.

He came at last, just before New Year's. It was the middle of a fine afternoon, and Alice and her father had gone in the sleigh to Carra-carra. Ellen had chosen to stay behind, but Margery did not know this, and of course did not tell John. After paying a visit to her in the kitchen, he had come back to the empty sitting-room, and was thoughtfully walking up and down the floor, when the door of Alice's room slowly opened and Ellen appeared. It was never her way, when she could help it, to show violent feeling before other people ; so she had been trying to steel herself to meet John without crying, and now came in with her little grave face prepared not to give way. His first look had like to overset it all.

" Ellie !" said he ;—" I thought everybody was gone. My dear Ellie !—"

Ellen could hardly stand the tone of these three words, and she bore with the greatest difficulty the kiss that followed them ; it took but a word or two more, and a glance at the old look and smile, to break down entirely all her guard. According to her usual fashion she was rushing away ; but John held her fast, and though gently drew her close to him.

" I will not let you forget that I am your brother, Ellie," said he.

Ellen hid her face on his shoulder, and cried as if she had never cried before.

" Ellie," said he after a while, speaking low and tenderly, " the

Bible says, 'We have known and believed the love that God hath toward us;'—have you remembered and believed this lately?"

Ellen did not answer.

"Have you remembered that God loves every sinner that has believed in his dear Son?—and loves them so well that he will let nothing come near them to harm them?—and loves them never better than when he sends bitter trouble on them? It is wonderful! but it is true. Have you thought of this, Ellie?"

She shook her head.

"It is not in anger he does it;—it is not that he has forgotten you;—it is not that he is careless of your trembling little heart,—never, never! If you are his child, all is done in love and shall work good for you; and if we often cannot see how, it is because we are weak and foolish, and can see but a very little way."

Ellen listened, with her face hid on his shoulder.

"Do you love Christ, Ellen?"

She nodded, weeping afresh.

"Do you love him less since he has brought you into this great sorrow?"

"No," sobbed Ellen;—"*more.*"

He drew her closer to his breast and was silent a little while.

"I am very glad to hear you say that!—then all will be well. And haven't you the best reason to think that all *is* well with your dear mother?"

Ellen almost shrieked. Her mother's name had not been spoken before her in a great while, and she could hardly bear to hear it now. Her whole frame quivered with hysterical sobs.

"Hush, Ellie!" said John, in a tone that, low as it was, somehow found its way through all her agitation, and calmed her like a spell;—"have you not good reason to believe that all is well with her?"

"Oh, yes!—oh, yes!"

"She loved and trusted him too; and now she is with him—she has reached that bright home where there is no more sin, nor sorrow, nor death."

"Nor parting either," sobbed Ellen, whose agitation was excessive.

"Nor parting!—and though *we* are parted from them, it is but for a little; let us watch and keep our garments clean, and soon we shall be all together, and have done with tears for ever. *She* has done with them now.—Did you hear from her again?"

"Oh, no—not a word!"

"That is a hard trial.—But in it all, believe, dear Ellie, the love that God hath toward us;—remember that our dear Saviour is near us, and feels for us, and is the same at all times.—And don't cry so, Ellie."

He kissed her once or twice, and begged her to calm herself. For it seemed as if Ellen's very heart was flowing away in her tears; yet they were gentler and softer far than at the beginning. The conversation had been a great relief. The silence between her and Alice on the thing always in her mind, a silence neither of them dared to break, had grown painful. The spell was taken off; and though at first Ellen's tears knew no measure, she was easier even then; as John soothed her and went on with his kind talk, gradually leading it away from their first subject to other things, she grew not only calm but more peaceful at heart than months had seen her. She was quite herself again before Alice came home.

" You have done her good already," exclaimed Alice as soon as Ellen was out of the room;—" I knew you would; I saw it in her face as soon as I came in."

" It is time," said her brother. " She is a dear little thing!"

The next day, in the middle of the morning, Ellen, to her great surprise, saw Sharp brought before the door with the side-saddle on, and Mr. John carefully looking to the girth and shortening the stirrup.

" Why, Alice," she exclaimed,—" what is Mr. John going to do?"

" I don't know, Ellie, I am sure; he does queer things sometimes. What makes you ask?"

Before she could answer he opened the door.

" Come, Ellen—go and get ready. Bundle up well, for it is rather frosty. Alice, has she a pair of gloves that are warm enough? Lend her yours, and I'll see if I can find some at Thirlwall."

Ellen thought she would rather not go; to anybody else she would have said so. Half a minute she stood still—then went to put on her things.

" Alice, you will be ready by the time we get back?—in half an hour."

Ellen had an excellent lesson, and her master took care it should not be an easy one. She came back looking as she had not done all winter. Alice was not quite ready; while waiting for her John went to the bookcase and took down the first volume of " Rollin's Ancient History;" and giving it to Ellen, said he would talk with her to-morrow about the first twenty pages. The consequence was, the hour and a half of their absence instead of being moped away was spent in hard study. A pair of gloves was bought at Thirlwall; Jenny Hitchcock's pony was sent for; and after that, every day when the weather would at all do they took a long ride. By degrees reading and drawing and all her studies were added to the history, till Ellen's time was well filled with business again. Alice had endeavoured to bring this about before, but fruitlessly. What she asked of her Ellen indeed *tried* to do ; what John told her *was done*. She grew a different creature. Appetite came back ; the colour sprang again to her cheek ; hope—meek and sober as it was,— relighted her eye. In her eagerness to please and satisfy her teacher her whole soul was given to the performance of whatever he wished her to do. The effect was all that he looked for.

The second evening after he came, John called Ellen to his side, saying he had something he wanted to read to her. It was before candles were brought, but the room was full of light from the blazing wood fire. Ellen glanced at his book as she came to the sofa ; it was a largish volume in a black leather cover a good deal worn ; it did not look at all interesting.

" What is it ?" she asked.

" It is called," said John, " ' The Pilgrim's Progress from this world to a better.' "

Ellen thought it did not *sound* at all interesting. She had never been more mistaken in her life, and that she found almost as soon as he begun. Her attention was nailed ; the listless, careless mood in which she sat down was changed for one of rapt delight ; she devoured every word that fell from the reader's lips ; indeed, they were given their fullest effect by a very fine voice and singularly fine reading. Whenever any thing might not be quite clear to Ellen, John stopped to make it so ; and with his help, and without it, many a lesson went home. Next day she looked a long time for the book ; it could not be found ; she was forced to wait until evening. Then to her great joy, it was brought out again, and John asked her if she wished to hear some more of it. After that, every evening while he was at home they spent an hour with the " Pilgrim." Alice would leave her work and come to the sofa too ; and with her head on her brother's shoulder, her hand in his, and Ellen's face leaning against his other arm, that was the common way they placed themselves to see and hear. No words can tell Ellen's enjoyment of those readings. They made her sometimes laugh and sometimes cry ; they had much to do in carrying on the cure which John's wisdom and kindness had begun.

They came to the place where Christian loses his burden at the cross ; and as he stood looking and weeping, three shining ones came to him. The first said to him, " Thy sins be forgiven thee ;" the second stripped him of his rags and clothed him with a change of raiment ; the third also set a mark on his forehead.

John explained what was meant by the rags and the change of raiment.

" And the mark in his forehead ?" said Ellen.

" That is the mark of God's children—the change wrought in

them by the Holy Spirit,—the change that makes them different from others, and different from their old selves."

" Do all Christians have it ?"

" Certainly. None can be a Christian without it ."

" But how can one tell whether one has it or no ?" said Ellen, very gravely.

" Carry your heart and life to the Bible and see how they agree. The Bible gives a great many signs and descriptions by which Christians may know themselves,—know both what they are and what they ought to be. If you find your own feelings and manner of life at one with these Bible words, you may hope that the Holy Spirit has changed you and set his mark upon you."

" I wish you would tell me of one of those places," said Ellen.

" The Bible is full of them. ' To them that believe *Christ is precious,*'—there is one. ' If ye love me, *keep my commandments ;*' —' He that saith he abideth in him ought himself also *so to walk even as he walked ;*'—' O how *love I thy law!*' The Bible is full of them, Ellie ; but you have need to ask for great help when you go to try yourself by them ; the heart is deceitful."

Ellen looked sober all the rest of the evening, and the next day she pondered the matter a good deal.

" I think I am changed," she said to herself at last. " I didn't use to like to read the Bible, and now I do very much ;—I never liked praying in old times, and now, oh, what should I do without it !—I didn't love Jesus at all, but I am sure I do now. I don't keep his commandments, but I do *try* to keep them ;—I *must* be changed a little. Oh, I wish mamma had known it before——."

Weeping with mixed sorrow and thankful joy, Ellen bent her head upon her little Bible to pray that she might be *more* changed ; and then, as she often did, raised the cover to look at the texts in the beloved handwriting.

" I love them that love me, and they that seek me early shall find me."

Ellen's tears were blinding her. " That has come true," she thought.

" I will be a God to thee and to thy seed after thee."

" That has come true too !" she said, almost in surprise,—" and mamma believed it would."—And then, as by a flash, came back to her mind the time it was written ; she remembered how when it was done her mother's head had sunk upon the open page ; she seemed to see again the thin fingers tightly clasped ;—she had not understood it then ; she did now ! " She was praying for me," thought Ellen,—" she was praying for me ! she believed that would come true."

The book was dashed down, and Ellen fell upon her knees in a perfect agony of weeping.

Even this, when she was calm again, served to steady her mind. There seemed to be a link of communion between her mother and her that was wanting before. The promise, written and believed in by the one, realized and rejoiced in by the other, was a dear something in common, though one had in the mean while removed to heaven, and the other was still a lingerer on the earth. Ellen bound the words upon her heart.

Another time, when they came to the last scene of Christian's journey, Ellen's tears ran very fast. John asked if he should pass it over? if it distressed her? She said, oh, no, it did not distress her; she wanted him to go on;—and he went on, though himself much distressed, and Alice was near as bad as Ellen. But the next evening, to his surprise, Ellen begged that before he went on to the second part he would read that piece over again. And when he lent her the book, with only the charge that she should not go further than he had been, she pored over that scene with untiring pleasure till she almost had it by heart. In short, never was a child more comforted and contented with a book than Ellen was with the " Pilgrim's Progress." That was a blessed visit of John's. Alice said he had come like a sunbeam into the house; she dreaded to think what would be when he went away.

She wrote him, however, when he had been gone a few weeks, that his will seemed to carry all before it, present or absent. Ellen went on steadily mending; at least she did not go back any. They were keeping up their rides, also their studies, most diligently; Ellen was untiring in her efforts to do whatever he had wished her, and was springing forward, Alice said, in her improvement.

CHAPTER XXXV.

I keep his house, and I wash, wring, brew, bake, scour, dress meat, and make the beds, and do all myself.—SHAKSPEARE.

THE spring had come; and Alice and Ellen were looking forward to pleasanter rides and walks after the sun should have got a little warmth and the snow should be gone; when one morning in the early part of March Mr. Van Brunt made his appearance. Miss Fortune was not well, and had sent him to beg that Ellen would come back to her. He was sorry, he said;—he knew Ellen was in the best place; but her aunt wanted her, and " he s'posed she'd have to go." He did not know what was the matter with Miss Fortune; it was a little of one thing and a little of another; " he s'posed she'd overdid, and it was a wonder, for he didn't know she *could* do it. *She* thought she was as tough as a piece of shoe-leather, but even that could be wore out."

Ellen looked blank. However, she hurriedly set herself to get her things together, and with Alice's help in half an hour she was ready to go. The parting was hard. They held each other fast a good while, and kissed each other many times without speaking.

"Good-by, dear Ellie," whispered Alice at last,—"I'll come and see you soon. Remember what John said when he went away."

Ellen did not trust herself to speak. She pulled herself away from Alice, and turned to Mr. Van Brunt, saying by her manner that she was ready; he took her bundle and they went out of the house together.

Ellen made a manful effort all the way down the hill to stifle the tears that were choking her. She knew they would greatly disturb her companion, and she did succeed though with great difficulty in keeping them back. Luckily for her, he said hardly any thing during the whole walk; she could not have borne to answer a question. It was no fault of Mr. Van Brunt's that he was so silent; he was beating his brains the whole way to think of something it would do to say, and could not suit himself. His single remark was, "that it was like to be a fine spring for the maple, and he guessed they'd make a heap of sugar."

When they reached the door he told her she would find her aunt up stairs, and himself turned off to the barn. Ellen stopped a minute upon the threshold to remember the last time she had crossed it,—and the *first* time; how changed every thing now!— and the thought came, was *this* now to be her home for ever? She had need again to remember John's words. When bidding her good-by he had said, "My little pilgrim, I hope you will keep the straight road, and win the praise of the servant who was faithful over a few things." "I will try!" thought poor Ellen; and then she passed through the kitchen and went up to her own room. Here, without stopping to think, she took off her things, gave one strange look at the old familiar place and her trunk in the corner, fell on her knees for one minute, and then went to her aunt's room.

"Come in!" cried Miss Fortune when Ellen had knocked. "Well, Ellen, there you are. I am thankful it is you; I was afraid it might be Mimy Lawson or Sarah Lowndes, or some of the rest of the set; I know they'll all come scampering here as soon as they hear I'm laid up."

"Are you very sick, aunt Fortune?" said Ellen.

"La! no, child; I shall be up again to-morrow; but I felt queer this morning somehow, and I thought I'd try lying down. I expect I've caught some cold."

There was no doubt of this, but this was not all. Besides catching cold, and doing her best to bring it about, Miss Fortune had overtasked her strength; and by dint of economy, housewifery, and *smartness*, had brought on herself the severe punishment of lying idle and helpless for a much longer time than she at first reckoned on.

" What can I do for you, aunt Fortune ?" said Ellen.

" Oh, nothing, as I know," said Miss Fortune,—" only let me alone and don't ask me any thing, and keep people out of the house. Mercy ! my head feels as if it would go crazy ! Ellen, look here," said she, raising herself on her elbow,—" I won't have any body come into this house,—if I lie here till doomsday, I won't ! Now, you mind me. I ain't a going to have Mimy Lawson, nor nobody else, poking all round into every hole and corner, and turning every cheese upside down to see what's under it. There ain't one of 'em too good for it, and they shan't have a chance. They'll be streaking here, a dozen of 'em, to help take care of the house ; but I don't care what becomes of the house—I won't have any body in it. Promise me you won't let Mr. Van Brunt bring any one here to help ; I know I can trust you to do what I tell you ; promise me !"

Ellen promised, a good deal gratified at her aunt's last words ; and once more asked if she could do any thing for her.

" Oh, I don't know !" said Miss Fortune, flinging herself back on her pillow ;—" I don't care what you do, if you only keep the house clear. There's the clothes in the basket under the table down stairs—you might begin to iron 'em ; they're only rough dry. But don't you come asking me about any thing ; I can't bear it. —Ellen, don't let a soul go into the buttery except yourself.—And Ellen ! I don't care if you make me a little catnip tea ;—the catnip's up in the store-room,—the furthest door in the back attic— here's the keys. Don't go fussing with any thing else there."

Ellen thought the prospect before her rather doleful when she reached the kitchen. It was in order, to be sure, and clean ; but it looked as if the mistress was away. The fire had gone out, the room was cold ; even so little a matter as catnip tea seemed a thing far off and hard to come by. While she stood looking at the great logs in the fireplace, which she could hardly move, and thinking it was rather a dismal state of things, in came Mr. Van Brunt with his good-natured face, and wanted to know if he could do anything for her. The very room seemed more comfortable as soon as his big figure was in it. He set about kindling the fire forthwith, while Ellen went up to the store-room. A well-filled store-room ! Among other things, there hung at least a dozen bunches of dried herbs from one of the rafters. Ellen thought she knew catnip, but after smelling of two or three she became utterly puzzled and was fain to carry a leaf of several kinds down to Mr. Van Brunt to find out which was which. When she came down again she found he had hung on the kettle for her, and swept up the hearth; so Ellen, wisely thinking it best to keep busy, put the ironing blanket on the table, and folded the clothes, and set the irons to the fire. By this time the kettle boiled. How to make catnip tea Ellen did not exactly know, but supposed it must follow the same rules as black tea, in the making of which she felt herself very much at home. So she put a pinch or two of catnip leaves into the pot, poured a little water on them, and left it to draw. Meanwhile came in kind Mr. Van Brunt with an armful or two of small short sticks for the fire, which Ellen could manage.

"I wish I could stay here and take care of you all the while," said he; "but I'll be round. If you want any thing you must come to the door and holler."

Ellen began to thank him.

"Just don't say any thing about that," said he, moving his hands as if he were shaking her thanks out of them; "I'd back all the wood you could burn every day for the pleasure of having you hum again, if I didn't know you was better where you was; but I can't help that. Now, who am I going to get to stay with you? Who would you like to have."

"Nobody, if you please, Mr. Van Brunt," said Ellen; "aunt Fortune don't wish it, and I had rather not, indeed."

He stood up and looked at her in amazement.

"Why, you don't mean to say," said he, "that you are thinking, or she is thinking, you can get along here alone without help?"

"I'll get along somehow," said Ellen. "Never mind, please let me, Mr. Van Brunt; it would worry aunt Fortune very much to have any body; don't say any thing about it."

"Worry her!' said he; and he muttered something Ellen did not quite understand, about "bringing the old woman to reason."

However he went off for the present; and Ellen filled up her tea-pot and carried it up stairs. Her old grandmother was awake; before, when Ellen was in the room, she had been napping; now she showed the greatest delight at seeing her; fondled her, kissed her, cried over her, and finally insisted on getting up directly and going down stairs. Ellen received and returned her caresses with great tenderness, and then began to help her to rise and dress.

"Yes, do," said Miss Fortune; "I shall have a little better chance of sleeping. My stars! Ellen, what do you call this?"

"Isn't it catnip?" said Ellen, alarmed.

"Catnip! it tastes of nothing but the teakettle. It's as weak as dish-water. Take it down and make some more. How much did you put in? you want a good double handful, stalks and all;

make it strong. I can't drink such stuff as that. I think if I could get into a sweat I should be better."

Ellen went down, established her grandmother in her old corner, and made some more tea. Then, her irons being hot, she began to iron; doing double duty at the same time, for Mrs. Montgomery had one of her talking fits on, and it was necessary to hear and answer a great many things. Presently the first visitor appeared in the shape of Nancy.

"Well, Ellen!" said she; "so Miss Fortune is really sick for once, and you are keeping house. Ain't you grand!"

"I don't feel very grand," said Ellen. "I don't know what is the matter with these clothes; I *cannot* make 'em look smooth."

"Irons ain't hot," said Nancy.

"Yes they are, too hot. I've scorched a towel already."

"My goodness, Ellen! I guess you have. If Miss Fortune was down you'd get it. Why, they're bone dry!" said Nancy, plunging her hand into the basket;—"you haven't sprinkled 'em, have you?"

"To be sure," said Ellen, with an awakened face, "I forgot it!"

"Here, get out of the way, *I'll* do it for you," said Nancy, rolling up her sleeves and pushing Ellen from the table; "you just get me a bowl of water, will you? and we'll have 'em done in no time. Who's a coming to help you?"

"Nobody."

"Nobody!—you poor chicken; do you think you're a going to do all the work of the house yourself?"

"No," said Ellen, "but I can do a good deal, and the rest will have to go."

"You ain't going to do no such thing; I'll stay myself."

"No you can't, Nancy," said Ellen, quietly.

"I guess I will if I've a mind to. I should like to know how you'd help it; Miss Fortune's abed."

"I could help it though," said Ellen; "but I am sure you won't when I ask you not."

"I'll do any thing you please," said Nancy, "if you'll get Miss Fortune to let me stay. Come do, Ellen! It will be splendid; and I'll help you finely, and I won't bother you neither. Come! go ask her; if you don't I will."

"I can't, Nancy; she don't want any body; and it worries her to talk to her. I can't go and ask her."

Nancy impatiently flung down the cloth she was sprinkling and ran up stairs. In a few minutes she came down with a triumphant face and bade Ellen go up to her aunt.

"Ellen," said Miss Fortune, "if I let Nancy stay will you take care of the keys, and keep her out of the buttery?"

"I'll try to, ma'am, as well as I can."

"I'd as lief have her as any body," said Miss Fortune, "if
she'd behave;—she was with me a little in the winter; she is
smart and knows the ways;—if I was sure she would behave herself, but I am afraid she will go rampaging about the house like
a wild cat."

"I think I could prevent that," said Ellen, who, to say truth,
was willing to have any body come to share what she felt would

be a very great burden.   "She knows I could tell Mr. Van Brunt
if she didn't do right, and she would be afraid of that."

"Well," said Miss Fortune, disconsolately, "let her stay then.
Oh, dear, to lie here! but tell her if she don't do just what you tell
her, I'll have Mr. Van Brunt turn her out by the ears.   And don't

let her come near me, for she drives me mad. And, Ellen! put the keys in your pocket. Have you got a pocket in that dress?"

"Yes, ma'am."

"Put 'em in there and don't take 'em out. Now go."

Nancy agreed to the conditions with great glee; and the little housekeeper felt her mind a good deal easier; for though Nancy herself was somewhat of a charge, she was strong and willing and ready, and if she liked any body liked Ellen. Mr. Van Brunt privately asked Ellen if she chose to have Nancy stay; and told her if she gave her any trouble to let him know, and he would make short work with her. The young lady herself also had a hint on the subject.

"I'll tell you what," said Nancy, when this business was settled, —"we'll let the men go off to Miss Van Brunt's to meals; we'll have enough to do without 'em. That's how Miss Fortune has fixed herself,—she would have Sam and Johnny in to board; they never used to, you know, afore this winter."

"The men may go," said Ellen, "but I had a great deal rather Mr. Van Brunt would stay than not,—if we can only manage to cook things for him; we should have to do it at any rate for ourselves, and for grandma."

"Well—*I* ain't as fond of him as all that," said Nancy, "but it'll have to be as you like I suppose. We'll feed him somehow."

Mr. Van Brunt came in to ask if they had any thing in the house for supper. Ellen told him "plenty," and would have him come in just as usual. There was nothing to do but to make tea; cold meat and bread and butter and cheese were all in the buttery; so that evening went off very quietly.

When she came down the next morning the fire was burning nicely, and the kettle on and singing. Not Nancy's work; Mr. Van Brunt had slept in the kitchen, whether on the table, the floor, or the chairs, was best known to himself; and before going to his work had left every thing he could think of ready done to her hand; wood for the fire, pails of water brought from the spout, and some matters in the lower kitchen got out of the way. Ellen stood warming herself at the blaze, when it suddenly darted into her head that it was milking time. In another minute she had thrown open the door and was running across the chip-yard to the barn. There, in the old place, were all her old friends, both four-legged and two-legged; and with great delight she found Dolly had a fine calf and Streaky another superb one, brindled just like herself. Ellen longed to get near enough to touch their little innocent heads, but it was impossible; and recollecting the business on her hands she too danced away.

"Whew!" said Nancy, when Ellen told her of the new inmates

of the barn-yard;—" there'll be work to do! Get your milk-pans ready, Ellen;—in a couple of weeks we'll be making butter."

" Aunt Fortune will be well by that time, I hope," said Ellen.

" She won't then, so you may just make up your mind to it. Dr. Gibson was to see her yesterday forenoon, and he stopped at Miss Lowndes on his way back; and he said it was a chance if she got up again in a month and more. So that's what it is, you see."

" A month and more." It was all that. Miss Fortune was not dangerously ill; but part of the time in a low nervous fever, part of the time encumbered with other ailments, she lay from week to week; bearing her confinement as ill as possible, and making it as disagreeable and burdensome as possible for Ellen to attend upon her. Those were weeks of trial. Ellen's patience and principle and temper were all put to the proof. She had no love, in the first place, for household work, and now her whole time was filled up with it. Studies could not be thought of. Reading was only to be had by mere snatches. Walks and rides were at an end. Often when already very tired she had to run up and down stairs for her aunt, or stand and bathe her face and hands with vinegar, or read the paper to her when Miss Fortune declared she was so nervous she should fly out of her skin if she didn't hear something besides the wind. And very often when she was not wanted up stairs, her old grandmother would beg her to come and read to *her*,—perhaps at the very moment when Ellen was busiest. Ellen did her best. Miss Fortune never could be put off; her old mother sometimes could, with a kiss and a promise; but not always; and then, rather than she should fret, Ellen would leave every thing and give half an hour to soothing and satisfying her. She loved to do this at other times; now it was sometimes burdensome. Nancy could not help her at all in these matters, for neither Miss Fortune nor the old lady would let her come near them. Besides all this there was a measure of care constantly upon Ellen's mind; she felt charged with the welfare of all about the house; and under the effort to meet the charge, joined to the unceasing bodily exertion, she grew thin and pale. She was tired with Nancy's talk; she longed to be reading and studying again; she longed, oh, how she longed! for Alice's and John's company again; and it was no wonder if she sometimes cast very sad longing looks further back still. Now and then an old fit of weeping would come. But Ellen remembered John's words; and often in the midst of her work, stopping short with a sort of pang of sorrow and weariness, and the difficulty of doing right, she would press her hands together and say to herself, " I will try to be a good pilgrim!" Her morning hour of prayer was very precious now; and her Bible grew more and more dear. Little Ellen found its words a mighty refreshment; and often when reading it she loved to recall what Alice had said at this and the other place, and John, and Mr. Marshman, and before them her mother. The passages about heaven, which she well remembered reading to her one particular morning, became great favourites; they were joined with her mother in Ellen's thoughts; and she used to go over them till she nearly knew them by heart.

"What *do* you keep reading that for, the whole time?" said Nancy one day.

"Because I like to," said Ellen.

"Well, if you do, you're the first one ever I saw that did."

"Oh, Nancy!" said Ellen;—"your grandma?"

"Well she does I believe," said Nancy,—"for she's always at it; but all the rest of the folks that ever I saw are happy to get it out of their hands, *I* know. They think they must read a little, and so they do, and they are too glad if something happens to break 'em off. You needn't tell *me;* I've seen 'em."

"I wish *you* loved it, Nancy," said Ellen.

"Well, what do you love it for? come, let's hear; maybe you'll convert me."

"I love it for a great many reasons," said Ellen, who had some difficulty in speaking of what she felt Nancy could not understand.

"Well—I ain't any wiser yet."

"I like to read it because I want to go to heaven, and it tells me how."

"But what's the use?" said Nancy;—"you ain't going to die yet; you are too young; you've time enough."

"Oh, Nancy!—little John Dolan, and Eleanor Parsons, and Mary Huff,—all younger than you and I; how can you say so?"

"Well," said Nancy,—"at any rate, that ain't reading it because you love it;—it's because you must, like other folks."

"That's only one of my reasons," said Ellen, hesitating and speaking gravely;—"I like to read about the Saviour, and what he has done for me, and what a friend he will be to me, and how he forgives me. I had rather have the Bible, Nancy, than all the other books in the world."

"That ain't saying much," said Nancy;—"but how come you to be so sure you are forgiven?"

"Because the Bible says, 'He that believeth on him shall not be ashamed,' and I believe in him;—and that he will not cast out any one that comes to him, and I have come to him;—and that he loves those that love him, and I love him. If it did not speak so very plainly I should be afraid, but it makes me happy to read such verses as these. I wish you knew, Nancy, how happy it makes me."

This profession of faith was not spoken without starting tears. Nancy made no reply.

As Miss Fortune had foretold, plenty of people came to the

house with proffers of service. Nancy's being there made it easy for Ellen to get rid of them all. Many were the marvels that Miss Fortune should trust her house "to two girls like that," and many the guesses that she would rue it when she got up again. People were wrong. Things went on very steadily and in an orderly manner; and Nancy kept the peace as she would have done in few houses. Bold and insolent as she sometimes was to others, she regarded Ellen with a mixed notion of respect and protection, which led her at once to shun doing any thing that would grieve her, and to thrust her aside from every heavy or difficult job, taking the brunt herself. Nancy might well do this, for she was at least twice as strong as Ellen; but she would not have done it for every body.

There were visits of kindness as well as visits of officiousness. Alice and Mrs. Van Brunt and Margery, one or the other every day. Margery would come in and mix up a batch of bread; Alice would bring a bowl of butter, or a basket of cake; and Mrs. Van Brunt sent whole dinners. Mr. Van Brunt was there always at night, and about the place as much as possible during the day; when obliged to be absent, he stationed Sam Larkens to guard the house, also to bring wood and water, and do whatever he was bid. All the help, however, that was given from abroad could not make Ellen's life an easy one; Mr. Van Brunt's wishes that Miss Fortune would get up again began to come very often. The history of one day may serve for the history of all those weeks.

It was in the beginning of April. Ellen came down stairs early, but come when she would she found the fire made and the kettle on. Ellen felt a little as if she had not quite slept off the remembrance of yesterday's fatigue; however, that was no matter; she set to work. She swept up the kitchen, got her milk strainer and pans ready upon the buttery shelf, and began to set the table. By the time this was half done, in came Sam Larkens with two great pails of milk, and Johnny Low followed with another. They were much too heavy for Ellen to lift, but true to her charge she let no one come into the buttery but herself; she brought the pans to the door, where Sam filled them for her, and as each was done she set it in its place on the shelf. This took some time, for there were eight of them. She had scarce wiped up the spilt milk and finished setting the table when Mr. Van Brunt came in.

"Good-morning!" said he. "How d'ye do to-day?"

"Very well, Mr. Van Brunt."

"I wish you'd look a little redder in the face. Don't you be too busy? Where's Nancy?"

"Oh, she's busy, out with the clothes."

"Same as ever up stairs?—What are you going to do for breakfast, Ellen?"

" I don't know, Mr. Van Brunt; there isn't any thing cooked in the house; we have eaten every thing up."

" Cleaned out, eh ?   Bread and all ?"

" Oh, no, not bread; there's plenty of that, but there's nothing else."

" Well never mind ;—you bring me a ham and a dozen of eggs, and I'll make you a first-rate breakfast."

Ellen laughed, for this was not the first time Mr. Van Brunt had acted as cook for the family.   While she got what he had asked for, and bared a place on the table for his operations, he went to the spout and washed his hands.

" Now a sharp knife, Ellen, and the frying-pan, and a dish,—and that's all I want of you."

Ellen brought them, and while he was busy with the ham she made the coffee and set it by the side of the fire to boil; got the cream and butter, and set the bread on the table; and then set herself down to rest, and amuse herself with Mr. Van Brunt's cookery.   He was no mean hand; his slices of ham were very artist-like, and frying away in the most unexceptionable manner. Ellen watched him and laughed at him, till the ham was taken out and all the eggs broke in; then after seeing that the coffee was right she went up stairs to dress her grandmother—always the last thing before breakfast.

" Who's frying ham and eggs down stairs ?" inquired Miss Fortune.

" Mr. Van Brunt," said Ellen.

This answer was unexpected.   Miss Fortune tossed her head over in a dissatisfied kind of way, and told Ellen to " tell him to be careful."

" Of what ?" thought Ellen ; and wisely concluded with herself not to deliver the message; very certain she should laugh if she did, and she had running in her head an indistinct notion of the command, " Honor thy father and thy mother."

Breakfast was ready but no one there when she got down stairs. She placed her grandmother at table, and called Nancy, who all this time had been getting the clothes out of the rinsing water and hanging them out on the line to dry ; said clothes having been washed the day before by Miss Sarah Lowndes, who came there for the purpose.   Ellen poured out the coffee, and then in came Mr. Van Brunt with a head of early lettuce which he had pulled in the garden and washed at the spout.   Ellen had to jump up again to get the salt and pepper and vinegar; but she always jumped willingly for Mr. Van Brunt.   The meals were pleasanter during those weeks than in all the time Ellen had been in Thirlwall before ; or she thought so.   That sharp eye at the head of the table was pleasantly missed.   They with one accord sat longer at meals ; more talking and laughing went on ; nobody felt afraid of being snapped up. Mr. Van Brunt praised Ellen's coffee (he had taught her how to make it), and she praised his ham and eggs. Old Mrs. Montgomery praised every thing, and seemed to be in particular comfort ; talked as much as she had a mind, and was respectfully attended to. Nancy was in high feather ; and the clatter of knives and forks and tea-cups went on very pleasantly. But at last chairs were pushed from the table, and work began again.

Nancy went back to her tubs. Ellen supplied her grandmother with her knitting and filled her snuff-box ; cleared the table and put up the dishes ready for washing. Then she went into the buttery to skim the cream. This was a part of the work she liked. It was heavy lifting the pans of milk to the skimming shelf before the window, but as Ellen drew her spoon round the edge of the cream she liked to see it wrinkle up in thick yellow leathery folds, showing how deep and rich it was ; it looked half butter already. She knew how to take it off now very nicely. The cream was set by in a vessel for future churning, and the milk, as each pan was skimmed, was poured down the wooden trough at the left of the window through which it went into a great hogshead at the lower kitchen door.

This done Ellen went up stairs to her aunt. Dr. Gibson always came early, and she and her room must be put in apple-pie order first. It was a long wearisome job. Ellen brought the basin for her to wash her face and hands ; then combed her hair and put on her clean cap. That was always the first thing. The next was to make the bed ; and for this, Miss Fortune, weak or strong, wrapped herself up and tumbled out upon the floor. When she was comfortably placed again, Ellen had to go through a laborious dusting of the room and all the things in it, even taking a dust-pan and brush to the floor if any speck of dust or crumbs could be seen there. Every rung of every chair must be gone over, though ever so clean ; every article put up or put out of the way ; Miss Fortune made the most of the little province of housekeeping that was left her ; and a fluttering tape escaping through the crack of the door would have put her whole spirit topsy-turvy. When all was to her mind, and not before, she would have her breakfast. Only gruel and biscuit, or toast and tea, or some such trifle, but Ellen must prepare it and bring it up stairs, and wait till it was eaten. And very particularly it must be prepared, and very faultlessly it must be served, or with an impatient expression of disgust Miss Fortune would send it down again. On the whole Ellen always thought herself happy when this part of her day was well over.

When she got down this morning she found the kitchen in nice order, and Nancy standing by the fire in a little sort of pause, having just done the breakfast dishes.

" Well !" said Nancy,—" what are you going to do now ?"

" Put away these dishes, and then churn," said Ellen.

" My goodness ! so you are. What's going to be for dinner, Ellen ?"

" That's more than I know," said Ellen laughing. " We have eaten up Mrs. Van Brunt's pie and washed the dish ;—there's nothing but some cold potatoes."

" *That* won't do," said Nancy. " I tell you what, Ellen,—we'll just boil pot for to-day ; somebody else will send us something by to-morrow most likely."

" I don't know what you mean by ' boil pot,' " said Ellen.

" Oh, you don't know every thing yet, by half. *I* know—I'll fix it. You just give me the things, Miss Housekeeper, that's all you've got to do ; I want a piece of pork and a piece of beef, and all the vegetables you've got."

" All ?" said Ellen.

" Every soul on 'em. Don't be scared, Ellen ! you shall see what I can do in the way of cookery ; if you don't like it you needn't eat it. What have you got in the cellar ?"

" Come and see, and take what you want, Nancy ; there is plenty of potatoes and carrots and onions, and beets I believe ; the turnips are all gone."

" Parsnips out in the yard, ain't there ?"

" Yes, but you'll have to do with a piece of pork, Nancy, I don't know any thing about beef."

While Nancy went round the cellar gathering in her apron the various roots she wanted, Ellen uncovered the pork barrel, and after looking a minute at the dark pickle she never loved to plunge into, bravely bared her arm and fished up a piece of pork.

" Now, Nancy, just help me with this churn out of the cellar, will you ? and then you may go."

" My goodness ! it is heavy," said Nancy. " You'll have a time of it, Ellen ; but I can't help you."

She went off to the garden for parsnips, and Ellen quietly put in the dasher and the cover, and began to churn. It was tiresome work. The churn was pretty full, as Nancy had said ; the cream was rich and cold, and at the end of half an hour grew very stiff. It spattered and sputtered up on Ellen's face and hands and apron, and over the floor ; legs and arms were both weary ; but still that pitiless dasher must go up and down, hard as it might be to force it either way ; she must not stop. In this state of matters she heard a pair of thick shoes come clumping down the stairs, and beheld Mr. Van Brunt.

" Here you are !" said he. " Churning !—Been long at it ?"

"A good while," said Ellen, with a sigh.

"Coming?"

"I don't know when."

Mr. Van Brunt stepped to the door and shouted for Sam Larkens. He was ordered to take the churn and bring the butter; and Ellen, very glad of a rest, went out to amuse herself with feeding the chickens, and then up stairs to see what Nancy was doing.

"Butter come?" said Nancy.

"No, Sam has taken it. How are you getting on? Oh, I am tired!"

"I'm getting on first-rate; I've got all the things in."

"In what?"

"Why, in the pot!—in a pot of water, boiling away as fast as they can; we'll have dinner directly. Hurra! who comes there?"

She jumped to the door. It was Thomas, bringing Margery's respects, and a custard-pie for Ellen.

"I declare," said Nancy, "it's a good thing to have friends, ain't it? I'll try and get some.—Hollo? what's wanting?—Mr. Van Brunt's calling you, Ellen."

Ellen ran down.

"The butter's come," said he. "Now do you know what to do with it?"

"Oh, yes," said Ellen smiling; "Margery showed me nicely."

He brought her a pail of water from the spout, and stood by with a pleased kind of look, while she carefully lifted the cover and rinsed down the little bits of butter which stuck to it and the dasher; took out the butter with her ladle into a large wooden bowl, washed it, and finally salted it.

"Don't take too much pains," said he ;—" the less of the hand it gets the better. That will do very well."

"Now are you ready?" said Nancy, coming down stairs, "'cause dinner is. My goodness! ain't that a fine lot of butter? there's four pounds, ain't there?"

"Five," said Mr. Van Brunt.

"And as sweet as it can be," said Ellen. "Beautiful, isn't it? Yes, I'm ready, as soon as I set this in the cellar and cover it up."

Nancy's dish,—the pork, potatoes, carrots, beets, and cabbage, all boiled in the same pot together,—was found very much to every body's taste except Ellen's. She made her dinner off potatoes and bread, the former of which she declared, laughing, were very porky and cabbagy; her meal would have been an extremely light one, had it not been for the custard-pie.

After dinner new labours began. Nancy had forgotten to hang on a pot of water for the dishes; so after putting away the eatables in the buttery, while the water was heating, Ellen warmed some gruel and carried it with a plate of biscuit up stairs to her aunt. But Miss Fortune said she was tired of gruel and couldn't eat it; she must have some milk porridge; and she gave Ellen very particular directions how to make it. Ellen sighed only once as she went down with her despised dish of gruel, and set about doing her best to fulfil her aunt's wishes. The first dish of milk she burnt;—another sigh and another trial;—better care this time had better success, and Ellen had the satisfaction to see her aunt perfectly suited with her dinner.

When she came down with the empty bowl Nancy had a pile of dishes ready washed, and Ellen took the towel to dry them. Mrs. Montgomery, who had been in an uncommonly quiet fit all day, now laid down her knitting and asked if Ellen would not come and read to her.

" Presently, grandma,—as soon as I have done here."

" I know somebody that's tired," said Nancy. " I tell you what, Ellen,—you had better take to liking pork; you can't work on potatoes. I ain't tired a bit. There's somebody coming to the door again ! Do run and open it, will you ? my hands are wet. I wonder why folks can't come in without giving so much trouble."

It was Thomas again, with a package for Ellen which had just come, he said, and Miss Alice thought she would like to have it directly. Ellen thanked her, and thanked him, with a face from which all signs of weariness had fled away. The parcel was sealed up, and directed in a hand she was pretty sure she knew. Her fingers burned to break the seal; but she would not open it there, neither leave her work unfinished; she went on wiping the dishes with trembling hands and a beating heart.

" What's that ?" said Nancy ; " what did Thomas Grimes want ? what have you got there ?"

" I don't know," said Ellen smiling ;—" something good, I guess."

" Something good ? is it something to eat ?"

" No," said Ellen,—" I didn't mean any thing to eat when I said something good; I don't think those are the best things."

To Ellen's delight she saw that her grandmother had forgotten about the reading and was quietly taking short naps with her head against the chimney. So she put away the last dish, and then seized her package and flew up stairs. She was sure it had come from Doncaster; she was right. It was a beautiful copy of the " Pilgrim's Progress,"—on the first leaf written, " To my little sister Ellen Montgomery, from J. H.;" and within the cover lay a letter. This letter Ellen read in the course of the next six days at least twice as many times ; and never without crying over it.

" Alice has told me" (said John), " about your new troubles.

There is said to be a time ' when the clouds return after the rain.'
I am sorry, my little sister, this time should come to you so early.
I often think of you, and wish I could be near you. Still, dear
Ellie, the good Husbandman knows what his plants want ; do you
believe that, and can you trust him ? They should have nothing
but sunshine if that was good for them. He knows it is not; so
there come clouds and rains, and ' stormy wind fulfilling his will.'
And what is it all for ?—' Herein is my Father glorified, *that ye bear
much fruit ;'* do not disappoint his purpose, Ellie. We shall have
sunshine enough by and by,—but I know it is hard for so young a
one as my little sister to look much forward ; so do not look forward, Ellie ; look up ! look off unto Jesus,—from all your duties,
troubles, and wants ; he will help you in them all. The more you
look up to him the more he will look down to you ; and he especially said, ' Suffer *little children* to come unto me ;' you see you are
particularly invited."

Ellen was a long time up stairs, and when she came down it was
with red eyes.

Mrs. Montgomery was now awake and asked for the reading
again; and for three-quarters of an hour Ellen and she were
quietly busy with the Bible. Nancy meanwhile was down stairs
washing the dairy things. When her grandmother released her
Ellen had to go up to wait upon her aunt ; after which she went
into the buttery, and skimmed the cream, and got the pans ready
for the evening milk. By this time it was five o'clock, and Nancy
came in with the basket of dry clothes ; at which Ellen looked
with the sorrowful consciousness that they must be sprinkled and
folded by and by, and ironed to-morrow. It happened, however,
that Jane Huff came in just then with a quantity of hot short-
cake for tea ; and seeing the basket she very kindly took the business of sprinkling and folding upon herself. This gave Ellen
spirits to carry out a plan she had long had, to delight the whole
family with some eggs scrambled in Margery's fashion ; after the
milk was strained and put away she went about it, while Nancy
set the table. A nice bed of coals was prepared ; the spider set
over them ; the eggs broken in, peppered and salted ; and she began carefully to stir them as she had seen Margery do. But instead of acting right the eggs maliciously stuck fast to the spider
and burned. Ellen was confounded.

" How much butter did you put in ?" said Mr. Van Brunt, who
had come in, and stood looking on.

" Butter !" said Ellen looking up,—" oh, I forgot all about it !—
I ought to have put that in, oughtn't I !—I'm sorry !"

" Never mind," said Mr. Van Brunt,—" 'tain't worth your being
sorry about. Here, Nancy—clean us off this spider, and we'll try
again."

At this moment Miss Fortune was heard screaming; Ellen ran up.

"What did she want?" said Mr. Van Brunt when she came down again.

"She wanted to know what was burning."

"Did you tell her?"

"Yes."

"Well, what did she say?"

"Said I mustn't use any more eggs without asking her."

"That ain't fair play," said Mr. Van Brunt;—"you and I are the head of the house now, I take it. You just use as many on 'em as you've a mind; and all you spile I'll fetch you again from hum. That's you, Nancy! Now, Ellen, here's the spider; try again; let's have plenty of butter in this time, and plenty of eggs too."

This time the eggs were scrambled to a nicety, and the supper met with great favour from all parties.

Ellen's day was done when the dishes were. The whole family went early to bed. She was weary; but she could rest well. She had made her old grandmother comfortable; she had kept the peace with Nancy; she had pleased Mr. Van Brunt; she had faithfully served her aunt. Her sleep was uncrossed by a dream, untroubled by a single jar of conscience. And her awaking to another day of labour, though by no means joyful, was yet not unhopeful or unhappy.

She had a hard trial a day or two after. It was in the end of the afternoon, she had her big apron on, and was in the buttery skimming the milk, when she heard the kitchen door open, and footsteps enter the kitchen. Out went little Ellen to see who it was, and there stood Alice and old Mr. Marshman! He was going to take Alice home with him the next morning, and wanted Ellen to go too; and they had come to ask her. Ellen knew it was impossible, that is, that it would not be right, and she said so; and in spite of Alice's wistful look, and Mr. Marshman's insisting, she stood her ground. Not without some difficulty, and some glistening of the eyes. They had to give it up. Mr. Marshman then wanted to know what she meant by swallowing herself up in an apron in that sort of way? so Ellen had him into the buttery and showed him what she had been about. He would see her skim several pans, and laughed at her prodigiously; though there was a queer look about his eyes, too, all the time. And when he went away, he held her in his arms, and kissed her again and again; and said that "some of these days he would take her away from her aunt, and she should have her no more." Ellen stood and looked after them till they were out of sight, and then went up stairs and had a good cry.

The butter-making soon became quite too much for Ellen to manage; so Jane Huff and Jenny Hitchcock were engaged to come by turns and do the heavy part of it; all within the buttery being still left to Ellen, for Miss Fortune would have no one else go there. It was a great help to have them take even so much off her hands; and they often did some other little odd jobs for her. The milk however seemed to increase as fast as the days grew longer, and Ellen could not find that she was much less busy. The days were growing pleasant too; soft airs began to come; the grass was of a beautiful green; the buds on the branches began to swell, and on some trees to put out. When Ellen had a moment of time she used to run across the chip-yard to the barn, or round the garden, or down to the brook, and drink in the sweet air and the lovely sights which never had seemed quite so lovely before. If once in a while she could get half an hour before tea, she used to take her book and sit down on the threshold of the front door, or on the big log under the apple-tree in the chip-yard. In those minutes the reading was doubly sweet; or else the loveliness of earth and sky was such that Ellen could not take her eyes from them; till she saw Sam or Johnny coming out of the cowhouse door with the pails of milk, or heard their heavy tramp over the chips;—then she had to jump and run. Those were sweet half hours. Ellen did not at first know how much reason she had to be delighted with her " Pilgrim's Progress;" she saw to be sure that it was a fine copy, well bound, with beautiful cuts. But when she came to look further, she found all through the book, on the margin or at the bottom of the leaves, in John's beautiful handwriting, a great many notes—simple, short, plain, exactly what was needed to open the whole book to her and make it of the greatest possible use and pleasure. Many things she remembered hearing from his lips when they were reading it together; there was a large part of the book where all was new; the part he had not had time to finish. How Ellen loved the book and the giver when she found these beautiful notes, it is impossible to tell. She counted it her greatest treasure next to her little red Bible.

CHAPTER XXXVI.

Oh, what will I do wi' him, quo' he,
   What will I do wi' him?
What will I do wi' him, quo' he,
   What will I do wi' him?

OLD SONG.

IN the course of time Miss Fortune showed signs of mending; and, at last, toward the latter end of April, she was able to come down stairs. All parties hailed this event for different reasons; even Nancy was growing tired of her regular life, and willing to have a change. Ellen's joy was, however, soon diminished by the terrible rummaging which took place. Miss Fortune's hands were yet obliged to lie still, but her eyes did double duty; *they* were never known to be idle in the best of times, and it seemed to Ellen now as if they were taking amends for all their weeks of forced rest. Oh, those eyes! Dust was found where Ellen never dreamed of looking for any; things were said to be dreadfully "in the way" where she had never found it out; disorder and dirt were groaned over, where Ellen did not know the fact or was utterly ignorant how to help it; waste was suspected where none had been, and carelessness charged where rather praise was due. Impatient to have things to her mind, and as yet unable to do any thing herself, Miss Fortune kept Nancy and Ellen running, till both wished her back in bed; and even Mr. Van Brunt grumbled that " to pay Ellen for having grown white and poor, her aunt was going to work the little flesh she had left off her bones." It was rather hard to bear, just when she was looking for ease too; her patience and temper were more tried than in all those weeks before. But if there was small pleasure in pleasing her aunt, Ellen did earnestly wish to please God; she struggled against ill temper, prayed against it; and though she often blamed herself in secret, she did so go through that week as to call forth Mr. Van Brunt's admiration, and even to stir a little the conscience of her aunt. Mr. Van Brunt comforted her with the remark that " it is darkest just before day," and so it proved. Before the week was at an end Miss Fortune began, as she expressed it, to "take hold;" Jenny Hitchcock and Jane Huff were excused from any more butter-making; Nancy was sent away; Ellen's labours were much lightened; and the house was itself again.

The third of May came. For the first time in near two months Ellen found in the afternoon she could be spared awhile; there was no need to think twice what she would do with her leisure. Perhaps Margery could tell her something of Alice! Hastily and joyfully she exchanged her working frock for a merino, put on nice shoes and stockings and ruffle again, and taking her bonnet and gloves to put on out of doors, away she ran. Who can tell how pleasant it seemed, after so many weeks, to be able to walk abroad again, and to walk to the mountain! Ellen snuffed the sweet air, skipped on the green sward, picked nosegays of grass and dandelions, and at last unable to contain herself set off to run. Fatigue soon brought this to a stop; then she walked more leisurely on, enjoying. It was a lovely spring day. Ellen's eyes were gladdened by it; she felt thankful in her heart that God had made every thing so beautiful; she thought it was pleasant to think *he* had made them; pleasant to see in them everywhere so much of the wisdom and power and goodness of him she looked up to with joy as her best friend. She felt quietly happy, and sure he would take care of her. Then a thought of Alice came into her head; she set off to run again, and kept it up this time till she got to the old house and ran round the corner. She stopped at the shed door and went through into the lower kitchen.

"Why, Miss Ellen dear!" exclaimed Margery,—"if that isn't you! Aren't you come in the *very* nick of time! How *do* you do? I am *very* glad to see you—uncommon glad to be sure. What witch told you to come here just now? Run in, run into the parlour and see what you'll find there."

"Has Alice come back?" cried Ellen. But Margery only laughed and said, "Run in!"

Up the steps, through the kitchen, and across the hall, Ellen ran,—burst open the parlour door,—and was in Alice's arms. There were others in the room; but Ellen did not seem to know it, clinging to her and holding her in a fast glad embrace, till Alice bade her look up and attend to somebody else. And then she was seized round the neck by little Ellen Chauncey!—and then came her mother, and then Miss Sophia. The two children were overjoyed to see each other, while their joy was touching to see, from the shade of sorrow in the one, and of sympathy in the other. Ellen was scarcely less glad to see kind Mrs. Chauncey; Miss Sophia's greeting too was very affectionate. But Ellen returned to Alice, and rested herself in her lap with one arm round her neck, the other hand being in little Ellen's grasp.

"And now you are happy, I suppose?" said Miss Sophia when they were thus placed.

"Very," said Ellen, smiling.

"Ah, but you'll be happier by and by," said Ellen Chauncey.

"Hush, Ellen!" said Miss Sophia;—"what curious things children are!—You didn't expect to find us all here, did you, Ellen Montgomery?"

"No indeed, ma'am," said Ellen, drawing Alice's cheek nearer for another kiss.

"We have but just come, Ellie," said her sister. "I should not have been long in finding you out. My child, how thin you have got."

"Oh, I'll grow fat again now," said Ellen.

"How is Miss Fortune?"

"Oh, she is up again and well."

"Have you any reason to expect your father home, Ellen?" said Mrs. Chauncey.

"Yes, ma'am;—aunt Fortune says perhaps he will be here in a week."

"Then you are very happy in looking forward, aren't you?" said Miss Sophia, not noticing the cloud that had come over Ellen's brow.

Ellen hesitated,—coloured—coloured more,—and finally with a sudden motion hid her face against Alice.

"When did he sail, Ellie?" said Alice gravely.

"In the Duc d'Orleans—he said he would——"

"*When?*"

"The fifth of April.—Oh, I can't help it!" exclaimed Ellen, failing in the effort to control herself; she clasped Alice as if she feared even then the separating hand. Alice bent her head down and whispered words of comfort.

"Mamma!" said little Ellen Chauncey under her breath, and looking solemn to the last degree,—"don't Ellen want to see her father?"

"She's afraid that he may take her away where she will not be with Alice any more; and you know she has no mother to go to."

"Oh!" said Ellen with a very enlightened face;—"but he won't, will he?"

"I hope not; I think not."

Cheered again, the little girl drew near and silently took one of Ellen's hands.

"We shall not be parted, Ellie," said Alice,—"you need not fear. If your father takes you away from your aunt Fortune, I think it will be only to give you to me. You need not fear yet."

"Mamma says so too, Ellen," said her little friend.

This was strong consolation. Ellen looked up and smiled.

"Now come with me," said Ellen Chauncey, pulling her hand, —"I want you to show me something; let's go down to the garden,—come! exercise is good for you."

"No, no," said her mother smiling,—"Ellen has had exercise enough lately; you mustn't take her down to the garden now; you would find nothing there. Come here!"

A long whisper followed, which seemed to satisfy little Ellen and she ran out of the room. Some time passed in pleasant talk and telling all that had happened since they had seen each other; then little Ellen came back and called Ellen Montgomery to the glass door, saying she wanted her to look at something.

"It is only a horse we brought with us," said Miss Sophia. "Ellen thinks it is a great beauty, and can't rest till you have seen it."

Ellen went accordingly to the door. There to be sure was Thomas before it holding a pony bridled and saddled. He was certainly a very pretty little creature; brown all over except one white forefoot; his coat shone it was so glossy; his limbs were fine; his eye gentle and bright; his tail long enough to please the children. He stood as quiet as a lamb, whether Thomas held him or not.

"Oh, what a beauty!" said Ellen;—"what a lovely little horse!"

"Ain't he!" said Ellen Chauncey;—"and he goes so beautifully besides, and never starts nor nothing; and he is as good-natured as a little dog."

"As a *good-natured* little dog, she means, Ellen," said Miss Sophia,—"there are little dogs of very various character."

"Well he looks good-natured," said Ellen. "What a pretty head!—and what a beautiful new side-saddle, and all. I never saw such a dear little horse in my life. Is it yours, Alice?"

"No," said Alice, "it is a present to a friend of Mr. Marshman's."

"She'll be a very happy friend, I should think," said Ellen.

"That's what I said," said Ellen Chauncey, dancing up and down,—"that's what I said. I said you'd be happier by and by, didn't I?"

"I?" said Ellen colouring.

"Yes, you,—you are the friend it is for; it's for you, it's for you! you are grandpa's friend, aren't you?" she repeated, springing upon Ellen, and hugging her up in an ecstasy of delight.

"But it isn't really for me, is it?" said Ellen, now looking almost pale;—"Oh, Alice!—"

"Come, come," said Miss Sophia,—"what will papa say if I tell him you received his present so?—come, hold up your head! Put on your bonnet and try him;—come, Ellen! let's see you."

Ellen did not know whether to cry or laugh,—till she mounted the pretty pony; that settled the matter. Not Ellen Chauncey's unspeakable delight was as great as her own. She rode slowly up and down before the house, and once a-going would not have known how to stop if she had not recollected that the pony had travelled thirty miles that day and must be tired. Ellen took not another turn after that. She jumped down, and begged Thomas to take the tenderest care of him; patted his neck; ran into the kitchen to beg of Margery a piece of bread to give him from her hand; examined the new stirrup and housings, and the pony all over a dozen times; and after watching him as Thomas led him off, till he was out of sight, finally came back into the house with a

face of marvellous contentment. She tried to fashion some message of thanks for the kind giver of the pony; but she wanted to express so much that no words would do. Mrs. Chauncey however smiled and assured her she knew exactly what to say.

"That pony has been destined for you, Ellen," she said, "this

year and more; but my father waited to have him thoroughly well
broken. You need not be afraid of him; he is perfectly gentle
and well-trained; if he had not been sure of that my father would
never have sent him;—though Mr. John *is* making such a horse-
woman of you."

"I wish I could thank him," said Ellen;—"but I don't know
how."

"What will you call him, Ellen," said Miss Sophia. "My
father has dubbed him 'George Marshman;'—he says you will like
that, as my brother is such a favourite of yours."

"He didn't *really*, did he?" said Ellen, looking from Sophia to
Alice. "I needn't call him that, need I?"

"Not unless you like," said Miss Sophia laughing,—"you may
change it; but what *will* you call him?"

"I don't know," said Ellen very gravely,—"he must have a
name to be sure."

"But why don't you call him that?" said Ellen Chauncey;—
"George is a very pretty name;—I like that; I should call him
'Uncle George.'"

"Oh, I couldn't!" said Ellen,—"I couldn't call him so; I
shouldn't like it at all."

"George Washington?" said Mrs. Chauncey.

"No indeed!" said Ellen. "I guess I wouldn't!"

"Why, is it too good, or not good enough?" said Miss Sophia.

"Too good! A great deal too good for a horse! I wouldn't
for any thing."

"How would Brandywine do then, since you are so patriotic?"
said Miss Sophia, looking amused.

"What is 'patriotic?'" said Ellen.

"A patriot, Ellen," said Alice smiling,—"is one who has a
strong and true love for his country."

"I don't know whether I am patriotic," said Ellen, "but I
won't call him Brandywine. Why, Miss Sophia!"

"No, I wouldn't either," said Ellen Chauncey;—"it isn't a pretty
name. Call him Seraphine!—like Miss Angell's pony—that's
pretty."

"No, no,—'Seraphine!' nonsense!" said Miss Sophia;—"call
him Benedict Arnold, Ellen; and then it will be a relief to your
mind to whip him."

"Whip him!" said Ellen,—"I don't want to whip him, I am
sure; and I should be afraid to besides."

"Hasn't John taught you that lesson yet?" said the young lady;
—"he is perfect in it himself. Do you remember, Alice, the chas-
tising he gave that fine black horse of ours we called the 'Black
Prince?'—a beautiful creature he was,—more than a year ago?—
My conscience! he frightened me to death."

" I remember," said Alice; " I remember I could not look on."

" What did he do that for ? " said Ellen.

" What's the matter, Ellen Montgomery ?" said Miss Sophia, laughing,—" where did you get that long face ? Are you thinking of John or the horse ? "

Ellen's eyes turned to Alice.

" My dear Ellen," said Alice smiling, though she spoke seriously,—" it was necessary ; it sometimes is necessary to do such things. You do not suppose John would do it cruelly or unnecessarily ? "

Ellen's face shortened considerably.

" But what had the horse been doing ? "

" He had not been doing any thing ; he would *not* do,—that was the trouble ; he was as obstinate as a mule."

" My dear Ellen," said Alice, " it was no such terrible matter as Sophia's words have made you believe. It was a clear case of obstinacy. The horse was resolved to have his own way and not do what his rider required of him ; it was necessary that either the horse or the man should give up ; and as John has no fancy for giving up, he carried his point,—partly by management, partly, I confess, by a judicious use of the whip and spur ; but there was no such furious flagellation as Sophia seems to mean, and which a good horseman would scarce be guilty of."

" A very determined ' use,' " said Miss Sophia. " I advise you, Ellen, not to trust your pony to Mr. John ; he will have no mercy on him."

"Sophia is laughing, Ellen," said Alice. " You and I know John, do we not ? "

" Then he did right ? " said Ellen.

" Perfectly right—except in mounting the horse at all, which I never wished him to do. No one on the place would ride him."

" He carried John beautifully all the day after that though," said Miss Sophia, " and I dare say he might have ridden him to the end of the chapter if you would have let papa give him to him. But he was of no use to any body else. Howard couldn't manage him—I suppose he was too lazy. Papa was delighted enough that day to have given John any thing. And I can tell you Black Prince the second is spirited enough ; I am afraid you won't like him."

" John has a present of a horse too, Ellen," said Alice.

" Has he ?—from Mr. Marshman ? "

" Yes."

" I'm very glad ! Oh, what rides we can take now, can't we, Alice ? We shan't want to borrow Jenny's pony any more. What kind of a horse is Mr. John's ? "

" Black,—perfectly black."

" Is he handsome ?"

" Very."

" Is his name Black Prince ?"

" Yes."

Ellen began to consider the possibility of calling her pony the
Brown Princess, or by some similar title—the name of John's two
chargers seeming the very most striking a horse could be known by.

" Don't forget, Alice," said Mrs. Chauncey, " to tell John to
stop for him on his way home. It will give us a chance of seeing
him, which is not a common pleasure, in any sense of the term."

They went back to the subject of the name, which Ellen pondered with uneasy visions of John and her poor pony flitting
through her head. The little horse was very hard to fit, or else
Ellen's taste was very hard to suit; a great many names were proposed, none of which were to her mind, Charley, and Cherry, and
Brown, and Dash, and Jumper,—but she said they had " John"
and " Jenny" already in Thirlwall, and she didn't want a " Charley ;" " Brown" was not pretty, and she hoped he wouldn't " dash"
at any thing, nor be a "jumper" when she was on his back.
Cherry she mused awhile about, but it wouldn't do.

" Call him Fairy," said Ellen Chauncey ;—" that's a pretty
name. Mamma says she used to have a horse called Fairy. Do,
Ellen ! call him Fairy."

" No," said Ellen ; " he can't have a lady's name—that's the
trouble."

" I have it, Ellen !" said Alice ;—" I have a name for you,—call
him the Brownie."

" The ' Brownie ?' " said Ellen.

" Yes—brownies are male fairies ; and brown is his colour ; so
how will that do ?"

It was soon decided that it would do very well. It was simple,
descriptive, and not common ; Ellen made up her mind that " The
Brownie" should be his name. No sooner given, it began to grow
dear. Ellen's face quitted its look of anxious gravity and came
out into the broadest and fullest satisfaction. She never showed
joy boisterously ; but there was a light in her eye which brought
many a smile into those of her friends as they sat round the tea-
table.

After tea it was necessary to go home, much to the sorrow of all
parties. Ellen knew however it would not do to stay ; Miss
Fortune was but just got well, and perhaps already thinking herself ill-used. She put on her things.

" Are you going to take your pony home with you ?" said Miss
Sophia.

" Oh, no, ma'am, not to-night. I must see about a place for
him ; and besides, poor fellow, he is tired I dare say."

" I do believe you would take more care of his legs than of your own," said Miss Sophia.

" But you'll be here to-morrow early, Ellie ?"

" Oh, won't I !" exclaimed Ellen, as she sprang to Alice's neck ; —" as early as I can, at least; I don't know when aunt Fortune will have done with me."

The way home seemed as nothing. If she was tired she did not know it. The Brownie! the Brownie!—the thought of him carried her as cleverly over the ground as his very back would have done. She came running into the chip-yard.

" Hollo !" cried Mr. Van Brunt, who was standing under the apple-tree cutting a piece of wood for the tongue of the ox-cart, which had been broken,—" I'm glad to see you *can* run. I was afeard you'd hardly be able to stand by this time ; but there you come like a young deer !"

" Oh, Mr. Van Brunt," said Ellen, coming close up to him and speaking in an under tone,—" you don't know what a present I have had ! What do you think Mr. Marshman has sent me from Ventnor ?"

" Couldn't guess," said Mr. Van Brunt, resting the end of his pole on the log and chipping at it with his hatchet ;—" never guessed any thing in my life ;—what is it ?"

" He has sent me the most beautiful little horse you ever saw ! —for my own—for me to ride ; and a new beautiful saddle and bridle ; you never saw any thing so beautiful, Mr. Van Brunt; he is all brown, with one white forefoot, and I've named him the ' Brownie ;' and oh, Mr. Van Brunt ! do you think aunt Fortune will let him come here ?"

Mr. Van Brunt chipped away at his pole, looking very good-humoured.

" Because you know I couldn't have half the good of him if he had to stay away from me up on the mountain. I shall want to ride him every day. Do you think aunt Fortune will let him be kept here, Mr. Van Brunt ?"

" I guess she will," said Mr. Van Brunt soberly, and his tone said to Ellen, " *I* will, if she don't."

" Then will you ask her and see about it ?—if you please Mr. Van Brunt ! I'd rather you would. And you won't have him put to plough or any thing, will you, Mr. Van Brunt? Miss Sophia says it would spoil him."

" I'll plough myself first," said Mr. Van Brunt with his half smile ;—" there shan't be a hair of his coat turned the wrong way. *I'll* see to him—as if he was a prince."

" Oh, thank you, dear Mr. Van Brunt ! How good you are. Then I shall not speak about him at all till you do, remember. I am *very* much obliged to you, Mr. Van Brunt !"

Ellen ran in. She got a chiding for her long stay, but it fell upon ears that could not hear. The Brownie came like a shield between her and all trouble. She smiled at her aunt's hard words as if they had been sugar-plums. And her sleep that night might have been prairie land, for the multitude of horses of all sorts that chased through it.

"Have you heerd the news?" said Mr. Van Brunt, when he had got his second cup of coffee at breakfast next morning.

"No," said Miss Fortune. "What news?"

"There ain't as much news as there used to be when I was young," said the old lady;—"'seems to me I don't hear nothing now-a-days."

"You might if you'd keep your ears open, mother. *What* news, Mr. Van Brunt?"

"Why, here's Ellen's got a splendid little horse sent her a present from some of her great friends,—Mr. Marshchalk,—"

"Mr. Marshman," said Ellen.

"Mr. Marshman. There ain't the like in the country, as I've heerd tell; and I expect next thing she'll be flying over all the fields and fences like smoke."

There was a meaning silence. Ellen's heart beat.

"What's going to be done with him, do you suppose?" said Miss Fortune. Her look said, "If you think I am coming round you are mistaken."

"Humph!" said Mr. Van Brunt slowly,—"I s'pose he'll eat grass in the meadow,—and there'll be a place fixed for him in the stables."

"Not in *my* stables," said the lady shortly.

"No,—in mine," said Mr. Van Brunt half smiling;—"and I'll settle with you about it by and by,—when we square up our accounts."

Miss Fortune was very much vexed; Ellen could see that; but she said no more, good or bad, about the matter; so the Brownie was allowed to take quiet possession of meadow and stables; to his mistress's unbounded joy.

Any body that knew Mr. Van Brunt would have been surprised to hear what he said that morning; for he was thought to be quite as keen a looker after the main chance as Miss Fortune herself, only somehow it was never laid against him as it was against her. However that might be, it was plain he took pleasure in keeping his word about the pony. Ellen herself could not have asked more careful kindness for her favourite than the Brownie had from every man and boy about the farm.

CHAPTER XXXVII.

Thou must run to him; for thou hast stayed so long that going will scarce serve the turn.—SHAKSPEARE.

CAPTAIN MONTGOMERY did *not* come the next week, nor the week after; and what is more, the Duck Dorleens, as his sister called the ship in which he had taken passage, was never heard of from that time. She sailed duly on the fifth of April, as they learned from the papers; but whatever became of her she never reached port. It remained a doubt whether Captain Montgomery had actually gone in her; and Ellen had many weeks of anxious watching, first for himself, and then for news of him in case he were still in France. None ever came. Anxiety gradually faded into uncertainty; and by midsummer no doubt of the truth remained in any mind. If Captain Montgomery had been alive, he would certainly have written, if not before, on learning the fate of the vessel in which he had told his friends to expect him home.

Ellen rather felt that she was an orphan than that she had lost her father. She had never learned to love him, he had never given her much cause. Comparatively a small portion of her life had been passed in his society, and she looked back to it as the least agreeable of all; and it had not been possible for her to expect with pleasure his return to America and visit to Thirlwall; she dreaded it. Life had nothing now worse for her than a separation from Alice and John Humphreys; she feared her father might take her away and put her in some dreadful boarding-school, or carry her about the world wherever he went, a wretched wanderer from every thing good and pleasant. The knowledge of his death had less pain for her than the removal of this fear brought relief.

Ellen felt sometimes, soberly and sadly, that she was thrown upon the wide world now. To all intents and purposes so she had been a year and three-quarters before; but it was something to have a father and mother living even on the other side of the world. Now Miss Fortune was her sole guardian and owner. However, she could hardly realize that, with Alice and John so near at hand. Without reasoning much about it, she felt tolerably secure that they would take care of her interests, and make good their claim to interfere if ever need were.

Ellen and her little horse grew more and more fond of each other. This friendship, no doubt, was a comfort to the Brownie; but to his mistress it made a large part of the pleasure of her every-day life. To visit him was her delight, at all hours, early and late ; and it is to the Brownie's credit that he always seemed as glad to see her as she was to see him. At any time Ellen's voice would bring him from the far end of the meadow where he was allowed to run. He would come trotting up at her call, and stand to have her scratch his forehead or pat him and talk to him ; and though the Brownie could not answer her speeches he certainly seemed to hear them with pleasure. Then throwing up his head he would bound off, take a turn in the field, and come back again to stand as still as a lamb as long as she stayed there herself. Now and then, when she had a little more time, she would cross the fence and take a walk with him ; and there, with his nose just at her elbow, wherever she went the Brownie went after her. After a while there was no need that she should call him ; if he saw or heard her at a distance it was enough ; he would come running up directly. Ellen loved him dearly.

She gave him more proof of it than words and caresses. Many were the apples and scraps of bread hoarded up for him ; and if these failed, Ellen sometimes took him a little salt to show that he was not forgotten. There were not certainly many scraps left at Miss Fortune's table; nor apples to be had at home for such a purpose, except what she gathered up from the poor ones that were left under the trees for the hogs; but Ellen had other sources of supply. Once she had begged from Jenny Hitchcock a waste bit that she was going to throw away ; Jenny found what she wanted to do with it, and after that many a basket of apples and many a piece of cold shortcake was set by for her. Margery, too, remembered the Brownie when disposing of her odds and ends; likewise did Mrs. Van Brunt ; so that among them all Ellen seldom wanted something to give him. Mr. Marshman did not know what happiness he was bestowing when he sent her that little horse. Many, many, were the hours of enjoyment she had upon his back. Ellen went nowhere but upon the Brownie. Alice made her a riding-dress of dark gingham ; and it was the admiration of the country to see her trotting or cantering by, all alone, and always looking happy. Ellen soon found that if the Brownie was to do her much good she must learn to saddle and bridle him herself. This was very awkward at first, but there was no help for it. Mr. Van Brunt showed her how to manage, and after a while it became quite easy. She used to call the Brownie to the bar-place, put the bridle on, and let him out; and then he would stand motionless before her while she fastened the saddle on ; looking round sometimes as if to make sure that it was she herself, and giving a little kind of satisfied neigh when he saw that it was. Ellen's heart began to dance as soon as she felt him moving under her ; and once off and away on the docile and spirited little animal, over the roads, through the lanes, up and down the hills, her horse her only companion, but having the most perfect understanding with him, both Ellen and the Brownie cast care to the winds. " I do believe," said Mr. Van Brunt, "that critter would a *leetle* rather have Ellen on his back than not." He was the Brownie's next best friend. Miss Fortune never said any thing to him or of him.

Ellen however reaped a reward for her faithful steadiness to duty while her aunt was ill. Things were never after that as they had been before. She was looked on with a different eye. To be sure Miss Fortune tasked her as much as ever, spoke as sharply, was as ready to scold if any thing went wrong;—all that was just as it used to be ; but beneath all that Ellen felt with great satisfaction that she was trusted and believed. She was no longer an interloper, in every body's way ; she was not watched and suspected ; her aunt treated her as one of the family and a person to be depended on. It was a very great comfort to little Ellen's life. Miss Fortune even owned that " she believed she was an honest child and meant to do right,"—a great deal from her ; Miss Fortune was never over forward to give any one the praise of *honesty*. Ellen now went out and came in without feeling she was an alien. And though her aunt was always bent on keeping herself and every body else at work, she did not now show any particular desire for breaking off Ellen from her studies ; and was generally willing when the work was pretty well done up that she should saddle the Brownie and be off to Alice or Mrs. Vawse.

Though Ellen was happy, it was a sober kind of happiness ;— the sun shining behind a cloud. And if others thought her so, it was not because she laughed loudly or wore a merry face.

" I can't help but think," said Mrs. Van Brunt, " that that child has something more to make her happy than what she gets in this world."

There was a quilting party gathered that afternoon at Mrs. Van Brunt's house.

" There is no doubt of that, neighbour," said Mrs. Vawse ; " nobody ever found enough here to make him happy yet."

" Well I don't want to see a prettier girl than that," said Mrs. Lowndes ;—" you'll never catch her, working at home or riding along on that handsome little critter of hers, that she ha'n't a pleasant look and a smile for you, and as pretty behaved as can be. I never see her look sorrowful but once."

" Ain't that a pretty horse ?" said Mimy Lawson.

" *I've* seen her look sorrowful though," said Sarah Lowndes ; " I've been up at the house when Miss Fortune was hustling every body round, and as sharp as vinegar, and you'd think it would take Job's patience to stand it ;—and for all there wouldn't be a bit of crossness in that child's face,—she'd go round, and not say a word that wasn't just so ;—you'd ha' thought her bread was all spread with honey ; and every body knows it ain't. I don't see how she could do it, for my part. I know *I* couldn't.''

" Ah, neighbour," said Mrs. Vawse, " Ellen looks higher than to please her aunt; she tries to please her God ; and one can bear people's words or looks when one is pleasing him.—She is a dear child !"

" And there's 'Brahm," said Mrs. Van Brunt,—" he thinks the hull world of her. I never see him take so to any one. There ain't an airthly thing he wouldn't do to please her. If she was his own child I've no idee he could set her up more than he does."

" Very well !" said Nancy coming up,—" good reason ! Ellen don't set *him* up any, does she ? I wish you'd just seen her once, the time when Miss Fortune was abed,—the way she'd look out for him ! Mr. Van Brunt's as good as at home in that house sure enough ; whoever's down stairs."

" Bless her dear little heart !" said his mother.

" A good name is better than precious ointment."

August had come, and John was daily expected home. One morning Miss Fortune was in the lower kitchen, up to the elbows in making a rich fall cheese; Ellen was busy up stairs, when her aunt shouted to her to " come and see what was all that splashing and crashing in the garden." Ellen ran out.

" Oh, aunt Fortune," said she,—" Timothy has broken down the fence and got in."

" Timothy !" said Miss Fortune,—" what Timothy ?"

" Why Timothy, the near ox," said Ellen laughing ;—" he has knocked down the fence over there where it was low, you know."

" The near ox !" said Miss Fortune,—" I wish he warn't quite so near this time. Mercy ! he'll be at the corn and over every thing. Run and drive him into the barnyard, can't you ?"

But Ellen stood still and shook her head. " He wouldn't stir for me," she said ;—" and besides I am as afraid of that ox as can be. If it was Clover I wouldn't mind."

" But he'll have every bit of the corn eaten up in five minutes ! Where's Mr. Van Brunt ?"

" I heard him say he was going home till noon," said Ellen.

" And Sam Larkens is gone to mill—and Johnny Low is laid up with the shakes. Very careless of Mr. Van Brunt!" said Miss Fortune, drawing her arms out of the cheese-tub wringing off the whey,—" I wish he'd mind his own oxen. There was no business to be a low place in the fence ! Well come along ! you ain't afraid with me, I suppose."

Ellen followed, at a respectful distance. Miss Fortune however feared the face of neither man nor beast ; she pulled up a bean pole, and made such a show of fight that Timothy after looking at her a little, fairly turned tail, and marched out at the breach he had made. Miss Fortune went after, and rested not till she had driven him quite into the meadow ;—get him into the barnyard she could not.

"You ain't worth a straw, Ellen !" said she when she came back ;—"couldn't you ha' headed him and driv' him into the barnyard ? Now that plaguy beast will just be back again by the time I get well to work. He ha'n't done much mischief yet— there's Mr. Van Brunt's salary he's made a pretty mess of; I'm glad on't! He should ha' put potatoes, as I told him. I don't know what's to be done—I can't be leaving my cheese to run and mind the garden every minute, if it was full of Timothys; and *you'd* be scared if a mosquito flew at you;—you had better go right off for Mr. Van Brunt and fetch him straight home—serve him right! he has no business to leave things so. Run along,— and don't let the grass grow under your feet !"

Ellen wisely thought her pony's feet would do the business quicker. She ran and put on her gingham dress and saddled and bridled the Brownie in three minutes; but before setting off she had to scream to her aunt that Timothy was just coming round the corner of the barn again ; and Miss Fortune rushed out to the garden as Ellen and the Brownie walked down to the gate.

The weather was fine, and Ellen thought with herself it was an ill wind that blew no good. She was getting a nice ride in the early morning, that she would not have had but for Timothy's lawless behaviour. To ride at that time was particularly pleasant and rare ; and forgetting how she had left poor Miss Fortune between the ox and the cheese-tub, Ellen and the Brownie cantered on in excellent spirits.

She looked in vain as she passed his grounds to see Mr. Van Brunt in the garden or about the barn. She went on to the little gate of the courtyard, dismounted, and led the Brownie in. Here she was met by Nancy who came running from the way of the barnyard.

"How d'ye do, Nancy?" said Ellen ;—"where's Mr. Van Brunt ?"

"Goodness ! Ellen !—what do you want ?"

"I want Mr. Van Brunt,—where is he ?"

"Mr. Van Brunt !—he's out in the barn,—but he's used himself up."

"Used himself up ! what do you mean ?"

"Why he's fixed himself in fine style ; he's fell through the trap-door and broke his leg."

"Oh, Nancy !" screamed Ellen,—"he hasn't ! how could he ?"

"Why easy enough if he didn't look where he was going,— there's so much hay on the floor. But it's a pretty bad place to fall."

" How do you know his leg is broken ?"

" 'Cause he says so, and any body with eyes can see it must be. I'm going over to Hitchcock's to get somebody to come and help in with him ; for you know me and Mrs. Van Brunt ain't Samsons."

" Where is Mrs. Van Brunt ?"

" She's out there—in a terrible to do."

Nancy sped on to the Hitchcock's; and greatly frightened and distressed Ellen ran over to the barn, trembling like an aspen. Mr.

Van Brunt was lying in the lower floor, just where he had fallen ; one leg doubled under him in such a way as left no doubt it must be broken. He had lain there some time before any one found him; and on trying to change his position when he saw his mother's distress, he had fainted from pain. She sat by weeping most bitterly. Ellen could bear but one look at Mr. Van Brunt ; that one sickened her. She went up to his poor mother and getting down on her knees by her side put both arms round her neck.

" *Don't* cry so, dear Mrs. Van Brunt," (Ellen was crying so she could hardly speak herself,)—" pray don't do so !—he'll be better —Oh, what shall we do ?"

" Oh, ain't it dreadful !" said poor Mrs. Van Brunt ;—" oh, 'Brahm ! 'Brahm ! my son !—the best son that ever was to me—oh, to see him there—ain't it dreadful ? he's dying !"

"Oh, no he isn't," said Ellen,—" oh, no he isn't !—what shall we do, Mrs. Van Brunt ?—what shall we do ?"

" The doctor !" said Mrs. Van Brunt,—" he said ' send for the doctor ;'—but I can't go, and there's nobody to send. Oh, he'll die !—oh, my dear 'Brahm ! I wish it was me !"

" What doctor ?" said Ellen ;—" I'll find somebody to go ; what doctor ?"

" Dr. Gibson, he said ; but he's away off to Thirlwall ; and he's been lying here all the morning a'ready !—nobody found him—he couldn't make us hear. Oh, isn't it dreadful !"

" Oh, don't cry so, dear Mrs. Van Brunt," said Ellen, pressing her cheek to the poor old lady's ; " he'll be better—he will ! I've got the Brownie here and I'll ride over to Mrs. Hitchcock's and get somebody to go right away for the doctor. I won't be long,— we'll have him here in a little while ! *don't* feel so bad !"

" You're a dear blessed darling !" said the old lady, hugging and kissing her,—" if ever there was one. Make haste dear, if you love him !—he loves you."

Ellen stayed but to give her another kiss. Trembling so that she could hardly stand she made her way back to the house, led out the Brownie again, and set off full speed for Mrs. Hitchcock's. It was well her pony was sure-footed, for letting the reins hang, Ellen bent over his neck crying bitterly, only urging him now and then to greater speed ; till at length the feeling that she had something to do came to her help. She straightened herself, gathered up her reins, and by the time she reached Mrs. Hitchcock's was looking calm again, though very sad and very earnest. She did not alight, but stopped before the door and called Jenny. Jenny came out, expressing her pleasure.

" Dear Jenny," said Ellen,—" isn't there somebody here that will go right off to Thirlwall for Dr. Gibson ? Mr. Van Brunt has broken his leg, I am afraid, and wants the doctor directly."

" Why dear Ellen," said Jenny, " the men have just gone off this minute to Mrs. Van Brunt's. Nancy was here for them to come and help move him in a great hurry. How did it happen ? I couldn't get any thing out of Nancy."

" He fell down through the trap-door. But dear Jenny, isn't there *any body* about ? Oh," said Ellen clasping her hands,—" I want somebody to go for the doctor *so* much !"

" There ain't a living soul !" said Jenny ; " two of the men and all the teams are 'way on the other side of the hill ploughing, and pa and June and Black Bill have gone over, as I told you; but I don't believe they'll be enough. Where's his leg broke?"

" I didn't meet them," said Ellen;—" I came away only a little while after Nancy."

" They went 'cross lots I guess,—that's how it was, and that's the way Nancy got the start of you."

" What shall I do?" said Ellen. She could not bear to wait till they returned; if she rode back she might miss them again, besides the delay; and then a man on foot would make a long journey of it. Jenny told her of a house or two where she might try for a messenger; but they were strangers to her; she could not make up her mind to ask such a favour of them. Her friends were too far out of the way.

" I'll go myself!" she said suddenly. " Tell 'em, dear Jenny, will you, that I have gone for Dr. Gibson and that I'll bring him back as quick as ever I can. I know the road to Thirl-wall."

" But Ellen! you mustn't," said Jenny;—" I am afraid to have you go all that way alone. Wait till the men come back,—they won't be long."

" No I can't, Jenny," said Ellen,—" I can't wait; I must go. You needn't be afraid. Tell 'em I'll be as quick as I can."

" But see, Ellen!" cried Jenny as she was moving off,—" I don't like to have you!"

" I must, Jenny. Never mind."

" But see, Ellen!" cried Jenny again,—" if you *will* go—if you don't find Dr. Gibson just get Dr. Marshchalk,—he's every bit as good and some folks think he's better;—he'll do just as well. Good-by!"

Ellen nodded and rode off. There was a little fluttering of the heart at taking so much upon herself; she had never been to Thirl-wall but once since the first time she saw it. But she thought of Mr. Van Brunt, suffering for help which could not be obtained, and it was impossible for her to hesitate. " I am sure I am doing right," she thought,—" and what is there to be afraid of? If I ride two miles alone, why shouldn't I four?—And I am doing right—God will take care of me." Ellen earnestly asked him to do so; and after that she felt pretty easy. " Now dear Brownie," said she, patting his neck,—" you and I have work to do to-day; behave like a good little horse as you are." The Brownie answered with a little cheerful kind of neigh, as much as to say, Never fear me!—They trotted on nicely.

But nothing could help that's being a disagreeable ride. Do what she would, Ellen felt a little afraid when she found herself on a long piece of road where she had never been alone before. There were not many houses on the way; the few there were looked strange; Ellen did not know exactly where she was, or how near the end of her journey; it seemed a long one. She felt rather lonely;—a little shy of meeting people, and yet a little unwilling to have the intervals between them so very long. She repeated to herself, "I am doing right—God will take care of me,"—still there was a nervous trembling at heart. Sometimes she would pat her pony's neck and say, "Trot on, dear Brownie! we'll soon be there!"—by way of cheering herself; for certainly the Brownie needed no cheering, and was trotting on bravely. Then the thought of Mr. Van Brunt as she had seen him lying on the barn-floor, made her feel sick and miserable; many tears fell during her ride when she remembered him. "Heaven will be a good place," thought little Ellen as she went;—"there will be no sickness, no pain, no sorrow; but Mr. Van Brunt!—I wonder if he is fit to go to heaven?"—This was a new matter of thought and uneasiness, not now for the first time in Ellen's mind; and so the time passed till she crossed the bridge over the little river and saw the houses of Thirlwall stretching away in the distance. Then she felt comfortable.

Long before, she had bethought her that she did not know where to find Dr. Gibson, and had forgotten to ask Jenny. For one instant Ellen drew bridle, but it was too far to go back, and she recollected any body could tell her where the doctor lived. When she got to Thirlwall however Ellen found that she did not like to ask *any body;* she remembered her old friend Mrs. Forbes of the Star inn, and resolved she would go there in the first place. She rode slowly up the street, and looking carefully till she came to the house. There was no mistaking it; there was the very same big star over the front door that had caught her eye from the coach-window, and there was the very same boy or man, Sam, lounging on the side-walk. Ellen reigned up and asked him to ask Mrs. Forbes if she would be so good as to come out to her for one minute. Sam gave her a long Yankee look and disappeared, coming back again directly with the landlady.

"How d'ye do, Mrs. Forbes?" said Ellen, holding out her hand; —"don't you know me? I am Ellen Montgomery—that you were so kind to, and gave me bread and milk,—when I first came here,—Miss Fortune's——"

"Oh, bless your dear little heart," cried the landlady; "don't I know you! and ain't I glad to see you! I must have a kiss. Bless you! I couldn't mistake you in Jerusalem, but the sun was in my eyes in that way I was a'most blind. But ain't you grown though! Forget you? I guess I ha'n't! there's one o' your friends wouldn't let me do that in a hurry; if I ha'n't seen you I've heered on you. But what are you sitting there in the sun for? come in—come in

—and I'll give you something better than bread and milk this time. Come! jump down."

"Oh, I can't, Mrs. Forbes," said Ellen,—"I am in a great hurry;—Mr. Van Brunt has broken his leg, and I want to find the doctor."

"Mr. Van Brunt!" cried the landlady. "Broken his leg! The land's sakes! how did he do that? *he* too!"

"He fell down through the trap-door in the barn; and I want to get Dr. Gibson as soon as I can to come to him. Where does he live, Mrs. Forbes?"

"Dr. Gibson? you won't catch him to hum, dear; he's flying round somewheres. But how come the trap-door to be open? and how happened Mr. Van Brunt not to see it afore he put his foot in it? Dear! I declare I'm real sorry to hear you tell. How happened it, darlin'? I'm cur'ous to hear."

"I don't know, Mrs. Forbes," said Ellen,—"but oh, where shall I find Dr. Gibson? Do tell me!—he ought to be there now;—oh, help me! where shall I go for him?"

"Well, I declare," said the landlady stepping back a pace,—"I don' know as I can tell—there ain't no sort o' likelihood that he's to hum at this time o' day—Sam! you lazy feller, you ha'n't got nothing to do but to gape at folks, ha' you seen the doctor go by this forenoon?"

"I seen him go down to Mis' Perriman's," said Sam,—"Mis' Perriman was a dyin'—Jim Barstow said."

"How long since?" said his mistress.

But Sam shuffled and shuffled, looked every way but at Ellen or Mrs. Forbes, and "didn' know."

"Well then," said Mrs. Forbes turning to Ellen,—"I don' know but you might about as well go down to the post-office—but if *I* was you, I'd just get Dr. Marshchalk instead! he's a smarter man than Dr. Gibson any day in the year; and he ain't quite so awful high neither, and that's something. *I'd* get Dr. Marshchalk; they say there ain't the like o' him in the country for settin' bones; it's quite a gift;—he takes to it natural like."

But Ellen said Mr. Van Brunt wanted Dr. Gibson, and if she could she must find him.

"Well," said Mrs. Forbes, "every one has their fancies;—*I* wouldn't let Dr. Gibson come near me with a pair of tongs;—but any how if you must have him, your best way is to go right straight down to the post-office and ask for him there,—maybe you'll catch him."

"Thank you, ma'am," said Ellen;—"where is the post-office?"

"It's that white-faced house down street," said the landlady, pointing with her finger where Ellen saw no lack of white-faced houses,—"you see that big red store with the man standing out in front ?—the next white house below that is Mis' Perriman's ; just run right in and ask for Dr. Gibson. Good-by, dear, I'm real sorry you can't come in ;—that first white house."

Glad to get free, Ellen rode smartly down to the post-office. Nobody before the door ; there was nothing for it but to get off here and go in ; she did not know the people either. "Never mind ! wait for me a minute, dear Brownie, like a good little horse as you are !"

No fear of the Brownie. He stood as if he did not mean to budge again in a century. At first going in Ellen saw nobody in the post-office ; presently, at an opening in a kind of boxed-up place in one corner a face looked out and asked what was wanted.

" Is Dr. Gibson here ?"

" No," said the owner of the face, with a disagreeable kind of smile.

" Isn't this Miss Perriman's house ?"

" You are in the right box, my dear, and no mistake," said the young man,—" but then it ain't Dr. Gibson's house, you know."

" Can you tell me, sir, where I can find him ?"

" Can't indeed—the doctor never tells me where he is going, and I never ask him. I am sorry I didn't this morning, for your sake."

The way, and the look, made the words extremely disagreeable, and furthermore Ellen had an uncomfortable feeling that neither was new to her. Where *had* she seen the man before? she puzzled herself to think. Where but in a dream had she seen that bold ill-favoured face, that horrible smile, that sandy hair,—she knew ! It was Mr. Saunders, the man who had sold her the merino at St. Clair and Fleury's. She knew him; and she was very sorry to see that he knew her. All she desired now was to get out of the house and away ; but on turning she saw another man, older and respectable-looking, whose face encouraged her to ask again if Dr. Gibson was there. He was not, the man said ; he had been there and gone.

" Do you know where I should be likely to find him, sir ?"

" No, I don't," said he ;—" who wants him ?"

" I want to see him, sir."

" For yourself ?"

" No, sir ; Mr. Van Brunt has broken his leg and wants Dr. Gibson to come directly and set it."

" Mr. Van Brunt !" said he,—" Farmer Van Brunt that lives down toward the Cat's back ? I'm very sorry ! How did it happen ?"

Ellen told as shortly as possible, and again begged to know where she might look for Dr. Gibson.

" Well," said he, " the best plan I can think of will be for you —How did you come here ?"

" I came on horseback, sir."

"Ah—well—the best plan will be for you to ride up to his house; maybe he'll have left word there, and any how *you* can leave word for him to come down as soon as he gets home. Do you know where the doctor lives?"

"No, sir."

"Come here," said he, pulling her to the door,—"you can't see it from here; but you must ride up street till you have passed two churches, one on the right hand first, and then a good piece beyond you'll come to another red brick one on the left hand;—and Dr. Gibson lives in the next block but one after that, on the other side;—any body will tell you the house. Is that your horse?"

"Yes, sir. I'm very much obliged to you."

"Well I will say!—if you ha'n't the prettiest fit out in Thirlwall—shall I help you? will you have a cheer?"

"No, I thank you, sir; I'll bring him up to this step; it will do just as well. I am *very* much obliged to you, sir."

He did not seem to hear her thanks; he was all eyes; and with his clerk stood looking after her till she was out of sight.

Poor Ellen found it a long way up to the doctor's. The postoffice was near the lower end of the town and the doctor's house was near the upper; she passed one church, and then the other, but there was a long distance between, or what she thought so. Happily the Brownie did not seem tired at all; his little mistress *was* tired and disheartened too. And there, all this time, was poor Mr. Van Brunt lying without a doctor! She could not bear to think of it.

She jumped down when she came to the block she had been told of, and easily found the house where Dr. Gibson lived. She knocked at the door. A grey-haired woman with a very dead-and-alive face presented herself. Ellen asked for the doctor.

"He ain't to hum."

"When will he be at home?"

"Couldn't say."

"Before dinner?"

The woman shook her head—"Guess not till late in the day."

"Where is he gone?"

"He is gone to Babcock—gone to ' attend a consummation,' I guess, he told me—Babcock is a considerable long way."

Ellen thought a minute.

"Can you tell me where Dr. Marshchalk lives?"

"I guess you'd better wait till Dr. Gibson comes back, ha'n't you?" said the woman coaxingly;—"he'll be along by and by. If you'll leave me your name I'll give it to him."

"I cannot wait," said Ellen,—"I am in a dreadful hurry. Will you be so good as to tell me where Dr. Marshchalk lives?"

" Well—if so be you're in such a takin' you can't wait—you know where Miss Forbes lives ?''

" At the inn ?—the Star—yes.''

" He lives a few doors this side o' her'n ; you'll know it the first minute you set your eyes on it—it's painted a bright yaller.''

Ellen thanked her, once more mounted, and rode down the street.

CHAPTER XXXVIII.

And he had ridden o'er dale and down
By eight o'clock in the day,
When he was ware of a bold Tanner,
Came riding along the way.
OLD BALLAD. .

THE yellow door, as the old woman had said, was not to be mistaken. Again Ellen dismounted and knocked ; then she heard a slow step coming along the entry, and the pleasant kind face of Miss Janet appeared at the open door. It was a real refreshment, and Ellen wanted one.

" Why it's dear little—ain't it ?—her that lives down to Miss Fortune Emerson's ?—yes, it is :—come in, dear ; I'm very glad to see you. How's all at your house ?''

" Is the doctor at home, ma'am ?''

" No dear, he ain't to home just this minute, but he'll be in directly ; Come in ;—is that your horse ?—just hitch him to the post there so he won't run away, and come right in. Who did you come along with ?''

" Nobody, ma'am ; I came alone,'' said Ellen while she obeyed Miss Janet's directions.

" Alone !—on that 'ere little skittish creeter ?—he's as handsome as a picture too—why do tell if you warn't afraid ? it a'most scares me to think of it.''

" I was a little afraid,'' said Ellen, as she followed Miss Janet along the entry,—" but I couldn't help that. You think the doctor will soon be in, ma'am ?''

" Yes, dear, sure of it,'' said Miss Janet, kissing Ellen and taking off her bonnet ;—" he won't be five minutes, for it's a'most dinner time. What's the matter dear ? is Miss Fortune sick again ?''

" No, ma'am,'' said Ellen sadly,—" Mr. Van Brunt has fallen through the trap-door in the barn and broken his leg.''

" Oh !'' cried the old lady with a face of real horror,—" you don't tell me ! Fell through the trap-door ! and he ain't a light weight neither;—oh, that is a lamentable event! And how is the poor old mother, dear?"

"She is very much troubled, ma'am," said Ellen, crying at the remembrance;—"and he has been lying ever since early this morning without anybody to set it; I have been going round and round for a doctor this ever so long."

"Why, warn't there nobody to come but you, you poor lamb?" said Miss Janet.

"No, ma'am; nobody quick enough; and I had the Brownie there, and so I came."

"Well, cheer up, dear! the doctor will be here now and we'll send him right off; he won't be long about his dinner, I'll engage. Come and set in this big cheer—do!—it'll rest you; I see you're a'most tired out, and it ain't a wonder. There—don't that feel better? now I'll give you a little sup of dinner, for you won't want to swallow.it at the rate Leander will his'n. Dear! dear!—to think of poor Mr. Van Brunt. He's a likely man too;—I'm very sorry for him and his poor mother. A kind body she is as ever the sun shined upon."

"And so is he," said Ellen.

"Well, so I dare say," said Miss Janet,—"but I don't know so much about him; howsever he's got everybody's good word as far as I know;—he's a likely man."

The little room in which Miss Janet had brought Ellen was very plainly furnished indeed, but as neat as hands could make it. The carpet was as crumbless and lintless as if meals were never taken there nor work seen; and yet a little table ready set for dinner forbade the one conclusion, and a huge basket of naperies in one corner showed that Miss Janet's industry did not spend itself in housework alone. Before the fire stood a pretty good-sized kettle, and a very appetizing smell came from it to Ellen's nose. In spite of sorrow and anxiety her ride had made her hungry. It was not without pleasure that she saw her kind hostess arm herself with a deep plate and tin dipper, and carefully taking off the pot-cover so that no drops might fall on the hearth, proceed to ladle out a goodly supply of what Ellen knew was that excellent country dish called pot-pie. Excellent it is when well made. and that was Miss Janet's. The pieces of crust were white and light like new bread; the very tit-bits of the meat she culled out for Ellen; and the soup gravy poured over all would have met even Miss Fortune's wishes, from its just degree of richness and exact seasoning. Smoking hot it was placed before Ellen on a little stand by her easy chair, with some nice bread and butter; and presently Miss Janet poured her out a cup of tea; "for," she said, "Leander never could take his dinner without it." Ellen's appetite needed no silver fork. Tea and pot-pie were never better liked; yet Miss

Janet's enjoyment was perhaps greater still. She sat talking and looking at her little visitor with secret but immense satisfaction.

" Have you heard what fine doings we're a going to have here by and by ?" said she. " The doctor's tired of me; he's going to get a new housekeeper ;—he's going to get married some of these days."

" Is he !" said Ellen. " Not to Jenny !"

" Yes indeed he is—to Jenny—Jenny Hitchcock; and a nice little wife she'll make him. You're a great friend of Jenny, I know."

" How soon ?" said Ellen.

" Oh, not just yet—by and by—after we get a little smarted up, I guess ;—before a great while. Don't you think he'll be a happy man ?"

Ellen could not help wondering, as the doctor just then came in and she looked up at his unfortunate three-cornered face, whether Jenny would be a happy woman ? But as people often do, she only judged from the outside; Jenny had not made such a bad choice after all.

The doctor said he would go directly to Mr. Van Brunt after he had been over to Mrs. Sibnorth's ; it wouldn't be a minute. Ellen meant to ride back in his company ; and having finished her dinner waited now only for him. But the one minute passed—two minutes—ten—twenty—she waited impatiently, but he came not.

" I'll tell you how it must be," said his sister,—" he's gone off without his dinner calculating to get it at Miss Hitchcock's,—he'd be glad of the chance. That's how it is, dear; and you'll have to ride home alone; I'm real sorry. S'pose you stop till evening, and I'll make the doctor go along with you. But oh, dear ! maybe he wouldn't be able to neither; he's got to go up to that tiresome Mrs. Robin's; it's too bad. Well, take good care of yourself, darling ; —couldn't you stop till it's cooler ?—well, come and see me as soon as you can again, but don't come without some one else along ! Good-by ! I wish I could keep you."

She went to the door to see her mount, and smiled and nodded her off.

Ellen was greatly refreshed with her rest and her dinner; it grieved her that the Brownie had not fared as well. All the refreshment that kind words and patting could give him, she gave ; promised him the freshest of water and the sweetest of hay when he should reach home ; and begged him to keep up his spirits and hold on for a little longer. It may be doubted whether the Brownie understood the full sense of her words, but he probably knew what the kind tones and gentle hand meant. He answered cheerfully ; threw up his head and gave a little neigh, as much as to say, *he* wasn't going to mind a few hours of sunshine ; and trotted on as if he knew his face was toward home,—which no doubt he did.

Luckily it was not a very hot day ; for August, it was remarkably cool and beautiful ; indeed, there was little very hot weather ever known in Thirlwall. Ellen's heart felt easier, now that her business was done ! and when she had left the town behind her and was again in the fields, she was less timid than she had been before ; she was going toward home ; that makes a great difference ; and every step was bringing her nearer. " I am glad I came after all," she thought ;—" but I hope I shall never have to do such a thing again. But I am glad I came."

She had no more than crossed the little bridge, however, when she saw what brought her heart into her mouth. It was Mr. Saunders, lolling under a tree. What could he have come there for at that time of day ? A vague feeling crossed her mind that if she could only get past him she should pass a danger ; she thought to ride by without seeming to see him, and quietly gave the Brownie a pat to make him go faster. But as she drew near Mr. Saunders rose up, came to the middle of the road, and taking hold of her bridle, checked her pony's pace so that he could walk alongside ; to Ellen's unspeakable dismay.

" What's kept you so long ?" said he ;—" I've been looking out for you this great while. Had hard work to find the doctor ?"

" Won't you please to let go of my horse," said Ellen, her heart beating very fast ;—" I am in a great hurry to get home ;— please don't keep me."

" Oh, I want to see you a little," said Mr. Saunders ;—" you ain't in such a hurry to get away from me as that comes to, are you ?"

Ellen was silent.

" It's quite a long time since I saw you last," said he ;—" how have the merinoes worn ?"

Ellen could not bear to look at his face and did not see the expression which went with these words, yet she *felt* it.

" They have worn very well," said she, " but I want to get home very much—*please* let me go."

" Not yet—not yet," said he,—" oh, no, not yet. I want to talk to you ; why, what are you in such a devil of a hurry for ? I came out on purpose ; do you think I am going to have all my long waiting for nothing ?"

Ellen did not know what to say ; her heart sprang with a nameless pang to the thought, if she ever got free from this ! Meanwhile she was not free.

" Whose horse is that you're on ?"

" Mine," said Ellen.

" Your'n ! that's a likely story. I guess he ain't your'n, and so you won't mind if I touch him up a little ;—I want to see how well you can sit on a horse."

Passing his arm through the bridle as he said these words, Mr. Saunders led the pony down to the side of the road where grew a clump of high bushes; and with some trouble cut off a long stout sapling. Ellen looked in every direction while he was doing this, despairing, as she looked, of aid from any quarter of the broad quiet open country. Oh, for wings! But she could not leave the Brownie if she had them.

Returning to the middle of the road, Mr. Saunders amused himself as they walked along with stripping off all the leaves and little twigs from his sapling, leaving it when done a very good imitation of an ox-whip in size and length, with a fine lash-like point. Ellen watched him in an ecstasy of apprehension, afraid alike to speak or to be silent.

"There! what do you think of that?" said he, giving it two or three switches in the air to try its suppleness and toughness;— "don't that look like a whip? Now we'll see how he'll go!"

"Please don't do any thing with it," said Ellen earnestly;—"I never touch him with a whip,—he doesn't need it,—he isn't used to it; pray, pray do not!"

"Oh, we'll just tickle him a little with it," said Mr. Saunders coolly,—"I want to see how well you'll sit him;—just make him caper a little bit."

He accordingly applied the switch lightly to the Brownie's heels, enough to annoy without hurting him. The Brownie showed signs of uneasiness, quitted his quiet pace, and took to little starts and springs and whisking motions, most unpleasing to his rider.

"Oh, do not!" cried Ellen, almost beside herself,—"he's very spirited, and I don't know what he will do if you trouble him."

"You let me take care of that," said Mr. Saunders;—"if he troubles *me* I'll give it to him! If he rears up, only you catch hold of his mane and hold on tight, and you won't fall off;—I want to see him rear."

"But you'll give him bad tricks!" said Ellen. "Oh, pray don't do so! Its very bad for him to be teased. I am afraid he will kick if you do so, and he'd be ruined if he got a habit of kicking. Oh, *please* let us go!" said she with the most acute accent of entreaty,—"I want to be home."

"You keep quiet," said Mr. Saunders coolly;—"if he kicks I'll give him such a lathering as he never had yet; he won't do it but once. I ain't a going to hurt him, but I am a going to make him rear;—no, I won't,—I'll make him leap over a rail, the first bar-place we come to; that'll be prettier."

"Oh, you musn't do that," said Ellen;—"I have not learned to leap yet; I couldn't keep on; you musn't do that if you please."

"You just hold fast and hold your tongue. Catch hold of his ears, and you'll stick on fast enough; if you can't you may get down, for I am going to make him take the leap whether you will or no."

Ellen feared still more to get off and leave the Brownie to her tormentor's mercy than to stay where she was and take her chance. She tried in vain, as well as she could, to soothe her horse; the touches of the whip coming now in one place and now in another, and some of them pretty sharp, he began to grow very frisky indeed; and she began to be very much frightened for fear she should suddenly be jerked off. With a good deal of presence of mind, though wrought up to a terrible pitch of excitement and fear, Ellen gave her best attention to keeping her seat as the Brownie sprang and started and jumped to one side and the other; Mr. Saunders holding the bridle as loose as possible so as give him plenty of room. For some little time he amused himself with this game, the horse growing more and more irritated. At length a smart stroke of the whip upon his haunches made the Brownie spring in a way that brought Ellen's heart into her mouth, and almost threw her off.

"Oh, don't!" cried Ellen, bursting into tears for the first time, —she had with great effort commanded them back until now;— "poor Brownie!—How can you! Oh, please let us go!—please let us go!"

For one minute she dropped her face in her hands.

"Be quiet!" said Mr. Saunders. "Here's a bar-place—now for the leap!"

Ellen wiped away her tears, forced back those that were coming, and began the most earnest remonstrance and pleading with Mr. Saunders that she knew how to make. He paid her no sort of attention. He led the Brownie to the side of the road, let down all the bars but the lower two, let go the bridle, and stood a little off prepared with his whip to force the horse to take the spring.

"I tell you I shall fall," said Ellen, reining him back. "How can you be so cruel!—I want to go home!"

"Well, you ain't a going home yet. Get off, if you are afraid."

But though trembling in every nerve from head to foot, Ellen fancied the Brownie was safer so long as he had her on his back; she would not leave him. She pleaded her best, which Mr. Saunders heard as if it was amusing, and without making any answer kept the horse capering in front of the bars, pretending every minute he was going to whip him up to take the leap. His object however was merely to gratify the smallest of minds by teasing a child he had a spite against; he had no intention to risk breaking her bones by a fall from her horse; so in time he had enough of the bar-place; took the bridle again and walked on. Ellen drew breath a little more freely.

"Did you hear how I handled your old gentleman after that time?" said Mr. Saunders.

Ellen made no answer.

"No one ever affronts me that don't hear news of it afterwards, and so he found to his cost. *I* paid him off, to my heart's content. I gave the old fellow a lesson to behave in future. I forgive him now entirely. By the way I've a little account to settle with you —didn't you ask Mr. Perriman this morning if Dr. Gibson was in the house?"

"I don't know who it was," said Ellen.

"Well, hadn't I told you just before he warn't there?"

Ellen was silent.

"What did you do that for, eh? Didn't you believe me?"

Still she did not speak.

"I say!" said Mr. Saunders, touching the Brownie as he spoke, —"did you think I told you a lie about it?—eh?"

"I didn't know but he might be there," Ellen forced herself to say.

"Then you didn't believe me?" said he, always with that same smile upon his face; Ellen knew that.

"Now that warn't handsome of you—and I'm a going to punish you for it, somehow or 'nother; but it ain't pretty to quarrel with ladies, so Brownie and me'll settle it together. You won't mind that I dare say."

"What are you going to do?" said Ellen, as he once more drew her down to the side of the fence.

"Get off and you'll see," said he, laughing;—"get off and you'll see."

"What do you want to do?" repeated Ellen, though scarce able to speak the words.

"I'm just going to tickle Brownie a little, to teach you to believe honest folks when they speak the truth; get off!"

"No I won't," said Ellen, throwing both arms round the neck of her pony;—"poor Brownie!—you shan't do it. He hasn't done any harm, nor I either; you are a bad man!"

"Get off!" repeated Mr. Saunders.

"I will not!" said Ellen, still clinging fast.

"Very well," said he coolly,—"then I will take you off; it don't make much difference. We'll go along a little further till I find a nice stone for you to sit down upon. If you had got off then I wouldn't ha' done much to him, but I'll give it to him now! If he hasn't been used to a whip he'll know pretty well what it means by the time I have done with him; and then you may go home as fast as you can."

It is very likely Mr. Saunders would have been as good, or as bad, as his word. His behaviour to Ellen in the store at New

York, and the measures taken by the old gentleman who had be-
friended her, had been the cause of his dismissal from the employ
of Messrs. St. Clair and Fleury. Two or three other attempts to
get into business had come to nothing, and he had been obliged to
return to his native town. Ever since, Ellen and the old gentleman had lived in his memory as objects of the deepest spite;—the
one for interfering, the other for having been the innocent cause;
and he no sooner saw her in the post-office than he promised himself revenge, such revenge as only the meanest and most cowardly
spirit could have taken pleasure in. His best way of distressing
Ellen, he found, was through her horse; he had almost satisfied
himself; but very naturally his feeling of spite had grown stronger
and blunter with indulgence, and he meant to wind up with such a
treatment of her pony, real or seeming, as he knew would give
great pain to the pony's mistress. He was prevented.

As they went slowly along, Ellen still clasping the Brownie's
neck and resolved to cling to him to the last, Mr. Saunders making
him caper in a way very uncomfortable to her, one was too busy
and the other too deafened by fear to notice the sound of fast-ap-
proaching hoofs behind them. It happened that John Humphreys
had passed the night at Ventnor; and having an errand to do for
a friend at Thirlwall had taken that road, which led him but a few
miles out of his way, and was now at full speed on his way home.
He had never made the Brownie's acquaintance, and did not recognise Ellen as he came up; but in passing them some strange
notion crossing his mind he wheeled his horse round directly in
front of the astonished pair. Ellen quitted her pony's neck, and
stretching out both arms toward him exclaimed, almost shrieked,
" Oh, John ! John ! send him away ! make him let me go !"

" What are you about, sir ?" said the new-comer sternly.

" It's none of your business !" answered Mr. Saunders, in whom
rage for the time overcame cowardice.

" Take your hand off the bridle !"—with a slight touch of the
riding-whip upon the hand in question.

" Not for you, brother," said Mr. Saunders sneeringly;—" I'll
walk with any lady I've a mind to. Look out for yourself !"

" We will dispense with your further attendance," said John
coolly. " Do you hear me ?—do as I order you !"

The speaker did not put himself in a passion, and Mr. Saunders,
accustomed for his own part to make bluster serve instead of
prowess, despised a command so calmly given.—Ellen, who knew
the voice, and still better could read the eye, drew conclusions very
different. She was almost breathless with terror. Saunders was
enraged and mortified at an interference that promised to baffle
him; he was a stout young man, and judged himself the stronger
of the two, and took notice besides that the stranger had nothing

in his hand but a slight riding-whip. He answered very insolently and with an oath; and John saw that he was taking the bridle in his left hand and shifting his sapling whip so as to bring the club end of it uppermost. The next instant he aimed a furious blow at his adversary's horse. The quick eye and hand of the rider disappointed that with a sudden swerve. In another moment, and Ellen hardly saw how, it was so quick,—John had dismounted, taken Mr. Saunders by the collar, and hurled him quite over into the gully at the side of the road, where he lay at full length without stirring.

"Ride on, Ellen!" said her deliverer.

She obeyed. He stayed a moment to say to his fallen adversary a few words of pointed warning as to ever repeating his offence; then remounted and spurred forward to join Ellen. All her power of keeping up was gone, now that the necessity was over. Her head was once more bowed on her pony's neck, her whole frame shaking with convulsive sobs; she could scarce with great effort keep from crying out aloud.

"Ellie!"—said her adopted brother, in a voice that could hardly be known for the one that had last spoken. She had no words, but as he gently took one of her hands, the convulsive squeeze it gave him showed the state of nervous excitement she was in. It was very long before his utmost efforts could soothe her, or she could command herself enough to tell him her story. When at last told, it was with many tears.

"Oh, how could he! how could he!" said poor Ellen;—"how could he do so!—it was very hard!"——

An involuntary touch of the spurs made John's horse start.

"But what took you to Thirlwall alone?" said he;—"you have not told me that yet."

Ellen went back to Timothy's invasion of the cabbages, and gave him the whole history of the morning.

"I thought when I was going for the doctor, at first," said she, —"and then afterwards when I had found him, what a good thing it was that Timothy broke down the garden fence and got in this morning; for if it had not been for that I should not have gone to Mr. Van Brunt's;—and then again after that I thought, if he only hadn't!"

"Little things often draw after them long trains of circumstances," said John,—"and that shows the folly of those people who think that God does not stoop to concern himself about trifles;— life, and much more than life, may hang upon the turn of a hand. But Ellen, you must ride no more alone.—Promise me that you will not."

"I will not to Thirlwall, certainly," said Ellen,—"but mayn't I to Alice's?—how can I help it?"

"Well—to Alice's—that is a safe part of the country;—but I should like to know a little more of your horse before trusting you even there."

"Of the Brownie?" said Ellen;—"Oh, he is as good as he can be; you need not be afraid of him; he has no trick at all; there never was such a good little horse."

John smiled. "How do you like mine?" said he.

"Is that your new one? Oh, what a beauty!—Oh, me, what a beauty! I didn't look at him before. Oh, I like him very much! he's handsomer than the Brownie;—do you like him?"

"Very well!—this is the first trial I have made of him. I was at Mr. Marshman's last night, and they detained me this morning, or I should have been here much earlier. I am very well satisfied with him, so far."

"And if you had *not* been detained!"—said Ellen.

"Yes, Ellie—I should not have fretted at my late breakfast and having to try Mr. Marshman's favourite mare, if I had known what good purpose the delay was to serve. I wish I could have been here half an hour sooner, though."

"Is his name the Black Prince?" said Ellen, returning to the horse.

"Yes, I believe so; but you shall change it, Ellie, if you can find one you like better."

"Oh, I cannot!—I like that very much. How beautiful he is! Is he good?"

"I hope so," said John, smiling;—"if he is not I shall be at the pains to make him so. We are hardly acquainted yet."

Ellen looked doubtfully at the black horse and his rider, and patting the Brownie's neck, observed with great satisfaction that *he* was very good.

John had been riding very slowly on Ellen's account; they now mended their pace. He saw however that she still looked miserably, and exerted himself to turn her thoughts from every thing disagreeable. Much to her amusement he rode round her two or three times, to view her horse and show her his own; commended the Brownie; praised her bridle hand; corrected several things about her riding; and by degrees engaged her in a very animated conversation. Ellen roused up; the colour came back to her cheeks; and when they reached home and rode round to the glass door she looked almost like herself.

She sprang off as usual without waiting for any help. John scarce saw that she had done so, when Alice's cry of joy brought him to the door, and from that together they went in to their father's study. Ellen was left alone on the lawn. Something was the matter; for she stood with swimming eyes and a trembling lip, rubbing her stirrup, which really needed no polishing, and forgetting the tired horses, which would have had her sympathy at any other time. What *was* the matter? Only—that Mr. John had forgotten the kiss he always gave her on going or coming. Ellen was jealous of it as a pledge of sistership, and could not want it; and though she tried as hard as she could to get her face in order, so that she might go in and meet them, somehow it seemed to take a great while. She was still busy with her stirrup, when she suddenly felt two hands on her shoulders, and looking up received the very kiss the want of which she had been lamenting. But John saw the tears in her eyes, and asked her, she thought with somewhat of a comical look, what the matter was? Ellen was ashamed to tell, but he had her there by the shoulders, and besides, whatever that eye demanded she never knew how to keep back, so with some difficulty she told him.

"You are a foolish child, Ellie," said he gently, and kissing her again. "Run in out of the sun while I see to the horses."

Ellen ran in, and told her long story to Alice; and then feeling very weary and weak she sat on the sofa and lay resting in her arms in a state of the most entire and unruffled happiness. Alice however after a while transferred her to bed, thinking with good reason that a long sleep would be the best thing for her.

CHAPTER XXXIX.

Now is the pleasant time,
The cool, the silent, save where silence yields
To the night-warbling bird; that now awake,
Tunes sweetest her love-laboured song   now reigns
Full orbed the moon, and with more pleasing light
Shadowy, sets off the face of things.

MILTON.

WHEN Ellen came out of Alice's room again it was late in the afternoon. The sun was so low that the shadow of the house had crossed the narrow lawn and mounted up near to the top of the trees; but on them he was still shining brightly, and on the broad landscape beyond, which lay open to view through the gap in the trees. The glass door was open; the sweet summer air and the sound of birds and insects and fluttering leaves floated into the room, making the stillness musical. On the threshold pussy sat crouched, with his forefeet doubled under his breast, watching with intense gravity the operations of Margery, who was setting the table on the lawn just before his eyes. Alice was paring peaches.

"Oh, we are going to have tea out of doors, aren't we!" said

Ellen. "I'm very glad. What a lovely evening, isn't it? Just look at pussy, will you, Alice? don't you believe he knows what Margery is doing?—Why didn't you call me to go along with you after peaches?"

"I thought you were doing the very best thing you possibly could, Ellie, my dear. How do you do?"

"Oh, nicely now! Where's Mr. John? I hope he won't ask for my last drawing to-night,—I want to fix the top of that tree before he sees it."

"*Fix* the top of your tree, you little Yankee?" said Alice;— "what do you think John would say to that?—*un*fix it you mean; it is too stiff already, isn't it?"

"Well, what *shall* I say?" said Ellen laughing. "I am sorry that is Yankee, for I suppose one must speak English.—I want to do something to my tree, then.—Where is he, Alice?"

"He is gone down to Mr. Van Brunt's, to see how he is, and to speak to Miss Fortune about you on his way back."

"Oh, how kind of him!—he's *very* good; that is just what I want to know; but I am sorry, after this long ride——"

"He don't mind *that*, Ellie. He'll be home presently."

"How nice those peaches look;—they are as good as straw-berries, don't you think so?—better,—I don't know which is best; —but Mr. John likes these best, don't he? Now you've done!— shall I set them on the table?—and here's a pitcher of splendid cream, Alice!"

"You had better not tell John so, or he will make you define *splendid*."

John came back in good time, and brought word that Mr. Van Brunt was doing very well, so far as could be known; also, that Miss Fortune consented to Ellen's remaining where she was. He wisely did not say, however, that her consent had been slow to gain till he had hinted at his readiness to provide a substitute for Ellen's services; on which Miss Fortune had instantly declared she did not want her and she might stay as long as she pleased. This was all that was needed to complete Ellen's felicity.

"Wasn't your poor horse too tired to go out again this after-noon, Mr. John?"

"I did not ride him, Ellie; I took yours."

"The Brownie!—did you?—I'm very glad! How did you like him? But perhaps *he* was tired a little, and you couldn't tell so well to-day."

"He was not tired with any work you had given him, Ellie;— perhaps he may be a little now."

"Why?" said Ellen, somewhat alarmed.

"I have been trying him; and instead of going quietly along the road we have been taking some of the fences in our way. As

I intend practising you at the bar, I wished to make sure in the first place that he knew his lesson."

" Well, how did he do ?"

" Perfectly well—I believe he is a good little fellow. I wanted to satisfy myself if he was fit to be trusted with you ; and I rather think Mr. Marshman has taken care of that."

The whole wall of trees was in shadow when the little family sat down to table ; but there was still the sun-lit picture behind ; and there was another kind of sunshine in every face at the table. Quietly happy the whole four, or at least the whole three, were ; first, in being together,—after that, in all things besides. Never was tea so refreshing, or bread and butter so sweet, or the song of birds so .delightsome. When the birds were gone to their nests, the cricket and grasshopper and tree-toad and katy-did, and name-less other songsters, kept up a concert,—nature's own,—in deli-cious harmony with woods and flowers, and summer breezes and evening light. Ellen's cup of enjoyment was running over. From one beautiful thing to another her eye wandered,—from one joy to another her thoughts went,—till her full heart fixed on the God who had made and given them all, and that Redeemer whose blood had been their purchase-money. From the dear friends beside her, the best-loved she had in the world, she thought of the one dearer yet from whom death had separated her ;—yet living still,—and to whom death would restore her, thanks to Him who had burst the bonds of death and broken the gates of the grave, and made a way for his ransomed to pass over. And the thought of Him was the joyfullest of all !

" You look happy, Ellie," said her adopted brother.

" So I am," said Ellen, smiling a very bright smile.

" What are you thinking about ?"

But John saw it would not do to press his question.

" You remind me," said he, " of some old fairy story that my childish ears received, in which the fountains of the sweet and bitter waters of life were said to stand very near each other, and to mingle their streams but a little way from their source. Your tears and smiles seem to be brothers and sisters ;—whenever we see one we may be sure the other is not far off."

" My dear Jack," said Alice, laughing,—" what an unhappy simile ! Are brothers and sisters always found like that ?"

" I wish they were," said John, sighing and smiling ;—" but my last words had nothing to do with my simile as you call it."

When tea was over, and Margery had withdrawn the things and taken away the table, they still lingered in their places. It was far too pleasant to go in. Mr. Humphreys moved his chair to the side of the house, and throwing a handkerchief over his head to defend him from the mosquitoes, a few of which were buzzing about, he either listened, meditated, or slept;—most probably one of the two latter; for the conversation was not very loud nor very lively; it was happiness enough merely to breathe so near each other. The sun left the distant fields and hills; soft twilight stole through the woods, down the gap, and over the plain; the grass lost its green; the wall of trees grew dark and dusky; and very faint and dim showed the picture that was so bright a little while ago. As they sat quite silent, listening to what nature had to say to them, or letting fancy and memory take their way, the silence was broken— hardly broken—by the distinct far-off cry of a whip-poor-will. Alice grasped her brother's arm, and they remained motionless, while it came nearer, nearer,—then quite near,—with its clear, wild, shrill, melancholy note sounding close by them again and again,—strangely, plaintively, then leaving the lawn, it was heard further and further off, till the last faint " whip-poor-will," in the far distance, ended its pretty interlude. It was almost too dark to read faces, but the eyes of the brother and sister had sought each other and remained fixed till the bird was out of hearing; then Alice's hand was removed to his, and her head found its old place on her brother's shoulder.

" Sometimes, John," said Alice, " I am afraid I have one tie too strong to this world. I cannot bear—as I ought—to have you away from me."

Her brother's lips were instantly pressed to her forehead.

" I may say to you, Alice, as Colonel Gardiner said to his wife, ' we have an eternity to spend together !' "

" I wonder," said Alice, after a pause,—" how those can bear to love or be loved, whose affection can see nothing but a blank beyond the grave."

" Few people, I believe," said her brother, " would come exactly under that description; most flatter themselves with a vague hope of reunion after death."

" But that is a miserable hope—very different from ours."

" Very different indeed !—and miserable; for it can only deceive; but ours is sure. ' Them that sleep in Jesus will God bring with him.' "

" Precious !" said Alice. " How exactly fitted to every want and mood of the mind are the sweet Bible words."

" Well ! said Mr. Humphreys, rousing himself,—" I am going in ! These mosquitoes have half eaten me up. Are you going to sit there all night ?"

" We are thinking of it, papa," said Alice cheerfully.

He went in, and was heard calling Margery for a light.

They had better lights on the lawn. The stars began to peep out through the soft blue, and as the blue grew deeper they came out more and brighter, till all heaven was hung with lamps. But that was not all. In the eastern horizon, just above the low hills that bordered the far side of the plain, a white light, spreading and growing and brightening, promised the moon, and promised that she would rise very splendid; and even before she came began to throw a faint lustre over the landscape. All eyes were fastened, and exclamations burst, as the first silver edge showed itself, and the moon rapidly rising looked on them with her whole broad bright face; lighting up not only their faces and figures but the wide country view that·was spread out below, and touching most beautifully the trees in the edge of the gap, and faintly the lawn; while the wall of wood stood in deeper and blacker shadow than ever.

" Isn't that beautiful !'' said Ellen.

" Come round here, Ellie,'' said John ;—" Alice may have you all the rest of the year, but when I am at home you belong to me. What was your little head busied upon a while ago ?''

" When ?'' said Ellen.

" When I asked you——''

" Oh, I know,—I remember. I was thinking——''

" Well ?''—

" I was thinking—do you want me to tell you ?''

" Unless you would rather not.''

" I was thinking about Jesus Christ,'' said Ellen in a low tone.

" What about him, dear Ellie ?'' said her brother, drawing her closer to his side.

" Different things,—I was thinking of what he said about little children—and about what he said, you know,—' In my Father's house are many mansions ;'—and I was thinking that mamma was there ; and I thought—that we all——''

Ellen could get no further.

" ' He that believeth in him shall not be ashamed,' '' said John softly. " ' This is the promise that he hath promised us, even eternal life ; and who shall separate us from the love of Christ ? Not death, nor things present, nor things to come. But he that hath this hope in him purifieth himself even as he is pure ;'—let us remember that too.''

" Mr. John,'' said Ellen presently,—" don't you like some of the chapters in the Revelation very much ?''

" Yes—very much. Why ?—do you ?''

" Yes. I remember reading parts of them to mamma, and that is one reason, I suppose ; but I like them very much. There is a great deal I can't understand, though.''

" There is nothing finer in the Bible than parts of that book,'' said Alice.

" Mr. John,'' said Ellen,—" what is meant by the ' white stone ?' ''

" ' And in the stone a new name written ?' "—

" Yes—that I mean."

" Mr. Baxter says it is the sense of God's love in the heart; and indeed that is it ' which no man knoweth saving him that receiveth it.' This, I take it, Ellen, was Christian's certificate, which he used to comfort himself with reading in, you remember ?"

" Can a child have it?" said Ellen thoughtfully.

" Certainly—many children have had it—you may have it. Only seek it faithfully. ' Thou meetest him that rejoiceth and worketh righteousness, those that remember thee in thy ways.'—And Christ said, ' he that loveth me shall be loved of my Father, and I will love him, and I will manifest myself to him !' There is no failure in these promises, Ellie ; he that made them is the same yesterday, to-day, and for ever."

For a little while each was busy with his own meditations. The moon meanwhile, rising higher and higher, poured a flood of light through the gap in the woods before them, and stealing among the trees here and there lit up a spot of ground under their deep shadow. The distant picture lay in mazy brightness. All was still, but the ceaseless chirrup of insects and gentle flapping of leaves ; the summer air just touched their cheeks with the lightest breath of a kiss, sweet from distant hay-fields, and nearer pines and hemlocks, and other of nature's numberless perfume-boxes. The hay-harvest had been remarkably late this year.

" This is higher enjoyment," said John,—" than half those who make their homes in rich houses and mighty palaces have any notion of."

" But cannot rich people look at the moon ?" said Ellen.

" Yes, but the taste for pure pleasures is commonly gone when people make a trade of pleasure."

" Mr. John,"—Ellen began.

" I will forewarn you," said he,—" that Mr. John has made up his mind he will do nothing more for you. So if you have any thing to ask, it must lie still,— unless you will begin again."

Ellen drew back. He looked grave, but she saw Alice smiling.

" But what shall I do?" said she, a little perplexed and half laughing. " What do you mean, Mr. John ? What does he mean, Alice ?"

" You could speak without a ' Mr.' to me this morning when you were in trouble."

" Oh !" said Ellen laughing,—" I forgot myself then."

" Have the goodness to forget yourself permanently for the future."

" Was that man hurt this morning, John ?" said his sister.

" What man ?"

" That man you delivered Ellen from."

" Hurt? no—nothing material; I did not wish to hurt him. He richly deserved punishment, but it was not for me to give it."

" He was in no hurry to get up," said Ellen.

" I do not think he ventured upon that till we were well out of the way. He lifted his head and looked after us as we rode off."

" But I wanted to ask something," said Ellen,—" Oh! what is the reason the moon looks so much larger when she first gets up than she does afterwards?"

" Whom are you asking?"

" You."

" And who is you? Here are two people in the moonlight."

" Mr. John Humphreys,—Alice's brother, and that Thomas calls ' the young master,' " said Ellen laughing.

" You are more shy of taking a leap than your little horse is," said John smiling,—" but I shall bring you up to it yet. What is the cause of the sudden enlargement of my thumb?"

He had drawn a small magnifying glass from his pocket and held it between his hand and Ellen.

" Why it is not enlarged," said Ellen, " it is only magnified."

" What do you mean by that?"

" Why, the glass makes it look larger."

" Do you know how, or why?"

" No."

He put up the glass again.

" But what do you mean by that?" said Ellen,—" there is no magnifying glass between us and the moon to make *her* look larger."

" You are sure of that?"

" Why yes!" said Ellen;—" I am perfectly sure; there is nothing in the world. There she is, right up there, looking straight down upon us, and there is nothing between."

" What is it that keeps up that pleasant fluttering of leaves in the wood?"

" Why, the wind."

" And what is the wind?"

" It is air—air moving, I suppose."

" Exactly. Then there *is* something between us and the moon."

" The air! But, Mr. John, one can see quite clearly through the air; it doesn't make things look larger or smaller."

" How far do you suppose the air reaches from us toward the moon?"

" Why all the way, don't it?

" No—only about forty miles. If it reached all the way there would indeed be no magnifying glass in the case."

" But how is it?" said Ellen. " I don't understand."

" I cannot tell you to-night, Ellie. There is a long ladder of knowledge to go up before we can get to the moon, but we will begin to mount to-morrow, if nothing happens. Alice, you have that little book of Conversations on Natural Philosophy, which you and I used to delight ourselves with in old time ?"

"Safe and sound in the bookcase," said Alice. "I have thought of giving it to Ellen before, but she has been busy enough with what she had already."

"I have done Rollin now, though," said Ellen ;—" that is lucky. I am ready for the moon."

This new study was begun the next day, and Ellen took great delight in it. She would have run on too fast in her eagerness but for the steady hand of her teacher; he obliged her to be very thorough. This was only one of her items of business. The weeks of John's stay were as usual not merely weeks of constant and varied delight, but of constant and swift improvement too.

A good deal of time was given to the riding-lessons. John busied himself one morning in preparing a bar for her on the lawn ; so placed that it might fall if the horse's heels touched it. Here Ellen learned to take first standing, and then running, leaps. She was afraid at first, but habit wore that off; and the bar was raised higher and higher, till Margery declared she " couldn't stand and look at her going over it." Then John made her ride without the stirrup, and with her hands behind her, while he, holding the horse by a long halter, made him go round in a circle, slowly at first, and afterwards trotting and cantering, till Ellen felt almost as secure on his back as in a chair. It took a good many lessons however to bring her to this, and she trembled very much at the beginning. Her teacher was careful and gentle, but determined ; and whatever he said she did, tremble or no tremble ; and in general loved her riding lessons dearly.

Drawing too went on finely. He began to let her draw things from nature ; and many a pleasant morning the three went out together with pencils and books and work, and spent hours in the open air. They would find a pretty point of view, or a nice shady place where the breeze came, and where there was some good old rock with a tree beside it, or a piece of fence, or the house or barn in the distance, for Ellen to sketch ; and while she drew and Alice worked, John read aloud to them. Sometimes he took a pencil too, and Alice read ; and often, often, pencils, books, and work were all laid down ; and talk,—lively, serious, earnest, always delightful,—took the place of them. When Ellen could not understand the words, at least she could read the faces ; and that was a study she was never weary of. At home there were other studies and much reading ; many tea drinkings on the lawn, and even breakfastings, which she thought pleasanter still.

As soon as it was decided that Mr. Van Brunt's leg was doing

well, and in a fair way to be sound again, Ellen went to see him ;
and after that rarely let two days pass without going again. John
and Alice used to ride with her so far, and taking a turn beyond
while she made her visit, call for her on their way back. She had
a strong motive for going in the pleasure her presence always gave,
both to Mr. Van Brunt and his mother. Sam Larkens had been
to Thirlwall and seen Mrs. Forbes, and from him they had heard
the story of her riding up and down the town in search of the
doctor ; neither of them could forget it. Mrs. Van Brunt poured
out her affection in all sorts of expressions whenever she had
Ellen's ear ; her son was not a man of many words ; but Ellen
knew his face and manner well enough without them, and read
there whenever she went into his room what gave her great
pleasure.

"How do you do, Mr. Van Brunt?" she said on one of these
occasions.

"Oh, I'm getting along, I s'pose," said he ;—"getting along as
well as a man can that's lying on his back from morning to night;
—prostrated, as 'Squire Dennison said his corn was t'other day."

"It is very tiresome, isn't it ?" said Ellen.

"It's the tiresomest work that ever was, for a man that has two
arms to be a doing nothing, day after day. And what bothers me
is the wheat in the ten-acre lot, that *ought* to be prostrated too,
and ain't, nor ain't like to be, as I know, unless the rain comes
and does it. Sam and Johnny 'll make no head-way at all with it
—I can tell as well as if I see 'em."

"But Sam is good, isn't he ?" said Ellen.

"Sam's as good a boy as ever was ; but then Johnny Low is
mischievous, you see, and he gets Sam out of his tracks once in a
while. I never see a finer growth of wheat. I had a sight rather
cut and harvest the hull of it than to lie here and think of it getting spoiled. I'm a'most out o' conceit o' trap doors, Ellen."

Ellen could not help smiling.

"What can I do for you, Mr. Van Brunt?"

"There ain't nothing," said he ;—"I wish there was. How are
you coming along at home ?"

"I don't know," said Ellen ;—"I am not there just now, you
know ; I am staying up with Miss Alice again."

"Oh, ay ! while her brother's at home. He's a splendid man,
that young Mr. Humphreys, ain't he ?"

"Oh, *I* knew that a great while ago," said Ellen, the bright
colour of pleasure overspreading her face.

"Well, *I* didn't, you see, till the other day, when he came here,
very kindly, to see how I was getting on. I wish something would
bring him again. I never heerd a man talk I liked to hear so
much."

Ellen secretly resolved something *should* bring him ; and went on with a purpose she had had for some time in her mind.

"Wouldn't it be pleasant, while you are lying there and can do nothing,—wouldn't you like to have me read something to you, Mr. Van Brunt ? *I* should like to, very much."

"It's just like you," said he gratefully,—"to think of that ; but I wouldn't have you be bothered with it."

"It wouldn't indeed. I should like it very much."

"Well, if you've a mind," said he ;—"I can't say but it would be a kind o' comfort to keep that grain out o' my head a while. Seems to me I have cut and housed it all three times over already. Read just whatever you have a mind to. If you was to go over a last year's almanac, it would be as good as a fiddle to me."

"I'll do better for you than that, Mr. Van Brunt," said Ellen, laughing in high glee at having gained her point. — She had secretly brought her Pilgrim's Progress with her, and now with marvellous satisfaction drew it forth.

"I ha'n't been as much of a reader as I had ought to," said Mr. Van Brunt, as she opened the book and turned to the first page ;—"but, however, I understand my business pretty well ; and a man can't be every thing to once. Now let's hear what you've got there."

With a throbbing heart, Ellen began ; and read, notes and all, till the sound of tramping hoofs and Alice's voice made her break off. It encouraged and delighted her to see that Mr. Van Brunt's attention was perfectly fixed. He lay still, without moving his eyes from her face, till she stopped ; then thanking her he declared that was a "first-rate book," and he "should like mainly to hear the hull on it."

From that time Ellen was diligent in her attendance on him. That she might have more time for reading than the old plan gave her, she set off by herself alone some time before the others, of course riding home with them. It cost her a little sometimes, to forego so much of their company ; but she never saw the look of grateful pleasure with which she was welcomed without ceasing to regret her self-denial. How Ellen blessed those notes as she went on with her reading ! They said exactly what she wanted Mr. Van Brunt to hear, and in the best way, and were too short and simple to interrupt the interest of the story. After a while she ventured to ask if she might read him a chapter in the Bible. He agreed very readily ; owning "he hadn't ought to be so long without reading one as he had been." Ellen then made it a rule to herself, without asking any more questions, to end every reading with a chapter in the Bible ; and she carefully sought out those that might be most likely to take hold of his judgment or feelings. They took hold of her own very deeply, by the means ; what was strong, or tender, before, now seemed to her too mighty to be withstood; and Ellen read not only with her lips but with her whole heart the precious words, longing that they might come with their just effect upon Mr. Van Brunt's mind.

Once as she finished reading the tenth chapter of John, a favourite chapter, which between her own feeling of it and her strong wish for him had moved her even to tears, she cast a glance at his face to see how he took it. His head was a little turned to one side, and his eyes closed; she thought he was asleep. Ellen was very much disappointed. She sank her head upon her book and prayed that a time might come when he would know the worth of those words. The touch of his hand startled her.

" What is the matter?" said he. " Are you tired?"

" No," said Ellen looking hastily up ;—" Oh, no! I'm not tired."

" But what ails you?" said the astonished Mr. Van Brunt; " what have you been a crying for? what's the matter?"

" Oh, never mind," said Ellen, brushing her hand over her eyes, —" it's no matter."

" Yes, but I want to know," said Mr. Van Brunt ;—" you shan't have any thing to vex you that *I* can help; what is it?"

" It is nothing, Mr. Van Brunt," said Ellen, bursting into tears again,—" only I thought you were asleep—I—I thought you didn't care enough about the Bible to keep awake—I want *so* much that you should be a Christian!"

He half groaned and turned his head away.

" What makes you wish that so much?" said he after a minute or two.

" Because I want you to be happy," said Ellen,—" and I know you can't without."

" Well, I am pretty tolerable happy," said he ;—" as happy as most folks I guess."

" But I want you to be happy when you die, too," said Ellen ;— " I want to meet you in heaven "

" I hope I will go there, surely," said he gravely,—" when the time comes."

Ellen was uneasily silent, not knowing what to say.

" I ain't as good as I ought to be," said he presently, with a half sigh ;—" I ain't good enough to go to heaven—I wish I was. *You* are, I do believe."

" I! oh, no, Mr. Van Brunt, do not say that ;—I am not good at all—I am full of wrong things."

" Well I wish I was full of wrong things too, in the same way," said he.

" But I am," said Ellen,—" whether you will believe it or not. Nobody is good, Mr. Van Brunt. But Jesus Christ has died for us,—and if we ask him he will forgive us, and wash away our sins, and teach us to love him, and make us good, and take us to be with him in heaven. Oh, I wish you would ask him!" she repeated with an earnestness that went to his heart. "I don't believe any one can be very happy that doesn't love him."

"Is that what makes *you* happy?" said he.

"I have a great many things to make me happy," said Ellen soberly,—"but that is the greatest of all. It always makes me happy to think of him, and it makes every thing else a thousand times pleasanter. I wish you knew how it is, Mr. Van Brunt."

He was silent for a little, and disturbed Ellen thought.

"Well!" said he at length,—"'tain't the folks that thinks themselves the best that *is* the best always ;—if you ain't good I should like to know what goodness is. *There's* somebody that thinks you be," said he a minute or two afterwards, as the horses were heard coming to the gate.

"No, she knows me better than that," said Ellen.

"It isn't any *she* that I mean," said Mr. Van Brunt.—"There's somebody else out there, ain't there?"

"Who?" said Ellen,—"Mr. John?—Oh, no indeed he don't. It was only this morning he was telling me of something I did that was wrong."—Her eyes watered as she spoke.

"He must have mighty sharp eyes, then," said Mr. Van Brunt, —"for it beats all *my* powers of seeing things."

"And so he has," said Ellen, putting on her bonnet,—"he always knows what I am thinking of just as well as if I told him. Good-by!"

"Good-by," said he ;—"I ha'n't forgotten what you've been saying, and I don't mean to."

How full of sweet pleasure was the ride home!

The "something wrong," of which Ellen had spoken, was this. The day before, it happened that Mr. John had broken her off from a very engaging book to take her drawing-lesson ; and as he stooped down to give a touch or two to the piece she was to copy, he said, "I don't want you to read any more of that, Ellie ; it is not a good book for you." Ellen did not for a moment question that he was right, nor wish to disobey ; but she had become very much interested, and was a good deal annoyed at having such a sudden stop put to her pleasure. She said nothing, and went on with her work. In a little while Alice asked her to hold a skein of cotton for her while she wound it. Ellen was annoyed again at the interruption ; the harp-strings were jarring yet, and gave fresh discord to every touch. She had, however, no mind to let her vexation be seen ; she went immediately and held the cotton, and as soon as it was done sat down again to her drawing. Before ten minutes had passed Margery came to set the table for dinner ; Ellen's papers and desk must move.

THE WIDE, WIDE WORLD. 415

"Why, it is not dinner-time yet this great while, Margery," said she;—"it isn't much after twelve."

"No, Miss Ellen," said Margery under her breath, for John was in one corner of the room reading,—"but by and by I'll be busy with the chops and frying the salsify, and I couldn't leave the kitchen;—if you'll let me have the table now."

Ellen said no more, and moved her things to a stand before the window; where she went on with her copying till dinner was ready. Whatever the reason was, however, her pencil did not work smoothly; her eye did not see true; and she lacked her usual steady patience. The next morning, after an hour and more's work and much painstaking, the drawing was finished. Ellen had quite forgotten her yesterday's trouble. But when John came to review her drawing, he found several faults with it; pointed out two or three places in which it had suffered from haste and want of care; and asked her how it had happened. Ellen knew it happened yesterday. She was vexed again, though she did her best not to show it; she stood quietly and heard what he had to say. He then told her to get ready for her riding lesson.

"Mayn't I just make this right first?" said Ellen;—"it won't take me long."

"No," said he,—"you have been sitting long enough; I must break you off. The Brownie will be here in ten minutes."

Ellen was impatiently eager to mend the bad places in her drawing, and impatiently displeased at being obliged to ride first. Slowly and reluctantly she went to get ready; John was already gone; she would not have moved so leisurely if he had been any where within seeing distance. As it was, she found it convenient to quicken her movements; and was at the door ready as soon as he and the Brownie. She was soon thoroughly engaged in the management of herself and her horse; a little smart riding shook all the ill-humour out of her, and she was entirely herself again. At the end of fifteen or twenty minutes they drew up under the shade of a tree to let the Brownie rest a little. It was a warm day and John had taken off his hat and stood resting too, with his arm leaning on the neck of the horse. Presently he looked round to Ellen, and asked her with a smile, if she felt right again?

"Why?" said Ellen, the crimson of her cheeks mounting to her forehead. But her eye sunk immediately at the answering glance of his. He then in a very few words set the matter before her, with such a happy mixture of pointedness and kindness, that while the reproof, coming from him, went to the quick, Ellen yet joined with it no thought of harshness or severity. She was completely subdued however; the rest of the riding-lesson had to be given up;

and for an hour Ellen's tears could not be stayed. But it was, and John had meant it should be, a strong check given to her besetting sin. It had a long and lasting effect.

<hr>

CHAPTER XL.

Speed. But tell me true, will 't be a match?
Laun. Ask my dog; if he say, ay, it will; if he say, no, it will; if he shake his tail and say nothing, it will.—Two Gentlemen of Verona.

In due time Mr. Van Brunt was on his legs again, much to every body's joy, and much to the advantage of fields, fences, and grain. Sam and Johnny found they must "spring to," as their leader said; and Miss Fortune declared she was thankful she could draw a long breath again, for do what she would she couldn't be everywhere. Before this John and the Black Prince had departed, and Alice and Ellen were left alone again.

"How long will it be, dear Alice," said Ellen, as they stood sorrowfully looking down the road by which he had gone,—"before he will be through that—before he will be able to leave Doncaster?"

"Next summer."

"And what will he do then?"

"Then he will be ordained."

"Ordained?—what is that?"

"He will be solemnly set apart for the work of the ministry, and appointed to it by a number of clergymen."

"And then will he come and stay at home, Alice?"

"I don't know what then, dear Ellen," said Alice, sighing;— "he may for a little; but papa wishes very much that before he is settled anywhere he should visit England and Scotland and see our friends there. Though I hardly think John will do it unless he sees some further reason for going. If he do not, he will probably soon he called somewhere—Mr. Marshman wants him to come to Randolph. I don't know how it will be."

"Well!" said Ellen, with a kind of acquiescing sigh—"at any rate now we must wait until next Christmas."

The winter passed with little to mark it except the usual visits to Ventnor; which, however, by common consent, Alice and Ellen had agreed should *not* be when John was at home. At all other times they were much prized and enjoyed. Every two or three months Mr. Marshman was sure to come for them, or Mr. Howard, or perhaps the carriage only with a letter; and it was bargained that Mr. Humphreys should follow to see them home. It was not always that Ellen could go, but the disappointments were seldom ; she too had become quite domesticated at Ventnor, and was sincerely loved by the whole family. Many as were the times she had been there, it had oddly happened that she had never met her old friend of the boat again ; but she was very much attached to old Mr. and Mrs. Marshman, and Mrs. Chauncey and her daughter ; the latter of whom reckoned all the rest of her young friends as nothing compared with Ellen Montgomery. Ellen, in her opinion, did every thing better than any one else of her age.

" She has good teachers," said Mrs. Chauncey.

" Yes, indeed ! I should think she had. Alice,—I should think any body would learn well with her ;—and Mr. John—I suppose he's as good, though I don't know so much about him ; but he must be a great deal better teacher than Mr. Sandford, mamma, for Ellen draws *ten times* as well as I do !''

" Perhaps that is your fault and not Mr. Sandford's," said her mother,—" though I rather think you overrate the difference.''

" I am sure I take pains enough, if that's all," said the little girl ;—" what more can I do, mamma ? But Ellen is so pleasant about it always ; she never seems to think she does better than I ; and she is always ready to help me and take ever so much time to show me how to do things ;—she is *so* pleasant ; isn't she, mamma ? I know I have heard you say she is very polite.''

" She is certainly that," said Mrs. Gillespie,—" and there is a grace in her politeness that can only proceed from great natural delicacy and refinement of character ;—how she can have such manners, living and working in the way you say she does, I confess is beyond my comprehension.''

" One would not readily forget the notion of good-breeding in the society of Alice and John Humphreys," said Miss Sophia.

" And Mr. Humphreys," said Mrs. Chauncey.

" There is no society about him," said Miss Sophia ;—" he don't say two dozen words a day.''

" But she is not with them," said Mrs. Gillespie.

" She is with them a great deal, aunt Matilda," said Ellen Chauncey,—" and they teach her every thing, and she does learn ! She must be very clever ; don't you think she is, mamma ? Mamma, she beats me entirely in speaking French, and she knows all about English history ; and arithmetic !—and did you ever hear her sing, mamma ?''

" I do not believe she beats you, as you call it, in generous estimation of others," said Mrs. Chauncey, smiling, and bending forward to kiss her daughter ;—" but what is the reason Ellen is so much better read in history than you ?''

" I don't know, mamma, unless—I wish I wasn't so fond of reading stories.''

"Ellen Montgomery is just as fond of them, I'll warrant," said Miss Sophia.

"Yes,—oh, I know she is fond of them; but then Alice and Mr. John don't let her read them, except now and then one."

"I fancy she does it though when their backs are turned," said Mrs. Gillespie.

"She! oh, aunt Matilda! she wouldn't do the least thing they don't like for the whole world. I know she never reads a story when she is here, unless it is my Sunday books, without asking Alice first."

"She is a most extraordinary child!" said Mrs. Gillespie.

"She is a *good* child!" said Mrs. Chauncey.

"Yes, mamma, and that is what I wanted to say;—I do not think Ellen is so polite because she is so much with Alice and John, but because she is so sweet and good. I don't think she could *help* being polite."

"It is not that," said Mrs. Gillespie;—"mere sweetness and goodness would never give so much elegance of manner. As far as I have seen, Ellen Montgomery is a *perfectly* well-behaved child."

"That she is," said Mrs. Chauncey;—"but neither would any cultivation or example be sufficient for it without Ellen's thorough good principle and great sweetness of temper."

"That's exactly what *I* think, mamma," said Ellen Chauncey.

Ellen's sweetness of temper was not entirely born with her; it was one of the blessed fruits of religion and discipline. Discipline had not done with it yet. When the winter came on, and the house-work grew less, and with renewed vigour she was bending herself to improvement in all sorts of ways, it unluckily came into Miss Fortune's head that some of Ellen's spare time might be turned to account in a new line. With this lady, to propose and to do were two things always very near together. The very next day Ellen was summoned to help her down stairs with the big spinning-wheel. Most unsuspiciously, and with her accustomed pleasantness, Ellen did it. But when she was sent up again for the rolls of wool; and Miss Fortune after setting up the wheel, put one of them into her hand and instructed her how to draw out and twist the thread of yarn, she saw all that was coming. She saw it with dismay. So much yarn as Miss Fortune might think it well she should spin, so much time must be taken daily from her beloved reading and writing, drawing and studying; her very heart sunk with her. She made no remonstrance, unless her disconsolate face might be thought one; she stood half a day at the big spinning-wheel, fretting secretly, while Miss Fortune went round with an inward chuckle visible in her countenance, that in spite of herself increased Ellen's vexation. And this was not the annoyance of a day; she must expect it day after day through the whole winter. It was a grievous trial. Ellen cried for a great while when she got to her own room, and a long hard struggle was necessary before she could resolve to do her duty. "To be patient and quiet! —and spin nobody knows how much yarn—and my poor history and philosophy and drawing and French and reading"—Ellen cried very heartily. But she knew what she ought to do; she prayed long, humbly, earnestly, that "her little rushlight might shine bright;"—and her aunt had no cause to complain of her. Sometimes, if overpressed, Ellen would ask Miss Fortune to let her stop; saying, as Alice had advised her, that *she* wished to have her do such and such things. Miss Fortune never made any objection; and the hours of spinning that wrought so many knots of yarn for her aunt, wrought better things yet for the little spinner: patience and gentleness grew with the practice of them; this wearisome work was one of the many seemingly untoward things which in reality bring out good. The time Ellen *did* secure to herself was held the more precious and used the more carefully. After all it was a very profitable and pleasant winter to her.

John's visit came as usual at the holidays, and was enjoyed as usual; only that every one seemed to Ellen more pleasant than the last. The sole other event that broke the quiet course of things, (beside the journeys to Ventnor) was the death of Mrs. Van Brunt. This happened very unexpectedly and after a short illness, not far from the end of January. Ellen was very sorry; both for her own sake and Mr. Van Brunt's, who she was sure felt much, though according to his general custom he said nothing. Ellen felt for him none the less. She little thought what an important bearing this event would have upon her own future well-being.

The winter passed and the spring came. One fine mild pleasant afternoon early in May, Mr. Van Brunt came into the kitchen and asked Ellen if she wanted to go with him and see the sheep salted. Ellen was seated at the table with a large tin pan in her lap, and before her a huge heap of white beans which she was picking over for the Saturday's favourite dish of pork and beans. She looked up at him with a hopeless face.

"I should like to go very much indeed, Mr. Van Brunt, but you see I can't. All these to do!"

"Beans, eh?" said he, putting one or two in his mouth. "Where's your aunt?"

Ellen pointed to the buttery. He immediately went to the door and rapped on it with his knuckles.

"Here, ma'am!" said he,—"can't you let this child go with me? I want her along to help feed the sheep."

To Ellen's astonishment her aunt called to her through the closed door to "go along and leave the beans till she came back." Joy-

fully Ellen obeyed. She turned her back upon the beans, careless
of the big heap which would still be there to pick over when she
returned; and ran to get her bonnet. In all the time she had been
at Thirlwall something had always prevented her seeing the sheep
fed with salt, and she went eagerly out of the door with Mr. Van
Brunt to a new pleasure.

They crossed two or three meadows back of the barn to a low
rocky hill covered with trees. On the other side of this they came
to a fine field of spring wheat. Footsteps must not go over the
young grain; Ellen and Mr. Van Brunt coasted carefully round by
the fence to another piece of rocky woodland that lay on the far
side of the wheat-field. It was a very fine afternoon. The grass
was green in the meadow; the trees were beginning to show their
leaves; the air was soft and spring-like. In great glee Ellen
danced along, luckily needing no entertainment from Mr. Van
Brunt, who was devoted to his salt-pan. His natural taciturnity
seemed greater than ever; he amused himself all the way over the
meadow with turning over his salt and tasting it, till Ellen laughingly told him she believed he was as fond of it as the sheep were;
and then he took to chucking little bits of it right and left, at any
thing he saw that was big enough to serve for a mark. Ellen
stopped him again by laughing at his wastefulness; and so they
came to the wood. She left him then to do as he liked, while she
ran hither and thither to search for flowers. It was slow getting
through the wood. He was fain to stop and wait for her.

"Aren't these lovely?" said Ellen as she came up with her
hands full of anemones,—"and look—there's the liverwort. I
thought it must be out before now—the dear little thing!—but I
can't find any blood-root, Mr. Van Brunt."

"I guess they're gone," said Mr. Van Brunt.

"I suppose they must," said Ellen. "I am sorry; I like them
so much. Oh, I believe I did get them earlier than this two years
ago when I used to take so many walks with you. Only think of
my not having been to look for flowers before this spring."

"It hadn't ought to ha' happened so, that's a fact," said Mr.
Van Brunt. "I don't know how it has."

"Oh, there are my yellow bells!" exclaimed Ellen;—"oh, you
beauties! Aren't they, Mr. Van Brunt?"

"I won't say but what I think an ear of wheat's handsomer,"
said he with his half smile.

"Why Mr. Van Brunt! how can you?—but an ear of wheat's
pretty too. Oh, Mr. Van Brunt, what *is* that? Do you get me
some of it, will you, please? Oh, how beautiful!—what is it?"

"That's black birch," said he;—"'*tis* kind o' handsome;—stop,
I'll find you some oak blossoms directly.—There's some Solomon's
seal—do you want some of that?"

Ellen sprang to it with exclamations of joy, and before she could rise from her stooping posture discovered some cowslips to be scrambled for. Wild columbine, the delicate corydalis, and more uvularias, which she called yellow bells, were added to her handful, till it grew a very elegant bunch indeed. Mr. Van Brunt looked complacently on, much as Ellen would at a kitten running round after its tail.

" Now I won't keep you any longer, Mr. Van Brunt," said she, when her hands were as full as they could hold ;—" I have kept you a great while ; you are very good to wait for me."

They took up their line of march again, and after crossing the last piece of rocky woodland came to an open hill-side, sloping gently up, at the foot of which were several large flat stones.

" But where are the sheep, Mr. Van Brunt," said Ellen.

" I guess they ain't fur," said he. " You keep quiet, 'cause they don't know you; and they are mighty scary. Just stand still there by the fence.—Ca-nan ! ca-nan ! Ca-nan, nan, nan, nan nan, nan, nan !"

This was the sheep call, and raising his voice Mr. Van Brunt made it sound abroad far over the hills. Again and again it sounded ; and then Ellen saw the white nose of a sheep at the edge of the woods on the top of the hill. On the call's sounding again the sheep set forward, and in a long train they came running along a narrow footpath down toward where Mr. Van Brunt was standing with his pan. The soft tramp of a multitude of light hoofs in another direction turned Ellen's eyes that way, and there were two more single files of sheep running down the hill from different points in the woodland. The pretty things came scampering along, seeming in a great hurry, till they got very near ; then the whole multitude came to a sudden halt, and looked very wistfully and doubtfully indeed at Mr. Van Brunt and the strange little figure standing so still by the fence. They seemed in great doubt, every sheep of them, whether Mr. Van Brunt were not a traitor, who had put on a friend's voice and lured them down there with some dark evil intent, which he was going to carry out by means of that same dangerous-looking stranger by the fence. Ellen almost expected to see them turn about and go as fast as they had come. But Mr. Van Brunt gently repeating his call, went quietly up to the nearest stone and began to scatter the salt upon it, full in their view. Doubt was at an end ; he had hung out the white flag ; they flocked down to the stones, no longer at all in fear of double-dealing, and crowded to get at the salt ; the rocks where it was strewn were covered with more sheep than Ellen would have thought it possible could stand upon them. They were like pieces of floating ice heaped up with snow, or queen-cakes with an immoderately thick frosting. It was one scene of pushing and crowding; those which had not had their share of the feast forcing themselves up to get at it, and shoving others off in consequence. Ellen was wonderfully pleased. It was a new and pretty sight, the busy hustling crowd of gentle creat-

ures; with the soft noise of their tread upon grass and stones, and the eager devouring of the salt. She was fixed with pleasure, looking and listening; and did not move till the entertainment was over, and the body of the flock were carelessly scattering here and there, while a few that had perhaps been disappointed of their part still lingered upon the stones in the vain hope of yet licking a little saltness from them.

" Well," said Ellen, " I never knew what salt was worth before. How they do love it ! Is it good for them, Mr. Van Brunt ?"

" Good for them ?" he said,—" to be sure it is good for them. There ain't a critter that walks, as I know, that it ain't good for, —'cept chickens, and it's very queer it kills them."

They turned to go homeward. Ellen had taken the empty pan to lay her flowers in, thinking it would be better for them than the heat of her hand ; and greatly pleased with what she had come to see, and enjoying her walk as much as it was possible, she was going home very happy ; yet she could not help missing Mr. Van Brunt's old sociableness. He was uncommonly silent, even for him, considering that he and Ellen were alone together ; and she wondered what had possessed him with a desire to cut down all the young saplings he came to that were large enough for walking sticks. He did not want to make any use of them, that was certain, for as fast as he cut and trimmed out one he threw it away and cut another. Ellen was glad when they got out into the open fields where there were none to be found.

" It is just about this time a year ago," said she, " that aunt Fortune was getting well of her long fit of sickness."

" Yes !" said Mr. Van Brunt, with a very profound air ;— " something is always happening most years."

Ellen did not know what to make of this philosophical remark.

" I am very glad nothing is happening this year," said she ;— " I think it is a great deal pleasanter to have things go on quietly."

" Oh, something might happen without hindering things going on quietly, I s'pose,—mightn't it ?"

" I don't know," said Ellen, wonderingly ; — " why Mr. Van Brunt what *is* going to happen ?"

" I declare," said he, half laughing,—" you're as cute as a razor ; I didn't say there was any thing going to happen, did I ?"

" But is there ?" said Ellen.

" Ha'n't your aunt said nothing to you about it ?"

" Why no," said Ellen,—" she never tells me any thing ; what is it ?"

" Why the story is," said Mr. Van Brunt,—" at least I know, for I've understood as much from herself, that—I believe she's going to be married before long."

" She !" exclaimed Ellen. " Married !—aunt Fortune !"

" I believe so," said Mr. Van Brunt, making a lunge at a tuft of tall grass and pulling off two or three spears of it, which he carried to his mouth.

There was a long silence, during which Ellen saw nothing in earth, air, or sky, and knew no longer whether she was passing through woodland or meadow. To frame words into another sentence was past her power. They came in sight of the barn at length. She would not have much more time.

" Will it be soon, Mr. Van Brunt?"

" Why pretty soon, as soon as next week, I guess; so I thought it was time you ought to be told. Do you know to who?"

" I don't *know*," said Ellen in a low voice;—" I couldn't help guessing."

" I reckon you've guessed about right," said he, without looking at her.

There was another silence, during which it seemed to Ellen that her thoughts were tumbling head over heels, they were in such confusion.

" The short and the long of it is," said Mr. Van Brunt, as they rounded the corner of the barn,—" we have made up our minds to draw in the same yoke; and we're both on us pretty go-ahead folks, so I guess we'll contrive to pull the cart along. I had just as lieve tell you, Ellen, that all this was as good as settled a long spell back, —'afore ever you came to Thirlwall; but I was never agoing to leave my old mother without a home; so I stuck to her, and would, to the end of time, if I had never been married. But now she is gone, and there is nothing to keep me to the old place any longer. So now you know the hull on it, and I wanted you should."

With this particularly cool statement of his matrimonial views, Mr. Van Brunt turned off into the barnyard, leaving Ellen to go home by herself. She felt as if she were walking on air while she crossed the chip-yard, and the very house had a seeming of unreality. Mechanically she put her flowers in water, and sat down to finish the beans; but the beans might have been flowers and the flowers beans for all the difference Ellen saw in them. Miss Fortune and she shunned each other's faces most carefully for a long time; Ellen felt it impossible to meet her eyes; and it is a matter of great uncertainty which in fact did first look at the other. Other than this there was no manner of difference in any thing without or within the house. Mr. Van Brunt's being absolutely speechless was not a *very* uncommon thing.

CHAPTER XLI.

Poor little, pretty, fluttering thing,
  Must we no longer live together?
And dost thou prune thy trembling wing
  To take thy flight thou knowest not whither?
PRIOR.

As soon as she could Ellen carried this wonderful news to Alice, and eagerly poured out the whole story, her walk and all. She was somewhat disappointed at the calmness of her hearer.

" But you don't seem half as surprised as I expected, Alice; I thought you would be so much surprised."

" I am not surprised at all, Ellie."

" Not !—aren't you ?—why, did you know any thing of this before ?"

" I did not *know*, but I suspected. I thought it was very likely. I am *very* glad it is so."

" Glad! are you glad? I am so sorry ;—why are you glad, Alice ?"

" Why are you sorry, Ellie ?"

" Oh, because !—I don't know—it seems so queer !—I don't like it at all. I am very sorry indeed."

" For your aunt's sake, or for Mr. Van Brunt's sake ?"

" What do you mean ?"

" I mean, do you think he or she will be a loser by the bargain ?"

" Why he, to be sure ; I think he will ; I don't think she will. I think he is a great deal too good. And besides—I wonder if he wants to really :—it was settled so long ago—maybe he has changed his mind since."

" Have you any reason to think so, Ellie ?" said Alice smiling.

" I don't know—I don't think he seemed particularly glad."

" It will be safest to conclude that Mr. Van Brunt knows his own mind, my dear ; and it is certainly pleasanter for us to hope so."

" But then, besides," said Ellen with a face of great perplexity and vexation,—" I don't know—it don't seem right! How can I ever—must I, do you think I shall have to call him any thing but Mr. Van Brunt ?"

Alice could not help smiling again.

" What is your objection, Ellie ?"

" Why, because I *can't !*—I couldn't do it, somehow. It would seem so strange. Must I, Alice ?—Why in the world are you glad, dear Alice ?"

"It smooths my way for a plan I have had in my head; you will know by and by why I am glad, Ellie."

"Well I am glad if you are glad," said Ellen sighing;—"I don't know why I was so sorry, but I couldn't help it; I suppose I shan't mind it after a while."

She sat for a few minutes, musing over the possibility or impossibility of ever forming her lips to the words "uncle Abraham," "uncle Van Brunt," or barely "uncle;" her soul rebelled against all three. "Yet if he should think me unkind,—then I must,—oh, rather fifty times over than that!" Looking up, she saw a change in Alice's countenance, and tenderly asked,

"What is the matter, dear Alice? what are you thinking about?"

"I am thinking, Ellie, how I shall tell you something that will give you pain."

"Pain! you needn't be afraid of giving me pain," said Ellen fondly, throwing her arms around her,—"tell me, dear Alice; is it something I have done that is wrong? what is it?"

Alice kissed her, and burst into tears.

"What is the matter, oh, dear Alice!" said Ellen, encircling Alice's head with both her arms;—"oh, don't cry! do tell me what it is!"

"It is only sorrow for you, dear Ellie."

"But why?" said Ellen in some alarm;—"why are you sorry for me? I don't care, if it don't trouble you, indeed I don't! Never mind me; is it something that troubles you, dear Alice?"

"No—except for the effect it may have on others."

"Then I can bear it," said Ellen;—"you need not be afraid to tell me dear Alice;—what is it? don't be sorry for me!"

But the expression of Alice's face was such that she could not help being afraid to hear; she anxiously repeated "what is it?"

Alice fondly smoothed back the hair from her brow, looking herself somewhat anxiously and somewhat sadly upon the uplifted face.

"Suppose Ellie," she said at length,—"that you and I were taking a journey together—a troublesome dangerous journey—and that *I* had a way of getting at once safe to the end of it;—would you be willing to let me go, and you do without me for the rest of the way?"

"I would rather you should take me with you," said Ellen, in a kind of maze of wonder and fear;—"why where are you going, Alice?"

"I think I am going home, Ellie,—before you."

"Home?" said Ellen.

"Yes,—home I feel it to be; it is not a strange land; I thank God it is my *home* I am going to."

Ellen sat looking at her, stupefied.

" It is your home too, love, I trust, and believe," said Alice tenderly ;—" we shall be together at last. I am not sorry for myself ; I only grieve to leave you alone,—and others,—but God knows best. We must both look to him."

" Why Alice," said Ellen starting up suddenly,—" what do you mean ? what do you mean ?—I don't understand you—what do you mean ?"

" Do you not understand me, Ellie ?"

" But Alice !—but Alice—*dear* Alice—what makes you say so ? is there any thing the matter with you ?"

" Do I look well, Ellie ?"

With an eye sharpened to painful keenness, Ellen sought in Alice's face for the tokens of what she wished and what she feared. It *had* once or twice lately flitted through her mind that Alice was very thin, and seemed to want her old strength, whether in riding, or walking, or any other exertion ; and it *had* struck her that the bright spots of colour in Alice's face were just like what her mother's cheeks used to wear in her last illness. These thoughts had just come and gone ; but now as she recalled them and was forced to acknowledge the justness of them, and her review of Alice's face pressed them home anew,—hope for a moment faded. She grew white, even to her lips.

" My poor Ellie ! my poor Ellie !" said Alice, pressing her little sister to her bosom,—" it must be ! We *must* say ' the Lord's will be done ;'—we must not forget he does all things well."

But Ellen rallied ; she raised her head again ; she could not believe what Alice had told her. To her mind it seemed an evil *too great to happen ;* it could not be ! Alice saw this in her look, and again sadly stroked her hair from her brow. " It must be, Ellie, she repeated."

" But have you seen somebody ?—have you asked somebody ?" said Ellen ;—" some doctor ?"

" I have seen, and I have asked," said Alice ;—" it was not necessary, but I have done both. They think as I do."

" But these Thirlwall doctors——"

" Not them ; I did not apply to them. I saw an excellent physician at Randolph, the last time I went to Ventnor."

" And he said——"

" As I have told you."

Ellen's countenance fell—fell.

" It is easier for me to leave you than for you to be left,—I know that, my dear little Ellie ! You have no reason to be sorry for me —I *am* sorry for you ; but the hand that is taking me away is one that will touch neither of us but to do us good ;—I know that too. We must both look away to our dear Saviour, and not for a moment doubt his love. I do not—you must not. Is it not said that 'he loved Martha, and her sister, and Lazarus?' "

" Yes," said Ellen, who never stirred her eyes from Alice's.

" And might he not—did it not rest with a word of his lips, to keep Lazarus from dying, and save his sisters from all the bitter sorrow his death caused them?"

Again Ellen said, " yes," or her lips seemed to say it.

" And yet there were reasons, good reasons, why he should not, little as poor Martha and Mary could understand it.—But had he at all ceased to *love them* when he bade all that trouble come? Do you remember, Ellie—oh, how beautiful those words are!—when at last he arrived near the place, and first one sister came to him with the touching reminder that he might have saved them from this, and then the other,—weeping and falling at his feet, and repeating ' Lord, if thou hadst been here !'—when he saw their tears, and more, saw the torn hearts that tears could not ease,—he even wept with them too ! Oh, I thank God for those words! He saw reason to strike, and his hand did not spare ; but his love shed tears for them ! and he is just the same now."

Some drops fell from Alice's eyes, not sorrowful ones; Ellen had hid her face.

" Let us never doubt his love, dear Ellie, and surely then we can bear whatever that love may bring upon us. I do trust it. I do believe it shall be well with them that fear God. I believe it will be well for me when I die,—well for you my dear, dear Ellie,— well even for my father——"

She did not finish the sentence, afraid to trust herself.—But oh, Ellen knew what it would have been ; and it suddenly startled into life all the load of grief that had been settling heavily on her heart. Her thoughts had not looked that way before ;—now when they did, this new vision of misery was too much to bear. Quite unable to contain herself, and unwilling to pain Alice more than she could help, with a smothered burst of feeling she sprang away, out of the door, into the woods, where she would be unseen and unheard.

And there in the first burst of her agony, Ellen almost thought she should die. Her grief had not now indeed the goading sting of impatience ; she knew the hand that gave the blow, and did not raise her own against it ; she believed too what Alice had been saying, and the sense of it was, in a manner, present with her in her darkest time. But her spirit died within her ; she bowed her head as if she were never to lift it up again ; and she was ready to say with Job, " what good is my life to me ?"

It was long, very long after, when slowly and mournfully she came in again to kiss Alice before going back to her aunt's. She would have done it hurriedly and turned away ; but Alice held her and looked sadly for a minute into the woe-begone little face, then clasped her close and kissed her again and again.

"Oh, Alice," sobbed Ellen on her neck,—"aren't you mistaken? maybe you are mistaken."

"I am not mistaken, my dear Ellie, my own Ellie," said Alice's clear sweet voice ;—"nor sorry, except for others. I will talk with you more about this. You will be sorry for me at first, and then I hope you will be glad. It is only that I am going home a little before you. Remember what I was saying to you a while ago. Will you tell Mr. Van Brunt I should like to see him for a few minutes some time when he has leisure ?—And come to me early to-morrow, love."

Ellen could hardly get home. Her blinded eyes could not see where she was steppin ; and again and again her fulness of heart got the better of every thing else, and unmindful of the growing twilight she sat down on a stone by the wayside or flung herself on the ground to let sorrows have full sway. In one of these fits of bitter struggling with pain, there came on her mind, like a sunbeam across a cloud, the thought of Jesus weeping at the grave of Lazarus. It came with singular power. Did he love them so well ? thought Ellen—and is he looking down upon us with the same tenderness even now ?—She felt that the sun was shining still, though the cloud might be between ; her broken heart crept to His feet and laid its burden there, and after a few minutes she rose up and went on her way, keeping that thought still close to her heart. The unspeakable tears that were shed during those few minutes were that softened out-pouring of the heart that leaves it eased. Very, very sorrowful as she was, she went on calmly now and stopped no more.

It was getting dark, and a little way from the gate, on the road, she met Mr. Van Brunt.

"Why I was beginning to get scared about you," said he. "I was coming to see where you was. How come you so late?"

Ellen made no answer, and as he now came nearer and he could see more distinctly, his tone changed.

"What's the matter?" said he,—"you ha'n't been well ! what has happened? what ails you, Ellen?"

In astonishment and then in alarm, he saw that she was unable to speak, and anxiously and kindly begged her to let him know what was the matter, and if he could do any thing. Ellen shook her head.

"Ain't Miss Alice well ?" said he ;—"you ha'n't heerd no bad news up there on the hill, have you ?"

Ellen was not willing to answer this question with yea or nay. She recovered herself enough to give him Alice's message.

" I'll be sure and go," said he,—" but you ha'n't told me yet what's the matter ! Has any thing happened ?"

" No," said Ellen ;—" don't ask me—she'll tell you—don't ask me."

" I guess I'll go up the first thing in the morning then," said he, —" before breakfast."

" No," said Ellen ;—" better not—perhaps she wouldn't be up so early."

" After breakfast then,—I'll go up right after breakfast. I was a going with the boys up into that 'ere wheat lot, but anyhow I'll do that first. They won't have a chance to do much bad or good before I get back to them, I reckon."

As soon as possible she made her escape from Miss Fortune's eye and questions of curiosity which she could not bear to answer, and got to her own room. There the first thing she did was to find the eleventh chapter of John. She read it as she never had read it before ;—she found in it what she never had found before ; one of those cordials that none but the sorrowing drink. On the love of Christ, as there shown, little Ellen's heart fastened ; and with that one sweetening thought amid all its deep sadness, her sleep that night might have been envied by many a luxurious roller in pleasure.

At Alice's wish she immediately took up her quarters at the parsonage, to leave her no more. But she could not see much difference in her from what she had been for several weeks past ; and with the natural hopefulness of childhood, her mind presently almost refused to believe the extremity of the evil which had been threatened. Alice herself was constantly cheerful, and sought by all means to further Ellen's cheerfulness ; though careful at the same time, to forbid, as far as she could, the rising of the hope she saw Ellen was inclined to cherish.

One evening they were sitting together at the window, looking out upon the same old lawn and distant landscape, now in all the fresh greenness of the young spring. The woods were not yet in full leaf ; and the light of the setting sun upon the trees bordering the other side of the lawn showed them in the most exquisite and varied shades of colour. Some had the tender green of the new leaf, some were in the red or yellow browns of the half-opened bud ; others in various stages of forwardness mixing all the tints between, and the evergreens standing dark as ever, setting off the delicate hues of the surrounding foliage. This was all softened off in the distance ; the very light of the spring was mild and tender compared with that of other seasons ; and the air that stole round the corner of the house and came in at the open window was laden with aromatic fragrance. Alice and Ellen had been for some time silently breathing it and gazing thoughtfully on the loveliness that was abroad.

" I used to think," said Alice, "that it must be a very hard thing to leave such a beautiful world. Did you ever think so, Ellie ?"

" I don't know," said Ellen faintly,—" I don't remember."

" I used to think so," said Alice. " But I do not now, Ellie ; my feeling has changed.—Do *you* feel so now, Ellie ?"

" Oh, why do you talk about it, dear Alice ?"

" For many reasons, dear Ellie. Come here and sit in my lap again."

" I am afraid you cannot bear it."

" Yes I can. Sit here, and let your head rest where it used to :" —and Alice laid her cheek upon Ellen's forehead ;—" you are a great comfort to me, dear Ellie."

" Oh, Alice, don't say so—you'll kill me !" exclaimed Ellen in great distress.

" Why should I not say so, love ?" said Alice soothingly. " I like to say it, and you will be glad to know it by and by. You are a *great* comfort to me."

" And what have you been to me !" said Ellen weeping bitterly.

" What I cannot be much longer ; and I want to accustom you to think of it, and to think of it rightly. I want you to know that if I am sorry at all in the thought, it is for the sake of others, not myself. Ellie, you yourself will be glad for me in a little while ;—you will not wish me back."

Ellen shook her head.

" I know you will not—after a while ;—and I shall leave you in good hands—I have arranged for that, my dear little sister !"

The sorrowing child neither knew nor cared what she meant, but a mute caress answered the *spirit* of Alice's words.

" Look up Ellie—look out again. Lovely—lovely ! all that is, —but I know heaven is a great deal more lovely. Feasted as our eyes are with beauty, I believe that eye has not seen, nor heart imagined the things that God has prepared for them that love him. *You* believe that, Ellie ; you must not be so *very* sorry that I have gone to see it a little before you."

Ellen could say nothing.

" After all, Ellie, it is not beautiful things nor a beautiful world that make people happy—it is loving and being loved ; and that is the reason why I am happy in the thought of heaven. I shall, if he receives me—I shall be with my Saviour ; I shall see him and know him, without any of the clouds that come between here. I am often forgetting and displeasing him now,—never serving him well nor loving him right. I shall be glad to find myself where all that will be done with for ever. I shall be like him !—Why do you cry so, Ellie ?" said Alice tenderly.

" I can't help it, Alice."

" It is only my love for you—and for two more—that could make me wish to stay here,—nothing else ;—and I give all that up, because I do not know what is best for you or myself. And I look to meet you all again before long. Try to think of it as I do, Ellie."

" But what shall I do without you ?" said poor Ellen.

" I will tell you, Ellie. You must come here and take my place, and take care of those I leave behind ; will you ?—and they will take care of you."

" But,"—said Ellen, looking up eagerly,—" aunt Fortune——"

" I have managed all that. Will you do it, Ellen ? I shall feel easy and happy about you, and far easier and happier about my father, if I leave you established here, to be to him as far as you can, what I have been. Will you promise me, Ellie ?"

In words it was not possible ; but what silent kisses, and the close pressure of the arms round Alice's neck could say was said.

" I am satisfied, then," said Alice presently. " My father will be your father—think him so, dear Ellie,—and I know John will take care of you. And my place will not be empty. I am very, very glad."

Ellen felt her place surely would be empty, but she could not say so.

" It was for this I was so glad of your aunt's marriage, Ellie," Alice soon went on. " I foresaw she might raise some difficulties in my way,—hard to remove perhaps ;—but now I have seen Mr. Van Brunt, and he has promised me that nothing shall hinder your taking up your abode and making your home entirely here. Though I believe, Ellie, he would truly have loved to have you in his own house."

" I am sure he would," said Ellen, — " but oh, how much rather——"

" He behaved very well about it the other morning,—in a very manly, frank, kind way,—showed a good deal of feeling I think, too. He gave me to understand that for his own sake he should be extremely sorry to let you go ; but he assured me that nothing over which he had any control should stand in the way of your good."

" He is *very* kind—he is *very* good—he is always so," said Ellen. " I love Mr. Van Brunt very much. He always was as kind to me as he could be."

They were silent for a few minutes, and Alice was looking out of the window again. The sun had set, and the colouring of all without was graver. Yet it was but the change from one beauty to another. The sweet air seemed still sweeter than before the sun went down.

" You must be happy, dear Ellie, in knowing that I am. I am

happy now. I enjoy all this, and I love you all,—but I can leave it and can leave you,—yes, both,—for I would see Jesus! He who has taught me to love him will not forsake me now. Goodness and mercy have followed me all the days of my life, and I shall dwell in the house of the Lord for ever. I thank him! Oh, I thank him!"

Alice's face did not belie her words, though her eyes shone through tears.

" Ellie, dear,—you must love him with all your heart, and live constantly in his presence. I know if you do he will make you happy, in any event. He can always give more than he takes away. Oh, how good he is!—and what wretched returns we make him!—I was miserable when John first went away to Doncaster; I did not know how to bear it. But now, Ellie, I think I can see it has done me good, and I can even be thankful for it. All things are ours—all things;—the world, and life, and death too."

" Alice," said Ellen, as well as she could,—" you know what you were saying to me the other day?"

" About what, love?"

" That about—you know,—that chapter——'

" About the death of Lazarus?"

" Yes. It has comforted me very much."

" So it has me, Ellie. It has been exceeding sweet to me at different times. Come sing to me,—' How firm a foundation.' "

From time to time Alice led to this kind of conversation, both for Ellen's sake and her own pleasure. Meanwhile she made her go on with her usual studies and duties; and but for these talks Ellen would have scarce known how to believe that it could be true which she feared.

The wedding of Miss Fortune and Mr. Van Brunt was a very quiet one. It happened at far too busy a time of year, and they were too cool calculators, and looked upon their union in much too business-like a point of view, to dream of such a wild thing as a wedding-tour, or even resolve upon so troublesome a thing as a wedding-party. Miss Fortune would not have left her cheese and butter-making to see all the New Yorks and Bostons that ever were built; and she would have scorned a trip to Randolph. And Mr. Van Brunt would as certainly have wished himself all the while back among his furrows and crops. So one day they were quietly married at home, the Rev. Mr. Clark having been fetched from Thirlwall for the purpose. Mr. Van Brunt would have preferred that Mr. Humphreys should perform the ceremony; but Miss Fortune was quite decided in favor of the Thirlwall gentleman, and of course he it was.

The talk ran high all over the country on the subject of this marriage, and opinions were greatly divided; some congratulating Mr. Van Brunt on having made himself one of the richest land-holders "in town" by the junction of another fat farm to his own; some pitying him for having got more than his match within doors, and "guessing he'd missed his reckoning for once."

"If he has, then," said Sam Larkens, who heard some of these condoling remarks,—"it's the first time in his life, I can tell you. If *she* ain't a little mistaken, I wish I mayn't get a month's wages in a year to come. I tell you, you don't know Van Brunt; he's as easy as any body as long as he don't care about what you're doing; but if he once takes a notion you can't make him gee nor haw no more than you can our near ox Timothy when he's out o' yoke; and he's as ugly a beast to manage as ever I see when he ain't yoked up. Why bless you! there ha'n't been a thing done on the farm this five years but just what he liked—*she* don't know it. I've heerd her," said Sam chuckling,—"I've heerd her a telling him how she wanted this thing done, and t'other, and he'd just not say a word and go and do it right t'other way. It'll be a wonder if somebody ain't considerably startled in her calculations 'afore summer's out."

CHAPTER XLII.

She enjoys sure peace for evermore,
As weather-beaten ship arrived on happy shore.
SPENSER.

IT was impossible at first to make Mr. Humphreys believe that Alice was right in her notion about her health. The greatness of the evil was such that his mind refused to receive it, much as Ellen's had done. His unbelief however lasted longer than hers. Constantly with Alice as she was, and talking to her on the subject, Ellen slowly gave up the hope she had clung to; though still, bending all her energies to the present pleasure and comfort of her adopted sister, her mind shrank from looking at the end. Daily and hourly, in every way, she strove to be what Alice said she was, a comfort to her, and she succeeded. Daily and hourly Alice's look and smile and manner said the same thing over and over. It was Ellen's precious reward, and in seeking to earn it she half the time earned another in forgetting herself. It was different with Mr. Humphreys. He saw much less of his daughter; and when he was with her, it was impossible for Alice, with all her efforts, to speak to him as freely and plainly as she was in the habit of speaking to Ellen. The consequences were such as grieved her, but could not be helped.

As soon as it was known that her health was failing, Sophia Marshman came and took up her abode at the parsonage. Ellen was almost sorry; it broke up in a measure the sweet and peaceful way of life she and Alice had held together ever since her own coming. Miss Sophia could not make a third in their conversations. But as Alice's strength grew less and she needed more attendance and help, it was plain her friend's being there was a happy thing for both Alice and Ellen. Miss Sophia was active, cheerful, untiring in her affectionate care, always pleasant in manner and temper; a very useful person in a house where one was ailing. Mrs. Vawse was often there too, and to her Ellen clung, whenever she came, as to a pillar of strength. Miss Sophia could do nothing to help *her;* Mrs. Vawse could, a great deal.

Alice had refused to write or allow others to write to her brother. She said he was just finishing his course of study at Doncaster; she would not have him disturbed or broken off by bad news from home. In August he would be quite through; the first of August he would be home.

Before the middle of June, however, her health began to fail much more rapidly than she had counted upon. It became too likely that if she waited for his regular return at the first of August she would see but little of her brother. She at last reluctantly consented that Mrs. Chauncey should write to him; and from that moment counted the days.

Her father had scarcely till now given up his old confidence respecting her. He came into her room one morning when just about to set out for Carra-carra to visit one or two of his poor parishioners.

"How are you to day, my daughter?" he asked tenderly.

"Easy, papa,—and happy," said Alice.

"You are looking better," said he. "We shall have you well again among us yet."

There was some sorrow for him in Alice's smile, as she looked up at him and answered, "Yes, papa,—in the land where the inhabitant shall no more say 'I am sick.'"

He kissed her hastily and went out.

"I almost wish I was in your place, Alice," said Miss Sophia. "I hope I may be half as happy when my time comes."

"What right have you to hope so, Sophia?" said Alice, rather sadly.

"To be sure," said the other, after a pause, "you have been ten times as good as I. I don't wonder you feel easy when you look back and think how blameless your life has been."

"Sophia, Sophia!" said Alice,—"you know it is not that. I

never did a good thing in all my life that was not mixed and spoiled with evil.   I never came up to the full measure of duty in any matter."

"But surely," said Miss Sophia,—"if one does the best one can, it will be accepted?"

"It won't do to trust to that, Sophia.   God's law requires perfection; and nothing less than perfection will be received as payment of its demand.   If you owe a hundred dollars, and your creditor will not hold you quit for any thing less than the whole sum, it is of no matter of signification whether you offer him ten or twenty."

"Why according to that," said Miss Sophia. "it makes no difference what kind of life one leads."

Alice sighed and shook her head.

"The fruit shows what the tree is.   Love to God *will* strive to please him—always."

"And is it of no use to strive to please him?"

"Of no manner of use, if you make that your *trust*."

"Well I don't see what one *is* to trust to," said Miss Sophia,—"if it isn't a good life."

"I will answer you," said Alice, with a smile in which there was no sorrow,—"in some words that I love very much, of an old Scotchman, I think;—' I have taken all my good deeds and all my bad, and have cast them together in a heap before the Lord; and from them all I have fled to Jesus Christ, and in him alone I have sweet peace.'"

Sophia was silenced for a minute by her look.

"Well," said she, "I don't understand it; that is what George is always talking about; but I can't understand him."

"I am *very* sorry you cannot," said Alice gravely.

They were both silent for a little while.

"If all Christians were like you," said Miss Sophia, "I might think more about it; but they are such a dull set ; there seems to be no life nor pleasure among them."

Alice thought of these lines,—

> Their pleasures rise to things unseen,
>   Beyond the bounds of time;
> Where neither eyes nor ears have been,
>   Nor thoughts of mortals climb.

"You judge," said she, "like the rest of the world, of that which they see not.   After all, *they* know best whether they are happy.   What do you think of Mrs. Vawse?"

"I don't know what to think of her; she is wonderful to me; she is past my comprehension entirely.   Don' t make *her* an example."

" No, religion has done that for me. What do you think of your brother ?"

" George—*He* is happy,—there is no doubt of that ; he is the happiest person in the family, by all odds ; but then—I think he has a natural knack at being happy ;—it is impossible for any thing to put him out."

Alice smiled and shook her head again.

" Sophistry, Sophia. What do you think of *me ?*"

" I don't see what reason you have to be any thing but happy."

" What have I to make me so ?"

Sophia was silent. Alice laid her thin hand upon hers.

" I am leaving all I love in this world. Should I be happy if I were not going to somewhat I love better ? Should I be happy if I had no secure prospect of meeting with them again ?—or if I were doubtful of my reception in that place whither I hope to go ?"

Sophia burst into tears. " Well I don't know," said she ; " I suppose you are right ; but I don't understand it."

Alice drew her face down to hers and whispered something in her ear.

Undoubtedly Alice had much around as well as within her to make a declining life happy. Mrs. Vawse and Miss Marshman were two friends and nurses not to be surpassed, in their different ways. Margery's motherly affection, her zeal, and her skill, left nothing for heart to wish in her line of duty. And all that affection, taste, and kindness, which abundant means could supply, was at Alice's command.—Still her greatest comfort was Ellen. Her constant thoughtful care ; the thousand tender attentions, from the roses daily gathered for her table to the chapters she read and the hymns she sung to her ; the smile that often covered a pang ; the pleasant words and tone that many a time came from a sinking heart ; they were Alice's daily and nightly cordial. Ellen had learned self-command in more than one school ; affection, as once before, was her powerful teacher now, and taught her well. Sophia openly confessed that Ellen was the best nurse ; and Margery, when nobody heard her, muttered blessings on the child's head.

Mr. Humphreys came in often to see his daughter, but never stayed long. It was plain he could not bear it. It might have been difficult too for Alice to bear, but she wished for her brother. She reckoned the time from Mrs. Chauncey's letter to that when he might be looked for ; but some irregularities in the course of the post-office made it impossible to count with certainty upon the exact time of his arrival. Meanwhile her failure was very rapid. Mrs. Vawse began to fear he would not arrive in time.

The weeks of June ran out ; the roses, all but a few late kinds, blossomed and died ; July came.

One morning when Ellen went into her room, Alice drew her close to her and said, "You remember, Ellie, in the Pilgrim's Progress, when Christiana and her companions were sent to go over the river?—I think the messenger has come for me. You mustn't cry, love;—listen—this is the token he seems to bring me,—'I have loved thee with an everlasting love.' I am sure of it, Ellie; I have no doubt of it;—so don't cry for me. You have been my dear comfort, my blessing—we shall love each other in heaven, Ellie."

Alice kissed her earnestly several times, and then Ellen escaped from her arms and fled away. It was long before she could come

back again. But she came at last; and went on through all that day as she had done for weeks before. The day seemed long, for every member of the family was on the watch for John's arrival, and it was thought his sister would not live to see another. It wore away; hour after hour passed without his coming; and the night fell. Alice showed no impatience, but she evidently wished and watched for him; and Ellen, whose affection read her face and knew what to make of the look at the opening door,—the eye turned toward the window,—the attitude of listening,—grew feverish with her intense desire that she should be gratified.

From motives of convenience, Alice had moved up stairs to a room that John generally occupied when he was at home; directly over the sitting-room, and with pleasant windows toward the east. Mrs. Chauncey, Miss Sophia, and Mrs. Vawse, were all there. Alice was lying quietly on the bed, and seemed to be dozing ; but Ellen noticed, after lights were brought, that every now and then she opened her eyes and gave an inquiring look round the room. Ellen could not bear it ; slipping softly out she went down stairs and seated herself on the threshold of the glass door, as if by watching there she could be any nearer the knowledge of what she wished for.

It was a perfectly still summer night. The moon shone brightly on the little lawn and poured its rays over Ellen, just as it had done one well-remembered evening near a year ago. Ellen's thoughts went back to it. How like and how unlike ! All around was just the same as it had been then ; the cool moonlight upon the distant fields, the trees in the gap lit up, as then, the lawn a flood of brightness. But there was no happy party gathered there now ; — they were scattered. One was away ; one a sorrowful watcher alone in the moonlight ;—one waiting to be gone where there is no need of moon or stars for evermore. Ellen almost wondered they could shine so bright upon those that had no heart to rejoice in them ; she thought they looked down coldly and un-feelingly upon her distress. She remembered the whip-poor-will ; none was heard to-night, near or far ; she was glad of it ; it would have been too much ;—and there were no fluttering leaves ; the air was absolutely still. Ellen looked up again at the moon and stars. They shone calmly on, despite the reproaches she cast upon them ; and as she still gazed up toward them in their purity and stead-fastness, other thoughts began to come into her head of that which was more pure still, and more steadfast. How long they have been shining, thought Ellen ;—going on just the same from night to night and from year to year,—as if they never would come to an end. But they *will* come to an end—the time *will* come when they stop shining—bright as they are ; and then, when all they are swept away, then heaven will be only begun ; that will never end !—never. And in a few years we who were so happy a year ago and are so sorry now, shall be all glad together there,—this will be all over !—And then as she looked, and the tears sprang to her thoughts, a favorite hymn of Alice's came to her remembrance.

> Ye stars are but the shining dust
>   Of my divine abode ;
> The pavements of those heavenly courts
>   Where I shall see my God.

> The Father of eternal lights
>   Shall there his beams display ;
> And not one moment's darkness mix
>   With that unvaried day.

"Not one moment's darkness!" "Oh," thought little Ellen,— "there are a great many here!"—Still gazing up at the bright calm heavens, while the tears ran fast down her face, and fell into her lap, there came trooping through Ellen's mind many of those words she had been in the habit of reading to her mother and Alice, and which she knew and loved so well.

"And there shall be no night there; and they need no candle, neither light of the sun; for the Lord God giveth them light: and they shall reign for ever and ever. And there shall be no more curse, but the throne of God and of the Lamb shall be in it; and his servants shall serve him; and they shall see his face; and his name shall be in their foreheads. And God shall wipe away all tears from their eyes; and there shall be no more death, neither sorrow, nor crying, neither shall there be any more pain: for the former things have passed away.

"And if I go and prepare a place for you, I will come again and receive you unto myself; that where I am, there ye may be also."

While Ellen was yet going over and over these precious things, with a strong sense of their preciousness in all her throbbing grief, there came to her ear through the perfect stillness of the night the faint, far-off, not-to-be-mistaken sound of quick-coming horse's feet,—nearer and nearer every second. It came with a mingled pang of pain and pleasure, both very acute; she rose instantly to her feet, and stood pressing her hand to her heart while the quick-measured beat of hoofs grew louder and louder, until it ceased at the very door. The minutes were few, but they were moments of intense bitterness. The tired horse stooped his head, as the rider flung himself from the saddle and came to the door where Ellen stood fixed. A look asked, and a look answered, the question that lips could not speak. Ellen only pointed the way, and uttered the words, "up stairs;" and John rushed thither. He checked himself however at the door of the room, and opened it and went in as calmly as if he had but come from a walk. But his caution was very needless. Alice knew his step, she knew *his horse's step* too well; she had raised herself up and stretched out both arms toward him before he entered. In another moment they were round his neck, and she was supported in his. There was a long, long silence.

"Are you happy, Alice?" whispered her brother.

"Perfectly. This was all I wanted. Kiss me, dear John."

As he did so, again and again, she felt his tears on her cheek, and put up her hands to his face to wipe them away; kissed him then, and then once again laid her head on his breast. They remained so a little while without stirring; except that some whispers were exchanged too low for others to hear, and once more she raised her face to kiss him. A few minutes after those who could look saw his colour change, he felt the arms unclasp their hold; and as he laid her gently back on the pillow they fell languidly down; the will and the power that had sustained them were gone. *Alice* was gone; but the departing spirit had left a ray of brightness on its earthly house; there was a half smile on the sweet face, of most entire peace and satisfaction. Her brother looked for a moment,—closed the eyes,—kissed, once and again, the sweet lips, —and left the room.

Ellen saw him no more that night, nor knew how he passed it. For her, wearied with grief and excitement, it was spent in long heavy slumber. From the pitch to which her spirits had been wrought by care, sorrow, and self-restraint, they now suddenly and completely sank down; naturally and happily, she lost all sense of trouble in sleep.

When sleep at last left her, and she stole down stairs into the sitting-room in the morning, it was rather early. Nobody was stirring about the house but herself. It seemed deserted; the old sitting-room looked empty and forlorn; the stillness was oppressive. Ellen could not bear it. Softly opening the glass door she went out upon the lawn where every thing was sparkling in the early freshness of the summer morning. How could it look so pleasant without, when all pleasantness was gone within?—It pressed upon Ellen's heart. With a restless feeling of pain, she went on, round the corner of the house, and paced slowly along the road till she came to the foot-path that led up to the place on the mountain John had called the Bridge of the Nose. Ellen took that path, often travelled and much loved by her; and slowly, with slow-dripping tears, made her way up over moss wet with the dew, and the stones and rocks with which the rough way was strewn. She passed the place where Alice had first found her,—she remembered it well;—there was the very stone beside which they had kneeled together, and where Alice's folded hands were laid. Ellen knelt down beside it again, and for a moment laid her cheek to the cold stone while her arms embraced it, and a second time it was watered with tears. She rose up again quickly and went on her way, toiling up the steep path beyond, till she turned the edge of the mountain and stood on the old place where she and Alice that evening had watched the setting sun. Many a setting sun they had watched from thence; it had been a favourite pleasure of them both to run up there for a few minutes before or after tea and see the sun go down at the far end of the long valley. It seemed to Ellen one of Alice's haunts; she missed her there; and the thought went keenly home that there she would come with her no more. She sat down on the stone she called her own, and leaning her head on Alice's which was close by, she wept bitterly, yet not very long;

she was too tired and subdued for bitter weeping; she raised her head again, and wiping away her tears looked abroad over the beautiful landscape. Never more beautiful than then.

The early sun filled the valley with patches of light and shade. The sides and tops of the hills looking toward the east were bright with the cool brightness of the morning; beyond and between them deep shadows lay. The sun could not yet look at that side of the mountain where Ellen sat, nor at the long reach of ground it screened from his view, stretching from the mountain foot to the other end of the valley; but to the left, between that and the Cat's back, the rays of the sun streamed through, touching the houses of the village, showing the lake, and making every tree and barn and clump of wood in the distance stand out in bright relief. Deliciously cool, both the air and the light, though a warm day was promised. The night had swept away all the heat of yesterday. Now, the air was fresh with the dew and sweet from hayfield and meadow; and the birds were singing like mad all around. There was no answering echo in the little human heart that looked and listened. Ellen loved all these things too well not to notice them even now; she felt their full beauty; but she felt it sadly. "*She* will look at it no more!" she said to herself. But instantly came an answer to her thought;—"Behold I create new heavens, and a new earth; and the former shall not be remembered, nor come into mind. Thy sun shall no more go down; neither shall thy moon withdraw itself: for the Lord shall be thine everlasting light, and the days of thy mourning shall be ended."

"She is there now," thought Ellen,—"she is happy,—why should I be sorry for her? I am not; but oh! I must be sorry for myself—Oh, Alice!—dear Alice!"

She wept; but then again came sweeping over her mind the words with which she was so familiar,—"the days of thy mourning shall be ended;" and again with her regret mingled the consciousness that it must be for herself alone. And for herself,— "Can I not trust Him whom she trusted?" she thought. Somewhat soothed and more calm, she sat still looking down into the brightening valley or off to the hills that stretched away on either hand of it; when up through the still air the sound of the little Carra-carra church bell came to her ear. It rang for a minute and then stopped.

It crossed Ellen's mind to wonder what it could be ringing for at that time of day; but she went back to her musings and had entirely forgotten it, when again, clear and full through the stillness the sound came pealing up.

"One—two!"

Ellen knew now! It went through her very heart.

It is the custom in the country to toll the church bell upon occasion of the death of any one in the township or parish. A few strokes are rung by way of drawing attention; these are followed after a little pause by a single one if the knell is for man, or two for a woman. Then another short pause. Then follows the number of the years the person has lived, told in short, rather slow strokes, as one would count them up. After pausing once more the tolling begins, and is kept up for some time; the strokes following in slow and sad succession, each one being permitted to die quite away before another breaks upon the ear.

Ellen had been told of this custom, but habit had never made it familiar. Only once she had happened to hear this notice of death given out; and that was long ago; the bell could not be heard at Miss Fortune's house. It came upon her now with all the force of novelty and surprise. As the number of the years of Alice's life was sadly tolled out, every.stroke was to her as if it fell upon a raw nerve. Ellen hid her face in her lap and tried to keep from counting, but she could not; and as the tremulous sound of the last of the twenty-four died away upon the air, she was shuddering from head to foot. A burst of tears relieved her when the sound ceased.

Just then a voice close beside her said low, as if the speaker might not trust its higher tones,—" I will lift up mine eyes unto the hills, from whence cometh my help !"

How differently *that* sound struck upon Ellen's ear ! With an indescribable air of mingled tenderness, weariness, and sorrow, she slowly rose from her seat and put both her arms round the speaker's neck. Neither said a word; but to Ellen the arm that held her was more than all words; it was the dividing line between her and the world,—on this side every thing, on that side nothing.

No word was spoken for many minutes.

" My dear Ellen," said her brother softly,—" how came you here ?"

" I don't know," whispered Ellen,—" there was nobody there—I couldn't stay in the house."

" Shall we go home now ?"

" Oh, yes—whenever you please.

But neither moved yet. Ellen had raised her head; she still stood with her arm upon her brother's shoulder; the eyes of both were on the scene before them; the thoughts of neither. He presently spoke again.

" Let us try to love our God better, Ellie, the less we have left to love in this world ;—that is his meaning—let sorrow but bring us closer to him. Dear Alice is well—she is well,—and if *we* are made to suffer, we know and we love the hand that has done it,—do we not Ellie ?"

Ellen put her hands to her face; she thought her heart would break. He gently drew her to a seat on the stone beside him, and still keeping his arm round her, slowly and soothingly went on—

"Think that she is happy;—think that she is safe;—think that she is with that blessed One whose face we seek at a distance,—satisfied with his likeness instead of wearily struggling with sin;—think that sweetly and easily she has got home; and it is our home too. We must weep, because we are left alone; but for her—'I heard a voice from heaven saying unto me, Blessed are the dead that die in the Lord!'"

As he spoke in low and sweet tones, Ellen's tears calmed and stopped; but she still kept her hands to her face.

"Shall we go home, Ellie?" said her brother after another silence. She rose up instantly and said yes. But he held her still, and looking for a moment at the tokens of watching and grief and care in her countenance, he gently kissed the pale little face, adding a word of endearment which almost broke Ellen's heart again. Then taking her hand they went down the mountain together.

CHAPTER XLIII.

I have seen angels by the sick one's pillow;
  Theirs was the soft tone and the soundless tread,
Where smitten hearts were drooping like the willow,
  They stood 'between the living and the dead.'

UNKNOWN.

THE whole Marshman family arrived to-day from Ventnor; some to see Alice's loved remains, and all to follow them to the grave. The parsonage could not hold so many; the two Mr. Marshmans, therefore, with Major and Mrs. Gillespie, made their quarters at Thirlwall. Margery's hands were full enough with those that were left.

In the afternoon however she found time for a visit to the room, *the* room. She was standing at the foot of the bed, gazing on the sweet face she loved so dearly, when Mrs. Chauncey and Mrs. Vawse came up for the same purpose. All three stood some time in silence.

The bed was strewn with flowers, somewhat singularly disposed. Upon the pillow, and upon and about the hands which were folded on the breast, were scattered some of the rich late roses,—roses and rose-buds, strewn with beautiful and profuse carelessness. A single stem of white lilies lay on the side of the bed; the rest of the flowers, a large quantity, covered the feet, seeming to have been flung there without any attempt at arrangement. They were of various kinds, chosen however with exquisite taste and feeling. Besides the roses, there were none that were not either white or distinguished for their fragrance. The delicate white verbena, the pure feverfew, mignonette, sweet geranium, white myrtle, the rich-scented heliotrope, were mingled with the late-blossoming damask and purple roses; no yellow flowers, no purple except those mentioned; even the flaunting petunia, though white, had been left out by the nice hand that had culled them. But the arranging of these beauties seemed to have been little more than attempted; though indeed it might be questioned whether the finest heart could have bettered the effect of what the over-tasked hand of affection had left half done. Mrs. Chauncey however after a while began slowly to take a flower or two from the foot and place them on other parts of the bed.

"Will Mrs. Chauncey pardon my being so bold," said Margery then, who had looked on with no pleasure while this was doing,—"but if she had seen when those flowers were put there,—it wouldn't be her wish, I am sure it wouldn't be her wish, to stir one of them."

Mrs. Chauncey's hand, which was stretched out for a fourth, drew back.

"Why who put them there?" she asked.

"Miss Ellen, ma'am."

"Where is Ellen?"

"I think she is sleeping, ma'am. Poor child! she's the most wearied of us all with sorrow and watching," said Margery weeping.

"You saw her bring them up, did you?"

"I saw her, ma'am. Oh, will I ever forget it as long as I live!"

"Why?" said Mrs. Chauncey gently.

"It's a thing one should have seen, ma'am, to understand. I don't know as i can tell in well."

Seeing however that Mrs. Chauncey still looked her wish, Margery went on, half under her breath.

"Why, ma'am, the way it was,—I had come up to get some linen out of the closet, for I had watched my time; Mrs. Chauncey sees, I was afeard of finding Mr. John here, and I knew he was lying down just then, so——"

"Lying down, was he?" said Mrs. Vawse. "I did not know he had taken any rest to-day."

"It was very little he took, ma'am, indeed, though there was need enough I am sure;—he had been up with his father the live-long blessed night. And then the first thing this morning he was away after Miss Ellen, poor child! wherever she had betaken herself to; I happened to see her before any body was out, going round the corner of the house, and so I knew when he asked me for her."

" Was she going after flowers *then ?*" said Mrs. Chauncey.

" Oh, no, ma'am,—it was a long time after ; it was this morning
some time.—I had come up to the linen closet, knowing Mr. John
was in his room, and I thought I was safe ; and I had just taken
two or three pieces on my arm, you know, ma'am, when somehow
I forgot myself, and forgot what I had come for, and leaving what
I should ha' been a doing, I was standing there, looking out this
way at the dear features I never thought to see in death—and I
had entirely forgotten what I was there for, ma'am,—when I heard
Miss Ellen's little footstep coming softly up stairs.   I didn't want
her to catch sight of me just then, so I had just drew myself back
a bit, so as I could see her without her seeing me back in the closet
where I was.   But it had like to have got the better of me entirely,
ma'am, when I see her come in with a lap full of them flowers,
and looking so as she did too ! but with much trouble I kept quiet.
She went up and stood by the side of the bed, just where Mrs.
Chauncey is standing, with her sweet sad little face,—it's the
hardest thing to see a child's face look so,—and the flowers all
gathered up in her frock.   It was odd to see her, she didn't cry,—
not at all—only once I saw her brow wrinkle, but it seemed as if she
had a mind not to, for she put her hand up to her face and held it
a little, and then she began to take out the flowers one by one, and
she'd lay a rose here and a rose-bud there, and so ; and then she
went round to the other side and laid the lilies, and two or three
more roses there on the pillow.   But I could see all the while it
was getting too much for her ; I see very soon she wouldn't get
through ; she just placed two or three more, and one rose there in
that hand, and that was the last.   I could see it working in her
face ; she turned as pale as her lilies all at once, and just tossed up
all the flowers out of her frock on the bed-foot there,—that's just
as they fell,—and down she went on her knees, and her face in her
hands on the side of the bed.   I thought no more about my linen,"
said Margery weeping,—" I couldn't do any thing but look at that
child kneeling there, and her flowers,—and all beside her she used
to call her sister, and that couldn't be a sister to her no more ; and
she's without a sister now to be sure, poor child !"

" She has a brother, unless I am mistaken," said Mrs. Chauncey,
when she could speak.

" And that's just what I was going to tell you, ma'am.   She had
been there five or ten minutes without moving, or more—I am sure
I don't know how long it was, I didn't think how time went,—when
the first thing I knew I heard another step, and Mr. John came in.
I thought, and expected, he was taking some sleep ; but I suppose,"
said Margery sighing, " he couldn't rest. I knew his step and just
drew myself back further.   He came just where you are, ma'am,
and stood with his arms folded a long time looking.   I don't know

how Miss Ellen didn't hear him come in; but however she didn't;
—and they were both as still as death, one on one side, and the
other on the other side. And I wondered he didn't see her; but
her white dress and all—and I suppose he had no thought but for
one thing. I knew the first minute he did see her, when he looked
over and spied her on the other side of the bed;—I see his colour
change; and then his mouth took the look it always did whenever
he sets himself to do any thing. He stood a minute, and then he
went round and knelt down beside of her, and softly took away one
of her hands from under her face, and held it in both of his own,
and then he made such a prayer!—Oh," said Margery, her tears
falling fast at the recollection,—"I never heard the like! I never
did! He gave thanks for Miss Alice, and he had reason enough
to be sure,—and for himself and Miss Ellen—I wondered to hear
him!—and he prayed for them too, and others,—and—oh, I thought
I couldn't stand and hear him; and I was afeard to breathe the
whole time, lest he would know I was there. It was the beauti-
fullest prayer I did ever hear, or ever shall, however."

"And how did Ellen behave?" said Mrs. Chauncey, when she
could speak.

"She didn't stir, nor make the least motion nor sound, till he had
done, and spoke to her. They stood a little while then, and Mr.
John put the rest of the flowers up there round her hands and the
pillow,—Miss Ellen hadn't put more than half a dozen;—I noticed how he kept hold of Miss Ellen's hand all the time. I heard
her begin to tell him how she didn't finish the flowers, and he told
her, 'I saw it all, Ellie,' he said; and he said 'it didn't want finishing.' I wondered how he should see it, but I suppose he did,
however. *I* understood it very well. They went away down stairs
after that."

"He is beautifully changed," said Mrs. Vawse.

"I don't know, ma'am," said Margery,—"I've heard that said
afore, but I can't say as I ever could see it. He always was the
same to me—always the honourablest, truest, noblest—my husband
says he was a bit fiery, but I never could tell that the one temper
was sweeter than the other; only every body always did whatever
Mr. John wanted, to be sure; but he was the perfectest gentleman,
always."

"I have not seen either Mr. John or Ellen since my mother came,"
said Mrs. Chauncey.

"No, ma'am," said Margery,—"they were out reading under
the trees for a long time; and Miss Ellen came in the kitchen-way
a little while ago and went to lie down."

"How is Mr. Humphreys?"

"Oh, I can't tell you, ma'am,—he is worse than any one knows
of I am afraid, unless Mr. John; you will not see him, ma'am; he

has not been here once, nor don't mean to, I think. It will go hard with my poor master, I am afraid," said Margery weeping;— "dear Miss Alice said Miss Ellen was to take her place; but it would want an angel to do that."

"Ellen will do a great deal," said Mrs. Vawse;—"Mr. Humphreys loves her well now, I know."

"So do I, ma'am, I am sure; and so does every one; but still—"

Margery broke off her sentence and sorrowfully went down stairs. Mrs. Chauncey moved no more flowers.

Late in the afternoon of the next day Margery came softly into Ellen's room.

"Miss Ellen, dear, you are awake, aren't you?"

"Yes, Margery," said Ellen, sitting up on the bed;—"come in. What is it?"

"I came to ask Miss Ellen if she *could* do me a great favour; —there's a strange gentleman come, and nobody has seen him yet, and it don't seem right. He has been here this some time."

"Have you told Mr. John?"

"No, Miss Ellen; he's in the library with my master; and somehow I durstn't go to the door; mayhap they wouldn't be best pleased. *Would* Miss Ellen mind telling Mr. John of the gentleman's being here?"

Ellen would mind it very much, there was no doubt of that; Margery could hardly have asked her to put a greater force upon herself; she did not say so.

"You are sure he is there, Margery?"

"I am quite sure, Miss Ellen. I am very sorry to disturb you; but if you wouldn't mind—I am ashamed to have the gentleman left to himself so long."

"I'll do it, Margery."

She got up, slipped on her shoes, and mechanically smoothing her hair, set off to the library. On the way she almost repented her willingness to oblige Margery; the errand was marvellous disagreeable to her. She had never gone to that room except with Alice; never entered it uninvited. She could hardly make up her mind to knock at the door. But she had promised; it must be done.

The first fearful tap was too light to arouse any mortal ears. At the second, though not much better, she heard some one move, and John opened the door. Without waiting to hear her speak he immediately drew her in, very unwillingly on her part, and led her silently up to his father. The old gentleman was sitting in his great study-chair with a book open at his side. He turned from it as she came up, took her hand in his, and held it for a few moments without speaking. Ellen dared not raise her eyes.

"My little girl," said he very gravely, though not without a tone of kindness too,—" are you coming here to cheer my loneliness ?"

Ellen in vain struggled to speak an articulate word ; it was impossible ; she suddenly stooped down and touched her lips to the hand that lay on the arm of the chair. He put the hand tenderly upon her head.

" God bless you," said he, " abundantly, for all the love you showed *her*. Come,—if you will,—and be, as far as a withered heart will let you, all that she wished. All is yours—except what will be buried with her."

Ellen was awed and pained very much. Not because the words and manner were sad and solemn ; it was the *tone* that distressed her. There was no tearfulness in it ; it trembled a little ; it seemed to come indeed from a withered heart. She shook with the effort she made to control herself. John asked her presently what she had come for.

"A gentleman," said Ellen,—" there's a gentleman—a stranger—"

He went immediately out to see him, leaving her standing there. Ellen did not know whether to go too or stay ; she thought from his not taking her with him he wished her to stay ; she stood doubtfully. Presently she heard steps coming back along the hall— steps of two persons—the door opened, and the strange gentleman came in. No stranger to Ellen ! she knew him in a moment ; it was her old friend, her friend of the boat,—Mr. George Marshman.

Mr. Humphreys rose up to meet him, and the two gentlemen shook hands in silence. Ellen had at first shrunk out of the way to the other side of the room, and now when she saw an opportunity she was going to make her escape ; but John gently detained her ; and she stood still by his side, though with a kind of feeling that it was not there the best place or time for her old friend to recognise her. He was sitting by Mr. Humphreys and for the present quite occupied with him. Ellen thought nothing of what they were saying ; with eyes eagerly fixed upon Mr. Marshman she was reading memory's long story over again. The same pleasant look and kind tone that she remembered so well came to comfort her in her first sorrow,—the old way of speaking, and even of moving an arm or hand, the familiar figure and face ; how they took Ellen's thoughts back to the deck of the steamboat, the hymns, the talks ; the love and kindness that led and persuaded her so faithfully and effectually to do her duty ;—it was all present again ; and Ellen gazed at him as at a picture of the past, forgetting for the moment every thing else. The same love and kindness were endeavouring now to say something for Mr. Humphreys' relief ; it was a hard task. The old gentleman heard and answered, for the most part briefly, but so as to show that his friend laboured in vain ; the bitterness and hardness of grief were unallayed yet. It was not till John made some slight remark that Mr. Marshman turned his head that way; he looked for a moment in some surprise, and then said, his countenance lightening, "Is that Ellen Montgomery?"

Ellen sprang across at that word to take his out-stretched hand. But as she felt the well-remembered grasp of it, and met the old look the thought of which she had treasured up for years,—it was too much. Back as in a flood to her heart, seemed to come at once all the thoughts and feelings of the time since then;—the difference of this meeting from the joyful one she had so often pictured to herself; the sorrow of that time mixed with the sorrow now; and the sense that the very hand that had wiped those first tears away was the one now laid in the dust by death. All thronged on her heart at once; and it was too much. She had scarce touched Mr. Marshman's hand when she hastily withdrew her own, and gave way to an overwhelming burst of sorrow. It was infectious. There was such an utter absence of all bitterness or hardness in the tone of this grief; there was so touching an expression of submission mingled with it, that even Mr. Humphreys was overcome. Ellen was not the only subdued weeper there; not the only one whose tears came from a broken-up heart. For a few minutes the silence of stifled sobs was in the room, till Ellen recovered enough to make her escape; and then the colour of sorrow was lightened, in one breast at least.

"Brother," said Mr. Humphreys,—" I can hear you now better than I could a little while ago. I had almost forgotten that God is good. 'Light in the darkness;'—I see it now. That child has given me a lesson."

Ellen did not know what had passed around her, nor what had followed her quitting the room. But she thought when John came to the tea-table he looked relieved. If his general kindness and tenderness of manner toward herself *could* have been greater than usual, she might have thought it was that night; but she only thought he felt better.

Mr. Marshman was not permitted to leave the house. He was a great comfort to every body. Not himself overburdened with sorrow, he was able to make that effort for the good of the rest which no one yet had been equal to. The whole family, except Mr. Humphreys, were gathered together at this time; and his grave cheerful unceasing kindness made that by far the most comfortable meal that had been taken. It was exceeding grateful to Ellen to see and hear him, from the old remembrance as well as the present effect. And he had not forgotten his old kindness for her; she saw it in his look, his words, his voice, shown in every way; and the feeling that she had got her old friend again and should never lose him now gave her more deep pleasure than any thing else could possibly have done at that time. His own family too had not seen him in a long time, so his presence was matter of general satisfaction.

Later in the evening Ellen was sitting beside him on the sofa, looking and listening,—he was like a piece of old music to her,—when John came to the back of the sofa and said he wanted to speak to her. She went with him to the other side of the room.

"Ellie," said he in a low voice, "I think my father would like to hear you sing a hymn,—do you think you could?"

Ellen loooked up, with a peculiar mixture of uncertainty and resolution in her countenance, and said yes.

"Not if it will pain you too much,—and not unless you think you can surely go through with it, Ellen," he said gently.

"No," said Ellen ;—"I will try."

"Will it not give you too much pain? do you think you can?"

"No—I will try," she repeated.

As she went along the hall she said and resolved to herself that she *would* do it. The library was dark ; coming from the light Ellen at first could see nothing. John placed her in a chair, and went away himself to a little distance where he remained perfectly still. She covered her face with her hands for a minute, and prayed for strength ; she was afraid to try.

Alice and her brother were remarkable for beauty of voice and utterance. The latter Ellen had in part caught from them ; in the former she thought herself greatly inferior. Perhaps she underrated herself ; her voice, though not indeed powerful, was low and sweet and very clear ; and the entire simplicity and feeling with which she sang hymns was more effectual than any higher qualities of tone and compass. She had been very much accustomed to sing with Alice, who excelled in beautiful truth and simplicity of expression ; listening with delight, as she had often done, and often joining with her, Ellen had caught something of her manner.

She thought nothing of all this now ; she had a trying task to go through. Sing!—then, and there ! — And what should she sing? All that class of hymns that bore directly on the subject of their sorrow must be left on one side ; she hardly dared think of them. Instinctively she took up another class, that without baring the wound would lay the balm close to it. A few minutes of deep stillness were in the dark room ; then very low, and in tones that trembled a little, rose the words,

> How sweet the name of Jesus sounds
> In a believer's ear ;
> It soothes his sorrows, heals his wounds,
> And drives away his fear.

The tremble in her voice ceased, as she went on,—

> It makes the wounded spirit whole,
>   And calms the troubled breast;
> 'Tis manna to the hungry soul,
>   And to the weary, rest.
>
> By him my prayers acceptance gain,
>   Although with sin defiled;
> Satan accuses me in vain,
>   And I am owned a child.
>
> Weak is the effort of my heart,
>   And cold my warmest thought,--
> But when I see thee as thou art,
>   I'll praise thee as I ought.
>
> Till then I would thy love proclaim
>   With every lab'ring breath;
> And may the music of thy name
>   Refresh my soul in death.

Ellen paused a minute. There was not a sound to be heard in the room. She thought of the hymn, "Loving Kindness;" but the tune, and the spirit of the words, was too lively. Her mother's favourite, "'Tis my happiness below," but Ellen could not venture that; she strove to forget it as fast as possible. She sang, clearly and sweetly as ever now,

> Hark my soul, it is the Lord,
> 'Tis thy Saviour, hear his word;—
> Jesus speaks, and speaks to thee,
> "Say, poor sinner, lovest thou me?
>
> "I delivered thee when bound,
> And when bleeding healed thy wound;
> Sought thee wandering, set thee right,
> Turned thy darkness into light.
>
> "Can a mother's tender care
> Cease toward the child she bare?
> Yea—*she* may forgetful be,
> Yet will I remember thee.
>
> "Mine is an unchanging love;
> Higher than the heights above,
> Deeper than the depths beneath,
> Free and faithful, strong as death.
>
> "Thou shalt see my glory soon,
> When the work of life is done,
> Partner of my throne shalt be,—
> Say, poor sinner, lovest thou me?"
>
> Lord, it is my chief complaint
> That my love is weak and faint;
> Yet I love thee and adore,—
> Oh, for grace to love thee more!

Ellen's task was no longer painful, but most delightful. She hoped she was doing some good; and that hope enabled her, after the first trembling beginning, to go on without any difficulty. She was not thinking of herself. It was very well she could not see the effect upon her auditors. Through the dark her eyes could only just discern a dark figure stretched upon the sofa and another standing by the mantel-piece. The room was profoundly still, except when she was singing. The choice of hymns gave her the greatest trouble. She thought of " Jerusalem, my happy home," but it would not do; she and Alice had too often sung it in strains of joy. Happily came to her mind the beautiful,

" How firm a foundation, ye saints of the Lord," &c.

She went through all the seven long verses. Still when Ellen paused at the end of this, the breathless silence seemed to invite her to go on. She waited a minute to gather breath. The blessed words had gone down into her very heart; did they ever seem half so sweet before? She was cheered and strengthened, and thought she could go through with the next hymn, though it had been much loved and often used, both by her mother and Alice.

> Jesus, lover of my soul,
> Let me to thy bosom fly,
> While the billows near me roll,
> While the tempest still is nigh.
> Hide me, O my Saviour, hide,
> Till the storm of life be past :—
> Safe into the haven guide,—
> O receive my soul at last !
>
> Other refuge have I none,
> Hangs my helpless soul on thee—
> Leave, ah ! leave me not alone !
> Still support and comfort me.
> All my trust on thee is stayed,
> All my help from thee I bring ;—
> Cover my defenceless head
> Beneath the shadow of thy wing.
>
> Thou, O Christ, art all I want ;
> More than all in thee I find ;
> Raise the fallen, cheer the faint,
> Heal the sick, and lead the blind.
> Just and holy is thy name,
> I am all unrighteousness ;
> Vile and full of sin I am,
> Thou art full of truth and grace.

Still silence ;—" silence that spoke !" Ellen did not know what it said, except that her hearers did not wish her to stop. Her next was a favourite hymn of them all.

" What are these in bright array," &c.

Ellen had allowed her thoughts to travel too far along with the words, for in the last lines her voice was unsteady and faint. She was fain to make a longer pause than usual to recover herself. But in vain; the tender nerve was touched; there was no stilling its quivering.

"Ellen"—said Mr. Humphreys then after a few minutes. She rose and went to the sofa. He folded her close to his breast.

"Thank you, my child," he said presently;—"you have been a comfort to me. Nothing but a choir of angels could have been sweeter."

As Ellen went away back through the hall her tears almost choked her; but for all that there was a strong throb of pleasure at her heart.

"I have been a comfort to him," she repeated. "Oh, dear Alice!—so I will."

CHAPTER XLIV.

A child no more!—a maiden now—
A graceful maiden with a gentle brow;
A cheek tinged lightly, and a dove-like eye,
And all hearts bless her as she passes by.
                                        MARY HOWITT.

THE whole Marshman family returned to Ventnor immediately after the funeral, Mr. George excepted; he stayed with Mr. Humphreys over the Sabbath, and preached for him; and much to every one's pleasure lingered still a day or two longer; then he was obliged to leave them. John also must go back to Doncaster for a few weeks; he would not be able to get home again before the early part of August. For the month between and as much longer indeed as possible, Mrs. Marshman wished to have Ellen at Ventnor; assuring her that it was to be her home always whenever she chose to make it so. At first neither Mrs. Marshman nor her daughters would take any denial; and old Mr. Marshman was fixed upon it. But Ellen begged with tears that she might stay at home and begin at once, as far as she could, to take Alice's place. Her kind friends insisted that it would do her harm to be left alone for so long, at such a season. Mr. Humphreys at the best of times kept very much to himself, and now he would more than ever; she would be very lonely. "But how lonely *he* will be if I go away!" said Ellen;—"I can't go." Finding that her heart was set upon it, and that it would be a real grief to her to go to Ventnor, John at last joined to excuse her; and he made an arrangement with Mrs. Vawse instead that she should come and stay with

Ellen at the parsonage till he came back. This gave Ellen great satisfaction; and her kind Ventnor friends were obliged unwillingly to leave her.

The first few days after John's departure were indeed sad days —very sad to every one; it could not be otherwise. Ellen drooped miserably. She had, however, the best possible companion in her old Swiss friend. Her good sense, her steady cheerfulness, her firm principle were always awake for Ellen's good, ever ready to comfort her, to cheer her, to prevent her from giving undue way to sorrow, to urge her to useful exertion. Affection and gratitude, to the living and the dead, gave powerful aid to these efforts. Ellen rose up in the morning and lay down at night with the present pressing wish to do and be for the ease and comfort of her adopted father and brother all that it was possible for her. Very soon, so soon as she could rouse herself to any thing, she began to turn over in her mind all manner of ways and means for this end. And in general, whatever Alice would have wished, what John did wish, was law to her.

"Margery," said Ellen one day, "I wish you would tell me all the things Alice used to do; so that I may begin to do them, you know, as soon as I can."

"What things, Miss Ellen?"

"I mean, the things she used to do about the house, or to help you,—don't you know?—all sorts of things. I want to know them all, so that I may do them as she did. I want to very much."

"Oh, Miss Ellen, dear," said Margery, tearfully, "you are too little and tender to do them things;—I'd be sorry to see you, indeed!"

"Why no, I am not, Margery," said Ellen; "don't you know how I used to do at aunt Fortune's? Now tell me—please, dear Margery! If I can't do it, I won't you know."

"Oh, Miss Ellen, she used to see to various things about the house;—I don't know as I can tell 'em all directly; some was to help me; and some to please her father or Mr. John, if he was at home; she thought of every one before herself, sure enough."

"Well what, Margery? what are they? Tell me all you can remember."

"Why, Miss Ellen,—for one thing,—she used to go into the library every morning, to put it in order, and dust the books and papers and things; in fact she took the charge of that room entirely; I never went into it at all, unless once or twice in the year, or to wash the windows."

Ellen looked grave; she thought with herself there might be a difficulty in the way of her taking this part of Alice's daily duties; she did not feel that she had the freedom of the library.

"And then," said Margery, "she used to skim the cream for me, most mornings, when I'd be busy; and wash up the breakfast things,—"

"Oh, I forgot all about the breakfast things!" exclaimed Ellen, —"how could I! I'll do them to be sure, after this. I never thought of them, Margery. And I'll skim the cream too."

"Dear Miss Ellen, I wouldn't want you to; I didn't mention it for that, but you was wishing me to tell you—I don't want you to trouble your dear little head about such work. It was more the thoughtfulness that cared about me than the help of all she could do, though that wasn't a little;—I'll get along well enough!—"

"But I should like to,—it would make me happier; and don't you think *I* want to help you too, Margery?"

"The Lord bless you, Miss Ellen," said Margery, in a sort of desperation, setting down one iron and taking up another, "don't talk in that way, or you'll upset me entirely.—I ain't a bit better than a child," said she, her tears falling fast on the sheet she was hurriedly ironing.

"What else, dear Margery?" said Ellen presently. "Tell me what else?"

"Well, Miss Ellen," said Margery, dashing away the water from either eye,—"she used to look over the clothes when they went up from the wash; and put them away; and mend them if there was any places wanted mending."

"I am afraid I don't know how to manage that," said Ellen very gravely.—"There is one thing I can do,—I can darn stockings very nicely; but that's only one kind of mending. I don't know much about the other kinds."

"Ah, well, but *she* did, however," said Margery, searching in her basket of clothes for some particular pieces. "A beautiful mender she was to be sure! Look here, Miss Ellen,—just see that patch—the way it is put on—so evenly by a thread all round; and the stitches, see—and see the way this rent is darned down;—oh, that was the way she did every thing!"

"I can't do it so," said Ellen sighing,—"but I can learn;—that I can do. You will teach me, Margery, won't you?"

"Indeed, Miss Ellen, dear, it's more than I can myself; but I will tell you who will; and that's Mrs. Vawse. I am thinking it was her she learned of in the first place,—but I ain't certain. Any how she's a first-rate hand."

"Then I'll get her to teach me," said Ellen;—"that will do very nicely. And now, Margery, what else?"

"Oh, dear, Miss Ellen,—I don't know,—there was a thousand little things that I'd only recollect at the minute; she'd set the table for me when my hands was uncommon full; and often she'd come out and make some little thing for the master when I wouldn't have the time to do the same myself;—and I can't tell—one can't think of those things but just at the minute. Dear Miss Ellen, I'd be sorry indeed to see you a trying your little hands to do all that she done.''

"Never mind, Margery,'' said Ellen, and she threw her arms round the kind old woman as she spoke,—"I won't trouble you—and you won't be troubled if I am awkward about any thing at first, will you?''

Margery could only throw down her holder to return most affectionately as well as respectfully Ellen's caress and press a very hearty kiss upon her forehead.

Ellen next went to Mrs. Vawse to beg her help in the mending and patching line. Her old friend was very glad to see her take up any thing with interest, and readily agreed to do her best in the matter. So some old clothes were looked up; pieces of linen, cotton, and flannel gathered together; a large basket found to hold all these rags of shape and no shape; and for the next week or two Ellen was indefatigable. She would sit making vain endeavours to arrange a large linen patch properly, till her cheeks were burning with excitement; and bend over a darn, doing her best to make invisible stitches, till Mrs. Vawse was obliged to assure her it was quite unnecessary to take *so much* pains. Taking pains, however, is the sure way to success. Ellen could not rest satisfied till she had equalled Alice's patching and darning; and though when Mrs. Vawse left her she had not quite reached that point, she was bidding fair to do so in a little while.

In other things she was more at home. She could skim milk well enough, and immediately began to do it for Margery. She at once also took upon herself the care of the parlour cupboard and all the things in it, which she well knew had been Alice's office; and thanks to Miss Fortune's training, even Margery was quite satisfied with her neat and orderly manner of doing it. Ellen begged her when the clothes came up from the wash, to show her where every thing went, so that for the future she might be able to put them away; and she studied the shelves of the linen closet, and the chests of drawers in Mr. Humphreys' room, till she almost knew them by heart. As to the library, she dared not venture. She saw Mr. Humphreys at meals and at prayers,—only then. He had never asked her to come into his study since the night she sang to him, and as for *her* asking—nothing could have been more impossible. Even when he was out of the house, out by the hour, Ellen never thought of going where she had not been expressly permitted to go.

When Mr. Van Brunt informed his wife of Ellen's purpose to desert her service and make her future home at the parsonage, the lady's astonishment was only less than her indignation; the latter

not at all lessened by learning that Ellen was to become the adopted
child of the house.   For a while her words of displeasure were
poured forth in a torrent; Mr. Van Brunt meantime saying very
little, and standing by like a steadfast rock that the waves dash
past, not *upon*.   She declared this was " the cap-sheaf of Miss
Humphreys' doing; she *might* have been wise enough to have expected as much ; she wouldn't have been such a fool if she had!
This was what she had let Ellen go there for ! a pretty return !''   But
she went on.   " She wondered who they thought they had to deal
with ; did they think she was going to let Ellen go in that way ?
she had the first and only right to her ; and Ellen had no more
business to go and give herself away than one of her oxen ; they
would find it out, she guessed, pretty quick ; Mr. John and all ;
she'd have her back in no time !''   What were her thoughts and
feelings, when after having spent her breath she found her husband
quietly opposed to this conclusion, words cannot tell.   *Her* words
could not ; she was absolutely dumb, till he had said his say ; and
then, appalled by the serenity of his manner she left indignation
on one side for the present and began to argue the matter.   But
Mr. Van Brunt coolly said he had promised ; she might get as many
help as she liked, he would pay for them and welcome ; but Ellen
would have to stay where she was.   He had promised Miss Alice ;
and he wouldn't break his word " for kings, lords, and commons.''
A most extraordinary expletive for a good republican,—which Mr.
Van Brunt had probably inherited from his father and grandfather.
What can waves do against a rock ?   The whilome Miss Fortune
disdained a struggle which must end in her own confusion, and
wisely kept her chagrin to herself, never even approaching the subject afterwards, with him or any other person.   Ellen had left the
whole matter to Mr. Van Brunt, expecting a storm and not wishing
to share it.   Happily it all blew over.

As the month drew to an end, and indeed long before, Ellen's
thoughts began to go forward eagerly to John coming home.   She
had learned by this time how to mend clothes; she had grown
somewhat wonted to her new round of little household duties; in
every thing else the want of him was felt.   Study flagged ; though
knowing what his wish would be, and what her duty was, she faithfully tried to go on with it.   She had no heart for riding or walking
by herself.   She was lonely ; she was sorrowful ; she was weary; all
Mrs. Vawse's pleasant society was not worth the mere knowledge
that *he* was in the house ; she longed for his coming.

He had written what day they might expect him.   But when it
came, Ellen found that her feeling had changed; it did not look
the bright day she had expected it would.   Up to that time she
had thought only of herself ; now she remembered what sort of a
coming home this must be to him ; and she dreaded almost as much

as she wished for the moment of his arrival. Mrs. Vawse was surprised to see that her face was sadder that day than it had been for many past ; she could not understand it. Ellen did not explain. It was late in the day before he reached home, and her anxious watch of hope and fear for the sound of his horse's feet grew very painful. She busied herself with setting the tea-table ; it was all done ; and she could by no means do any thing else. She could not go to the door to listen there ; she remembered too well the last time ; and she knew he would remember it.

He came at last. Ellen's feeling had judged rightly of his, for the greeting was without a word on either side ; and when he left the room to go to his father, it was very, very long before he came back. And it seemed to Ellen for several days that he was more grave and talked less than even the last time he had been at home. She was sorry when Mrs. Vawse proposed to leave them. But the old lady wisely said they would all feel better when she was gone ; and it was so. Truly as she was respected and esteemed, on all sides, it was felt a relief by every one of the family when she went back to her mountain-top. They were left to themselves ; they saw what their numbers were ; there was no restraint upon looks, words, or silence. Ellen saw at once that the gentlemen felt easier, that was enough to make her so. The extreme oppression that had grieved and disappointed her the first few days after John's return, gave place to a softened gravity ; and the household fell again into all its old ways ; only that upon every brow there was a chastened air of sorrow, in everything that was said a tone of remembrance, and that a little figure was going about where Alice's used to move as mistress of the house.

Thanks to her brother, that little figure was an exceeding busy one. She had in the first place, her household duties, in discharging which she was perfectly untiring. From the cream skimmed for Margery, and the cups of coffee poured out every morning for Mr. Humphreys and her brother, to the famous mending which took up often one half of Saturday, whatever she did was done with her best diligence and care ; and from love to both the dead and the living, Ellen's zeal never slackened. These things however filled but a small part of her time, let her be as particular as she would ; and Mr. John effectually hindered her from being too particular. He soon found a plenty for both her and himself to do.

Not that they ever forgot or tried to forget Alice ; on the contrary. They sought to remember her, humbly, calmly, hopefully, thankfully ! By diligent performance of duty, by Christian faith, by conversation and prayer, they strove to do this ; and after a time succeeded. Sober that winter was, but it was very far from being an unhappy one.

"John," said Ellen one day, some time after Mrs. Vawse had

left them,—" do you think Mr. Humphreys would let me go into his study every day when he is out, to put it in order and dust the books ?"

" Certainly.   But why does not Margery do it ?"

" She does, I believe, but she never used to ; and I should like to do it very much if I was sure he would not dislike it.   I would be careful not to disturb any thing ; I would leave every thing just as I found it."

" You may go when you please, and do what you please there, Ellie."

" But I don't like to—I couldn't without speaking to him first ; I should be afraid he would come back and find me there, and he might think I hadn't had leave."

" And you wish *me* to speak to him,—is that it ?   Cannot you muster resolution enough for that, Ellie ?"

Ellen was satisfied, for she knew by his tone he would do what she wanted.

" Father," said John, the next morning at breakfast ;—" Ellen wishes to take upon herself the daily care of your study, but she is afraid to venture without being assured it will please you to see her there."

The old gentleman laid his hand affectionately on Ellen's head, and told her she was welcome to come and go when she would ;— the whole house was hers.

The grave kindness and tenderness of the tone and action spoiled Ellen's breakfast.   She could not look at any body nor hold up her head for the rest of the time.

As Alice had anticipated, her brother was called to take the charge of a church at Randolph, and at the same time another more distant was offered him.   He refused them both, rightly judging that his place for the present was at home.   But the call from Randolph being pressed upon him very much, he at length agreed to preach for them during the winter ; riding thither for the purpose every Saturday, and returning to Carra-carra on Monday.

As the winter wore one, a grave cheerfulness stole over the household.   Ellen little thought how much she had to do with it. She never heard Margery tell her husband, which she often did with great affection, " that that blessed child was the light of the house."   And those who felt it the most said nothing.   Ellen was sure, indeed, from the way in which Mr. Humphreys spoke to her, looked at her, now and then laid his hand on her head, and some- times, very rarely, kissed her forehead, that he loved her and loved to see her about ; and that her wish of supplying Alice's place was in some little measure fulfilled.   Few as those words and looks were, they said more to Ellen than whole discourses would from other people; the least of them gladdened her heart with the feeling that she was a comfort to him. But she never knew how much. Deep as the gloom still over him was, Ellen never dreamed how much deeper it would have been, but for the little figure flitting round and filling up the vacancy; how much he reposed on the gentle look of affection, the pleasant voice, the watchful thoughtfulness that never left any thing undone that she could do for his pleasure. Perhaps he did not know it himself. She was not sure he even noticed many of the little things she daily did or tried to do for him. Always silent and reserved, he was more so now than ever; she saw him little, and very seldom long at a time, unless when they were riding to church together; he was always in his study or abroad. But the trifles she thought he did not see were noted and registered, and repaid with all the affection he had to give.

As for Mr. John, it never came into Ellen's head to think whether she was a comfort to him ; he was a comfort to *her ;* she looked at it in quite another point of view. He had gone to his old sleeping-room up stairs, which Margery had settled with herself he would make his study ; and for that he had taken the sitting-room. This was Ellen's study too, so she was constantly with him ; and of the quietest she thought her movements would have to be.

" What are you stepping so softly for ?" said he, one day, catching her hand as she was passing near him.

" You were busy—I thought you were busy," said Ellen.

" And what then ?"

" I was afraid of disturbing you."

" You never disturb me," said he ;—" you need not fear it. Step as you please, and do not shut the doors carefully. I see you and hear you ; but without any disturbance."

Ellen found it was so. But she was an exception to the general rule ; other people disturbed him, as she had one or two occasions of knowing.

Of one thing she was perfectly sure, whatever he might be doing,—that he saw and heard her ; and equally sure that if any thing were not right she should sooner or later hear of it. But this was a censorship Ellen rather loved than feared. In the first place, she was never misunderstood ; in the second, however ironical and severe he might be to others, and Ellen knew he could be both when there was occasion, he never was either to her. With great plainness always, but with an equally happy choice of time and manner, he either said or looked what he wished her to understand. This happened indeed only about comparative trifles ; to have seriously displeased him, Ellen would have thought the last great evil that could fall upon her in this world.

One day Margery came into the room with a paper in her hand.

" Miss Ellen," said she in a low tone,—" here is Anthony Fox again—he has brought another of his curious letters that he wants to know if Miss Ellen will be so good as to write out for him once more. He says he is ashamed to trouble you so much."

Ellen was reading, comfortably ensconced in the corner of the wide sofa. She gave a glance, a most ungratified one, at the very original document in Margery's hand. Unpromising it certainly looked.

" Another ! Dear me !—I wonder if there isn't somebody else he could get to do it for him, Margery ? I think I have had my share. You don't know what a piece of work it is, to copy out one of those scrawls. It takes me ever so long in the first place to find what he has written, and then to put it so that any one else can make sense of it—I've got about enough of it. Don't you suppose he could find plenty of other people to do it for him ?"

" I don't know, Miss Ellen,—I suppose he could."

" Then ask him, do ; won't you, Margery ? I'm so tired of it ! and this is the third one ; and I've got something else to do. Ask him if there isn't somebody else he can get to do it ;—if there isn't, I will ;—tell him I am busy."

Margery withdrew and Ellen buried herself again in her book. Anthony Fox was a poor Irishman, whose uncouth attempts at a letter Ellen had once offered to write out and make straight for him, upon hearing Margery tell of his lamenting that he could not make one fit to send *home* to his mother.

Presently Margery came in again, stopping this time at the table which Mr. John had pushed to the far side of the room to get away from the fire.

" I beg your pardon, sir," she said,—" I am ashamed to be so troublesome,—but this Irish body, this Anthony Fox, has begged me, and I didn't know how to refuse him, to come in and ask for a sheet of paper and a pen for him, sir,—he wants to copy a letter, —if Mr. John would be so good ; a quill pen, sir, if you please ; he cannot write with any other."

" No," said John coolly. " Ellen will do it."

Margery looked in some doubt from the table to the sofa, but Ellen instantly rose up and with a burning cheek came forward and took the paper from the hand where Margery still held it.

" Ask him to wait a little while, Margery," she said hurriedly, —" I'll do it as soon as I can,—tell him in half an hour."

It was not a very easy nor quick job. Ellen worked at it patiently, and finished it well by the end of the half hour ; though with a burning cheek still ; and a dimness over her eyes frequently obliged her to stop till she could clear them. It was done, and she carried it out to the kitchen herself.

The poor man's thanks were very warm ; but that was not what Ellen wanted. She could not rest till she had got another word from her brother. He was busy ; she dared not speak to him ; she sat fidgeting and uneasy in the corner of the sofa till it was time to get ready for riding. She had plenty of time to make up her mind about the right and the wrong of her own conduct.

During the ride he was just as usual, and she began to think he did not mean to say any thing more on the matter. Pleasant talk and pleasant exercise had almost driven it out of her head, when as they were walking their horses over a level place, he suddenly began,

" By the by, you are too busy, Ellie," said he. " Which of your studies shall we cut off ?"

" *Please*, Mr. John," said Ellen blushing,—" don't say any thing about that ! I was not studying at all—I was just amusing myself with a book—I was only selfish and lazy."

" *Only*—I would rather you were too busy, Ellie."

Ellen's eyes filled.

" I was wrong," she said,—" I knew it at the time,—at least as soon as you spoke I knew it; and a little before ;—I was very wrong !"

And his keen eye saw that the confession was not out of compliment to him merely ; it came from the heart.

" You are right now," he said smiling. " But how are your reins ?"

Ellen's heart was at rest again.

"Oh, I forgot them," said she gayly,—" I was thinking of something else."

" You must not talk when you are riding, unless you can contrive to manage two things at once ; and no more lose command of your horse than you would of yourself."

Ellen's eye met his with all the contrition, affection, and ingenuousness that even he wished to see there ; and they put their horses to the canter.

This winter was in many ways a very precious one to Ellen. French gave her now no trouble ; she was a clever arithmetician ; she knew geography admirably, and was tolerably at home in both English and American history ; the way was cleared for the course of improvement in which her brother's hand led and helped her. He put her into Latin ; carried on the study of natural philosophy they had begun the year before, and which with his instructions was perfectly delightful to Ellen ; he gave her some works of stronger reading than she had yet tried, besides histories in French and English, and higher branches of arithmetic. These things were not crowded together so as to fatigue, nor hurried through so as to overload. Carefully and thoroughly she was obliged to put her mind through every subject they entered upon; and just at that age, opening as her understanding was, it grappled eagerly with all that he gave her, as well from love to learning as from love to him. In reading too, she began to take new and strong delight. Especially two or three new English periodicals, which John sent for on purpose for her, were mines of pleasure to Ellen. There was no fiction in them either; they were as full of instruction as of interest. At all times of the day and night, in her intervals of business, Ellen might be seen with one of these in her hand; nestled among the cushions of the sofa, or on a little bench by the side of the fireplace in the twilight, where she could have the benefit of the blaze, which she loved to read by as well as ever. Sorrowful remembrances were then flown, all things present were out of view, and Ellen's face was dreamingly happy.

It was well there was always somebody by, who whatever he might himself be doing, never lost sight of her. If ever Ellen was in danger of bending too long over her studies or indulging herself too much in the sofa-corner, she was sure to be broken off to take an hour or two of smart exercise, riding or walking, or to recite some lesson (and their recitations were very lively things), or to read aloud, or to talk. Sometimes if he saw that she seemed to be drooping or a little sad, he would come and sit down by her side or call her to his, find out what she was thinking about; and then, instead of slurring it over, talk of it fairly and set it before her in such a light that it was impossible to think of it again gloomily, for that day at least. Sometimes he took other ways; but never when he was present allowed her long to look weary or sorrowful. He often read to her, and every day made her read aloud to him. This Ellen disliked very much at first, and ended with as much liking it. She had an admirable teacher. He taught her how to manage her voice and how to manage the language; in both which he excelled himself, and was determined that she should; and besides this their reading often led to talking that Ellen delighted in. Always when he was making copies for her she read to him, and once at any rate in the course of the day.

Every day when the weather would permit, the Black Prince and the Brownie with their respective riders might be seen abroad in the country far and wide. In the course of their rides Ellen's horsemanship was diligently perfected. Very often their turning-place was on the top of the Cat's back, and the horses had a rest and Mrs. Vawse a visit before they went down again. They had long walks too, by hill and dale; pleasantly silent or pleasantly talkative,—all pleasant to Ellen!

Her only lonely or sorrowful time was when John was gone to Randolph. It began early Saturday morning, and perhaps ended with Sunday night; for all Monday was hope and expectation. Even Saturday she had not much time to mope ; that was the day for her great week's mending. When John was gone and her morning affairs were out of the way, Ellen brought out her work-basket, and established herself on the sofa for a quiet day's sewing without the least fear of interruption. But sewing did not always hinder thinking. And then certainly the room did seem very empty and very still; and the clock, which she never heard the rest of the week, kept ticking an ungracious reminder that she was alone. Ellen would sometimes forget it in the intense interest of some nice little piece of repair which must be exquisitely done in a wristband or a glove ; and then perhaps Margery would softly open the door and come in.

"Miss Ellen, dear, you're lonesome enough; isn't there something I can do for you? I can't rest for thinking of your being here all by yourself."

"Oh, never mind, Margery," said Ellen smiling,—" I am doing very well. I am living in hopes of Monday. Come and look here, Margery,—how will that do?—don't you think I am learning to mend ?"

"It's beautiful, Miss Ellen ! I can't make out how you've learned so quick. I'll tell Mr. John some time who does these things for him."

"No, indeed, Margery ! don't you. *Please* not, Margery. I like to do it very much indeed, but I don't want he should know it, nor Mr. Humphreys. Now you won't, Margery, will you ?"

"Miss Ellen, dear, I wouldn't do the least little thing as would be worrisome to you for the whole world. Aren't you tired sitting here all alone?"

"Oh, sometimes, a little," said Ellen sighing. "I can't help that, you know."

"I feel it even out there in the kitchen," said Margery ;—" I feel it lonesome hearing the house so still ; I miss the want of Mr. John's step up and down the room. How fond he is of walking so, to be sure ! How do you manage, Miss Ellen, with him making his study here ? don't you have to keep uncommon quiet ?"

"No," said Ellen,—" no quieter than I like. I do just as I have a mind to."

"I thought, to be sure," said Margery, "he would have taken up stairs for his study, or the next room, one or t'other ; he used to be mighty particular in old times ; he didn't like to have any body round when he was busy ; but I am glad he is altered however ; it is better for you, Miss Ellen, dear, though I didn't know how you was ever going to make out at first."

Ellen thought for a minute, when Margery was gone, whether it could be that John was putting a force upon his liking for her sake, bearing her presence when he would rather have been without it. But she thought of it only a minute; she was sure, when she recollected herself, that however it happened, she was no hinderance to him in any kind of work; that she went out and came in, and as he had said, he saw and heard her without any disturbance. Besides he had said so; and that was enough.

Saturday evening she generally contrived to busy herself in her books. But when Sunday morning came with its calmness and brightness; when the business of the week was put away, and quietness abroad and at home invited to recollection, then Ellen's thoughts went back to old times, and then she missed the calm sweet face that had agreed so well with the day. She missed her in the morning, when the early sun streamed in through the empty room. She missed her at the breakfast-table, where John was not to take her place. On the ride to church, where Mr. Humphreys was now her silent companion, and every tree in the road and every opening in the landscape seemed to call for Alice to see it with her. Very much she missed her in church. The empty seat beside her,—the unused hymn-book on the shelf,—the want of her sweet voice in the singing,—oh, how it went to Ellen's heart. And Mr. Humphreys' grave steadfast look and tone kept it in her mind; she saw it was in his. Those Sunday mornings tried Ellen. At first they were bitterly sad; her tears used to flow abundantly whenever they could unseen. Time softened this feeling.

While Mr. Humphreys went on to his second service in the village beyond, Ellen stayed at Carra-carra and tried to teach a Sunday school. She determined as far as she could to supply beyond the home circle the loss that was not felt only there. She was able however to gather together but her own four children whom she had constantly taught from the beginning, and two others. The rest were scattered. After her lunch, which having no companion but Margery was now a short one, Ellen went next to the two old women that Alice had been accustomed to attend for the purpose of reading, and what Ellen called preaching. These poor old people had sadly lamented the loss of the faithful friend whose place they never expected to see supplied in this world, and whose kindness had constantly sweetened their lives with one great pleasure a week. Ellen felt afraid to take so much upon herself, as to try to do for them what Alice had done; however she resolved; and at the very first attempt their gratitude and joy far overpaid her for the effort she had made. Practice and the motive she had, soon enabled Ellen to remember and repeat faithfully the greater part of Mr. Humphreys' morning sermon. Reading the Bible to Mrs. Blockson was easy; she had often done that; and to repair the loss of Alice's pleasant comments and explanations she bethought her of her Pilgrim's Progress. To her delight the old woman heard it greedily, and seemed to take great comfort in it; often referring to what Ellen had read before and begging to hear such a piece over again. Ellen generally went home pretty thoroughly tired, yet feeling happy; the pleasure of doing good still far overbalanced the pains.

Sunday evening was another lonely time; Ellen spent it as best she could. Sometimes with her Bible and prayer, and then she

ceased to be lonely; sometimes with so many pleasant thoughts that had sprung up out of the employments of the morning that she could not be sorrowful; sometimes she could not help being both. In any case, she was very apt when the darkness fell to take to singing hymns; and it grew to be a habit with Mr. Humphreys when he heard her to come out of his study and lie down upon the sofa and listen, suffering no light in the room but that of the fire. Ellen never was better pleased than when her Sunday evenings were spent so. She sung with wonderful pleasure when she sung for him ; and she made it her business to fill her memory with all the beautiful hymns she ever knew or could find, or that he liked particularly.

With the first opening of her eyes on Monday morning came the thought, " John will be at home to-day !" That was enough to carry Ellen pleasantly through whatever the day might bring. She generally kept her mending of stockings for Monday morning, because with that thought in her head she did not mind any thing. She had no visits from Margery on Monday ; but Ellen sang over her work, sprang about with happy energy, and studied her hardest ; for John in what he expected her to do made no calculations for work of which he knew nothing. He was never at home till late in the day ; and when Ellen had done all she had to do, and set the supper-table with punctilious care, and a face of busy happiness it would have been a pleasure to see if there had been any one to look at it, she would take what happened to be the favourite book and plant herself near the glass door ; like a very epicure, to enjoy both the present and the future at once. Even then the present often made her forget the future ; she would be lost in her book, perhaps hunting the elephant in India or fighting Nelson's battles over again, and the first news she would have of what she had set herself there to watch for would be the click of the door-lock or a tap on the glass, for the horse was almost always left at the further door. Back then she came, from India or the Nile ; down went the book ; Ellen had no more thought but for what was before her.

For the rest of that evening the measure of Ellen's happiness was full. It did not matter whether John were in a talkative or a thoughtful mood ; whether he spoke to her and looked at her or not ; it was pleasure enough to feel that he was there. She was perfectly satisfied merely to sit down near him, though she did not get a word by the hour together.

CHAPTER XLV.

Ne in all the welkin was no cloud.
CHAUCER.

ONE Monday evening, John being tired, was resting in the corner of the sofa. The silence had lasted a long time. Ellen thought so, and standing near, she by and by put her hand gently into one of his which he was thoughtfully passing through the locks of his hair. Her hand was clasped immediately, and quitting his abstracted look he asked what she had been doing that day? Ellen's thoughts went back to toes of stockings and a long rent in her dress; she merely answered, smiling, that she had been busy.

"Too busy, I'm afraid. Come round here and sit down. What have you been busy about?"

Ellen never thought of trying to evade a question of his. She coloured and hesitated. He did not press it any further.

"Mr. John," said Ellen, when the silence seemed to have set in again,—"there is something I have been wanting to ask you this great while,"—

"Why hasn't it been *asked* this great while?"

"I didn't quite like to;—I didn't know what you would say to it."

"I am sorry I am at all terrible to you, Ellie."

"Why you are not!" said Ellen, laughing,—"how you talk! but I don't much like to ask people things."

"I don't know about that," said he smiling;—"my memory rather seems to say that you ask things pretty often."

"Ah, yes,—those things,—but I mean—I don't like to ask things when I am not quite sure how people will like it."

"You are right, certainly, to hesitate when you are doubtful in such a matter; but it is best not to be doubtful when I am concerned."

"Well," said Ellen,—"I wished very much—I was going to ask—if you would have any objection to let me read one of your sermons."

"None in the world, Ellie," said he, smiling,—"but they have never been written yet."

"Not written!"

"No—there is all I had to guide me yesterday."

"A half sheet of paper!—and only written on one side!—Oh, I can make nothing of this. What is *this?*—Hebrew?"

"Shorthand."

"And is that all! I cannot understand it," said Ellen, sighing as she gave back the paper.

"What if you were to go with me next time? They want to see you very much at Ventnor."

"So do I want to see them," said Ellen;—"very much indeed."

"Mrs. Marshman sent a most earnest request by me that you would come to her the next time I go to Randolph."

Ellen gave the matter a very serious consideration; if one might judge by her face.

"What do you say to it?"

"I should like to go—*very* much," said Ellen, slowly,—"but——"

"But you do not think it would be pleasant?"

" No, no," said Ellen laughing,—" I don't mean that; but I think I would rather not."

" Why?"

" Oh,—I have some reasons."

" You must give me very good ones, or I think I shall overrule your decision, Ellie."

" I have *very* good ones,—plenty of them,—only———"

A glance, somewhat comical in its keenness, overturned Ellen's hesitation.

" I have indeed," said she, laughing,—" only I did not want to tell you. The reason why I didn't wish to go was because I thought I should be missed. You don't know how much I miss you," said she with tears in her eyes.

" That is what I was afraid of! Your reasons make against you, Ellie."

" I hope not;—I don't think they ought."

" But Ellie, I am very sure my father would rather miss you once or twice than have you want what would be good for you."

" I know that! I am sure of that; but that don't alter my feeling, you know. And besides—that isn't all."

" Who else will miss you?"

Ellen's quick look seemed to say that he knew too much already, and that she did not wish him to know more. He did not repeat the question, but Ellen felt that her secret was no longer entirely her own.

" And what do you do, Ellie, when you feel lonely?" he went on presently.

Ellen's eyes watered at the tone in which these words were spoken; she answered, " Different things."

" The best remedy for it is prayer. In seeking the face of our best friend we forget the loss of others. That is what I try, Ellie, when I feel alone;—do you try it?" said he, softly.

Ellen looked up; she could not well speak at that moment.

" There is an antidote in that for every trouble. You know who said, ' he that cometh to me shall never hunger, and he that believeth on me shall never thirst.' "

" It troubles me," said he after a pause,—" to leave you so much alone. I don't know that it were not best to take you with me every week."

" Oh, no!" said Ellen,—" don't think of me. I do not mind it indeed. I do not always feel so—sometimes,—but I get along very well; and I would rather stay here, indeed I would. I am always happy as soon as Monday morning comes."

He rose up suddenly and began to walk up and down the room.

" Mr. John"—

" What, Ellie?"

" I do sometimes seek His face very much when I cannot find it."
She hid her face in the sofa-cushion. He was silent a few minutes, and then stopped his walk.

"There is something wrong then with you, Ellie," he said
gently. "How has it been through the week? If you can let
day after day pass without remembering your best friend, it may
be that when you feel the want you will not readily find him.
How is it daily, Ellie? is seeking his face your first concern? do
you give a sufficient time faithfully to your Bible and prayer?"

Ellen shook her head; no words were possible. He took up his
walk again. The silence had lasted a length of time and he was
still walking, when Ellen came to his side and laid her hand on
his arm.

"Have you settled that question with your conscience, Ellie?"
She weepingly answered yes. They walked a few turns up and
down.

"Will you promise me, Ellie, that every day when it shall be
possible, you will give an hour *at least* to this business?—whatever
else may be done or undone?"

Ellen promised; and then with her hand in his they continued
their walk through the room till Mr. Humphreys and the servants
came in. Her brother's prayer that night Ellen never forgot.

No more was said at that time about her going to Ventnor.
But a week or two after, John smilingly told her to get all her
private affairs arranged and to let her friends know they need not
expect to see her the next Sunday, for that he was going to take
her with him. As she saw he had made up his mind, Ellen said
nothing in the way of objecting; and now that the decision was
taken from her was really very glad to go. She arranged every
thing, as he had said; and was ready Saturday morning to set off
with a very light heart.

They went in the sleigh. In a happy quiet mood of mind,
Ellen enjoyed every thing exceedingly. She had not been to
Ventnor in several months; the change of scene was very grateful.
She could not help thinking, as they slid along smoothly and
swiftly over the hard-frozen snow, that it *was* a good deal pleasanter, for once, than sitting alone in the parlour at home with her
work-basket. Those days of solitary duty, however, had prepared
her for the pleasure of this one; Ellen knew that, and was ready
to be thankful for every thing. Throughout the whole way,
whether the eye and mind silently indulged in roving, or still better loved talk interrupted that, as it often did, Ellen was in a state
of most unmixed and unruffled satisfaction. John had not the
slightest reason to doubt the correctness of his judgment in bringing her. He went in but a moment at Ventnor, and leaving her
there, proceeded himself to Randolph.

Ellen was received as a precious lending that must be taken the greatest care of and enjoyed as much as possible while one has it. Mrs. Marshman and Mrs. Chauncey treated her as if she had been their own child. Ellen Chauncey overwhelmed her with joyful caresses, and could scarcely let her out of her arms by night or by day. She was more than ever Mr. Marshman's pet; but indeed she was well petted by all the family. It was a very happy visit.

Even Sunday left nothing to wish for. To her great joy not only Mrs. Chauncey went with her in the morning to hear her brother (for his church was not the one the family attended), but the carriage was ordered in the afternoon also; and Mrs. Chauncey and her daughter and Miss Sophia went with her again. When they returned, Miss Sophia, who had taken a very great fancy to her, brought her into her own room and made her lie down with her upon the bed, though Ellen insisted she was not tired.

"Well you ought to be, if you are not," said the lady. "*I* am. Keep away, Ellen Chauncey—you can't be any where without talking. You can live without Ellen for half an hour, can't ye? Leave us a little while in quiet. '

Ellen for her part was quite willing to be quiet. But Miss Sophia was not sleepy, and it soon appeared had no intention of being silent herself.

"Well how do you like your brother in the pulpit?" she began.

"I like him anywhere, ma'am," said Ellen smiling a very unequivocal smile.

"I thought he would have come here with you last night;—it is very mean of him! He never comes near us; he always goes to some wretched little lodging or place in the town there;—always; never so much as looks at Ventnor unless sometimes he may stop for a minute at the door."

"He said he would come here to-night," said Ellen.

"Amazing condescending of him! However, he isn't like anybody else; I suppose we must not judge him by common rules. How is Mr. Humphreys, Ellen?"

"I don't know, ma'am," said Ellen,—"it is hard to tell; he doesn't say much. I think he is rather more cheerful—if any thing—than I expected he would be."

"And how do you get along there, poor child! with only two such grave people about you?"

"I get along very well, ma'am," said Ellen, with what Miss Sophia thought a somewhat curious smile.

"I believe you will grow to be as sober as the rest of them," said she. "How does Mr. John behave?"

Ellen turned so indubitably curious a look upon her at this that Miss Sophia half laughed and went on.

"Mr. Humphreys was not always as silent and reserved as he is

now; I remember him when he was different;—though I don't
think he ever was much like his son. Did you ever hear about
it?"

"About what, ma'am?"

"Oh, all about his coming to this country, and what brought
him to Carra-carra?"

"No, ma'am."

"My father, you see, had come out long before, but the two
families had been always very intimate in England, and it was kept
up after he came away. He was a particular friend of an elder
brother of Mr. Humphreys; his estate and my grandfather's lay
very near each other; and besides, there were other things that
drew them to each other;—he married my aunt, for one. My
father made several journeys back and forth in the course of years,
and so kept up his attachment to the whole family, you know; and
he became very desirous to get Mr. Humphreys over here,—this
Mr. Humphreys, you know. He was the younger brother—younger
brothers in England generally have little or nothing; but you don't
know anything about that, Ellen. *He* hadn't any thing then but
his living, and that was a small one; he had some property left
him though, just before he came to America."

"But Miss Sophia"—Ellen hesitated,—"Are you sure they
would like I should hear all this?"

"Why yes, child!—of course they would; every body knows it.
Some things made Mr. Humphreys as willing to leave England
about that time as my father was to have him. An excellent
situation was offered him in one of the best institutions here, and
he came out. That's about—let me see—I was just twelve years
old and Alice was one year younger. She and I were just like
sisters always from that time. We lived near together, and saw
each other every day, and our two families were just like one. But
they were liked by every body. Mrs. Humphreys was a very fine
person,—very; oh, very! I never saw any woman I admired more.
Her death almost killed her husband; and I think Alice—I don't
know!—there isn't the least sign of delicate health about Mr.
Humphreys nor Mr. John,—not the slightest,—nor about Mrs.
Humphreys either. She was a very fine woman!"

"How long ago did she die?" said Ellen.

"Five,—six, seven,—seven years ago. Mr. John had been left
in England till a little before. Mr. Humphreys was never the
same after that. He wouldn't hold his professorship any longer;
he couldn't bear society; he just went and buried himself at
Carra-carra. That was a little after we came here."

How much all this interested Ellen! She was glad however
when Miss Sophia seemed to have talked herself out, for she
wanted very much to think over John's sermon. And as Miss

Sophia happily fell into a doze soon after, she had a long quiet time for it, till it grew dark, and Ellen Chauncey whose impatience could hold no longer came to seek her.

John came in the evening. Ellen's patience and politeness were severely tried in the course of it; for while she longed exceedingly to hear what her brother and the older members of the family were talking about,—animated, delightful conversation she was sure,—Ellen Chauncey detained her in another part of the room; and for a good part of the evening she had to bridle her impatience, and attend to what she did not care about. She did it, and Ellen Chauncey did not suspect it; and at last she found means to draw both her and herself near the larger group. But they seemed to have got through what they were talking about; there was a lull. Ellen waited; and hoped they would begin again.

"You had a full church this afternoon, Mr. John," said Miss Sophia.

He bowed gravely.

"Did you know whom you had among your auditors? the —— and —— were there;" naming some distinguished strangers in the neighbourhood.

"I think I saw them."

"You 'think' you did! Is that an excess of pride or an excess of modesty? Now do be a reasonable creature, and confess that you are not insensible to the pleasure and honour of addressing such an audience!"

Ellen saw something like a flash of contempt, for an instant in his face, instantly succeeded by a smile.

"Honestly, Miss Sophia, I was much more interested in an old woman that sat at the foot of the pulpit stairs."

"That old thing!" said Miss Sophia.

"I saw her," said Mrs. Chauncey;—"poor old creature! she seemed most deeply attentive when I looked at her."

"_I_ saw her!" cried Ellen Chauncey,—"and the tears were running down her cheeks several times."

"I didn't see her," said Ellen Montgomery, as John's eye met hers. He smiled.

"But do you mean to say," continued Miss Sophia, "that you are absolutely careless as to who hears you?"

"I have always one hearer, Miss Sophia, of so much dignity, that it sinks the rest into great insignificance."

"That is a rebuke," said Miss Sophia;—"but nevertheless I shall tell you that I liked you very much this afternoon."

He was silent.

"I suppose you will tell me next," said the young lady laughing, "that you are sorry to hear me say so."

"I am," said he gravely.

" Why ?—may I ask ?"

" You show me that I have quite failed in my aim, so far at least as one of my hearers was concerned."

" How do you know that ?"

" Do you remember what Louis the Fourteenth said to Massillon ?—Mon père, j'ai entendu plusieurs grands orateurs dans ma chapelle; j'en ai été fort content; pour vous, toutes les fois que je vous ai entendu, j'ai été très mécontent de moi-même !"

Ellen smiled. Miss Sophia was silent for an instant.

" Then you really mean to be understood, that provided you fail of your aim, as you say, you do not care a straw what people think of you ?"

" As I would take a bankrupt's promissory note in lieu of told gold. It gives me small gratification, Miss Sophia—very small indeed,—to see the bowing head of the grain that yet my sickle cannot reach."

" I agree with you most heartily," said Mr. George Marshman. The conversation dropped ; and the two gentlemen began another in an under tone, pacing up and down the floor together.

The next morning, not sorrowfully, Ellen entered the sleigh again and they set off homewards.

" What a sober little piece that is," said Mr. Howard.

" Oh !—sober !" cried Ellen Chauncey ;—" that is because you don't know her, uncle Howard. She is the cheerfullest, happiest girl that I ever saw,—always."

" Except Ellen Chauncey,—always," said her uncle.

" She is a singular child," said Mrs. Gillespie. " She is grave certainly, but she don't look moped at all, and I should think she would be, to death."

" There's not a bit of moping about her," said Miss Sophia. "She can laugh and smile as well as any body ; though she has sometimes that peculiar grave look of the eyes that would make a stranger doubt it. I think John Humphreys has infected her ; he has something of the same look himself."

" I am not sure whether it is the eyes or the mouth, Sophia," said Mr. Howard.

" It is both," said Miss Sophia. " Did you ever see the eyes look one way and the mouth another ?"

" And besides," said Ellen Chauncey, " she has reason to look sober, I am sure."

" She is a fascinating child," said Mrs. Gillespie. " I cannot comprehend where she gets the manner she has. I never saw a more perfectly polite child ; and there she has been for months with nobody to speak to her but two gentlemen and the servants. It is natural to her, I suppose ; she can have nobody to teach her."

" I am not so sure as to that," said Miss Sophia; " but I have noticed the same thing often. Did you observe her last night, Matilda, when John Humphreys came in? you were talking to her at the moment;—I saw her, before the door was opened,—I saw the colour come and her eye sparkle, but she did not look toward him for an instant till you had finished what you were saying to her and she had given, as she always does, her modest quiet answer; and then her eye went straight as an arrow to where he was standing."

" And yet," said Mrs. Chauncey, " she never moved toward him when you did, but stayed quietly on that side of the room with the young ones till he came round to them, and it was some time too."

" She is an odd child," said Miss Sophia, laughing,—" what do you think she said to me yesterday? I was talking to her and getting rather communicative on the subject of my neighbours' affairs; and she asked me gravely,—the little monkey!—if I was sure they would like her to hear it? I felt quite rebuked; though I didn't choose to let her know as much."

" I wish Mr. John would bring her every week," said Ellen Chauncey sighing; " it would be so pleasant to have her."

Toward the end of the winter Mr. Humphreys began to propose that his son should visit England and Scotland during the following summer. He wished him to see his family and to know his native country, as well as some of the most distinguished men and institutions in both kingdoms. Mr. George Marshman also urged upon him some business in which he thought he could be eminently useful. But Mr. John declined both propositions, still thinking he had more important duties at home. This only cloud that rose above Ellen's horizon, scattered away.

One evening, it was a Monday, in the twilight, John was as usual pacing up and down the floor. Ellen was reading in the window.

" Too late for you, Ellie."

" Yes," said Ellen,—" I know—I will stop in two minutes"—

But in a quarter of that time she had lost every thought of stopping, and knew no longer that it was growing dusk. Somebody else, however, had not forgotten it. The two minutes were not ended, when a hand came between her and the page and quietly drew the book away.

" Oh, I beg your pardon!" cried Ellen starting up. " I entirely forgot all about it!"

He did not look displeased; he was smiling. He drew her arm within his.

" Come and walk with me. Have you had any exercise to-day?"

" No."

" Why not ?"

" I had a good deal to do, and I had fixed myself so nicely on the sofa with my books; and it looked cold and disagreeable out of doors."

" Since when have you ceased to be a fixture ?"

" What!—Oh," said Ellen laughing,—" how shall I ever get rid of that troublesome word? What shall I say?—I had *arranged* myself, *established* myself, so nicely on the sofa."

" And did you think that a sufficient reason for not going out ?"

" No," said Ellen, " I did not; and I did not decide that I would not go; and yet I let it keep me at home after all;—just as I did about reading a few minutes ago. I meant to stop, but I forgot it, and I should have gone on I don't know how long if you had not stopped me. I very often do so."

He paused a minute, and then said,

" You must not do so any more, Ellie."

The tone, in which there was a great deal both of love and decision, wound round Ellen's heart, and constrained her to answer immediately,

" I will not—I will not."

" Never parley with conscience;—it is a dangerous habit."

" But then—it was only——"

" About trifles; I grant you; but the habit is no trifle. There will not be a just firmness of mind and steadfastness of action, where tampering with duty is permitted even in little things."

" I will try not to do it," Ellen repeated.

" No," said he smiling,—" let it stand as at first. '*I will not*,' means something; '*I will try*,' is very apt to come to nothing. ' I will keep thy precepts with my whole heart!'—not ' I will *try*.' Your reliance is precisely the same in either case."

" I will not, John," said Ellen smiling.

" What were you poring over so intently a while ago ?"

" It was an old magazine—Blackwood's Magazine, I believe, is the name of it—I found two great piles of them in a closet up stairs the other day; and I brought this one down."

" This is the first that you have read ?"

" Yes—I got very much interested in a curious story there;— why ?"

" What will you say, Ellie, if I ask you to leave the rest of the two piles unopened ?"

" Why, I will say that I will do it, of course," said Ellen, with a little smothered sigh of regret however;—" if you wish it."

" I do wish it, Ellie."

" Very well—I'll let them alone then. I have enough other reading ; I don't know how I happened to take that one up ; because I saw it there, I suppose."

" Have you finished Nelson yet?"

" Oh, yes !—I finished it Saturday night. Oh, I like it *very* much ! I am going all over it again though. I like Nelson very much ; don't you?"

" Yes—as well as I can like a man of very fine qualities without principle."

" Was he that ?" said Ellen.

" Yes ; did you not find it out ? I am afraid your eyes were blinded by admiration."

" Were they !" said Ellen. " I thought he was so very fine, in every thing ; and I should be sorry to think he was not."

" Look over the book again by all means, with a more critical eye ; and when you have done so you shall give me your cool estimate of his character."

" Oh, me !" said Ellen. " Well,—but I don't know whether I can give you a *cool* estimate of him ;—however I'll try. I cannot think coolly of him now, just after Trafalgar. I think it was a shame that Collingwood did not anchor as Nelson told him to ; don't you ? I think he might have been obeyed while he was living, at least."

" It is difficult," said John smiling, " to judge correctly of many actions without having been on the spot and in the circumstances of the actors. I believe you and I must leave the question of Trafalgar to more nautical heads."

" How pleasant this moonlight is !" said Ellen.

" What makes it pleasant?"

" What *makes* it pleasant !—I don't know ; I never thought of such a thing. It is *made* to be pleasant.—I can't tell *why ;* can any body ?"

" The eye loves light for many reasons, but all kinds of light are not equally agreeable. What makes the peculiar charm of these long streams of pale light across the floor ? and the shadowy brightness without ?"

" You must tell," said Ellen ; " I cannot."

" You know we enjoy any thing much more by contrast ; I think that is one reason. Night is the reign of darkness, which we do not love ; and here is light struggling with the darkness, not enough to overcome it entirely, but yet banishing it to nooks and corners and distant parts, by the side of which it shows itself in contrasted beauty. Our eyes bless the unwonted victory."

" Yes," said Ellen,—" we only have moonlight nights once in a while."

" But that is only one reason out of many, and not the greatest.

It is a very refined pleasure, and to resolve it into its elements is something like trying to divide one of these same white rays of light into the many various coloured ones that go to form it;—and not by any means so easy a task."

"Then it was no wonder I couldn't answer," said Ellen.

"No—you are hardly a full-grown philosopher yet, Ellie."

"The moonlight is so calm and quiet," Ellen observed admiringly.

"And why is it calm and quiet?—I must have an answer to that."

"Because *we* are generally calm and quiet at such times?" Ellen ventured after a little thought.

"Precisely!—we and the world. And association has given the moon herself the same character. Besides that her mild sober light is not fitted for the purposes of active employment, and therefore the more graciously invites us to the pleasures of thought and fancy."

"I am loving it more and more, the more you talk about it," said Ellen laughing.

"And there you have touched another reason, Ellie, for the pleasure we have, not only in moonlight, but in most other things. When two things have been in the mind together, and made any impression, the mind *associates* them; and you cannot see or think of the one without bringing back the remembrance or the feeling of the other. If we have enjoyed the moonlight in pleasant scenes, in happy hours, with friends that we loved,—though the sight of it may not always make us directly remember them, it yet brings with it a waft from the feeling of the old times,—sweet as long as life lasts!"

"And sorrowful things may be associated too?" said Ellen.

"Yes, and sorrowful things.—But this power of association is the cause of half the pleasure we enjoy. There is a tune my mother used to sing—I cannot hear it now without being carried swiftly back to my boyish days,—to the very spirit of the time; I *feel* myself spring over the greensward as I did then."

"Oh, I know that is true," said Ellen. "The camellia, the white camellia you know,—I like it so much ever since what you said about it one day. I never see it without thinking of it; and it would not seem half so beautiful but for that."

"What did I say about it?"

"Don't you remember? you said it was like what you ought to be, and what you should be if you ever reached heaven; and you repeated that verse in the Revelation about 'those that have not defiled their garments.' I always think of it. It seems to give me a lesson."

"How eloquent of beautiful lessons all nature would be to us," said John musingly, " if we had but the eye and the ear to take them in."

" And in that way you would heap associations upon associations ?"

" Yes ; till our storehouse of pleasure was very full."

" You do that now," said Ellen. " I wish you would teach me."

" I have read precious things sometimes in the bunches of flowers you are so fond of, Ellie. Cannot you ?"

" I don't know—I only think of themselves ; except—sometimes, they make me think of Alice."

" You know from any works we may form some judgment of the mind and character of their author ?"

" From their writings, I know you can," said Ellen ;—" from what other works ?"

" From any which are not mechanical ; from any in which the mind, not the hand, has been the creating power. I saw you very much interested the other day in the Eddystone lighthouse ; did it help you to form no opinion of Mr. Smeaton ?"

" Why yes, certainly," said Ellen,—" I admired him exceedingly for his cleverness and perseverance ; but what other works ?—I can't think of any."

" There is the lighthouse,—that is one thing. What do you think of the ocean waves that now and then overwhelm it ?"

Ellen half shuddered. " I shouldn't like to go to sea, John ! But you were speaking of men's works and women's works ?"

" Well, women's works,—I cannot help forming some notion of a lady's mind and character from the way she dresses herself."

" Can you ! do you !"

" I cannot help doing it. Many things appear in the style of a lady's dress that she never dreams of ;—the style of her thoughts among others."

" It is a pity ladies didn't know that," said Ellen, laughing ;—" they would be very careful."

" It wouldn't mend the matter, Ellie. That is one of the things in which people are obliged to speak truth. As the mind is, so it will show itself."

" But we have got a great way from the flowers," said Ellen.

" You shall bring me some to-morrow, Ellie, and we will read them together."

" There are plenty over there now," said Ellen, looking toward the little flower-stand, which was as full and as flourishing as ever, —" but we can't see them well by this light."

" A bunch of flowers seems to bring me very near the hand that made them. They are the work of his fingers ; and I cannot consider them without being joyfully assured of the glory and loveliness of their Creator. It is written as plainly to me in their delicate painting and sweet breath and curious structure, as in the very pages of the Bible; though no doubt without the Bible I could not read the flowers."

"I never thought much of that," said Ellen. "And then you find particular lessons in particular flowers?"

"Sometimes."

"Oh, come here!" said Ellen, pulling him toward the flower-stand,—"and tell me what this daphne is like—you need not see that, only smell it, that's enough;—do John, and tell me what it is like!"

He smiled as he complied with her request, and walked away again.

"Well, what is it?" said Ellen; "I know you have thought of something."

"It is like the fragrance that Christian society sometimes leaves upon the spirit; when it is just what it ought to be."

"My Mr. Marshman!" exclaimed Ellen.

John smiled again. "I thought of him, Ellie. And I thought also of Cowper's lines:—

> "'When one who holds communion with the skies,
> Has filled his urn where those pure waters rise,
> Descends and dwells among us meaner things,—
> It is as if an angel shook his wings!'"

Ellen was silent a moment from pleasure.

"Well, I have got an association now with the daphne!" she said joyously; and presently added, sighing,—"How much you see in every thing, that I do not see at all."

"Time, Ellie," said John;—"there must be time for that. It will come. Time is cried out upon as a great thief; it is people's own fault. Use him but well, and you will get from his hand more than he will ever take from you."

Ellen's thoughts travelled on a little way from this speech,— and then came a sigh, of some burden, as it seemed; and her face was softly laid against the arm she held.

"Let us leave all that to God," said John gently.

Ellen started. "How did you know—how could you know what I was thinking of?"

"Perhaps my thoughts took the same road," said he smiling. "But Ellie, dear, let us look to that one source of happiness that can never be dried up; it is not safe to count upon any thing else."

"It is not wonderful," said Ellen in a tremulous voice,—"if I——"

"It is not wonderful, Ellie, nor wrong. But we, who look up to God as our Father,—who rejoice in Christ our Saviour,—we are happy, whatever beside we may gain or lose. Let us trust him, and never doubt that, Ellie."

"But still"—said Ellen.

"But still, we will hope and pray alike in that matter. And while we do, and may, with our whole hearts, let us leave ourselves in our Father's hand. The joy of the knowledge of Christ! the joy the world cannot intermeddle with, the peace it cannot take away!—Let us make that our own, Ellie; and for the rest put away all anxious care about what we cannot control."

Ellen's hand however did not just then lie quite so lightly on his arm as it did a few minutes ago; he could feel that; and could see the glitter of one or two tears in the moonlight as they fell. The hand was fondly taken in his; and as they slowly paced up and down, he went on in low tones of kindness and cheerfulness with his pleasant talk, till she was too happy in the present to be anxious about the future; looked up again and brightly into his face, and questions and answers came as gayly as ever.

CHAPTER XLVI.

Who knows what may happen?   Patience and shuffle the cards? . . . Perhaps after all, I shall some day go to Rome, and come back St. Peter.

LONGFELLOW.

THE rest of the winter, or rather the early part of the spring, passed happily away. March, at Thirlwall, seemed more to belong to the former than the latter. Then spring came in good earnest; April and May brought warm days and wild flowers. Ellen refreshed herself and adorned the room with quantities of them; and as soon as might be she set about restoring the winter-ruined garden. Mr. John was not fond of gardening; he provided her with all manner of tools, ordered whatever work she wanted to be done for her, supplied her with new plants, and seeds, and roots, and was always ready to give her his help in any operations or press of business that called for it. But for the most part Ellen hoed, and raked, and transplanted, and sowed seeds, while he walked or read; often giving his counsel indeed, asked and unasked, and always coming in between her and any difficult or heavy job. The hours thus spent were to Ellen hours of unmixed delight. When he did not choose to go himself he sent Thomas with her, as the garden was some little distance down the mountain, away from the house and from every body; he never allowed her to go there alone.

As if to verify Mr. Van Brunt's remark, that "something is

always happening most years," about the middle of May there came letters that after all determined John's going abroad. The sudden death of two relatives, one after the other, had left the family estate to Mr. Humphreys; it required the personal attendance either of himself or his son; he could not, therefore his son

must, go. Once on the other side of the Atlantic, Mr. John thought it best his going should fulfil all the ends for which both Mr. Humphreys and Mr. Marshman had desired it; this would occasion his stay to be prolonged to at least a year, probably more. And he must set off without delay.

In the midst, not of his hurry, for Mr. John seldom was or seemed to be in a hurry about any thing; but in the midst of his business, he took special care of every thing that concerned or could possibly concern Ellen. He arranged what books she should read, what studies she should carry on; and directed that about these matters as well as about all others she should keep up a constant communication with him by letter. He requested Mrs. Chauncey to see that she wanted nothing, and to act as her general guardian in all minor things, respecting which Mr. Humphreys could be expected to take no thought whatever. And what Ellen thanked him for most of all, he found time for all his wonted rides, and she thought more than his wonted talks with her; endeavouring, as he well knew how, both to strengthen and cheer her mind in view of his long absence. The memory of those hours never went from her.

The family at Ventnor were exceeding desirous that she should make one of them during all the time John should be gone; they urged it with every possible argument. Ellen said little, but he knew she did not wish it; and finally compounded the matter by arranging that she should stay at the parsonage through the summer, and spend the winter at Ventnor, sharing all Ellen Chauncey's advantages of every kind. Ellen was all the more pleased with this arrangement that Mr. George Marshman would be at home. The church John had been serving were becoming exceedingly attached to him and would by no means hear of giving him up; and Mr. George engaged, if possible, to supply his place while he should be away. Ellen Chauncey was in ecstasies. And it was further promised that the summer should not pass without as many visits on both sides as could well be brought about.

Ellen had the comfort, at the last, of hearing John say that she had behaved unexceptionably well where he knew it was difficult for her to behave well at all. That *was* a comfort, from him, whose notions of unexceptionable behaviour she knew were remarkably high. But the parting, after all, was a dreadfully hard matter; though softened as much as it could be at the time and rendered very sweet to Ellen's memory by the tenderness, gentleness, and kindness, with which her brother without checking soothed her grief. He was to go early in the morning; and he made Ellen take leave of him the night before; but he was in no hurry to send her away; and when at length he told her it was very late, and she rose up to go, he went with her to the very door of her room and there bade her good-night.

How the next days passed Ellen hardly knew; they were unspeakably long.

Not a week after, one morning Nancy Vawse came into the kitchen, and asked in her blunt fashion,

"Is Ellen Montgomery at home?"

"I believe Miss Ellen is in the parlour," said Margery dryly.

"I want to speak to her."

Margery silently went across the hall to the sitting-room.

"Miss Ellen, dear," she said softly, "here is that Nancy girl wanting to speak with you,—will you please to see her?"

Ellen eagerly desired Margery to let her in, by no means displeased to have some interruption to the sorrowful thoughts she could not banish. She received Nancy very kindly.

"Well, I declare, Ellen!" said that young lady, whose wandering eye was upon every thing but Ellen herself,—"ain't you as fine as a fiddle? I guess you never touch your fingers to a file now-a-days,—do you?"

"A file!" said Ellen.

"You ha'n't forgot what it means, I s'pose," said Nancy somewhat scornfully,—"'cause if you think I'm a going to swallow that, you're mistaken. I've seen you file off tables down yonder a few times, ha'n't I?"

"Oh, I remember now," said Ellen smiling;—"it is so long since I heard the word that I didn't know what you meant. Margery calls it a dishcloth, or a floorcloth, or something else."

"Well, you don't touch one now-a-days, do you?"

"No," said Ellen, "I have other things to do."

"Well, I guess you have. You've got enough of books now, for once, ha'n't you? What a lot!—I say, Ellen, have you got to read all these?"

"I hope so, in time," said Ellen, smiling. "Why haven't you been to see me before?"

"Oh,—I don't know!"—said Nancy, whose roving eye looked a little as if she felt herself out of her sphere. "I didn't know as you would care to see me now."

"I am very sorry you should think so, Nancy; I would be as glad to see you as ever. I have not forgotten all your old kindness to me when aunt Fortune was sick."

"You've forgotten all that went before that, I'spose," said Nancy with a half laugh. "You beat all! Most folks remember and forget just t'other way exactly. But besides, I didn't know but I should catch myself in queer company."

"Well—I am all alone now," said Ellen, with a sigh.

"Yes, if you warn't I wouldn't be here, I can tell you. What do you think I have come for to-day, Ellen?"

"For any thing but to see me?"

Nancy nodded very decisively.

"What?"

"Guess."

" How can I possibly guess?   What have you got tucked up in
your apron there?"

" Ah!—that's the very thing," said Nancy.   " What *have* I
got, sure enough?"

" Well, I can't tell through your apron," said Ellen smiling.

" And *I* can't tell either;—that's more, ain't it?   Now listen,
and I'll tell you where I got it, and then you may find out what it
is, for I don't know.   Promise you won't tell any body."

" I don't like to promise that, Nancy."

" Why?"

" Because it might be something I ought to tell somebody
about."

" But it ain't."

" If it isn't I won't tell.   Can't you leave it so?"

" But what a plague!   Here I have gone and done all this just
for you, and now you must go and make a fuss.   What hurt would
it do you to promise?—it's nobody's business but yours and mine,
and somebody else's that won't make any talk about it I promise
you."

" I won't speak of it, certainly, Nancy, unless I think I ought;
can't you trust me?"

" I wouldn't give two straws for any body else's say so," said
Nancy;—" but as you're as stiff as the mischief I s'pose I'll have
to let it go.   I'll trust you!   Now listen.   It don't look like any
thing, does it?"

" Why no," said Ellen laughing; " you hold your apron so loose
that I cannot see any thing."

" Well, now listen.   You know I've been helping down at your
aunt's,—did you?"

" No."

" Well, I have,—these six weeks.   You never see any thing go on
quieter than they do, Ellen.   I declare it's fun.   Miss Fortune never
was so good in her days.   I don't mean she ain't as ugly as ever, you
know, but she has to keep it in.   All I have to do if I think any
thing is going wrong, I just let her think I am going to speak to
him about it;—only I have to do it very cunning for fear she would
guess what I am up to; and the next thing I know it's all straight.
He *is* about the coolest shaver," said Nancy, " I ever did see.   The
way he walks through her notions once in a while—not very often,
mind you, but when he takes a fancy,—it's fun to see!   Oh, I can
get along there first-rate now.   *You'd* have a royal time, Ellen."

" Well, Nancy—your story?"

" Don't you be in a hurry!   I am going to take my time.   Well
I've been there this six weeks; doing all sorts of things, you know;
taking your place, Ellen; don't you wish you was back in it?—
Well a couple of weeks since, Mrs. Van took it into her head

she would have up the wagon and go to Thirlwall to get herself some things; a queer start for her; but at any rate Van Brunt brought up the wagon and in she got and off they went. Now *she meant*, you must know, that I should be fast in the cellar-kitchen all the while she was gone, and she thought she had given me enough to keep me busy there; but I was up to her! I was as spry as a cricket, and flew round, and got things put up; and then I thought I'd have some fun. What do you think I did?—Mrs. Montgomery was quietly sitting in the chimney-corner and I had the whole house to myself. How Van Brunt looks out for her, Ellen; he won't let her be put out for any thing or any body."

"I am glad of it," said Ellen, her face flushing and her eyes watering; "it is just like him. I love him for it."

"The other night she was mourning and lamenting at a great rate because she hadn't you to read to her; and what do you think he does but goes and takes the book and sits down and reads to her himself. You should have seen Mrs. Van's face!"

"What book?" said Ellen.

"What book?—why your book,—the Bible,—there ain't any other book in the house, as I know. What on earth are you crying for, Ellen?—He's fetched over his mother's old Bible, and there it lays on a shelf in the cupboard; and he has it out every once in a while. Maybe he's coming round, Ellen. But do hold up your head and listen to me! I can't talk to you while you lie with your head in the cushion like that. I ha'n't more than begun my story yet."

"Well, go on," said Ellen.

"You see, I ain't in any hurry," said Nancy,—"because as soon as I've finished I shall have to be off; and it's fun to talk to you. What do you think I did, when I had done up all my chores?— where do you think I found this, eh? *you'd* never guess."

"What is it?" said Ellen.

"No matter what it is;—I don't know;—where do you think I found it?"

"How can I tell? I don't know."

"You'll be angry with me when I tell you."

Ellen was silent.

"If it was any body else," said Nancy,—"I'd ha' seen 'em shot afore I'd ha' done it, or told of it either; but you ain't like any body else. Look here!" said she, tapping her apron gently with one finger and slowly marking off each word,— "this—came out of—your—aunt's—box—in—the closet—up stairs—in—her room."

"Nancy!"

"Ay, Nancy! there it is. Now you look! 'Twon't alter it, Ellen; that's where it was, if you look till tea-time."

" But how came you there ?''

" 'Cause I wanted to amuse myself, I tell you. Partly to please myself, and partly because Mrs. Van would be so mad if she knew it.''

" Oh, Nancy !''

" Well—I don't say it was right,—but any how I did it; you ha'n't heard what I found yet.''

" You had better put it right back again, Nancy, the first time you have a chance.''

" Put it back again —I'll give it to you, and then *you* may put it back again, if you have a mind. I should like to see you. Why you don't know what I found.''

" Well, what did you find ?''

" The box was chuck full of all sorts of things, and I had a mind to see what was in it, so I pulled 'em out one after the other till I got to the bottom. At the very bottom was some letters and papers, and there,—staring right in my face,—the first thing I see was, ' Miss Ellen Montgomery.' ''

" Oh, Nancy !'' screamed Ellen,—" a letter for me ?''

" Hush !—and sit down, will you ?—yes, a whole package of letters for you. Well, thought I, Mrs. Van has no right to that any how, and she ain't a going to take the care of it any more ; so I just took it up and put it in the bosom of my frock while I looked to see if there was any more for you, but there warn't. There it is !''—

And she tossed the package into Ellen's lap. Ellen's head swam.

" Well, good-by !'' said Nancy rising ;—" I may go now I suppose, and no thanks to me.''

" Yes I do—I do thank you very much, Nancy,'' cried Ellen, starting up and taking her by the hand,—" I do thank you,—though it wasn't right ;—but oh, how could she ! how could she !''

" Dear me !'' said Nancy ; " to ask that of Mrs. Van ! she could do any thing. *Why* she did it, ain't so easy to tell.''

Ellen, bewildered, scarcely knew, only *felt*, that Nancy had gone. The outer cover of her package, the seal of which was broken, contained three letters ; two addressed to Ellen, in her father's hand, the third to another person. The seals of these had not been broken. The first that Ellen opened she saw was all in the same hand with the direction ; she threw it down and eagerly tried the other. And yes ! there was indeed the beloved character of which she never thought to have seen another specimen. Ellen's heart swelled with many feelings ; thankfulness, tenderness, joy, and sorrow, past and present ;—*that* letter was not thrown down, but grasped, while tears fell much too fast for eyes to do their work. It was long before she could get far in the letter. But when she had fairly begun it, she went on swiftly, and almost breathlessly, to the end.

"My dear, dear little Ellen,

"I am scarcely able—but I must write to you once more. *Once* more, daughter, for it is not permitted me to see your face again in this world. I look to see it, my dear child, where it will be fairer than ever here it seemed, even to me. I shall die in this hope and expectation. Ellen, remember it. Your last letters have greatly encouraged and rejoiced me. I am comforted, and can leave you quietly in that hand that has led me and I believe is leading you. God bless you, my child!

"Ellen, I have a mother living, and she wishes to receive you as her own when I am gone. It is best you should know at once why I never spoke to you of her. After your aunt Bessy married and went to New York, it displeased and grieved my mother greatly that I too, who had always been her favourite child, should leave her for an American home. And when I persisted, in spite of all that entreaties and authority could urge, she said she forgave me for destroying all her prospects of happiness, but that after I should be married and gone she should consider me as lost to her entirely, and so I must consider myself. She never wrote to me, and I never wrote to her after I reached America. She was dead to me. I do not say that I did not deserve it.

"But I have written to her lately and she has written to me. She permits me to die in the joy of being entirely forgiven, and in the further joy of knowing that the only source of care I had left is done away. She will take you to her heart, to the place I once filled, and I believe fill yet. She longs to have you, and to have you as entirely her own, in all respects; and to this, in considera-tion of the wandering life your father leads, and will lead,—I am willing and he is willing to agree. It is arranged so. The old happy home of my childhood will be yours, my Ellen. It joys me to think of it. Your father will write to your aunt and to you on the subject, and furnish you with funds. It is our desire that you should take advantage of the very first opportunity of proper persons going to Scotland who will be willing to take charge of you. Your dear friends, Mr. and Miss Humphreys, will, I dare say, help you in this.

"To them I could say much, if I had strength. But words are little. If blessings and prayers from a full heart are worth any thing, they are the richer. My love and gratitude to them can-not——"

The writer had failed here; and what there was of the letter had evidently been written at different times. Captain Montgomery's was to the same purpose. He directed Ellen to embrace the first opportunity of suitable guardians, to cross the Atlantic and repair to No. — Georges-street, Edinburgh ; and that Miss Fortune would give her the money she would need, which he had written to her to do, and that the accompanying letter Ellen was to carry with her and deliver to Mrs. Lindsay, her grandmother.

Ellen felt as if her head would split. She took up that letter, gazed at the strange name and direction which had taken such new and startling interest for her, wondered over the thought of what she was ordered to do with it, marvelled what sort of fingers they were which would open it, or whether it would ever be opened ;— and finally, in a perfect maze, unable to read, think, or even weep, she carried her package of letters into her own room, the room that had been Alice's, laid herself on the bed, and them beside her ; and fell into a deep sleep.

She woke up toward evening with the pressure of a mountain weight upon her mind. Her thoughts and feelings were a maze still ; and not Mr. Humphreys himself could be more grave and abstracted than poor Ellen was that night. So many points were to be settled,—so many questions answered to herself,—it was a good while before Ellen could disentangle them, and know what she did think and feel, and what she would do.

She very soon found out her own mind upon one subject,—she would be exceeding sorry to be obliged to obey the directions in the letters. But must she obey them ?

" I have promised Alice," thought Ellen ;—" I have promised Mr. Humphreys—I can't be adopted twice. And this Mrs. Lindsay,— my grandmother !—she cannot be nice or she wouldn't have treated my mother so. She cannot be a nice person ;—hard,—she must be hard ;—I never want to see her. My mother !—But then my mother loved her, and was very glad to have me go to her. Oh ! —oh ! how could she !—how could they do so !—when they didn't know how it might be with me, and what dear friends they might make me leave ! Oh, it was cruel !—But then they did *not* know, that is the very thing—they thought I would have nobody but aunt Fortune, and so it's no wonder—Oh, what shall I do ! What *ought* I to do ? These people in Scotland must have given me up by this time ; it's—let me see—it's just about three years now,— a little less,—since these letters were written. I am older now, and circumstances are changed ; I have a home and a father and a brother ; may I not judge for myself ?—But my mother and my father have ordered me,—what shall I do !—If John were only here—but perhaps he would make me go,—he might think it right. And to leave him,—and maybe never to see him again !—and Mr. Humphreys ! and how lonely he would be without me, I cannot ! I will not ! Oh, what *shall* I do ! What shall I do !"

Ellen's meditations gradually plunged her in despair; for she could not look at the event of being obliged to go, and she could not get rid of the feeling that perhaps it might come to that. She wept bitterly; it didn't mend the matter. She thought painfully, fearfully, long; and was no nearer an end. She could not endure to submit the matter to Mr. Humphreys; she feared his decision; and she feared also that he would give her the money Miss Fortune had failed to supply for the journey; how much it might be Ellen had no idea. She could not dismiss the subject as decided by circumstances, for conscience pricked her with the fifth commandment. She was miserable. It happily occurred to her at last to take counsel with Mrs. Vawse; this might be done she knew without betraying Nancy; Mrs. Vawse was much too honourable to press her as to how she came by the letters, and her word could easily be obtained not to speak of the affairs to any one. As for Miss Fortune's conduct, it must be made known; there was no help for that. So it was settled; and Ellen's breast was a little lightened of its load of care for that time; she had leisure to think of some other things.

Why had Miss Fortune kept back the letters? Ellen guessed pretty well, but she did not know quite all. The package, with its accompanying despatch to Miss Fortune, had arrived shortly after Ellen first heard the news of her mother's death, when she was refuged with Alice at the parsonage. At the time of its being sent Captain Montgomery's movements were extremely uncertain; and in obedience to the earnest request of his wife he directed that without waiting for his own return Ellen should immediately set out for Scotland. Part of the money for her expenses he sent; the rest he desired his sister to furnish, promising to make all straight when he should come home. But it happened that he was already this lady's debtor in a small amount, which Miss Fortune had serious doubts of ever being repaid; she instantly determined that if she had once been a fool in lending him money, she would not a second time in adding to the sum; if he wanted to send his daughter on a wild-goose-chase after great relations, he might come home himself and see to it; it was none of her business. Quietly taking the remittance to refund his own owing, she of course threw the letters into her box, as the delivery of them would expose the whole transaction. There they lay till Nancy found them.

Early next morning after breakfast Ellen came into the kitchen, and begged Margery to ask Thomas to bring the Brownie to the door. Surprised at the energy in her tone and manner, Margery gave the message and added that Miss Ellen seemed to have picked up wonderfully; she hadn't heard her speak so brisk since Mr. John went away.

The Brownie was soon at the door, but not so soon as Ellen, who had dressed in feverish haste. The Brownie was not alone; there was old John saddled and bridled, and Thomas Grimes in waiting.

"It's not necessary for you to take that trouble, Thomas," said Ellen;—"I don't mind going alone at all."

"I beg your pardon, Miss Ellen,—(Thomas touched his hat)— but Mr. John left particular orders that I was to go with Miss Ellen whenever it pleased her to ride; never failing."

"Did he!" said Ellen;—"but is it convenient for you now, Thomas? I want to go as far as Mrs. Vawse's."

"It's always convenient, Miss Ellen,—always; Miss Ellen need not think of that at all, I am always ready."

Ellen mounted upon the Brownie, sighing for the want of the hand that used to lift her to the saddle; and spurred by this recollection set off at a round pace.

Soon she was at Mrs. Vawse's; and soon finding her alone, Ellen had spread out all her difficulties before her and given her the letters to read. Mrs. Vawse readily promised to speak on the subject to no one without Ellen's leave; her suspicions fell upon Mr. Van Brunt, not her grand-daughter. She heard all the story, and read the letters before making any remark.

"Now, dear Mrs. Vawse," said Ellen anxiously, when the last one was folded up and laid on the table,—"what do you think?"

"I think, my child, you must go," said the old lady steadily.

Ellen looked keenly, as if to find some other answer in her face; her own changing more and more for a minute, till she sunk it in her hands.

"Cela vous donne beaucoup de chagrin,—je le vois bien," said the old lady tenderly. (Their conversations were always in Mrs. Vawse's tongue.)

"But," said Ellen presently, lifting her head again, (there were no tears)—"I cannot go without money."

"That can be obtained without any difficulty."

"From whom? I cannot ask aunt Fortune for it, Mrs. Vawse; I could not do it!"

"There is no difficulty about the money. Show your letters to Mr. Humphreys."

"Oh, I cannot!" said Ellen, covering her face again.

"Will you let me do it? I will speak to him if you permit me."

"But what use? *He* ought not to give me the money, Mrs. Vawse? It would not be right; and to show him the letters would be like asking him for it. Oh, I can't bear to do that!"

"He would give it you, Ellen, with the greatest pleasure."

"Oh, no, Mrs. Vawse," said Ellen, bursting into tears,—"he

would never be pleased to send me away from him! I know—I know—he would miss me. Oh, what shall I do?"

"Not *that*, my dear Ellen," said the old lady, coming to her and gently stroking her head with both hands. "You must do what is *right;* and you know it cannot be but that will be the best and happiest for you in the end."

"Oh, I wish—I wish," exclaimed Ellen from the bottom of her heart,—"those letters had never been found!"

"Nay, Ellen, *that* is not right."

"But I promised Alice, Mrs. Vawse; ought I go away and leave him? Oh, Mrs. Vawse, it is very hard! *Ought* I?"

"Your father and your mother have said it, my child."

"But they never would have said it if they had known?"

"But they did not know, Ellen; and here it is."

Ellen wept violently, regardless of the caresses and soothing words which her old friend lavished upon her.

"There is one thing!" said she at last, raising her head,—"I don't know of any body going to Scotland, and I am not likely to; and if I only do not before autumn,—that is not a good time to go, and then comes winter."

"My dear Ellen!" said Mrs. Vawse sorrowfully, "I must drive you from your last hope. Don't you know that Mrs. Gillespie is going abroad with all her family?—next month I think."

Ellen grew pale for a minute, and sat holding bitter counsel with her own heart. Mrs. Vawse hardly knew what to say next.

"You need not feel uneasy about your journeying expenses," she remarked after a pause;—"you can easily repay them, if you wish, when you reach your friends in Scotland."

Ellen did not hear her. She looked up with an odd expression of determination in her face, determination taking its stand upon difficulties.

"I shan't stay there, Mrs. Vawse, if I go!—I shall go, I suppose, if I must; but do you think any thing will keep me there? Never!"

"You will stay for the same reason that you go for, Ellen; to do your duty."

"Yes, till I am old enough to choose for myself, Mrs. Vawse, and then I shall come back; if they will let me."

"Whom do you mean by 'they?'"

"Mr. Humphreys and Mr. John."

"My dear Ellen," said the old lady kindly, "be satisfied with doing your duty now; leave the future. While you follow him, God will be your friend; is not that enough? and all things shall work for your good. You do not know what you will wish when the time comes you speak of. You do not know what new friends you may find to love."

Ellen had in her own heart the warrant for what she had said and what she saw by her smile Mrs. Vawse doubted; but she disdained to assert what she could bring nothing to prove. She took a sorrowful leave of her old friend and returned home.

After dinner, when Mr. Humphreys was about going back to his study, Ellen timidly stopped him and gave him her letters, and asked him to look at them some time when he had leisure. She told him also where they were found and how long they had lain there, and that Mrs. Vawse had said she ought to show them to him.

She guessed he would read them at once,—and she waited with a beating heart. In a little while she heard his step coming back along the hall. He came and sat down by her on the sofa and took her hand.

"What is your wish in this matter, my child?" he said gravely and cheerfully.

Ellen's look answered that.

"I will do whatever you say I must, sir," she said faintly.

"I dare not ask myself what *I* would wish, Ellen; the matter is taken out of our hands. You must do your parents' will, my child. I will try to hope that you will gain more than I lose. As the Lord pleases! If I am bereaved of my children, I am bereaved."

"Mrs. Gillespie," he said after a pause, "is about going to England;—I know not how soon. It will be best for you to see her at once and make all arrangements that may be necessary. I will go with you to-morrow to Ventnor if the day be a good one."

There was something Ellen longed to say, but it was impossible to get it out; she could not utter a word. She had pressed her hands upon her face to try to keep herself quiet; but Mr. Humphreys could see the deep crimson flushing to the very roots of her hair. He drew her close within his arms for a moment, kissed her forehead, Ellen *felt* it was sadly, and went away. It was well she did not hear him sigh as he went back along the hall; it was well she did not see the face of more settled gravity with which he sat down to his writing; she had enough of her own.

They went to Ventnor. Mrs. Gillespie with great pleasure undertook the charge of her and promised to deliver her safely to her friends in Scotland. It was arranged that she should go back to Thirlwall to make her adieus; and that in a week or two a carriage should be sent to bring her to Ventnor, where her preparations for the journey should be made, and whence the whole party would set off.

"So you are going to be a Scotchwoman after all, Ellen," said Miss Sophia.

"I had a great deal rather be an American, Miss Sophia."

" Why Hutchinson will tell you," said the young lady, " that it is infinitely more desirable to be a Scotchwoman than that."

Ellen's face, however, looked so little inclined to be merry that she took up the subject in another tone.

" Seriously, do you know," said she, " I have been thinking it is a very happy thing for you. I don't know what would become of you alone in that great parsonage house. You would mope yourself to death in a little while ; especially now that Mr. John is gone."

" He will be back," said Ellen.

" Yes but what if he is ? he can't stay at Thirlwall, child. He can't live thirty miles from his church you know. Did you think he would ? They think all the world of him already. I expect they'll barely put up with Mr. George while he is gone ;—they will want Mr. John all to themselves when he comes back, you may rely on that. What *are* you thinking of, child ?"

For Ellen's eyes were sparkling with two or three thoughts which Miss Sophia could not read.

" I should like to know what you are smiling at," she said with some curiosity. But the smile was almost immediately quenched in tears.

Notwithstanding Miss Sophia's discouraging talk, Ellen privately agreed with Ellen Chauncey that the Brownie should be sent to her to keep and use as her own, *till his mistress should come back ;* both children being entirely of opinion that the arrangement was a most unexceptionable one.

It was not forgotten that the lapse of three years since the date of the letters left some uncertainty as to the present state of affairs among Ellen's friends in Scotland ; but this doubt was not thought sufficient to justify her letting pass so excellent an opportunity of making the journey. Especially as Captain Montgomery's letter spoke of an *uncle,* to whom equally with her grandmother, Ellen was to be consigned. In case circumstances would permit it, Mrs. Gillespie engaged to keep Ellen with her, and bring her home to America when she herself should return.

And in little more than a month they were gone ; adieus and preparations and all were over. Ellen's parting with Mrs. Vawse was very tender and very sad ;—with Mr. Van Brunt, extremely and gratefully affectionate, on both sides ;—with her aunt, constrained and brief ;—with Margery, very sorrowful indeed. But Ellen's longest and most lingering adieu was to Captain Parry, the old grey cat. For one whole evening she sat with him in her arms ; and over poor pussy were shed the tears that fell for many better loved and better deserving personages, as well as those not a few that were wept for him. Since Alice's death Parry had transferred his entire confidence and esteem to Ellen ; whether from feeling a want, or because love and tenderness had taught her the touch and the tone that were fitted to win his regard. Only John shared it. Ellen was his chief favourite and almost constant companion. And bitterer tears Ellen shed at no time than that evening before she went away, over the old cat. She could not distress kitty with her distress, nor weary him with the calls upon his sympathy, though indeed it is true that he sundry times poked his nose up wonderingly and caressingly in her face. She had no remonstrance or interruption to fear; and taking pussy as the emblem and representative of the whole household, Ellen wept them all over him; with a tenderness and a bitterness that were somehow intensified by the sight of the grey coat, and white paws, and kindly face, of her unconscious old brute friend.

The old people at Carra-carra were taken leave of; the Brownie too, with great difficulty. And Nancy.

"I am real sorry you are going, Ellen," said she;—"you're the only soul in town I care about. I wish I'd thrown them letters in the fire after all! Who'd ha' thought it!"

Ellen could not help in her heart echoing the wish.

"I'm real sorry, Ellen," she repeated. "Ain't there something I can do for you when you are gone?"

"Oh, yes, dear Nancy," said Ellen, weeping,—"if you would only take care of your dear grandmother. She is left alone now. If you would only take care of her, and read your Bible, and be good, Nancy,—oh, Nancy, Nancy! do, do!"

They kissed each other, and Nancy went away fairly crying.

Mrs. Marshman's own woman, a steady excellent person, had come in the carriage for Ellen. And the next morning early after breakfast, when every thing else was ready, she went into Mr. Humphreys' study to bid the last dreaded good-by. She thought her obedience was costing her dear.

It was nearly a silent parting. He held her a long time in his arms; and there Ellen bitterly thought her place ought to be. "What have I to do to seek new relations?" she said to herself. But she was speechless; till gently relaxing his hold he tenderly smoothed back her disordered hair, and kissing her, said a very few grave words of blessing and counsel. Ellen gathered all her strength together then, for she had something that *must* be spoken.

"Sir," said she, falling on her knees before him and looking up in his face,—"this don't alter—you do not take back what you said, do you?"

"What that I said, my child?"

"That," said Ellen, hiding her face in her hands on his knee, and scarce able to speak with great effort,—"that which you said when I first came—that which you said about——"

"About what, my dear child?"

" My going away don't change any thing, does it, sir?   Mayn't
I come back, if ever I can?"

He raised her up and drew her close to his bosom again.

" My dear little daughter," said he, " you cannot be so glad to
come back as my arms and my heart will be to receive you.   I
scarce dare hope to see that day, but all in this house is yours, dear
Ellen, as well when in Scotland as here.   I take back nothing, my
daughter.   Nothing is changed."

A word or two more of affection and blessing, which Ellen was
utterly unable to answer in any way,—and she went to the carriage; with one drop of cordial in her heart, that she fed upon a
long while.   " He called me his daughter!—he never said that before since Alice died!   Oh, so I will be as long as I live, if I find
fifty new relations.   But what good will a daughter three thousand
miles off do him !"

CHAPTER XLVII.

Speed. Item. *She is proud.*
Laun. Out with that;—it was Eve's legacy, and cannot be ta'en from her.
                                                    SHAKSPEARE.

THE voyage was peaceful and prosperous; in due time the whole
party found themselves safe in London. Ever since they set out
Ellen had been constantly gaining on Mrs. Gillespie's good will;
the major hardly saw her but she had something to say about that
"best-bred child in the world." "Best-hearted too, I think," said
the major; and even Mrs. Gillespie owned that there was something more than good-breeding in Ellen's politeness. She had good
trial of it; Mrs. Gillespie was much longer ailing than any of the
party; and when Ellen got well, it was her great pleasure to de-
vote herself to the service of the only member of the Marshman
family now within her reach. She could never do too much. She
watched by her, read to her, was quick to see and perform all the
little offices of attention and kindness where a servant's hand is
not so acceptable; and withal never was in the way nor put herself
forward. Mrs. Gillespie's own daughter was much less helpful.
Both she and William, however, had long since forgotten the old
grudge, and treated Ellen as well as they did any body; rather
better. Major Gillespie was attentive and kind as possible to the
gentle, well-behaved little body that was always at his wife's pillow; and even Lester, the maid, told one of her friends "she was
such a sweet little lady that it was a pleasure and gratification to
do any thing for her." Lester acted this out; and in her kindly
disposition Ellen found very substantial comfort and benefit
throughout the voyage.

Mrs. Gillespie told her husband she should be rejoiced if it turned
out that they might keep Ellen with them and carry her back to
America; she only wished it were not for Mr. Humphreys but herself. As their destination was not now Scotland but Paris, it was
proposed to write to Ellen's friends to ascertain whether any change
had occurred, or whether they still wished to receive her. This
however was rendered unnecessary. They were scarcely established
in their hotel, when a gentleman from Edinburgh, an intimate
friend of the Ventnor family, and whom Ellen herself had more
than once met there, came to see them. Mrs. Gillespie bethought
herself to make inquiries of him.

"Do you happen to know a family of Lindsays, in Georges-street,
Mr. Dundas?"

"Lindsays? yes, perfectly well. Do you know them?"

" No ; but I am very much interested in one of the family. Is the old lady living ?"

" Yes, certainly ;—not very old either—not above sixty, or sixty-five ; and as hale and alert as at forty. A very fine old lady."

" A large family ?"

" Oh, no ; Mr. Lindsay is a widower this some years, with no children ; and there is a widowed daughter lately come home,—Lady Keith ;—that's all."

" Mr. Lindsay—that is the son ?"

" Yes. You would like them. They are excellent people—excellent family—wealthy—beautiful country seat on the south bank of the Tyne, some miles out of Edinburgh ; I was down there two weeks ago ;—entertain most handsomely and agreeably, two things that do not always go together. You meet a pleasanter circle nowhere than at Lindsay's."

" And that is the whole family ?" said Mrs. Gillespie.

" That is all. There were two daughters married to America some dozen or so years ago. Mrs. Lindsay took it very hard, I believe, but she bore up, and bears up now, as if misfortune had never crossed her path ; though the death of Mr. Lindsay's wife and son was another great blow. I don't believe there is a grey hair on her head at this moment. There is some peculiarity about them perhaps,—some pride too ;—but that is an amiable weakness," he added laughing, as he rose to go ;—" Mrs. Gillespie, I am sure will not find fault with them for it."

" That's an insinuation, Mr. Dundas ; but look here, what I am bringing to Mrs. Lindsay in the shape of a grand-daughter."

" What, my old acquaintance, Miss Ellen !—is it possible !—My dear madam, if you had such a treasure for sale, they would pour half their fortune into your lap to purchase it, and the other half at her feet."

" I would not take it, Mr. Dundas."

" It would be no mean price, I assure you, in itself, however it might be comparatively. I give Miss Ellen joy."

Miss Ellen took none of his giving.

" Ah, Ellen, my dear," said Mrs. Gillespie when he was gone,—" we shall never have you back in America again. I give up all hopes of it. Why do you look so solemn, my love ? You are a strange child ; most girls would be delighted at such a prospect opening before them."

" You forget what I leave, Mrs. Gillespie."

" So will you, my love, in a few days ; though I love you for remembering so well those that have been kind to you. But you don't realize yet what is before you."

" Why you'll have a good time, Ellen," said Marianne :—" I wonder you are not out of your wits with joy. *I* should be."

" You may as well make over the Brownie to me, Ellen," said William ;—" I expect you'll never want him again."

" I cannot, you know, William ; I lent him to Ellen Chauncey."

"*Lent* him !—that's a good one. For how long ?"

Ellen smiled, though sighing inwardly to see how very much narrowed was her prospect of ever mounting him again. She did not care to explain herself to those around her. Still, at the very bottom of her heart lay two thoughts, in which her hope refuged itself. One was a peculiar assurance that whatever her brother pleased, nothing could hinder him from accomplishing ; the other, a like confidence that it would not please him to leave his little sister unlooked-after. But all began to grow misty, and it seemed now as if Scotland must henceforth be the limit of her horizon.

Leaving their children at a relation's house, Major and Mrs. Gillespie accompanied her to the north. They travelled post, and arriving in the evening at Edinburgh, put up at a hotel in Prince's-street. It was agreed that Ellen should not seek her new home till the morrow ; she should eat one more supper and breakfast with her old friends, and have a night's rest first. She was very glad of it. The major and Mrs. Gillespie were enchanted with the noble view from their parlour windows ; while they were eagerly conversing together, Ellen sat alone at the other window, looking out upon the curious Old Town. There was all the fascination of novelty and beauty about that singular picturesque mass of buildings, in its sober colouring, growing more sober as the twilight fell ; and just before outlines were lost in the dusk, lights began feebly to twinkle here and there, and grew brighter and more as the night came on, till their brilliant multitude were all that could be seen where the curious jumble of chimneys and house-tops and crooked ways had shown a little before. Ellen sat watching this lighting up of the Old Town, feeling strangely that she was in the midst of new scenes indeed, entering upon a new stage of life; and having some difficulty to persuade herself that she was really Ellen Montgomery. The scene of extreme beauty before her seemed rather to increase the confusion and sadness of her mind. Happily, joyfully, Ellen remembered, as she sat gazing over the darkening city and its brightening lights, that there was One near her who could not change ; that Scotland was no remove from him ; that his providence as well as his heaven was over her there ; that there, not less than in America, she was his child. She rejoiced, as she sat in her dusky window, over his words of assurance, " I am the good shepherd, and know my sheep, and am known of mine ;" and she looked up into the clear sky (that at least was home-like), in tearful thankfulness, and with earnest prayer that she might be kept from evil. Ellen guessed she might have special need to offer that prayer. And as again her eye wandered over the singular bright spectacle that kept reminding her she was a stranger in a strange place, her heart joyfully leaned upon another loved sentence, —"This God is our God for ever and ever; he will be our guide even unto death."

She was called from her window to supper.

"Why how well you look," said Mrs. Gillespie; "I expected you would have been half tired to death. Doesn't she look well?"

"As if she was neither tired, hungry, nor sleepy," said Major Gillespie kindly;—"and yet she must be all three."

Ellen was all three. But she had the rest of a quiet mind.

In the same quiet mind, a little fluttered and anxious now, she set out in the post-chaise the next morning with her kind friends to No. — Georges-street. It was their intention, after leaving her, to go straight on to England. They were in a hurry to be there; and Mrs. Gillespie judged that the presence of a stranger at the meeting between Ellen and her relations would be desired by none of the parties. But when they reached the house they found the family were not at home; they were in the country—at their place on the Tyne. The direction was obtained, and the horses' heads turned that way. After a drive of some length, through what kind of a country Ellen could hardly have told, they arrived at the place.

It was beautifully situated; and through well-kept grounds they drove up to a large, rather old-fashioned, substantial-looking house. "The ladies were at home;" and that ascertained, Ellen took a kind leave of Mrs. Gillespie, shook hands with the major at the door, and was left alone for the second time in her life, to make her acquaintance with new and untried friends. She stood for one second looking after the retreating carriage,—one swift thought went to her adopted father and brother far away,—one to her Friend in heaven,—and Ellen quietly turned to the servant and asked for Mrs. Lindsay.

She was shown into a large room where nobody was, and sat down with a beating heart while the servant went up stairs; looking with a strange feeling upon what was to be her future home. The house was handsome, comfortably, luxuriously furnished; but without any attempt at display. Things rather old-fashioned than otherwise; plain, even homely in some instances; yet evidently there was no sparing of money in any line of use or comfort; nor were reading and writing, painting and music, strangers there. Unconsciously acting upon her brother's principle of judging of people from their works, Ellen, from what she saw gathered around her, formed a favourable opinion of her relations; without thinking of it, for indeed she was thinking of something else.

A lady presently entered, and said that Mrs. Lindsay was not very well. Seeing Ellen's very hesitating look, she added, " shall I carry her any message for you ?"

This lady was well-looking and well-dressed ; but somehow there was something in her face or manner that encouraged Ellen to an explanation ; she could make none. She silently gave her her father's letter, with which the lady left the room.

In a minute or two she returned and said her mother would see Ellen up stairs, and asked her to come with her. This then must be Lady Keith !—but no sign of recognition ? Ellen wondered, as her trembling feet carried her up stairs, and to the door of a room where the lady motioned her to enter ; she did not follow herself.

A large pleasant dressing-room ; but Ellen saw nothing but the dignified figure and searching glance of a lady in black, standing in the middle of the floor. At the look which instantly followed her entering, however, Ellen sprang forward, and was received in arms that folded her as fondly and as closely as ever those of her own mother had done. Without releasing her from their clasp, Mrs. Lindsay presently sat down ; and placing Ellen on her lap, and for a long time without speaking a word, she overwhelmed her with caresses,—caresses often interrupted with passionate bursts of tears. Ellen herself cried heartily for company, though Mrs. Lindsay little guessed why. Along with the joy and tenderness arising from the finding a relation that so much loved and valued her, and along with the sympathy that entered into Mrs. Lindsay's thoughts, there mixed other feelings. She began to know, as if by instinct, what kind of a person her grandmother was. The clasp of the arms that were about her said as plainly as possible, " I will never let you go !" Ellen felt it ; she did not know in her confusion whether she was most glad or most sorry ; and this uncertainty mightily helped the flow of her tears.

When this scene had lasted some time Mrs. Lindsay began with the utmost tenderness to take off Ellen's gloves, her cape (her bonnet had been hastily thrown off long before), and smoothing back her hair, and taking the fair little face in both her hands, she looked at it and pressed it to her own, as indeed something most dearly prized and valued. Then saying, " I must lie down ; come in here, love,"—she led her into the next room, locked the door, made Ellen stretch herself on the bed : and placing herself beside her drew her close to her bosom again, murmuring, " My own child—my precious child—my Ellen—my own darling—why did you stay away so long from me ?—tell me ?"

It was necessary to tell ; and this could not be done without revealing Miss Fortune's disgraceful conduct. Ellen was sorry for that ; she knew her mother's American match had been unpopular with her friends ; and now what notions this must give them of one at least of the near connections to whom it had introduced her. She winced under what might be her grandmother's thoughts. Mrs. Lindsay heard her in absolute silence, and made no comment; and at the end again kissed her lips and cheeks, embracing her, Ellen *felt*, as a recovered treasure that would not be parted with. She was not satisfied till she had drawn Ellen's head fairly to rest on her breast, and then her caressing hand often touched her cheek, or smoothed back her hair, softly now and then asking slight questions about her voyage and journey; till exhausted from excitement more than fatigue Ellen fell asleep.

Her grandmother was beside her when she awoke, and busied herself with evident delight in helping her to get off her travelling clothes and put on others; and then she took her down stairs and presented her to her aunt.

Lady Keith had not been at home, nor in Scotland, at the time the letters passed between Mrs. Montgomery and her mother; and the result of that correspondence, respecting Ellen, had been known to no one except Mrs. Lindsay and her son. They had long given her up; the rather as they had seen in the papers the name of Captain Montgomery among those lost in the ill-fated Duc d'Orleans. Lady Keith therefore had no suspicion who Ellen might be. She received her affectionately, but Ellen did not get rid of her first impression.

Her uncle she did not see until late in the day, when he came home. The evening was extremely fair, and having obtained permission, Ellen wandered out into the shrubbery; glad to be alone, and glad for a moment to exchange new faces for old; the flowers were old friends to her, and never had looked more friendly than then. New and old both were there. Ellen went on softly from flower-bed to flower-bed, soothed and rested, stopping here to smell one, or there to gaze at some old favourite or new beauty, thinking curious thoughts of the past and the future, and through it all taking a quiet lesson from the flowers;—when a servant came after her with a request from Mrs. Lindsay that she would return to the house. Ellen hurried in; she guessed for what, and was sure as soon as she opened the door and saw the figure of a gentleman sitting before Mrs. Lindsay. Ellen remembered well she was sent to her uncle as well as her grandmother, and she came forward with a beating heart to Mrs. Lindsay's outstretched hand, which presented her to this other ruler of her destiny. He was very different from Lady Keith,—her anxious glance saw that at once— more like his mother. A man not far from fifty years old; finelooking and stately like her. Ellen was not left long in suspense; his look instantly softened as his mother's had done; he drew her to his arms with great affection, and evidently with very great pleasure; then held her off for a moment while he looked at her changing colour and downcast eye, and folded her close in his arms again, from which he seemed hardly willing to let her go, whispering as he kissed her, "you are my own child now,—you are my little daughter,—do you know that, Ellen? I am your father henceforth;—you belong to me entirely, and I belong to you;—my own little daughter!"

"I wonder how many times one may be adopted," thought Ellen that evening;—"but to be sure, my father and my mother have quite given me up here,—that makes a difference; they had a right to give me away if they pleased. I suppose I do belong to my uncle and grandmother in good earnest, and I cannot help myself. Well! but Mr. Humphreys seems a great deal more like my father than my uncle Lindsay. I cannot help that—but how they would be vexed if they knew it?"

That was profoundly true!

Ellen was in a few days the dear pet and darling of the whole household, without exception and almost without limit. At first, for a day or two, there was a little lurking doubt, a little anxiety, a constant watch, on the part of all her friends, whether they were not going to find something in their newly acquired treasure to disappoint them; whether it could be that there was nothing behind to belie the first promise. Less keen observers, however, could not have failed to see very soon that there was no *disappointment* to be looked for; Ellen was just what she seemed, without the shadow of a cloak in any thing. Doubts vanished; and Ellen had not been three days in the house when she was taken home to two hearts at least in unbounded love and tenderness. When Mr. Lindsay was present he was not satisfied without having Ellen in his arms or close beside him; and if not there she was at the side of her grandmother.

There was nothing, however, in the character of this fondness, great as it was, that would have inclined any child to presume upon it. Ellen was least of all likely to try; but if her will, by any chance, had run counter to theirs, she would have found it impossible to maintain her ground. She understood this from the first with her grandmother; and in one or two trifles since had been more and more confirmed in the feeling that they would do with her and make of her precisely what they pleased, without the smallest regard to her fancy. If it jumped with theirs, very well; if not, it must yield. In one matter Ellen had been roused to plead very hard, and even with tears, to have her wish, which she verily thought she ought to have had. Mrs. Lindsay smiled and kissed her, and went on with the utmost coolness in what she was doing, which she carried through, without in the least regarding Ellen's distress or showing the slightest discomposure; and the same thing was repeated every day, till Ellen got used to it. Her uncle she had never seen tried; but she knew it would be the same with him. When Mr. Lindsay clasped her to his bosom Ellen felt it was as *his own;* his eye always seemed to repeat, "*my own* little daughter;" and in his whole manner love was mingled with as much authority. Perhaps Ellen did not like them much the worse for this, as she had no sort of disposition to displease them in any thing; but it gave rise to sundry thoughts however, which she kept to herself; thoughts that went both to the future and the past.

Lady Keith, it may be, had less *heart* to give than her mother and brother, but pride took up the matter instead; and according to her measure Ellen held with her the same place she held with Mr. and Mrs. Lindsay; being the great delight and darling of all three and with all three, seemingly, the great object in life.

A few days after her arrival, a week or more, she underwent one evening a kind of catechising from her aunt, as to her former manner of life;—where she had been and with whom since her mother left her; what she had been doing; whether she had been to school, and how her time was spent at home, &c., &c. No comments whatever were made on her answers, but a something in her aunt's face and manner induced Ellen to make her replies as brief and to give her as little information in them as she could. She did not feel inclined to enlarge upon any thing, or to go at all further than the questions obliged her; and Lady Keith ended without having more than a very general notion of Ellen's way of life for three or four years past. This conversation was repeated to her grandmother and uncle.

"To think," said the latter the next morning at breakfast,— "to think that the backwoods of America should have turned us out such a little specimen of——"

"Of what, uncle?" said Ellen, laughing.

"Ah, I shall not tell you that," said he.

"But it is extraordinary," said Lady Keith,—"how after living among a parcel of thick-headed and thicker-tongued Yankees she could come out and speak pure English in a clear voice;—it is an enigma to me."

"Take care, Catherine," said Mr. Lindsay laughing,—"you are touching Ellen's nationality;—look here," said he, drawing his fingers down her cheek.

"She must learn to have no nationality but yours," said Lady Keith somewhat shortly.

Ellen's lips were open, but she spoke not.

"It is well you have come out from the Americans, you see, Ellen," pursued Mr. Lindsay;—"your aunt does not like them."

"But why, sir?"

"Why," said he gravely,—"don't you know that they are a

parcel of rebels who have broken loose from all loyalty and fealty, that no good Briton has any business to like?"

"You are not in earnest, uncle?"

"*You* are, I see," said he, looking amused. "Are you one of those that make a saint of George Washington?"

"No," said Ellen,—"I think he was a great deal better than some saints. But I don't think the Americans were rebels."

"You are a little rebel yourself. Do you mean to say you think the Americans were right?"

"Do you mean to say you think they were wrong, uncle?"

"I assure you," said he, "if I had been in the English army I would have fought them with all my heart."

"And if I had been in the American army I would have fought *you* with all my heart, uncle Lindsay."

"Come, come," said he laughing;—"*you* fight! you don't look as if you would do battle with a good-sized mosquito."

"Ah, but I mean if I had been a man," said Ellen.

"You had better put in that qualification. After all, I am inclined to think it may be as well for you on the whole that we did not meet. I don't know but we might have had a pretty stiff encounter, though."

"A good cause is stronger than a bad one, uncle."

"But Ellen,—these Americans forfeited entirely the character of good friends to England and good subjects to King George."

"Yes, but it was King George's fault, uncle; he and the English forfeited their characters first."

"I declare," said Mr. Lindsay laughing, "if your sword had been as stout as your tongue, I don't know how I might have come off in that same encounter."

"I hope Ellen will get rid of these strange notions about the Americans," said Lady Keith discontentedly.

"I hope not, aunt Keith," said Ellen.

"Where did you get them?" said Mr. Lindsay.

"What, sir?"

"These notions."

"In reading, sir; reading different books;—and talking."

"Reading!—So you did read in the backwoods?"

"Sir!" said Ellen, with a look of surprise.

"What have you read on this subject?"

"Two lives of Washington, and some in the Annual Register, and part of Graham's United States; and one or two other little things."

"But those gave you only one side, Ellen; you should read the English account of the matter."

"So I did, sir; the Annual Register gave me both sides; the bills and messages were enough."

" What Annual Register ?"

" I don't know, sir ;—it is English ;—written by Burke, I believe."

" Upon my word !   And what else have you read ?"

" I think that's all about America," said Ellen.

" No, but about other things ?"

" Oh, I don't know, sir," said Ellen smiling ;—" a great many books ;—I can't tell them all."

" Did you spend all your time over your books ?"

" A good deal, sir, lately ;—not so much before."

" How was that ?"

" I couldn't, sir.   I had a great many other things to do."

" What else had you to do ?"

" Different things," said Ellen, hesitating from the remembrance of her aunt's manner the night before.

" Come, come ! answer me."

" I had to sweep and dust," said Ellen colouring,—" and set tables,—and wash and wipe dishes,—and churn,—and spin,— and——"

Ellen *heard* Lady Keith's look in her, " Could you have conceived it !"

" What shall we do with her ?" said Mrs. Lindsay ;—" send her to school or keep her at home ?"

" Have you never been to school, Ellen ?"

" No, sir ; except for a very little while, more than three years ago."

" Would you like it ?"

" I would a *great* deal rather study at home, sir,—if you will let me."

" What do you know now ?"

" Oh, I can't tell, sir," said Ellen ;—" I don't know any thing very well,—unless——"

" Unless what ?" said her uncle laughing ;—" come ! now for your accomplishments."

" I had rather not say what I was going to, uncle ; please don't ask me."

" Yes, yes," said he ;—" I shan't let you off.   Unless what ?"

" I was going to say, unless riding," said Ellen colouring.

" Riding !—And pray how did you learn to ride ?   Catch a horse by the mane and mount him by the fence and canter off bare-backed ? was that it ? eh ?"

" Not exactly, sir," said Ellen laughing.

" Well, but about your other accomplishments.   You do not know any thing of French, I suppose ?"

" Yes I do, sir."

" Where did you get that?"

" An old Swiss lady in the mountains taught me."

" Country riding and Swiss French," muttered her uncle.

" Did she teach you to speak it?"

" Yes, sir."

Mr. Lindsay and his mother exchanged glances, which Ellen interpreted, " Worse and worse."

" One thing at least can be mended," observed Mr. Lindsay. " She shall go to De Courcy's riding-school as soon as we get to Edinburgh."

" Indeed, uncle, I don't think that will be necessary."

" Who taught you to ride, Ellen?" asked Lady Keith.

" My brother."

" Humph!—I fancy a few lessons will do you no harm," she remarked.

Ellen coloured and was silent.

" You know nothing of music, of course?"

" I cannot play, uncle."

" Can you sing?"

" I can sing hymns."

" Sing hymns! That's the only fault I find with you, Ellen,— you are too sober. I should like to see you a little more gay,— like other children."

" But uncle, I am not unhappy because I am sober."

" But I am," said he. " I do not know precisely what I shall do with you; I must do something!"

" Can you sing nothing but hymns?" asked Lady Keith.

" Yes, ma'am," said Ellen, with some humour twinkling about her eyes and mouth,—" I can sing ' Hail Columbia!' "

" Absurd!" said Lady Keith.

" Why, Ellen," said her uncle laughing,—" I did not know you could be so stubborn; I thought you were made up of gentleness and mildness. Let me have a good look at you,—there's not much stubbornness in those eyes," he said fondly.

" I hope you will never salute *my* ears with your American ditty," said Lady Keith.

" Tut, tut," said Mr. Lindsay, " she shall sing what she pleases, and the more the better."

" She has a very sweet voice," said her grandmother.

" Yes, in speaking, I know; I have not heard it tried otherwise; and very nice English it turns out. Where did you get your English, Ellen?"

" From my brother," said Ellen, with a smile of pleasure.

Mr. Lindsay's brow rather clouded.

" Whom do you mean by that?"

" The brother of the lady that was so kind to me." Ellen disliked to speak the loved names in the hearing of ears to which she knew they would be unlovely.

"How was she so kind to you?"

"Oh, sir!—in every thing—I cannot tell you;—she was my friend when I had only one beside; she did every thing for me."

"And who was the other friend? your aunt?"

"No, sir."

"This brother?"

"No, sir; that was before I knew him."

"Who then?"

"His name was Mr. Van Brunt."

"Van Brunt!—Humph!—And what was he?"

"He was a farmer, sir."

"A Dutch farmer, eh? how came you to have any thing to do with *him?*"

"He managed my aunt's farm, and was a great deal in the house."

"He was! And what makes you call this other *your brother?*"

"His sister called me her sister—and that makes me his."

"It is very absurd," said Lady Keith, "when they are nothing at all to her, and ought not to be."

"It seems then you did not find a friend in your aunt, Ellen? —eh?"

"I don't think she loved me much," said Ellen in a low voice.

"I am very glad we are clear of obligation on *her* score," said Mrs. Lindsay.

"Obligation!—And so you had nothing else to depend on, Ellen, but this man—this Van something—this Dutchman? what did he do for you?"

"A great deal, sir;"—Ellen would have said more, but a feeling in her throat stopped her.

"Now just hear that, will you?" said Lady Keith. "Just think of her in that farm house, with that sweeping and dusting woman and a Dutch farmer, for these three years!"

"No," said Ellen,—"not all the time; this last year I have been,——"

"Where, Ellen?"

"At the other house, sir."

"What house is that?"

"Where that lady and gentleman lived that were my best friends."

'Well it's all very well," said Lady Keith,—"but it is past now; it is all over; you need not think of them any more. We will find you better friends than any of these Dutch Brunters or Grunters."

" Oh, aunt Keith !" said Ellen,—" if you knew"—But she burst into tears.

" Come, come," said Mr. Lindsay, taking her into his arms,—" I will not have that. Hush, my daughter. What is the matter, Ellen ?"

But Ellen had with some difficulty contained herself two or three times before in the course of the conversation, and she wept now rather violently.

" What is the matter, Ellen ?"

" Because," sobbed Ellen, thoroughly roused,—" I love them dearly ! and I ought to love them with all my heart. I cannot forget them, and never shall ; and I can never have better friends —never !—it's impossible—oh, it's impossible."

Mr. Lindsay said nothing at first except to soothe her ; but when she had wept herself into quietness upon his breast, he whispered,

" It is right to love these people if they were kind to you, but as your aunt says, that is past. It is not necessary to go back to it. Forget that you were American, Ellen,—you belong to me ; your name is not Montgomery any more,—it is Lindsay ;—and I will not have you call me ' uncle'—I am your father ;—you are my own little daughter, and must do precisely what I tell you. Do you understand me ?"

He would have a " yes" from her, and then added, " Go and get yourself ready and I will take you with me to Edinburgh."

Ellen's tears had been like to burst forth again at his words ; with great effort she controlled herself and obeyed him.

" I shall do precisely what he tells me of course," she said to herself as she went to get ready ;—" but there are some things he cannot command ; nor I neither ;—I am glad of that ! Forget indeed !"

She could not help loving her uncle ; for the lips that kissed her were very kind as well as very peremptory ; and if the hand that pressed her cheek was, as she felt it was, the hand of power, its touch was also exceeding fond. And as she was no more inclined to despite his will than he to permit it, the harmony between them was perfect and unbroken.

CHAPTER XLVIII.

Bear a lily in thy hand:
Gates of brass cannot withstand
One touch of that magic wand.
                                        LONGFELLOW.

MR. LINDSAY had some reason that morning to wish that Ellen would look merrier; it was a very sober little face he saw by his side as the carriage rolled smoothly on with them toward Edinburgh; almost pale in its sadness. He lavished the tenderest kindness upon her, and without going back by so much as a hint to the subjects of the morning, he exerted himself to direct her attention to the various objects of note and interest they were passing. The day was fine, and the country, also the carriage and the horses; Ellen was dearly fond of driving; and long before they reached the city Mr. Lindsay had the satisfaction of seeing her smile break again, her eye brighten, and her happy attention fixing on the things he pointed out to her, and many others that she found for herself on the way,—his horses first of all. Mr. Lindsay might relax his efforts and look on with secret triumph; Ellen was in the full train of delighted observation.

" You are easily pleased, Ellen," he said, in answer to one of her simple remarks of admiration.

" I have a great deal to please me," said Ellen.

" What would you like to see in Edinburgh ?"

" I don't know, sir ; any thing you please."

" Then I will show you a little of the city in the first place."

They drove through the streets of Edinburgh, both the Old and the New Town, in various directions; Mr. Lindsay extremely pleased to see that Ellen was so, and much amused at the curiosity shown in her questions, which however were by no means as free and frequent as they might have been had John Humphreys filled her uncle's place.

" What large building is that over there ?" said Ellen.

" That ?—that is Holyrood House."

" Holyrood !—I have heard of that before ;—isn't that where Queen Mary's rooms are ? where Rizzio was killed ?"

" Yes; would you like to see them ?"

" Oh, *very* much !"

" Drive to the Abbey—So you have read Scottish history as well as American, Ellen ?"

" Not very much, sir ; only the Tales of a Grandfather yet. But what made me say that,—I have read an account of Holyrood House somewhere. Uncle——"

"Ellen!"

"I beg your pardon, sir;—I forgot;—it seems strange to me," said Ellen, looking distressed.

"It must not seem strange to you, my daughter; what were you going to say?"

"I don't know, sir,—Oh, I was going to ask if the silver cross is here now, to be seen?"

"What silver cross?"

"That one from which the Abbey was named,—the silver rood that was given, they pretended, to—I forget now what king,—"

"David First, the founder of the Abbey? No, it is not here, Ellen; David the Second lost it to the English. But why do you say *pretended*, Ellen? It was a very real affair; kept in England for a long time with great veneration."

"Oh, yes, sir; I know the *cross* was real;—I mean, it was pretended that an angel gave it to King David when he was hunting here."

"Well, how can you tell but that was so? King David was made a saint, you know."

"Oh, sir," said Ellen laughing, "I know better than that; I know it was only a monkish trick."

"Monkish trick! what do you mean? the giving of the cross, or the making the king a saint?"

"Both, sir," said Ellen, still smiling.

"At that rate," said Mr. Lindsay, much amused, "if you are such a skeptic, you will take no comfort in any thing at the Abbey, —you will not believe any thing is genuine."

"I will believe what you tell me, sir."

"Will you? I must be careful what I say to you then, or I may run the risk of losing my own credit."

Mr. Lindsay spoke this half jestingly, half in earnest. They went over the palace.

"Is this very old, sir?" asked Ellen.

"Not very; it has been burnt and demolished and rebuilt, till nothing is left of the old Abbey of King David but the ruins of the chapel, which you shall see presently. The oldest part of the House is that we are going to see now, built by James Fifth, Mary's father, where her rooms are."

At these rooms Ellen looked with intense interest. She pored over the old furniture, the needle-work of which she was told was at least in part the work of the beautiful Queen's own fingers; gazed at the stains in the floor of the bed-chamber, said to be those of Rizzio's blood; meditated over the trap-door in the passage, by which the conspirators had come up; and finally sat down in the room and tried to realize the scene which had once been acted there. She tried to imagine the poor Queen and her attendant and her favourite Rizzio sitting there at supper, and how that door, that very door,—had opened, and Ruthven's ghastly figure, pale and weak from illness, presented itself, and then others; the alarm of the moment; how Rizzio knew they were come for him and fled to the Queen for protection; how she was withheld from giving it, and the unhappy man pulled away from her and stabbed with a great many wounds before her face; and there, there!—no doubt, —his blood fell!

"You are tired;—this doesn't please you much," said Mr. Lindsay, noticing her grave look.

"Oh, it pleases me *very* much?" said Ellen, starting up;—" I do not wonder she swore vengeance."

"Who?" said Mr. Lindsay laughing.

"Queen Mary, sir."

"Were you thinking of her all this while? I am glad of it. I spoke to you once without getting a word. I was afraid this was not amusing enough to detain your thoughts."

"Oh, yes it was," said Ellen;—" I have been trying to think about all that. I like to look at old things very much."

"Perhaps you would like to see the Regalia."

"The what, sir?"

"The Royal things—the old diadem and sceptre, &c., of the Scottish kings. Well come," said he, as he read the answer in Ellen's face,—" we will go; but first let us see the old chapel."

With this Ellen was wonderfully pleased. This was much older still than Queen Mary's rooms. Ellen admired the wild melancholy look of the gothic pillars and arches springing from the green turf, the large carved window empty of glass, the broken walls;— and looking up to the blue sky, she tried to imagine the time when the gothic roof closed overhead, and music sounded through the arches, and trains of stoled monks paced through them, where now the very pavement was not. Strange it seemed, and hard, to go back and realize it; but in the midst of this, the familiar face of the sky set Ellen's thoughts off upon a new track, and suddenly they were *at home*,—on the lawn before the parsonage. The monks and the abbey were forgotten; she silently gave her hand to her uncle and walked with him to the carriage.

Arrived at the Crown room, Ellen fell into another fit of grave attention; but Mr. Lindsay, taught better, did not this time mistake rapt interest for absence of mind. He answered questions and gave her several pieces of information, and let her take her own time to gaze and meditate.

"This beautiful sword," said he, " was a present from Pope Julius Second to James Fourth."

"I don't know any thing about the Popes," said Ellen. "James Fourth?—I forget what kind of a king he was."

"He was a very good king;—he was the one that died at Flodden."

"Oh, and wore an iron girdle because he had fought against his father,—poor man!"

"Why ' poor man,' Ellen? he was a very royal prince; why do you say ' poor man?' "

"Because he didn't know any better, sir."

"Didn't know any better than what?"

"Than to think an iron girdle would do him any good."

"But why wouldn't it do him any good?"

"Because, you know, sir, that is not the way we can have our sins forgiven."

"What *is* the way?"

Ellen looked at him to see if he was in jest or earnest. Her look staggered him a little, but he repeated his question. She cast her eyes down and answered,

"Jesus Christ said, ' I am the way, the truth, and the life; no man cometh unto the Father but by me.' "

Mr. Lindsay said no more.

"I wish that was the Bruce's crown," said Ellen after a while. "I should like to see any thing that belonged to him."

"I'll take you to the field of Bannockburn some day; that belonged to him with a vengeance. It lies over yonder."

"Bannockburn! will you? and Stirling castle!—Oh, how I should like that!"

"Stirling castle," said Mr. Lindsay, smiling at Ellen's clasped hands of delight,—"what do you know of Stirling castle?"

"From the history, you know, sir; and the Lord of the Isles;—

"Old Stirling's towers arose in light——"

"Go on," said Mr. Lindsay.

"And twined in links of silver bright
Her winding river lay."

"That's this same river Forth, Ellen. Do you know any more?"

"Oh, yes, sir."

"Go on and tell me all you can remember."

"*All;* that would be a great deal, sir."

"Go on till I tell you to stop."

Ellen gave him a good part of the battle, with the introduction to it.

"You have a good memory, Ellen," he said, looking pleased.

"Because I like it, sir; that makes it easy to remember. I like the Scots people."

"Do you!" said Mr. Lindsay much gratified;—"I did not know you liked any thing on this side of the water. Why do you like them?"

"Because they never would be conquered by the English."

"So," said Mr. Lindsay, half amused and half disappointed,—"the long and the short of it is, you like them because they fought the enemies you were so eager to have a blow at."

"Oh, no, sir," said Ellen laughing, "I do not mean that at all; the French were England's enemies too, and helped us besides, but I like the Scots a great deal better than the French. I like them because they would be free."

"You have an extraordinary taste for freedom! And pray, are all the American children as strong republicans as yourself?"

"I don't know, sir; I hope so."

"Pretty well, upon my word!—Then I suppose even the Bruce cannot rival your favourite Washington in your esteem?"

Ellen smiled.

"Eh?" said Mr. Lindsay.

"I like Washington better, sir, of course; but I like Bruce very much."

"Why do you prefer Washington?"

"I should have to think to tell you that, sir."

"Very well, think, and answer me."

"One reason, I suppose, is because he was an American," said Ellen.

"That is not reason enough for so reasonable a person as you are, Ellen; you must try again, or give up your preference."

"I like Bruce, very much indeed," said Ellen musingly,—"but he did what he did for *himself*,—Washington didn't."

"Humph!—I am not quite sure as to either of your positions," said Mr. Lindsay.

"And besides," said Ellen, "Bruce did one or two wrong things. Washington always did right."

"He did, eh? What do you think of the murder of Andre?"

"I think it was right," said Ellen firmly.

"Your reasons, my little reasoner?"

"If it had not been right, Washington would not have done it."

"Ha! ha!—so at that rate you may reconcile yourself to any thing that chances to be done by a favourite."

"No, sir," said Ellen, a little confused, but standing her ground, —"but when a person *always* does right, if he happen to do something that I don't know enough to understand, I have good reason to think it is right, even though I cannot understand it."

" Very well! but apply the same rule of judgment to the Bruce, can't you?"

" Nothing could make me think the murder of the Red Comyn right, sir. Bruce didn't think so himself."

" But remember, there is a great difference in the times; those were rude and uncivilized compared to these; you must make allowance for that."

" Yes, sir, I do; but I like the civilized times best."

" What do you think of this fellow over here,—what's his name, —whose monument I was showing you,—Nelson!"

" I used to like him very much, sir."

" And you do not now?"

" Yes, sir, I do; I cannot help liking him."

" That is to say, you would if you could?"

" I don't think, sir, I ought to like a man merely for being great unless he was good. Washington was great and good both."

" Well, what is the matter with Nelson?" said Mr. Lindsay, with an expression of intense amusement,—" I ' used to think,' as you say, that he was a very noble fellow."

" So he was, sir; but he wasn't a good man."

" Why not?"

" Why you know, sir, he left his wife; and Lady Hamilton persuaded him to do one or two other very dishonourable things; it was a great pity!"

" So you will not like any great man that is not good as well. What is your definition of a good man, Ellen?"

" One who always does right because it is right, no matter whether it is convenient or not," said Ellen, after a little hesitation.

" Upon my word, you draw the line close. But opinions differ as to what is right; how shall we know?"

" From the Bible, sir," said Ellen quickly, with a look that half amused and half abashed him.

" And you, Ellen,—are you yourself *good* after this nice fashion?"

" No, sir; but I wish to be."

" I do believe that. But after all, Ellen, you might like Nelson; those were only the spots in the sun."

" Yes, sir; but can a man be a truly great man who is not master of himself?"

" That is an excellent remark."

" It is not mine, sir," said Ellen blushing;—" it was told me; I did not find out all that about Nelson myself; I did not see it all the first time I read his life; I thought he was perfect."

" I know who *I* think is," said Mr. Lindsay kissing her.

They drove now to his house in Georges-street. Mr. Lindsay had some business to attend to and would leave her there for an hour or two. And that their fast might not be too long unbroken, Mrs. Allen the housekeeper was directed to furnish them with some biscuits in the library, whither Mr. Lindsay led Ellen.

She liked the looks of it very much. Plenty of books, old-looking comfortable furniture ; pleasant light ; all manner of etceteras around which rejoiced Ellen's heart. Mr. Lindsay noticed her pleased glance passing from one thing to another. He placed

her in a deep easy chair, took off her bonnet and threw it on the sofa, and kissing her fondly asked her if she felt at home. "Not yet," Ellen said ; but her look said it would not take long to make her do so. She sat enjoying her rest, and munching her biscuit with great appetite and satisfaction, when Mr. Lindsay poured her out a glass of sweet wine.

That glass of wine looked to Ellen like an enemy marching up to attack her. Because Alice and John did not drink it, she had always, at first without other reason, done the same; and she was determined not to forsake their example now. She took no notice of the glass of wine, though she had ceased to see any thing else in the room, and went on, seemingly as before, eating her biscuit, though she no longer knew how they tasted.

"Why don't you drink your wine, Ellen?"

"I do not wish any, sir."

"Don't you like it?"

"I don't know, sir; I have never drunk any."

"No! Taste it and see."

"I would rather not, sir, if you please. I don't care for it."

"Taste it, Ellen!"

This command was not to be disobeyed. The blood rushed to Ellen's temples as she just touched the glass to her lips and set it down again.

"Well?" said Mr. Lindsay.

"What, sir?"

"How do you like it?"

"I like it very well, sir, but I would rather not drink it."

"Why?"

Ellen coloured again at this exceedingly difficult question, and answered as well as she could, that she had never been accustomed to it, and would rather not.

"It is of no sort of consequence what you have been . accustomed to," said Mr. Lindsay. "You are to drink it all, Ellen."

Ellen dared not disobey. When biscuits and wine were disposed of, Mr. Lindsay drew her close to his side, and encircling her fondly with his arms, said,

"I shall leave you now for an hour or two, and you must amuse yourself as you can. The bookcases are open—perhaps you can find something there; or there are prints in those portfolios; or you can go over the house and make yourself acquainted with your new home. If you want any thing ask Mrs. Allen. Does it look pleasant to you?"

"Very," Ellen said.

"You are at home here, daughter; go where you will and do what you will. I shall not leave you long. But before I go— Ellen—let me hear you call me father."

Ellen obeyed, trembling, for it seemed to her that it was to set her hand and seal to the deed of gift her father and mother had made. But there was no retreat; it was spoken; and Mr. Lindsay folding her close in his arms kissed her again and again.

"Never let me hear you call me any thing else, Ellen. You are mine own now—my own child—my own little daughter. You shall do just what pleases me in every thing, and let by-gones be by-gones. And now lie down there and rest, daughter, you are trembling from head to foot ;—rest and amuse yourself in any way you like till I return."

He left the room.

" I have done it now !" thought Ellen, as she sat in the corner of the sofa where Mr. Lindsay had tenderly placed her ;—" I have called him my father—I am bound to obey him after this. I wonder what in the world they will make me do next. If he chooses to make me drink wine every day, I must do it !—I cannot help myself. That is only a little matter. But what if they were to want me to do something wrong ?—they might ;—John never did—I could not have disobeyed *him*, possibly !—but I could them, if it was necessary,—and if it is necessary, I will !—I should have a dreadful time—I wonder if I could go through with it. Oh, yes, I could, if it was right,—and besides would rather bear any thing in the world from them than have John displeased with me ;—a great deal rather ! But perhaps after all they will not want any thing wrong of me. I wonder if this is really to be my home always, and if I shall never get home again ?—John will not leave me here !—but I don't see how in the world he can help it, for my father and my mother, and I myself—I know what he would tell me if he was here, and I'll try to do it. God will take care of me if I follow him ; it is none of my business."

Simply and heartily commending her interests to his keeping, Ellen tried to lay aside the care of herself. She went on musing ; how very different and how much greater her enjoyment would have been that day if John had been with her. Mr. Lindsay, to be sure, had answered her questions with abundant kindness and sufficient ability ; but his answers did not, as those of her brother often did, skilfully draw her on from one thing to another, till a train of thought was opened which at the setting out she never dreamed of ; and along with the joy of acquiring new knowledge she had the pleasure of discovering new fields of it to be explored, and the delight of the felt exercise and enlargement of her own powers, which were sure to be actively called into play. Mr. Lindsay told her what she asked, and there left her. Ellen found herself growing melancholy over the comparison she was drawing ; and wisely went to the bookcases to divert her thoughts. Finding presently a history of Scotland, she took it down, resolving to refresh her memory on a subject which had gained such new and strange interest for her. Before long, however, fatigue and the wine she had drunk effectually got the better of studious thoughts ; she stretched herself on the sofa and fell asleep.

There Mr. Lindsay found her a couple of hours afterwards under the guard of the housekeeper.

" I cam in, sir," she said whispering,—" it's mair than an hour back, and she's been sleeping just like a baby ever syne; she hasna stirred a finger. Oh, Mr. Lindsay, it's a bonny bairn, and a gude. What a blessing to the house!"

"You're about right there, I believe, Maggie; but how have you learned it so fast?"

"I canna be mista'en, Mr. George,—I ken it as weel as if we had a year auld acquentance; I ken it by thae sweet mouth and een, and by the look she gied me when you tauld her, sir, I had been in the house near as long's yoursel. An' look at her eenow. There's heaven's peace within, I'm a'maist assured."

The kiss that wakened Ellen found her in the midst of a dream. She thought that John was a king of Scotland, and standing before her in regal attire. She offered him, she thought, a glass of wine, but raising the sword of state, silver scabbard and all, he with a tremendous swing of it dashed the glass out of her hands; and then as she stood abashed, he went forward with one of his old grave kind looks to kiss her. As the kiss touched her lips Ellen opened her eyes to find her brother transformed into Mr. Lindsay, and the empty glass standing safe and sound upon the table.

"You must have had a pleasant nap," said Mr. Lindsay, "you wake up smiling. Come—make haste—I have left a friend in the carriage.—Bring your book along if you want it."

The presence of the stranger, who was going down to spend a day or two at "the Braes," prevented Ellen from having any talking to do. Comfortably placed in the corner of the front seat of the barouche, leaning on the elbow of the carriage, she was left to her own musings. She could hardly realize the change in her circumstances. The carriage rolling fast and smoothly on—the two gentlemen opposite to her, one her father!—the strange, varied, beautiful scenes they were flitting by,—the long shadows made by the descending sun,—the cool evening air,—Ellen, leaning back in the wide easy seat, felt as if she were in a dream. It was singularly pleasant; she could not help but enjoy it all very much; and yet it seemed to her as if she were caught in a net from which she had no power to get free; and she longed to clasp that hand that could she thought draw her whence and whither it pleased. "But Mr. Lindsay opposite?—I have called him my father—I have given myself to him," she thought;—"but I gave myself to somebody else first;—I can't undo that—and I never will!" Again she tried to quiet and resign the care of herself to better wisdom and greater strength than her own. "This may all be arranged, easily, in some way I could never dream of," she said to herself; "I have no business to be uneasy. Two months ago, and I was quietly at home and seemed to be fixed there for ever; and now, and without any thing extraordinary happening, here I am,—

just as fixed. Yes, and before that, at aunt Fortune's,—it didn't seem possible that I could ever get away from being her child; and yet how easily all that was managed. And just so in some way that I cannot imagine, things may open so as to let me out smoothly from this." She resolved to be patient, and take thankfully what she at present had to enjoy; and in this mood of mind the drive home was beautiful; and the evening was happily absorbed in the history of Scotland.

It was a grave question in the family that same evening whether Ellen should be sent to school. Lady Keith was decided in favour of it; her mother seemed doubtful; Mr. Lindsay, who had a vision of the little figure lying asleep on his library sofa, thought the room had never looked so cheerful before, and had near made up his mind that she should be its constant adornment the coming winter. Lady Keith urged the school plan.

"Not a boarding-school," said Mrs. Lindsay;—"I will not hear of that."

"No, but a day-school; it would do her a vast deal of good I am certain; her notions want shaking up very much. And I never saw a child of her age so much a child."

"I assure you *I* never saw one so much a woman. She has asked me to-day, I suppose," said he smiling, "a hundred questions or less; and I assure you there was not one foolish or vain one among them; not one that was not sensible, and most of them singularly so."

"She was greatly pleased with her day," said Mrs. Lindsay.

"I never saw such a baby face in my life," said Lady Keith,— "in a child of her years."

"It is a face of uncommon intelligence!" said her brother.

"It is both," said Mrs. Lindsay.

"I was struck with it the other day," said Lady Keith,—"the day she slept so long upon the sofa up stairs after she was dressed; she had been crying about something, and her eyelashes were wet still, and she had that curious grave innocent look you only see in infants; you might have thought she was fourteen months instead of fourteen years old; fourteen and a half she says she is."

"Crying?" said Mr. Lindsay;—"what was the matter?"

"Nothing," said Mrs. Lindsay, "but that she had been obliged to submit to me in something that did not please her."

"Did she give you any cause of displeasure?"

"No,—though I can see she has strong passions. But she is the first child I ever saw that I think I could not get angry with."

"Mother's heart half misgave her, I believe," said Lady Keith laughing;—"she sat there looking at her for an hour."

"She seems to me perfectly gentle and submissive," said Mr. Lindsay.

" Yes, but don't trust too much to appearances," said his sister.
" If she is not a true Lindsay after all I am mistaken. Did you
see her colour once or twice this morning when something was said
that did not please her ?"

" You can judge nothing from that," said Mr. Lindsay,—" she
colours at every thing. You should have seen her to-day when I
told her I would take her to Bannockburn."

" Ah, she has got the right side of you ; you will be able to discern no faults in her presently."

" She has used no arts for it, sister ; she is a straightforward
little hussy, and that is one thing I like about her ; though I was
as near as possible being provoked with her once or twice to-day.
There is only one thing I wish was altered,—she has her head filled
with strange notions—absurd for a child of her age—I don't know
what I shall do to get rid of them."

After some more conversation it was decided that school would
be the best thing for this end, and half decided that Ellen should
go.

But this half decision Mr. Lindsay found it very difficult to keep
to, and circumstances soon destroyed it entirely. Company was
constantly coming and going at " the Braes," and much of it of a
kind that Ellen exceedingly liked to see and hear ; intelligent, cultivated, well-informed people, whose conversation was highly agreeable and always useful to her. Ellen had nothing to do with the
talking, so she made good use of her ears.

One evening Mr. Lindsay, a M. Villars, and M. Muller, a Swiss
gentleman and a noted man of science, very much at home in Mr.
Lindsay's house, were carrying on, in French, a conversation in
which the two foreigners took part against their host. M. Villars
began with talking about Lafayette ; from him they went to the
American Revolution, and Washington, and from them to other
patriots and other republics, ancient and modern ;—MM. Villars
and Muller taking the side of freedom and pressing Mr. Lindsay
hard with argument, authority, example, and historical testimony.
Ellen as usual was fast by his side, and delighted to see that he
could by no means make good his ground. The ladies at the other
end of the room would several times have drawn her away, but
happily for her, and also as usual, Mr. Lindsay's arm was around
her shoulders, and she was left in quiet to listen. The conversa
tion was very lively, and on a subject very interesting to her ; for
America had been always a darling theme ;. Scottish struggles for
freedom were fresh in her mind ; her attention had long ago been
called to Switzerland and its history by Alice and Mrs. Vawse, and
French history had formed a good part of her last winter's reading.
She listened with the most eager delight, too much engrossed to
notice the good-humoured glances that were every now and then

given her by one of the speakers. Not Mr. Lindsay ;—though his hand was upon her shoulder or playing with the light curls that fell over her temples, *he* did not see that her face was flushed with interest, or notice the quick smile and sparkle of the eye that followed every turn in the conversation that favoured her wishes or foiled his ;—it was M. Muller. They came to the Swiss, and their famous struggle for freedom against Austrian oppression. M. Muller wished to speak of the noted battle in which that freedom was made sure, but for the moment its name had escaped him.

"Par ma foi," said M. Villars,—"il m'a entièrement passé !"

Mr. Lindsay could not or would not help him out. But M. Muller suddenly turned to Ellen, in whose face he thought he saw a look of intelligence, and begged of her the missing name.

"Est-ce Morgarten, monsieur ?" said Ellen blushing.

"Morgarten ! c'est ça !" said he with a polite, pleased bow of thanks. Mr. Lindsay was little less astonished than the Duke of Argyle when his gardener claimed to be the owner of a Latin work on mathematics.

The conversation presently took a new turn with M. Villars ; and M. Muller withdrawing from it addressed himself to Ellen. He was a pleasant-looking elderly gentleman ; she had never seen him before that evening.

"You know French well then ?" said he, speaking to her in that tongue.

"I don't know, sir," said Ellen modestly.

"And you have heard of the Swiss mountaineers ?"

"Oh, yes, sir ; a great deal."

He opened his watch and showed her in the back of it an exquisite little painting, asking her if she knew what it was.

"It is an Alpine châlet, is it not, sir ?"

He was pleased and went on, always in French, to tell Ellen that Switzerland was his country ; and drawing a little aside from the other talkers, he entered into a long and to her most delightful conversation. In the pleasantest manner he gave her a vast deal of very entertaining detail about the country and the manners and habits of the people of the Alps, especially in the Tyrol, where he had often travelled. It would have been hard to tell whether the child had most pleasure in receiving, or the man of deep study and science most pleasure in giving, all manner of information. He saw, he said, that she was very fond of the heroes of freedom, and asked if she had ever heard of Andrew Hofer, the Tyrolese peasant who led on his brethren in their noble endeavours to rid themselves of French and Bavarian oppression. Ellen had never heard of him.

"You know William Tell ?"

"Oh, yes," Ellen said,—she knew him.

" And Bonaparte?"

" Yes, very well."

He went on then to give her in a very interesting way the history of Hofer;—how when Napoleon made over his country to the rule of the King of Bavaria, who oppressed them, they rose in mass; overcame army after army that were sent against them in their mountain fastnesses, and freed themselves from the hated Bavarian government; how years after Napoleon was at last too strong for them; Hofer and his companions defeated, hunted like wild beasts, shot down like them; how Hofer was at last betrayed by a friend, taken, and executed, being only seen to weep at parting with his family. The beautiful story was well told, and the speaker was animated by the eager deep attention and sympathy of his auditor, whose changing colour, smiles, and even tears, showed how well she entered into the feelings of the patriots in their struggle, triumph, and downfall; till as he finished she was left full of pity for them and hatred of Napoleon. They talked of the Alps again. M. Muller put his hand in his pocket, and pulled out a little painting in mosaic to show her, which he said had been given him that day. It was a beautiful piece of pietra dura work—Mont Blanc. He assured her the mountain often looked exactly so. Ellen admired it very much. It was meant to be set for a brooch or some such thing, he said, and he asked if she would keep it and sometimes wear it, to " remember the Swiss, and to do him a pleasure."

" Moi, monsieur!" said Ellen, colouring high with surprise and pleasure,—" je suis bien obligée—mais, monsieur, je ne saurais vous remercier!"

He would count himself well paid, he said, with a single touch of her lips.

" Tenez, monsieur!" said Ellen, blushing, but smiling, and tendering back the mosaic.

He laughed and bowed and begged her pardon, and said she must keep it to assure him she had forgiven him; and then he asked by what name he might remember her.

" Monsieur, je m'appelle Ellen M——"

She stopped short, in utter and blank uncertainty what to call herself; Montgomery she dared not; Lindsay stuck in her throat.

" Have you forgotten it?" said M. Muller, amused at her look, " or is it a secret?"

" Tell M. Muller your name, Ellen," said Mr. Lindsay, turning round from a group where he was standing at a little distance. The tone was stern and displeased. Ellen felt it keenly, and with difficulty and some hesitation still, murmured,

" Ellen Lindsay."

" Lindsay? Are you the daughter of my friend Mr. Lindsay?"

Again Ellen hesitated, in great doubt how to answer, but finally, not without starting tears, said,

"Oui, monsieur."

"Your memory is bad to-night," said Mr. Lindsay, in her ear, —"you had better go where you can refresh it."

Ellen took this as a hint to leave the room, which she did immediately, not a little hurt at the displeasure she did not thin' she had deserved; she loved Mr. Lindsay the best of all her relations, and really loved him. She went to bed and to sleep again that night with wet eyelashes.

Meanwhile M. Muller was gratifying Mr. Lindsay in a high degree by the praises he bestowed upon his daughter,—her intelligence, her manners, her modesty, and her *French*. He asked if she was to be in Edinburgh that winter and whether she would be at school; and Mr. Lindsay declaring himself undecided on the latter point, M. Muller said he should be pleased, if she had leisure, to have her come to his rooms two or three times a week to read with him. This offer, from a person of M. Muller's standing and studious habits, Mr. Lindsay justly took as both a great compliment and a great promise of advantage to Ellen. He at once and with much pleasure accepted it. So the question of school was settled.

Ellen resolved the next morning to lose no time in making up her difference with Mr. Lindsay, and schooled herself to use a form of words that she thought would please him. Pride said indeed, "Do no such thing; don't go to making acknowledgements when you have not been in the wrong; you are not bound to humble yourself before unjust displeasure." Pride pleaded powerfully. But neither Ellen's heart nor her conscience would permit her to take this advice. "He loves me very much," she thought,—"and perhaps he did not understand me last night; and besides, I owe him—yes, I do!—a child's obedience now. I ought not to leave him displeased with me a moment longer than I can help. And besides I couldn't be happy so. God gives grace to the humble—I will humble myself."

To have a chance for executing this determination she went down stairs a good deal earlier than usual; she knew Mr. Lindsay was generally there before the rest of the family, and she hoped to see him alone. It was too soon even for him, however; the rooms were empty; so Ellen took her book from the table, and being perfectly at peace with herself, sat down in the window and was presently lost in the interest of what she was reading. She did not know of Mr. Lindsay's approach till a little imperative tap on her shoulder startled her.

"What were you thinking of last night? what made you answer M. Muller in the way you did?"

Ellen started up, but to utter her prepared speech was no longer possible.

"I did not know what to say," she said, looking down.

"What do you mean by that?" said he angrily. "Didn't you know what I wished you to say?"

"Yes—but—do not speak to me in that way!" exclaimed Ellen, covering her face with her hands. Pride struggled to keep back the tears that wanted to flow.

"I shall choose my own method of speaking. Why did you not say what you knew I wished you to say?"

"I was afraid—I didn't know—but he would think what wasn't true."

"That is precisely what I wish him and all the world to think. I will have no difference made, Ellen, either by them or you. Now lift up your head and listen to me," said he, taking both her hands, —"I lay my commands upon you, whenever the like questions may be asked again, that you answer simply according to what I have told you, without any explanation or addition. It is true, and if people draw conclusions that are not true, it is what I wish. Do you understand me?"

Ellen bowed.

"Will you obey me?"

She answered again in the same mute way.

He ceased to hold her at arm's length, and sitting down in her chair drew her close to him, saying more kindly,

"You must not displease me, Ellen."

"I had no thought of displeasing you, sir," said Ellen bursting into tears,—"and I was very sorry for it last night. I did not mean to disobey you—I only hesitated——"

"Hesitate no more. My commands may serve to remove the cause of it. You are my daughter, Ellen, and I am your father. Poor child!" said he, for Ellen was violently agitated,—"I don't believe I shall have much difficulty with you."

"If you will only not speak and look at me so," said Ellen,— "it makes me very unhappy——"

"Hush!" said he kissing her;—"do not give me occasion."

"I did not give you occasion, sir?"

"Why, Ellen!" said Mr. Lindsay, half displeased again,—"I shall begin to think your aunt Keith is right, that you are a true Lindsay. But so am I,—and I will have only obedience from you —without either answering or argumenting."

"You shall," murmured Ellen. "But do not be displeased with me, father."

Ellen had schooled herself to say that word; she knew it would greatly please him; and she was not mistaken; though it was spoken so low that his ears could but just catch it. Displeasure was entirely overcome. He pressed her to his heart, kissing her with great tenderness, and would not let her go from his arms till he had seen her smile again; and during all the day he was not willing to have her out of his sight.

It would have been easy that morning for Ellen to have made a breech between them that would not readily have been healed. One word of humility had prevented it all, and fastened her more firmly than ever in Mr. Lindsay's affection. She met with nothing from him but tokens of great and tender fondness; and Lady Keith told her mother apart that there would be no doing any thing with George; she saw he was getting bewitched with that child.

CHAPTER XLIX.

My heart is sair, I dare nae tell,
    My heart is sair for somebody;
I could wake a winter night
    For the sake of somebody.
        Oh-hon! for somebody!
        Oh hey! for somebody!
I wad do—what wad I not,
    For the sake of somebody.

SCOTCH SONG.

IN a few weeks they moved to Edinburgh, where arrangements were speedily made for giving Ellen every means of improvement that masters and mistresses, books and instruments, could afford.

The house in Georges-street was large and pleasant. To Ellen's great joy, a pretty little room opening from the first landing-place of the private staircase was assigned for her special use as a study and work-room; and fitted up nicely for her with a small bookcase, a practising piano, and various etceteras. Here her beloved desk took its place on a table in the middle of the floor, where Ellen thought she would make many a new drawing when she was by herself. Her work-box was accommodated with a smaller stand near the window. A glass door at one end of the room opened upon a small iron balcony; this door and balcony Ellen esteemed a very particular treasure. With marvellous satisfaction she arranged and rearranged her little sanctum till she had all things to her mind, and it only wanted, she thought, a glass of flowers. " I will have that too some of these days," she said to herself; and resolved to deserve her pretty room by being very busy there. It was hers alone, open indeed to her friends when they chose to keep her company; but lessons were taken elsewhere; in the library, or the music-room, or more frequently her grandmother's dressing-room. Wherever, or whatever, Mrs. Lindsay or Lady Keith was always present.

Ellen was the plaything, pride, and delight of the whole family. Not so much however Lady Keith's plaything as her pride ; while pride had a less share in the affection of the other two, or rather perhaps was more overtopped by it. Ellen felt however that all their hearts were set upon her, felt it gratefully, and determined

she would give them all the pleasure she possibly could. Her love for other friends, friends that they knew nothing of, *American* friends, was, she knew, the sore point with them ; she resolved not to speak of those friends, nor allude to them, especially in any way that should show how much of her heart was out of Scotland. But this wise resolution it was very hard for poor Ellen to keep. She was unaccustomed to concealments ; and in ways that she could neither foresee nor prevent, the unwelcome truth would come up, and the sore was not healed.

One day Ellen had a headache and was sent to lie down. Alone, and quietly stretched on her bed, very naturally Ellen's thoughts went back to the last time she had had a headache, *at home*, as she always called it to herself. She recalled with a straitened heart the gentle and tender manner of John's care for her; how nicely he had placed her on the sofa; how he sat by her side bathing her temples, or laying his cool hand on her forehead, and once, she remembered, his lips. "I wonder," thought Ellen, "what I ever did to make him love me so much, as I know he does?" She remembered how, when she was able to listen, he still sat beside her, talking such sweet words of kindness and comfort and amusement, that she almost loved to be sick to have such tending, and looked up at him as at an angel. She felt it all over again. Unfortunately, after she had fallen asleep, Mrs. Lindsay came in to see how she was, and two tears, the last pair of them, were slowly making their way down her cheeks. Her grandmother saw them, and did not rest till she knew the cause. Ellen was extremely sorry to tell, she did her best to get off from it, but she did not know how to evade questions; and those that were put to her indeed admitted of no evasion.

A few days later, just after they came to Edinburgh, it was remarked one morning at breakfast that Ellen was very straight and carried herself well.

"It is no thanks to me," said Ellen smiling,—"they never would let me hold myself ill."

"Who is 'they?'" said Lady Keith.

"My brother and sister."

"I wish, George," said Lady Keith discontentedly, "that you would lay your commands upon Ellen to use that form of expression no more. My ears are absolutely sick of it."

"You do not hear it very often, aunt Keith," Ellen could not help saying.

"Quite often enough; and I know it is upon your lips a thousand times when you do not speak it."

"And if Ellen does, we do not," said Mrs. Lindsay, "wish to claim kindred with all the world."

"How came you to take up such an absurd habit?" said Lady Keith. "It isn't like you."

"They took it up first," said Ellen;—"I was too glad——"

"Yes, I dare say they had their reasons for taking it up," said her aunt;—"they had acted from interested motives I have no doubt; people always do."

"You are very much mistaken, aunt Keith," said Ellen, with uncontrollable feeling;—"you do not in the least know what you are talking about!"

Instantly, Mr. Lindsay's fingers tapped her lips. Ellen coloured painfully, but after an instant's hesitation she said,

"I beg your pardon, aunt Keith, I should not have said that."

"Very well!" said Mr. Lindsay. "But understand, Ellen, however you may have taken it up,—this habit,—you will lay it down for the future. Let us hear no more of brothers and sisters. I cannot, as your grandmother says, fraternize with all the world, especially with unknown relations."

"I am very glad you have made that regulation," said Mrs. Lindsay.

"I cannot conceive how Ellen has got such a way of it," said Lady Keith.

"It is very natural," said Ellen, with some huskiness of voice, "that I should say so, because I feel so."

"You do not mean to say," said Mr. Lindsay, "that this Mr. and Miss Somebody—these people—I don't know their names——"

"There is only one now, sir."

"This person you call your brother—do you mean to say you have the same regard for him as if he had been born so?"

"No," said Ellen, cheek and eye suddenly firing,—"but a thousand times more!"

She was exceedingly sorry the next minute after she had said this; for she knew it had given both pain and displeasure in a great degree. No answer was made. Ellen dared not look at any body, and needed not; she wished the silence might be broken; but nothing was heard except a low "whew!" from Mr. Lindsay, till he rose up and left the room. Ellen was sure he was very much displeased. Even the ladies were too much offended to speak on the subject; and she was merely bade to go to her room. She went there, and sitting down on the floor, covered her face with her hands. "What shall I do? what shall I do?" she said to herself. "I never shall govern this tongue of mine. Oh, I wish I had not said that! they never will forgive it. What *can* I do to make them pleased with me again?—Shall I go to my father's study and beg him——but I can't ask him to forgive me—I haven't done wrong—I can't unsay what I said. I can do nothing,—I can only go in the way of my duty and do the best I can,—and maybe they will come round again. But oh, dear!"—

A flood of tears followed this resolution.

Ellen kept it; she tried to be blameless in all her work and behaviour, but she sorrowfully felt that her friends did not forgive her. There was a cool air of displeasure about all they said and did; the hand of fondness was not laid upon her shoulder, she was not wrapped in loving arms, as she used to be a dozen times a day; no kisses fell on her brow or lips. Ellen felt it, more from Mr. Lindsay than both the others; her spirits sunk;—she had been forbidden to speak of her absent friends, but that was not the way to make her forget them ; and there was scarce a minute in the day when her brother was not present to her thoughts.

Sunday came; her first Sunday in Edinburgh. All went to church in the morning; in the afternoon Ellen found that nobody was going; her grandmother was lying down. She asked permission to go alone.

" Do you want to go because you think you must? or for pleasure?" said Mrs. Lindsay.

" For pleasure !" said Ellen's tongue and her opening eyes at the same time.

" You may go."

" With eager delight Ellen got ready, and was hastening along the hall to the door, when she met Mr. Lindsay.

" Where are you going ?"

" To church, sir."

" Alone ! What do you want to go for ! No, no, I shan't let you. Come in here—I want you with me ;—you have been once to-day already, haven't you? You do not want to go again ?"

" I do indeed, sir, very much," said Ellen, as she reluctantly followed him into the library,—" if you have no objection. You know I have not seen Edinburgh yet."

" Edinburgh ! that's true, so you haven't," said he, looking at her discomfited face. " Well go, if you want to go so much."

Ellen got as far as the hall door, no further ; she rushed back to the library.

" I did not say right when I said that," she burst forth ;—" that was not the reason I wanted to go.—I will stay, if you wish me, sir."

" I don't wish it," said he in surprise ;—" I don't know what you mean—I am willing you should go if you like it. Away with you ! it is time."

Once more Ellen set out, but this time with a heart full ; much too full to think of any thing she saw by the way. It was with a singular feeling of pleasure that she entered the church alone. It was a strange church to her, never seen but once before, and as she softly passed up the broad aisle she saw nothing in the building or the people around her that was not strange,—no familiar face, no familiar thing. But it was a church, and she was alone, quite alone in the midst of that crowd ; and she went up to the empty pew and ensconced herself in the far corner of it, with a curious feeling of quiet and of being at home. She was no sooner seated, however, than leaning forward as much as possible to screen herself from observation, bending her head upon her knees, she burst into an agony of tears. It was a great relief to be able to weep freely ; at home she was afraid of being seen or heard or questioned ;

now she was alone and free, and she poured out her very heart in weeping that she with difficulty kept from being loud weeping.

" Oh, how could I say that how could I say that Oh, what *would* John have thought of me if he had heard it!—Am I beginning already to lose my truth ? am I going backward already ? Oh, what shall I do ! what will become of me if I do not watch over myself—there is no one to help me or lead me right—not a single one—all to lead me wrong! what will become of me ?—But there is One who has promised to keep those that follow him—he is sufficient, without any others—I have not kept near enough to him ! that is it ;—I have not remembered nor loved him—' If ye love me, keep my commandments,'—I have not! I have not! Oh, but I will !—I will ; and he will be with me, and help me and bless me, and all will go right with me."

With bitter tears Ellen mingled as eager prayers, for forgiveness and help to be faithful. She resolved that nothing, come what would, should tempt her to swerve one iota from the straight line of truth ; she resolved to be more careful of her private hour; she thought she had scarcely had her full hour a day lately ; she resolved to make the Bible her only and her constant rule of life in every thing ;—and she prayed, such prayers as a heart thoroughly in earnest can pray, for the seal to these resolutions. Not one word of the sermon did Ellen hear ; but she never passed a more profitable hour in church in her life.

All her tears were not from the spring of these thoughts and feelings ; some were the pouring out of the gathered sadness of the week ; some came from recollections, oh, how tender and strong! of lost and distant friends. Her mother—and Alice—and Mr. Humphreys—and Margery—and Mr. Van Brunt—and Mr. George Marshman ;—and she longed, with longing that seemed as if it would have burst her heart, to see her brother. She longed for the pleasant voice, the eye of thousand expressions, into which she always looked as if she had never seen it before, the calm look that told he was satisfied with her, the touch of his hand, which many a time had said a volume. Ellen thought she would give any thing in the world to see him and hear him speak one word. As this could not be, she resolved with the greatest care to do what would please him ; that when she did see him he might find her all he wished.

She had wept herself out ; she had refreshed and strengthened herself by fleeing to the stronghold of the prisoners of hope ; and when the last hymn was given out she raised her head and took the book to find it. To her great surprise she saw Mr. Lindsay sitting at the other end of the pew, with folded arms, like a man not thinking of what was going on around him. Ellen was startled, but obeying the instinct that told her what he would like, she immediately moved down the pew and stood beside him while the last hymn was singing ; and if Ellen had joined in no other part of the service that afternoon, she at least did in that with all her heart. They walked home then without a word on either side. Mr. Lindsay did not quit her hand till he had drawn her into the library. There he threw off her bonnet and wrappers, and taking her in his arms, exclaimed,

" My poor little darling ! what was the matter with you this afternoon ?"

There was so much of kindness again in his tone, that over-joyed, Ellen eagerly returned his caress, and assured him that there was nothing the matter with her now.

" Nothing the matter !" said he, tenderly pressing her face against his own,—" nothing the matter ! with these pale cheeks and wet eyes ? nothing *now*, Ellen ?"

" Only that I am so glad to hear you speak kindly to me again, sir."

" Kindly ? I will never speak any way but kindly to you, daughter ;—come ! I will not have any more tears—you have shed enough for to-day I am sure; lift up your face and I will kiss them away. What was the matter with you, my child ?"

But he had to wait a little while for an answer.

" What was it, Ellen ?"

" One thing," said Ellen,—" I was sorry for what I had said to you, sir, just before I went out."

" What was that ? I do not remember any thing that deserved to be a cause of grief."

" I told you, sir, when I wanted you to let me go to church, that I hadn't seen Edinburgh yet."

" Well ?"

" Well, sir, that wasn't being quite true ; and I was very sorry for it !"

" Not true ? yes it was ; what do you mean ? you had *not* seen Edinburgh."

" No, sir, but I mean—*that* was true, but I said it to make you believe what wasn't true."

" How ?"

" I meant you to think, sir, that that was the reason why I wanted to go to church—to see the city and the new sights—and it wasn't at all."

" What was it then ?"

Ellen hesitated.

" I always love to go, sir,—and besides I believe I wanted to be alone."

" And you were not, after all," said Mr. Lindsay, again pressing her cheek to his,—" for I followed you there. But Ellen, my child, you were troubled without reason; you had said nothing that was false."

"Ah, sir, but I had made you believe what was false."

"Upon my word," said Mr. Lindsay, "you are a nice reasoner. And are you always true upon this close scale?"

"I wish I was, sir, but you see I am not. I am sure I hate every thing else!"

"Well, I will not quarrel with you for being true," said Mr. Lindsay;—"I wish there was a little more of it in the world. Was this the cause of all those tears this afternoon?"

"No, sir—not all."

"What beside, Ellen?"

Ellen looked down, and was silent.

"Come—I must know."

"Must I tell you all, sir?"

"You must indeed," said he smiling; "I will have the whole, daughter."

"I had been feeling sorry all the week because you and grandmother and aunt Keith were displeased with me."

Again Mr. Lindsay's silent caress in its tenderness seemed to say that she should never have the same complaint to make again.

"Was that all, Ellen?" as she hesitated.

"No, sir."

"Well?"

"I wish you wouldn't ask me further; please do not!—I shall displease you again."

"I will not be displeased."

"I was thinking of Mr. Humphreys," said Ellen in a low tone.

"Who is that?"

"You know, sir,—you say I must not call him——"

"What were you thinking of him?"

"I was wishing very much I could see him again."

"Well you *are* a truth-teller," said Mr. Lindsay,—"or bolder than I think you."

"You said you would not be displeased, sir."

"Neither will I, daughter; but what shall I do to make you forget these people?"

"Nothing, sir; I cannot forget them; I shouldn't deserve to have you love me a bit if I could. Let me love them, and do not be angry with me for it!"

"But I am not satisfied to have your body here and your heart somewhere else."

"I must have a poor little kind of heart," said Ellen, smiling amidst her tears, "if it had room in it for only one person."

"Ellen," said Mr. Lindsay inquisitively, "did you *insinuate* a falsehood there?"

" No, sir!"

" There is honesty in those eyes," said he, " if there is honesty anywhere in the world. I am satisfied—that is half satisfied. Now lie there, my little daughter, and rest," said he, laying her upon the sofa ; " you look as if you needed it."

"I don't need any thing now," said Ellen, as she laid her cheek upon the grateful pillow, " except one thing—if grandmother would only forgive me too."

" You must try not to offend your grandmother, Ellen, for she does not very readily forgive ; but I think we can arrange this matter. Go you to sleep."

" I wonder," said Ellen, smiling as she closed her eyes, " why every body calls me 'little ;' I don't think I am very little. Every body says ' little.' "

Mr. Lindsay thought he understood it when a few minutes after he sat watching her as she really had fallen asleep. The innocent brow, the perfect sweet calm of the face, seemed to belong to much younger years. Even Mr. Lindsay could not help recollecting the housekeeper's comment, " Heaven's peace within ;" scarcely Ellen's own mother ever watched over her with more fond tenderness than her adopted father did now.

For several days after this he would hardly permit her to leave him. He made her bring her books and study where he was ; he went out and came in with her ; and kept her by his side whenever they joined the rest of the family at meals or in the evening. Whether Mr. Lindsay intended it or not, this had soon the effect to abate the displeasure of his mother and sister. Ellen was almost taken out of their hands, and they thought it expedient not to let him have the whole of her. And though Ellen could better bear their cold looks and words since she had Mr. Lindsay's favour again, she was very glad when they smiled upon her too, and went dancing about with quite a happy face.

She was now very busy. She had masters for the piano and singing and different branches of knowledge ; she went to Mr. Muller regularly twice a week ; and soon her riding-attendance began. She had said no more on the subject, but went quietly, hoping they would find out their mistake before long. Lady Keith always accompanied her.

One day Ellen had ridden near her usual time, when a young lady with whom she attended a German class, came up to where she was resting. This lady was several years older than Ellen, but had taken a fancy to her.

" How finely you got on yesterday," said she,—" making us all ashamed. Ah, I guess M. Muller helped you."

" Yes," said Ellen, smiling, " he did help me a little ; he helped me with those troublesome pronunciations."

" With nothing else, I suppose ? Ah. well, we must submit to be stupid. How do you do to-day ?"

" I am very tired, Miss Gordon."

" Tired ? Oh, you're not used to it."

" No it isn't that," said Ellen ;—" I *am* used to it—that is the reason I am tired. I am accustomed to ride up and down the country at any pace I like ; and it is very tiresome to walk stupidly round and round for an hour."

" But do you know how to manage a horse? I thought you were only just beginning to learn."

" Oh, no—I have been learning this great while ;—only they don't think I know how, and they have never seen me. Are you just come, Miss Gordon ?"

" Yes, and they are bringing out Sophronisbe for me—do you know Sophronisbe ?—look—that light grey—isn't she beautiful? she's the loveliest creature in the whole stud."

" Oh, I know !" said Ellen ; " I saw you on her the other day ; she went charmingly. How long shall I be kept walking here, Miss Gordon ?"

" Why I don't know—I should think they would find out—what does De Courcy say to you ?"

" Oh, he comes and looks at me and says, ' très bien—très bien,' and ' allez comme ça,' and then he walks off."

" Well I declare that is too bad," said Miss Gordon laughing. " Look here—I've got a good thought in my head—suppose you mount Sophronisbe in my place, without saying any thing to any body, and let them see what you are up to. Can you trust yourself ? she's very spirited."

" I could trust myself," said Ellen ; " but, thank you, I think I had better not."

" Afraid ?"

" No, not at all ; but my aunt and father would not like it."

" Nonsense ! how should they dislike it—there's no sort of danger, you know. Come !—I thought you sat wonderfully for a beginner. I am surprised De Courcy hadn't better eyes. I guess you have learned German before Ellen ?—Come, will you ?"

But Ellen declined, preferring her plodding walk round the ring to any putting of herself forward. Presently Mr. Lindsay came in. It was the first time he had been there. His eyes soon singled out Ellen.

" My daughter sits well," he remarked to the riding-master.

" A merveille !—Mademoiselle Lindesay does ride remarquablement pour une beginner—qui ne fait que commencer. Would it be possible that she has had no lessons before ?"

" Why, yes—she has had lessons—of what sort I don't know," said Mr. Lindsay, going up to Ellen. " How do you like it, Ellen ?"

" I don't like it at all, sir."

" I thought you were so fond of riding."

" I don't call this riding, sir."

" Ha! what *do* you call riding? Here, M. De Courcy—won't you have the goodness to put this young lady on another horse and see if she knows any thing about handling him."

" With great pleasure!" M. De Courcy would do any thing that was requested of him. Ellen was taken out of the ring of walkers and mounted on a fine animal, and set by herself to have her skill tried in as many various ways as M. De Courcy's ingenuity could point out. Never did she bear herself more erectly; never were her hand and her horse's mouth on nicer terms of acquaintanceship; never, even to please her master, had she so given her whole soul to the single business of managing her horse and herself perfectly well. She knew as little as she cared that a number of persons besides her friends were standing to look at her; she thought of only two people there, Mr. Lindsay and her aunt; and the riding-master, as his opinion might affect theirs.

" C'est très bien,—c'est très bien," he muttered,—c'est par-faite-ment—Monsieur, mademoiselle votre fille has had good lessons—voilà qui est entièrement comme il faut."

" Assez bien," said Mr. Lindsay smiling. " The little gypsy!"

" Mademoiselle," said the riding-master as she paused before them,—" pourquoi, wherefore have you stopped in your canter tantôt—a little while ago—et puis récommencé?"

" Monsieur, he led with the wrong foot."

" C'est ça—justement!" he exclaimed.

" Have you practised leaping, Ellen?"

" Yes, sir."

" Try her, M. De Courcy. Ho · high will you go, Ellen?"

" As high as you please, sir," said Ellen, leaning over and patting her horse's neck to hide her smile.

" How you look, child!" said Mr. Lindsay in a pleased tone. " So *this* is what you call riding?"

" It is a little more like it, sir."

Ellen was tried with standing and running leaps, higher and higher, till Mr. Lindsay would have no more of it; and M. De Courcy assured him that his daughter had been taught by a very accomplished rider, and there was little or nothing left for him to do; il n'y pouvait plus;—but he should be very happy to have her come there to practise, and show an example to his pupils.

The very bright colour in Ellen's face as she heard this might have been mistaken for the flush of gratified vanity: it was noth-ing less. Not one word of this praise did she take to herself, nor had she sought for herself;—it was all for somebody else; and perhaps so Lady Keith understood it, for she looked rather dis-

comfited. But Mr. Lindsay was exceedingly pleased; and promised Ellen that as soon as the warm weather came she should have
a horse and rides to her heart's content.

CHAPTER L.

She was his care, his hope, and his delight,
Most in his thought, and ever in his sight.
                                        DRYDEN.

ELLEN might now have been in some danger of being spoiled,—
not indeed with over-indulgence, for that was not the temper of
the family,—but from finding herself a person of so much consequence. She could not but feel that in the minds of every one of
her three friends she was the object of greatest importance; their
thoughts and care were principally occupied with her. Even Lady
Keith was perpetually watching, superintending, and admonishing;
though she every now and then remarked with a kind of surprise,
that "really she scarcely ever had to say any thing to Ellen; she
thought she must know things by instinct." To Mr. Lindsay and
his mother she was the idol of life; and except when by chance
her will might cross theirs, she had what she wished and did what
she pleased.

But Ellen happily had two safeguards which effectually kept her
from pride or presumption.

One was her love for her brother and longing remembrance of
him. There was no one to take his place, not indeed in her affections, for that would have been impossible, but in the daily course
of her life. She missed him in every thing. She had abundance
of kindness and fondness shown her, but the *sympathy* was wanting. She was talked *to*, but not *with*. No one now knew always
what she was thinking of, nor if they did would patiently draw out
her thoughts, canvass them, set them right or show them wrong.
No one now could tell what she was *feeling*, nor had the art sweetly,
in a way she scarce knew how, to do away with sadness, or dulness,
or perverseness, and leave her spirits clear and bright as the noon-
day. With all the petting and fondness she had from her new
friends, Ellen felt alone. She was petted and fondled as a darling
possession—a dear plaything—a thing to be cared for, taught, governed, disposed of, with the greatest affection and delight; but
John's was a higher style of kindness, that entered into all her innermost feelings and wants; and his was a higher style of authority too, that reached where theirs could never attain; an authority

Ellen always felt it utterly impossible to dispute; it was sure to be exerted on the side of what was right; and she could better have borne hard words from Mr. Lindsay than a glance of her brother's eye. Ellen made no objection to the imperativeness of her new guardians; it seldom was called up so as to trouble her, and she was not of late particularly fond of having her own way; but she sometimes drew comparisons.

"I could not any sooner—I could not as soon—have disobeyed John;—and yet he never would have spoken to me as they do if I had."

"*Some* pride perhaps?" she said, remembering Mr. Dundas's words;—"I should say a great deal—John isn't proud;—and yet —I don't know—he isn't proud as they are; I wish I knew what kinds of pride are right and what wrong—he would tell me if he was here."

"What are you in a 'brown study' about, Ellen?" said Mr. Lindsay?

"I was thinking, sir, about different kinds of pride—I wish I knew the right from the wrong—or is there any good kind?"

"All good, Ellen—all good," said Mr. Lindsay,—"provided you do not have too much of it."

"Would you like me to be proud, sir?"

"Yes," said he, laughing and pinching her cheek, "as proud as you like; if you only don't let *me* see any of it."

Not very satisfactory; but that was the way with the few questions of any magnitude Ellen ventured to ask; she was kissed and laughed at, called metaphysical or philosophical, and dismissed with no light on the subject. She sighed for her brother. The hours with M. Muller were the best substitute she had; they were dearly prized by her, and, to say truth, by him. He had no family, he lived alone; and the visits of his docile and intelligent little pupil became very pleasant breaks in the monotony of his home-life. Truly kind-hearted and benevolent, and a true lover of knowledge, he delighted to impart it. Ellen soon found she might ask him as many questions as she pleased, that were at all proper to the subject they were upon; and he, amused and interested, was equally able and willing to answer her. Often when not particularly busy he allowed her hour to become two. Excellent hours for Ellen. M. Muller had made his proposition to Mr. Lindsay, partly from grateful regard for him, and partly to gratify the fancy he had taken to Ellen on account of her simplicity, intelligence, and good manners. This latter motive did not disappoint him. He grew very much attached to his little pupil; an attachment which Ellen faithfully returned, both in kind, and by every trifling service that it could fall in her way to render him. Fine flowers and fruit, that it was her special delight to carry to

M. Muller ; little jobs of copying, or setting in order some disorderly
matters in his rooms, where he soon would trust her to do any
thing ; or a book from her father's library ; and once or twice
when he was indisposed, reading to him as she did by the hour
patiently, matters that could neither interest nor concern her.   On
the whole, and with good reason, the days when they were to
meet were hailed with as much pleasure perhaps by M. Muller as
by Ellen herself.

Her other safeguard was the precious hour alone which she had
promised John never to lose when she could help it.   The only
time she could have was the early morning before the rest of the
family were up.   To this hour, and it was often more than an
hour, Ellen was faithful.   Her little Bible was extremely precious
now ; Ellen had never gone to it with a deeper sense of need ; and
never did she find more comfort in being able to disburden her
heart in prayer of its load of cares and wishes.   Never more than
now had she felt the preciousness of that Friend who draws closer
to his children the closer they draw to him ; she had never realized more the joy of having him to go to.   It was her special
delight to pray for those loved ones she could do nothing else for ;
it was a joy to think that He who hears prayer is equally present
with all his people, and that though thousands of miles lie between
the petitioner and the petitioned for, the breath of prayer may span
the distance and pour blessings on the far-off head.   The burden
of thoughts and affections gathered during the twenty-three hours,
was laid down in the twenty-fourth ; and Ellen could meet her
friends at the breakfast-table with a sunshiny face.   Little they
thought where her heart had been, or where it had got its sunshine.

But notwithstanding this, Ellen had too much to remember and
regret than to be otherwise than sober,—soberer than her friends
liked.   They noticed with sorrow that the sunshine wore off as the
day rolled on ;—that though ready to smile upon occasion, her face
always settled again into a gravity they thought altogether unsuit-
able.   Mrs. Lindsay fancied she knew the cause, and resolved to
break it up.

From the first of Ellen's coming her grandmother had taken the
entire charge of her toilet.   Whatever Mrs. Lindsay's notions in
general might be as to the propriety of young girls learning to
take care of themselves, Ellen was much too precious a plaything
to be trusted to any other hands, even her own.   At eleven o'clock
regularly every day she went to her grandmother's dressing-room
for a very elaborate bathing and dressing ; though not a very long
one, for all Mrs. Lindsay's were energetic.   Now, without any hint
as to the reason, she was directed to come to her grandmother an
hour before the breakfast time, to go through then the course of

cold-water, sponging, and hair-gloving, that Mrs. Lindsay was accustomed to administer at eleven. Ellen heard in silence, and obeyed, but made up her hour by rising earlier than usual, so as to have it before going to her grandmother. It was a little difficult at first, but she soon got into the habit of it, though the mornings were dark and cold. After a while it chanced that this came to Mrs. Lindsay's ears, and Ellen was told to come to her as soon as she was out of bed in the morning.

"But grandmother," said Ellen,—"I am up a great while before you; I should find you asleep; don't I come soon enough?"

"What do you get up so early for?"

"You know, ma'am—I told you some time ago. I want some time to myself."

"It is not good for you to be up so long before breakfast, and in these cold mornings. Do not rise in future till I send for you."

"But grandmother,—that is the only time for me—there isn't an hour after breakfast that I can have regularly to myself; and I cannot be happy if I do not have some time."

"Let it be as I said," said Mrs. Lindsay.

"Couldn't you let me come to you at eleven o'clock again, ma'am? *do*, grandmother!"

Mrs. Lindsay touched her lips; a way of silencing her that Ellen particularly disliked, and which both Mr. Lindsay and his mother was accustomed to use.

She thought a great deal on the subject, and came soberly to the conclusion that it was her duty to disobey. "I promised John," she said to herself,—"I will never break that promise! I'll do any thing rather. And besides, if I had not, it is just as much my duty—a duty that no one here has a right to command me against. I will do what I think right, come what may."

She could not without its coming to the knowledge of her grandmother. A week or rather two after the former conversation, Mrs. Lindsay made inquiries of Mason, her woman, who was obliged to confess that Miss Ellen's light was always burning when she went to call her.

"Ellen," said Mrs. Lindsay the same day,—"have you obeyed me in what I told you the other morning?—about lying in bed till you are sent for?"

"No, ma'am."

"You are frank! to venture to tell me so. Why have you disobeyed me?"

"Because, grandmother, I thought it was right."

"You think it is right to disobey, do you?"

"Yes, ma'am, if——"

"If what?"

" I mean, grandmother, there is One I must obey even before you."

" If what?" repeated Mrs. Lindsay.

" Please do not ask me, grandmother; I don't want to say that."

" Say it at once, Ellen!"

" I thing it is right to disobey if I am told to do what is wrong," said Ellen in a low voice.

" Are you to be the judge of right and wrong?"

" No, ma'am."

" Who then?"

" The Bible."

" I do not know what is the reason," said Mrs. Lindsay, "that I cannot be very angry with you. Ellen, I repeat the order I gave you the other day. Promise me to obey."

" I cannot, grandmother; I *must* have that hour; I cannot do without it."

" So must I be obeyed, I assure you, Ellen. You will sleep in my room henceforth."

Ellen heard her in despair; she did not know what to do. *Appealing* was not to be thought of. There was, as she said, no time she could count upon after breakfast. During the whole day and evening she was either busy with her studies or masters, or in the company of her grandmother or Mr. Lindsay; and if not there, liable to be called to them at any moment. Her grandmother's expedient for increasing her cheerfulness had marvellous ill success. Ellen drooped under the sense of wrong, as well as the loss of her greatest comfort. For two days she felt and looked forlorn; and smiling now seemed to be a difficult matter. Mr. Lindsay happened to be remarkably busy those two days, so that he did not notice what was going on. At the end of them, however, in the evening, he called Ellen to him, and whisperingly asked what was the matter.

" Nothing, sir," said Ellen, " only grandmother will not let me do something I cannot be happy without doing."

" Is it one of the things you want to do because it is right, whether it is convenient or not?" he asked smiling. Ellen could not smile.

" Oh, father," she whispered, putting her face close to his, " if you would only get grandmother to let me do it!"

The words were spoken with a sob, and Mr. Lindsay felt her warm tears upon his neck. He had, however, far too much respect for his mother to say any thing against her proceedings while Ellen was present; he simply answered that she must do whatever her grandmother said. But when Ellen had left the room, which she did immediately, he took the matter up. Mrs. Lindsay explained, and insisted that Ellen was spoiling herself for life and the world by a set of dull religious notions that were utterly unfit for a child; that she would very soon get over thinking about her habit of morning prayer, and would then do much better. Mr. Lindsay looked grave; but with Ellen's tears yet wet upon his cheek, he could not dismiss the matter so lightly, and persisted in desiring that his mother should give up the point, which she utterly refused to do.

Ellen meanwhile had fled to her own room. The moonlight was quietly streaming in through the casement; it looked to her like an old friend. She threw herself down on the floor, close by the glass, and after some tears, which she could not help shedding, she raised her head and looked thoughtfully out. It was very seldom now that she had a chance of the kind; she was rarely alone but when she was busy.

"I wonder if that same moon is this minute shining in at the glass door at home?—no, to be sure it can't this minute—what am I thinking of?—but it was there or will be there—let me see—east —west—it was there some time this morning I suppose; looking right into our old sitting-room. Oh, moon, I wish I was in your place for once, to look in there too! But it is all empty now—there's nobody there—Mr. Humphreys would be in his study—how lonely, how lonely he must be! Oh, I wish I was back there with him!—John isn't there though—no matter—he will be,—and I could do so much for Mr. Humphreys in the meanwhile. He must miss me. I wonder where John is—nobody writes to me; I should think some one might. I wonder if I am ever to see them again. Oh, he will come to see me surely before he goes home!—but then he will have to go away without me again—I am fast now—fast enough—but oh! am I to be separated from them for ever! Well! —I shall see them in heaven!"

It was a "Well" of bitter acquiescence, and washed down with bitter tears.

"Is it my bonny Miss Ellen?" said the voice of the housekeeper coming softly in;—"is my bairn sitting a' her lane i' the dark? Why are ye no wi' the rest o' the folk, Miss Ellen?"

"I like to be alone, Mrs. Allen, and the moon shines in here nicely."

"Greeting!" exclaimed the old lady, drawing nearer,—"I ken it by the sound o' your voice;—greeting eenow! Are ye no weel, Miss Ellen? What vexes my bairn? Oh, but your father would be vexed an he kenned it!"

"Never mind, Mrs. Allen," said Ellen; "I shall get over it directly; don't say any thing about it."

"But I'm wae to see you," said the kind old woman, stooping down and stroking the head that again Ellen had bowed on her knees;—"will ye no tell me what vexes ye? Ye suld be as blithe as a bird the lang day."

" I can't, Mrs. Allen, while I am away from my friends."

" Friends! and wha has mair frinds than yoursel, Miss Ellen, or better frinds?—father and mither and a' ; where wad ye find thae that will love you mair."

" Ah, but I haven't my brother !'' sobbed Ellen.

" Your brither, Miss Ellen? An' wha's he ?''

" He's every thing, Mrs. Allen ! he's every thing ! I shall never be happy without him !—never ! never !''

" Hush, *dear* Miss Ellen ! for the love of a' that's gude ;— dinna talk that gate ! and dinna greet sae ! your father wad be sair vexed to hear ye or to see ye.''

" I cannot help it," said Ellen ;—" it is true.''

" It may be sae ; but dear Miss Ellen, dinna let it come to your father's ken ; ye're his very heart's idol ; he disna merit aught but gude frae ye.''

" I know it, Mrs. Allen," said Ellen weeping, and so I *do* love him—better than any body in the world, except two. But oh ! I want my brother !—I don't know how to be happy or good either without him. I want him all the while.''

" Miss Ellen, I kenned and loved your dear mither weel for mony a day—will ye mind if I speak a word to her bairn ?''

" No, dear Mrs. Allen—I'll thank you ;—did you know my mother ?''

" Wha suld if I didna ? she was brought up in my arms, and a dear lassie. Ye're no muckle like her, Miss Ellen ;—ye're mair bonny than her; and no a' thegither sae frack ;—though she was douce and kind too.''

" I wish''—Ellen began, and stopped.

" My dear bairn, there is Ane abuve wha disposes a' things for us ; and he isna weel pleased when his children fash themselves wi' his dispensations. He has ta'en and placed you here, for your ain gude I trust,—I'm sure it's for the gude of us a',—and if ye haena a' things ye wad wish, Miss Ellen, ye hae Him ; dinna forget that, my ain bairn.''

Ellen returned heartily and silently the embrace of the old Scotchwoman, and when she left her, set herself to follow her advice. She tried to gather her scattered thoughts and smooth her ruffled feelings, in using this quiet time to the best advantage. At the end of half an hour she felt like another creature ; and began to refresh herself with softly singing some of her old hymns.

The argument which was carried on in the parlour sunk at length into silence without coming to any conclusion.

" Where is Miss Ellen ?'' Mrs. Lindsay asked of a servant that came in.

" She is up in her room, ma'am, singing.''

" Tell her I want her."

" No—stop," said Mr. Lindsay :—" I'll go myself."

Her door was a little ajar, and he softly opened it without disturbing her. Ellen was still sitting on the floor before the window, looking out through it, and in rather a low tone singing the last verse of the hymn " Rock of Ages."

> While I draw this fleeting breath,—
> When my eyelids close in death,—
> When I rise to worlds unknown,
> And behold thee on thy throne,—
> Rock of Ages, cleft for me,
> Let me hide myself in thee !

Mr. Lindsay stood still at the door. Ellen paused a minute, and then sung " Jerusalem my happy home." Her utterance was so distinct that he heard every word. He did not move till she had finished, and then he came softly in.

" Singing songs to the moon, Ellen ?"

Ellen started and got up from the floor.

" No, sir ; I was singing them to myself."

" Not entirely, for I heard the last one. Why do you make yourself sober singing such sad things ?"

" I don't, sir ; they are not sad to me ; they are delightful. I love them dearly."

" How came you to love them ? it is not natural for a child of your age. What do you love them for, my little daughter ?"

" Oh, sir, there are a great many reasons,—I don't know how many."

" I will have patience, Ellen ; I want to hear them all."

" I love them because I love to think of the things the hymns are about,—I love the tunes, dearly,—and I like both the words and the tunes better, I believe, because I have sung them so often with friends."

" Humph ! I guessed as much. Isn't that the strongest reason of the three ?"

" I don't know, sir ; I don't think it is."

" Is all your heart in America, Ellen, or have you any left to bestow on us ?"

" Yes, sir."

" Not very much !"

" I love *you*, father," said Ellen, laying her cheek gently alongside of his.

" And your grandmother, Ellen ?" said Mr. Lindsay, clasping his arms around her.

" Yes, sir."

But he well understood that the " yes" was fainter.

" And your aunt ?—speak, Ellen."

" I don't love her as much as I wish I did," said Ellen ;—" I love her a little, I suppose. Oh, why do you ask me such a hard question, father ?"

" That is something you have nothing to do with," said Mr. Lindsay, half laughing. " Sit down here," he added, placing her on his knee, " and sing to me again."

Ellen was heartened by the tone of his voice, and pleased with the request. She immediately sang with great spirit a little Methodist hymn she had learned when a mere child. The wild air and simple words singularly suited each other.

> O Canaan—Bright Canaan—
> I am bound for the land of Canaan.
> O Canaan ! it is my happy, happy home—
> I am bound for the land of Canaan.

" Does that sound sad, sir ?"

" Why yes,—I think it does, rather, Ellen. Does it make you feel merry ?"

" Not *merry*, sir,—it isn't *merry ;* but I like it very much."

" The tune or the words ?"

" Both, sir."

" What do you mean by the land of Canaan ?"

" Heaven, sir."

" And do you like to think about that ? at your age ?"

" Why certainly, sir ! Why not ?"

" Why *do* you ?"

" Because it is a bright and happy place," said Ellen, gravely ; —" where there is no darkness, nor sorrow, nor death, neither pain nor crying ;—and my mother is there, and my dear Alice, and my Saviour is there ; and I hope I shall be there too."

" You are shedding tears now, Ellen."

" And if I am, sir, it is not because I am unhappy. It doesn't make me unhappy to think of these things—it makes me glad ; and the more I think of them the happier I am."

" You are a strange child. I am afraid your grandmother is right, and that you are hurting yourself with poring over serious matters that you are too young for."

" She would not think so if she knew," said Ellen, sighing. " I should not be happy at all without that, and you would not love me half so well, nor she either. Oh, father," she exclaimed, pressing his hand in both her own and laying her face upon it,— " do not let me be hindered in that ! forbid me any thing you please, but not that ! the better I learn to please my best Friend, the better I shall please you."

" Whom do you mean by ' your best friend ?' "

" The Lord my Redeemer."

" Where did you get these notions?" said Mr. Lindsay, after a short pause.

" From my mother, first, sir."

" She had none of them when I knew her."

" She had afterwards, then, sir; and oh !''—Ellen hesitated,— " I wish every body had them too !"

" My little daughter," said Mr. Lindsay, affectionately kissing the cheeks and eyes which were moist again,—" I shall indulge you in this matter. But you must keep your brow clear, or I shall revoke my grant. And you belong to me now; and there are some things I want you to forget, and not remember,—you understand ? Now don't sing songs to the moon any more to-night— good-night, my daughter."

" They think religion is a strange melancholy thing," said Ellen to herself as she went to bed ;—" I must not give them reason to think so—I must let my rushlight burn bright—I must take care —I never had more need !"

And with an earnest prayer for help to do so, she laid her head on the pillow.

Mr. Lindsay told his mother he had made up his mind to let Ellen have her way for a while, and begged that she might return to her old room and hours again. Mrs. Lindsay would not hear of it. Ellen had disobeyed her orders, she said ;—she must take the consequences.

" She is a bold little hussy to venture it," said Mr. Lindsay,— " but I do not think there is any naughtiness in her heart."

" No, not a bit. I could not be angry with her. It is only those preposterous notions she has got from somebody or other."

Mr. Lindsay said no more. Next morning he asked Ellen privately what she did the first thing after breakfast. Practise on the piano for an hour, she said.

" Couldn't you do it at any other time ?"

" Yes, sir, I could practise in the afternoon, only grandmother likes to have me with her."

" Let it be done then, Ellen, in future."

" And what shall I do with the hour after breakfast, sir ?"

" Whatever you please," said he smiling.

Ellen thanked him in the way she knew he best liked, and gratefully resolved he should have as little cause as possible to complain of her. Very little cause indeed did he or any one else have. No fault could be found with her performance of duty ; and her cheerfulness was constant and unvarying. She remembered her brother's recipe against loneliness and made use of it ; she remembered Mrs. Allen's advice and followed it ; she grasped the promises, " he that cometh to me shall never hunger,"—and " seek and ye shall find," —precious words that never yet disappointed any one ; and though tears might often fall that nobody knew of, and she might not be so *merry* as her friends would have liked to see her; though her cheerfulness was touched with sobriety, they could not complain; for her brow was always unruffled, her voice clear, her smile ready.

After a while she was restored to her own sleeping-room again, and permitted to take up her former habits.

CHAPTER LI.

Other days come back on me
With recollected music.

BYRON.

THOUGH nothing could be smoother than the general course of her life, Ellen's principles were still now and then severely tried.

Of all in the house, next to Mr. Lindsay, she liked the company of the old housekeeper best. She was a simple-minded Christian, a most benevolent and kind-hearted, and withal sensible and respectable person; devotedly attached to the family, and very fond of Ellen in particular. Ellen loved, when she could, to get alone with her, and hear her talk of her mother's young days; and she loved furthermore, and almost as much, to talk to Mrs. Allen of her own. Ellen could to no one else lisp a word on the subject; and without dwelling directly on those that she loved, she delighted to tell over to an interested listener the things she had done, seen, and felt, with them.

" I wish that child was a little more like other people," said Lady Keith one evening in the latter end of the winter.

" Humph!" said Mr. Lindsay,—" I don't remember at this moment any one that I think she could resemble without losing more than she gained."

" Oh, it's of no use to talk to you about Ellen, brother! You can take up things fast enough when you find them out, but you never will see with other people's eyes."

" What do your eyes see, Catherine ?"

" She is altogether too childish for her years; she is really a baby."

" I don't know," said Mr. Lindsay smiling; " you should ask M. Muller about that. He was holding forth to me for a quarter of an hour the other day, and could not stint in her praises. She will go on, he says, just as fast as he pleases to take her."

" Oh, yes—in intelligence and so on, I know she is not wanting; that is not what I mean."

" She is perfectly lady-like always," said Mrs. Lindsay.

" Yes, I know that,—and perfectly child-like too."

"I like that," said Mr. Lindsay; "I have no fancy for your grown-up little girls."

"Well!" said Lady Keith in despair, "you may like it; but I tell you she is too much of a child nevertheless,—in other ways. She hasn't an idea of a thousand things. It was only the other day she was setting out to go, at mid-day,—through the streets with a basket on her arm—some of that fruit for M. Muller I believe."

"If she has any fault," said Mr. Lindsay, "it is want of pride, —but I don't know—I can't say I wish she had more of it."

"Oh, no, of course! I suppose not. And it doesn't take any thing at all to make the tears come in her eyes; the other day I didn't know whether to laugh or be vexed at the way she went on with a kitten, for half an hour or more. I wish you had seen her! I am not sure she didn't cry over that. Now I suppose the next thing, brother, you will go and make her a present of one."

"If you have no heavier charges to bring," said Mr. Lindsay smiling, "I'll take breath and think about it."

"But she isn't like any body else,—she don't care for young companions,—she don't seem to fancy any one out of the family unless it is old Mrs. Allen, and she is absurd about her. You know she is not very well lately, and Ellen goes to see her I know every day, regularly; and there are the Gordons and Carpenters and Murrays and McIntoshes—she sees them continually, but I don't think she takes a great deal of pleasure in their company. The fact is, she is too sober."

"She has as sweet a smile as I ever saw," said Mr. Lindsay,— "and as hearty a laugh, when she does laugh; she is none of your gigglers."

"But when she does laugh," said Lady Keith, "it is not when other people do. I think she is generally grave when there is most merriment around her."

"I love to hear her laugh," said Mrs. Lindsay; "it is in such a low sweet tone, and seems to come so from the very spring of enjoyment. Yet I must say I think Catherine is half right."

"With half an advocate," said Lady Keith, "I shall not effect much."

Mr. Lindsay uttered a low whistle. At this moment the door opened, and Ellen came gravely in, with a book in her hand.

"Come here, Ellen," said Mr. Lindsay holding out his hand,— "here's your aunt says you don't like any body—how is it? are you of an unsociable disposition?"

Ellen's smile would have been a sufficient apology to him for a much graver fault.

"Any body out of the house, I meant," said Lady Keith.

"Speak, Ellen, and clear yourself," said Mr. Lindsay.

"I like some people," said Ellen smiling;—"I don't think I like a great many people *very* much."

"But you don't like young people," said Lady Keith,—"that is what I complain of; and it's unnatural. Now there's the other day, when you went to ride with Miss Gordon and her brother, and Miss MacPherson and her brother—I heard you say you were not sorry to get home. Now where will you find pleasanter young people?"

"Why don't you like them, Ellen?" said Mrs. Lindsay.

"I do like them, ma'am, tolerably."

"What does 'tolerably' mean?"

"I should have liked my ride better the other day," said Ellen, "if they had talked about sensible things."

"Nonsense!" said Lady Keith. "Society cannot be made up of M. Mullers."

"What did they talk about, Ellen?" said Mr. Lindsay, who seemed amused.

"About partners in dancing,—at least the ladies did,—and dresses, and different gentlemen, and what this one said and the other one said,—it wasn't very amusing to me."

Mr. Lindsay laughed. "And the gentlemen, Ellen; how did you like them?"

"I didn't like them particularly, sir."

"What have you against *them*, Ellen?"

"I don't wish to say any thing against them, aunt Keith."

"Come, come,—speak out."

"I didn't like their talking, sir, any better than the ladies, and besides that, I don't think they are very polite."

"Why not?" said Mr. Lindsay, highly amused.

"I don't think it was very polite," said Ellen, "for them to sit still on their horses when I went out, and let Brocklesby help me to mount. They took me up at M. Muller's, you know, sir; M. Muller had been obliged to go out and leave me."

Mr. Lindsay threw a glance at his sister which she rather resented.

"And pray what do you expect, Ellen?" said she. "You are a mere child—do you think you ought to be treated as a woman?"

"I don't wish to be treated as any thing but a child, aunt Keith."

But Ellen remembered well one day at home when John had been before the door on horseback and she had run out to give him a message,—his instantly dismounting to hear it. "And I was more a child then," she thought,—" and he wasn't a stranger."

"Whom *do* you like, Ellen?" inquired Mr. Lindsay, who looked extremely satisfied with the result of the examination.

"I like M. Muller, sir."

"Nobody else?"

" Mrs. Allen."

" There !'' exclaimed Lady Keith.

" Have you come from her room just now ?"

" Yes, sir."

" What's your fancy for going there ?"

" I like to hear her talk, sir, and to read to her ; it gives her a great deal of pleasure ;—and I like to talk to her."

" What do you talk about ?"

" She talks to me about my mother"—

" And you ?"

" I like to talk to her about old times," said Ellen, changing colour.

" Profitable conversation !" said Mrs. Lindsay.

" You will not go to her room any more, Ellen," said Mr. Lindsay.

In great dismay at what Mrs. Allen would think, Ellen began a remonstrance. But only one word was uttered ; Mr. Lindsay's hand was upon her lips. He next took the book she still held.

" Is this what you have been reading to her ?"

Ellen bowed in answer.

" Who wrote all this ?"

Before she could speak he had turned to the front leaf and read, " To my little sister." He quietly put the book in his pocket ; and Ellen as quietly left the room.

" I am glad you have said that," said Lady Keith. " You are quick enough when you see any thing for yourself, but you never will believe other people."

" There is nothing wrong here," said Mr. Lindsay,—" only I will not have her going back to those old recollections she is so fond of. I wish I could make her drink Lethe !"

" What is the book ?" said Mrs. Lindsay.

" I hardly know," said he, turning it over,—" except it is from that person that seems to have obtained such an ascendency over her—it is full of his notes—it is a religious work."

" She reads a great deal too much of that sort of thing," said Mrs. Lindsay. " I wish you would contrive to put a stop to it. You can do it better than any one else ; she is very fond of you."

That was not a good argument. Mr. Lindsay was silent ; his thoughts went back to the conversation held that evening in Ellen's room, and to certain other things ; and perhaps he was thinking that if religion had much to do with making her what she was, it was a tree that bore good fruits.

" I think," said Lady Keith, " that is one reason why she takes so little to the young people she sees. I have seen her sit perfectly grave when they were all laughing and talking around her—it really looks singular—I don't like it—I presume she would have thought it wicked to laugh with them. And the other night;—I missed her from the younger part of the company, where she should have been, and there she was in the other room with M. Muller and somebody else,—gravely listening to their conversation!''

"I saw her," said Mr. Lindsay smiling,—"and she looked any thing but dull or sober. I would rather have her gravity, after all, Catherine, than any body else's merriment I know."

"I wish she had never been detained in America after the time when she should have come to us," said Mrs. Lindsay.

"I wish the woman had what she deserves that kept back the letters!" said Mr. Lindsay.

"Yes indeed!" said his sister;—"and I have been in continual fear of a visit from that very person that you say gave Ellen the book."

"He isn't here!" said Mr. Lindsay.

"I don't know where he is;—but he *was* on this side of the water, at the time Ellen came on; so she told me."

"I wish he was in Egypt!"

"I don't intend he shall see her if he comes," said Lady Keith, "if I can possibly prevent it. I gave Porterfield orders, if any one asked for her, to tell me immediately, and not her upon any account; but nobody has come hitherto, and I am in hopes none will."

Mr. Lindsay rose and walked up and down the room with folded arms in a very thoughtful style.

Ellen with some difficulty bore herself as usual throughout the next day and evening, though constantly on the rack to get possession of her book again. It was not spoken of nor hinted at. When another morning came she could stand it no longer; she went soon after breakfast into Mr. Lindsay's study, where he was writing. Ellen came behind him and laying both her arms over his shoulders, said in his ear,

"Will you let me have my book again, father?"

A kiss was her only answer. Ellen waited.

"Go to the bookcases," said Mr. Lindsay presently, "or to the bookstore, and choose out any thing you like, Ellen, instead."

"I wouldn't exchange it for all that is in them!" she answered with some warmth, and with the husky feeling coming in her throat. Mr. Lindsay said nothing.

"At any rate," whispered Ellen after a minute, "you will not destroy it, or do any thing to it?—you will take care of it and let me have it again, won't you, sir?"

"I will try to take care of you, my daughter."

Again Ellen paused; and then came round in front of him to plead to more purpose.

" I will do any thing in the world for you, sir," she said earnestly, " if you will give me my book again."

" You must do any thing in the world for me," said he, smiling
and pinching her cheek,—" without that."

" But it is mine !" Ellen ventured to urge, though trembling.

" Come, come !" said Mr. Lindsay, his tone changing,—" and
you are mine, you must understand."

Ellen stood silent, struggling, between the alternate surgings of
passion and checks of prudence and conscience. But at last the
wave rolled too high and broke. Clasping her hands to her face,
she exclaimed, not indeed violently, but with sufficient energy of
expression, " Oh, it's not right !—it's not right !"

" Go to your room and consider of that," said Mr. Lindsay. " I
do not wish to see you again to-day, Ellen."

Ellen was wretched. Not from grief at her loss merely ; that
she could have borne ; that had not even the greatest share in her
distress ; she was at war with herself. Her mind was in a perfect
turmoil. She had been a passionate child in earlier days ; under
religion's happy reign that had long ceased to be true of her ; it
was only very rarely that she or those around her were led to remember or suspect that it had once been the case. She was surprised and half frightened at herself now, to find the strength of
the old temper suddenly roused. She was utterly and exceedingly
out of humour with Mr. Lindsay, and consequently with every
body and every thing else ; consequently, conscience would not
give her a moment's peace ; consequently, that day was a long and
bitter fight betwixt right and wrong. Duties were neglected, because she could not give her mind to them ; then they crowded
upon her notice at undue times ; all was miserable confusion. In
vain she would try to reason and school herself into right feeling ;
at one thought of her lost treasure passion would come flooding up
and drown all her reasonings and endeavours. She grew absolutely
weary.

But the day passed and the night came, and she went to bed
without being able to make up her mind ; and she arose in the
morning to renew the battle.

" How long is this miserable condition to last !" she said to herself. " Till you can entirely give up your feeling of resentment,
and apologize to Mr. Lindsay," said conscience. " Apologize !—
but I haven't done wrong." " Yes, you have," said conscience ;
" you spoke improperly ; he is justly displeased ; and you must
make an apology before there can be any peace." " But I said the
truth—it is *not* right—it is not right ! it is wrong ; and am *I* to go
and make an apology !—I can't do it." " Yes, for the wrong you
have done," said conscience,—" that is all your concern. And he
has a right to do what he pleases with you and yours, and he may

have his own reasons for what he has done ; and he loves you
very much, and you ought not to let him remain displeased with
you one moment longer than you can help—he is in the place of
a father to you, and you owe him a child's duty.''

But pride and passion still fought against reason and conscience,
and Ellen was miserable. The dressing-bell rang.

" There, I shall have to go down to breakfast directly, and they
will see how I look,—they will see I am angry and ill-humoured.
Well I *ought* to be angry ! But what will they think then of my
religion ?—is my rushlight burning bright? am I honouring Christ
now ?—is *this* the way to make his name and his truth lovely in
their eyes ? Oh, shame ! shame ! — I have enough to humble
myself for. And all yesterday, at any rate, they know I was
angry.''

Ellen threw herself upon her knees ; and when she rose up the
spirit of pride was entirely broken, and resentment had died with
self-justification.

The breakfast-bell rang before she was quite ready. She was
afraid she could not see Mr. Lindsay until he should be at the
table. " But it shall make no difference,'' she said to herself,—
" they know I have offended him—it is right they should hear
what I have to say.''

They were all at the table. But it made no difference. Ellen
went straight to Mr. Lindsay, and laying one hand timidly in his
and the other on his shoulder, she at once humbly and frankly
confessed that she had spoken as she ought not the day before,
and that she was very sorry she had displeased him, and begged
his forgiveness. It was instantly granted.

" You are a good child, Ellen,'' said Mr. Lindsay as he fondly
embraced her.

" Oh, no, sir !—don't call me so—I am every thing in the world
but that.''

" Then all the rest of the world are good children. Why didn't
you come to me before ?''

" Because I couldn't, sir ;—I felt wrong all day yesterday.''

Mr. Lindsay laughed and kissed her, and bade her sit down and
eat her breakfast.

It was about a month after this that he made her a present of a
beautiful little watch. Ellen's first look was of great delight ; the
second was one of curious doubtful expression, directed to his face,
half tendering the watch back to him as she saw that he understood her.

" Why,'' said he smiling, " do you mean to say you would
rather have that than this ?''

" A great deal !''

" No,'' said he, hanging the watch round her neck,—" you shall not have it ; but you may make your mind easy, for I have it safe, and it shall come back to you again some time or other."

With this promise Ellen was obliged to be satisfied.

The summer passed in the enjoyment of all that wealth, of purse and of affection both, could bestow upon their darling. Early in the season the family returned to the Braes. Ellen liked it there much better than in the city ; there was more that reminded her of old times. The sky and the land, though different from those she best loved, were yet but another expression of nature's face ; it was the same face still ; and on many a sunbeam Ellen travelled across the Atlantic.* She was sorry to lose M. Muller, but she could not have kept him in Edinburgh ; he quitted Scotland about that time.

Other masters attended her in the country, or she went to Edinburgh to attend them. Mr. Lindsay liked that very well ; he was often there himself, and after her lesson he loved to have her with him in the library and at dinner and during the drive home. Ellen liked it because it was so pleasant to him ; and besides, there was a variety about it, and the drives were always her delight, and she chose his company at any time rather than that of her aunt and grandmother. So, many a happy day that summer had she and Mr. Lindsay together ; and many an odd pleasure in the course of them did he find or make for her. Sometimes it was a new book, sometimes a new sight, sometimes a new trinket. According to his promise, he had purchased her a fine horse ; and almost daily Ellen was upon his back, and with Mr. Lindsay in the course of the summer scoured the country far and near. Every scene of any historic interest within a good distance of " the Braes" was visited, and some of them again and again. Pleasures of all kinds were at Ellen's disposal ; and to her father and grandmother she was truly the light of the eyes.

And Ellen was happy ; but it was not all these things, nor even her affection for Mr. Lindsay, that made her so. He saw her calm sunshiny face and busy happy demeanour, and fancied, though he had sometimes doubts about it, that she did not trouble herself much with old recollections, or would in time get over them. It was not so. Ellen never forgot ; and sometimes when she seemed busiest and happiest, it was the thought of an absent and distant friend that was nerving her energies and giving colour to her cheek. Still, as at first, it was in her hour alone that Ellen laid down care and took up submission ; it was that calmed her brow and brightened her smile. And though now and then she shed bitter tears, and repeated her despairing exclamation, " Well ! I will see him in

---

* " Then by a sunbeam I will climb to thee."—GEORGE HERBERT.

heaven !"—in general she lived on hope, and kept at the bottom of her heart some of her old feeling of confidence.

Perhaps her brow grew somewhat meeker and her smile less bright as the year rolled on. Months flew by, and brought her no letters. Ellen marvelled and sorrowed in vain. One day mourning over it to Mrs. Allen, the good housekeeper asked her if her friends knew her address? Ellen at first said "to be sure," but after a few minutes' reflection was obliged to confess that she was not certain about it. It would have been just like Mr. Humphreys to lose sight entirely of such a matter, and very natural for her, in her grief and confusion of mind and inexperience, to be equally forgetful. She wrote immediately to Mr. Humphreys and supplied the defect; and hope brightened again. Once before she had written, on the occasion of the refunding her expenses. Mr. Lindsay and his mother were very prompt to do this, though Ellen could not tell what the exact amount might be; they took care to be on the safe side, and sent more than enough. Ellen's mind had changed since she came to Scotland; she was sorry to have the money go; she understood the feeling with which it was sent, and it hurt her.

Two or three months after the date of her last letter, she received at length one from Mr. Humphreys, a long, very kind, and very wise one. She lived upon it for a good while. Mr. Lindsay's bills were returned. Mr. Humphreys declined utterly to accept them, telling Ellen that he looked upon her as his own child up to the time that her friends took her out of his hands, and that he owed her more than she owed him. Ellen gave the money, she dared not give the whole message, to Mr. Lindsay. The bills were instantly and haughtily re-enclosed and sent back to America.

Still nothing was heard from Mr. John. Ellen wondered, waited, wept; sadly quieted herself into submission, and as time went on, clung faster and faster to her Bible and the refuge she found there.

CHAPTER LII.

Hon.—Why didn't you show him up, blockhead ?
Butler.—Show him up, sir ? With all my heart, sir.
Up or down, all's one to me.
GOOD-NATURED MAN.

ONE evening, it was New Year's eve, a large party was expected at Mr. Lindsay's. Ellen was not of an age to go abroad to parties, but at home her father and grandmother never could bear to do without her when they had company. Generally, Ellen liked it very much ; not called upon to take any active part herself, she had leisure to observe and enjoy in quiet; and often heard music, and often by Mr. Lindsay's side listened to conversation, in which she took great pleasure. To-night, however, it happened that Ellen's thoughts were running on other things ; and Mrs. Lindsay's woman, who had come in to dress her, was not at all satisfied with her grave looks and the little concern she seemed to take in what was going on.

"I wish, Miss Ellen, you'd please hold your head up, and look somewhere—I don't know when I'll get your hair done if you keep it down so."

"Oh, Mason, I think that'll do—it looks very well—you needn't do any thing more."

"I beg your pardon, Miss Ellen, but you know it's your grandmother that must be satisfied, and she will have it just so ;—there,—now that's going to look lovely ;—but indeed Miss Ellen she won't be pleased if you carry such a soberish face down stairs,—and what will the master say ! Most young ladies would be as bright as a bee at being going to see so many people, and indeed it's what you should."

"I had rather see one or two persons than one or two hundred," said Ellen, speaking half to herself and half to Mrs. Mason.

"Well, for pity's sake, Miss Ellen, dear, if you can, don't look as if it was a funeral it was. There ! 'tain't much trouble to fix you, anyhow—if you'd only care a little more about it, it would be a blessing. Stop till I fix this lace. The master will call you his white rose-bud to-night, sure enough."

"That's nothing new," said Ellen, half smiling.

Mason left her ; and feeling the want of something to raise her spirits, Ellen sorrowfully went to her Bible, and slowly turning it over, looked along its pages to catch a sight of something cheering before she went down stairs.

"*This God is our God for ever and ever : he will be our guide even unto death.*"

"Isn't that enough?" thought Ellen, as her eyes filled in answer. "It ought to be—John would say it was—oh ! where is he !"

She went on turning leaf after leaf.

"*O Lord of hosts, blessed is the man that trusteth in thee !*"

"That is true surely," she thought. "And I do trust in him— I am blessed—I am happy, come what may. He will let nothing come to those that trust in him but what is good for them—if he is my God I have enough to make me happy—I ought to be happy—I will be happy !—I will trust him, and take what he gives me ; and try to leave, as John used to tell me, my affairs in his hand."

For a minute tears flowed; then they were wiped away; and the smile she gave Mr. Lindsay when she met him in the hall was not less bright than usual.

The company were gathered, but it was still early in the evening, when a gentleman came who declined to enter the drawing-room, and asked for Miss Lindsay.

"Miss Lindsay is engaged."

"An' what for suld ye say sae, Mr. Porterfield?" cried the voice of the housekeeper, who was passing in the hall,— "when ye ken as weel as I do that Miss Ellen——"

The butler stopped her with saying something about "my lady," and repeated his answer to the gentleman.

The latter wrote a word or two on a card which he drew from his pocket, and desired him to carry it to Miss Ellen. He carried it to Lady Keith.

"What sort of a person, Porterfield?" said Lady Keith, crumpling the paper in her fingers; and withdrawing a little from the company.

"Uncommon fine gentleman, my lady," Porterfield answered in a low tone.

"A gentleman?" said Lady Keith inquiringly.

"Certain, my lady!—and as up and down spoken as if he was a prince of the blood; he's somebody that is not accustomed to be said 'no' to, for sure."

Lady Keith hesitated. Recollecting however that she had just left Ellen safe in the music-room, she made up her mind; and desired Porterfield to show the stranger in. As he entered, unannounced, her eyes unwillingly verified the butler's judgment; and to the inquiry whether he might see Miss Lindsay she answered very politely, though with regrets that Miss Lindsay was engaged.

"May I be pardoned for asking," said the stranger, with the slightest possible approach to a smile, "whether that decision is imperative? I leave Scotland to-morrow—my reasons for wishing to see Miss Lindsay this evening are urgent."

Lady Keith could hardly believe her ears, or command her countenance to keep company with her expressions of "sorrow that it was impossible—Miss Lindsay could not have the pleasure that evening."

"May I beg then to know at what hour I may hope to see her to-morrow?"

Hastily resolving that Ellen should on the morrow accept a long-given invitation, Lady Keith answered that "she would not be in town—she would leave Edinburgh at an early hour."

The stranger bowed and withdrew; that was all the bystanders saw. But Lady Keith, who had winced under an eye that she could not help fancying read her too well, saw that in his parting look which made her uneasy; beckoning a servant who stood near, she ordered him to wait upon that gentleman to the door.

The man obeyed; but the stranger did not take his cloak and made no motion to go.

" No, sir! not that way," he said sternly, as the servant laid his hand on the lock ;—" show me to Miss Lindsay !"

" Miss Ellen ?" said the man doubtfully, coming back, and thinking from the gentleman's manner that he must have misunderstood Lady Keith ;—" where is Miss Ellen, Arthur ?"

The person addressed threw his head back towards the door he had just come from on the other side of the hall.

" This way, sir, if you please,—what name, sir ?"

" No name —stand back !" said the stranger as he entered.

There were a number of people gathered round a lady who was at the piano singing. Ellen was there in the midst of them. The gentleman advanced quietly to the edge of the group and stood there without being noticed; Ellen's eyes were bent on the floor. The expression of her face touched and pleased him greatly; it was precisely what he wished to see. Without having the least shadow of sorrow upon it, there was in all its lines that singular mixture of gravity and sweetness that is never seen but where religion and discipline have done their work well; the writing of the wisdom that looks soberly, and the love that looks kindly, on all things. He was not sure at first whether she were intently listening to the music, or whether her mind was upon something far different and far away; he thought the latter. He was right. Ellen at the moment had escaped from the company and the noisy sounds of the performer at her side; and while her eye was curiously tracing out the pattern of the carpet, her mind was resting itself in one of the verses she had been reading that same evening. Suddenly, and as it seemed, from no connection with any thing in or out of her thoughts, there came to her mind the image of John as she had seen him that first evening she ever saw him, at Carra-carra, when she looked up from the boiling chocolate and espied him,— standing in an attitude of waiting near the door. Ellen at first wondered how that thought should have come into her head just then ; the next moment, from a sudden impulse, she raised her eyes to search for the cause and saw John's smile.

It would not be easy to describe the change in Ellen's face. Lightning makes as quick and as brilliant an illumination, but lightning does not stay. With a spring she reached him, and seizing both his hands drew him out of the door near which they were standing; and as soon as they were hidden from view threw herself into his arms in an agony of joy. Before however either of them could say a word, she had caught his hand again, and led him back along the hall to the private staircase ; she mounted it rapidly to *her room;* and there again she threw herself into his arms, exclaiming, " Oh, John!—my dear John! my dear brother!"

But neither smiles nor words would do for the overcharged heart. The tide of joy ran too strong, and too much swelled from the open sources of love and memory, to keep any bounds. And it kept none. Ellen sat down, and bowing her head on the arm of the sofa wept with all the vehement passion of her childhood, quivering from head to foot with convulsive sobs. John might guess from the outpouring now how much her heart had been secretly gather-

ing for months past. For a little while he walked up and down the room; but this excessive agitation he was not willing should continue. He said nothing; sitting down beside Ellen on the sofa, he quietly possessed himself of one of her hands; and when in her excitement the hand struggled to get away again, it was not permitted. Ellen understood that very well and immediately checked herself. Better than words, the calm firm grasp of his hand quieted her. Her sobbing stilled; she turned from the arm of the sofa, and leaning her head upon him took his hand in both hers and pressed it to her lips as if she were half beside herself. But that was not permitted to last either, for his hand quickly imprisoned hers again. There was silence still. Ellen could not look up yet, and neither seemed very forward to speak; she sat gradually quieting down into fulness of happiness.

"I thought you never would come, John," at length Ellen half whispered, half said.

"And I cannot stay now. I must leave you to-morrow, Ellen." Ellen started up and looked up now.

"Leave me! For how long? Where are you going?"

"Home."

"To America!"—Ellen's heart died within her. Was *this* the end of all her hopes? did her confidence end *here?* She shed no tears now. He could see that she grew absolutely still from intense feeling.

"What's the matter, Ellie?" said the low gentle tones she so well remembered;—"I am leaving you but for a time. I *must* go home now, but if I live you will see me again."

"Oh, I wish I was going with you!" Ellen exclaimed, bursting into tears.

"My dear Ellie!" said her brother in an altered voice, drawing her again to his arms,—"you cannot wish it more than I!"

"I never thought you would leave me here, John."

"Neither would I, if I could help it; neither will I a minute longer than I can help; but we must both wait, my own Ellie. Do not cry so, for my sake!"

"Wait?—till when?" said Ellen, not a little reassured.

"I have no power now to remove you from your legal guardians, and you have no right to choose for yourself."

"And when shall I?"

"In a few years."

"A few years!—But in the meantime, John, what shall I do without you?—If I could see you once in a while—but there is no one here—not a single one—to help me to keep right; no one talks to me as you used to; and I am all the while afraid I shall go wrong in something; what shall I do?"

"What the weak must always do, Ellie,—seek for strength where it may be had."

"And so I do, John," said Ellen weeping,—"but I want you,— oh how much!"

"Are you not happy here?"

"Yes—I am happy—at least I thought I was half an hour ago, —as happy as I can be. I have every thing to make me happy, except what would do it."

"We must both have recourse to our old remedy against sorrow and loneliness—you have not forgotten the use of it, Ellie?"

" No, John," said Ellen, meeting his eyes with a tearful smile.

" They love you here, do they not?"

" Very much—too much."

" And you love them?"

" Yes."

" That's a doubtful ' yes.' "

" I do love my father,—very much ; and my grandmother too, though not so much. I cannot help loving them,—they love me so. But they are so unlike you !"

" That is not much to the purpose, after all," said John smiling. " There are varieties of excellence in the world."

" Oh, yes, but that isn't what I mean ; it isn't a variety of excellence. They make me do every thing that they have a mind,—I don't mean," she added smiling, " that *that* is not like you,—but you always had a reason ; they are different. My father makes me drink wine every now and then,—I don't like to do it, and he knows I do not, and I think that is the reason I have to do it."

" That is not a matter of great importance, Ellie, provided they do not make you do something wrong."

" They could not do that I hope : and there is another thing they cannot make me do.'

" What is that?"

" Stay here when you will take me away."

There was a few minutes' thoughtful pause on both sides.

" You are grown, Ellie," said John,—" you are not the child I left you."

" I don't know," said Ellen smiling,—" it seems to me I am just the same."

" Let me see—look at me !"

She raised her face, and amidst smiles and tears its look was not less clear and frank than his was penetrating. " Just the same," was the verdict of her brother's eyes a moment afterwards. Ellen's smile grew bright as she read it there.

" Why have you never come or written before, John?"

" I did not know where you were. I have not been in England for many months till quite lately, and I could not get your address. I think my father was without it for a long time, and when at last he sent it to me, the letter miscarried—never reached me—there were delays upon delays."

" And when did you get it?"

" I preferred coming to writing."

" And now you must go home so soon !"

" I must, Ellie. My business has lingered on a great while, and it is quite time I should return. I expect to sail next week—Mrs. Gillespie is going with me—her husband stays behind till spring."

Ellen sighed.

" I made a friend of a friend of yours whom I met in Switzerland last summer—M. Muller."

" M. Muller! did you! Oh, I'm very glad! I am very glad
you know him—he is the best friend I have got here, after my
father. I don't know what I should have done without him."

" I have heard him talk of you," said John smiling.

" He has just come back; he was to be here this evening."

There was a pause again.

" It does not seem right to go home without you, Ellie," said
her brother then. " I think you belong to me more than to any
body."

" That is exactly what I think !" said Ellen with one of her
bright looks, and then bursting into tears ;—" I am very glad you
think so too! I will always do whatever you tell me—just as I
used to—no matter what any body else says."

" Perhaps I shall try you in two or three things, Ellie."

" Will you! in what? Oh, it would make me so happy—so
much happier—if I could be doing something to please you. I
wish I was at home with you again !"

" I will bring that about, Ellie, by and by, if you make your
words good."

" I shall be happy then," said Ellen, her old confidence standing
stronger than ever—" because I know you will if you say so.
Though how you will manage it I cannot conceive. My father
and grandmother and aunt cannot bear to hear me speak of
America. I believe they would be glad if there wasn't such a
place in the world. They would not even let me think of it if
they could help it ; I never dare mention your name, or say a word
about old times. They are afraid of my loving any body I
believe. They want to have me all to themselves."

" What will they say to you then, Ellie, if you leave them to
give yourself to me?"

" I cannot help it," replied Ellen,—" they must say what they
please ;"—and with abundance of energy, and not a few tears, she
went on ;—" I love them, but I had given myself to you a great
while ago ; long before I was his daughter, you called me your
little sister—I can't undo that, John, and I don't want to—it
doesn't make a bit of difference that we were not born so !"

John suddenly rose and began to walk up and down the room.
Ellen soon came to his side, and leaning upon his arm as she had
been used to do in past times, walked up and down with him, at
first silently.

" What is it you wanted me to do, John ?" she said gently at
length ; " you said ' two or three things.' "

" One is that you keep up a regular and full correspondence
with me."

"I am very glad that you will let me do that," said Ellen,— "that is exactly what I should like, but——"

"What?"

"I am afraid they will not let me."

"I will arrange that."

"Very well," said Ellen joyously,—"then it will do. Oh, it would make me so happy! And you will write to me?"

"Certainly!"

"And I will tell you every thing about myself; and you will tell me how I ought to do in all sorts of things? that will be next best to being with you. And then you will keep me right."

"I won't promise you that, Ellie," said John smiling;—"you must learn to keep yourself right."

"I know you will, though, however you may smile. What next?"

"Read no novels."

"I never do, John. I knew you did not like it, and I have taken good care to keep out of the way of them. If I had told any body why, though, they would have made me read a dozen."

"Why Ellie!" said her brother,—"you must need some care to keep a straight line where your course lies now."

"Indeed I do, John," said Ellen, her eyes filling with tears,— "oh how I have felt that sometimes! And then how I wanted you!"

Her hand was fondly taken in his, as many a time it had been of old, and for a long time they paced up and down; the conversation running sometimes in the strain that both loved and Ellen now never heard; sometimes on other matters; such a conversation as those she had lived upon in former days, and now drank in with a delight and eagerness inexpressible. Mr. Lindsay would have been in dismay to have seen her uplifted face, which, though tears were many a time there, was sparkling and glowing with life and joy in a manner he had never known it. She almost forgot what the morrow would bring, in the exquisite pleasure of the instant, and hung upon every word and look of her brother as if her life were there.

"And in a few weeks," said Ellen at length, "you will be in our old dear sitting-room again, and riding on the Black Prince!— and I shall be here!—and it will be——"

"It will be empty without you, Ellie;—but we have a friend that is sufficient; let us love him and be patient."

"It is very hard to be patient," murmured Ellen. "But dear John, there was something else you wanted me to do? what is it? you said 'two or three' things."

"I will leave that to another time."

"But why? I will do it whatever it be—pray tell me."

" No," said he smiling,—"not now,—you shall know by and by
—the time is not yet. Have you heard of your old friend Mr.
Van Brunt?"

" No—what of him?"

" He has come out before the world as a Christian man."

" Has he!"

John took a letter from his pocket and opened it.

" You may see what my father says of him; and what he says
of you too Ellie;—he has missed you much."

" Oh, I was afraid he would," said Ellen,—" I was sure he
did!"

She took the letter, but she could not see the words. John told
her she might keep it to read at her leisure.

" And how are they all at Ventnor? and how is Mrs. Vawse?
and Margery?"

" All well. Mrs. Vawse spends about half her time at my
father's."

" I am very glad of that!"

" Mrs. Marshman wrote me to bring you back with me if I
could, and said she had a home for you always at Ventnor."

" How kind she is," said Ellen;—" how many friends I find
everywhere. It seems to me, John, that everybody almost loves
me."

" That *is* a singular circumstance! However, I am no exception
to the rule, Ellie."

" Oh, I know that," said Ellen laughing. " And Mr. George?"

" Mr. George is well."

" How much I love him!" said Ellen. " How much I would
give to see him. I wish you could tell me about poor Captain and
the Brownie, but I don't suppose you have heard of them. Oh,
when I think of it all at home, how I want to be there!—Oh,
John! sometimes lately I have almost thought I should only see
you again in heaven."

" My dear Ellie! I shall see you there, I trust; but if we live
we shall spend our lives here together first. And while we are
parted we will keep as near as possible by praying for and writing
to each other. And what God orders let us quietly submit to."

Ellen had much ado to command herself at the tone of these
words and John's manner, as he clasped her in his arms and kissed
her brow and lips. She strove to keep back a show of feeling that
would distress and might displease him. But the next moment
her fluttering spirits were stilled by hearing the few soft words of
a prayer that he breathed over her head. It was a prayer for her
and for himself, and one of its petitions was that they might be
kept to see each other again. Ellen wrote the words on her
heart.

" Are you going?"

He showed his watch.

" Well, I shall see you to-morrow!"

" Shall you be here?"

" Certainly—where else should I be? What time must you set out?"

" I need not till afternoon, but—How early can I see you?"

" As early as you please. Oh, spend all the time with me you can, John!"

So it was arranged.

" And now, Ellie, you must go down stairs and present me to Mr. Lindsay."

" To my father!"

For a moment Ellen's face was a compound of expressions. She instantly acquiesced however, and went down with her brother, her heart it must be confessed going very pit-a-pat indeed. She took him into the library which was not this evening thrown open to company; and sent a servant for Mr. Lindsay. While waiting for his coming, Ellen felt as if she had not the fair use of her senses. Was that John Humphreys quietly walking up and down the library? Mr. Lindsay's library? and was she about to introduce her brother to the person who had forbidden her to mention his name? There was something however in Mr. John's figure and air, in his utter coolness, that insensibly restored her spirits. Triumphant confidence in him overcame the fear of Mr. Lindsay; and when he appeared, Ellen with tolerable composure met him, her hand upon John's arm, and said, " Father, this is Mr. Humphreys," —*my brother* she dared not add.

" I hope Mr. Lindsay will pardon my giving him this trouble," said the latter;—" we have one thing in common which should forbid our being strangers to each other. I, at least, was unwilling to leave Scotland without making myself known to Mr. Lindsay."

Mr. Lindsay most devoutly wished the " thing in common" had been any thing else. He bowed, and was " happy to have the pleasure," but evidently neither pleased nor happy. Ellen could see that.

" May I take up five minutes of Mr. Lindsay's time to explain, perhaps to apologize," said John, slightly smiling,—" for what I have said?"

A little ashamed, it might be, to have his feeling suspected, Mr. Lindsay instantly granted the request, and politely invited his unwelcome guest to be seated. Obeying a glance from her brother which she understood, Ellen withdrew to the further side of the room, where she could not hear what they said. John took up the history of Ellen's acquaintance with his family, and briefly gave it to Mr. Lindsay, scarce touching on the benefits by them conferred on her, and skilfully dwelling rather on Ellen herself and setting forth what she had been to them. Mr. Lindsay could not be unconscious of what his visitor delicately omitted to hint at, neither could he help making secretly to himself some most unwilling admissions; and though he might wish the speaker at the antipodes, and doubtless did, yet the sketch was too happily given, and his fondness for Ellen too great, for him not to be delightedly interested in what was said of her. And however strong might have been his desire to dismiss his guest in a very summary manner, or to treat him with haughty reserve, the graceful dignity of Mr. Humphreys' manners made either expedient impossible. Mr. Lindsay felt constrained to meet him on his own ground—the ground of high-bred frankness; and grew secretly still more afraid that his real feelings should be discerned.

Ellen from afar, where she could not hear the words, watched the countenances with great anxiety and great admiration. She could see that while her brother spoke with his usual perfect ease, Mr. Lindsay was embarrassed. She half read the truth. She saw the entire politeness where she also saw the secret discomposure, and she felt that the politeness was forced from him. As the conversation went on, however, she wonderingly saw that the cloud on his brow lessened,—she saw him even smile; and when at last they rose, and she drew near, she almost thought her ears were playing her false when she heard Mr. Lindsay beg her brother to go in with him to the company and be presented to Mrs. Lindsay. After a moment's hesitation this invitation was accepted, and they went together into the drawing-room.

Ellen felt as if she was in a dream. With a face as grave as usual, but with an inward exultation and rejoicing in her brother impossible to describe, she saw him going about among the company,—talking to her grandmother,—yes and her grandmother did not look less pleasant than usual,—recognizing M. Muller, and in conversation with other people whom he knew. With indescribable glee Ellen saw that Mr. Lindsay managed most of the time to be of the same group. Never more than that night did she triumphantly think that Mr. John could do any thing. He finished the evening there. Ellen took care not to seem too much occupied with him; but she contrived to be near when he was talking with M. Muller, and to hang upon her father's arm when *he* was in Mr. John's neighbourhood. And when the latter had taken leave, and was in the hall, Ellen was there before he could be gone. And there came Mr. Lindsay too behind her!

"You will come early to-morrow morning, John?"

"Come to breakfast, Mr. Humphreys, will you?" said Mr. Lindsay, with sufficient cordiality.

But Mr. Humphreys declined this invitation, in spite of the

timid touch of Ellen's fingers upon his arm, which begged for a different answer.

"I will be with you early, Ellie," he said however.

"And oh! John," said Ellen suddenly, "order a horse and let us have one ride together; let me show you Edinburgh."

"By all means," said Mr. Lindsay,—"let us show you Edinburgh; but order no horses, Mr. Humphreys, for mine are at your service."

Ellen's other hand was gratefully laid upon her father's arm as this second proposal was made and accepted.

"Let *us* show you Edinburgh," said Ellen to herself, as she and Mr. Lindsay slowly and gravely went back through the hall. "So there is an end of my fine morning!—But however, how foolish I am! John has his own ways of doing things—he can make it pleasant in spite of every thing."

She went to bed, not to sleep indeed, for a long time, but to cry for joy and all sorts of feelings at once.

Good came out of evil, as it often does, and as Ellen's heart presaged it would when she arose the next morning. The ride was preceded by half an hour's chat between Mr. John, Mr. Lindsay, and her grandmother; in which the delight of the evening before was renewed and confirmed. Ellen was obliged to look down to hide the too bright satisfaction she felt was shining in her face. She took no part in the conversation, it was enough to hear. She sat with charmed ears, seeing her brother overturning all her father's and grandmother's prejudices, and making his own way to their respect at least, in spite of themselves. Her marvelling still almost kept even pace with her joy. "I knew he would do what he pleased," she said to herself,—"I knew they could not help that; but I did not dream he would ever make them *like* him,—that I never dreamed!"

On the ride again, Ellen could not wish that her father were not with them. She wished for nothing; it was all a maze of pleasure, which there was nothing to mar but the sense that she would by and by wake up and find it was a dream. And no, not that either. It was a solid good and blessing, which though it must come to an end, she should never lose. For the present there was hardly any thing to be thought of but enjoyment. She shrewdly guessed that Mr. Lindsay would have enjoyed it too, but for herself; there was a little constraint about him still, she could see. There was none about Mr. John; in the delight of his words and looks and presence, Ellen half the time forgot Mr. Lindsay entirely; she had enough of them; she did not for one moment wish Mr. Lindsay had less.

At last the long beautiful ride came to an end; and the rest of the morning soon sped away, though as Ellen had expected she was not permitted to spend any part of it alone with her brother. Mr. Lindsay asked him to dinner, but this was declined.

Not till long after he was gone did Ellen read Mr. Humphreys' letter. One bit of it may be given.

" Mr. Van Brunt has lately joined our little church. This has given me great pleasure. He had been a regular attendant for a long time before. He ascribes much to your instrumentality; but says his first thoughts (earnest ones) on the subject of religion were on the occasion of a tear that fell from Ellen's eye upon his hand one day when she was talking to him about the matter. He never got over the impression. In his own words, ' it scared him !' That was a dear child ! I did not know how dear till I had lost her. I did not know how severely I should feel her absence ; nor had I the least notion when she was with us of many things respecting her that I have learnt since. I half hoped we should yet have her back, but that will not be. I shall be glad to see you, my son."

The correspondence with John was begun immediately, and was the delight of Ellen's life. Mrs. Lindsay and her daughter wished to put a stop to it ; but Mr. Lindsay dryly said that Mr. Humphreys had frankly spoken of it before him, and as he made no objection then he could not now.

Ellen puzzled herself a little to think what could be the third thing John wanted of her ; but whatever it were, she was very sure she would do it !

For the gratification of those who are never satisfied, one word shall be added, to wit, that

The seed so early sown in little Ellen's mind, and so carefully tended by sundry hands, grew in course of time to all the fair structure and comely perfection it had bid fair to reach—storms and winds that had visited it did but cause the root to take deeper hold ;—and at the point of its young maturity it happily fell again into those hands that had of all been most successful in its culture.—In other words, to speak intelligibly, Ellen did in no wise disappoint her brother's wishes, nor he hers. Three or four more years of Scottish discipline wrought her no ill ; they did but serve to temper and beautify her Christian character ; and then, to her unspeakable joy, she went back to spend her life with the friends and guardians she best loved, and to be to them, still more than she had been to her Scottish relations, " the light of the eyes."

THE END.

APPENDIX

UNPUBLISHED CHAPTER

One afternoon, it is of no sort of consequence whether it was fair or cloudy, for nobody cared; but, however, it was a calm and lovely spring day—a carriage stopped at a house in one of our pleasantest, though not one of our largest cities. A gentleman and lady alighted.

"Is my father at home?"

"No, Sir."

"Tell Mrs. Grimes I want to see her."

It was a corner house, and the large parlour or sitting-room, which the travellers entered, having windows on two sides, was remarkably cheerful and pleasant. It would have seemed so to any, but Ellen immediately uttered an exclamation of surprise and fond pleasure. Around her, on every hand, were the very loved things she had been used to see at the Carra-Carra parsonage, and as near as possible in the same arrangement. There stood the dear old book-case with its books—the sofas, the cupboard, the pictures,—yes, even Alice's cabinet of curiosities,—the same table in the middle of the floor. Ellen stood fixed, with clasped hands of pleasure and tender recollection, and eyes that were making too feeling a recognition of its objects. These indeed were intermixed with new ones. Large additions of whatever was convenient or desirable had been made to the old stock. It was rather a curious looking room—everything rather than fashionable or formal. Its look was of substantial and elegant comfort, without any fastidious regard to the wood of the furniture or the covering of the cushions or to one thing's matching another.

"You are looking for the flower stand—that is in your room. It is empty but you will soon fill it."

"My room?"

"Yes—your private room—your study," said he smiling, "next to mine. There is a door between that you may set open whenever you please—you know I have an old habit of not being disturbed by you."

"And Mr. Humphreys?"

"You mustn't call him so anymore, Ellie."

"No and I don't wish it indeed. How glad I should have been in old times to have changed that if I could. There is one comfort—you will not touch my lips if I say anything you do not like."

"Touch your lips?"

"No, no!" said Ellen, laughing and blushing—"You know what I mean. But you didn't answer me?"

"About what?"

"About—my father."

"He has the library, just as he used to," said John smiling.

At this instant another door opened and Margery's voice was heard in joyful tones of welcome, speaking to "dear Mr. John." But that gentleman had walked out as she walked in leaving Ellen alone to greet her astonished eyes. If he had undergone transformation before them they could hardly have looked more astonished or more incredulous. Ellen's joyful greeting soon gave her the evidence of more senses than one. She seized the old lady's hand, kissed her and fairly threw herself upon her neck. Margery found tongue, though she could hardly return the embrace.

"Miss Ellen!—Miss Ellen dear!—is it possible it is your own self? O stand up and let me look at you."

"Don't I look as I used to, Margery?" said Ellen, laughing and crying.

"It is! It is!" exclaimed the old woman, clasping her now to her heart.—"It's my dear little Miss Ellen—it's your own dear self in this house again!—O what a day!"—and then she released her, to sob and cry more freely, as from time to time she went on. Ellen attempted no answer.

"O the master, how glad he will be! You've not seen him yet? O Miss Ellen, dear Miss Ellen, I never thought in this wide world to

see you back again—I never expected it. And we'll keep you now,
won't we? And you're not changed—no," said Margery, holding her
back to look at her,—"you are just the very same! the very same!—
I see you are Miss Ellen in everything—they haven't spoiled you; I
can see it. And how uncommon well you are looking to be sure!—
And tall you have growed, too. Oh it makes me young again to see
you. But will we keep you now? How did you get away from those
new friends of yours in Scotland? I thought they would never let
you go, to be sure; and have they? Did some of them come out with
you, Miss Ellen, or how is it?"

Ellen's cheeks grew rosy.

"Not Miss Ellen, Margery," said another person joining them.

"Mr. John!"

Margery glanced with a changed countenance first at one and
then at the other, and then with an "Oh!" of most mixed and
inexplicable character, threw her apron over her face and hurried
off to her own premises; whither Ellen after one look at John
immediately followed her.

There he found them, a quarter of an hour afterwards, sitting
together. Tears and smiles were yet fresh on Margery's face.
Ellen's was not visible; a large grey cat, the veritable old Captain
Parry, now aged thirteen or fourteen years, yet in tolerable use of
all of his faculties, was in her lap; over him Ellen half-embracing
leaned, and she was sobbing in hearty good earnest; while poor
pussy's unconscious head was stroked with the tenderest of all
affectionate fingers. Margery rose up as her master entered, but it
was a little while before Ellen could recover herself and do the
same.

"Come," said he drawing her arm through his—"Can you stand a
third meeting? I don't know," he added, stopping and smiling,
"whether I ought to permit it today."

"Never mind," said Ellen, looking down from the keen eyes that
seemed she thought to see every spot of weakness there was in her
composition—they saw it good-humouredly too—"I must be foolish
sometimes, you know."

"Foolish," said he in another tone. "Then I am glad you are not
very wise, Ellie. Margery, I wish you would take that key and see
that the room between mine be opened and put in order."

"The room next to your study, sir?"

"Yes—immediately—I have advanced Margery, you see," said he

as they went along the hall—"to the dignity and responsibility of a housekeeper's place."

"I am glad of it—she deserves it."

But Ellen was not thinking of what she was saying. John was leading her back to the room she had first been in and she could hardly go fast enough, she scarce waited to enter the door before she quitted his arm to spring to those of Mr. Humphreys.

That was a meeting!—the pleasure and promise of which future times were never to see belied, a meeting in half a minute of which Ellen lived over half her life. Mr. Humphreys was as speechless as she, save the one single exclamation that came, Ellen felt, from his heart,—"My very own dear little daughter!" How much she understood in those five words. How well the remembrance that at their parting he had commanded himself perfectly, and knew how it was that he could not now. Silently he pressed her again and again to his bosom, kissing her brow and cheeks and then abruptly released her from his arms and quitted the room. How well Ellen felt that the old wound was healed at last.

After a while Ellen went to see if the library looked like itself. It looked much more like itself than the sitting-room; the old familiar books and bookshelves and library furniture being unmixed with new or strange things. The dining-room was adjoining the library on the other side of the hall. After the library John proposed that Ellen should visit *her room.*

"My father's sleeping-room, you see, is there on the same floor; he never goes higher."

Up a low staircase and along a wide, pleasant hall John led her into his study, and through it into the room he called hers.

There was a strong contrast here to all the other parts of the house. They indeed bespoke easy circumstances and refined habits, but also an utter carelessness of display; the appliances of comfort and ease and literary and studious wants,—no luxury or parade. But here apparently nothing had been spared which wealth could provide or taste delight in, or curious affection contrive for its object. There was no more formality than appeared in the sitting-room; elegance reigned in all the seemingly careless arrangements; but *here* there was no mixture of incongruous things; all was in keeping though nothing was like anything else. Splendour was not here certainly for the wealth of the room must be found by degrees; and though luxuriously comfortable, luxury was not its characteristic; or if, it was the luxury of the mind. *That* had been catered for. For that nothing had been spared. A few very fine old paintings hung on the walls in lights that showed them well; in the glow of that warm afternoon they showed marvellously. A number of engravings by the best hands were disposed to the best advantage. Beautiful bits of statuary, in various kinds—precious pieces of antiquity—curiosities of art—relics of nature—mementoes of times or scenes of historical or other peculiar interest—copies of some of those wonders of the world which are the property of ages; and likenesses in colours, marble and bronze, of those other wonders whom ages adore. On every side, at every point, things to seize the eye and lead off the wandering thought upon some track of pleased fancy or useful research or stirring remembrance. And all disposed with such perfection that though full the room hardly seemed so. The furniture was in harmony with the rest—curious and tasteful. Cabinets and tables and bureaus of various material and structure;—a little antique book-case in one corner, an old-fashioned but extremely handsome escritoire in another; and easy chairs, footstools and lounges, formed everyone of them for the perfect delight and satisfaction of its occupier.

In one of them Ellen was silently and tenderly placed by the hands that had led her there. Her face had sobered with surprise at first entering; and as her eye passed along the room from one thing to another, her look grew more sober still, till it ended at the eyes that were fixed on her; and then she covered her face with her hands.

"Come," said he, gently drawing them down—"you musn't take it so, Ellie."

"How could you do so much for me?"

"So much?" said he smiling. "Because, to tell the truth, I did not precisely know what further would better it,—that is the reason it is *so* much, and not more, Ellie."

Ellen answered not except by her looks. "Not that additions cannot be made with advantage; but it will be for you to do from time to time."

Ellen shook her head. "I shall never wish to do that. How perfect. How perfectly beautiful!—I do not deserve it. You make me ashamed of my own unworthiness."

"I am not ashamed of it, Ellie."

"You mean me to be a luxurious-liver at my ease."

"I mean no such thing. If you show any symptoms of such a character it will rouse me to a most vigorous opposition, I assure you."

"I am glad of that," said Ellen smiling;—"I may enjoy myself in perfect security that you will see the beginning of mischief and put a stop to it. I am not sure but I have got a little spoiled in Scotland. But indeed I should be inexcusable if I could be unfaithful to duty *here.*"

Again Ellen's eye wandered over the room, and as it noted the multiplied evidences of affection in the thoughtfulness, care, taste and profusion on every hand displayed, her countenance changed again; she exclaimed with flushing cheek and watering eye—

"You have given me too much, John!"

His quick eye answered that. Ellen understood, but her look in return! There was in it a life-long of feeling and memory; it seemed in its self-renunciation to gather up all the past and lay it and herself with it at his feet. When he spoke it was to answer another thought that was working in Ellen's mind.

"It is no more my purpose," he said, gently putting back the hair from her forehead, first on one side and then on the other—"no more my purpose than I suppose it is yours to make life as one of our friends says a jaunt of pleasure!' If ever we could have formed such a rash design, I trust we should not have been permitted to carry it out. No—we will try to do the work of life together and help each other to be faithful. Come!—you are looking pale, Ellie," he said smiling;—"I shall be tempted to try Mr. Lindsay's remedy for something I do not like."

But Ellen's head found its old resting-place and there was a long, long silence. And then they took together that course which of all others best strengthens, fortifies and quiets the mind. And then Ellen was herself again, except only a little more grave and a little more tender than her usual wont. She took her station by one of the open windows where the warm spring air came pleasantly in.

"What a delicious place for reading! and I have read so little lately."

"How was that?"

"Because I had not time. I could not help it," said Ellen seriously—"They filled up my days and nights with engagements which I had no means of avoiding, unless I would have provoked scenes that would have done them and me more hurt than any loss I was suffering."

"You can make up for lost time now."

"Yes, and I hardly call it lost time, for I would a great deal rather read next door to you; you will help me out when I am in a puzzle."

"Do you get into puzzles, still?" said he smiling.

"Not exactly a puzzle, perhaps—or if I do I commonly work it out—but I often launch out upon a sea where I dare not trust my own navigation, and am fain to lower sail and come humbly back to the shore; but now I will take the pilot along," she said joyously,— "and sail every whither."

"Have with you," said he smiling—"to the world's end!"

"How delightfully private this room is—having no entrance but through other rooms where no one can intrude. Any one else would have put all these beauties downstairs, and so lost half the good of them for the enjoyment of other people's envy and admiration."

"A wife that would have wished them there, Ellie, I would never have married. With splendours we have no concern. Whatever has to do with the highest perfection of body and mind I will seek and have, both for you and myself. Accordingly I have desired a friend in whose judgement I can trust, to send me out as good a riding-horse for you as can be had."

The grateful touch of Ellen's hand upon his arm spoke her answer.

"My poor old Brownie," she said presently, "I wonder what has become of him."

"He will soon be an old Brownie in good earnest. We may as well let him remain Ellen Chauncey's delight, which he has been ever since you committed him to her care."

"She can't love him better than I did, nor have half the pleasure on his back, I am sure, that I had. You must introduce me won't you, John, in particular as well as in general to your work here— some time when you have leisure. I don't want to look at these things without you."

"That door is always open," said he,—"except when you choose to lock it."

"Ay," said Ellen laughing—"that is for you to walk in here. Not for me to walk in there."

"Both, I assure you," said he. "I shall make you understand that. But come—let us begin at once."

They began with two little pictures hanging in a beautiful light over the window. The first was a fine copy of Correggio's recumbent Magdalen.

"I have seen that before," said Ellen, after a few minutes of silent pleasure,—"in an engraving—not in colours. How exquisite! Can anything surpass the perfect graceful repose of that whole figure? There is not a muscle strained. What a wonderful art!"

"There is beautiful management of light."

"Beautiful—and beauty of drawing. But the attitude—it seems to me nothing could exceed the gracefulness of it—the entire, natural abandonment of every limb. How that head rests upon the hand!—I like that very much. I am very glad it is here."

He smiled and silently drew her before the other picture. And there Ellen stood a good while to look, without speaking a word or giving any other expression of opinion than by a long breath.

It was merely two heads, the Madonna and child, in a little antique heavily carved oval frame, that just enclosed them. Nothing but the two heads—yet how much! The mother's face in calm beauty bent over that of the infant as if about to give the kiss her lips were already pouting for; the expression of grave maternal dignity and love; but in the child's uplifted deep blue eye there was a perfect heaven of affection, while the little mouth was parted, it might be either for a kiss or a smile, ready for both.

"How do you like that?"

Ellen drew another long breath as she said, "I have no words!"

He smiled again. "What do you think of this as compared with the other?"

"There is no comparison, I think."

"Yes, you may compare them—this is moral beauty, that is merely physical; *there* is only the material outside, with indeed all the beauty of delineation, *here* is the immaterial soul."

"I am sure here is the beauty of delineation too," said Ellen, with her eyes fixed on the picture.

"Delineation of something else. Beauty of feature does not make the charm of *this* picture—it serves but the purpose of a clear glass through which what is behind may be the more easily and perfectly seen."

"That is not all?" said Ellen, her eyes still fixed.

"It is the greatest part. What makes these very features so lovely but the exceeding loveliness of that which shines through them?"

"And you think it is only when we can read the one that we see the other? I am apt to think there is an eternity of the beautiful as well as of the true."

"Well—with all my heart—but they are inseparably wedded together; and in this, and I believe in all worlds, it is the true that makes the beautiful—using *true* in its largest sense of conformity with the eternal model of right."

"But surely there is a beauty and a deformity of feature with which the mind has nothing to do?"

"I will not take it upon me to say how far. Perfection of mind certainly *tends* to perfection of body, and perhaps all the varieties of uncomeliness with which our eyes are familiar have come from the near or remote workings of evil. Recollect how intellect, refinement, peace, and love write their characters on the countenance and in the course of generations change the very conformation of men?"

"That is true. That is a pleasant thought. And in the utter disarrangement of every thing since the fall, the inward and outward beautiful are not always found together. They will be beautiful in heaven!"

"There is no doubt of that."

"And the beauty of the mind can now glorify even a homely set of features, without waiting for the course of generations. But *here*, as you said, there is beauty of both minds. What an expression of peace on that brow!"

"How fine the look of grave happiness in the whole face. How very rarely you see that look in real life! The happiness and the affection you sometimes find, but the *gravity* is wanting. I never saw it but in a very few."

"I was going to ask," said Ellen,—"if true happiness were not always grave; but I remember you make a distinction between *gravity* and sobriety."

"*Sobriety* gives but a part of the meaning of the other word. *True* happiness *is* always grave, Ellie."

"I wonder," said Ellen,—"if that is what people mean by the *divinity* in a face—an expression with which I have been sundry times puzzled. I never could make out anything but *humanity* when they cried *divinity!*"

"It is humanity, I think," said John smiling,—"but refined from human impurity—pure humanity."

"And not knowing what to make of it they call it divinity, I suppose. One would think the painter of that ought to have been a good man; he must have understood and felt so much of the good and the true."

"They generally manage to give something of that refined calm look to their Madonnas. I am afraid they were not much the better for it themselves. Look at that child's eye!—it has the deep purity and gravity of Heaven's own blue."

"What a grave face the face of the sky is to be sure!" said Ellen, "But that little face—I cannot talk about that."

"How fine the foreshortening."

"Wonderful!—You should not have hung this picture so near the other, John; I shall never be able to see but the one."

"There is a lesson in them, though. There you have the beauty that fades—the beauty of earth; here is that which endures. Charity never faileth!"

"Well let them hang," said Ellen smiling—"I would not have them moved now. I am glad this is just over where my flowers will be; there is nothing of earth about them either, except their origin. This is the best corner of my room, John?"

"Let us see; you are judging somewhat too soon."

They passed on. But they had hardly proceeded a step beyond the door when something struck out a train of conversation which held them fast before the article they had been looking at till they were called down to tea.

"At this rate," said Ellen laughing—"I shall become acquainted with my new premises in about two months."

The evening after that was quietly, serenely happy, disturbed only by extreme difficulty Ellen found in calling Mr. Humphreys anything. *He* shared no such feeling. Miss Sophia would have said she never saw him so like his old self; and Ellen certainly had never known his cheerfulness so unclouded, his eye so bright or his reserve so scattered. The name that some years ago he had so seldom and so hardly spoken now seemed a delight to his lips. A great part of the evening he sat beside Ellen on the sofa with her hand in his.

"You are the same child you used to be Ellen," he said, looking at her fondly, "the same—only grown and improved. A little pale—not now indeed," he added smiling.

"I have hardly forgotten the ship yet, sir."

"We travelled as fast as we could from Edinburgh to America," said John. "Ellen was sick during the whole voyage; and she has not had much time to rest since we landed, for I was in haste to get home."

"And how could that Scotch uncle of yours,—that Mr. Lindsay— how could he let you go, Ellen?"

"Because he could not help it, sir, I believe," said Ellen smiling. "He hardly has, for he has promised me and himself that he will spend half of his time near me."

"He is welcome," said Mr. Humphreys,—"since we have you fast now."

And then drawing her again to his breast he said, what he had said once before and with a strong tenderness of accent that Ellen well interpreted, "My own dear little daughter!" before he let her go, whispering, "something *is* changed, after all Ellen!"

After a long talk with Mr. Humphreys the next morning, the first she had ever had with him in her life, Ellen went up to *her room*. Business had taken Mr. John out for an hour or two. On his return he found her there, quietly seated in one of the easy chairs with her little red Bible on the table before her, looking very thoughtful.

"What are you doing?"

"Thinking—hard," said Ellen smiling. "This room *only* wants to have my flower-stand filled to be absolute perfection. Only that. They will do for it what nothing but flowers can."

"What were you thinking about?"

"I was thinking—I was trying to think—what I ought to be and do—what I ought to be presently busy about."

"Shall I help you?"

Ellen's look was answer enough. A conversation followed thereupon, at some length, which left her brow and heart clear of all shadows of doubt or care. Many a time as she had known John do the same thing for her, she always admired anew and with some marvel the happy skill with which he invariably found the very knot of her thoughts and gently untied it. He paused at length in the walk which according to custom they had been pursuing up and down the room, before the old escritoire.

The flower-stand stood in the corner of the room next the windows, between them and the study door. The opposite corner, between them and the corresponding door, was occupied by the above-mentioned escritoire. It was quite a large piece of furniture. John unlocked it and showed and explained to Ellen its various and curious internal arrangements, with its beautiful workmanship and costly antique garniture.

"Where did you get all this roomful of things, John?"

"Some of them I picked up in the course of my wanderings, in France, Switzerland and Italy;—some are old heirlooms and came to me with our family property a few years ago; this is one of them. Here," said he, opening and showing her how to open the peculiar lock of a certain concealed drawer, well lined with gold and silver pieces and bank bills—"here, Ellie, you will always find what you want in this kind. I shall never ask you how you spend it—you are a steward, and must give an account of your stewardship, but not to me."

"Money!" said Ellen; "what am I to do with it?"

"That I leave entirely to you," said he smiling.

"But I do not want anything. That would last me for years."

"Hardly. You are to be my steward in all that concerns the interior arrangements of the household. I will not have your time taken up with petty details—Margery is to keep the house—but you must keep both house and housekeeper. Here you will always find your supply, both for that and for all other purposes to which you may wish to apply it."

"But I don't know how much I ought to spend? The whole expenses of the house!—I should be afraid of doing too much or too little."

"If I see you going very far out of the way in anything I will let you know."

He smiled.

"I assure you I would a great deal rather you should know what I do."

"I assure you I would a great deal rather not. No—Ellie—I leave it to you. If your arithmetic gets bewildered, or if anybody gives you trouble, in either case you may come to me; I will make short work for you."

"Very well—as you please. But how can you trust me so far?" said Ellen smiling; "You do not know me?"

"Perfectly!"

The warm blood came from Ellen's very heart to her cheeks at the look and smile which accompanied this one word. She was silent a moment.

"Well," she then said laughingly, "you are pretty secure, for I have not the slightest idea that I could spend a dollar of this foolishly without its coming to your knowledge."

"I think that is, very probable," said he smiling—"you would tell me yourself, Ellie."

"No, but if I didn't."

"A hopeless if! Never depend upon it, my dear Ellie. If not with words, you would tell me without them."

"How?"

"You would not look at me as you are doing now. Eyes and mouth have their own language."

"Well," said Ellen presently—"I am very glad of it! You will tell me if I do anything wrong, and it will be just like old times. How I have longed for those old times! Oh!" and she covered her face with her hands, "sometimes I am almost afraid I am too happy."

The answer to this need not be described.

"Not too happy, dear Ellie," he said presently after, "for our happiness has a foundation and may stretch into the future far forward as faith can look."

"Yes," said Ellen tremblingly—"I shall have you then."

There was another few minutes silence.

"This piece of furniture," said John, "belonged to my father's mother and grandmother and great-grandmother, and now it has come to your hands."

"How long such an insignificant thing," said Ellen thoughtfully—"outlasts its more dignified possessors."

"No," said John smiling;—"He that doeth the will of God abideth forever:

This life of mortal breath
Is but the suburb of that life elysian
Whose portal we call Death—

And them that sleep in Jesus will God bring with him."

"I am satisfied," said Ellen softly, nestling again to his side;—"that is enough. I want no more."

AFTERWORD

When *The Wide, Wide World* first appeared in 1850, it caused a sensation in the literary marketplace. No novel written in the United States had ever sold so well. It went through fourteen editions in two years and became one of the best-selling novels of the nineteenth century both in this country and in England.[1] While critics praised it in the pages of the *North American Review*, *The Nation*, and the *Literary World* (Henry James compared Warner's realism to Flaubert's), most of Warner's contemporaries probably shared the feelings of a man from Philadelphia who wrote in a fan letter:

> When I say that your books give me exquisite pleasure, I deny them their highest and truest praise. They have done me good. They have made me a wiser and a better man—more strengthened to duty, more reconciled to suffering.[2]

Most twentieth-century readers do not expect novels to do them good in the sense intended by the man from Philadelphia. We want to be instructed and entertained but not, as a rule, "strengthened to duty" or "reconciled to suffering." The values that made *The Wide, Wide World* a popular and critical success in its own time have changed so much in a hundred years that one might suppose Warner's novel would have become tedious or unintelligible. Yet the book remains compulsively readable, absorbing, and provoking to an extraordinary degree, though not in the same way or for the same reasons that it was for Warner's contemporaries.

The reason the novel has the power to move readers now lies in our contradictory relationship to its heroine and the heritage she represents. *The Wide, Wide World* is the Ur-text of the nineteenth-century United States. More than any other book of its time, it embodies, uncompromisingly, the values of the Victorian era. Its ideology of duty, humility, and submission to circumstance, and its insistence on the imperative of self-sacrifice, are infuriating to some readers, for these doctrines challenge everything the twentieth century has stood for in politics, psychology, and morals. The novel's ethic of submission violates everything the feminist movement has taught women about the need for self-assertion. It negates modern psychology's emphasis on the dangers of repressed anger. It rejects totally the liberal belief in self-determination and freedom of choice, performs a strange inversion of the capitalist's faith in individual enterprise, and implicitly denies the Marxist claim that collective action to reshape economic structures can improve the lives of the exploited. In an age in which self-development and self-realization are ultimate goals, *The Wide, Wide World* seems a bizarre throwback, almost medieval in its conception of human destiny; yet at the same time, it is impossible to put the story down. Something about it refuses to let go.

For one thing, the heroine's psycho-political situation is just as relevant today as it was in 1850. Ellen Montgomery is a vulnerable, powerless, and innocent person victimized by those in authority over her. Since we have all at one time or another been in her position, we cannot help sharing her emotional point of view. We sympathize with Ellen's loneliness in strange surroundings, share her dislike for the boring, unfamiliar tasks she is forced to do, yearn along with her for the affection and understanding she craves, and hate the petty tyrannies and downright cruelty of her masters. Even her efforts to subdue her angry feelings are absorbing, because Warner's registration of psychic turmoil is so excruciatingly precise. And though Ellen's belief in submissiveness and self-abnegation may horrify us, we cannot help siding with her in her efforts to do what she believes is right. For, and this is the point at which the essential conflict surfaces, there is always the possibility that she *is* right, that self-sacrifice *is* better than self-actualization, acceptance wiser than protest. We are, after all, the children of the nineteenth century; we, too, believe in charity and service to others.

The usefulness of *The Wide, Wide World* to a modern audience is that it forces us to recognize within our own systems of belief conflicts, such as that between Christian and Freudian versions of the self, that we have been unaccustomed to face. Indeed, Warner's novel may have more to say to a modern audience than "classic" novels of the nineteenth century. Texts like *Moby-Dick* and *The Scarlet Letter* have been domesticated for us by a critical tradition that sees moral and epistemological ambiguity as the benchmark of literary merit. Warner's text, on the other hand, intends no such ambiguities. Its moral assertions, like them or not, are crystal clear. The novel's didacticism, combined with its emotional drawing power, compels the reader to make certain choices, and thus to recognize contradictions, such as those between an ideal of service and an ideal of self-actualization, that literary modernism with its fetishization of complexity has left untouched. The conflicts that *The Wide, Wide World* produces in modern readers, however, do not all belong to the twentieth century. Some are rooted in the conditions that produced the novel itself, particularly the conditions of Susan Warner's life, which were, in the directest possible way, the inspiration for her work.

I

The endlessly demanding attempt to achieve self-sacrifice that is the principle of Ellen's education in *The Wide, Wide World* also governed Susan Warner's life. While self-sacrifice was certainly the universal prescription for moral development in the antebellum era, Susan Warner and her sister, Anna, had a special reason to adopt it as their own, since circumstances seemed peculiarly arranged to thwart their desires. Though born into a world of wealth and privilege, they spent most of their lives learning to cope with want and deprivation. The struggle between an imperious desire for luxury and sway and a felt obligation to submit herself to God's will is the central drama of Susan Warner's life.

The preface to Anna Warner's biography of her sister captures perfectly both the tone and content of their moral striving.

> If ever this book is printed and read, at two things, I doubt not some people will wonder. First, at our strange, exceptional life, and then that I should be willing to tell it so freely.
> I was *not* willing. I am by nature a terribly secretive person, and

it goes hard with me to tell anybody what is nobody's business. Furthermore, our home life was so unendingly precious, that it hurts me to have it gazed at by cold and careless eyes; this also is true.

But a faithful chronicler must not please himself. I could not truly set forth my sister's character, without giving the surroundings among which it took shape and strength.

For the rest, I have no call to be sensitive. New England blood is never ashamed of any work that ought to be done; and no believer has cause to cover his face, in any spot where his dear Lord sees fit to bid him dwell; for work, for service, or for the mere polishing attrition. (iii)

Anna's preface, typically, places duty before self. By nature terribly secretive, Anna nevertheless reveals the Warners' home life to strangers. The act of writing the biography is a version of her whole life in miniature—and of her sister's, too—as she sees it: an act of self-abnegation. Susan and Anna are the "believers" who have had to dwell where the Lord saw fit (in a "poor-looking" house far from the society they were accustomed to), leading lives that were not their own but his, every moment given over to the Lord's service, whether actively (writing, day and night, books that would bring people to Jesus), or, in Anna's telling phrase, through "the mere polishing attrition"—simply being worn by the frustrations of daily life to greater spiritual refinement.

Susan and Anna were the children of Anna Bartlett, stepdaughter of Cornelius Bogert, a wealthy New York lawyer, and of Henry Whiting Warner, a prosperous lawyer whose father had served in the New York State legislature. Susan was born (in 1819) to the couple after their first child had died and so was doubly precious to her parents, becoming more so when, after her birth, they lost two more children in succession. She was eight years old when Anna was born, and, according to Anna, somewhat spoiled. "Love of power was born with her," Anna writes, "and a great relish for the right of way" (75).

Susan had the right of way as a child, in every sense, as Anna's picture of her being taken to her grandmother Bogert's house in Jamaica, New York, suggests.

The old family coach, with sleek horses and coloured coachman; my grandmother on the back seat; and on the whole of the front seat the little Queen. Feet against one side of the coach, head against the other; perhaps a paper of candied orange peel or ginger—or ginger-cakes—on her lap for light refreshment; and in her hand a volume of Plutarch's Lives, in which she read steadily all the nine miles to Jamaica.(78)

Join this picture to another that Anna provides, and the backdrop for what is to come begins to take shape:

She was a bit of a Sybarite by nature; liking ease and warmth and bright colours (especially red, which she was fond of wearing) and dainty fare. . . . Quite ready always to use Mr. Hale's prescription for a long life, and do nothing herself that she could get someone else to do for her. . . . Her particular delight was to have a low seat at the corner of the hearth and read by firelight; but all her life long she liked to have someone else keep up the fire. (88)

Susan's absorption in books, linked in both the carriage description and in this one to her love of ease, was, according to Anna, the "master passion" of her young life. She loved to read and to make up stories, and shunned the out-of-doors, excercise, and physical adventure.[3] She would read:

. . . with a perfectly absorbed face, and ear regardless of calls, demands, and questions. Whatever the book might be, she was never ready to lay it down. The carriage waited for her, breakfast began without her. But no such trifles disturbed her mind, or indeed I think found their way far into her thoughts; the latest page of her beloved book held her fast in dreamland. (91)

It was reality that Susan shrank from, at least that part of it that demanded responsiveness to others' needs and providing for her own. When she was nine years old, her mother died, and she clung to her father, whose long absences on trips to Albany made her frantic. (Anna clung to her Aunt Fanny, Henry Warner's sister, who devoted her life to caring for her brother and his children.) Still, until the age of nineteen, Susan enjoyed the perogatives of a genteel, affluent upbringing. Piano lessons, singing lessons, dancing lessons, Italian lessons, and French lessons studded her weekly calendar. She learned to draw and sew, was tutored in history, mathematics, grammar, literature, and geography, and was made acquainted with the masterpieces of European art. While Susan was in her teens her father, who was making a great deal of money in real estate, purchased a Domenichino print of St. Cecilia, a Murillo St. Sebastian, and a Sir Joshua Reynolds portrait of young Hannibal. Susan's diary records visits to art galleries, concerts, and the opera. She bought clothes and took tea and was "in twenty minds" about whether she liked her new piano. The fashionable world she moved in bred in her a strong sense of social superiority:

> One thing annoys me much. The girls who come to help her in harvest time will call Aunt Fanny by her Christian name, and will come into the front room and sit down as if they were equals. This worries me and makes me angry, though Aunty says it is foolish. (109)

Susan's sense of superiority to hired help received a shock in 1838 when, because of a drastic change in financial circumstances, Henry Warner sold the fashionable townhouse on St. Mark's Place and moved the family to Constitution Island, across from West Point, in order to economize. Having lost most of his money in the panic of 1837, he agreed to buy the island, which he could ill afford, when his brother Thomas backed out of a deal he had made to purchase it for development as a family estate and resort. After trying to drain some meadowlands that lay between the island and the mainland, Henry was sued by a neighbor; he countersued, and ended up losing what little capital he had remaining.[4] Meanwhile, the family farm he had inherited in Canaan, New York (where the hired girls were so impertinent), was sold to cover the interest on the mortgage and to make payments toward Constitution Island, while most of the rest of Henry Warner's real estate holdings fell prey to law suits. Apparently, he had failed to protect his interests in writing, as he had failed to do in securing the loan to buy the island. Consequently, when the heirs of the man from whom he originally borrowed the money decided to foreclose, the Warners were saved from total destitution only by some friends who stepped in at the last moment to assume the debt.

They moved, as Anna puts it, from "crimson cushions and tall mirrors . . . greenhouse, carriage, and a corps of servants" to a revolutionary war farmhouse where the wind rattled the window sashes and sometimes there was no one but themselves to gather wood to heat the house. At first, the more rustic and self-dependent life seems to have been a lark. Judging from her diary entries, Susan enjoyed sawing and chopping wood, rowing on the Hudson, and churning butter. But gradually the tone changes. "I do not study Italian, I play but very little on the piano, I do not read much, I do not even write every day. I do not sing at all, except on Sundays" (192). "I do not like to wash dishes, nor dust furniture, nor to sweep rooms, nor to set the table." "I should like to see the day when I need not work" (189–90).

Harder than the household drudgery was the isolation. Anna writes: "from dainty silks and laces, we came down to calicoes, fashioned by our own fingers," "but the banishment of silk dresses entailed a much heavier loss; that of intercourse with other people. If you have 'nothing to wear,' few want you; while some think it kind not to invite you, because of course (in such case) you cannot want to come! and for a good while we had little to do with visits or visitors."[5] Susan was nineteen, "in the bloom of her young womanhood." "I think," says Anna, "it tried my sister more than anyone guessed" (176–77). Though they spent winters in rooms in the city, the relative absence of money and clothes, and the accompanying loss of social standing, meant that Susan and Anna would never marry into the social circles for which their education and tastes had fitted them. "Thus," Anna continues, "the young life opened into young womanhood, with all the setting changed, and only herself the same. For still she loved power, and ease, and dreams; and still would have had the work of the world go on without her" (199).

What happened next in Warner's life could have been predicted, given what had gone before; the way it happened is like something from a novel she might have written:

Walking up Waverley Place one day, she met an acquaintance who just then was counted a leader of fashion. And as they passed, this woman's bow was so slight and cool, that it had almost the air of a rebuff. Whether so meant or not does not matter; it seemed so to my sister. And as she walked on, with that sense of check that is so painful to a young person, all her nerves astir at the supposed slight, she said in her heart that she would put her happiness in a safer place, beyond the reach of scornful fingers. She would have something that should stand, though the whole world went to pieces. (200–201)

In 1844, six years after the move to the island, she and Anna became members of the Mercer Street Presbyterian Church, an event which changed the course of their lives. The first thing it changed was their relationship to each other. Whereas before Susan had wanted to distinguish herself from Anna in every way (one senses that she thought she was Anna's superior), "now," says Anna, "we were on ground where neither years nor knowledge went for much." As they stood side by side and recited the covenant that made them church members, giving themselves "'solemnly . . . away, . . . to be his willing servants forever,' the bond was knit . . . which should outlast all time . . ." (204).[6]

There were other changes as well. Before her conversion Susan's journal entries, as Mary Kelley has astutely observed, reveal a person "struggling . . . to hold together the pieces of an existence that refused to coalesce. The compulsion to do, and thus to wonder what to do, appears continually threatened by an underlying question, why do it?"[7] Dedication to Christ supplied the answers to such questions by giving her work: Sunday school teaching, proselytizing among the poor, and sewing and collecting money for the foreign missions. But perhaps more important, it gave her a reason for living. The disappointments of life in society paled before the importance of serving God and doing his will. Behavior came to be judged by a new norm, holiness, and accomplishment measured by the degree to which one did *not* seek recognition for accomplishments.

Given the conditions of life in the nineteenth century for women like the Warner sisters, religious conversion was both a necessary strategy for survival and a real alternative to married life. Their religion gave them dignity in a world where they suffered social humiliation, a sense of purpose in a society in which unmarried women frequently had no functional place.[8] In addition, it made them matter to themselves. Cut off from intercourse with their own social circle, they found in Christian belief daily assurance that there was one who was watching and caring for them. At the same time, their faith provided them with a source of emotional experience—feelings of joy, wonder, and gratitude—and with hope when circumstances were grim. The Reverend Thomas Skinner, the rector at Mercer Street whom Susan idolized, preached that "religion is . . . a struggle, a race, requiring self-denial and the most arduous exertions" but that "Christ makes it delightful to use self-denial and do everything which in itself may be difficult and painful" (218–19).

This doctrine must have helped to support a life already difficult and painful. Certainly, it prompted Warner actively to place new demands upon herself. As a Visiter[9] for the New York City Tract Society, she ventured into neighborhoods where no one else would go (220); as a collector for the mission fund, she waited in the vestibules of socially prominent people who had once been her friends. There was even a period when she denied herself proper food on the assumption that *anything* she enjoyed must be forsworn (212–13). But despite these self-mortifications, or perhaps in part because of them, her letters and her journal in the years following her conversion seem happier than before, more purposeful, forthright, and determined. Highly critical of herself and other people, Warner knew her own mind and stuck to her principles unapologetically; while learning to reconcile herself to deprivations, she retained a capacity for enjoying life. On a rare visit to Boston, she exclaims in her letters how much she loves railroad travelling ("the novelty, excitement, and adventure"), Boston ("much better than New York"), and good sermons ("borne up on eagle's wings towards the sky") (236). But what Warner liked most about Boston was the intellectual life. "How I like to see and hear intelligent people!" (242). "I feel . . . a rousing and exciting effect upon my mind from the intercourse I have with different persons" (247). "I am glad of the practice in *arguing* I have enjoyed in this place" (251).

The Warners' worsening financial situation put an end to such visits for some time. In 1848 a mortgage on one of Henry Warner's remaining properties came due, and there was nothing to pay it with. The Warners' furniture, books, prints, paintings, and piano had to be sold to make up the sum, and the four of them—Henry, Fanny, Anna, and Susan—watched "like mice in a cage of rattlesnakes" while their possessions were auctioned off.[10] At night, they huddled in the firelight around the furniture that was left and wondered where the money to buy lamp oil would come from. That was the year Anna made up a children's game called "Robinson Crusoe's Farmyard," which put bread on the table for a while; and that was the year that Susan, prompted by her aunt, began writing a story that became one of the all-time best sellers in the United States. She was twenty-nine years old.

II

The bitter circumstances that led to the writing of *The Wide, Wide World* contributed to the novel's phenomenal success. By reproducing her own situation in that of her heroine, Warner managed to reproduce the situation of most her contemporaries. Or rather, she mirrored the way they felt about themselves. The belief that one does not control the circumstances of one's life but must learn instead to become reconciled to them informed the outlook of many people in the antebellum era. "In popular thought of the pre-Civil War period," writes Lewis Saum, "no theme was more pervasive or philosophically fundamental than the providential view. Simply put, that view held that, directly or indirectly, God controlled all things."[11] Learning to resign oneself to the will of God was not regarded as cowardly or defeatist behavior but as a realistic way of meeting the facts of life. Contrary to the modern critical view that popular women's novels were escapist and unable to deal with grim facts, the strength of such novels lay precisely in showing what it is like to face facts you cannot change and live with them day by day. Ellen Montgomery says to her aunt early in the novel that if she were free to do what she wanted she would run away—and spends the rest of the novel learning to extirpate that impulse from her being. One cannot run away in the world of nineteenth-century women's fiction, any more than the Warner sisters in real life could have run away from Constitution Island. Women writers of that era, unlike their male counterparts, could not walk out the door and become Mississippi riverboat captains, go off on whaling voyages, or build themselves cabins in the woods. Escape, consequently, is the one thing their novels never offer; on the contrary, they teach their readers that the only way to overcome adversity is through overcoming the enemy within.

The fact that Ellen is not even allowed to protest against injustice, much less escape from it, but learns instead to practice humility and acceptance of the divine will, was a cause of her enormous popularity. While not everybody in the culture believed in submission rather than protest—the year that Warner began to write the novel was also the year of the first women's rights convention—, most readers found the doctrine familiar and persuasive, for it belonged to the ideology of the evangelical reform movement that had molded the consciousness of the nation in the years before the Civil War.

The conception of reality on which the reform movement was based is dramatically illustrated in the activities of the New York City Tract Society, to which the Warner sisters belonged. The purpose of the society was to help the city's poor by distributing a religious tract to every family once a month. Tract Visiters believed that the only real help one could offer another person, rich or poor, was not material but spiritual, and the Directions that guided them in their work insisted on this: "Be much in prayer," the Directions said. "Endeavor to feel habitually and deeply that all your efforts will be in vain unless accompanied by the Holy Ghost. And this blessing you can expect only in answer to prayer. Pray, therefore, without ceasing. Go from your closet to your work and from your work return again to the closet."[12] To understand what made these Directions meaningful and effective for the people who carried them out is to understand the power of what has been labelled pejoratively, and in retrospect, "sentimental" fiction. "Sentimental" novels take place, metaphorically and literally, in the "closet." Their heroines rarely get beyond the confines of a private space—the kitchen, the parlor, the upstairs chamber— and most of what they do takes place inside the "closet" of the heart.

For what the word "sentimental" means as applied to these novels is that the arena of human action, as in the Tract Society Directions, has been defined not as the world but as the human heart. This fiction shares with the reform movement a belief that all true action is not material but spiritual, that one obtains spiritual power through prayer, and that those who know how, in the privacy of their closets, to struggle for possesion of their souls will one day possess the world through the power given to them by God. This theory of power makes itself felt, in the mid-nineteenth century, not simply in the explicit assertions of religious propaganda, nor in personal declarations of faith, but as a principle of interpretation that gave form to experience itself.

One Tract Visiter, for example, records that a young woman who was dying of pulmonary consumption became concerned at the eleventh hour about the condition of her soul and asked for spiritual help:

Shc was found by the Visiter, [the report reads] supplied with a number of tracts, and kindly directed to the Saviour of sinners. . . . For some time clouds hung over her mind, but they were at length dispelled by the sun of righteousness. . . . As she approached the hour which tries men's souls, her strength failed fast; her friends gathered around her; . . . and while they were engaged in a hymn her soul seemed to impart unnatural energy to her emaciated and dying body. To the astonishment of all, she said to her widowed mother, who bent anxiously over her, 'Don't weep for me, I shall soon be in the arms of my Saviour.' She prayed fervently, and fell asleep in Jesus.[13]

The facts of this anecdote do not correspond to what a twentieth-century observer would have recorded had he or she been at the scene: the furniture of the sick room, the kind of house the woman lived in, her neighborhood, her socio-economic background, the symptoms of her illness, its history and course of treatment. Instead of all this, the Tract Visiter sees a spiritual predicament: the women's initial "alarm," God's action on her heart, the turn from sin to righteousness. Whereas the modern observer would have structured the events in a downward spiral, as the woman's condition deteriorated from serious to critical, and ended with her death, the report reverses that progression. Its movement is upward, from "thoughtlessness" to "conviction" to "great tranquility, joy, and triumph." The events the Visiter records are structured by assumptions about the nature of reality that bear little relation to a contemporary perspective on the scene.

The story of the young woman's death from pulmonary consumption is exactly the kind of exemplary tale that had formed the consciousness of the nation in the early years of the nineteenth century. Such stories were the staple of pulpit oratory and filled the religious publications, which were distributed in astoundingly large quantities (the American Tract Society alone claims to have published thirty-seven million tracts at a time when the entire population of the country was only eleven million), and were the backbone of the McGuffey's readers and other primers on which virtually the entire nation had been schooled. They appeared in manuals of social behavior and in instructional literature of every variety, filled the pages of popular magazines, and appeared even in the daily newspapers.

When one turns from tract society reports, primers, etiquette books, journal entries, magazine stories, and pulpit homilies to the fiction of writers like Susan Warner, one finds the same assumptions at work. Her novels are motivated by the same commitments; they are hortatory and instructional in the same way, depend upon the same rhetorical conventions, and they take for granted the same relationship between the daily activities of humble people and the spiritual destiny of humankind. The popular fiction written by women of the mid-nineteenth century has been dismissed by modern critics primarily because it follows from assumptions about the shape and meaning of existence that we no longer hold. But once one understands the coherence and force of those assumptions, the literature that helped to shape the world in their image no longer seems thoughtless or trivial. Rather, novels like *The Wide, Wide World* which enunciate this vision in narrative terms lent dignity and purpose to lives that otherwise would have been impossibly narrow and stultifying. The conviction that human events are, ultimately and inevitably, shaped by secret prayer produces a view of society in which orphan girls like Ellen Montgomery, and writers like Susan Warner, can hope to change the world.[14]

To say that Susan Warner hoped to change the world through writing fiction is misleading to the extent that it implies a desire on her part to transform political and economic structures. Although Warner believed in giving material aid to the poor and in relieving suffering, the sources of oppression and injustice, as she sees them, do not lie in social arrangements. Evil is disobedience to the will of God. Doing good, therefore, means helping human beings to become receptive to God's will, which is accomplished through religious conversion. While Warner's failure to confront questions of property and class directly leads, as we shall see, to certain contradictions within her own practice as a Christian writer, she gave herself wholly to the pursuit of her ideals as she understood them. Warner wrote novels in order to save souls and hence to save herself. When the man from Philadelphia said that the "highest and truest praise" of her books was that "they have done . . . good," her told her, in effect, that she had accomplished her purpose.

III

The question is, what are we to make of such an enterprise now? While it is crucially important to recognize that novels like *The Wide, Wide World* helped women—and men—in the nineteenth century to make sense of their lives, it is also necessary to ask what they can do for us. If we do not share a belief in the ultimate reality of God in Jesus Christ, or expect to become more reconciled to suffering for having read these novels, how can we enter imaginatively into their fictional world? Why should anyone in the late twentieth century *care* about the perils of a pious orphan and her masochistic ways?

The answer, I think, is that Warner's heroine cannot be dismissed because she *is* us. Although Ellen Montgomery's submissive behavior may enrage us, we follow her adventures with bated breath because we feel, or have felt at some time, our own relation to the world to be like hers. It is not only that as children we have felt powerless and overwhelmed by circumstance, but that as adults we share, or have shared, with Ellen a whole range of character traits and psychological needs. The sense that our difficulties are undeserved, our efforts to overcome them heroic, our merits exceptional, and our misfortunes unique makes it much easier than we might have supposed to inhabit the consciousness of this blameless, persecuted orphan. At one time or another we feel (or have felt) that we, too, are innocent, have only the best intentions, are insufficiently armed against the world, easily injured, unable to hide our emotions, and in need of love and attention.

The enormous amount of attention Ellen receives is one of the most seductive features of her story. People are always talking about her when she isn't present and can't take their eyes off her when she is. Alice and Mr. John continually ask her to reveal her innermost thoughts, and seize upon every tremulous word. What tasks Ellen most about Aunt Fortune is not that she makes Ellen churn butter when she would rather be learning French, it is that Ellen is not the primary focus of her aunt's thoughts. To read *The Wide, Wide World* is to experience life as if everything that happened to you, every thought that passed through your mind, every feeling you ever had, deserved the most minute consideration. Warner knows how to make a story out of anything—leaving a party early, catching a cold. Her ability to register, through Ellen's inner turmoil, the intensity and range of emotion aroused in people's daily lives by the tiniest occurrences makes the novel at times absolutely riveting.

Moreover, Ellen's predicament—subjugation to a series of authorities over which she has no control—springs from hierarchies of power that still structure most people's experience: I mean the authoritarian relationships that obtain between parents and children, men and women, teachers and pupils. What makes Ellen's situation so highly charged for modern readers is that, instead of rebelling against the injustice of her masters, she is forced by others and learns to force herself to submit to them. The whole weight of the novel, every ounce of rhetoric it contains, is calculated to drive this lesson home: "though we *must* sorrow," Ellen's mother teaches her, "we must not rebel."

The Wide, Wide World draws us irresistibly and intimately into the mind of a character who affirms and acts on beliefs that, in many respects, violate our innermost sense of what a human being can be. Indeed, it is a kind of bildungsroman in reverse. Instead of initiating her into society, the heroine's experience teaches her how to withdraw into the citadel of herself. The Christian precepts she internalizes teach her not how to succeed in the marketplace, or implement her purposes in the world, but how to become a saint who makes herself malleable to the will of others. Under the guidance of her mentors, she undergoes repeated trials in the course of mastering the principles of her vocation—which is to forget self. As the novel progresses, and the trials that befall her grow more severe, she is required to show an equanimity more unperturbed and a humility more complete. At the endpoint of the disciplinary process, the heroine does not exist for herself at all any more but only for others. Sanctified by the sacrifice of her will, Ellen becomes, like her friend Alice, "a person who supplied what was wanting everywhere; like the transparent glazing which painters use to spread over the dead color of their pictures; unknown, it was she gave life and harmony to the whole." The ideal to which the novel educates its heroine and its readers is the opposite of self-development and self-realization, it is to become empty of self, an invisible transparency that nevertheless is miraculously responsible for the life in everything.

That is why the novel provokes such powerfully conflicted reactions now. If Ellen is right, *we* are doomed, and yet we cannot write her off because she is part of us. Not only are her vulnerability, her inner turmoil, and her victimization familiar, but so are the Christian values she affirms. It is impossible not to admire Ellen's treatment of other people—her kindness to her grandmother, her patience with Nancy Vawse, her affection for Mr. Van

Brunt—nor is the selflessness she strives for altogether foreign to a modern conception of ideal behavior. Ellen incarnates ideals of charity and service to others that remain integral to the Judeo-Christian tradition of our culture. We are, literally, the grandchildren of the nineteenth century, lineal descendants of people just like Ellen whose values and beliefs survive in us alongside the teachings of Nietzsche, Marx, and Freud.

In fact, it is when you look at *The Wide, Wide World* in terms of the issues that preoccupied these thinkers—the issues of power and sexuality—that the novel reveals the source of its strongest and most disturbing appeal. The love of power even when it is not our own, the love of seeing power displayed, power triumphant, crushing everything in its path, even—and perhaps especially—when what it crushes happens to be us is at the core of the novel's attraction. At this level, *The Wide, Wide World* is a chronicle of violence. For all its exaltation of passivity and turning the other cheek, its central situation, repeated over and over again, is the violation of one human being by another. To see ourselves as the objects of acts of domination as we read about Ellen's successive humiliations is to be in the position of master at the same time as we are identifying with the victim. Witnessing the process of subjugation, not once, but time after time, we lend ourselves, emotionally, to it even as we are horrified.

The novel's dramatization of domination and submission, moreover, is sexualized from the start. At the same time that Ellen's self-immolations are excruciatingly painful, they are also, and for the same reason, titillating. While the tears Ellen sheds on every page are tears of repressed anger, they are also tears of orgasmic release, spilling again and again in situations where she is being psychically stripped. These scenes replicate what Susan Griffin has called the basic pornographic situation, in which one person is robbed by another of everything that makes him or her a human being and is reduced to the status of an object.[15] The thrill of abandoning the self completely, of giving one's self over to the power of another, as when Mr. John says to Ellen "be humbled in the dust before Him—the more the better," suggests a relationship between punishment and sexual pleasure that recalls nothing so much as the *The Story of O*, another education in submission in which the heroine undergoes ever more painful forms of self-effacement, until finally she asks "permission" to die. In its ruthless suppression of Ellen's outrage and pain, *The Wide, Wide World* reenacts, as pornography does, the primal initiation of the child into a culture that denies the body and its feelings.[16] It is the memory of that subjugation in ourselves, more than anything else, that keeps us turning the pages of Warner's book.

On the other hand, the tears that flow when Ellen is embraced by her mother and Alice Humphreys, and the physical intimacy that subsists between her and them, hint at an alternative to the brutal sexuality embodied in her male masters, Uncle Lindsay and, especially, Mr. John, whose prowess as a horse-beater is Warner's oblique acknowledgment of the sexual style he represents. The affection and closeness that women share in the sheltered spaces of domestic fiction and the homely sacraments (often the taking of food and tea) through which they offer tenderness, nourishment, and support to one another, embody an intimacy that takes the place of heterosexual love. Combining sensual delight, emotional comfort, and spiritual communion, these rituals offer moments of wholeness and fulfillment that compensate the female characters for the renunciations that are their daily portion.

Those renunciations, which guarantee the complementarity of male and female roles, also underline their similarity. As Joanne Dobson points out, Mr. John has raised Ellen to be his wife—he educates her, molds her mind, prescribes her behavior and makes her will completely malleable to his.[17] Thus the roles of men and women in this fiction are interdigitated, he will command, she will obey. Yet at the same time, the heroine's role is not so much the antithesis of the hero's as a transformation of it. Whether one's salvation is material or spiritual, the recipe for achieving it is the same. Ellen's long journey toward sainthood imitates the traditional male model of striving for worldly success in that both are based on the Protestant idea that self-denial, discipline, and hard work will pay off eventually. Though Ellen's "success" is the extinction of her personality, and thus is the inversion of a man's, her reward, in the end, is also the same as his. All of Ellen's material losses, like Job's, are finally returned to her a hundredfold—in contemporary terms, she "has it all." According to this scenario, which amalgamates capitalist striving with Christian self-effacement, the meek really do inherit the earth.[18]

The conflicts expressed in the novel between body and spirit, between Christian dedication to selflessness and middle-class materialism, between a woman's desire for independence and her desire for male protection, emerge most strikingly in the last chapter. In the poverty and isolation of Constitution Island, amidst unremitting efforts to trust in God's goodness, Warner dreamed of luxury and access to the world.

IV

In the final chapter, Warner gives her heroine everything that she herself wanted and couldn't get: city living, wealth and position, relief from household cares, people who adore her, and marriage to an all-powerful protector. In the construction of this paradise, Warner's longing for old times struggles with her newfound dedication to the Lord. She yearns for the sheltered existence she led before her father lost his money, and to be free from burdens that young women of her class were neither expected nor prepared to shoulder. In fact, reinfantilization, along with luxury and ease, is Ellen's reward for years of suffering and discipline. She is entirely free of responsibility, and entirely dependent on others. Although she is married, her life still has the character of a preadolescent fantasy (sex is alluded to in embarrassed blushes and silences). Her relationship to Mr. John is still that of pupil to teacher. He will be her "pilot" as she navigates the seas of thought, and her moral preceptor, whose "eyes . . . see every spot of weakness in her composition." "You will tell me if I do anything wrong," says Ellen to her husband, "and it will be just like old times." In Mr. John's house there is no kindling to gather; there are no tables to set or dishes to wash: "I will not have your time taken up with petty details," says Mr. John. "Margery is to keep the house." Best of all, there is money to burn. The final treasure John bestows on Ellen is a drawerful of cash totally at Ellen's disposal. This is the paradise of someone who had written in her diary: "I wish one thing—that father would give each of us an allowance" (233).

Susan Warner's desire to have a man shield her from the world is symbolized by the position of Ellen's room, which stands, as John puts it, "between mine." The inner sanctum, an emblem of Ellen herself, unites the values left over from the old New York society life with those acquired as a convert to evangelical Christianity. It is the room of a sybarite who has given herself to Jesus. Expensive works of art and other evidences of good taste symbolizing wealth and prestige serve as sacramental objects belonging to a religion in which cultivation of the intellect and imagination is felt to be identical with spiritual elevation. The opulence of the treasures Mr. John has collected—paintings, engravings, pieces of statuary, relics of antiquity, copies of the old masters—is justified by their power to awaken the higher faculties. They are "things to seize the eye and lead off the wandering thought upon some track of pleased fancy or useful research or stirring remembrance." The luxury of the room, if it is there at all, is not material but a "luxury of the mind."[19]

The contradiction between Warner's commitment to a life of selfless service to the Lord and her desire for sensual and intellectual gratification, as well as for the power and position conferred by the ownership of expensive commodities, expresses itself most markedly in the discussion between Ellen and Mr. John comparing the paintings of a recumbent Magdalen and a Madonna and child which are the pièces de résistance of Ellen's room. Hanging side by side, their purpose is to illustrate the difference between physical and moral beauty.[20] As Mr. John pontificates:

> *"There* is only the material outside . . . *here* is the immaterial soul. . . . Beauty of feature does not make the charm of *this* picture [alluding, of course, to the Madonna]—it serves but the purpose of a clear glass through which what is behind may be the more easily and perfectly seen. . . . What makes these features so lovely but the exceeding loveliness of that which shines through them? . . . There you have the beauty that fades—the beauty of the earth; here is that which endures. Charity never faileth!"

The passage reflects Warner's anxiety about her own looks (hence the "loveliness" that "shines *through*" the physical features), her ambivalent relation to her body and its craving for pleasure (the recumbent Magdalen); the resolution (that was being forced upon her) to renounce sexual fulfillment by emulating the Virgin; and her determination, in the absence of more tangible supports, to rely on divine love. The passage also points to the contradiction between Ellen's obvious delight in owning such costly and precious objects and the lesson of those objects which is, ironically, that treasures are nothing, charity all. In using the last chapter to supply herself, in imagination, with the luxury and the protection she longed for, Warner has become aware, at some level, that the dream of wealth and comfort does not jibe with her hard-won resolve to accept the Lord's will. In turning the reward she has invented for Ellen into an elaborate rationalization of her own desire, a desire to which she had been socialized by her upbringing, Warner only makes more obvious a split she does not see and therefore cannot acknowledge within her culture and within herself.

But if Susan Warner was not yet ready, at the age of twenty-nine, to accept a life of hardship without at least imagining an alternative, it is hard to blame her. The old days never did return in reality, as opposed to fiction. Though her first novel was a stunning success, and her second, *Queechy* almost as popular, the need to repurchase Constitution Island in 1857, because the friend who held the mortgage couldn't make the final payment, wiped out all their reserves. She and Anna started work on a novel together, *Say and Seal*, which received mixed notices, and they began to grade papers for a local school to supplement their earnings. Susan's diary entries in this period reveal low spirits and poor health—the farmhouse was freezing in winter; it was 28 degrees in the parlor one day—but she never ceased struggling to accept what the Lord withheld, as she put it, as well as what he gave. Eventually she came to accept her celibacy and solitude, though not without spells of anxiety and depression.[21] "By now," Mabel Baker writes, "even to the most optimistic of spirits hope for any real change on any level—social, financial, romantic—would have seemed patently naive."[22]

Because they needed the steadier income a stable audience could provide, after 1860 the sisters switched from the New York-based commercial publisher, G.P. Putnam's Sons, to R. Carter and Brothers, a religious publishing house, and their work grew progressively more didactic. Sometimes they had to sell their books outright because they needed money immediately and couldn't wait for royalties. They turned out homiletic tales on the Beatitudes (the Golden Ladder series); tried editing a children's magazine, *The Little American*, which failed to make a profit; Susan composed a series of stories on the Lord's prayer; and together they wrote a collection of books about the Bible. "I have been thinking," Susan wrote in her diary in 1869, "if this great loneliness and isolation is to make us do more work or do it better, with more entireness of heart or strength of desire—why, I am content. I feel the isolation and the loneliness very great indeed" (459).

That loneliness was mitigated when, after her father died in 1875, Warner began to hold Bible classes for West Point cadets, who would row over to the island on Sunday afternoons and be served refreshments by Susan and Anna when instruction was over. The teaching was a source of great pleasure and satisfaction to Susan, as it apparently was to the students as well; the letters they sent her from all over the world testify to the influence she exerted on their lives.[23]

Until her death in 1885, Susan Warner continued to teach and to write novels and religious texts (over thirty in all) that explicitly emphasize the need to renounce worldly desires and find fulfillment in faith and good works.[24] Her last novel, *Daisy Plains* (1885), contains a passage that clearly expresses her feelings about herself:

> If you enter upon the service of the Lord Jesus, you must remember that you are not your own. You must live to do his service and accept his will, whatever it may cost; and there must be no half-way work. It is a continued service, hour by hour and minute by minute; it means, not living to one's self, and being separate from the world; it means loving him best.[25]

Though learning to do the Lord's service and accept his will was never easy, Warner's journals and letters indicate that her religious beliefs afforded her moments of great joy, and a sense of peace and fulfillment. That they enabled her and her sister to lead lives that made a difference to those who knew them is suggested by the existence of the Constitution Island Association, a group of local people who have preserved the house where the Warners lived and are dedicated to keeping their memory alive. The Warner sisters believed in something, gave themselves to it wholly, and never wavered in their commitment. They tried to help other people according to their lights, and they loved and cared for one another. Of the many memorable images that Anna records in her biography, this one, describing the sisters' early morning routine in the days when they wrote desperately for a living, is among the most compelling. The scene evokes the combination of self-discipline and delectation that marks both their writing and their lives:

> At tea the night before, we prepared our little plate of bread and butter, saw that our kindling basket was full, and had our small tea-kettle filled and ready. I was generally up by half past four; and by the time my sister came down, the fire was burning, the kettle was boiling . . . and the green-shaded student lamp gave out its invitation to write. A delicious cup of tea and the . . . relished bread and butter came first; and then two silent, busy pens kept company in the delightful work. The fire sang and snapped, the coals dropped slowly, and the noiseless pens covered sheet after sheet. (381–82)

JANE TOMPKINS
Duke University
Durham, North Carolina

NOTES

1. Edward Halsey Foster, *Susan and Anna Warner* (Boston: Twayne Publishers, n.d.), 35, 49. Foster's book and Mabel Baker's *Light in the Morning* (West Point, N.Y.: The Constitution Island Association Press, 1978) are the only modern accounts of Susan Warner's life and both are very useful. Anyone really interested in Warner should read Anna Warner's biography of her sister, cited below.

2. As quoted by Anna B. Warner in *Susan Warner* (New York: G.P. Putnam's Sons, 1909), 354. Page numbers for future citations from the biography will be given in parentheses in the text.

3. Susan writes in her journal: "This evening all but me went round to visit Mrs. Alden and Mrs. Wheldon. I shut the doors and windows of the front parlour to keep out bats and insects, and sat there reading 'The Betrothed' till they came back" (118). Anna comments: "Afraid of storms, burglars, steamboats, and horses, and cattle; of worms, snakes, mice, bats, and caterpillars, . . . she would try the bedroom door at intervals through the night to see if it was locked; and I have known her many a time to get up in the perfect darkness and creep all about under her bed, to make sure there was no one there. She was timid on ice, on a foot bridge, on a gangway; with imagination always at work; and in time of public sickness or disturbance, the papers were kept from her. (119)

All quotations from Susan's journal are from quotations in Anna's biography.

4. Anna Warner's biography says that the Warners did not have to pay damages and that the other party had to pay costs, but Mabel Baker says that in exchange for being allowed to drain the meadows, Henry Warner had to pay court costs and was consequently left with no capital to carry out his project (*Susan Warner*, 198; *Light in the Morning*, 28–29).

5. One of the most touching things in Anna's biography is her memory, down to the last detail, of three dresses that Susan wore as a girl. Her total recall on this point testifies more than any explicit acknowledgment could the degree to which the loss of fine clothes mattered to them. Anna spends quite a bit of time explaining that they were helped by the fact that they "had never heard dress *talked*," but her preoccupation with the issue shows how deep it went (176–77).

6. Anna seems almost to have merged her identity with Susan's by the time she wrote the biography. The passage continues: "Still I find myself questioning what she would have me do; still unconsciously, I say 'we,' and 'ours.' And if I write on the fly leaf of a book, it is often the two names together, as they used to be" (204–205).

7. Mary Kelley, *Private Woman, Public Stage: Literary Domesticity in Nineteenth-Century America* (New York: Oxford University Press, 1984), 88, 87.

8. For an account of spinsterhood as a respectable alternative to marriage and motherhood after the Revolution, see Lee Chambers-Schiller, *A Better Husband: Single Women in America, The Generations of 1740–1820* (New Haven: Yale University Press, 1984).

9. The terms *Visiter* and *Tract Visiter* are no longer in use; I am following the nineteenth-century spelling and capitalization.

10. The quoted phrase is from Anna Warner's novel *Dollars and Cents*, which, according to Grace Overmeyer, gives an account of a sheriff's sale that parallels what happened to the Warners themselves ("Hudson River Bluestockings—The Warner Sisters of Constitution Island," *New York History* 40, no. 2 (April 1959): 147.

11. Lewis Saum, *The Popular Mood of Pre-Civil War America* (Westport, Conn.: Greenwood Press, 1980), 3.

12. New York City Tract Society, *Eleventh Annual Report* (New York: New York City Tract Society, 1837), back cover.

13. *Eleventh Annual Report*, 51–52.

14. For an expanded discussion of this and other aspects of *The Wide, Wide World*'s cultural context, see Jane Tompkins, *Sensational Designs: The Cultural Work of American Fiction, 1790–1860* (New York: Oxford University Press, 1985), 147–85.

15. Susan Griffin, *Pornography and Silence: Culture's Revenge Against Nature* (New York: Harper & Row, 1981).

16. See *Pornography and Silence*, 144–54.

17. Joanne Dobson, "The Hidden Hand: Subversion of Cultural Ideology in Three Mid-Nineteenth-Century American Women Writers," *American Quarterly,* forthcoming. This essay, which deals with Susan Warner, A.D.T. Whitney, and E.D.E.N. Southworth takes a somewhat different view of *The Wide, Wide World* from the one offered here. For other useful discussions of Warner's work, see Nina Baym, *Women's Fiction: 1820–1870* (Ithaca: Cornell University Press, 1978); *Private Woman, Public Stage*; and *Sensational Designs.*

18. I am grateful to Susan Getze for pointing out to me the structural similarity in male and female roles.

19. Warner's insistence that Ellen prefers to keep her treasures in an upstairs room to avoid the appearance of display is a coded way of indicating her social class.

20. The attitude toward art this passage displays, in which the objects exist only to negate their own materiality, reflects the theory of painting put forward in 1850 by the *Christian Examiner*: "When art expresses to the world pure and ennobling thought, then her mute language is the language of heaven, and she becomes one of the chief instrumentalities in spiritualizing mankind."

The use of the pronoun "she" signals the special connection between women and art in antebellum thought. Women, in the pre-Civil War era, were seen as instruments of spiritual and moral refinement, existing to ennoble and spiritualize men. Thus, they share with works of art the status of vehicles of inspiration, existing not as ends in themselves but as elevating influences. When works of art depict a beautiful, holy woman, they are triply sacramental. As art they represent the "mute language of heaven"; as depictions of women, they represent woman's role as spiritual mediator; and as depictions of holy women (such as the Virgin Mary), they are the purest earthly embodiments of the eternal spirit. For the source of this discussion, and of the passage quoted above, see Elizabeth Garrity Ellis, "The 'Intellectual and Moral Made Visible': The 1839 Washington Allston Exhibition and Unitarian Taste in Boston," *Prospects* 10 (1985): 39–75.

21. The struggle to accept the Lord's will, to live contentedly, to "die to self," to "be all God's," is the leitmotif of the passages Anna quotes from her sister's journal. See for example, pages 391, 396, 397, 398, 400–401, 424, 427–28, 439, 446, 463, 464.

22. *Light in the Morning,* 77. In a passage that indicates that Warner has accepted her celibacy she refers to marriage, movingly, as "that vision of great gladness" that "has merely looked in at our windows and passed us by." In what follows, however, she makes it clear that she is glad to have remained single (477).

23. For an account of the Warner sisters' relation to West Point, see

William A. McIntosh, "Constitution Island: The Warners' Living Legacy," *Assembly* 45, no. 1 (June 1986): 12–13, 34–35.

24. For a complete listing of Susan Warner's works, and Anna's as well, see Foster, *Susan and Anna Warner*, 129–131.

25. As quoted in *Susan and Anna Warner*, 102, from Susan Warner, *Daisy Plains* (New York: R. Carter and Brothers, 1885), 85.